Anonymus

The Midland Monthly

Anonymus

The Midland Monthly

ISBN/EAN: 9783741195747

Manufactured in Europe, USA, Canada, Australia, Japa

Cover: Foto ©Andreas Hilbeck / pixelio.de

Manufactured and distributed by brebook publishing software
(www.brebook.com)

Anonymus

The Midland Monthly

THE MIDLAND
MONTHLY

ILLUSTRATED.

VOLUME IV.   JULY - DECEMBER.

 1895

JOHNSON BRIGHAM, PUBLISHER,
DES MOINES, IOWA.

INDEX

TO

THE MIDLAND MONTHLY

VOLUME IV

PROSE

POETRY.

FROM PHOTOGRAPH BY F. W. WEBSTER, DES MOINES.

TYPES OF MIDLAND BEAUTY. I.

THE MIDLAND MONTHLY.

VOLUME IV.   JULY, 1895.   NUMBER 1.

A NATURALIST'S VOYAGE DOWN THE MACKENZIE.

BY FRANK RUSSELL.

WE REACHED Fort Resolution from Fort Rae on the fifteenth of December. I could not induce the men engaged for the buffalo hunt to start before New Year's Day, as that is the principal holiday in their calendar. At that time all the hands within a hundred miles of the fort came in to attend the festivities, while the more distant Yellow Knives, Dog Ribs, Chippewyans, Slaveys and Hares sent in couriers with reports of their fall hunt and to get a few supplies.

The day was celebrated by drinking a hundred gallons of tea, and eating all the small stock of flour in the company store besides an enormous quantity of meat. The program closed with a grand ball in the "Big House," or clerk's residence, for those able to dance the jigs and reels of the half-breeds, while the Indians in one of the smaller shanties danced, or rather stamped and swayed their bodies, to the time of sagwa chants and improvised songs.

The supply of fish was nearly exhausted and all the dogs were starving. I had no little difficulty in securing provisions for our trip. After many delays, agreeing to pay double wages, I at last induced Little Francois and Henri, two Chippewyan Indians, to start for the interior of the unexplored buffalo country lying southwest of us.

We had no trail after the first day, but plowed through the soft snow of small lakes, or cut our way through the unbroken forest. We followed the course of a small stream for a few miles, which saved time and labor; but, as it was strongly impregnated with minerals and only partially frozen over, we frequently broke through. The sleds had to be scraped every few rods, the ice forming on the bottoms making them drag heavily. Our snow-shoes filled with ice. Our moose-skin moccasins absorbed water like sponges, and then froze stiff. We could not run to keep warm at any time on the trip owing to the load and the soft snow; but we kept up the circulation by pushing the sleds.

Though we went beyond the point at which the buffalo had been killed in previous winters, we found no trace of them. Our provisions gave out and we were compelled to turn back, reaching the fort after an absence of fourteen days.

I returned at once to Fort Rae, where I spent the month of February attending a line of traps thirty miles in length, which made a long round for one day's work.

On the fourth of March, assisted by the missionary and the clerk of the post, I succeeded in persuading a petty chief to allow me to accompany him into the Barren Ground after musk-ox. Money or its equivalent would not overcome their superstition. They said that they, born and bred to such a life, found the trip difficult and dangerous, so that I, a white man, need not hope to reach the musk-ox. Johnnie Cohoyla finally agreed to permit me to accompany him if I would pay two skins, or one dollar a day, and supply the tea, "and you will see musk-ox," said he, in conclusion. The force of his remark I afterward understood when I found he was doing his best to prevent my killing any. Johnnie had been employed by the company in his younger days and had then acquired a limited vocabulary of Red River French and an unlimited amount of impudence.

Their camp was located about two hundred miles northeast from Fort Rae, near the edge of the Barrens. Here we remained twenty days, the Dog Ribs always waiting until after the Easter festa before starting upon the hunt. Caribou were killed and the meat dried, both for the hunters and for the women and children left behind. The bones were pounded and boiled for grease.

A pair of snow-shoes about three feet and a half in length, smaller than ordinarily used, was made by each hunter. The dogs were well cared for,—that is, fed two or three times a week. New lines were braided for the sleds, and a half dozen pairs of new moccasins were made for each man.

On the evening of the twenty-eighth my dogs were not to be found at feeding time.

"*Tekah il mangaient vos chiens assoir,*" said Johnnie.

"*Yazzy tekah thlokn,*" said the others.

"The wolves will eat your dogs to-night."

"Yes, indeed, the wolves are very numerous."

Without the dogs I could do nothing. Missing this opportunity, I must remain another year in the country or go back to the States without accomplishing the main object of the expedition. With these thoughts in mind I passed an anxious night. After scouring the country the next day in search of them, I found them all by the middle of the afternoon, where they had been feasting on a wounded deer which they had found. An hour later we had started from camp. The eleven Indians took seven sleds, drawn by twenty-eight of the most villainous-looking curs.

These Indian dogs are a different breed from the woolly, sharp-eared Eskimo dog. They are called giddies in the North, and are smaller than the dogs used by the company. They are carried in the small canoes in summer, but usually have to shift for themselves at that season. This summer's starvation is their preparation for the winter's work, in which heavy hauling and heavier mauling soon termi-

OUR PACKET LEAVING FORT RAE.

A SLAVEY CAMP.

nate their career. They are of a variety of colors, but all have a wolfish appearance. Many of them had at least half the hair burned from their bodies from lying in the hot ashes of the camp-fire. A giddy with half his tail singed off and yellow spots burned into his coat here and there, his back arched from hunger, his tread that of an animal that expects to have a club thrown at him if he approaches anything edible, does not present a dignified appearance.

Three days of rapid travel brought us to the Coppermine River, where a little clump of low twisted pines, far out from the main woods, afforded an opportunity to load our sleds for the Barren Ground.

"Jimmie the Chief" was leader of the band, and by far the most intelligent man among them. As we were about to start after loading our sleds with wood, Jimmie, after a long look eastward, said to me : "A—ye letchin bady, nitzy nitchaw, yazzy edsah." "Not a stick out there as

large as my finger ; the winds are strong ; it will be terribly cold."

We relied upon our rifles for provision ; the country being so open we could not approach the caribou readily, and we depended on chasing them until their curiosity brought them to a halt within range.

When a caribou was killed one man would be detailed to cut it up, which he would do skilfully and quickly. Jimmie would divide the spoils as fairly as possible among his followers. In this allotment Hakkahwe always had his share and with a repeating rifle did his share of the hunting. They used single or double barreled muzzle-loading smooth-bores, carrying shot or a heavy ball. These weapons were much lighter than mine, which circumstance became a serious item when it came to a long-distance race after musk-ox. It has been said that they can fire as rapidly as with repeaters, which is of course an exaggeration, though they do load with wonderful rapidity when pursuing caribou and musk-ox.

The shoulders and thighs would be cut up at once and given to the dogs, the men, fortunate enough to get them, eating the tendons before they froze and cracking the long bones for that greatest of Dog Rib luxuries — the marrow. This fresh marrow seemed to satisfy our thirst which we could not quench with water during the day. Frozen marrow is a rare treat and if roasted is beyond praise.

Our supply of wood was so small that no fire could be made at midday, so only two meals a day were eaten. At night two deerskin lodges sheltered the party from the piercing wind. There was no pine brush to spread our blankets on, no fire to warm our hands and feet or dry our perspiration-soaked garments. Our frozen moccasins and pieces of blanket used for socks were placed next our shirts where the warmth of our bodies would dry them during the night.

Our fire was only large enough to boil a kettle of meat for a few minutes; this gave us very cold fingers when eating the half raw viands. As the last man rolled up in his blanket at night the Indian giddies all came inside the lodge. The twelve just filled it. At first they searched for meat through and over everything, and quarreled over the bones about the fireplace. Then a few would lie down on top of us, and from that time on until they were driven out in the morning they kept up a continual snarling and fighting. A dog would move up as close to a desirable place as he dared, then sit down and growl. The dog occupying that place would reply in emphatic terms; the growls would grow louder; the newcomer would keep edging closer, until a conflict ensued. I am unable to furnish statistics as to the number of fights occurring within the limits of the lodge each night, but I remember that the number taking place over me was on an average three.

As they lay upon my robe the heat of their bodies would melt the snow, which

FORT GOOD HOPE.

FORT SIMPSON.

blew in to a depth of from one to six inches each night. This immediately froze when they left it; and, as there was no fire to thaw it, my robe and single blanket became as stiff as a board.

On the tenth day a northeast gale filled the air with fine blinding snow obscuring all land-marks and making travel impossible. It was bitterly cold and as we had no fuel to warm the lodge we spent the day rolled up in the blankets, only boiling one kettle of meat at noon and a little tea at night. The next day showed no change in the storm outside and we were unable to move. The day following proved clear and we pushed on. Mr. Cohoyla set off alone on a course parallel to that of the others so as to cover more ground.

Soon afterward we discovered a large band of thirty or forty musk-ox about three miles away. The cry of "Etjerer" (musk-ox) brought up the lagging trains. The dogs were released from their harness and set off in bands of three or four as soon as they discovered the trail of the fleeing animals. Some trotted placidly along at their masters' heels.

The musk-ox can run faster than man, though they are soon overtaken by the dogs, when they halt and form in a circle with an unbroken front of sharp and dangerous horns presented outward.

We chased them unavailingly for six miles. Our clothing became saturated with perspiration which froze as we walked back to the sleds with the dogs, which had to be gathered in on account of the wolves. It was after nightfall when we put up the lodge that night, tired, thirsty and hungry. We were out of tea and must quench our thirst with the greasy bouillon in which the meat was boiled.

A blizzard set in that night causing us much anxiety about Johnnie Cohoyla, who had not been seen since morning. I was awakened at dawn by the monotonous wailing of his brother, Esyuh, who was chanting the virtues of the lost reprobate and entreating the fates in general and the North Wind in particular to spare him. The fine snow covered everything inside the lodge, in places to a depth of two feet. The wind swept by with a rush that would nearly take one off his feet. It was impossible to search for the lost man until the day following, when he was found in a snow-drift, safely and warmly rolled up in a couple of musk-ox skins which he had secured and without which he must certainly have perished.

Late in the afternoon the next day I killed three musk-ox. My fingers were frozen before I finished skinning them by the faint light of the moon. The two following days were too stormy to travel, so that I had an opportunity to skin the heads of the animals, and to split the skulls so that they could be packed on the sled, which was only fifteen inches wide and eight feet long. As the skins had been left over night wrapped around the heads, they froze in great awkward balls which could not be loaded in the wrapper, but must be lashed on top, which made the load topheavy. I now had as many skins as the Hudson's Bay people told me would be possible to bring out.

Again we discovered a large band of musk-ox, of which I killed four. I could put but two of these on the sled, making a load nearly as high as my shoulder and reaching out over both ends of the sled. Then I tried to hire the Indians to carry out a head and a skeleton for me, but could not induce them to do so at any price.

My load weighed at least five hundred pounds, two hundred pounds more than the dogs could haul without constant forcing. I pushed on the sled and carried a load on my back to help them as much as possible.

When we turned back we traveled from twelve to sixteen and a half hours per day without eating or drinking from morning till night. On the fourth day our carefully hoarded supply of wood was exhausted, and we were compelled to burn our lodge poles.

It was nearly midnight on the twenty-third of April when we again reached the Coppermine River. We had burned our last lodge pole and were nearly without food. We were all too exhausted to cut much brush, and we fell asleep in a little hole scooped in the deep snow, to be awakened five hours later by Jimmie shouting in Dog Rib, "It's a long way to camp yet, there are no deer, and we've got to hurry ourselves."

We had been twenty-two days in the Barren Ground, and I had anticipated enjoying a good rest and a huge fire on reaching the woods once more. Three days of rapid travel, with five hours' rest each night, brought us to the camps. On the last day, though I was suffering from *mal de raquette*, and straining constantly

A GIUINIE PUP.

A GIODIB IN ACTIVE SERVICE.

to assist the dogs, I could
scarcely keep awake. The
last two days were much
warmer : the snow soft-
ened, so that lumps of ice
formed between the foot
and snow-shoe in walking
a few yards. This blis-
tered the bottoms of my
feet wherever the ball or
heel sustained any weight,
—not in a few small blis-
ters, but on the entire
surface. The nails of the
smaller toes dropped off.

The hunt had taken
twenty-eight days. All
had returned safely with
full loads. We had worn
goggles constantly to
avoid snow-blindness.

From the Iowa State University Collection

MUSK-OX HEAD.

I reached Fort Rae on
the night of May 4th, with
five complete skins and skulls of musk-
ox. I had been absent sixty days and
traveled over eight hundred miles on
snow-shoes. No white man had heretofore reached the musk-ox from Fort
Rae. No American museum has a series
of these animals equalling that secured by
this expedition for the State University
of Iowa.

As I was unable to employ Indians who
would risk their precious lives in descending the Coppermine, and as there were no
good collecting grounds for the ornithol-
ogist near Rae, I decided to descend the
Mackenzie, and return home by way of
the Arctic Ocean, Behring Straits and
San Francisco.

A few travelers have gone down the
Mackenzie to Peel River, one hundred
and sixty miles from the Arctic Ocean,
then, following the regular Hudson's Bay
Company's route across the mountains
to the Yukon River, have reached civilization through Behring Sea ; but no one
had ever before passed down the Mackenzie to its mouth and around Alaska.

To follow this plan I was compelled to
leave Rae immediately and cross the
Great Slave Lake before the ice broke up.
The snow was melting rapidly, making the
Portage road to Providence impassable.

Again I found it necessary to travel
alone. I was unable to travel during the
day owing to the snow being too soft to
sustain the weight of the dogs and sled,
but pushed on at night instead.

In going ashore to "drink tea," as
camping for a meal is called, it was necessary to wade and drag the sled through
a broad strip of water, or slush, from six
inches to a foot in depth, which lay along
shore, just outside the heavy drifts. In
starting out in the evening I had to pass
through this water, which soaked through
my moccasins and heavy blanket foot-
wrappings. These soon froze stiff on the
outside, making them anything but warm,
and very heavy. I found it necessary to
wear more on my feet than in midwinter,
as the snow-shoes more easily blistered
them when continually wet. The snow-
shoes themselves, becoming water-soaked
so often, stretched and broke, so that new
lacing was required each day.

In driving dogs on long trips the animals become bewildered and disheart-

ened if there is no one to run before them. A team that has been apparently worn out, and which pays no attention to the whip but to lie down and yell, will start off at a brisk trot and strain at the collar to keep up if a boy runs before them. I had to direct mine with the whip and voice alone. They were too heavily loaded to keep moving if I went before them, and there was, of course, no track. The supply of dog-fish was exhausted on the sixth day. I traveled that night as usual; but, instead of stopping next day, I pushed on until midnight, when, in the darkness, I ran into a field of rotten ice and had to wait for daylight before getting ashore. This was just at the head of the Mackenzie, and I had some difficulty in getting ashore at all.

There is a productive fishery here about which half-breeds and Indians were said to be always encamped. I expected to find men to take me forty miles down the river to Providence in a canoe and, of course, to find plenty of fish for myself and the dogs.

Much to my surprise, chagrin and disgust, I found the place abandoned! Releasing the dogs, I tried to get a little rest before continuing.

The following day, after a fruitless search for Indians, I started over the rotten river ice toward Providence. The dogs soon gave out, whereupon I cached the load on an island, upon a scaffold high enough to keep the wolves from destroying it, and the next morning set off to gain the north bank of the river and follow it down to the fort. By wading a broad channel I reached the shore, and after a couple of hours' hard work found a camp of Slavey Indians.

They were living in lodge-shaped enclosures covered with willows and reeds, which afforded no protection from the elements. The men were dressed in the ordinary clothing obtained at the trading station, though a few still retained their

FORT WRIGLEY.

winter capotes of woven rabbit skin, than which there is no warmer garment made. The women wore dresses of cheap print, utterly unsuited to the climate and their mode of living.

They at once boiled a large kettle of jack-fish — their only food — and all gathered to see the stranger and to drink tea. They understood neither French nor English, and their dialect differed considerably from that of the Dog Ribs with which I was becoming somewhat acquainted, so that it was some time before I could induce them to assist me to reach the post.

The next day my sled was brought to the camp and loaded in a large canoe paddled by two Slaveys. My dogs were to be fed and brought down as soon as the river opened.

It was not without regret that I parted from these faithful friends, the dogs that had accompanied me over 2,200 miles of snow on wind-swept lakes and dismal barrens. They, with intelligent and expressive faces, beside the camp fire, were always more companionable and friendly to me than the chattering Indians who, I knew, would desert me for a trifling cause. Poor fellows! Many a time had they been beaten into the snow when exhausted and hungry. Many a time had they been harnessed in the morning too weak and stiff to start the heavy load and to answer the heavy whip with their piteous whine. Nudjuk, Treff, Major, and Corbeau, we have hunted, eaten and slept together for the last time. Farewell!

Twelve miles above Providence the narrow channel which we were following terminated in an ice jam and we had to make the last stage of the journey through the trackless bush. I reached the fort on the evening of the eleventh day after leaving Rae.

On the second of June, though the river was full of running ice, I left Providence in a birch canoe with an Indian guide, and before night reached the steamer "Wrigley," which is laid up each winter twenty miles below the fort. A half hour later we were steaming toward Good Hope, which is seven hundred miles down the Mackenzie.

LE GRAND SIEUR (1792).

BENEATH her low-hung balconies
He waits, gay velvet lover;
The dusk lurks in the poplar trees;
She flings a rose unto the breeze;
Night soon their joy will cover.

Back, rabble, from the chateau walls!
Back, hunger-driven masses!
He feasts within his splendid halls!
The bitter tumult of your calls
Is drowned in clinking glasses.

He comes! Ah, citizens, no fear
Lurks 'neath those haughty graces.
He smiles as flash your poniards near;
'Tis now he holds them doubly dear —
France, honor, love,— his laces!

WORCEST, MASS.

Josette Gertrude Menard.

THE RIVER BEND.

WHAT joy, upon the dancing stream,
    Under the sweeping paddle's play,
'Neath tinted sky from sunset's gleam,
Where water-lilies lie and dream,
    Awaiting the soft touch of day,—
To voyage in a light canoe,
    In which there's only room for two!

Where purling streams wind in and out,
    In wastefulness and wanton glee,
Where willows dip their thirsty boughs,
And lovers 'change undying vows
    Beneath the well known trysting tree,
We linger in our light canoe,
    In which there's only room for two!

The robin sings; or sweet brown thrush
    On topmost bough in evening air,
With heaving breast and swelling throat
Pours out his heart with every note;
    The while, we sit in silence there,
Concealed from the musician's view,
    Entranced, within the light canoe:

THE RIVER BEND.

Or idly float, 'neath silent stars,
　　While sprinkled thickly on the stream
Their bright reflected faces show;
With stars above and stars below,
　　It all seems like a passing dream.
With thoughts too deep for words, we two
　　Sit voiceless, in our light canoe!

Oh, Golden Silence! When two hearts
　　Are throbbing with responsive beat!
When trembling on the lips are hung
The sweetest words of mortal tongue,
　　Which lovers falt'ringly repeat:
"I love you!" who would not be true
　　To plighted troth in light canoe?

Dear River Bend, with light and shade!
　　With fringed willows by the score,
Festooned with wild grape blossoms sweet,
While lipping waves thy name repeat
　　In whispered ripples 'long the shore;
Sad day, when we shall bid adieu
　　To thee, and to our swift canoe!

And when down Life's long stream we glide
　　To where Styx' waters darkly roll,
And meet old Charon, gaunt and grim,
To his demandings say to him:
　"Insist not on our paying toll;
For, if it's just the same to you,
　　We'll cross o'er in our staunch canoe!"

DES MOINES.　　　　　　　　　　　　TACITUS HUSSEY.

A MOUNTAIN DEER HUNT.

BY L. H. FULLER.

"IS THIS Mr. Emsley, the taxidermist?" I asked, as I stepped into a large room filled with handsome rugs, noble heads, and other evidences of that great game country which lies around Missoula, Montana. Answered in the affirmative by a man who was busily engaged in putting the finishing touches on an eight-point elk's head, I told him I wanted to put in four days hunting to the best possible advantage.

Calling up a keen-eyed man, he introduced me to Mr. Martin Spencer,* familiarly called "Nelse," who, he said, would take me out for any length of time. A plan was soon settled upon, and in two hours we were bidding Missoula goodbye, each astride of one of the much-abused cayuses, our camping outfit strapped on behind, our rifles across the saddles.

Crossing Rattlesnake Creek as we left the town, we proceeded to follow that

* Formerly of Manchester, Iowa.

beautiful stream up to the head, where, as "Nelse" told me, we would surely find a bear or a deer, or perhaps a mountain goat, or a "big-horn," and would enjoy some of the most beautiful scenery in the state.

As evening drew near, our spirits and ambitions were somewhat dampened by a cold rain and fog, but the prospect of a shot at a "white-tail" modified the unpleasantness. Ten miles up the Rattlesnake we camped, and after supper, while our clothes were steaming from the hot pine fire, I felt the first exhilarating effects of camp life.

The next morning found the heavy fog and rain still on, and the prospect gloomy. Leaving the trail we started up the mountains, the steep sides covered with a heavy growth of pine trees, the bushes dripping wet. I began to wonder if I had not been a bit over-ambitious. All day long we wandered through these woods, sometimes riding, sometimes

ON THE FLATHEAD RESERVATION. ST. MARY'S LAKE.

ON THE FLATHEAD RESERVATION —" HOME OF THE MOUNTAIN GOAT."

walking, picking our way around rocks and logs, almost ready to "bush." Every now and then a great mountain grouse would whirr up through the wet bushes and perch herself on a neighboring bough, watching us with great curious eyes, until one of Nelse's bullets would leave her headless. No other signs of life did we meet all day long.

Late at night we camped high up on the mountain, and soon the resinous pine was shooting flames up into the black night-fog. Bacon, baked potatoes and hard flap-jacks mysteriously disappeared. A full-sized appetite in the big woods of the Montana mountains is not discriminating. Articles that would make hollow-eyed dyspepsia laugh with glee, and that in civilization would not be eaten or allowed on any table, are eaten and digested without a qualm.

"We ought to see something to-morrow sure," said Spencer. And then I began to ply him with questions as to the way to look for game, the way to shoot a bear (afraid I would see one, and afraid I would not), and before bedtime he had posted me for the most difficult shooting —theoretically. He is a splendid shot

and a master of woodcraft ; not a "sign" escapes him.

The second morning came bright and clear. We could see from our elevation over the tops of the smaller ranges, and the sight alone was well worth our hard trip. The great trees in the valleys and along the sides of the mountains, whose tops were turned to shining silver as they reflected the rays of the morning sun, formed beautiful shadows for nature's superb picture. For miles we could see the huge hills dividing the valleys which were filled with grand old pines and firs that opened here and there to let a small lake look up as if inviting us to rest upon its grassy banks.

We began our downward trip. The first hour's ride gave us a glimpse of a deer as he crashed down the mountain side. When Nelse said, "Here's a fresh bear track," I felt ready for any hardship. By noon camp was made and we were out looking for game. "Signs" were plenty. Bear-browsed huckleberry bushes, and the sound of a deer as he hurried away, told us that we were in a game country.

The next morning Nelse directed me to follow on down the range of mountains to the lower valley and around up the other side back to camp. This was my first trip alone. As I wandered on down over the steep rocks I began to realize how awful is solitude. My own voice seemed to startle me. But I found fresh signs and began to hunt with caution. Once I found a place where a bear had rested during the night, at the foot of a fallen tree. After following the huge

SCENE ON THE MISSOULA RIVER, NEAR MISSOULA.

tracks for a few rods I turned away satisfied with bear-hunting. There is nothing inspiring about a large-sized bear track when one is alone!

When noon came I was tired and disheartened. I had lost all hope of seeing any more game and was ready to quit. Swinging myself up on a ledge of rocks I suddenly became aware of something alive only a few feet away. My heart stopped beating and I was afraid to breathe. I could see long ears thrown forward, bright eyes looking into mine, each pair of eyes revealing curiosity and surprise. I could see those delicate nostrils quivering with excitement as they tried to scent from the air the possible danger. With a movement that was almost spasmodic, I threw my Winchester up to my shoulder and sent a "45" bullet — somewhere.

As I crouched under the smoke and

peered through, sure enough, not fifty feet away was my first deer thrashing around among the bushes in her death agony. A merciful bullet kindly ended all suffering, and I stood in the awful stillness wondering at what I had done. A feeling of guilt, almost shame, filled me and I looked around as if afraid someone had seen me.

I soon had the animal skinned and, with the "saddles" perched on my shoulders, worked my way to camp. The hind-quarters of a fat "black-tail" deer is no light load, and the sun was setting when I reached camp.

A feast followed that was fit for the gods, — venison fried in bacon fat, with the breast of grouse baked tender, roasted potatoes and cool spring water. Labor had made us hungry and at last we were rewarded. If the gods ever look with envy on earth-born man, it must be when a mountain appetite is waited upon by the rewards of the chase which is its *raison d' étre*.

The next morning, at sunrise, we were on our way home. We climbed up the peak of the range, and looked regretfully back upon those little lakes as they caught up the golden gleams and gilded the shadows of the grand old firs that fringed their borders.

ANOTHER SCENE ON THE MISSOULA.

THE SPIRIT LAKE MASSACRE.

By Hon. C. C. Carpenter,
Ex-Governor of Iowa

THE recent completion of a monument in commemoration of the massacre, in 1857, at Okoboji and Spirit Lakes, has revived interest in the bloodiest tragedy of Iowa history. Prior to 1856, Okoboji and Spirit Lakes were unknown to civilized people, except as they had been visited by the hunter, the explorer, and the surveyor. During all the centuries which had come and gone the waters of these lakes had been unruffled, except by the lazy paddle of the Indian navigator and by the fierce winds which swept down from the North. It is easy to imagine that these lakes possessed for the Indian a peculiar charm, and were regarded by him with almost superstitious interest. The enchanting loveliness of the scenery by which they were surrounded; the picturesque bluffs which broke the monotony of the surrounding prairie; the little bays indenting their shores; and the capes, reaching out into their silent waters, shaded by the gorgeous foliage of beautiful groves, could but strongly appeal to the imagination of these children of nature. Their waters were deeper than those of a great majority of fresh-water lakes of the Northwest. The fish with which they abounded were of greater variety and, owing to the purity of their waters, of a richer flavor than were found in the shallower lakes of the farther North. The Indian doubtless found at these lakes the same attraction, inviting him when wearied with the exertions and perhaps disappointments of the chase to seek their shady recesses for rest and recreation, that in later years has made them the resort of his civilized successor. In imagination he often saw the inviting blaze of the fire at his tepee, as he surmounted some distant ridge of the prairie when coming home from the weary hunt of the deer and the elk. So his Indian proclivities led him back to these old haunts, where in other days he had lounged in happy indolence, from the distant reservation to which he had been exiled by the necessities of a civilization he could not comprehend.

The vanguard of the population which rescued this beautiful portion of the state from the wilderness arrived in July, 1856. They were the representatives of a race always facing westward—a type of American citizenship which will become extinct with the disappearance of the frontier. Some of them had visited this outpost of the public domain the year before; had staked out their claims, and now came back accompanied by their families, with oxen, wagons, their domestic animals, breaking-plows, scythes, hay-rakes, axes, their scanty household furniture and a limited supply of provision, but with boundless hopes, strong arms, and resolute purposes.

The first arrival at the Lakes was the family of Rowland Gardner, consisting of himself, wife, two daughters, Eliza and Abigail, and a little son, Rowland, Jr. Also, as part of the same family, came a married daughter and her husband, Harvey Luce, and their two children. They had previously lived at Shell Rock and Clear Lake. Arriving on the sixteenth day of July, as soon as they had selected the place they wished to preëmpt, they set to work to erect a log-house—the first built at the lakes—which still stands as an interesting memorial of a family whose name will always be conspicuously mentioned among the pioneers of this bloody ground. They were soon followed by James Mattock, wife and five children, from Delaware county, who settled and built a cabin near the east side of the strait connecting East and West Okoboji. Then came Joel Howe, wife and six

17

children, together with a son-in-law, Alvin Noble, his wife and one child. In the same party were Joseph M. Thatcher, wife and one child. This entire party came from Hampton, Franklin county, and made their claims on the east side of East Okoboji. Finally there came from Linn county a Mr. Marble and his wife, who settled on the west side of Spirit Lake, several miles from the settlement at the Okobojis. In addition to these families there were several young men who from time to time found their way into the settlement. William Granger,

Yours very truly
Cyrus C. Carpenter

from Red Wing, Minnesota, reached the lakes about the time of the arrival of the Gardners, accompanied by his brother, Carl Granger, a Doctor Harriott and Bertell A. Snyder,—the three latter being young, single men. They built a cabin near the west side of the strait connecting the lakes, not far from what is now known as Smith's Point. After building their cabin, William Granger returned to Red Wing, to spend the winter with his family. The three young men remained during the winter. Morris Markham came in with the Howe family and lived during the winter in the Noble family. There also came with the Mattock family one Madison, accompanied by a son eighteen years old, the remainder of his family staying in Delaware county, whither he intended to return for them in the spring.

During the latter part of the summer and the early fall the people at the settlement were busy erecting their cabins, building stables to protect their cattle and horses during the forthcoming winter, and cutting hay, which was done by hand with the scythe. They were a happy and hopeful people, were all pleased with their new location and looked forward with joyful anticipations to a prosperous future.

Finally the winter was upon them. On the first day of December a fearful snowstorm ushered in one of the severest winters in the history of the state. For weeks one storm followed another in quick succession until the prairie was buried in snow from two to three feet in depth; and in ravines and depressions, where the drifting snow had lodged, it was frequently from six to ten feet deep. The half dozen families and the few young men constituting the settlement at the lakes, were almost as thoroughly cut off from the outside world as though they had been cast upon an island in mid-ocean. During these long and lonely weeks they had some apprehension that their slender stock of provision might vanish before they were able to reach the sources of supply. And they sometimes feared disease, requiring remedies which

could not be procured in the settlement, might strike down some member of a family. But the real fate which awaited them never disturbed their dreams or caused them a moment's anxiety.

The winter passed slowly away. Early in February Mr. Luce and Mr. Thatcher left with an ox-team to go to their old home for a load of provision. After incredible hardships they reached the settlements where, by constant use in more thickly settled neighborhoods, the roads were kept barely passable. They went to Hampton, Shell Rock, Cedar Falls and Waterloo. They secured a load of provision and started on their return, accompanied and reinforced by three young men who had not before visited the lakes—Jonathan Howe and Enoch Ryan—son and son-in-law of Joel Howe—and a young acquaintance named Robert Clark. After many days of toilsome traveling they reached Shippey's,—a family living in the southern part of Palo Alto county,—about twelve miles below the present town of Emmetsburg. Their oxen had become so exhausted that they determined to leave them for a few days' rest, Mr. Thatcher remaining to take care of them, while Luce and the three young men went forward to the lakes. They arrived at the lakes on the sixth day of March, just two days before the massacre.

During this long and lonely winter the few people at the lakes had formed the attachment for each other which results from common hardships, dangers, hopes and ambitions. The utmost good-will existed between them all. The great severity of the cold and almost impassable snow-drifts had prevented them from making frequent visits, but there was a friendly interest in one another and a neighborly fellowship which is unknown among people who have never experienced the loneliness of the frontier. Their scanty supplies of food were held in common. If the bottom of the meal-chest was reached at one of the cabins, the inmates always knew that so long as any remained in the neighbor's chest, it would be shared with them. The social fellowship between the settlers, when they were able to meet, helped to while away these weary weeks. They, however, longed for the coming spring, and when the first days of March had come, and the sun began to have a slight effect upon the vast snow-fields which surrounded their lonely cabins, the melting snow occasionally forming in icicles on the south side of the snow-covered roofs, new life and fresh hopes seemed to bring a brighter luster to the eye, to add elasticity to the footstep, and there was a more joyous expression on the face. But just as the people reached the threshold of these long-looked-for and happier days, the great calamity overwhelmed them.

In the early days of February a band of Sioux Indians, well known on the frontier by their repeated incursions into the northwestern portion of the state, appeared in the western part of Woodbury county. They were known as Ink-pa-du-ta's band. While the settlers at the various places which they had visited during the previous years did not particularly fear them, yet on account of their begging, thieving, and generally lawless propensities, they were most unwelcome visitors. It seemed, however, that they were unusually lawless, and even quarrelsome, as they made their way along the Little Sioux River, through Cherokee, Buena Vista and Clay counties, toward the lakes. The truth is, this particular band was outside of all wholesome restraints commonly recognized even among Indians.

The Indians, whose authority was acknowledged over a large portion of the Territory of Minnesota, prior to the Treaty of 1851, were known as the Wakpekuti Sioux. Their principal chiefs were Wamdesapa and Tasagi. The tradition is that Wamdesapa and his band were regarded as "toughs" even according to the code of Indian morals. Their predatory and lawless character had rendered them so unpopular with their Indian confederates that they were finally obliged to withdraw from the fraternity of the Wakpekuti

and make their headquarters on the Vermillion river, in the present state of South Dakota. Accordingly, when the Treaty of Mendota, in 1851, was made, by which a large portion of the Territory of Minnesota was ceded to the Government, they were not called into the councils, and had no share in its grants or its provisions. Thus this band of outlaws became a retreat for every Indian inclined to defy the restraints of the more law-abiding among their fellows. Ink-pa-du-ta was the lineal successor, both in authority and in deviltry, of Wamdesapa, and his followers were a remnant of Wamdesapa's band of outlaws. Their lawlessness, however, prior to 1857, had been confined principally to stealing, robbing and abusing families unarmed and remote from neighbors. It is probable that the long cold winter, the scarcity of game in the vicinity of their reservation in Dakota, and resistance to their demands in the more thickly settled portion of the Little Sioux Valley, south of Cherokee county, had excited their demoniacal propensities to an unusual pitch. So, as they moved northward their insolence increased. In Buena Vista county they robbed the house, shot the cattle, and shamefully abused a family by the name of Weaver. In Clay county, near the present town of Peterson, their outrages upon two families — Mead and Taylor — were even more bold and villainous. Finally, on the seventh day of March, they reached the Okoboji Lakes, when their pent-up savagery had become an insatiate thirst for blood. On the morning of the eighth, just as the Gardner family were about to breakfast, an Indian entered the cabin. He professed friendship, and the Gardners shared their breakfast with him. He was soon followed by several more, with their squaws and papooses, led by Ink-pa-du-ta himself. The family shared their scanty stores with all these hungry visitors. After they had eaten to satiety they began a series of insolent and menacing interferences with the family and their household goods. One demanded ammunition, and, when Mr. Gardner was taking some from a box to give him, he snatched the box; another attempted to take a powder-horn from the wall and was prevented by Mr. Luce, the son-in-law.

Mr. Gardner, who had learned something of Indian character by his experience with them while living at Clear Lake, in Cerro Gordo county, felt the gravity of the situation, and had suggested to Doctor Harriott and Mr. Snyder, who had called in the forenoon, that the settlers should be notified of the danger, and should assemble at his cabin, which was the largest and best situated for defense, and prepare for the conflict. The young men, however, did not think the situation serious; said it was a sullen mood of the Indians which would be only temporary, and went away toward their cabins. The Indians staid about the house until nearly noon, and finally left, after shooting some of the cattle and driving others before them. They went in the direction of the Mattock cabin, near which was the cabin of the young men, Harriott, Granger and Snyder. In the judgment of Mr. Gardner there was no longer any doubt as to the hostile purposes of the Indians. The situation was hastily canvassed. Mr. Gardner thought the two young men, Luce and Clark, who were at the house, should try immediately to reach the homes of the other settlers, notify them of the danger with the advice that they assemble at his house for defense. Although the family felt that the departure of these two men would weaken their force should the Indians immediately return, it was determined to try to save their neighbors as well as themselves. So they started on their perilous mission, never to return.

Their remains were found on the lake-shore the following summer.

About an hour after they had gone several gun-shots were heard by the Gardners, in quick succession, and in the direction of the Mattock house. This convinced them that the work of death had begun. Two hours passed, in which there was a faint hope that the two young men who had gone to arouse the neighbors might be able to reach some of them and return with reënforcements. Finally they discovered several Indians approaching the cabin. The impulse of Mr. Gardner was to barricade the door and at least sell his life as dearly as possible. But his wife, feeling the hopelessness of any attempt at defense, dissuaded him with the argument that, if there was any hope for the family, it was in trying to conciliate them. Meanwhile, they reached the house and, coming in, asked for flour, and when Mr. Gardner turned to get it for them, they shot him through the heart. Then one leveled a gun to shoot Mrs. Gardner. The daughter, Mrs. Luce, grabbed the gun and pulled down the muzzle, when the Indians seized both mother and daughter and beat them to death with the butts of their guns. They now snatched the helpless babe of Mrs. Luce from the arms of the girl of thirteen (now Mrs. Abigail Gardner Sharp), to whom were clinging with the instinct of terror, not only the babe, but her little six-year-old brother and another little child of Mrs. Luce. Snatching all three of these helpless little ones from the dazed and paralyzed girl, they carried them outside the house and beat them to death with sticks of wood. They now ransacked the cabin, taking such things as curiosity or their wants prompted, and then led away the helpless girl from the appalling scene toward the Mattock cabin.

Now, for the first time, Abigail began to realize that she was a captive. It is needless to attempt to record in words the indescribable terror of this young girl.

Arriving at the Mattock cabin, she found that the Indians had set up their tepees in the vicinity. The dead bodies of the family were scattered over the ground, the cabin was in flames, and two of the household had been left to perish in the fire. Here there had evidently been an attempt at defense. But the inmates had awakened to the danger when too late to organize. Near this house lay poor Harriott, dead, with his gun still in his hands.

Snyder also lay dead in the vicinity, showing that when the attack was made upon the Mattock family these two young men had, undoubtedly, crossed the straits from their own cabin to aid in the defense of their friends, and had died with their faces to the foe. It was now evening, and with savage intuition they celebrated the day's carnage with an Indian war-dance.

The writer has tried to imagine what must have been the feelings of a helpless captive girl in this camp of demons, during the orgies of this long night, with the picture of the horrors through which she had just passed burned into her bewildered brain. It cannot be imagined. It would be useless to try to describe it.

The next morning the savages, with appetites sharpened for blood, sallied forth on the war-path. The Howe family, living further north on the east side of East Okoboji, and the family of a son-in-law, Alvin Noble, and the Thatcher family, with whom also was stopping the young man Ryan, another son-in-law of Mr. Howe, all were entirely ignorant of the fate of their neighbors and of the presence in the neighborhood of Ink-pa-du-ta and his band. Mr. Howe had started to visit the Gardner cabin on an errand. When a short distance from his home he was met by the Indians, was shot, and his head was severed from his body. The savages then went to the cabin and soon murdered the remainder of the family, comprising the wife and six children — a young man, a young woman, and four younger children. They next visited the Noble cabin, in which were Noble, his wife and infant child, his brother-in-law Ryan, and also Mrs. Thatcher and infant child. As usual they feigned friendship on entering the house, and as soon as opportunity offered they shot both Noble and Ryan. Then seizing the two infant children from their mothers' arms, dashed their brains out against a tree at the door. After plundering the house, shooting several of the cattle and killing the poultry, they left with their booty, dragging the two helpless and horrified women — Mrs. Noble and Mrs. Thatcher — into captivity. On

the route to their camp they stopped at the cabin of the Howes, where Mrs. Noble was still more crushed and paralyzed to see the dead bodies of her mother, brothers and sisters. They then returned to their tepees, near the Mattock place. Upon their arrival, with two more captives, Abbie Gardner was placed for a time in the same tepee with her companions in captivity. The desolation of these three women, left by themselves to recount their woes and with the agony of despair endeavor to look into the future, is not a theme for words.

On the tenth of March they moved westward across West Okoboji. The next day, northward to Marble Grove, at Spirit Lake. Here another opportunity offered to slake their thirst in blood. Living alone, far from neighbors, were these two young people — Mr. and Mrs. Marble. Before they were aware of the presence of a human being besides themselves, the Indians were in and around their cabin. As usual, they pretended to be friends and made signs of goodwill. They invited Marble out to shoot at a mark. After a few shots, when his gun was empty, the target fell; they motioned him to set it up. His wife, sitting at a window, with a woman's instinct divined their purpose, and, as she suspected, the instant he turned his back to set up the target they shot him through the head. His wife in horror sprang from the house with the impulse to fly to her husband's relief, but was seized and borne to their camp a captive. Before leaving Marble Grove they again repeated the fiendish orgies of the war-dance.

After these events the Indians moved northwestward, with captives and booty. They moved by easy stages, camping at various groves along the route. On the twenty-sixth of March they were encamped at Heron Lake, about fifteen miles northwest of Springfield. They left early on the morning of the twenty-sixth, painted in their most demoniac hideousness. Like wild beasts, the taste of blood had only sharpened their appetite for more. The captives knew from their gesticulations and jargon, and the direction they took on leaving the camp, that their destination was Springfield (now Jackson) on the Des Moines River. The feelings of Abbie Gardner, the captive girl, can be partially imagined when it is understood that her elder sister, Eliza, was at Springfield. She had gone there with friends in the early fall, and owing to the severe weather and great depth of snow had been unable to return to the lakes, thus escaping the Indian barbarities at her father's house. The Indians were destined, however, to meet at Springfield an unexpected resistance.

It will be remembered that a man by the name of Morris Markham came to the lakes with the Howe family, and was spending the winter with the Nobles. The day on which the Indians reached the Howe and Noble cabins, and killed or carried into captivity their inmates, Markham had gone across to the Des Moines River, some fifteen miles east, to get a stray yoke of oxen. He returned late in the evening to the Gardner cabin, which he discovered to be a scene of desolation. He divined it to be the work of Indians, and started for the Mattock place, and was only prevented from running into the Indian camp — located as it was in timber and brush — by the barking of the Indian dogs. Keeping on the prairie to the right of the timber he finally reached the Howe place, only to find a desolate house and the mangled remains of a family who had been his best friends. Thence he went to the Noble cabin — his home — where again all was silent, dark and desolate. There was but one other house at the lakes he could hope to reach and that was the Marble cabin at Spirit Lake, and he reasoned that they had shared the fate of all the others. He had now traveled over thirty miles without food or rest. Remaining in the timber until daylight, he started, though nearly exhausted, for Springfield, some eighteen miles to the northward. Arriving at Springfield, half frozen and half-famished, he delivered his startling message.

On hearing Markham's story several families assembled at the house of Mr. Thomas, the largest in the place, and resolved to defend themselves to the end. They also dispatched two young men — Henry Tretts and Mr. Cliffen — to Fort Ridgeley, to represent the situation, and ask for protection of the United States troops. At first there were twenty two persons, old and young, in the Thomas house; and here most of them remained for seventeen days. Some of the citizens, however, did not move to this cabin. Three brothers, named Woods, from Mankato, were the original proprietors of the town. They kept a store and trading station. Two of them, William and George, were now there. They were so confident of their friendly influence with the Indians, who were their frequent customers, that they scouted the idea of danger, and remained at their store. They especially relied upon the apparent friendship of another band, under Chief Ishtahabah, or Sleepy-Eye, then camping in the vicinity. A man named Sheigley, with his little son, was also at his cabin. In the home of a Mr. Wheeler, near the Thomas house, were also two men, named Henderson and Smith, who had been so severely frozen that Henderson lost both his feet and Smith one of his. For lack of room in the Thomas house, they remained at the Wheelers'. Another family named Stewart, who at first went to the Thomas cabin, had returned to their own house, as the excitement was too intense for a person of the nervous temperament of Mrs. Stewart.

Such was the situation on the afternoon of March 26th. About three o'clock, a little eight-year-old son of the Thomases, who had been out in the yard, rushed to the door, saying, "The boys are coming!" referring to the two young men who had gone to Fort Ridgeley, and who were hourly expected. Quite a number of the people in the house came to the door, several stepping outside, when in an instant there sprang out from behind the stable, and from behind the neighboring trees, a score of Indians, all simultaneously firing into the bevy of people at the door. The little boy, William Thomas, who had been deceived by an Indian dressed in a white man's suit, and who had called them to the door, fell mortally wounded. Mr. Thomas himself was wounded in the wrist, eventually losing his arm. David Carver, one of the party, was wounded in the left arm, and Miss Drusilla Swanger in the shoulder. But in the excitement and rush for the door none of them realized that they were wounded, and little Willie, who had fallen

unnoticed, was left outside, where he soon died from his mortal wound.

Now began a fight for life. There were three men unwounded,—Jareb Palmer, Bradshaw and Markham. The two latter seized each a gun, and, knocking the chinking from between the logs to get sight of the enemy, began firing. Palmer, assisted by Mrs. Thomas, barricaded the door, pulling up puncheons from the floor with which to strengthen it and protect the inmates from bullets fired at the door. Miss Swanger, though wounded, with

MAJOR WILLIAM WILLIAMS,
Commanding the Spirit Lake Relief Expedition.

HON. JOHN F. DUNCOMBE.
Captain of Company B, of the Spirit Lake Relief Expedition.

Miss Gardner, worked at casting bullets, whilst Mrs. Louisa Church herself took a gun and stood at a port hole, firing at every Indian head she could see. And it is believed that she fired the only shot that really killed an Indian. Whilst this battle was in progress at the Thomas house, detachments of the Indians attacked the store, killing the Woodses, and carrying away their goods. It is said the band which had been camping near Springfield during the winter, and upon whose friendship the Woodses relied, were foremost in the attack upon them. Others had gone to Stewart's, killed him, his wife and two children, — one little boy of eight years saving himself by flight, and hiding behind a log. But, strange to say, in their contest at the Thomas house, where they remained until darkness put an end to the conflict, they overlooked the Wheeler cabin, where the two men were lying with frozen limbs, and also the Sheigley cabin, in which Sheigley and his little son were momentarily expecting an attack. At night all became quiet in the vicinity of the Thomas house. And now the inmates discussed the question of flight. It was finally resolved to make an effort to leave. There had been a yoke of oxen in the stable, and, if the Indians had not killed them, it was resolved to hitch them to a sled near the door and start for Fort Dodge. Then the question arose as to exploring the stable, to find whether the oxen were still living. Some of the people in the besieged house believed the quiet was only a ruse of the Indians to get them to expose themselves, when they would rush upon them from their hiding places. Morris Markham volunteered to make the exploration, and, taking his gun, which he was to fire if attacked, he went to the dark stable, loosened the oxen, felt around and found the yoke, hitched them to the sled and drove up to the door. They hastily loaded a few things and, taking on those unable to walk, about nine o'clock in the evening started upon their perilous journey. Dragging through the deep snow all night long, at great disadvantage, as there was no road to guide them, they found at daylight that they had only made about six miles; and, after continuing the journey the entire day, at night they reached the cabin of George Granger, only fifteen miles from where they started. After resting a few hours they continued their journey southward. And here, for the present, we turn to another chapter in this sad drama.

In the fall of 1856, Orlando C. Howe, R. A. Wheelock and B. F. Parmenter left Newton in Jasper county and visited Spirit Lake. They made the acquaintance of the few settlers at the lakes, and after making preëmptions returned to Newton and spent the winter. Early in March they left home again for the lakes. After great hardships they arrived on the fifteenth of March, within a few miles of the lakes, when their team had become so exhausted that they were obliged to leave their wagon and push forward without it. Late at night they arrived at one of the cabins, where they found the evidences

of death and desolation which the Indians had left in their trail some days before. The next morning, on further investigation, they were satisfied that the Indians had wiped out the settlement. They started for Fort Dodge to give the alarm.

They reached Fort Dodge the evening of the twenty-first of March. A public meeting was called and responded to by almost every able-bodied man in town. It was determined to raise two companies of volunteers to march to the scene of the massacre, with the hope of rescuing any of the settlers who might still be living, and if possible overtaking and punishing the Indians. The next morning the two companies organized as Company "A" and Company "B," and elected officers,—Company "A" electing Charles B. Richards as captain, and Company "B" electing John F. Duncombe, each with a sufficient corps of subordinate officers to complete their organization. Runners had been sent to Webster City to represent the situation and invite the people there to join the proposed expedition. On the twenty-third about thirty men marched across the prairie from Webster City, ready to join the command. After arriving at Fort Dodge they organized by electing J. C. Johnson captain, and a full corps of subordinate officers. The whole command numbered something over one hundred men.

As early as 1855 Major Williams had represented to Governor Grimes the danger of an Indian outbreak upon the frontier; and had been authorized by the governor, whenever the danger should seem imminent, to organize the citizens for defense. He was therefore looked upon as the natural leader of the battalion, and was cheerfully recognized as its commander. On the morning of March 24th the battalion started upon its long, difficult and arduous campaign. The difficulties of moving loaded teams, especially through an unsettled country, have been sufficiently indicated. The severe cold of the winter had just begun to moderate. The fact that the great snowdrifts had begun to soften in the March sun rendered the traveling more difficult and uncomfortable than during the intense cold. It was necessary to pull through the deep snow all day, and lie down to sleep at night in boots and clothes saturated with water. The command moved in light marching order. Three ox-teams, hauling the wagons, and three or four riding horses, constituted the transportation. The first day the command made about nine miles, and on the second arrived at Dakota City in Humboldt county. To fully realize the difficulties of the march, it is only necessary to say that, in crossing the great snow-drifts that filled ravines and depressions on the prairie, the entire command would frequently form in two files, about the distance apart of ordinary wagon tracks, and would march and countermarch across the drift, until they had beaten two tracks sufficiently hard to bear up the teams and wagons; when this experiment failed, they would tie a long rope to a wagon, a hundred men would stretch out the length of the rope and then all pull together, and in spite of the resisting banks of snow which would accumulate in front of the wagon, it was pulled through. Frequently oxen and horses were hauled across the snow-drifts by the main strength of from fifty to a hundred men. Each day's march and experience of hardships was but the repetition of its predecessor. On the morning of the third day of the campaign, three or four of the men were absolutely exhausted and ill, whilst two had become entirely snow-blind, so that it was necessary to discharge them. After these were discharged, Major Williams said to the command:

"You now understand this is not to be a holiday campaign, and every man in the battalion who feels that he has gone far enough is at liberty to return."

To the honor of American manhood, it may be said, that there were not more than two or three well men who turned their faces to the rear. The march was continued seven days without other incidents than have been mentioned, except that as the command moved northward the snow increased in depth and the roads became more difficult.

A little after noon, the thirtieth of March, when the advance guard were a few miles north of Medium Lake, they discovered to the northwest what at first they supposed to be Indians. But after moving forward a short distance, they saw a team, and knew they must be white people. On approaching nearer, they proved to be the refugees from Springfield, who now, on the fourth day of their flight, had scarcely made forty miles. They were a sad looking company. Women had waded through snow, and aided in shoveling roads through deep drifts, until their skirts were worn to fringes and their shoes were in shreds. Those who had been wounded in Springfield had not yet had their wounds dressed. They were absolutely destitute of food. Their joy on meeting the command was unbounded. A messenger was sent back to the main command, and the force, with the refugees, moved to the nearest timber and camped. The surgeon of the battalion, Doctor Bissell, dressed the wounds of the poor sufferers who had borne almost insufferable pain for four days and nights. The next morning they were furnished provisions from the scanty supply of the battalion and sent rejoicing on their way southward.

The command now moved forward with renewed vigor, believing that at Springfield they would find the Indians. On April 1st the battalion reached the Granger cabin in a grove on the Des Moines River, within about four miles of the Minnesota state line, and fifteen miles from Springfield. Here it was learned that Captain Bee, with a company of regular soldiers from Fort Ridgeley, had been at Spirit Lake and buried the body of Mr. Marble, and had moved thence to Springfield, and, finding no Indians, had, after a few hours' pursuit on their trail westward, started on their return to Fort Ridgeley.

The battalion now found itself with not over three days' rations on hand, and a hundred miles from the sources of supply. It was conceded by all that it was useless to move farther with the hope of overtaking the Indians. It was therefore determined by Major Williams to detail a small party to proceed to the lakes and bury the dead, supplying them with the larger portion of the provisions remaining, while the main command should return to Fort Dodge. On the morning of April 2d the detachment started for the lakes, and the main command faced about toward home. The third day of the return march, April 4th, the battalion left Medium Lake in a drizzling rain. About three o'clock in the afternoon it arrived at Cylinder Creek, twelve miles south. The march had been the most laborious and discouraging of any since leaving Fort Dodge. It was raining, the sloughs and depressions, which had to be crossed, were filled with snow-slush and were running over with water. Arriving at Cylinder Creek, which in ordinary stages of water is a mere thread meandering through a low bottom, it was found to be fully half a mile wide. The bottom was covered with water at least four feet deep, and the channel was ten or twelve feet deep. Various experiments were made to devise some method of crossing the command. It was determined to cork a wagon-box, two or three to cross in it, and, if possible, stretch a rope over the deep channel, by the help of which it was hoped the wagon-box might be swung back and forth over the channel, the men and teams reaching it by wading across the bottoms. The experiment was made. But when Captains Duncombe and Richards, with two others, had crossed over, barely escaping shipwreck in the passage, the current was so swift, and the wind having turned into the north, it was impossible to return with their ungainly craft, against a head wind. Major Williams was now urged to take the best team and a few wounded refugees and return to Medium Lake, where there were four or five Irish families. This he did. The great body of the men on the north side of the creek began to prepare for protecting themselves as best they could during the approaching night. In the meantime the weather was becoming intensely cold, so that their wet clothes were freezing. They took one of the wagons apart, placing the hind wheels and forward wheels some distance from each other, and over these stretched a wagon sheet, and a tent cloth, which they had with them, pinning them to the ground on the north, east and west. The wind was now sweeping down from the north, the rain had turned to snow, and the temperature was rapidly falling. In short, the Storm King had unleashed all the furies of his Arctic Empire. So, without food, without fire, without dry clothing, the men huddled under their improvised shelter for the night. As the snow increased, some of the more resolute went out and banked the shelter on the north, east and west. Here they remained not only through the night but through the next day and the next night, when the storm abated. But in the forty-eight hours of its continuance it had bridged the Cylinder, so that the entire command, with teams and horses, crossed on the ice. After getting something to eat at Shippey's, about two miles south of the creek, which had been provided for by Captains Duncombe and Richards, who had crossed Saturday in the wagon-box, each man pushed forward towards home.

————

As severe as were the sufferings of the main command, they did not equal those of the detachment which went to the lakes. It will be remembered that when the battalion started upon its return march a detachment started for the lakes, about fifteen miles distant. This detachment arrived at East Okoboji, and the Howe and Noble cabins, about three o'clock in the afternoon. They found the undisturbed dead, and the unbroken silence and desolation which had reigned since the departure of the Indians nearly a month before. They dug graves and buried the bodies, at the Howe and Noble cabins, that afternoon. The next morning they went to the Mattock place and buried the dead, also at the Granger cabin. They finally reached the Gardner house, where they buried the remains of the family. Remaining there through the night, on the following morning they prepared for their march across the prairie to the Des Moines River. As has been said, there was a drizzling rain and the clouds seemed to portend a storm. Quite a number thought it better not to leave that day. Their rations were getting scarce, but the wagon of Howe, Wheelock and Parmenter, which they left on the prairie some three miles east of the Gardner place, two weeks before, was still there, and was, in part, loaded with provision which they could go out and get. But the majority were in favor of going that day, and started in the early morning. R. A. Smith and Messrs. Howe, Wheelock and Parmenter, and one or two others remained. The party which left found a difficult and wearisome journey before them. They met the same impediments, only perhaps more difficult to overcome, that the main command met on its march from Medium Lake to Cylinder Creek. They had to cross streams in which the ice was breaking up, with water overflowing the banks, and sloughs full of snow-slush. In picking their way around sloughs, looking for crossings over streams, they were greatly delayed and wearied. Finally, as has been said, the mild weather of the morning turned to a blinding and pitiless blizzard. Night came on and they had not reached the river. The darkness and storm were so intense that they knew it would be impossible to keep the right course if they proceeded, so they stopped on the prairie. The stronger and more determined kept their feet all night. Among them were Wm. K. Laughlin and John N. Maxwell, who walked back and forth and kept constantly waking and arousing those who were becoming drowsy. Morning finally came. Some who had pulled off their water-soaked boots the night before, found it impossible to get them on in the morning, and had to cut their blankets and wrap their feet so that they could travel.

They could see the timber, however,

and made their way toward it. Coming to a slough too deep to wade, they differed as to the best route around it, and unfortunately some went one way and others took the opposite direction. Finally they began to reach the timber, but as yet found no human habitation. Mr. Laughlin, who was the wiriest, and who during the trying ordeal had maintained a cool judgment and unfailing nerve, gathered some dry leaves from under the trunk of an old tree, loaded his musket with some paper wadding, fired it into the leaves and started a fire. The detachment came straggling in, one after another, until all had reached the timber but two — Captain J. C. Johnson, who commanded the detachment, and William E. Burkholder. They still hoped that these might have reached the river above or below, and as soon as Major Williams, who was at Medium Lake, was made aware of the situation, he sent out men from the Irish colony with instructions to go up and down the river, and search the groves at which they would naturally reach it, still hoping to find them. But the search was vain.

Eleven years afterward, a settler hunting his cattle found their remains and, lying by them, the remnants of their guns, which had been spared by fire and rust. They had nearly reached the timber when, doubtless overcome with fatigue and drowsiness, they lay down to the sleep which knows no waking.

The death of these two young men under these sad conditions cast a shadow of regret and sorrow over the expedition. They were favorites with their comrades. Captain Johnson was a noble specimen of physical manhood ; was intelligent, frank and manly. Every man of his company felt his death to be a personal sorrow. William E. Burkholder was a most promising young man. He had but a few days before joining the command been elected treasurer of Webster county. The fact that his father's family had only arrived at Fort Dodge a few days prior to these events furnished him many reasons for wishing to remain at home ; but he was generous, manly and high-spirited, and could not see other young men going out to endure hardships and meet dangers which he was not willing to accept for himself. And who shall say it is not better to die such a death than to live a long and entirely selfish life !

Before dismissing this part of the story the writer must say a word respecting the officers. Major Williams was over sixty years old, and yet he met all the requirements and endured all the hardships of the campaign with a courage and cheerfulness which was an inspiration to every man under his command. Every officer of the battalion deserves honorable mention. They returned from the campaign with the respect and good-will of every man in the ranks. They could receive no higher tribute.

It only remains now to follow the captives to the end of their captivity. Those who would know the whole sad story will turn with interest to the sketch written from memory by Mrs. Abbie Gardner Sharp, the sole survivor of the massacre, to be published along with this account.

When the Indians returned to Heron Lake, where they had left the captives and their squaws during their raid upon Springfield, they hastily started on their journey northwestward. Day after day they pursued their weary march. The squaws, as is the Indian custom, bore such burdens as could not be packed upon their horses and ponies. The captives were made to carry burdens the same as the squaws. Mrs. Sharp was then a slight and delicate girl, and yet was made to carry a burden nearly as heavy as she was herself. The absolute hell through which these women passed may be faintly imagined when it is recalled that the melting snow in many places was waist deep, into which they would frequently sink to that depth, and at least to their knees at every step, all the while bending beneath the heavy packs which they were forced to carry. The Indians partially avoided much of this torture by their facility in wearing snow-shoes. Six weeks of this experience brought them

to the Big Sioux River. The wonder is that any of them lived to reach this river. Hard as was the experience of all of them, that of Mrs. Thatcher was the most heart-rending. Her nursing babe had been torn from her arms and killed. The repeated colds, which of necessity followed the hardships and exposures of her captivity, had resulted in the illnesses natural to her situation. But with patience and fortitude she endured all the pangs of a hundred deaths and, as the weather grew milder, had really begun to recover, when the inhuman monsters seized the occasion of crossing the Big Sioux on a bridge of brush and logs— which required the steadiest nerve to walk— to push her into the foaming current. She swam to the shore some distance down the stream, but was pushed back by one Indian and shot by another. This ended the captivity of Mrs. Thatcher. The sight of this barbarity climaxed the despair of the remaining captives.

Not long after this, early in May, while they were encamped at Skunk Lake, about thirty miles west of the Big Sioux, two Indians from the Yellow Medicine Agency came to the camp and, after being entertained for the night by Ink-pa-du-ta, they proposed to purchase Abbie Gardner, but were informed she was not for sale. Finally they made a bargain for Mrs. Marble and took her with them to the Yellow Medicine Agency in Minnesota. She and her purchasers gave full information as to the captivity of Mrs. Noble and Miss Gardner. Hon. Charles E. Flandreau, the government agent, and Governor Medary, with the two missionaries at the agency, Rev. Messrs. Riggs and Williamson, as also Colonel Alexander, who commanded at Fort Ridgeley, now put forth every effort to get some of the more friendly and intelligent Indians to proceed to Ink-pa-du-ta's camp and ransom them. It required weeks of negotiation to secure the proper Indians for the mission, and to supply them with the articles which would be likely to secure the ransom. And one of the results of a delay which could not be avoided was the tact that, but a few days before its consummation, a son of Ink-pa-du-ta, because he had not been obeyed in some demand upon Mrs. Noble, who was a most spirited and high-minded woman, had beaten her brains out with a club. When, a few days after the sad death of Mrs. Noble, three strange Indians came into the camp, then on the James River, in what is now Spink county, South Dakota, and seemed to have important business, Abbie Gardner knew that she was the subject of negotiation. After a day or two of talk and bantering she was turned over to the Agency Indians and was borne away to the Yellow Medicine Agency, and on to St. Paul, and to liberty.

————

This is the story commemorated by the monument. It was creditable to the Twenty-fifth General Assembly, after all these years, to have turned aside from the ordinary routine of the legislator to pay this tribute to the pioneer. The two most influential factors in securing this legislation were Senator Funk, of Dickinson county, and Mrs. Sharp. The monument is a beautiful shaft, about sixty feet high, built in alternate sections of rough and polished granite. The commission appointed by the Governor to superintend its building was fortunate in having as a member Mr. Duncombe, an able lawyer and man of experience and affairs, who was himself an actor in these events. After such a lapse of time, to gather the facts and dates, and secure the names, properly spelled, required extensive correspondence and patient investigation. Hon. Charles Aldrich was intrusted with this work, and performed it to the entire satisfaction of his associates. Mrs. Sharp also, by her memory of events and persons, was as efficient in the commission as she had been in securing the legislation for the monument. Hon. R. A. Smith, in the time he devoted to overseeing the erection, from foundation to apex, and in the removal and reburial of the remains, and in the beautifying of the grounds, rendered most important and intelligent service. As long as this granite shaft shall stand, the Okoboji and Spirit Lake Massacre will be a story of thrilling interest and pathetic sadness.

————————

QUATRAINS.

By CLARENCE HAWKES.

ENVIRONMENT.

A WONDROUS shell was thrown up from the deep,
  Where it had lain long centuries asleep,—
  But, in a day, the sunlight and the dew
  Had cracked and stained this shell of wondrous hue.

A CARESS.

A MBITION, where are all thy glories now,—
  The wealth, the fame that I did crave of yore?
  I'd rather feel her hand upon my brow
  Than any crown that monarch ever wore.

HADLEY, MASS.

THE SOLE SURVIVOR'S STORY OF THE MASSACRE.*

By Abigail Gardner Sharp.

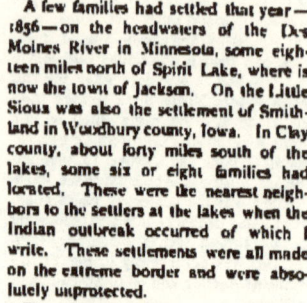

ABOUT the year of 1855 the wild and romantic region of Spirit and Okoboji Lakes began to be viewed as the "promised land" by the adventurous pioneer of that period. My father, Rowland Gardner, and his son-in-law, Harvey Luce, were the first white men to bring their families for settlement in this region. It was in July, 1856, that heavy emigrant wagons drawn by ox-teams brought their passengers to the shores of the Okoboji Lakes. The family consisted of father, mother, two sisters and one brother. My brother was six years old, and I was thirteen. My eldest sister was the wife of Harvey Luce and was the mother of two small children.

A few families had settled that year—1856—on the headwaters of the Des Moines River in Minnesota, some eighteen miles north of Spirit Lake, where is now the town of Jackson. On the Little Sioux was also the settlement of Smithland in Woodbury county, Iowa. In Clay county, about forty miles south of the lakes, some six or eight families had located. These were the nearest neighbors to the settlers at the lakes when the Indian outbreak occurred of which I write. These settlements were all made on the extreme border and were absolutely unprotected.

The winter of 1856-57 was one never to be forgotten by the early settlers of Iowa and Minnesota. The bitter cold, deep snow, and violent storms that winter rendered communication between the scattered settlements almost impossible. Lakes and rivers were frozen to a great depth, and the ground was covered with four feet or more of snow on the level, and in the drifts the snow was fifteen to twenty feet deep. The settlers remained in their log cabins, not daring to attempt the dreadful elements, even for a short journey, unless necessity compelled them to do so.

ABBIE GARDNER SHARP,
Sole Survivor of the Spirit Lake Massacre.

*About twenty-eight years after the tragic events vividly narrated in this paper, Mrs. Sharp published a history of the massacre. The little book was so well received that it has run through four editions and is still selling. Several years ago Mrs. Sharp bought back a portion of her father's homestead, the title of which reverted to the government after the massacre. On this tract stands the log cabin built by her father. This cabin is now that lady's home. It is thrown open to the public during the summer months and is well worth a visit. Its walls are decorated with oil paintings picturing scenes associated with the historic events of '57, also relics and mementoes of pioneer life in the lake region of Iowa. Mrs. Sharp herself receives all guests with unmistakable cordiality.

THE SPIRIT LAKE MASSACRE MONUMENT.
Erected by the State of Iowa, and to be dedicated July 25th.   The Spot where Mr. Gardner fell marked by the Pile of Stones in the Foreground.   The Gardner Cabin on the Right.

The eighth of March, 1857, dawned bright and fair. The rising sun never shed brighter beams than on that ill-fated morning. Spring, that had already come in theory, now seemed near at hand, and the long winter of our discontent to have passed away.

As our family was about to sit down to breakfast, a solitary Indian entered the house wearing the guise of friendship. After the family had partaken of the frugal meal, and the visitor had warmed himself by the fire, my mother prepared a place for him and he ate his breakfast at our table. This Indian was followed by others, until Ink-pa-du-ta and his band of savages, squaws and papooses had all entered the house. They all wanted something to eat, and food was freely given them.

They then asked for ammunition and numerous other things. While father was about giving them a few gun-caps, one of the band snatched the whole box from his hand. At the same time another one, as if by agreement, tried to seize a powder-horn which hung against the wall. He was prevented, however, by Mr. Luce, who now suspected their intentions were to get possession of our ammunition so that we might not be able to protect ourselves. The Indian then drew his gun and would have shot my brother-in-law, had not the latter prevented him by promptly seizing the weapon pointed at his head.

The Indians prowled about the house and yard until noon, when they went off toward our neighbor's, Mr. Mattock's. They drove away our cattle as they went, and shot them down by the roadside.

After the Indians had gone the matter was talked over by the family, as the situation was considered serious, and some measures should be taken for defense.

It was our desire to notify our neighbors

3

of the danger; but if any should go it would weaken the force at home, and the Indians were liable to return at any time.

It was decided that Mr. Luce and Mr. Clark should go to warn the others of the impending danger, while father should remain at home to defend the family. They started out about 2 P. M. An hour later we could hear the reports of fire-arms in rapid succession from the house of our nearest neighbors, the Mattocks. We were then no longer in doubt of the awful conspiracy. Two long hours we passed in this fearful anxiety and suspense, waiting and watching, with conflicting hope and fear, for the safety of Mr. Luce and Mr. Clark as well as for our defense-less settlement.

As the sun was setting father went out to reconnoiter. He hastily entered the house, saying,—"The Indians are coming and we are all doomed to die!"

His first thought was to barricade the door and return the fight with his two loaded guns. He said, "While they are killing all of us I will kill a few of them." But to this my mother, not having lost all faith in these savages, objected — she still had hopes that they would appreciate our kindness and spare our lives. "If we must die," said she, "let us go inno-cent of shedding blood."

Alas, for the faith placed in the stony-hearted savages! The Indians entered the house, and instantly shot my father through the heart. He fell dead. At the same time they seized my mother and my sister by the arms, beating them over the head with their guns and driving them out of doors; they there killed these de-fenseless women in the most shocking manner.

When the Indians entered the house, and during these awful scenes, I was seated in a chair holding my sister's babe, and her little boy and my brother were clinging to my side.

They next seized the children, tearing them from my arms one at a time. The little ones reached out their arms toward me, crying in terror for the protection that I was powerless to give them. Heed-less of their piteous cries the savages dragged them out of doors and killed them with sticks of stove-wood.

During these awful scenes I was both speechless and tearless; but now, alone in the midst of the dying and the dead, it seemed as though I could not wait for the missile of death to strike me, so I rushed forward to one of the band and begged him to "kill me, quick!" He then roughly seized me by the arm with his brawny hand and said something which I could not understand, but I well knew by his actions that I was to be taken captive.

Terrible as were the scenes through which I had just passed, others, if pos-sible even more horrible, awaited me. A tramp of a mile through the snow brought me to their camp, near the house of our neighbors, the Mattocks. Here the sights and sounds that met my eye and ear were appalling. The forest was lighted by their camp-fires and the burn-ing building; the air was rent with the hideous war-whoop of the savages, inter-mingled with the shrieks and groans of two helpless victims confined in the burn-ing cabin. Scattered upon the ground were the dead bodies of thirteen persons, — men, women and children.

Here, amid such scenes as these, in an Indian camp, I spent the first night of my captivity. No tongue or pen can portray the feelings and emotions I experienced during that long, sleepless night.

Early the next morning the warriors painted themselves black — which with the Sioux means war — and again sallied forth on the war-path.

Mr. Luce and Mr. Clark had the day before been overtaken and killed by the Indians a short distance from our home. The other settlers had consequently re-ceived no news of the outbreak while these terrible scenes were enacted in their very midst.

Throughout their whole course, the treacherous Indians got into the homes of their victims through professions of friendship and the claims of hospitality, taking the men by surprise so that they could not defend themselves and their families.

Of the forty persons who were then residents of the lake region at the time of the massacre there was not one left to tell the tale! Every one who was at home was killed except Mrs. Noble, Mrs. Thatcher, Mrs. Marble and myself, whom the Indians took with them as captives on their return to the North.

The massacre was first discovered by one Markham who, being absent from home, returned on the evening of the ninth of March. He found only the dead bodies of his friends and neighbors. He then proceeded to the settlement eighteen miles north of the lakes on the Des Moines river in Minnesota and carried the appalling news.

A rally was made and several families assembled at the house of Mr. Thomas for better protection. They also dispatched two men on snow-shoes across the bleak country a distance of about two hundred and fifty miles to Fort Ridgeley to ask that troops be sent to their rescue.

Meanwhile Ink-pa-du-ta's band, with booty and captives, was moving in a northwesterly direction, camping at night in the groves along the streams and by small lakes, hunting for human game in the person of defenseless settler or unwary traveler.

On the twenty-sixth of March we reached Heron Lake where the warriors left us in camp with their squaws and papooses. Painting themselves again in the most war-like fashion, with rifle in hand and scalping-knife in their belts, they went forth the second time on the war-path.

I leave to ex-Governor Carpenter the description of the events which followed, — the brave and successful defense of the twenty-one men, women and children in the log house of Mr. Thomas.

The assault made by our captors on the Thomas house was vigorously kept up and as vigorously resisted until sunset, when the Indians became weary of firing at blank walls, and ignorant of the number of inmates and not having the courage to charge on the works they returned to their camp bringing in the spoils. On their return they gave us captives to understand that they had met with a repulse from the whites.

I also leave to ex-Governor Carpenter the account of the expedition formed in the settlements to the south of us for the threefold purpose of burying our dead, relieving the survivors if any should be found, and punishing the Indians if they could be overtaken, part of which expedition he himself was — and no unimportant part, either.

Scarcely twenty-four hours had elapsed since the attack on the house of Mr. Thomas when a company of United States soldiers arrived from Fort Ridgeley, under command of Captain Bee. Like the volunteers from Fort Dodge, they had endured almost unheard of hardships and surmounted all conceivable difficulties. They buried the dead found at Jackson, also Mr. Marble, who was killed at Spirit Lake, and came so near overtaking us captors and captives that they reached at 3 P. M. the camping-ground left by us in the morning. When their presence was discovered by our captors, the wildest excitement reigned among them. The squaws extinguished the fires by pouring on water that the smoke might not be seen, tore down the tents and hastened from the camp down the creek, skulking like partridges among the willows and tall prairie grass.

We were encamped on a low piece of ground by the Little Sioux River. Between us and the soldiers was a high rolling prairie, so that the camp was not visible to the soldiers; but the Indians obtained a view from the higher ground, and could see all the movements of their pursuers. I observed one of the Indians creeping along the ground to the base of a tree, some rods from camp on higher ground. He then perched himself among its branches, where he could observe the movements of the troops.

One Indian was detailed to stand guard over us, and to kill us, they said, if there was an attack by the soldiers. The rest of the warriors prepared for battle. The company of United States troops above referred to had suffered much from exposure and fatigue in carrying out their orders to go to Spirit Lake and do what they could to suppress the Indians. When the lakes were reached the Indians were gone. Their trail led to the west, and this pursuit was made by a portion of the command, some mounted on mules and some afoot. An examination was made of the deserted camp and fires by their half-breed guide, and the pursuit was then and there abandoned on the declaration of the guide that the enemy was by their signs several days in advance. The guides being half-breeds, their interests might have been more with the Indians than with the whites; but whether they were true or false, it was like to us captives. Had an attack been made it would have been certain death to us.

After six weeks of incessant marching over the trackless prairies and through what is now known as Lake Madison in South Dakota, we were visited by two strange Indians. They remained over night in Ink-pa-du-ta's camp, and were entertained by pantomimic representation of the massacre. The next morning they ventured to ask for one of the women. Mrs. Marble was the fortunate one. They paid for her all they had.

Just before starting on the unknown journey, Mrs. Marble came to my tent to bid me good-bye. She told me she believed her purchasers intended to take her to the whites. She said if they did she would do all in her power for the rescue of Mrs. Noble and myself.

Though thirty-nine eventful years have passed since that memorable day, the picture of her departure is still vivid in my memory. I can see her yet, as she marched away from the Indian camp, with her purchasers following in Indian file. The last account I had of her was some ten years since, when she was living in California, the wife of Mr. S. M. Sibaugh. She was taken by her purchasers to the agency, and delivered to Charles E. Flandreau, United States In-

THE MASSACRE AT THE GARDNER CABIN.
Mrs. Sharp's Recollection of the Tragedy as embodied by her on an Oil Painting.

THE KILLING OF MRS. THATCHER.
Mrs. Sharp's Recollection of the Tragedy as embodied by her in an Oil Painting.

dian agent for the Sioux, the Indians receiving five hundred dollars each.

Ink-pa-du-ta's band were now far beyond the Big Sioux, in Dakota territory, and probably beyond where any white man had ever been. We passed through an Indian camp on one occasion, where the squaws had planted and raised a small patch of corn. Here about one-half a teacupful of corn was boiled and given to me, the first morsel of food I had eaten in three days. We were compelled to eat whatever was given us or dispose of it unknown to them. The Indians would frequently give me food that I could not swallow,—for instance, fish of which the flesh was so decomposed that it was falling from the bone.

Among the game killed for meat were wild geese, ducks, swans, brants, pelicans, cranes, beavers, otters, muskrats, skunks, etc. The beaver and otter were thrown on the fire and singed to free them of the thickest of the fur, then cut into pieces and pitched into a camp kettle and boiled. The fowls were prepared for cooking by merely pulling off the roughest of the feathers. They were then placed in a kettle without washing or dressing. They were eaten without salt, or seasoning of any kind.

Occasionally there would be a day so cold that even a Sioux would not travel. These days were even more dreaded by me than the wearisome marches.

Through the deep snow, across creeks, sloughs, rivers and lakes, we pushed on until we reached the Big Sioux River, on or about where is now the the town of Flandreau, in South Dakota. There we found a bridge made in time of floods by the trees,—tops, roots and all being borne downward by the current, forming a dam across the stream.

As Mrs. Thatcher and I were about to follow the Indians across one of these uncertain bridges, where a misstep might plunge us into the deep, cold water, an Indian approached us and, taking the pack which Mrs. Thatcher was carrying, placed it on his own back and ordered us to go on. This seeming kindness aroused our suspicions, as they had not offered us assistance under any circumstances whatever. It immediately occurred to Mrs. Thatcher, as well as to myself, that her time had come to die. She hastily bade me good-bye, and said, "If you are so fortunate as to ever escape, tell my husband and parents that I desired to live and escape for their sake."

Mr. Thatcher was one of the four who were away from home at the time of the massacre.

When we reached the center of the river, as we anticipated, the Indian pushed Mrs. Thatcher from the bridge into the swollen stream. By what seemed supernatural strength she breasted the torrent and, making a desperate struggle for life, reached the shore and was clinging to the roots of a tree at the bank when she was met by other members of the band, who were coming upon the scene. With long poles they shoved her back again into the angry stream. She was carried down by the strong current of the Big Sioux, while the Indians on either side of the river were running along the banks, whooping and yelling and throwing sticks and stones at her until she was carried beyond my sight. She was finally shot by one of the Indians in another division of the band, who was crossing on another bridge some distance below. Thus ended the sufferings, tortures and agonies of poor Mrs. Thatcher.

While making this journey through the unbroken wilderness of the Northwest we frequently met parties from the various bands of the Sioux Indians. On or about the first of May we encamped near Big Skunk Lake. We were crowded in the tepee among the young Indians with their dirty faces, who now had a good opportunity to show us their nature. They would fight, pull hair, scratch and bite until their faces were smeared with blood, the squaws not making any attempt to restrain them.

Some four weeks after the departure of Mrs. Marble we fell in with a party of Yankton Sioux. One of them, named Wanduskaihauke, or End-of-the-Snake, purchased Mrs. Noble and myself from the mercenary Ink-pa-du-ta.

One evening, a short time after we were sold, just as we supposed we were settled for the night after a weary march, Mrs. Noble and I were about to lie down to rest when a son of Ink-pa-du-ta came into the tent of the Yankton and ordered Mrs. Noble to go out. She shook her head as a signal that she would not go. No sooner did she refuse to obey than the Indian seized her by the arm with one hand, and, with a big war-club in the other, he dragged her just outside the tent door and there struck her three blows such as only an Indian can deal. The piteous groans of his victim came through the tent and pierced my ears — deep, sorrowful and awful to hear. I did not dare venture out to go to her side, I was so terror-stricken.

Now I was left alone with them — no one to talk to, no one to share with me this bitter cup. Gladly would I have given up my claim on this life ; but, for some unaccountable reason, I was spared.

It was now beautiful spring, indeed, and nature was arrayed in her fairest and freshest robes. As we journeyed across the vast prairies of Dakota, from the elevated points the scenes were really wonderful. Look in any direction, the grassy prai-

INTERIOR OF THE GARDNER CABIN.

rie was only bounded by the horizon. We traveled for weeks without seeing timber. The only things visible were antelope and buffalo and flocks of birds. We were moving farther and farther from civilization, and deeper into the heart of an unbroken wilderness.

A few days after the death of Mrs. Noble we reached the Jim River, in the northern part of South Dakota. Here was an encampment of two hundred lodges of the Yankton Sioux, a powerful branch of the Sioux nation.

I was probably the first white person these Indians had ever seen, and was, to them, a great curiosity. They gathered around my tepee door to look me over, wondering and commenting on my flaxen hair, blue eyes, and fair, though tanned, complexion.

We had been in this camp a few days only when, to me, a most interesting event occurred. By this time nearly all hope had departed, and I was completely overcome by the thought that there was no way of escaping this servitude.

On the thirtieth day of May there appeared in the camp of the Yanktons three Indians wearing coats and white shirts with starched bosoms. I was certain they were from the white settlements as I well knew no Indian women were skilled in the art of laundering white shirts. I soon discovered that I was the object of their conversation. Councils were held after the Indian custom. They sat on the ground, in a circle, and talked and smoked, passing the peace-pipe around. Each Indian took a whiff, then handed it to the next one who sat near him in the circle.

At the end of three days I was delivered over to the "Indians in coats," and the journey toward civilization began. I was ignorant, however, of their good intentions. The price paid for my ransom was two horses, twelve blankets, two kegs of powder, twenty pounds of tobacco, thirty-two yards of blue squaw-cloth, thirty-seven and a half yards of calico, and a quantity of ribbon, with which these Indians had been provided by United States Agent Flandreau. The names of the rescuing party were: Mazaintemani, Ho-ton-ho-washta, and Che-tan-maga. The last-named still survives, and has expressed his intention of being at Okoboji during the summer of 1895.

A deep interest in the fate of the captives had been manifested since the rescue of Mrs. Marble. The legislature of the territory of Minnesota was then in session and passed an act appropriating $10,000, or so much thereof as was necessary, to compass the rescue of the captives, but Agent Flandreau had fitted out the expedition on his own credit before the news of legislative action reached the frontier. Samuel Medary, then governor of the territory, turned the appropriation over to Agent Flandreau to use as he thought best, and to reimburse the outlay made by the agent, the traders, and the missionaries in fitting out the rescuing party and in making presents to the Indians who volunteered their services. Over three thousand dollars was expended by the then territory of Minnesota, under the Governor's and Agent Flandreau's direction, for the release from captivity of Mrs. Marble and myself.

A magnificent monument of granite, fifty-five feet in height and of graceful proportions, has recently been erected upon the site of the massacre by the grateful state of Iowa, at a cost of $5,000, to mark the spot of so much interest in our history. The dedication of the monument, with appropriate ceremonies, will take place on the twenty-sixth of July, 1895, and the occasion will be one of great interest to the people of Iowa, Minnesota, and South Dakota, and to all who are interested in our pioneer history.

IN JUNE.

T̶HOU hast from Heaven a gracious
*   boon,*
When youth and hope and summer noon
*   Possess thy soul in June!*
Glad and free the heart is beating,
Strong and sweet the fresh earth's greeting,
Life within new life is meeting,—
*   All the world's in tune!*
The glorious sun is in the sky,
Brave, youthful hopes are beating high,
The sap leaps free through blooming trees.
To serve anew banqueting bees.
The song of youth's a brief, bright lay,—
So brief, so bright as this fair day
*   In June!*

Thou hast from Heaven a wondrous boon,
When night and love and summer moon
*   Possess thy soul in June!*
Clear and true the bird's song swelling,
From the thrush, in rapture welling,
O'er the earth in rich notes dwelling,
*   Melody is strewn!*
In a kiss that throbs and thrills
The far blue sky meets purple hills ;
So close Heaven clasps the warming earth,
All life is joy, all life is mirth.
The song of love's a short, sweet lay,—
So short, so sweet as this fair day
*   In June!*
        FT. DODGE.

Thou hast from Heaven the dearest boon,
When poet's heart and poet's rune
*   Possess thy soul in June!*
Boughs above with music ringing,
Love, of love the summer's singing,
See thy heart sweet answers springing,
*   Though is gone life's noon.*
In fragrant beauty, stately pride,
With faint, enchanting blushes dyed,
Roses bloom for poet and bride.
The poet's day's a long, long day,
For love and youth will pass away,
A poet is poet for aye and aye,—
*   In June!*

                MARY A. KIRKUP.

EMMABURG AND ITS LEGEND.

BEFORE starting out for our afternoon at Emmaburg, let us recall the romantic legend of the castle. Part of the story, relating to the elopement of Emma, Charlemagne's daughter, with the Emperor's private secretary, Eginhard, was told in THE MIDLAND of November, in my paper entitled "Charlemagne in Legend and in History." The sequel to the story was then promised, and here it is.

Five years after Emma and Eginhard eloped from the imperial palace in Aix La Chapelle, Charlemagne was hunting in the woods south of the city. Noon came and, being hungry, he sought a shady slope near the little lake in the valley and, spreading out upon the grass the contents of his capacious sack, he ate his luncheon and drank his wine. This done, he became drowsy and, stretching himself out upon the grass, he was soon fast asleep. While he slept a little boy happened along and, seeing the Emperor's glittering scabbard, stealthily drew from it the sword and began playing soldier with it. The noise awakened the Emperor. At first angry, his wrath was soon turned to interest in the mock-heroic bearing of the little man. Calling the boy to him, he was so charmed with his frank face and manly manner that he accepted his invitation to go home with him and see his mother.

Hand in hand the hunter and his guide went through the forest to a hut on a rocky height overlooking the lake.

" Da ist meine mutter," exclaimed the child as the door opened and a stout, red-cheeked young woman appeared on the scene.

A moment more and Father Karl and his banished daughter, Emma, were locked in each other's arms, hugging and kissing and crying for joy,—the little fel-

THE LAKE VIEW FROM EMMABURG

low crying too, because he saw his mother in tears! The Emperor forgave his daughter for the crime of choosing her own husband, and Eginhard for the crime of wooing a maiden above his station. He proposed that they return with him to the city and make the palace their home. But they had learned to love their forest life; so with profuse thanks they declined his urgent invitation and Karl went back to Aix alone.

He directed his Italian builders to suspend work on the palace chapel and build a castle for his daughter on the site of the hut where the reconciliation had taken place. And so Emmaburg was built and there Emma and Eginhard and their children "lived happy ever after."

We are off at last for Emmaburg. It is Ascension Day, or, as the Germans term it, "Christihimmelfahrt." This is here a legal holiday. We find the station crowded with people who, like ourselves, are off for a day's pleasuring. When the train to Brussels comes in, there is a great rush for the cars, and though we have second-class tickets, the only seats we can find are in a third-class car.

We find ourselves packed into a compartment which holds altogether four women, three men and five children. While waiting at the station the fast train from Paris comes in. Looking out of the window we find ourselves face to face with a father and daughter, evidently Americans. They eye us with much interest. We fondly imagine them saying to each other, "Quite respectable looking Germans for third-class!" With a well-dressed and pretty German lady on each side of me, and a bright little German boy on my lap, I feel rather proud of my third-class surroundings; and my wife, sitting opposite, between two good-looking Germans, also rather enjoys the curiosity of the strangers.

We quietly slip out of the city and are soon in a long, dark tunnel under a spur of the Ardennes. We come out into a valley of rare beauty, with a small lake in the center.

At Ronheide, a popular resort, many get out. Our party of six, two of them children, have the car to ourselves, and we have great sport watching the boys and listening to their cries of delight as one and another object of beauty passes before us.

"Hegenrath!" cries the conductor, and we get out. The way to the castle is long and we first go to the Casino and take a lunch. We walk about half a mile down a winding roadway to the little lake. There are no fences in sight. Hedges are everywhere to be seen along the roadside and between the fields. We pass many pretty little homes, some built of brick, others of stone. They are whitened with fresh whitewash, or made golden with the rich gold-yellow paint made from the yellow ochre found here. To the left is Atenberg; to the right, Hegenrath. We take the road to the right. As we pass a group of country people, we note that the men touch their hats, or take them off. To us? O, no. Wherever two roads cross, in this part of Germany, a crucifix, large or small, has been set up along the roadside. Pious Catholics, be they peasants or barons, always do reverence to Christ as they pass the cross. As there are many cross-roads they are never long without a reminder of Christ's death.

We are now well out into the valley. Up on the hill yonder are two churches, one Catholic, the other Lutheran. Both are open. The bells are ringing. People are coming from every way to attend Ascension Day services.

Just ahead of us on the right is a big pile of rock surrounded by an iron railing. In the center of the largest rock facing the road is a marble slab. Let us see what it means. Upon the slab are graven the words:

DEN ANDENKEN AN DEN RUHMVOLLEN,
KRIEG VON 1870-1871.
UND DEINE
TAPFEREN STREITER VON PREUSS UND
DEUTM. MOHLARET.
ERRICHTET DEN 27 TEN MAERTZ 1874.
Es ist fruehling geworden,
Im Deutschen Vaterlande.

For the benefit of those who may not be able to more than guess at the meaning of these words, I will add that the tablet is "in memory of the glorious war of 1870-71, and the brave warriors of Prussia and Neutral Moresnet. Erected in March, 1874." Then follows this pretty sentiment : " It is become Spring in the German Fatherland."

The Casino, a pleasant resting-place, stands well up over the lake. Its porch and garden are filled with people eating and drinking and having a merry time. All are talking German except two Englishmen and an English woman, and a gay party of Belgians. Down below, a family party are starting out on the lake in a row-boat, and a little boy sits upon the bow with his feet hanging over into the water. The two boys with us are wild to go out on the lake ; but Die Mutter looks at a little cloud in the west, and says "Nein." That settles it, for as a rule German children have learned the lesson of obedience.

We eat our bread and drink our coffee, and walk around the lake to the south. Standing upon a little bridge we look up the ravine to the east, and there, upon a height south of the gorge, stands the castle of Emmaburg.

I used to think of castles as very grand and very large. Some are. Emmaburg is not. The way they have in Germany of building walls to connect dwellings with barns and stables, forming a courtyard inside, makes the smallest farm-house look much larger than it is.

Standing where you can see the side walls of the great court, with the tall watch-tower in the center, the castle seems immense. It is built of rough gray limestone. The main part is square but its round towers and turrets and queer-shaped iron-barred windows give it a beauty which no amount of modern paint and woodwork could give. A flag flies from the tall tower, giving us a welcome. We climb the steep hill and present ourselves at the arched gateway. No guard disputes our entrance. Things have changed. Once the near approach of anybody to this gate would have been the signal for alarm, and at the entrances and grated windows armed men would have appeared. Huge stones and winged arrows would have made short work of a party of six. Now the castle walls are in

EMMABURG, LOOKING FROM THE TOWN.

ruins and the only dweller in the castle is a little old German who, with his family to assist him, sells beer, coffee, hot milk, and bread and cheese, to all who visit the castle. I say "all," for all are expected to buy something of him, as that is the only way he has of making a living on the place. We enter the large courtyard and look about. The chickens look up at us and cluck and resume their poor pickings. We enter the tall round tower, and there perched upon poles are perhaps a hundred more chickens.

The old guards who a thousand or more years ago were wont to stand looking out of the little windows watching to see if all were well, would be speechless with indignation were they to come to life and see these chickens the sole dwellers in the old tower.

Across the court are the stables and carriage houses of a prince or noble whose name nobody seems to know, and whose crest above the entrance to the carriage house is now become quite dim. So much for fame! But the date, "A. D. 1700," is plainly seen. The barns on the south are a little more ancient. Over the arched entrance from the orchard and fields in the rear is the weather-worn date, "1648."

These buildings are quite youthful compared with the castle itself. The upper part and the roof are new, but the gray-black walls, in places sunken and in places bulging out, the little low-arched doorways, the dungeon-like cellar-way, the iron-barred windows with walls thicker than my cane is long, all tell the story of a time so far back in the past as to make the Landing of the Pilgrims at Plymouth Rock seem almost like an event of yesterday.

We enter. We climb the stone stairs worn nearly round by the feet of many thousand visitors. The little man who haunts the castle bows us into the banquet hall. Soon we are seated at a broad table, at one end of which are a merry party of students with their queer little green caps. At a table by themselves in an alcove sit several youths and maidens. Hot milk, coffee, beer and black bread are spread before the guests. There we sit and eat our "brod" and look out of the west window upon a scene of rare beauty,—the valley green with the new verdure; the lake, a molten mass of silver; the village reaching far up the hill from the north shore of the lake, and over all a sky of deepest blue, now without a cloud. We roam at will through the upper rooms and then down and out, taking a peep as we go into the kitchen where the fat wife of the little ghost of Eginhard warms over the coffee and heats the milk for those who come to see the castle.

It is getting late, and we hurry back, across the fields, to the station.

REPOSE.

THE night-winds sigh and stir the trembling leaves
　　To sweetest lullaby, o'er nodding flowers;
　The starry sky a shimmering garment weaves,
　　O'er prairies wide and iridescent bowers.

LETTS, IOWA.　　　　　　　　　　Albina Marilla Letts.

LINNIE HAGUEWOOD.*

By Bernard Murphy.

BUT few of our middle-western people knew, while reading of Laura Bridgman and Helen Keller, the past few years, that in their midst existed a child similarly afflicted. Yet such is the case.

The subject of this sketch, Linnie Haguewood, was born in Ida Grove, Iowa, October 12, 1879. She was in perfect health and in possession of all her senses until eighteen months old, when she was stricken with spinal fever. As a result of this fever the nerves of her eyes and ears became paralyzed, leaving her both blind and deaf. She did not fully recover her physical health for a long time, and was almost entirely helpless for many years.

At the age of fourteen years, her mother, with the aid of a deaf mute, had taught her about three hundred name words, so she could make many of her wants known. In November, 1893, her parents were persuaded to send her to the Iowa College for the Blind. Her case was thought by the principal to be utterly hopeless, but she was retained and entered as a student. She was placed in the kindergarten, and in a short time showed aptness to learn. During her first year she worked with clay, paper folding, paper cutting, sewing-cards and bead-work. During this year she clearly showed she possessed a good and bright mind. The loss of sight and hearing quickened her memory, and probably no child in Iowa possesses so retentive a memory. During this year, also, one of the pupils took great interest in her and partially taught her to read the "raised print" used by the blind.

At the close of the school year she went home with her teacher, Miss Dora Donald, who, during the vacation, gave her object lessons,—teaching her the use and names of numberless objects. This

*It was fitting that the originator of the movement for the education of this singularly afflicted and singularly gifted girl should be delegated to write for THE MIDLAND a sketch of her life. An additional editorial word may be timely, giving direction and point to the movement so well begun. Mr. R. Murphy, treasurer of the Linnie Haguewood fund (who, by the way, is editor and publisher of the Vinton, Iowa, Eagle), informs us that the trust fund now in his hands amounts to nearly $1,100, and that about $1,900 more will be needed to complete the proposed four years' course. The girl's father is a day laborer and unable to further assist her. The direct purpose of the movement is to give Linnie Haguewood special instruction under a teacher devoted solely to her, either in the Perkins Institute where special teachers are so employed, or under a special teacher in the Vinton College for the Blind. It is to be hoped the purpose so benevolently conceived and the movement so well begun may be further advanced, through contributions from the generous, well-to-do class,—to whom this note of suggestion is directly addressed. [ED.

LINNIE HAGUEWOOD.

was done by the use of the deaf manual. To explain this it is only necessary to say that the "operator" puts her hand against Linnie's, and Linnie catches the letters by sense of touch.

The past year Linnie has made rapid progress and has shown remarkable development of mind. Her memory is so retentive that she rarely has to be told anything more than once. In her beadwork she has learned numbers, and can carry combinations of numbers necessary in constructing bead-work in "chairs," "card cases," "watch cases," etc., in different colored beads. She has also become quite expert in knitting, crocheting and needle work, under the instruction of the fancy work teacher. She has also been taught to swing Indian clubs, remembering the changes and going through the evolutions almost faultlessly.

Linnie has graduated in the kinder-garten and is ready to take up higher studies. In order to do this it is necessary to place her in charge of a special teacher, as she cannot proceed with the regular classes.

By a thorough investigation the writer has become convinced that her mind is susceptible of as full development as any seeing child in the State. In all her work she has shown remarkable progress, and there is no reason apparent why this cannot be continued.

In physique Linnie is well developed for a child of her age; has a well shaped head, well formed features, finely shaped and beautiful hands and arms, and, as her picture indicates, is mentally as well as physically prepossessing.

The school year has closed and Linnie has gone to the home of her parents, who live in Delaware Center, Delaware County.

"WHO'S CRUM?"

By Ed. S. White.

ON MAY 25, at Berkeley Oval, New York City, Mr. John V. Crum, of the State University of Iowa, surprised the champions of all the Eastern universities. Yale and Harvard, *et al.*, had heard of a young Lochinvar coming out of the West, with a remarkable record for fast running. But they were confident that the inaccurate timers of the "omnivorous West" had overrated the boy's abilities. Yale said he couldn't beat Richards; Harvard hoped he could, but she was a doubting Thomas. Pennsylvania shook her head dubiously.

But when the preliminaries demonstrated that Crum was decidedly "in the push," there was an alarming drop in Yale and other Eastern stocks. And Richards dropped a tear from his bright blue eye when he discovered that the little fellow bearing the old gold of the "Corn-stalk" University of Iowa had

carried "old gold" past the theretofore invincible blue of Yale. Horror of horrors! The 100-yard dash had gone to "the Wild West!" And in 10 seconds! And this dire calamity was duplicated when a little later Herr Crum took the 220-yard run in 22 seconds! Yale protested, of course. She said John didn't run as they do in the East, and that his running was not pretty, and, *propterea quod*, he was a professional!

John V. Crum is not yet twenty-three years old. He was born in Bedford, Iowa, September 3, 1872. He is the son of a prominent lawyer and banker of that city. In 1890 he graduated from the Bedford High School, entering the State University of Iowa in the fall of that year. For a year he was not superior to at least fifteen sprinters in the University, and nobody, not even Crum himself, realized the fame in store for him. In his junior year he could defeat all but one man, Henry C. McCluskey, a well-known University athlete. In that year, at Des Moines, he seconded McCluskey nicely, both men defeating Swallum, Grinnell College's representative, in the Iowa State meet of college athletes.

As a senior collegiate Mr. Crum began to show himself a runner, winning at both the home and State meets, and making a record of 10 1-5 seconds on the 100 yards, and 23 seconds for the 220. Going to Chicago he won these runs in a field of forty entries, winning the 100-yard dash in 10 1-5 seconds, and the 220-yard dash in 22 3-5. This performance practically placed him at the head of collegiate runners west of the Alleghanies.

Entering the law department last fall, after graduation with the college class of '94, Crum has had an uninterrupted series of victories, at Iowa City, St. Louis (last fall), New York and Chicago.

He has broken many Iowa State records, not only in sprinting, but in hurdling, having done the 220-yard hurdles in 26 4-5 seconds.

He owns twenty-four medals, and, despite the Yale protest, will receive two Mott Haven laurels.

Mr. Crum is not only an athlete, but he is a gentleman and scholar. He has won renown by conscientious hard work. His efficient trainer, Mr. Ed. C. Moulton, is deserving of praise for his splendid work in developing "the Iowa Wonder." Mr. Crum is a member of Beta Theta Pi fraternity, and also owes allegiance to the Phi Delta Phi legal fraternity. He graduates from the University Law School

JOHN V. CRUM.

this year. If Cambridge and Oxford Universities accept the challenge of the American Intercollegiate Athletic Association, Crum will represent the universities of our great midland region. Crum doesn't smoke, drink, nor dissipate in any way. He believes in the intellectual and moral influence of athletic sports. He says that an athlete "gets so he can control himself at trying times, and a man should learn that he must treat his body well, or it will not return the compliment at the most critical time." Crum's success has a sermon in it.

JAMES F. WILSON.

A SKETCH OF SENATOR WILSON'S LIFE BY HIS TOWNSMAN, C. M. JUNKIN.—
A REVIEW OF HIS PUBLIC CAREER BY HIS COLLEAGUE, SENATOR
ALLISON.—TRIBUTES TO HIS ABILITY AND WORTH BY
OLD-TIME FRIENDS, EX-CONGRESSMAN CONGER,
LATE MINISTER TO BRAZIL, AND EX-
CONSUL-GENERAL BYERS.

Representative Men Series.*

JAMES F. WILSON was born at Newark, Ohio, October 19, 1828. On the death of his father, ten years later, the care of the widowed mother and two younger children was thrust upon him, and from the meager wages of a harness-maker's apprentice he ministered to their support and comfort. With a desire for an education and a love of books, through many long years of study supplemented by the instruction of friends who manifested an interest in the struggles of the brave lad, he acquired what was equivalent to a common school education of that day, with a considerable knowledge of Latin. He began the study of law while working at the bench, and Hon. William B. Woods, afterwards a Justice of the Supreme Court of the United States, gave the young student access to his library and became his preceptor.

Young Wilson was admitted to the bar in his native town in 1851, and enjoyed a year or more of successful practice, but he had determined to seek a newer and wider field. Immediately after his marriage to Mary A. K. Jewett, November 25, 1852, he removed to Iowa and located at Fairfield.

The ability of the man and his conscientious work early commanded recognition, and he soon took a high rank in his profession. But it was not as a practitioner that he was destined to attain the full measure of his success and prominence; and, whatever the promotions that might have been accorded him within the limits of his profession, they could not have been more satisfactory to him nor useful to the public than those coming from his service in the broader field of state and national organic and statutory lawmaking.

Political issues, then in a formative state, gave the young lawyer opportunity for a display of ability and integrity which won for him the confidence of his own people, and he was elected to the constitutional convention of Iowa when a resident of the State only three years, and, with one exception, was the youngest member of a body whose wisdom and concernment for the welfare of the people of a great commonwealth subsequent years have proved.

From a recent Photograph
SENATOR WILSON.

*This series includes "Father" Clarkson, January, '94; Samuel J. Kirkwood, February, '94; James Harlan, March, '94; James W. McDill April, 1894; Gen. George W. Jones, June, '94; Frank Hatton, September, '94, and will include many more prominent public men of the midland region.

48

In 1857 Mr. Wilson was appointed a member of the Des Moines River Improvement Commission. He was elected to the lower house of the General Assembly the same year. In 1859 he was promoted to the State Senate, and aided in the re-compilation of the statutes of Iowa known as the Revision of 1860. In 1861 he was chosen to fill the unexpired term of Gen. S. R. Curtis, in the Thirty-seventh Congress. He was thrice re-elected, his period of service extending from December 2, 1861, to March 3, 1869.

From that time until 1883, when he was elected to the United States Senate, Mr. Wilson was an active factor in the public and political affairs of his State, but held no official position except a membership in the government directory of the Union Pacific Railway Company. So strong was his determination to retire from public life at the close of his service in the House, so intense his desire to devote his time to the interests of his home and his family, that two offers of positions in the cabinet of President Grant were not sufficient to swerve him from his purpose.

Mr. Wilson was reëlected to the Senate in 1888, and had completed his term little more than a month before his death.

It is a remarkable fact that in every convention before which James F. Wilson was a candidate, his nomination was made by acclamation, and that both his retirements from public life were voluntary and announced long before his terms of office expired.

The records of the bodies in which he served bear sufficient evidence of the greatness of this man, the shrewdness of his judgment, the keenness of his fore-sight, the strength of his influence. No history of the legislation of the war period, or of the days of reconstruction, is complete without his name.

It was not as a public man, however, that James F. Wilson left the deepest impress upon the community in which he lived for nearly half a century. There was a loyalty to home about the man, a simplicity in his manner, a domesticity in his tastes, which endeared him to his own

JAMES F. WILSON
On entering the House of Representatives

people. Crowned as his life was with a series of political and professional successes, there was nothing in which he manifested so much sincere pleasure as the deep and tender regard which the friends and neighbors of his youth and manhood were wont to show him. And the purity of his life, his fidelity to every interest committed to his care, the sterling honesty and integrity of the man among all the temptations of public life, his splendid talents so wisely used, made him worthy the admiration of the common people as he was worthy "the love of Lincoln and the trust of Grant."

Mr. Wilson died on the 22d day of April at his home in Fairfield, whither he had gone as soon as his term in the Senate terminated. He had been in ill health for several years, with strength gradually but certainly failing. His remains were interred the Thursday following, and all Iowa contributed to the assemblage which gathered to pay a last tribute of respect to the great statesman and honored citizen.

All the surviving members of his family reside in Fairfield — his widow, his eldest son, Rollin J. Wilson, a prominent lawyer of southern Iowa, Miss Kittie, the only daughter, and James F. Wilson, junior, a promising young merchant.—C. M. JENNIN, *Editor of the Fairfield Ledger.*

SENATOR ALLISON'S ESTIMATE OF HIS PUBLIC CAREER.

Honorable James F. Wilson entered the House of Representatives December 2, 1861, having been elected to fill the vacancy created by the resignation of Honorable Samuel R. Curtis, who was reëlected, 1860, to the Thirty-seventh Congress, and resigned in the summer of 1861 to enter the army as brigadier-general of volunteers. Although Mr. Wilson at this time was only thirty-two years of age, he had served in the State Legislature, in the House and Senate; was a member of the Constitutional Convention of 1856, and aided in the code revision of 1860, and was, therefore, familiar with legislative methods and work. General William Vandever, the only other member of the House from Iowa, also entered the Union army as colonel of the Ninth Iowa Volunteer Infantry, although he did not resign his seat. Thus, during most of the period from 1861 to March, 1863, Mr. Wilson was the only member of the House serving at Washington, from Iowa. This situation imposed upon him great additional labor. Though Senators Harlan and Grimes deservedly occupied commanding positions in the Senate, they could not lighten the necessary routine work of their only colleague in the House, during the absence of General Vandever with his regiment. But this added responsibility gave Mr. Wilson at once great prominence with his colleagues, who learned to recognize his ability and value as a member.

Mr. Wilson was placed on the Judiciary committee during his first term, and was active and efficient in the work of the committee, so that, when the Thirty-eighth Congress was organized, in December, 1863, he was made chairman of the committee then regarded as second in importance, the Ways and Means only

above it in rank. Mr. Wilson remained its chairman during the remaining six years of his service in the House. This committee was compelled to consider the most difficult questions of constitutional and international law. Other important, intricate and novel questions arising out of the War were necessarily submitted to the committee, requiring great labor in their investigation, and its decisions were subjected to the most searching analysis and criticism. Mr. Wilson, as chairman of the committee, fully met the expectations of his friends, and his reports and speeches on the subjects committed to his care exhibited great research and learning, and commanded the respect and confidence of the House.

Mr. Blaine, in his "Twenty Years in Congress," speaking of the young men from the Northwest, entering Congress for the first time in 1861, says of Mr. Wilson: "A man of positive strength, destined to take a very prominent part in legislative proceedings." This statement of him was fully verified in his subsequent career.

Mr. Wilson took an active part in the discussion of all the War measures, and impressed his views upon the House from time to time as respects the organization and maintenance of the forces in the field and as respects the laws which should govern our treatment of the states in rebellion, and the treatment of the freedmen. After the close of the War he took an active part in all the great debates relating to loans, taxation, the raising of revenue and the public debt, as also the reconstruction of the states lately in rebellion, and their readmision into the Union, and other great questions arising out of the War period. Many of these questions, during the War and after its close, were considered of transcendent importance as respects their influence upon the success of the Union cause, bitterly contested then, but now acquiesced in by all as necessary to the faithful conduct of the War and to the restoration of the Union on the basis of justice to all. Most of these questions are now studied only historically as illustrating the wisdom of the men who dealt legislatively with the problems necessary for the restoration of the Union and in aid of the men who were valiantly fighting the battles of the Union in the field.

Of the many questions pressing for solution only two or three can be mentioned by way of illustration in the space allotted to me. First in importance and in point of time is the Thirteenth Amendment to the Constitution, abolishing slavery. Mr. Blaine, in his volumes, attributes to Mr. Ashley, of Ohio, the honor of first introducing this amendment — on the 14th of December, 1863. This is only technically true. Mr. Wilson offered the amendment on the same day, in like terms. These amendments were successively offered upon a call of the states by the Speaker, beginning with Maine. Thus, under the rules of the House, Ohio was called before Iowa, and Mr. Ashley's amendment appears first in the record, though both were offered practically at the same time. Both resolutions were referred to the Judiciary committee, and Mr. Wilson's amendment was reported back favorably by him from the committee and, on the 19th of March he advocated its adoption in a speech of great power. A similar amendment was offered in the Senate by Senator Henderson, of Missouri, in January, 1864, and it was reported in changed phraseology by Senator Trumbull, chairman of the Senate Judiciary committee, using the language now found in the constitution, and, after an exhaustive debate, the amendment passed the Senate on the 8th of April, 1864, with only six dissenting votes. This Senate amendment was taken up in the House, on motion of Mr. Wilson, without reference to his committee, and, after a lengthy debate, failed because a two-thirds vote could not be secured. A motion to reconsider was made by Mr. Ashley, who changed his vote to the negative for that purpose, which motion was not considered until January, 8, 1865, and after the fall election of 1864, when the necessary two-thirds voted for it, and it was submitted to the several states for ratification. It

may be truthfully said that to the joint efforts and perseverance of Messrs. Wilson and Ashley, sustained by all their Republican colleagues and by the earnest coöperation of President Lincoln, this constitutional minority of 1864 was converted into a constitutional majority in 1865. The importance of this amendment and its passage by the Thirty-eighth Congress, rather than later, cannot be overestimated, and the active and effective efforts of Mr. Wilson in its behalf entitle him to receive the lasting gratitude of his countrymen.

When the Thirty-ninth Congress convened, in December, 1865, it soon found itself in sharp conflict with President Johnson, who successively vetoed a series of measures intended to secure to the negro race the rights secured by the Thirteenth amendment, then ratified by three-fourths of the states, and also to protect those in the South who had remained true to the Union. The most important of these was the "Civil Rights Bill," so-called, which passed both houses by large majorities and was vetoed by the President, and again passed by a constitutional majority over the veto, and thus became a law on the 8th of April, 1866. Mr. Wilson had charge of this bill in the House, and, as chairman of the Judiciary committee, offered important amendments to the bill — previously passed the Senate — which were agreed to. Mr. Blaine says, "He supported the bill in a speech of great strength and legal research."

Mr. Wilson actively participated in the preliminary steps to secure the adoption of the Fourteenth amendment.

Late in this Congress, the subject of the impeachment of President Johnson was submitted to Mr. Wilson's committee, the examination to continue during the Fortieth Congress. The investigation was a protracted one, and Mr. Wilson, though entering upon the examination of the question with a belief that the law and practice respecting impeachments rested substantially in the judgment of the Senate as to the character of the offensive acts, after careful study of the law and the precedents, was forced to the conclusion that, at least under our constitution, no federal officer could be impeached for any offense not named in the constitution, or which was not a criminal offense under the laws of Congress. Mr. Wilson made a minority report against impeachment, under the evidence then taken, supporting his decision with an elaborate review of the evidence and of the history of impeachments. This report forms an interesting and valuable treatise on the whole subject. This first attempt failed because a majority of the House sustained the view of Mr. Wilson. Later new charges were made involving the violation of penal statutes. Mr. Wilson, believing that these statutes had been knowingly and intentionally violated, reported from the Judiciary committee a resolution in favor of the impeachment of the President, which was adopted by a large majority, and he was selected as one of the managers by vote of the House, and faithfully represented the House at the bar of the Senate. After a lengthy trial, presided over by Chief Justice Chase, the President was acquitted.

These illustrations show how active and influential he was in the House of Representatives during the exciting period of the War and the acrimonious and turbulent period of reconstruction that followed.

That Mr. Wilson brought to the consideration of these great subjects a clear intellect, a well stored mind, great industry, conscientious devotion to public duty, and exalted patriotism, appears from an impartial view of his work in the House of Representatives.

Mr. Wilson had so impressed himself upon the country and the public men of his time, that General Grant offered him the first place in his cabinet when he entered upon the Presidency. Mr. Wilson's great labors in the House, and his continuous work there, had impaired his physical strength, and for this reason, chiefly, he declined the arduous but highly honorable service proffered. He retired from public life in 1869, but continued deeply interested, and actively participated as a private citizen in the affairs of his state and country.

Twelve years later, in 1883, Mr. Wilson entered the Senate. But in these twelve years great changes had taken place in our country and in the character of the public questions brought forward for consideration; the animosities of the War had partially passed away; the exciting public questions, hotly contested during his former period of service dividing political parties, were now largely acquiesced in by all parties, and questions of a material character chiefly occupied the public mind. It is true that in portions of the South the constitutional guarantees, and laws to secure their observance, which Mr. Wilson had aided in passing during his former period of service, were disregarded, but the situation was such that these conditions could not easily be overcome by statutory enactments.

Mr. Wilson brought with him into the Senate the great name he had achieved in the House and a mind ripened and matured by close study and attention to public affairs during the interval, and he soon achieved a commanding position in the Senate. He was placed upon its important committees. As soon as there was a vacancy he was placed on the Judiciary, and became a valuable working member of that important committee.

Mr. Wilson had been instrumental, whilst a member of the House, in passing a law which fully asserted the power of Congress to regulate commerce among the states, and, as a member of the newly created committee on interstate commerce, he actively aided in shaping and framing the Interstate Commerce Act of 1887.

Until his working power was impaired by increasing ill health, Mr. Wilson assiduously performed his labors in the Senate and in the committee room. He commanded the full respect and esteem of his associates on both sides of the chamber, which is the best test of the usefulness of a member of a legislative or other deliberative body. Although his career in the Senate was not as attractive and brilliant as in the House, it was one of continued usefulness to the Senate and to the country, and through it all he reflected great honor upon the State which gave him her generous confidence and support. Although not as demonstrative as some, he was a sincere, ardent and devoted friend, without deceit and without guile in his relations to friends and to the public.

It was my fortune to serve with him in the two houses for a period of eighteen years. During that period, we often differed as to measures and policies, but during all this period of service, and during our acquaintance of more than thirty years, our friendly relations were never in the slightest degree disturbed. His uniform kindness and helpfulness was appreciated by his colleagues, who always had the benefit of his knowledge and his judgment respecting men and affairs affecting the interests of our state and country. A character so well poised and so true and just will, I am sure, long be appreciated by those who knew him well, as also by those who study the history of the eventful period of his public service and useful life.— Hon. WILLIAM B. ALLISON, *Iowa's Senior Senator.*

TRIBUTE OF A CONGRESSIONAL COLLEAGUE.

I MET Senator James F. Wilson for the first time as a guest in my home, when in perfect health and in the strength and vigor of robust manhood. I met him for the last time at his own fireside, when the hand of disease had been laid heavily upon him. Twenty years of a busy, eventful life had sped meanwhile, but in all these years he had been my admired, loved and trusted friend.

Senator Wilson was one of Iowa's greatest men and the peer of any man in the nation. His early career in the House of Representatives was marked by a rapidity and brilliancy of development scarce equaled and never excelled by any service of equal length in the legislative history of our country. His later life in the United States Senate was marked by a power and influence exerted, and by an effectiveness of accomplishment surpassed by none. He was a model patriot and statesman, and all who knew him believed and trusted him.

He was in the Senate when I entered Congress, and I very early sought his advice. I shall never forget with what kindness, yet earnestness, he said to me, "If you simply want to get along easily here, and avoid criticism and opposition at home, then watch the course of Mr. —— (a member of long service, but a known trimmer and demagogue), and follow him. But if you want to do something, to be something, and accomplish something, then take the trouble to investigate for yourself, determine what is right, and then take the risk of standing by your own convictions."

This he always did. He used his own eyes, his own brain, and always fearlessly uttered his own thoughts, with a boldness and courage that made him an enviable example for all his colleagues. He never jumped at conclusions, but invariably approached them by a regular and systematic course of study and reasoning, and, when he reached a conclusion, it was to him as clear and satisfactory as a demonstrated mathematical problem, and upon it he rested immovable; and, utterly regardless of popular censure or applause, he held his course as true to the line of his convictions as the needle to the pole. He had the courage to do that which he believed to be right, always and under all circumstances.

There is no place in the world where the measure of a man is more quickly and accurately taken than on the floor of either branch of Congress. This measurement placed James F. Wilson high up on the roll, and marked him a veritable giant.

Congressional work is so varied and so overwhelming that it is utterly impossible for any one man to thoroughly investigate or grasp it all, hence it is parceled out to various committees, and often each must necessarily depend for his information upon the research and judgment of some

other. Senator Wilson's grasp of questions was so quick and comprehensive,
and his judgment so clear and unerring,
that no man's advice was oftener sought
and followed than his. All knew that
when he rose to speak, it was because he
had something to say,—something that
was the result of work, of thought, of
conviction; something that was worth
hearing, and worth heeding. Such faith
had his brother senators in his wisdom,
integrity and patriotism, that he had only
to ask their aid to insure their support for
any bill he might propose or advocate.
This fact, supplemented by his great ability as a speaker, gave almost universal
success to every measure that he earnestly
espoused or championed.

As a citizen, he was of the highest type;
as a friend, he was ever kind and true;
as a husband, he was tender and thoughtful; as a father, most loving and indul-
gent. His family circle was truly, and in
the strictest sense, a home. He always
gave every spare moment from his professional and public duties to his family,
and was idolized by every member of it.
His children and —

"His loving wife beguiled him more than
    Fame's emblazoned zeal,
And one sweet note of tenderness than Tri-
    umph's loudest peal."

In the kindness of his great heart, in
the depth and strength of his friendship,
in the tenderness and trustfulness of his
love, in his devotion to duty, in the incomparable power and unstinted reverence of his intellect, in his faith that
over all is God, blessed and blessing forever,—he came up to the full measure of
the noblest manhood. A splendid type
of those men who have given strength
and glory to the past, and promise security and perpetuity for the future of our
republic.

Of course he had his faults. He must
have had, else he could not have been
human. But I did not know them, and
now, as I reflect upon his life and work,
I still fail to find them.

Some characters attain their greatest
stature during this life, and the light of
example begins even to diminish at their

death. But the reputation and character of James F. Wilson will continue to
grow, and the more it is studied and the
better it is understood the more refulgent
will be the light of its example.

The memory and influence of his pure
and positive life will live when the chisel-
ings of marble have been effaced and
when the emblems of mortal greatness
have decayed forever.

It is indeed an inestimable blessing for
Iowa and the nation that such a man has
lived, and it is a most happy fortune for
our youth everywhere that such a standard of high character has been left them;
and that such a model of superb statesmanship, splendid citizenship and ideal
manhood is thus their priceless heritage.
May they properly appreciate it and emu-
late it.— HON. E. H. CONGER, Ex-Mem-
ber of Congress and Late Minister to
Brazil.

TRIBUTE OF AN OLD-TIME FRIEND.

JAMES F. WILSON is quietly lying among
the trees and blossoms that he loved so
much, down at Fairfield. He was a true
friend of nature. Not one public man in
a million gets so much out of the woods
and flowers and green grasses. Was it
not this constant communion with nature that made him so good a man? Senator Wilson *was* a good man; a good
friend, a good patriot. He could have
been nothing else. He was by nature
true, simple, kind. His great political
success in life was as much due to his
constant sincerity as it was to his native
ability. What a character to possess!
Everybody trusted James F. Wilson's
word. Every man and woman who had
to do with him knew him to be honest.
He pretended nothing. All was open
sincerity with him, and he never looked
in two directions at the same time. He
hated shams, and he despised political
trickery. His whole life was summed up
in the practice of common sincerity.

Of ambition, in its ordinary sense, he
possessed none at all. To him a good
deed was its own reward, and he permitted no one to rush to the newspapers

to tell what good thing he had done, or what he might politically have deserved. He was true to his party,—true to his State,—but, above all, he was true to himself. Had he desired open reward for benefits he conferred on legislation, good government and party honor, he could have had it without the seeking, and in the highest degree. It is not every public man who can decline great promotions when urged on him. Mr. Wilson could do that. He was great enough to do it. In all his career he was never a self-seeker. His hand and his heart were forever open to others. Absolute unselfishness is the surest road to friends and honor in any country. Senator Wilson traveled that road all his life.

It matters little whether he died in office, or out of office; In his seat in the Senate, or on his beautiful farm among the flowers. Those who knew him best honored his life for what it was, not for the accident of place or fortune. They loved and honored the kind, simple man with the warm heart and the strong head. His judgment was nearly infallible in political things. He studied them for what they were, and not for their mere time-serving uses. He was a statesman, not a politician. The eclipse to his bodily health, in recent years, was a sorrowful loss to the State he loved. With his time out in the Senate, he hoped to spend the years left him among his trees and with his friends,—and then, suddenly, came the end, and he was laid away among the blossoms.

His funeral was a notable one. At two o'clock of that beautiful April day it seemed as if all the men and women in all the county were wending their way to the saddened home to have one last look on a face that had been familiar and honored among them for forty years. Senator Wilson, the statesman, was not thought of. It was "Mr. Wilson, our

friend and neighbor." The loss seemed absolutely personal to the whole community. A stronger test of true greatness could not be imagined. What matters it what the public or the politicians may think of us when we are dead? What did those who had most to do with us think of us? That is the test. And Mr. Wilson's character stood that test to the very end. The day was such a one as he would have chosen, for he was so in tune with nature all his life. Never had Iowa seen so many blossoms. The roadsides to the cemetery were one grand bouquet of fragrance; the grave itself was lined with delicate flowers. On every hand was heard the expression, "Oh, if he could only have seen these blossoms, and this beautiful day!"

They put him away to sleep among the flowers, and, so rounded out and perfect was his life, they will forget that he is dead.

The town was in grief. All business was suspended; flags hung at half-mast; people spoke in low tones, and sorrow was on every face. Whatever the world may have thought, his friends said, "We have buried a noble man."

Senator Wilson was, in the true sense, a great man. He built with his own hands the ladder on which he climbed to national success. Good men honored him, and all men gave him their confidence. What more can a noble man want? He died lamented. His monument will be his name. On the way to the cemetery the great procession passed by the draped library building, which he had helped endow, and which owed its very existence to his constant labor and friendship. It, too, will be his monument; and so long as Iowa honors noble character, unselfish life, and self-made fame, the name of James F. Wilson will not be forgotten.—MAJOR S. H. M. BYERS, *Late Consul-General to St. Gall, Switzerland.*

MIDLAND WAR SKETCHES. IX.

TRUE STORY OF A MOTHER'S LOVE AND DEVOTION.

By Captain J. E. Duncan.

ANENT the sad tragedy of Private John Tompkins, Seventy-seventh Illinois Volunteer Infantry, related in the December MIDLAND, the following sketch may not be uninteresting.

The 4th day of August, 1862, was Blue Monday. Alone in my office, I sat drumming mechanically on my desk, thinking of the precious lives that had been sacrificed in the effort to maintain the Federal Union. Without, the day was cold and cheerless; the air and mist drove us for warmth to the fireside; the clouds were dull and heavy, and a fog hid the beautiful Pecatonic River from view. Suddenly the door opened, and my friend Waring entered. I eagerly exclaimed, "Charley, let's raise a company and don the blue!"

From photo taken [illegible]

CAPT. J. E. DUNCAN,
Co. B, Twenty-third Wisconsin Infantry.

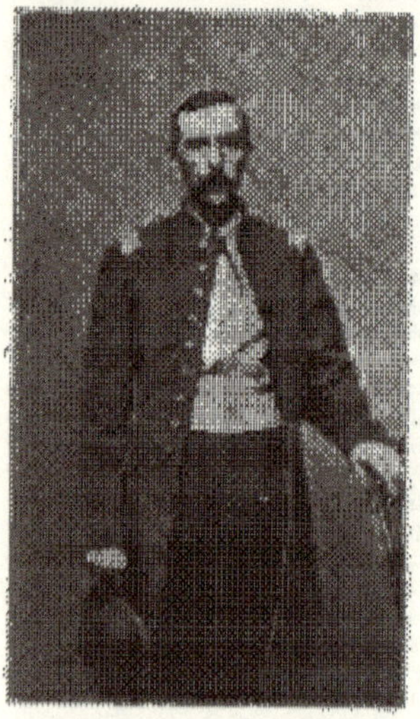

"Agreed!" said he, with equal animation. "I feel that History is being made," continued Waring, with earnestness, as he came and stood at my elbow, "and I have no part in it."

Two weeks later we had enlisted two hundred stalwart young men, divided them into two company organizations, elected officers, and tendered the commands to the government. Before the close of the month Company B was enrolled in the Twenty-third Wisconsin Volunteer Infantry and mustered into the United States service, — Waring captain.

Among our number was a young man named George Ray, son of a widow who resided among the willows, in the vicinity of the recruiting station. Mrs. Ray was a woman of deep piety and patriotic impulses, and a devoted mother. George was her pride, and Mrs. Ray's consent to his enlistment was only obtained after frequent appeals to her patriotism. She finally threw her arms around her son's neck and, with tearful eyes, bade him go, breathing a prayer for the protection of her boy. George was an intelligent, manly young fellow; his life had been devoted to his mother. Her comfort and happiness were his first care, and the most enjoyable part of his youth was found in unselfish contributions to her welfare. George's character was fashioned by the prayers and pious admonitions of Christian parents. His life was honorable and upright. To a pleasant face he added an agreeable manner and a kind heart. To his comrades he was gentle and courteous; and he rapidly won the respect and confidence of his

MOTHER AND SON — MRS. RAY AND HER SON, GEORGE.

superiors. To his lovable qualities was added a courage that knew not fear.

We left Madison, Wisconsin, early in September, and, after a holiday in Kentucky, December found us in Memphis, and Christmas and the new year in the Yazoo bottoms, north of Vicksburg, with "Uncle Billy Sherman."

We failed to capture the Gibraltar of the South. Charge as frequently, impetuously and fearlessly as we would, the blue coats could not scale the palisades of the Walnut in the face of a fire that swept them down to a man. We retired with honor and waving flags, but without the coveted victory.

Our ranks were thinned daily by battle, disease, and the hardships incident to a campaign in a country filled with malaria. Captain Waring was sent to hospital at Memphis immediately on leaving the poisonous atmosphere of the Yazoo — the River of Death. Two short months thereafter we received news of his demise. He had made his contribution to

history with his life. Our hearts were bowed with sorrow when we learned that a life so full of patriotic energy, so filled with heroic fervor, had gone out. Only with their lives will die the love which Company B bore for the genial, kind and gentle officer, whom they honored with their unanimous suffrages for their commander.

The Federal forces, under command of General John A. McClernand, landed three miles south of Arkansas Post on the evening of Saturday, January 10, 1863, while the gunboats "De Kalb" and "Louisville" forged ahead and engaged Fort Hindman. The Twenty-third Wisconsin made its bed that night on the ooze and sodden ground near the fort, and at early sunrise debouched from the timber into the open, which was swept by the enemy's artillery and sharpshooters. Nearly all day the conflict raged, and with heavy loss on the part of our forces, which were always exposed, while the enemy was sheltered by breastworks.

At 4 P. M. the Twenty-third Wisconsin swept over the Confederate rifle-pits and into Fort Hindman in a magnificent charge, headed by Gen. S. G. Burbridge. The works were ours, with four thousand prisoners; and the beautiful flag of the Twenty-third was the first to be unfurled in the Confederate stronghold.

Our loss had been heavy—Company B suffering more severely than the other company organizations.

Among the first to fall was George Ray, shot through the lungs. Though his wounds were mortal, he had sufficient strength to drag himself from the line of battle into the timber. And there, making a pillow of his knapsack, he lay down to sleep—to die—calm, peaceful and serene, his life work done. We found him after the battle, his eyes and lips closed, and his hands folded across his breast. There was no evidence of suffering; his was a gentle, peaceful, painless passing to the other shore.

The night was closing about us when

From an old photo taken in New Orleans, 1860.
CAPT. C. B. WARING.

the body was discovered, and hastily we prepared our comrade for interment. Under the swaying forest pines we dug his grave, and in a rough coffin we placed his mortal remains. While the winds whistled a mournful dirge, and the stars hid their faces, and the storm-clouds scurried above us, and the thunder and lightning mocked our sorrow, we knelt above him in prayer, and then, tearfully, filled the grave with earth and returned to the fort.

———

With considerate tenderness we gently broke to the stricken mother the sad news of her son's death. It came to her, as we had anticipated, like the sudden crash of a great ship upon an unseen rock. She seemed paralyzed by the severity of the blow; she sank down as if crushed by an unseen hand. But she rallied,—with wonderful vitality,—and at once began preparations for a journey to Arkansas Post to recover the body of her son and bring it back to her Wisconsin home.

Making all needful preparations for the journey before her, Mrs. Ray left her home in February following the capture. At Memphis she purchased a mule, harness and cart, and, crossing the Mississippi, she proceeded on her long and lonely journey. By the highways, uncertain paths and devious byways that she was compelled to pursue, Arkansas Post was distant several hundred miles. It would be needless to accompany her day after day, as she wended her solitary and perilous way. With no direct route that she could follow with measurable certainty, she nevertheless pushed forward with remarkable speed. No obstacle seemed to daunt her. In a strange and unknown country, among a people hostile and bitterly antagonistic, physically helpless if attacked, and dependent upon the inhabitants for food for herself and beast, camping at night alone, and frequently far from habitation, with the cry of the wolf and wild-cat breaking her rest and kept at bay only by the flickering blaze of her camp-fire; through wood and marsh and thicket, over swift-running streams with treacherous quicksand, by obscure paths, through fields of mire and slush, in rain and sleet and snow, in storm and sunshine — on — on — and on, this frail, feeble mother pursued her way, with one object in view and one purpose in mind.

She neared the end of her journey, and hope lightened her heart and hastened her step. A restful smile played upon her sad face. But, alas! how soon were all her hopes and anticipations to be dashed to the ground! The hardships and perils encountered by this courageous soul were to go for naught.

Mrs. Ray was within a few miles of her destination, when she encountered a band of ruffians who not only refused to permit her to complete her trip, but also confiscated her outfit and drove her back. All her prayers for permission to continue her journey to the end fell upon hearts of stone, and she was ruthlessly, and with violence, turned back and forced to retrace her steps.

In course of time this heart-broken mother reached her Wisconsin home — sick and weary, and well-nigh the end of life's journey. She had proven herself a heroine worthy the name. Could frail, feeble woman do more! Had not her sacrifices been great, her courage beyond her strength, her efforts heroic!

Her purpose, however, was unshaken. She did not for a moment surrender her intention. Naturally feeble and prostrated by her unusual exertions and the hardships she had endured and obstacles she had to overcome, she waited only until she had recruited her health and was physically able to again make the attempt to reach the Post. Then she prepared for a second journey. The arguments and pleadings of family and friends availed nothing; nor did the dangers, privations and hardships previously experienced affect her purpose. A mother's love! — to what depths will it not descend — to what heights will it not

rise! To what can we liken its power! Who can record its intensity!

Another journey by rail and steamer to Memphis; another purchase of mule, harness and cart; across the Mississippi River into Arkansas; and once more the start is made for the Post. It is now the early springtime. The rains descend and swell the streams; the roads are deep in mud; paths are obliterated; and here and there and nearly everywhere on the route she encounters the rough riders of the Confederacy. But the dear old mother, her heart swelling with hope, pushes on. She encounters unexpected obstacles on her way. At one time the mad current sweeps her down stream, and at another she narrowly escapes a watery grave. — mired in apparently unfathomable sloughs, sinking deep into marshes, and almost buried in treacherous quicksands. But she had never known the word *fail.*

She was weeks on the road, and had arrived at a point on the Arkansas River not far distant from the place of landing of the Federal troops on the 10th of the previous January. She was within hearing distance from the battle-field. She could almost see the very tree-tops under which reposed all that was mortal of her son. And from her heart welled up prayers of gratitude that her long and perilous journey was at an end, and she was about to realize the object of her mission.

Alas! we propose and plan and toil in vain! From out the deep, dark wood issued the same body of Confederates that had before crossed her path and stood between her and the realization of all for which she had so heroically striven. Why pursue the sad tale further? Her tears were vain; her sobs and prayers and pleadings fell on callous hearts. With cruelty that has few parallels she was driven back, with the loss of all she had. Discouraged, disheartened, weary of life, a few years later she joined the idol of her mother-heart.

JIM HENRY.

I DOTE on frisky horses, grand military men,
And big volcanic characters that wrestle with the pen;
But matrimony 'pears to be a game of pitch and toss,
An' she who plays the winnin' hand has got to be the boss!

So I set my stakes in airly life an', carryin' out my plan,
I lighted on Jim Henry, a meek an' lowly man;
He was tol'able good-lookin', an' fairly well-to-do,
With an easy disposition, like a stretched-out rubber shoe.

It was leap-year when Jim Henry first visited our town,
He was shy as a spring chicken till I promptly ran him down,
An' some folks hed the cheek to say 'twas me that popped the question,
But 'twasn't so! I merely smiled and gave him a suggestion!

We just was spliced an' settled when the War come on to stay,
An' men was musterin' companies an' marchin' 'em away;
I didn't think Jim Henry would ever want to fight,
Or I never should have trusted him a minute out of sight!

It struck me like a typhoon, or a fit of gastric cramp,
When I found he hed enlisted an' was goin' off to camp,
I raved, an' he was speechless; I biled, an' he was ca'm,
An' while I was exhortin' he was happy as a clam.

The voice of patriotism fur me hed little charm,
When I wanted my Jim Henry to stay and work the farm;
An' he couldn't sharp-shoot rebels, sevin' how he lacked the sense
To bit a brahmy chicken on the nearest barn-yard fence!

But he went an' saw the circus, with all its smoke and noise,
As' I guess his courage averaged with the other soldier-boys;
He fit an' marched and manœuvred, eat hard-tack an' salt beef,
Till a shell exploded in his ear an' made him awful deef.

Then, after the fights was over, after the Rebs was thrashed,
After the boys come marchin' home, king-hearted and mustached,
Many a gentle pardner, toughened by army rule,
Was, like my meek Jim Henry, as stubborn as a mule.

He was just as slow an' easy as in the days gone by,
His talk was plain an' comf'table; but when he saw me try
To drive him or to scold him, his hand went to his ear,
An' the more I screamed an' shouted, the more he wouldn't hear!

Bymeby he got a pension, an' then I thought 'twas time
To claim my rights; an' so I writ the President a line.
I said: "Dear sir,— I take this chance to state my case in brief:
Jim Henry is a pensioner, an' he is dreful deef.

"I'm a dependent relative, his poor, afflicted wife,
An' the desperate situation is a-wearin' out my life!
My tongue is dry as leather, my voice can't raise a note,
An' I've got 'bronchitis' in my chest, an' quinsy in my throat.

"All these hev come from shoutin' through the holler of his hand,
An' what he doesn't relish he won't try to understand!
All these is disabilities; Jim Henry is their cause,
An' I hope you'll try to shape 'em so's to fit the pension laws.

"But if no rulin' hits me, bein' how my cause is just,
Jest pass it on to congress—a strictly private trust;—
An' git up something special, as a bright act of your life,
A bill made to 'identify' Jim Henry's patient wife!"

I sent this on to Washington as soon as the ink was dry,
With postage stamps inside of it to bring me a reply,
It came too soon to suit me; 'twas my letter backward fired,
With these words scrawled upon it: "No answer is required."

That clinched the female question furever more fur me!
I yearned to swing the ballot-box an' set all 'mankind free,'
Jim Henry fought fur liberty an' generous pension drew,
While I, who've yelled fur liberty, could never git thar, too!

An' so a sufferin' suffragist is what I call myself,
With bitter disappointments laid by on Time's broad shelf;
Still shoutin' to Jim Henry in life's sere and yellow leaf,
I find a meek and lowly man's a terror when he's deef!

SUMNER, IOWA.   *Emma Eggleson.*

COL: DE JARNETTE:
An Incident
OF
PIONEER DAYS
in DAKOTA

By John Drake.

A DOZEN years ago a number of men were gathered at the depot of a little Dakota town awaiting the arrival of the daily train from the East. Does the reader know anything of the Dakota of those days? The country was new, very new, and the great sea of prairie that stretched away from the railway which had been pushed through to the Missouri River, was then unbroken by the habitation of the pioneer, except in the vicinity of those few places where towns had been located. In those early days the population of the country was composed almost wholly of men, creating a condition that cannot well be described in story, a personal experience being necessary to a full understanding of the peculiarities that characterize men in such a state. In the town of which we write no woman had ever set foot. Its business men were young, shrewd, and, as a rule, well edu-

cated; in fact, the kind who are always first to grow tired of the prosy old towns of the East, and who possess the nerve to go west to help build cities in harmony with their own ideas. It was by such as these that Mirage City had been platted, boomed and built up. But, for all their courage and hardihood, the new condition developed a feeling of homesickness that was general. Letters from the States were anxiously awaited, and the traveler hailing from the East who stopped off in Mirage City found himself the object of cordial attention. Even the train from the East was looked upon as a messenger from a beloved land, and it seldom pulled into the little depot that it was not met by a large representation of citizens. Indeed, so generally was that practice observed that the engineer learned to expect every citizen to be occupying his accustomed place on the platform, and the absence of one brought an inquiry as to the cause. On the day of which we speak an old gentleman was the only passenger to alight. His was a queer, pathetic figure

—thin, haggard, forlorn, and yet he had an indescribable dignity. The smile that occasionally lit up his pale face, and for the moment drove away its sadness, was mysterious, inscrutable. His single piece of baggage was a queer-shaped box which he kept constantly in his arms, as though afraid of losing it. Without addressing anyone in the crowd, he walked across the vacant lots between the depot and the town, and entered a building over the door of which was the sign "Hamlin County Bank," in prodigious letters of yellow, the purpose of the imitation of gold being, no doubt, to impress the community with the stability of the institution. To the cashier the newcomer introduced himself as M. de Jarnette, Charlotte, S. C. He was a perfect type of the old school of aristocracy which existed in the South before the War. His education was manifest by the beauty and purity of his language, his culture by his gracious and polite mannerisms, and his aristocracy by that air of refined dignity and pleasing rather than objectionable independence which marks the blue-blooded Southerner.

One by one the residents of the town dropped into the bank, ostensibly on business, but in reality to learn something of the stranger. They were curious to know, when told from whence he had come, what had caused the man, so far advanced in years, to leave a land of sunshine and flowers to journey to a region where reverse conditions might be expected, — but on that point the Southerner was silent. However, they were to be gratified concerning the queer-shaped piece of baggage. After being placed in possession of such bits of information as a stranger in a strange land would naturally seek, the old gentleman opened the box. It contained a model of a machine the character and use of which the Mirage City-ites could not even conjecture. It was removed and placed carefully upon the counter, and the old gentleman, in a finely modulated voice, began :

"Gentlemen, this is not a solution of the problem of perpetual motion ; not a conglomeration of superannuated clock-work, but a machine that will demonstrate a new principle in mechanics. To claim perpetual motion would be to insult your intelligence, hence I ask you to examine what I term a self-sustaining motor. In this machine gravity is not only overcome, but is made to furnish a share of the power desired. Added to that is centrifugal force, and from that combination we have the new power that leaves to steam the ruling of the wave, but snatches from her grasp her long-held supremacy on land," etc., etc.

It was evident to his audience that the old gentleman had labored upon the contrivance until his mind had suffered. He was a victim of the perpetual motion delusion, albeit like others he professed to believe the notion to be a mechanical absurdity.

The model was in the shape of a top, the small end working in a socket, the large end describing a circle in its movement. Around the model, extending from bottom to top, was a spiral railway. By placing an iron ball on the lower end of this railway and moving the upper end as described, the ball would travel toward the top and yet be moving on a downward incline. It was thus that "gravity was overcome." The centrifugal force was obtained by the increasing speed of the ball as it traveled around the circle. But like all machines of its kind before it, the self-sustaining motor lacked something. It was not quite finished. The wheel that would start it in motion had yet to be made and placed in position.

Joe Catlett, the mechanical genius of the town, was first to examine the machine, the others gracefully acknowledging his title to that distinction by remaining in the background : and, although he gave it as his opinion that the thing wasn't worth a tinker's malediction, so far as its practical utility was concerned, he promptly bought and paid for a share of stock in the Self-Sustaining Motor Company, which by that time the old gentleman had organized. This action of

Joe's, and also the care-worn appearance of the aged inventor, touched the sympathies of the men, and soon the Self-Sustaining Motor Company had a number of new shareholders. An arrangement followed by which the old gentleman was to use a house located on a hill to the north of the town for a workshop in which to build a motor. Work on the machine was begun at once, and soon the whole community became interested in it. On Sundays the shop was thrown open for inspection of the work, and crowds of visitors called regularly to note the progress made. On various occasions the inventor gave lectures in the grain elevator,—it was there all public meetings were held,—and they were always well attended. The fact was, the residents had no faith whatever in the success of the motor, but they sympathized with the deluded old man, and his talks were interesting because of his eloquence and evident sincerity. When his rations got low, a shopping tour always resulted in a replenished larder, although no cash ever changed hands. The butcher, the grocer and the baker all accepted the stock of the Self-Sustaining Motor Company in exchange for goods, and thus the same became, so far as he was concerned, a recognized legal tender in the town. With this condition of affairs the pinched and haggard look finally left the face of the old man, his step quickened, and color took the place of pallor in his cheek.

It occurred to "Doc" Hess — Doc was from Missouri, and a Missouri democrat of the old school — that George Loar, an exasperating republican, with whom he regularly argued politics, would probably have his ideas of the "late unpleasantness" corrected should he hear the inventor's story of the War and its causes, but the old gentleman evidenced his fine sense of propriety by politely declining to talk upon the subject. Doc tried harder than ever to induce the old Southerner to reopen the issues that had been dead for a quarter of a century, when he saw one day an epauleted gray

coat among the articles which the old man treasured; but a simple though interesting account of a meeting with General Grant was the only war reminiscence he could be prevailed upon to narrate.

"It was early in November of '61," said he, "following Grant's capture of Belmont. I was a colonel of the Confederate forces through which the Federals had to cut their way to reach the transports, and was one of the few prisoners taken by Grant in that affair. That evening I was taken before the General, who evidently hoped to learn something of the plans of the enemy. My gray hairs must have touched him, for, on looking me over, his demeanor became so courteous, if not to say kind, that the conversation which followed was anything but that to be expected between captor and captured. When the General had become convinced that to further question and cross-question me would be useless, he turned to broader phases of the strife, and appeared to be anxious to get at the opinions and feelings of the common soldier of the Southern army. Kentucky was then wavering between secession and loyalty to the Union, and Grant was much concerned for the outcome. 'Colonel,' said he earnestly, 'I have great hopes for Kentucky.' 'So have I, General,' I replied courteously, yet enthusiastically, my zeal for the cause of the Confederacy refusing to be curbed. Instead of taking umbrage at this retort the General was visibly affected and said that such a spirit was commendable in a Confederate soldier, but that it boded ill for the much desired ending of the struggle. When the interview was over, much to my surprise, I was given a safe passport through the lines."

The long June days wore away and the rich grasses of the prairie withered and turned brown under a midsummer sun. Autumn came with its haze which mellowed old Sol's rays like the spreading of a huge canvas, and still the old man worked on. The sweet notes from his flute were regularly borne down over the little town on the evening zephyrs, for he was a master of that soulful instrument. That the program always ended with "Dixie" was exasperating to George Loar and correspondingly satisfactory to Hess. But when the white frosts made their appearance, and fast-flitting clouds hid the sun throughout the day, the cheerless aspect of his surroundings began to tell upon the old man. The sounds of the flute became irregular and mournful, and finally ceased altogether. The holders of Self-Sustaining Motor stock quickly noted the change in the old man, and by dint of questioning, in a manner not to offend, discovered that he was homesick for the sunny Southland and for the only relative he had in the world — his wife.

Within a few hours a public meeting was in session in the grain warehouse, and Fred Carruth, the postmaster, editor, attorney and real estate dealer of the town, was telling the story of the inventor's longings for a sight of the aged wife who was in a far-off Southern state. When he had finished a highly-colored dissertation on the feasibility of the motor (he didn't have the least particle of faith in its success, nor did his hearers), and had actually shed tears in his appeal to those who

were themselves, even then, feeling the pangs of homesickness, and had expatiated upon the notoriety that would be given their town by reason of it being the only one in the county to possess a woman, he offered Motor stock for sale in quantities to suit purchasers. Every man in the audience took a share, and even John Dunn, who already had a pigeon-hole in his safe devoted exclusively to that character of paper, increased his holdings. When the meeting adjourned, enough money was piled up on the little pine table to purchase transportation for one from Charlotte to Mirage City, with enough to spare to fit up a little home for the aged couple. The old man's face was a study as he watched the proceedings. His gratitude was beyond expression in words, and he only smiled in his mysterious way and returned to his workshop on the hill.

A letter was one day received saying the transportation had reached Charlotte, and that Mrs. de Jarnette would start for Mirage City on the following day. The time of her arrival was calculated upon, and it was determined to make the event a notable one. Hand-bills were struck and sent to neighboring towns advertising the fact that the first woman to set

foot upon that part of the territory would arrive on a certain date, and would, of course, land at Mirage City. No more complete program would have been arranged had the occasion been the celebration of a national holiday. To add to the importance of the event, it was announced that on that day the working model of the motor would be finished; that at that time the last wheel would be placed in position which was to start in motion a machine that would revolutionize affairs on two-fifths of the earth's surface. Early and

"Within a few hours a public meeting was in session in the grain warehouse, and Fred Carruth, the postmaster, editor, attorney and real estate dealer of the town, was telling the story," etc.

late the old inventor worked, and far into the night were heard the dulcet notes of his flute.

When the great day finally came the leaden sky gave evidence of approaching winter. It is characteristic of Dakota that the delightful days of a long-drawn-out fall are usually brought to an end by a blizzard,—sudden, howling, awful. A softly-falling snow in a bright morning sun is before night whirled and driven on a wind that shrieks and roars and cuts like a knife. The sun becomes hid in a sky of ice, and the snow moves in blinding drifts across the prairies like ocean billows in a storm. But no attention was paid to the frowning elements. Men came from far and near and the town was filled. The old man had the different parts of his intricate machine finished, and nothing remained to do but place them in position. The little depot was crowded at train time, but the telegraph instrument clicked off the information that the train was snow-bound. An early darkness settled down and still the crowd remained. The storm finally broke upon them like a wild beast, and the electric instrument ceased its ticking. The wires had gone down. For two days the winds howled and shrieked and the snow piled itself into mountains. The cold was so intense that the prisoners suffered although the little depot stove was piled high with fuel. The imprisoned ones had no food, and to attempt to reach the town, only a few blocks away, would have been suicidal.

But the storm broke away as suddenly as it came, and the sun shone brightly through the frosty air. The people turned out with shovels, the blockade was removed, and again was the crowd awaiting the arrival of the snow-bound train. When the smoke from the engine was first sighted, miles away across the glistening expanse of snow, a mighty cheer went up. The old inventor joined not in the shout, but the tears that

" Men wrapped in furs cleared the way with shovels before the sled which bore two rough boxes."

coursed down his cheeks told their own story. The ice-covered cars stopped at last before the platform, and the committee got aboard to meet and welcome the distinguished traveler. The first coach was gone through, then the next and the next, but the object of their search was not there. When the searchers returned to the platform the look of eager expectancy on the face of the old man gave way to one of painful disappointment. At that juncture the trainmen were seen to unload a rough box from the baggage car, and the sight of it sent a shock through the assemblage. Instinctively all eyes were turned toward the pale face of the old man. A deeper ashen hue overspread his countenance, and with a groan, an outburst of the agony that filled his soul, he fell into the arms of Catlett—dead.

A funeral cortege moved slowly up the hill to the north of the little town. Men wrapped in furs cleared the way with shovels before the sled which bore two rough boxes. Fine snow filled the air and at times shut out the melancholy view. Sun-dogs as bright as the headless orb they had followed across a strangely tinted sky cast their sickening light into the grave that was to hold two bodies, and the gale swept great clouds of snow into the faces of the workers as they dropped the frozen clods upon the coffins.

The working model of the Self-Sustaining Motor lies scattered about the workshop on the hill where the old inventor left it; the stock of the company long since ceased to be a legal tender;

the furnished home has been presented to the woman who was first to reach the town alive, and a pipe-stone shaft on the hill, at whose feet the Big Sioux sparkles and splashes in summer and lies still and dead In winter, marks the resting place of the couple that made a cemetery a necessity in Mirage City.

THE POET'S ART.

I HAVE not skill to sweep with fingers swift,
   In ready rote, as learned of men and books,
The tuned strings of guitars, nor yet the gift
   To voice, mimetic, chortling birds and brooks
As some mechanic toy; but, ah! I know
   The soundless melody of lips and looks.

Tell me, oh master, by thy harp of gold,
   Canst render me the laughter of a child?
Canst thou the prayers interpret of the old,
   The misery of maidenhood defiled?
Or by one trick of fingers known to thee
   Express the pity of the Christ reviled?

Canst thou, I ask, with all thy Old World art,
   Evolve the joy of liberty's first breath,
Or yet the love of one pure, faithful heart,
   That knoweth martyrdom for love, and death?
Canst from the strings evoke one hallowed note
   As sweet as words the tender mother saith?

And what are words, mere words, and pleasing sound?
   'Tis something more than strain of lute, or word,
That stirs in us emotions so profound
   We feel that higher kinship He conferred;
The grandest things God gave to mortal man
   Have ne'er by mortal man been seen or heard.

A smile is sweeter than a Delphic reed,
   And beauty is more dulcet than a flute;
There's more than trumpet's blast in Valor's deed;
   The night hath music without lyre or lute;
The flowers are hymns; a madrigal the morn,
   And all Earth's sweetest melody is mute.

My music all in grandest silence rolls,
   Too high and holy for irreverent ears:
I ken the pealing anthem of all souls,
   The solemn diapason of the spheres,
The glorious chanson of all life and love,
   The calm, sweet interludes of years.

A tender cadence echoes from the Past
   And swells the Future's martial melody;
The stars, glad minstrels of the silent vast,
   In chorus join in joyous jubilee;
And most sublime of all *Te Deums* I hear,
   The *De Profundis* of Infinity!

NEW YORK.   *Arthur Grissom.*

JAMES WILMOT SCOTT.*

By LEIGH LESLIE, OF THE CHICAGO RECORD.

WHEN James Wilmot Scott died, American journalism lost one of its masterful spirits, the great city of Chicago lost one of its best citizens, and the world lost a man richly endowed with the sweeter, choicer attributes of humanity.

There was an element of peculiar sadness in the taking off of the distinguished publisher. It may be said that death came literally in the hour of his greatest triumph. The prime ambition of his life had been to own and control a great newspaper. Toward the realization of this most worthy aspiration all his best energies had been bent. He had just acquired possession of the two journals to the building of which he had given years of intelligent thought and exacting labor, when he was cut down, almost without warning. The cares and trials incident to the negotiations resulting in the purchase of a controlling interest in these great properties — a transaction involving hundreds of thousands of dollars — had weighed heavily upon him, and, tired, but looking confidently to the future, he had gone East in quest of a few weeks' rest. That he should have been stricken upon the very threshold of his enlarged career is, from our human viewpoint, deplorable indeed. Only two days before his death he said : "I never before felt so happy, except when I was married. I have reached my highest ambition."

James Wilmot Scott was great as a journalist ; he was yet greater as a man. He was cheery, generous, sympathetic. He loved all that was good and true and beautiful. He disliked cordially all that was false. He was liberal-minded and progressive. He believed that the world was growing better,— that humanity was becoming purer and nobler. He had faith in God, and he had faith in human nature. All the influences that went out from his life were sweet and wholesome.

Good men were his friends because he was honest, valorous, genial and gracious. In all the relations of life he was just and charitable. He was never recreant to duty. His conscience was his guide. He was not vindictive, nor was he intolerant. He was modest, and his tastes were simple. In him the poor, the weak and the unfortunate had a friend. He found his greatest delight in alleviating human suffering. Appeals to him for help were never unanswered. He was unostentatious in his charities, believing, with Johnson, that he who would have his virtue published is not the servant of virtue, but of glory. His heart was full of tenderness and compassion. It was the philosophy of his life to use all the faculties that God had given him to the accomplishment of noble purposes.

Mr. Scott was a self-made man in the best and truest sense. The record of his achievements is an inspiration ; it will ever hold out a hope to worthy ambition. In nothing else are exemplified more signally the possibilities that lie before every American youth of energy, perseverance and good mental equipment.

His boyhood days were spent in the quaint old town of Galena. He was the son of a journalist. It was in the dingy office of his father, D. Wilmot Scott, who was engaged in the publishing business there for thirty-five years, that he learned the printer's trade. He was a bright, healthy, active boy, with rosy cheeks, chubby fists, and short, fat legs. He was called "Jimmy" in those days, and he was "Jimmy" thereafter to every man, woman and child in that town. He ever cherished a tender sentiment for all that pertained to his boyhood. In his later years he enjoyed nothing else more than to go back to his old home, where everybody

*Born in Walworth county, Wisconsin, June, 1849; died in New York, April 14, 1895.

67

knew and loved and admired him, to spend a few days among the rugged hills over which he used to climb and about which clustered so many precious memories.

Journalists, like poets, are born, not made. This boy possessed the true journalistic instinct. While working over the forms and cases he resolved, when he should attain his majority, to go to some big city and build a great daily journal. He didn't confide this secret ambition to George Swift, or "the Kohlsaat boys," or his other companions, lest they should ridicule him for being such an impossible fellow. He was so frank and generous that they all loved him, but it is quite likely they *would* have thought it preposterous that he should expect to do such great things. He worked on and clung to his high hope.

JAMES WILMOT SCOTT.

When he had learned all there was to be learned in that old-fashioned office about type-setting, he entered Beloit College, taking a two years' course in this institution. Then he went to New York to engage in the newspaper business in earnest. Having no influential friends in the great metropolis, he did not succeed in getting an acceptable position there, so he turned his attention temporarily to floriculture, meanwhile contributing valuable papers to publications devoted to that art. Subsequently he took a position in the government printing office at Washington, where he gained serviceable knowledge. In 1872 he went to Prince George county, Maryland, to start a weekly newspaper. This venture was not a financial success, and he soon abandoned it and returned to Galena. He remained there for several years, assisting his father in the publication of a weekly journal called *The Press.* In 1875, dissatisfied with so limited a field, and confident that he had capacity to succeed in a larger one, he went to Chicago. He had met with nothing but disappointments thus far, but he was still ambitious. *The Daily National Hotel Reporter* was for sale, and he bought a controlling interest in it, his partner being Mr. F. Willis Rice, the present manager of the paper.

In May, 1881, *The Chicago Herald* was founded by a stock company of which Mr. Scott was the head. In 1883, John R. Walsh, the rich banker, purchased a controlling interest in the paper, Mr. Scott remaining with the next interest, and continuing as publisher. In April, 1890, Mr. Scott, in conjunction with Mr.

Walsh, founded *The Evening Post.* Last winter Mr. Scott acquired all of Mr. Walsh's stock in these two papers, thereby coming into complete control of the properties. In March he purchased a controlling interest in *The Times,* and consolidated that aged and enfeebled journal with the more youthful and more buoyant *Herald.* These two stupendous transactions engrossed Mr. Scott's attention for several months, and it is probable that the extraordinary mental and nervous strain to which he was subjected during that period was the immediate cause of his death.

Mr. Scott once said that, in looking over the newspaper field in Chicago, he had found the average life of the managing editor in harness was only five years, and this had impressed upon him the futility of building up animosities and contentions and bitternesses, and the wisdom of cheerfulness and good-fellowship. Few of his contemporaries possessed in so great a degree the power of cultivating friendships. No other conspicuous newspaper man of his time had so many warm personal friends. He was admirably magnanimous and generous in all his impulses. He was highly considerate and appreciative of others, and always quick to recognize ability and faithfulness. He was an excellent judge of men. He was particularly loved and admired by those who were daily associated with him in the conduct of his papers. With his co-workers he kept in close and sympathetic touch, and to them his death came with the poignancy of a personal affliction.

Horace Greeley, Thurlow Weed, Henry J. Raymond and the elder Bennett, of the preceding generation, became noted as formulators and promoters of great public policies. Charles A. Dana, Henry Watterson, and a few other journalists of this era have also been thus distinguished. Mr. Scott will be remembered, not so much for the impress he made upon public life,—which, however, was not inconsiderable,—as for the impress he made upon the newspaper life of his time. He possessed positive genius as an organizer,

which, together with splendid administrative capacity, tireless energy, great steadfastness of purpose, a swift intuition, nice balancings of judgment, and exceptional fertility of resource, easily made him one of the most potent forces in his particular department of newspaper work. No one else of modern times has done so much to raise the standard of typographical excellence in journalism. He understood, as few others have understood, the art of newspaper-making. He was indeed a true representative of the modern type of newspaper man. He was for several years president of the Chicago Press Club, and was serving his fourth consecutive term as president of the American Newspaper Publishers' Association, the largest and most important newspaper organization in the world. He was for six years president of the United Press Association.

The social demands upon Mr. Scott in the later years of his life were greater, perhaps, than those upon any other man in Chicago. He was a member of no fewer than thirteen clubs in that city, besides having honorary membership in various social organizations in New York, Boston, Philadelphia, Paris and London. He was the founder and president of the Fellowship Club, and belonged also to the Union League, the Iroquois, the Chicago, the Union, the Wabansee, the Washington Park, the Twentieth Century, the Press, the Cycle and Saddle, the Contributors', the Chicago Athletic, and the University Clubs. He was the first non-resident of Philadelphia elected to membership in the famous Clover Club.

Mr. Scott's domestic life was ideal in its purity and its simplicity. In his hospitable home love and trust and good cheer reigned supreme. Although a prominent club man, Mr. Scott spent most of his evenings at his own fireside. The children of his wife's dead sister—four charming little girls—were reared by him and Mrs. Scott, and his love for them was as pure and deep and tender as is that of the true father for his own. The companionship of his dear ones in the home circle was more precious to him than was that of all others in the world. After a romp with the children in the evening, he was wont to retire to what he called his "nest," a bright, cozy room on the second floor of his house. Here he was free from all disturbance except when he was called up by telephone occasionally to answer some important question from the office, and here he frequently wrote and read till midnight. It was his habit to read every Chicago newspaper carefully, as well as the important matter in the leading dailies of other large cities. The walls of his "nest" were adorned with portraits of noted men and women of his acquaintance, and the floors were covered with beautiful rugs, most of which he had collected in his travels. It was no uncommon thing for him to do the day's work of an ordinary man in this room before going down town in the morning. He was generally at his desk in the *Herald* building at ten o'clock. He had capacity for much hard work, and accomplished a vast deal during business hours.

It is an interesting coincidence and a striking commentary on the mutability of human affairs, as well as on the American way of doing business, that within a week after the death of Mr. Scott, *The Times-Herald* and *The Post*, the former recognized for years as the leading exponent of democracy in the West, and at the time of the sale the only democratic morning paper in Chicago, should have passed into the hands of Hermann H. Kohlsaat, a friend of his boyhood in Galena, and that both papers should have been converted from the advocacy of democratic doctrine into Independent republican journals. Mr. Kohlsaat was Mr. Scott's most intimate personal friend. He is a gentleman of exceptional business capacity, great wealth, and high social standing. It remains to be seen whether he can take the place made vacant by Mr. Scott.

BELLE'S ROSES.* II.

BY E. HOUGH.

IV.

THE late train which rolled into Burlingame bore in its main coach but half a dozen passengers. These were a squat French-Canadian woman, black-haired, much encumbered by bird-cages, and talkative by reason of frequent applications to a certain black bottle kept well at hand; her husband, equally squat, equally black-haired, but taciturn by reason of similar applications to the same bottle; an old lady of New England garb and feature; her niece, fresh-starched, red-haired and pretty; and, lastly, a brown, sun-burned man, dressed in a checked suit of new "ready-made" clothing, a celluloid collar encircled by a red silk handkerchief, a soft slouch hat, and a pair of queer high-heeled, narrow-toed boots, such as to-day are rarely seen in the eastern or middle country, even in the most rural districts. Upon these boots he wore a pair of heavy spurs, which jingled as he stumped along the railway platform in his pigeon-toed walk. The total effect of this last traveler's appearance was such that he attracted attention from his fellow passengers and from the loungers present about the depot at that late hour. This man was accompanied by a rather fantastically clad and striking looking little child, apparently about four years of age, whose dark skin, black hair, and soft dark eyes gave her the look of one foreign to the land. Quiet, serious-faced, almost solemn in her mien, this little one watched every movement of her big protector and clung to him with the utmost solicitude.

Mr. Rufus Bascom gave a hurried

* Begun in the June MIDLAND, accompanied by portrait of the author.

glance at the recent debarkations as
he backed his one-horse Black Maria up
to the platform. "There's a dollar, or
mebbe a dollar'n a quarter in this here fer
me," he chuckled to himself; and then
called out aloud : " Right this way, folks,
'f you want to g' up the hill. Take ye
to the hotels 'r any part of the city. Cost
ye a quarter. Aint no other conveyance
daown here to-night. Better git right
in."

They all got in. The Canadian man
and woman wanted a hotel where they
could stay over night for a dollar, that
being the total of their fortune. The old
lady objected to paying twenty-five cents
apiece for herself and niece.

"I don't think y' ought to charge
more'n fifteen cents up to 'Nooski Avenue," said she. "Maria come up here
last summer, an' she said a man took her
up for fifteen cents. An' they's two of
us goes to the same place."

A compromise was finally effected by
which Mr. Bascom agreed to carry these
two passengers to their destination for
thirty-five cents. "They didn't git much
the best of me," he muttered to himself.
Of the Canadian couple he exacted full
tariff, and they stolidly agreed, since
their exchequer was so nearly exhausted
at best. There followed some incident
bags, bird-cages and bundles, and then
the vehicle started up the long hill toward
the town.

"Where d' you want to go, mister?"
asked Mr. Bascom of the sun-burned
man.

"To some good hotel ; I aint particular," replied the latter.

"'Bout a two dollar house, 'r a dollar'n
a halfer?" delicately inquired Mr. Bascom.

"I don't give a d—n," calmly replied
the stranger. At which the old lady and
her niece gave a jump, bumping their
heads against the roof of the hack. Mr.
Bascom coughed deprecatingly.

"Well, you see,—" he began in an
apologetic tone.

"Only, I draws the line on beans," resumed the stranger with equal calmness.

"Then I guess I'd better take ye to the
Grand," said Mr. Bascom thoughtfully.

The ride went on after that for some
moments in a silence broken only by the
wheezing of the broken-winded horse.
At length the stranger again spoke.

"My friend," said he. "ken you tell
me w'cther ther's a sort of lang'age
school, a studyin'-ranch, or somethin' or
other o' that sort, thet's runnin' here now?
— sort o' high-toned outfit, I reckon."

"D'ye mean P'fessor Gonfalso's Summer School of Langwitch ?"

"I expect thet's about it. Lots o'
young *moharries* comes to it, I 'low ?"

"Eh ?"

"Lots o' young wimmen. Come from
all over, I've heard."

"Oh, land! yes. They's more'n two
hundred in taown now. It's a good thing
fer the place, thet school is. I guess
every one o' them young wimmen must
hev to pay's much's four dollars a week
board, 'n they stay here nigh onto two
months. Eight times four's thirty-two,
an' two hunderd times thet is six thou-
sernd four hundred. To say nothin' 'bout
washin'. Besides, they's livery ! Why,
last summer I made more'n thirty-eight
dollars m'self with this here rig — an'
say,"(behind a confidential hand)"thet's
more'n I ever paid fer thet hoss. I got
him of old Deacon Eakins. We wuz on
the street one day, 'n says he to me, says
he—"

"I ax yore pardon, my friend," said
the stranger gravely, "but ken you tell
me where that school-ranch is located?"

"Where's the buildin'?"

"Yes, where the young wimmen comes
together."

"Oh, its th' old University buildin',
right up to th' top of th' hill. Street-car
runs right by it. In th' mornin' you jest
take the street-car to the corner o' Wy-
nooski Av'nue an' Ellum Street, an'
they'll kerry ye right up to it. Cost ye
'bout five cents."

"I reckon I ken raise it," remarked the
stranger sententiously. A little later he
and the child were disembarked at the
Grand Hotel, where he wrote laboriously

upon the hotel register to the effect that "J. b. Jenkins and Child, Noo York," were arrived.

Wrapped up in this shallow disguise, Jim took 'Nita on his knee, smoothed back her hair with rough tenderness, and drew the first breath half free from care and anxiety which he had known for many days. The nature of his mission had handicapped him, and he was a rough detective at best; yet with faithfulness he had kept his counsel, while from the Western city to the East, and through the East to this point, he followed the trail of his quarry under difficulties hardly to be imagined for one so absolutely unused to the ways of crowded towns, but with an energy and persistence not to be denied. The strain in all this had been intense. He was rejoiced to feel it relax, and to know himself well within the limits of the time assigned him.

The day was the 26th of June.

"To-morrer, 'Nita," said he, as he stroked her hair, "we gits you a mother, er we gits the reason why."

The child was sleepy and worn out, and, leaning her little head upon her burly guardian's shoulder, she fell fast asleep. Jim picked her up in his arms and carried her to bed. Throwing his own hat upon the floor, and carefully hanging up his spurs upon a hook behind the door, he stood looking at the child as she lay with one arm under her head and her dark hair tumbled across her face, breathing hard in the heavy slumber of tired infancy.

"In my 'pinion," muttered he, "this yer is a clar case w'ere a woman is needed. I aint fit to take no such care o' this yer child as Cap'n Jordan's baby orto have. Wot fools men is! Wot fools *everybody* is! Wot a blank, blanked fool I am myself! 'Cause, d—n me, whether I'm fit er not, I goes an' gits stuck on this child, an' I shore hates to give her up; spesh'ly to a woman not fit to be her mother. Come, Annie, *chiquit*, le'ss take yer clothes off, dearie, an' go to bed right."

The child stirred drowsily as he took her up, and threw her arms about his neck,

as, with the clumsy kindliness to which she was now accustomed, he assisted her with her garments.

"In the mornin', 'Nita," said Jim, going over to his weather-beaten valise and taking out some articles of finery which, under the pronounced standard of a taste formulated in Arizona, had seemed to him suitable for this very occasion, "in the mornin' we dresses you up fine. This yer new yaller an' red dress is about right, an' w'en you gits yore silver s'ord in yore hair, an' yore new red handkerchief on, I reckon yore new Maw is shore due to like ye, an' no mistake."

"Who, 'migo, Jim?" asked Anita, sleepily.

"Yore new Maw."

The child looked up at him with great, questioning eyes. With the instinct of childhood she knew that some change had befallen her guardian; that something, she knew not what, was about to happen. Few children so taciturn as Anita, or so sad. In her perplexity she became the more reserved.

"Wot's the matter, 'Nita?" asked Jim, looking at her closely. "Aint ye all right?" In his short tutelage as protector of the child he had, beyond belief for one who had never himself been a father, grown thoughtful and quick in all matters bearing on her welfare. "Ye aint sick, are ye, *muchacha?*"

Anita buried her face in his hands as he held them out. "No, 'migo," she said, in her slow, old way, "not sick, but in my side, here; and I am afraid. *Yo no quero* anyone. *Yo quero su, 'migo* Jim! I want to be with you."

Jim's voice shook with a miserable failure at gaiety as he sought to cheer her up. "Thar, thar, now, little un," he concluded, "we don't know nothin' about wot is goin to happen, an' we won't worry. The main thing is to git a good night's sleep. It's allus best to sleep hearty before goin' into a scrimmage of any kind. To-morrer we wins, er we knows why. She kaint help likin' you, darlin.' 'Nita, child"—and he folded her close in his arms—"I do wish't I could be yore paw always, but I kaint, an' I aint fit. You got to have a mother, dearie, an' to-morrer we finds one. Of co'se, they may be some few hitches, but all the same, to-morrer is shore goin' to be the day w'en we gits mothers, er we gits reasons! Come, chile, now go to sleep."

V.

Professor Barclay was the youngest assistant in the Gonsalso School of Language, and perhaps the ablest. At thirty-five he was a fairly good looking and well finished man, slightly bald, of very passable figure, and a face sensible and bright. He was a thinker besides being a linguist, and his reputation was far wider than his state. No man connected with the school was more popular than he, and daily his class-room was crowded with young ladies who for some reason seemed to prefer his instruction to that of many older men.

Professor Barclay had the faculty of assimilating and of imparting knowledge, and in his methods was bound by no cast-iron rules. Interested himself, he interested his students, and he kept himself interested by never allowing himself to fall into a groove of thought. Variety, that was his method. Thus, in his French classes he was as apt to talk French history as French pronouns, and on any morning one of these spirited prologues which he was wont to call his "little talks" might prolong itself quite through the regular hour, and this "talk" might be on some topic altogether remote from the questions of grammar or philology. Still, no one was ever heard to complain, either among the students or among the faculty.

This morning, Professor Barclay had found something which interested him more than usual. He appeared at class hour carrying a newspaper, a copy of the Sunday edition of one of the great metropolitan dailies, in whose customary more or less ill-assorted means of information he had found an article which set him to thinking, or at least to talking. Much of the thinking had been done already, for this article was nothing more nor less than

a symposium of the ideas of some of the most learned minds of the New World and of the Old. The title was, "What is the Perfect Man"?* Professor Barclay was deeply excited, and read aloud to running comment column after column of wise, shrewd, practical or absurd dissertation upon the qualities of the man without flaw or failing.

"We may set up our standard, and we may frame beliefs," said Professor Barclay, dashing his finger into the page, "but of what use is all that to humanity? Better plan some way to benefit the men actually alive, imperfect as they are. There is not any Perfect Man, unless we except Divinity incarnate. I load my knight with armor, cord on band, and netted links of steel so thick and heavy he cannot mount his horse, and can hardly stand alone. Of what use is he? Lance-proof he is, but still worthless to support a king or to defend a home. Perfection, or let me say perfectionism, is the worst of imperfection. We want no perfect men, for they are or would be worthless in society. We want human beings, good specimens of the species they represent in nature, and not good individuals alone. My rabbit on the campus yonder is a good rabbit. He is one of a species, and the species will live after him. Nature does not watch the individual, and does not care for him. She cares only for the species. For the little perfections of a mere lay figure she has no regard. She cares nothing for the dwarfed limb of a Hindoo priest, crippled through his fanatical devotion to his religious belief—that which he calls goodness—nor does she care for the magnificent physical development of a perfect athlete, devoted only to the perfection of his body. Does she care more for the intellectual giant than she does for you or me? What are Newton, Bacon, Aristotle—anybody? Pots! But the line of the species that produced them goes undulating on in infinite variety throughout life. —"

*Such a symposium was actually published a few years ago, though the story does not follow the ideas there shown.

Nature works only by broad laws. We must take our point of view at a distance if we would see her works. When we have done that, we shall not see merely the Individual. We are getting too far away from Nature to-day, and we are thinking too much of the Individual. Our culture and our refinement are too much sheer egotism. Our measures of manhood and womanhood are too often mere straws, held over-closely to the eye and looking larger than they are. We find no one perfect according to our absolute ideas, and so we say no one is so good as we are. We try to be yet better, we press and crowd each faculty to its utmost, training ourselves in body, in mind, in every external and showy way, so that we may pose before ourselves as types of this really mean and narrow doctrine of perfectionism. We lose sight of Nature, and try to be purely artificial, schooled, trained, cultured, developed, perfect. We lose sight of Nature, and after a while Nature will lose sight of us. We will be too good to live! That is the doctrine of the Individual, and that is what it amounts to. That is why such words as these, many of them from scientists of the highest ability, the profoundest intellectual power, are more entertaining and more curious than useful. They lay plans and measures for the perfect man, but they plan only for an impossibility. The perfect man does not and cannot exist. If perfect physically, he must, as one learned writer here remarks, be perfectly strong, perfectly beautiful, perfectly swift; yet if perfectly strong, he could be neither perfectly fleet nor perfectly comely. Mental perfection has its same drawbacks, self-existent. My philosopher cannot be my general; my poet cannot be my *bourgeois*. Morally it is the same also. If I am perfect morally, I can not go upon the streets and transact business, therefore I fall out of the race in the struggle for survival, and my perfection has made me most imperfect, because most far from Nature's broad plans for the species.

"To-day there is simply a struggle all through the land for the sake of the Individual. More learning, more culture, more self-improvement, is our cry. Very well for us to have an ideal and to follow it, but the danger to-day is that we shall take the ideal too seriously, and follow for a possibility what is only an illusion, and so land in a morass of doubt, bare of real happiness. This withdrawing into one's self for all the good of life, this introspection, this effort at self-satisfaction and this gaining only of discontent — what good is it doing us? What is our education in things external, things formal, things by the rule, doing for us and for the world? Charity, kindliness, the impulses of the heart, sympathy, forgiveness, tolerance, breadth, grasp — what are we learning about these things? What about the man as related to other men? What about the human ties which bind all earth together — what about the human sympathy which ought to be and grow? The ideal is well, but there is no law on earth or heaven binding us to absolutism. Rigidity is not in nature, but flexibility, change, variety, compensation — these are in nature. Sympathy — that is what we need. Love — that is what we ought to have. The Bible tells us 'Love is the fulfilling of the Law,' and in that the Bible never meant the cold and pulseless admiration of a Self!"

Professor Barclay fairly trembled with the nervous vehemence of his utterance, as he laid down the paper and concluded his little talk. Singularly enough, as he was closing his last sentence, his eyes wandered to that corner of the room where sat Belle Danvers, one of his most attentive listeners. Was Professor Barclay talking for all, or for just a few of his class in French? His gaze had often wandered toward this corner.

Belle Danvers carried out of the class-room that morning only one distinct or formulated thought, and that she did not understand, though time and again it wandered through her mind, until at length it took a recurrent, rhythmic form,

—"Love, love fulfills, love fulfills, love fulfills the Law!" What did that mean? There was considerable excitement created by the bold young teacher's discourse, and he was by many of the more pronounced disciples openly accused of treason to the cult, but Belle Danvers pondered not upon such treason. Only the lilt of the closing aphorism and the burden of its attendant question clung to her mind. She found herself asking again and again, "What does that mean?" —even when much later in the day she had retired to the quiet of her own apartments.

Belle was a woman endowed and schooled in a self-control which would have been more admirable had it been less intense. Her stoicism, as far as matters of her own personal feelings were concerned, was fairly pitiful. In ten years, not even a member of her own family had ever heard her mention the name of the man she once had loved. In her creed it was simply a duty to crucify the heart. In some vague way she thought that thereby she would be advancing the cause of Woman — an error as absolute as that of the dervish who mutilates his body to advance the glory of his cruel faith. Pitiable, almost unforgivable, such a life would be, if left unredeemed by any milder traits. Yet by a strange paradox, and one possible only with a being as inexplicable as a woman, Belle's friends knew her to be the softest-hearted woman in the world. And well enough Belle herself knew, once each year all the more keenly, in this month of June, that her heart was not dead, only suffering. Once each year in the ten, never later than this very day, the twenty-seventh of June, and often prompt upon that time, there had come to her, unsigned, unheralded, unexplained, from parts of the country as diverse as the years, yet following her in some mysterious way and with a sweet relentlessness finding her no matter where she might be, the offering of fresh red roses, whose sending and whose sender she could not mistake. Once every year there came a conflict which she dreaded

and yet for which she longed. Of that conflict or its cause, not one token had ever escaped her. And in all the years not one word had she ever sent to the sender of the roses.

Before now, Belle had sought to test the strength of this mysterious power which pursued and found her at its will. She had a faint and half superstitious belief that if she could evade these silent followers for but a single year she would thereafter be free from the spell of which they were the visible token. Vain hope! It was the power of Love. Each year, not later than this very day, the roses came and lay before her, fresh, bright, smiling, and sweet, sweet, sweet! In her bosom there was arising a plaintive protest that they had not come to-day. Could they come? Nothing from the express company, nothing in the mail. It was over. She had triumphed. Her plans had been such that only a few of her trusted friends knew her address. The roses could not find her this year! They would not come now. How could they come? Oh! would they not come?

Tired and troubled, Belle cast herself upon her couch and sought to sleep, her head a mere centrifugum of whirling thoughts which would obey no order. What did it all amount to, after all? she wearily questioned. What was the good of it all? Why did she live, and what was the good of living? Was sheer unhappiness the highest good a soul could know? Was she any better off for her efforts to elevate woman? Was Woman, or any woman, the better off for that? After all, had she been better or more useful than many another woman? Had she done any more good? Had she reached the Nirvana of her class? Was there any Nirvana, after all? — And would the roses come?

A reiterant refrain ran through her mind, and curiosity for the reason of it soothed her brain. She fell asleep and, sleeping, smiled; because, when Belle slept, she was out from under the iron whips of error, and was natural. Because, too, she dreamed now that she could understand the clarion pealing of the high harmonious music which rang so pleasing sweet and clear through all her soul : — " *Love fulfills, Love fulfills, Love fulfills the Law !* "

VI.

" Pardner," said Jim to the street car driver who was conveying himself and Anita up the hill toward the old University buildings, and with whom he had struck up a ready conversation ; " pard-ner, they's one thing I often noticed about mules, an' wich you don't seem to re-member — you can't force 'em along only about so fast, an' you don't need to try. 'Taint no stubbornness of the mule — that's a thing wich aint half understood by most folks — but it's the nacher'l make-up of the beast. A mule aint built to jog along only about just so fast, an' if you crowds 'em beyond that gait, you breaks 'em down a lot sooner'n you'd ort to. That's why they aint fit fer teamin' like this yer. Some folks is nacher'ly fit to drive mules, an' some aint. You're one of them 'at aint. I ken see that, 'cause you're bustin' up yer span, w'en they aint no more use ter do it, in this yer graveyard of a town, than they is to kerry worter w'en ye ken camp by it. You don't hev to make no grass nor wor-ter to-night, yet you pound yer span ez if't you wuz on the Jornada with yer can-teens empty. Say, w'eres yere extry ex? "

" My extra what ? " asked the driver, querulously, again automatically flicking his team with the whip, and looking askance at his singular passenger.

" Yore extra ex. Spusin' you break down on the trail, aint ye got no extry axle tree along, ner no extry wheel ? "

The driver gave a loud guffaw of laughter, but hastily checked himself as he reflected upon the possible character of the unique fare he was carrying. " Did ye want to git off 't the collidge build-in's ? " he asked. " That's them right yonder, top o' th' hill. The classes is mostly down stairs. Jest foller the walk right up ter the door, an' don't step on the flower-beds." With which parting shot

he rattled off alone in his rumbling yellow chariot, doubled up over the dashboard with convulsive laughter.

It was rather late in the day, for Anita had slept very soundly that morning, and Jim had been loath to awaken her, while the laborious details of the child's toilet, which he intended to be elaborate, had consumed yet more time. Everything about the great buildings seemed very quiet, and for a moment Jim was con-fused, as he stood, with Anita held fast by the hand, in the wide hall from which so many doors appeared to open out. All was silent. " Fer a school of lang-'ages, 'Nita," said he, " this yer ain't my idee at all. It's too blame quiet." He walked on down the hall, until at length a murmur of voices came to him from a room upon the left. He knocked at the door, and was answered by a young man, who softly opened the door and stepped out.

" Good mornin'," said Jim ; " is this Perfesser Gonfalso's school of lang-'ages ? "

" Yes, sir," replied the other, casting a querying gaze over the odd couple that stood before him.

" Ken you tell me w'ether they's a young woman here by the name of Dan-vers — Miss Belle Danvers ? "

" In what class was she, do you know ? "

" I don't know that."

" You will find Professor Barclay in the room at the end of the hall," said the young man, civilly. " He is the secretary of the school, and can tell whether or not any such name is enrolled. There are several hundred students here, you know, and in a number of different classes. Shall I show you to Professor Barclay ? "

" I wish you would, pardner," said Jim, quietly. And soon they stood at the door of the proper room. Professor Barclay was just upon the point of departure, having met his last class for the day. He cast a rather caustic glance upon his interlocutor and his strange little companion.

" We have such a name upon the rolls," said he, replying to Jim's question. " Miss

Danvers is in the French class. Do you wish to see her?"

"I should be glad to," replied Jim gravely, involuntarily tightening his grip upon Anita's hand. The child looked up into his face expectant. From the one to the other Professor Barclay glanced keenly. Something told him this errand was a serious one.

"Miss Danvers is not here at present," he said; "her class was dismissed some time ago. I can direct you to her place of residence. It is No. — Winooski Avenue, Mrs. Philpot's house."

Jim looked troubled. The ways of the towns were after all still hard for him. He knew more of the stars than of the streets. The Professor saw his hesitation and his face brightened. "You seem a stranger in the city," said he, "perhaps you would like to have me show you the way. I know it very well."

Professor Barclay was quite right about that. Indeed, he should have known it very well, since he had called at Mrs. Philpot's house every evening that week. And what better chance could he ask than this to call again that afternoon? He could take these two strangers along, gratify his fully normal sense of curiosity by learning why they came, and, after they had gone, sit down and talk with Miss Danvers, and learn what she thought of his talk that morning. Perhaps,—who knew?—there might come all the nearer the time when he could say to Miss Danvers something further which had been lying on his mind, about love and the fulfillment of the law. Surely he would pilot these two thither, and take all chance of being seen upon the street with them.

"I'd shore be obliged to ye if you'd go 'long with me," said Jim.

"Are you acquainted with Miss Danvers?" asked Professor Barclay, rather more suavely.

"I never saw her!" said Jim grimly.

"Ah? And you would like to meet her soon? Pardon me, I shall be with you in a moment, and shall be glad to accompany you."

A little later the trio had crossed the wide green campus, descended the long hill, and passed to the right up another beautifully embowered street. When they paused before the ample and comfortable looking square brick house which had been Belle Danvers' abode for the past few weeks, Professor Barclay knew no more of his companion's errand or intentions than he had known before they left the college buildings. "It's for Miss Danvers perticular," Jim had briefly replied to the sole question he had dared to ask outright, and beyond that no query could well be plied.

A straight brick walk, lined with prim flower-beds, led up to the front door. The yard, however, was wide, well shaded, and carpeted with a soft green turf. A trellis, supporting some flowering vines, ran across one corner to a quaint little summer-house, where a comfortable seat or two showed, pleasantly inviting. Jim paused beneath a tree, removed his hat, and wiped his forehead with his gaudy handkerchief. The day had been very warm.

"I aint used to this kind of hot weather, Mr. Barclay," said he. "In our country a feller don't never sweat any, no matter how hot it is. I can't hardly breathe inside a house here, I git so warm. Now, I'll tell ye. I've got some rather hard work to do, a-seein' of Miss Danvers, an' I'm shore I'd take it fer a great favor if you'd jest tell her 'at I'd be very glad if she'd jest as lieves come outside, an' talk out here w'ere they's more air. If you'll go in an' tell her that, me an' the child'll be waitin' just over yer, on them seats."

Professor Barclay was already too much perplexed by the enigmatical conduct of his odd convoy to feel much additional surprise at this slightly unconventional expression of preference in the matter of calling upon a lady who was still a perfect stranger. If he reflected upon anything at all, it was probably to the effect that the street was very quiet, and that no one would be likely to pass at that hour of the day. But never was a blanker face than his, as he went up the steps, pulled the bell and finally went within.

Jim went over to the summer-house and sat down, with Anita's hand clasped firmly in his. He looked straight on ahead of him, not daring to answer the appeal of the child's eyes, which he felt turned upon him. The delay seemed to him an age. He arose and took a long breath as he heard the door open and saw Professor Barclay appear, accompanied by a tall young lady who seemed to his eyes the most beautiful being the earth ever produced.

"What a singular child!" exclaimed Miss Danvers in a quiet aside as they descended the steps and left the walk.

"Yes, and what a remarkable man!" replied the Professor, with equally polite discretion, and gaze averted from the objects of discussion. "I will remain near, Miss Danvers, and if you wish me, I beg you will call."

Belle Danvers did not hear him. Faultlessly dressed, severely beautiful, half haughtily correct of carriage, she had not crossed half the fifty feet of intervening greensward before she felt a chill and knew a dread. The look on the rough borderman's face had in it a solemnity as potent as a restraining hand. All her hauteur broke down before it. No trace of awkwardness or embarrassment now lurked in the earnest and resolute purpose of that stern face before her.

"I beg yore pardon, ma'am," said Jim as he stepped forward from the arbor, "but are you Miss Belle Danvers?"

"I am," replied Belle, with a strange tightening at her heart. Then, with the instinct natural to her, she kept her case, and let the other do the talking.

"I am very glad to see you, ma'am," said Jim, still holding Anita by the hand. "I have come some ways to see you; from Arizony, Fort ——, Arizony. I have a letter for you, ma'am, w'ich wuz thought not best to put in the mails. An' I have a peckidge, w'ich I wuz to put in yore own hands. An' I have a little gal, w'ich I wish to interduce to you more speshal, w'en you've read the letter, an' have opened the peckidge, ma'am. The gal's name is 'Nita Jordan."

Belle Danver's lips closed sharp and hard. Her face was pale as she extended her hand to take the soiled and battered parcels which Haines produced from his pocket.

"You will excuse me a moment!" she said, as with hands none too steady she attempted to open the envelope. The address was nearly effaced. She could not tell the handwriting. But the name of the little girl — what could it all mean? Who was this man? Why did he come?

"Excuse me, ruther, ma'am," said Jim, a sort of pity breaking over his face in spite of himself as he gazed at her evident distress. "Excuse me, ma'am, but there's pretty tough news in that there letter yo're about to read, leastways tough for me to carry, an' likely hard enough for you, after all. I don't know how to do these things very well, but — It's *death* yo're goin' to read about!"

Whiter yet grew Belle Danvers' face. The truth flashed upon her, and as its keenness sank into her soul, she stood straight up, crowded both hands against her bosom, and looked about her blindly. To Professor Barclay it seemed time to interfere. He stepped up quickly.

"Miss Danvers—" he began.

"I must beg yore pardon, sir," said Jim, stepping to meet him, "but this is strickly private."

"Step back!" exclaimed the Professor, for the moment valiant in his eagerness. "Can't you see Miss Danvers is ill!" He attempted to pass. A heavy hand fell on his shoulder, and a gray eye looked coldly into his. "The orders give me," said Jim, "wuz to find this lady, to see her in private, me an' her, an' the child, an' no one else. This trouble is trouble of her own. She made it, not you. Now you go on away, or you'll make trouble for yourself."

"But then — but can't you see?"

"I see it all, but I can't argy. I have my orders. In my country one 'No' is all a gentleman expects. Go on away, now, or I'll show you, an' show you quick, w'ot follers 'No' in Arizony!"

Belle Danvers was upon the seat in the summer-house when Jim turned about. Her face was drawn and gray. The letter was open in her hand.

"*My Dearest Belle*," it began. Never but the one man on earth had ever so addressed her. Never, she knew, would that man's hand address her again. That little tawdry pasteboard box — how well she knew what it held! Belle's roses had found her again, and for the last time that could ever be. Yearly they had found her, every year in ten long years, and in those years not one word had ever gone from her. Her heart flamed up in sudden bitter agony that now it was too late for that one word. What had all her schooling done for this woman here — of what value was all this training in self-restraint, self-repression, emotion-destroying, since out of it all, and after it all, there remained only these two words, "My Dearest"? God knows, there is little enough in any of our lives beyond those two comforting small words. For a life dwarfed, instead of widened, by faculties suppressed, by false theories and a miserable pride of self, how wretched, how unspeakably wretched, to realize, when all too late, that all the training has been futile, idle, a wrong and a mistake! How terrifying, to this poor woman here, to realize, so late, the compelling significance of those words, whose repetition she had years ago forbidden!

Belle Danvers did not read. She held the blurred sheet before her eyes, and the fire of her brain photographed the words forever on her mind. Here was the reproach and the protest at his dismissal, and the rebellion at its injustice; yet, almost in the same lines came words attempting to justify her in her course, and speaking of things long past and now forgiven. Here was the story of his life, wild, reckless, careless, — so different from what he once had planned. Here was the bitter self-condemnation of a heart not schooled in ill-doing, but only fallen in with it. Here was his keen self-reproach for the wrong he had done himself and done to others. Here was the whole dreary, horrible story.

"I don't think any man is what his sweetheart thinks he is," said the letter, "and when a man starts wrong, with nothing to hold him back, he finds he isn't what he thought he was himself."

"I have missed you," continued the letter, "Oh, how I have missed you, and wanted you, and needed you, you, *you!* Will you believe now, are you now woman enough to understand, that with all my heart I loved you at the first, and with all my heart I have loved you all these years, even when no longer worthy of your love?"

And there was the brief and simple story of his extreme distress, the record of his efforts to get to her the old tokens of his love, even after he himself should no longer be alive. Here was all the indomitableness she once had known and dreaded, but which now she loved, since it had forced the very gates of death and made itself heard in its plea for justice, and for the sake of love. Here was the very last breath of what might have been a good and noble life, as well as a brave and reckless one, talking to her, speaking of a child motherless, pleading with her, — not accusing her, — and ending with a question which only the whole agony of a soul could ask or answer:

"I know life is worthless as I have lived it. It has all been empty, empty, without you. But will you now believe me, — that in life and in my dying hour I loved you with all the good and clean part of my heart, and if there is anything after this world, I'll love you there the same!"

Then came the last scattered, illegible, broken words, where the man was trying still to write on, though hand and mind were in the grip of the final Enemy, and only a splendid will, averse to yield itself beaten, even by that foe, flickered and struggled in the broken body and above the heart at least half clean. Oh, the pity, that such a man should die in such a way, alone, unstayed, uncomforted!

Belle Danvers arose, and with one groan snapped all the shackles of heredity and training. In all her adult life she had never wept. Shall we say, therefore, she had never before really known love? The infinite bitterness which turns to the supremest sweet had never touched her lips. But when this bronzed and rugged borderer, this faithful messenger of a faithful man, approached her and silently placed in her hands the faded and withered stems of what had been sweet-odored flowers, the roses of the rocky desert, he handed to her the mystic, awful cup of Love, and from it there passed the spirit of the one unquenchable and changeless element of the universe. To her lips, already trembling, she pressed the meager, faded blossoms, less beautiful, but more dear, than all the offerings of the years gone by. Regret, remorse, shame, scorn for him, then pity, understanding, forgiveness, love, all these swept on and through her bosom. Her heart strained and labored as a soul in the ultimate effort for forgiveness and salvation.

And she was saved. Rain, rain, good tears, and wash away the idle husk of this poor, wasted life! Rain tears, and water into blossoming the flowers of hope and immortality upon the shallow, sandy grave this woman's hands have dug!

———

Evening was approaching. The shadows grew longer across the silent and deserted street. At length Jim led Anita up to her. The child had plucked from the trellis a fresh blooming rose. She smiled and held it out. Belle Danvers caught her in her arms. "Oh, baby!" she sobbed; "Oh, baby, *baby!*"

———

THE "ATHENS" OF IOWA METHODISM.

By Ben. F. Clayton.

THE proud position of the Iowa literate has not been attained as an afterthought. It has not been a secondary consideration in the organization of our State government, nor has it been a spasmodic growth of a few years, alternately checked by political revolutions or restrained by financial disruptions. The germ of Iowa's advanced civilization was planted by the hardy frontiersman in the erection of the log school-house, and its culture and care has been the first consideration in the development of the State. The advanced ground taken by our first settlers in the establishment of schools, the universal desire that every child in Iowa should become an educated citizen fully equipped to confront the problems of life, the donation of public lands by the general government for educational purposes, the care with which our school laws have been formulated, and the lavish expenditure of time and of money to maintain private and corporate educational institutions within our border, all together lead us to hope for higher possibilities, until we reach the verge of ideal perfection in mental development.

Our commonwealth's high purpose to educate all our people has invited within our lines the best type of emigration from other states, and secured to us the better class of the foreign element that seek our shores to better their condition.

Sharing in the enthusiasm of those in the advance guard of our western civilization, the "newcomer" has been none the less energetic in expanding and in improving the original system, until it is justly conceded the most complete, comprehensive and liberal educational system known to any country.

As an introduction to an article of this kind it will not be improper, nor will it be wholly uninteresting, to briefly review the introduction of the school into Iowa, and to refer to the marvelous growth and development of schools in the state. Such an introduction will serve as a prelude to what we may say with reference to Simpson College, and the incentive that actuated the good people of Indianola and of the Des Moines Conference of the Methodist Episcopal Church in furnishing additional facilities for a higher education within its borders.

Professor T. S. Parvin, a venerable and honored citizen of Cedar Rapids and of the state, a man whom we follow in educational history with the greatest confidence, says the first school taught north of Missouri and west of the Mississippi was by one Jennings, in a log school-house in Lee county, in 1830. Mr. Jennings referred to it in after life as the largest "deestrict" in the world, extending to Canada on

BISHOP SIMPSON IN 1857.
When the College at Indianola was named after him.

the north and to the Pacific Ocean on the west !

It covered a territory much less known in that day, in its geography and in its topography, than is now known of Africa. The district in which Mr. Jennings taught, as he fixes the boundary, covered a territory out of which have been carved thirteen states. From that day until Iowa assumed the dignity of statehood, the hardy pioneer venturing "beyond the Mississippi" erected the log school-house, with puncheon floor and hewed seats, large fireplace and stick chimney, greased paper window and clapboard roof, and this " before they had money to operate them with." These people in shaping the destiny of a new commonwealth were actuated by the spirit of young " Erasmus," the classic German scholar of the Fourteenth Century, who declared "as soon as he got any money he would buy Greek books and then he would buy some clothes." With them the first determination was to lay a broad and a deep foundation for mental culture.

REV. ALEXANDER BURNS.
President, 1869-1879.

REV. T. A. BERRY,
President, 1879-1881.

doctrine which inspired the authors of the Declaration of Independence. Under the enthusiasm of James Harlan, M. L. Fisher, and Thomas H. Benton, with equally able colleagues, they in turn led by the warm Scotch-Irish blood of Gov. J. W. Grimes, the great aggressive leader and the bold advocate of "higher education, prohibition, and the non-extension of slavery," it is not strange that our political institutions were founded upon principles as firm as the everlasting hills. With the early pioneers the principle was firmly fixed that "governments are established for the protection of the governed." With them the greatest safety of a state or a nation was held to be in the education of her people to the highest civil, social, and intellectual plane — much more effective and permanent than any attempt to instill high aspirations and nobility of life through the enforcement of the cold provisions of criminal law.

They were acting under the correct theory that the property interests, as well as the material resources, of the state could be more effectually developed by the intelligent, educated citizen. The enabling act of the congress of the United States, under which the territory was organized, declared that the people of Iowa "shall enjoy all the rights, privileges, and immunities" that belong to a free people. That "religion, morality and knowledge being necessary to good government and to the happiness of mankind, schools and all the means of education shall be forever encouraged." From the classic hills of New England, from the commercial centers of the East, from the shops, the factory, and the field of the middle and western states, came the representatives of the professions, the arts, the mechanics, and the sturdy yeomanry, hailing with delight the advent of Iowa into the sisterhood of states, and with equal zeal advocating that sound political

The people of Indianola, the Des Moines Conference, and the friends of Simpson College, believed that such an institution would provide moral protection in addition to the safety secured by the body politic. With them the safest, cheapest and best way to perpetuate good government was through the channels of intellectual development.

The thought that inspired the originators of Simpson College was that education was the best preventive of pauperism and crime, and was much less expensive than to punish the one by the enforcement of law, or to relieve the other by the hand of charity. In common with the people of Iowa they believed that a higher education would foster truth, maintain justice, encourage philanthropy, promote public good, and make permanent the blessings of liberty.

The city of Indianola, and the county of Warren, popularly known as the "three-river country," was settled by the best

REV. B. L. PARKS,
President, 1880-1886.

REV. W. E. HAMILTON, D. D.,
President, 1886-1889.

for a campus were secured, the sum of $4,500 was subscribed, and later the school was opened with Professor W. E. Gray in charge and H. C. Cowles and S. W. Hanford as assistants, with a regular academic course of study and with 184 students.

During the War period the seminary was under the charge of Professor O. H. Baker (since a consul at Copenhagen) and his wife, and the name of the institution was changed to the "Des Moines Conference Seminary." During the year 1867 the seminary was raised to the grade of a college and given the name of "Simpson Centenary College," with Professor S. M. Vernan as its first president, who resigned a few months later and was succeeded by Rev. A. Burns, D. D. Following Doctor Burns, Simpson College has been ably presided over by Rev. T. S. Berry,

class of emigrants. Among its inhabitants can be found the Puritan and the shrewd New Englander; the liberality of the Middle and Western States; the chivalry of Virginia and of Kentucky; the sturdy English, and the quick-witted and positive Scotch-Irish, all combined in the onward march of the progressive young commonwealth. The vigor with which they have always opposed the saloon and kindred evils soon marked Indianola as the future "Athens of the Des Moines Conference" and the proper location for her educational institution.

The annual conference of 1860, convened at that place, recognized and encouraged the establishment of the "Male and Female Seminary of Indianola." The prime movers in the enterprise were Hon. George W. Griffs, Hon. George W. Jones and Rev. J. C. Reed. Ample grounds

Rev. E. L. Park, W. E. Hamilton,
D. D., Rev. E. M. Holmes, B. D.,
and Rev. Fletcher Brown, B. D.,—
all living except Doctor Berry,
whose name is revered by the College and the Church. The financial
struggle of Simpson College is but
the repetition of the financial history of similar institutions, save
possibly the fierce contest to remove it to the capital of the state.
A later conference gave it the name
of "Simpson College." Standing
in the tall maple grove of the
commodious and lovely campus is
the main college building, containing the chapel, the president's and
the secretary's offices, rooms for
the literary societies and for the
commercial department; also the
four-story science hall with its
printing office, library, chemical
and physical laboratory, rooms for
Latin and modern languages, art
gallery, museum and class recitation rooms, and the large and substantial Ladies' Hall with dining-
room and kitchen, bath and separate living rooms, all surrounded by ample
room and accommodation for the athletic
sports belonging to college life. The
blending together of the natural and the
artistic, the combination of nature and of
art, furnishes a view seldom seen, and

REV. E. M. HOLMES,
President, 1889-1892.

one that would charm the most critical
artist.

The value of the college plant is near
$100,000, and the endowment fund of the
institution is approximately the same,
which fund is being constantly increased
through the efforts of
President Brown. The
catalogue of the college
develops a course of study
equal to the older col-
leges East, and it far surpasses the study pursued
by Yale, Princeton and
Harvard at the end of
the first century of their
existence.

It is most difficult to
write of a meritorious
educational institution set
on foot by private enter-
prise and resist the temptation to follow a historic
vein with reference to

SIMPSON COLLEGE, INDIANOLA.

those who have been identified with it. The founders and up-builders of this college are all noble characters and each has made an impress that will live in the memory of the thousands of Simpson students. They have exerted an influence that will be felt in coming ages in the high type of our state citizenship. Among the worthy pioneer students of Simpson was Doctor Bradley, who for twenty years or more was in charge of the mission work in India, where he died a few years ago. He was a member of the first graduating class of the college. The class of '94 contained twenty-five members.

The Simpson students and alumni are found in the mission field and the educational work of nearly every country on the globe. They are prominent in state, on the rostrum and in the pulpit; they are in mechanics, the trades and the arts; they are in the professions, in literature, in music and in

REV. FLETCHER BROWN.
President, 1890-1895.

SCIENCE HALL.

poetry, and are eminently successful in every avocation of life.

The character and the mental
caliber of the Simpson student, we
presume, will compare favorably
with those of like institutions.
They are no better, probably no
worse. There are about as many
schemes to evade college discipline; as much "tick tacking the
town" and as many hazing parties; as much sharp practice on the
college authorities and the verdant
"new student"; as much moonlight rambling; as many fabrica-
tions in the form of pledges of
eternal fidelity between the sexes;
as many happy unions and as many
disappointments as the result of
college courtship; as many drones
and as many bright students as
may be found in the average college.

Like the graduates of all similar
institutions, Simpson's alumni are
most loyal to their Alma Mater.
To the gray-haired alumnus, a
visit to the college, where he can

HON. JOHN W. HENDERSON,
Secretary, Board of Trustees, Simpson.

LADIES' HALL.

live again the scenes of college life, and revive memories of the chapel, the class rooms, the corridor and the fields of athletic sports of other days, creates a feeling closely allied to the pleasure experienced by the weary pilgrim of the Arabian desert as he treads the streets of the Mecca of his heart's delight.

SIMPSON COLLEGE WHEEL CLUB.

THE RUNAWAY.

By Charles B. Acheson.

THE warm rays of the afternoon sun shone in through the open window of the little railway station and, glancing from the polished brass of the telegraph key on the table, threw a beam into the eyes of one of the two men sitting there, with chair tilted back and pipe in mouth.

"Gettin' on toward three o'clock, aint it, George?" he said, as he lazily changed his position for a more shady spot. "Number 9's later than usual to-day. Wonder what's up!"

"She left Rockford thirty-five minutes behind. Have to side-track here and wait for Number 13 to pass her."

George Kincaid was telegraph operator, ticket agent, station master and general man at one of the many small Missouri stations of the "R. & O." Railroad. Clifford as a town was nothing to speak of—some dozen or fifteen houses, a store and post-office combined, and the railway station, comprised the whole of it.

A dull, uninteresting little place with no life in it. Dull indeed George found it, coming from the lively, bustling little village of Kirksome, eight or nine miles up the road. But orders were orders,—and, too, situations were not found growing on every bush, so he had accepted the first one offered him.

The other occupant of the room was a young fellow from Clifford, who had found the station a good loafing place that hot afternoon. Besides, he was ambitious, this Jim. He had a "hankerin'" for a "soft snap," as he considered the position held by George. "Nothin' much to do, an' the pay aint so bad." So he spent much of his spare time in and about the depot, picking up a knowledge of the duties required of a station master and operator. It was barely five minutes since George had spoken when Number 9 came pulling up in front of the station, and then slowly backed onto the siding to wait for the express, Number 13, to pass. This was precisely at 2:56 and 13 was due Clifford at 3:11.

George went leisurely back to the office after he had seen 9 safely on the switch. As he entered he heard his office called on the sounder. Impatient and hurried the call seemed. Dropping into a chair he answered, and then took the message:

"*Look out for runaway engine — two cars. Just passed here.*"

The startling words ticked out clear and distinct. They came from Rockford, another small settlement about five miles west of Clifford.

George repeated and O. K'd mechanically before he clearly realized the meaning of the communication. Then it came home to him — "*Look out for runaway*" it had said.

He hastily looked at his watch — 2:59! No. 13 was due Kirk at 2:57 — and no station between Kirk and Clifford! Quick! It might possibly be a few minutes late. "My God, keep it back!" was his fervent prayer as he turned again to his key and called Kirk, —

"*Hold 13. Runaway train just passed Rockford. Number 9 on switch here. Kincaid.*"

His heart sank within him as the reply came ticking back, —

"*Number 13 passed here on time, 2:57.*"

He sat for a few seconds with bowed head, helpless. The situation was a terrible one. Number 13, with her six coaches well filled with human freight, and the runaway, rushing toward each other on the same track! What could he do! What *could* he do! The thought made him frantic. Suddenly he leaped to his feet. He must stop that runaway. He *must* do it. The lives of perhaps two hundred passengers depended on him. Again he looked at his watch. It marked one minute and a half after 3 o'clock. How the time had flown! "Here, Jim," he cried to his companion, "you know the code. Mind the wire till I come back — if I do come back," he added to himself. "If Keene, the conductor on Number 9, comes in, tell him there's a runaway between here and Rockford and I've gone down to meet it. I'll try my best to stop

it. It's my only way," — and he was gone, running down the track.

Not much more than a quarter of a mile of the way had he covered when the runaway engine came in sight, rocking from side to side, and tearing over the rails with terrible speed. "Wide open!" George muttered, and stopped still in the middle of the track,

To an observer it would have seemed sheer madness — suicide — to stand there directly in the path of an uncontrolled engine, tearing toward him at the rate of forty miles an hour. But there he stood, firm and unflinching, regaining his breath after the run he had had.

Now the engine is nearly on him! He seems to feel the hot breath scorching his cheek! He gathers himself, jumps high in the air and forward. Merciful heavens — he is ground under the wheels! No — he is safe, clinging to the guard! Yes, safe for the moment, but the blow is a terrible one. The engine struck him with murderous force and leaves him clinging there, stunned for the moment.

But only for a moment. Then, realizing that something must be done, and done at once, he painfully clambers back over the great, panting, throbbing machine to the cab, conscious only that he must stop the runaway at the earliest possible moment, and that there is terrible pain in his chest and side.

Faintness comes over him as he closes the throttle and applies the brakes. At any other time he would have fainted; but like a flood, the thought surges through his brain that his duty is but half done as yet. "A few minutes more — only a few minutes," he mutters between his closed, set teeth.

Slowly the engine comes to a stop, as if reluctant to give up its victims. Then its wheels begin to revolve again and it is soon speeding back over the way it came.

Meanwhile a stern fight is going on in the little cab. George stands upright, his hands clenched, his eyes strained, battling against a strong tendency to unconsciousness. As faintness steals over him he shakes it off with a supreme effort of his strong will. Will-power alone sustains him during the ordeal. The thought that he must keep at his post till the runaway is safely side-tracked surges through his brain like fire. This one idea and purpose is there. After that, no matter. Then he can yield to that numbness — that horrible sinking — and so glide down into oblivion.

An end must come to all things but the Infinite. And an end came to that awful ride. What seemed to him an eternity was in reality only a very few minutes, and soon the runaway was safe from harm-doing on the siding at Rockford.

The strain removed, George sank into a state of semi-consciousness. Strange images and fancies ranged through his head like specters. Again, in his dreams, he was in the quiet little station at Clifford. The sun shone through the open window and he could hear the birds outside. A smile was on his face as, proud in the realization of duty performed, he said, "Runaway safe on switch at Rockford."

How proud his friends would be of him! Had not his mother, when he had left her, laid her dear hand on his shoulder and bade him let duty to himself and God be his first thought? Had not his little sister loudly proclaimed her faith in his doing great things? His mother — if he could only see her again! Perhaps they would give him a few days' leave to go back to the old home. They might do it after this. The thought made him glad. If it were not for that strange feeling in his side he would be quite happy lying there in the sun-lit room. But what a strange feeling it was, and why did the faces leaning over him look so grave? Why did they not smile?

The pain is coming again, but this time it is less intense. He feels drowsy. It will be good to sleep. He closes his eyes and thinks again of his mother. Those bending over him see the poor boy's lips flutter for a moment, as if to give expression to a thought, and then close. The hastily summoned physician rises to his feet, removes his hand from over the lad's heart, straightens himself up, looks at the men in the room gravely and says, "It is over."

EDITORIAL COMMENT.

"LIFE AND LETTERS," by W. D. Howells, is an interesting feature recently added to that now decidedly "sporty" "Journal of Civilization," *Harper's Weekly*. In the issue of June 8 Mr. Howells discusses dialect. In his judgment "the general reader" is, "in a certain measure, and in a certain kind, perhaps the very highest kind," "not worth minding." There's a delicate touch of cynicism in this author's remark that "if there is anything clearly ascertained concerning the general reader it is that you never can tell what will please him. He is quite like a spoiled child in not knowing what he wants, but unhappily he is like a spoiled child also in knowing what he does not want." Mr. Howells' direct statement is clearly true, but isn't his simile a bad one? Isn't the public rather more like an editor than a spoiled child? The author never can tell what the editor wants until he experiments on him, and extorts from him an acceptance. When Mr. Howells was engaged in the business of passing upon manuscripts, he must have received many letters of inquiry as to whether a paper on this, that or the other subject would be acceptable, and his almost unvarying answer, with many variations, doubtless was that he didn't know, — that it was not articles *per se* that he wanted, but he would be pleased to pass upon the availability of any manuscript sent him. So with the general public.

Both editor and public are like the boarder whose landlady asked him if he was "fond of Dutch cheese." "My dear madam," said he, "I made a serious mistake once in saying in the presence of a lady friend that I never tired of Dutch cheese. It so happened that I became a regular Sunday diner at the lady's table and, regularly as Sunday came, I was forced to crowd down more or less of the rancidest stuff that ever passed for Dutch cheese. Ever since that painful experience I refuse to commit myself in advance on any such vital question."

Take another homely illustration. A lady once made a simple salad which delighted the palate of her guest. At another time, in honor of the self-same guest, she made a more elaborate salad. She knew it was the best she had ever made, and would have resented any suggestion to the contrary, or any comparison with her previous efforts in the same direction. The salad course was reached. The honored guest attempted the salad and retreated. He sought to cover his retreat with a brilliant fire of conversation. The hostess, not to be diverted from the subject next her heart, expressed regret that he didn't like her salad. The guest assured her that he did—that he had a most delightful recollection of the last salad he had eaten at her table, but the fact was his appetite hadn't been very sharp lately!

A Howells writes a charming little love story, such as "A Chance Acquaintance," or "Their Wedding Journey," and year after year the general public absurdly keep calling for it. But when Howells tempts the public with more pretentious work, into which the author weaves the finest brain material he is conscious of possessing, as, for instance, "Silas Lapham," or "Hazard of New Fortunes," or—what's the name of that story in which the heroine's one drop of negro blood is microscopically examined?—the public simply doesn't buy the last-named books,—and the author wonders what the reason is, and, unless he is very good to himself, he is liable to become just a trifle cynical over the whimsicalities of popular taste.

But,—returning to the subject,—we referred to Mr. Howells as having dialect under consideration, his conclusion being that this fitful, spoiled child, the general public, has "got tired" of dialect. His advice to writers is that if they persist in using dialect—and he doesn't know why they shouldn't—they must make up their minds that the general public will get along without them. Is our critic wholly right? Would it not be nearer truth to state that the public tires only of the excessive use of dialect? No one has equaled Mr. McClennan in the literary use made of "the French-English parlance of Canada." But, by the time the reader reaches the end of one of that author's stories of Canadian life, he feels a sense of relief somewhat similar to that experienced by one who has listened to a play rendered in a tongue with which he is not very familiar. If Mr. McClennan would drop the monologue style and tell his stories himself, giving his readers frequent rests from dialect, and reducing to the minimum the use of the vernacular, he might win us wandering sheep back to his fold. He may, however, be as indifferent as Howells to the approval of the general public. Thomas Nelson Page's "Marse Chan" and "Meh Lady" are loaded down with dialect; but, most fortunate would the Harpers be if they could repeat that author's early successes in dialect stories. Readers of Cable's "Old Creole Days" would be delighted with another volume as fresh and dialectful as was the first. The Skandinavian-English, in the hands of a Hamlin Garland, is an added charm to the admirable characterizations which that author has given us. Our judgment of that portion of the general public which extends far eastward and westward from the Mississippi, is that any attempted representation of Creole life, or Skandinavian-American life, or rural life in the North, or plantation life in the South, which should exclude a reproduction of the pronunciation of the personages introduced, would deprive the reader of one great charm in the characterization. Our "guess" at what the general public wants in the matter of dialect is: just as much of it as is necessary to give the reader a true conception of the "speech of people "—no more.

* *

PERSISTENCY finds splendid embodiment in Herbert Spencer. Eighteen years ago, at the age of fifty-seven, this man sat down to the great work of his life, the all-including "Principles of Sociology." Far from robust at the time, his health has since been steadily failing. But during all these years he has toiled on almost unremittingly; and now, at seventy-five, he is closing up the last installment of the work. It is probable that with the conclusion of the book will close the most brilliant distinctively intellectual career of our century.

* *

SPEAKING of the alleged "New Woman,"—the really strong, self-reliant, sympathetic, helpful woman,—what light might not history have thrown upon her claim that she is not new at all, had the early historians but grasped the Dionysian conception of history as "philosophy teaching by example," and not the mere chronicle of battles and sieges, of the crimes of kings and the uprisings of subjects ! But here and there a side-light has been thrown upon the life of people in ages past which reveals the fact that woman was then, as she is now, helpful in emergencies as in the every-day duties of life. Let us recall an instance — not the regulation illustration, such as Semiramis, or Zenobia, or Joan of Arc, but one that is comprehended and felt by the masses and is part of their cherished traditions. There is a pretty well authenticated tradition attached to the siege of Weinberg, in the Twelfth Century, which, whether truth or fiction, shows what might have been expected of woman in that day. The German Emperor, Conrad, in his war upon the Guelphs, lay siege to the Weinbergers. After a long and stubborn resistance, the besieged surrendered, the city gates were thrown open and the conquerors entered. Conrad was so incensed at the stubbornness of the resistance that he issued a mandate that every arms-bearing man in the captured city be

put to death. He considerately gave the women permission to quit the city, taking with them whatever they might individually carry away upon their backs. The city gates were again thrown open, this time by the conquerors, and a long line of women appeared, each bearing upon her back, not her goods and chattels, much as she longed to take them with her, but in their stead, a husband, or father, or son, or lover ! Brave as the Weinbergers had shown themselves in battle and siege, they thought it not beneath their dignity to thus receive back their forfeited lives from their wives, mothers, daughters and sweethearts. The Emperor was so nonplussed by the shrewd device of the women that, when his nephew protested against the escape of the men upon the shoulders of the women, he could only say, "The word of an Emperor is sacred."

The temptation is strong to tell that other story of the Bohemian women who, when a body of dismounted cavalrymen marched triumphantly through their streets, took off the kerchiefs which they were wont to wear upon their heads and threw them upon the ground. The bespurred soldiers were soon caught in the silken meshes prepared for them. Hopelessly entangled, they fell to the ground and were taken prisoners by the husbands of the shrewd women who had thus placed the besiegers at the mercy of the besieged.

Thus, in every age has woman been a helpmate, and thus she will continue to be to the end of time. She is now only readjusting herself to the altered conditions of our era.

* *

AMERICAN lovers of song whose memories go back to the Jenny Lind craze are wont to speak of the Swedish nightingale as birdlike, if not angelic, in nature ; but Dr. Hauslich, in his "*Aus Meinem Leben*," makes her appear quite otherwise. Invited to lunch at her house near London, he received a welcome so rude that her husband, Mr. Goldschmidt, felt compelled to half apologize for her conduct. Perhaps there was something wanting in the manner of her guest —or, perhaps, as musical critic, in commenting on her work he had not soared far enough above actual criticism to satisfy the much be-praised prima donna.

⁂

WILLIAM WATSON has just completed the longest lyrical poem he has yet written, "A Hymn to the Sea." This poem will go far toward determining whether its author be the true successor to Tennyson, or only one among the many rare verse-makers of the era who are doing much to make our ways delightful with their sweet singing.

AMONG THE MAGAZINES.

The June *Review of Reviews* follows its admirable "Progress of the World" with a paper by Willis J. Abbot on "Chicago Newspapers and Their Makers," which is not a paper to skip, as one might at first glance think. Mr. Abbot cleverly handles a hackneyed subject. His love of truth may possibly have been somewhat weakened by his evident good-fellowship, but not very much. What couldn't a man say in praise of Scott, Nixon, Medill, Stone, Lawson, Kohlsaat, Seymour, Hawley and the rest — the makers of the new journalism of Chicago! And this new journalism — what a subject to write upon! Old-time readers of and swearers at the Chicago *Times* of Storey's time have not got over their old habit of condemning Chicago journalism in toto. Ignorant of the vast quantities of salacious matter which the Chicago papers exclude and which at least one New York paper is wont to make its leading feature, the old-timer and his younger echo unite in condemning where they should commend. Mr. Abbot correctly notes the subordination of opinion-making to news-telling observable in the Chicago press. We of the farther West don't make up our judgments as much from the editorials as from the news pages of the great dailies. Relatively to circulation, the editorial pages of the home dailies of our smaller cities exert far more influence on the public mind than do the editorial pages in the Chicago press. The bad example of the wilful Storey finds no following in the Chicago journalists of to-day. All are bent on supplying the public with a basis for forming conclusions and not inclined to appeal, to dictate, or to scold. All have learned by rough experience and by shrewd observation that the man of the Middle-West whom they would serve carries his sovereignty under his hat; makes up his judgment as to general and national questions, and is disposed to go contrary when the Chicago journals assume to dictate his course.

The *Southern Magazine*, after our declination of its publisher's offer to consolidate with THE MIDLAND MONTHLY, last fall, suspended publication. It has since revived and taken the name *Mid-Continent*. It has not honored us with an exchange, but we learn that it is a handsome and well-edited magazine.

The delightfully inevitable Howells! Scarcely are we done with dissent from some one thing he has said before we are grown enthusiastic over some other work of his hand! The most charming paper which has appeared in the magazines in a long time is Howells' "Tribulations of a Cheerful Giver," in the June *Century*. It recalls the good old days of Addison and Steele. In fact, we may spend a half-day running back over the musty volumes of "The Spectator" and find nothing as finely humorous, as delicately purposeful, as this latest work of Howells.

GOSSIP ABOUT AUTHORS.

The author of "Belle's Roses,"* Mr. Emerson Hough, or "E. Hough," as he prefers to sign himself, was born of Virginian parents in the little city of Newton, Iowa. He graduated from the State University in 1880 and was admitted to the bar two years later. His fondness for travel and adventure soon won him from his law books and, though fairly successful at the bar, he early abandoned his practice for a mining camp in New Mexico. His experiences in camp have supplied material for sketches which have appeared in various periodicals. Then followed "some brutal days," as he terms them, when he was seeking the sort of foothold he desired for journalistic work. Adventurous by nature, and devoted to the sports of the field, he at length found himself identified with *Forest and Stream*, of New York City. Six years ago last fall he became manager of the western business of that periodical, with headquarters in Chicago. "I bless the day," he says, "when I stumbled into this work, for I like it and it gives me independence, and no amount of wealth can do more than that for a man." There are few of the wilder corners of the Union that have escaped the personal observation of this successful

<hr>

* See page 531 of the present number.

picturer of outdoor life. In the winter of '93-4, with Elwood Hofer, a mountain guide, and two privates of the regular army, he made one of the most daring trips known in the history of the Rocky Mountains. Leaving Fort Yellowstone with packs on their backs, the party traveled on snowshoes more than two hundred miles through the heart of the wild mountain country of the Yellowstone, sleeping out in the snow with the mercury at 21° below zero, fording rushing streams, and subjected to other perils. This trip Lieutenant Schwatka had previously attempted, but without success. Mr. Hough's vivid story of his adventures, published in *Forest and Stream* and syndicated in the great dailies, attracted much attention at the time. For five years Mr. Hough has done little pure literary work ; but he has now in press, and will issue during the early summer, his first book, to be entitled "The Singing Mouse Stories," which he describes as "studies of in-doors and out-of-doors." Of his scattered Western stories he could collect another volume, and we have a rumor of a collection of more recent and less local studies. The story, "Belle's Roses," concluded in this number, is said to be given first place in this latter work. Of one phase of it the author writes us,—

The New Woman is not a dangerous thing, for at heart she is the old Woman of Paradise, without whom there can be no paradise to-day. The maternal heart and the gentle soul of woman will always be with us, and will triumph over a multitude of fads and foolishness. The New Woman cannot escape the way of Nature. The danger is not in her, but in the strained and unnatural doctrines which may be promulgated in regard to her. Man can not make a better woman than God has already made, nor, indeed, can man much change her, nor can she change herself.

This thought evidently underlies the motive and furnishes the denouement of the story which Mr. Hough has so dramatically written.

SPEAKING of the astuteness of the Chinese, a MIDLAND contributor, Mrs. Clement, sends us from Japan a clipping from a Nanking correspondent of the China *Gazette* of February 25th, giving the details of "an excellent scheme for the annihilation of the Japanese." The story is that the Governor of Nanking recently issued a proclamation ordering everybody to devise some scheme for the destruction of the Japanese. A sage of high repute came to the Governor's *James*, bringing his scheme with him. The scheme was a remarkable one. Every soldier was to be armed with a sword, a long bamboo pole, and a bucket of water! The pole and the bucket should be held with the left hand, the sword in the right. On charging upon the foe, the buckets should be hurled at the opposing ranks, so as to wet their powder and so render their guns useless. The bamboo poles should then be thrust between the legs of the enemy and given a twist, which would cause the Japanese to topple over in confusion. After that it would be an easy matter to finish off the dripping and prostrate foe with the sword. The Governor did not think the plan was practicable.

Hon. George F. Parker, United States consul at Birmingham, England, whose contributions to THE MIDLAND are pleasantly recalled, has been elected president of the Birmingham Dramatic and Literary Club.

TALKS WITH CORRESPONDENTS.

Find enclosed an original poem composed for the exercises at this place ; but, on account of the rain, it was not delivered. Take it for what it is worth to you and forward me a copy of your magazine which it contains. Criticise it to your liking. I have not punctuated or done anything to perfect it.

This writer simply mistakes the nature of the magazine. THE MIDLAND is not a receptacle for manuscripts which have been unfortunate. It is reaching out after the choicest product of midland literature. Its embarrassment is one of riches in this respect. Far from wanting something to fill its pages with, its editor is continually questioning as to what is best for coming numbers, and what can, without loss of availability, be left over to make place for matter which, for various reasons, claims present attention. Now, viewing the question raised by this well-intending, but mistaken correspondent as to the availability of her poem, she herself must see what the inevitable answer must be. (1) As she herself says, it was written for a purely local occasion and with no thought of the forty or fifty thousand readers of THE MIDLAND. (2) Its author sends it to us without having punctuated it "or done anything to perfect it." Written for a purely local occasion, it is not of general interest. Its author having confessedly done nothing to perfect it, and poems having no power to perfect themselves, one need scarcely look at the poem to find it too faulty in construction to be available, even were the thought of the verse sufficiently de-localized to be acceptable for magazine use. Be self-critical.

I do not suppose it will make any difference in the verdict [of the judges in the June 30th competition] but I will add that I am a native of Iowa and the greater part of my life has been passed there.

Thus writes a Pacific-slope competitor for one of the three prizes in the recent competition. We emphatically answer *no;* nothing makes any difference in the verdict except the relative character of the contributions themselves. The judges may not render a just verdict but, our word for it, they purpose to do that thing and nothing else. We cannot guarantee the correctness of their separate judgments,—each judge acting separately and unknown to the other two,—but we can vouch for the honesty and honor of the judges and for their intelligent appreciation of the good in literature. The prize contributions themselves, thus far announced, show that no pent-up Iowa confines our competition — that the whole country is made tributary to THE MIDLAND. We find that the cash prizes awarded have found their way into the the four corners of Iowa, also into Illinois, Missouri, Kansas, Colorado, California, Idaho, South Dakota and Kentucky.

If you can do so, I will be pleased to have you give me a pointer as to where I can send my class of work, with hope of publication. If there are any who use such drivel. I don't want to keep pestering you. Yet I want to place my articles somewhere if I can.

This is an extract from a letter acknowledging receipt of a MS. returned. Taking the writer's own word for it,—that his MS. is "drivel," the answer is easy:— Nowhere. But the writer clearly doesn't mean what he says, for he is desirous to have it published, feeling that it has merit —as it certainly has. We often get inquiries of this kind, and desire to say that no one editor can tell what another editor wants, and no writer can tell where he

can get his MSS. published in any other than the old, laborious, disappointing way—offering them to the publishers he thinks most likely to want them.

The Editor tells us MSS. are not acceptable unless typewritten. Is it so?

No. Typewritten MSS. are preferable, for they are always readable. You write a plain hand and need not go to the expense of getting your MS. typewritten. But here before us is another MS., beautiful in appearance as a whole, but about as translatable as a page of Balzac to a first-termer in French. The author of that MS. should invest in a typewriter or patronize a typist. But the trouble lies right here: Said author doesn't know his writing is blind. His wife reads it; his clerks read it; his banker knows his signature far as he can see it. But the editor who hasn't grown up on it finds it very hard reading. He would rather run a lawn-mower back and forth across a good-sized lawn than read six pages of this man's elegantly written manuscript. The point is, gentle reader: If anybody has ever found it hard to read your MS., then somebody else is sure to find it at least equally hard. If that somebody else is asked to pass upon your work, and finds no pleasure in it, can you blame him if he sends it back to you unused? Another big advantage in the use of the typewriter is in that it enables one to see his own work somewhat as it would look in print. It thus frees us from many a blunder frees us,—and foolish notion.

Do the good MSS. which do not win prizes receive your consideration?

Yes, and if any are found available for our use in the near future, we open correspondence with the authors relative to them with a view to their publication.

THE MIDLAND BOOK TABLE.

Reviewers are wont to fight shy of the avowed purpose novel; but now and then they find one which compels their attention to the very last. "A Voice in the Wilderness," by Maria Weed,[*] is of this rare sort. Its introduction frankly informs the reader that the story is opportune as a voice raised against the morphine habit—"the greatest enemy that to-day menaces humanity." Can one get interested in a heroine addicted to the morphine habit? Yes. Helen Mathews not only deeply interests the reader, but commands the reader's active sympathy. The victim of a physician's excessive use of

the drug, she makes a brave but unavailing struggle against the power over her life. A Doctor Stanley, who has made a specialty of the opium habit, undertakes her case. The reader is quite ready to forgive and bless Doctor Stanley for throwing his whole heart and soul into this particular case — and therein lies the chief strength and beauty of the story. Two interesting minor characters hover about the principal actors — Marian, a noble young woman, who responds to Doctor Stanley's solicitation and serves his patient as a companion, and Horace Belknap, a devoted lover of Marian. The scenes and incidents are few. The psychological study developed by the story

[*] Laird & Lee, publishers, Chicago.

makes a strong impression. The proof-reading on the book was carelessly done, but otherwise the little work is attractive. It has several excellent drawings by Mr. Justice, a Chicago artist, formerly of Cedar Rapids. The author of the story is a lady prominent in the new movement for club federation in the Middle West and was the first treasurer of the Club Federation of Iowa. A paper from her pen, entitled "Mothers in Clubs," appeared in THE MIDLAND of April, 1894.

Oklahoma has thus early found her poet! She hasn't yet had time to place a laurel on his brow. She hasn't yet taken time to read the poems which immortalize her. But recognition is a mere circumstance; the fact alone concerns us. The brevet poet laureate of Oklahoma is Freeman E. Miller, A. M., professor of English language and literature in the Agricultural and Mechanical College of the territory. The foundation of his fame is a book of 127 pages, entitled, "Oklahoma, and Other Poems."* The title poem sounds the praises of the new territory in words as strong and free as are the winds that sweep over its prairies. The poet finds a surprising degree of greatness and goodness in her people and beauty in her situation. The best lines in "Oklahoma" are these:

Morning saw a desert sleeping,
Night beheld an empire leaping
Watch above the wilderness:

One of the strongest poems in the book is "The Race for Homes," descriptive of that memorable April 22, 1889, when at early morn

The legion waits
The turning of the desert gates,
That men of might may enter in.

And, when noon comes, the signal is given which figuratively swings open the gates and lets the home-seekers in. Then follows the mad rush, and it is vividly pictured.

Stronger still is the description of a similar scene at Perry, September 16, 1893. With the poet's aid we see—

Crowds! Crowds! Crowds!
Suddenly heroes if come from the clouds
That faded away as they came;
Mad cries of people aflame
With thirst for a morsel of land;
Wild hunters of fortune, whose game
Is ever escaping the hand;
Vast, countless, uncountable throngs
With restless, unresistable feet.

But out from the clouds,
Out from the agonized dust that en-shrouds,
True kings shall arise who shall reign
In homes on the populous plain!
Great cities shall gather and grow.

*Charles Wells Moulton, publisher, Buffalo, New York.

"The Banks o' Turkey Run," is a new version of the old longing for old scenes and old friends. Among the several sonnets is one which vividly pictures the long unbroken solitude of Oklahoma, "save when passed the bison herds, and savage hunters swept in thundering chaos."

Macmillan & Company are doing good service in republishing, with attractive illustrations, works of fiction that in their day were relatively great, but somehow failed to perpetuate themselves with the publishers. Reading these books as they appear, one cannot help wondering if, after all, literary greatness doesn't largely rest with publishers, or with the circumstances which raise in publishers' minds the question of availability. Take an illustration: "A Window in Thrums," by Barrie, has developed new interest in Scottish village life. A few old men and a few young men with fondness for old books went back from "A Window in Thrums" to "Annals of the Parish" and thought they saw in one a suggestion of the other—just as readers of "Annals of the Parish" in their time were sure they saw a suggestion of Goldsmith's "Vicar of Wakefield." To this association of thought we doubtless owe the pleasure we now have in reading John Galt's "Annals of the Parish,"* for, in the introduction to the book before us, Mr. Alfred Ainger says, "It is a noticeable circumstance that the present reprint coincides with a marked revival of interest in Scottish character and manners. We owe this largely to such admirable pictures of these as Mr. Barrie's, whose masterpiece, 'A Window in Thrums,' owes its success to the dominance of character over plot—character drawn with consummate humor and pathos." John Galt's two best works bound together—the one above mentioned and "The Ayrshire Legatees"—comprise about all their poor, hard-worked but ever cheery author wrote that is now worth reprinting. Story followed drama, and drama followed story in quick succession from the teeming brain of this indefatigable writer. Even Scott did not surpass him in industry. But alas, poor John Galt! If now conscious of the fate of his work while he was on earth, how regretful he must be that, with a world of material all about him,—his own little Ayrshire world with all its happenings, grave and gay, ranging all the way from tragedy to farce-comedy,—he persistently went outside that world and attempted to picture scenes he had not

*"Annals of the Parish" and "The Ayrshire Legatees," in one volume. Macmillan & Co., publishers, New York; $1.25

witnessed and characters which found no counterpart in the range of his own experience! The "Annals of the Parish" is the autobiography of the Reverend Micah Balwhidder, the minister of Delmailing. In this autobiography the minister unconsciously reveals himself a good-hearted, large-souled, not very clever man, full of little weaknesses, yet sound to the core in all the moral essentials. His simple narrative abounds in that most enjoyable kind of humor, the unconscious kind — for example, the refreshing complacency with which he regards his commonplace epitaph on his first wife, beginning,—

"A lovely Christian, spouse and friend."

"This," he writes, "was greatly thought of at the time, and Mr. Lorimore, who had a nerve for poesy himself in his younger years, was of opinion that it was so much to the purpose, and suitable withal, that he made his scholars write it out for their examination copies, at the reading whereof before the heritors the tear came into my eye and everyone present sympathized with me in my great affliction for the loss of the first Mrs. Balwhidder."

The story the parson tells is not simply humorous; it also gives a vivid picture of the interesting community-life along the west coast during the reign of George III., a picture drawn in simple colors and with few lines. The illustrations, by Charles E. Brock, are full of humor and have a strong suggestion of the Cruikshank touch which the reader associates with Dickens, Fielding and Smollett.

The author of "Esther Waters," Mr. George Moore, has been written up as a social reformer and written down as a caterer to a depraved popular taste for the scandalous. His new book, "Celibates,"* as was anticipated, throws some light upon the question of the author's purpose. If we were to judge the author by his "Mildred Lawson," the first of the three stories which make up the book, we could but condemn him as a low imitator of Du Maurier, the imitator thinking to sell his book by offering something more suggestive than "Trilby" descriptive of that unconventional artist life which Du Maurier has pictured. Mildred Lawson refuses to marry a man because she prefers to be his mistress and be free. She goes to Paris and studies the nude in art. She prefers to study in the men's class. She has the surface refinements of a lady, the instincts of a courtesan, the cold-blooded

* "Celibates," by George Moore, Macmillan & Co., New York, publishers; $1.50.

selfishness of a cat and the charms of a pleasing personality from which there is no escaping. It is not enough that the sorry failure of such a career should be shown. The suggestiveness of the descriptions and of the conversations running through the book reveal the unworthy purpose of the author.

"John Norton," the hero of the second story, is a straight-laced son and heir. He would be an anchorite against the wishes of his mother, who wants him to marry and settle down on the estate. Though he is abnormally averse to woman and to marriage, the pretty, gentle, delicate Kitty Hare wins his love, and then begins a war of love against fancied duty to his church. He seizes a pliant hour, or, rather, a witching hour seizes him, and he kisses her. Remorse follows his proposal of marriage and he comes back next day to withdraw the proposal. Meantime, a tramp has outraged Kitty and she, driven to madness by the outrage, flees from her morbid lover and, jumping out of a window, is killed. John fancies it was the stolen kiss that worked such madness in Kitty's brain and he determines to no more think of woman but to give his life to the church. Both Kitty and John are pure, and the story can hurt no one — nor do any one good.

"Agnes Lahens," the heroine of the third story, is pure as Kitty, and of a deeper, nobler nature. It may be that the picture of this beautiful character required the horrible setting given it; but greater artists than George Moore have not found it necessary to give more than a suggestion of the striking contrast. Aside from Agnes and her weak, half-crazy father and the priest who takes her back to the convent, all the characters are steeped in sin and brazenly shameless. Agnes' mother is Lord Chadwick's mistress, and with the knowledge and reluctant consent of her husband. The men who frequent her home are unfit for the society of a pure girl, and the women who meet them there are worse than the men. The splendid resistance of this pure young girl to the combined attempts of all these to break her into the ways of the world — their world — with the pathetic grief and unavailing attempts of the weak man whom she called father to shield his daughter from this hell in her own home — constitutes the strength of the story. A story with an excellent moral, and yet — who would introduce pure young womanhood to such a world for the purpose of strengthening virtue, or for any other purpose? Mr. Moore ought to do better work than he has yet done.

TYPES OF MIDLAND BEAUTY. II.

THE MIDLAND MONTHLY.

VOLUME IV.　　　　　AUGUST, 1895.　　　　　NUMBER 2.

THE DELLS OF THE WISCONSIN.

BY FANNY KENNISH EARL.

AVIS stopped rocking long enough to ask : "Well, what does he say?"

I read from the letter :

"—I have planned to take a few days off next week. Either here at M., or at L., or, if you will want to take the drive to the Dells, bring Flossie out and M. J., and I will go with you. I do not think we would need the two horses. Brown Betty is perfectly competent for the surrey. She is full of spirit and on good terms with life and the world in general.

"Here we have a comfortable house, here are all the books I value most; moreover, we command a view of 'the western possessions,' and even, when the clouds are not too thick, of the 'Castles in Spain'; here also is the beautiful lake — a landscape, framed by the library window, the equal of which was not to be found even in the Columbian gallery ; we have a boat, Betty and the surrey for the drives, and ample provision for ministering to our physical wants. At L. there

is the quiet of the village, a lake, also, for boating and bathing, and your vixenish pony on which to exercise one's temper and muscle.

"I have laid before you the possibilities of the vacation. Take your choice."

"I'm not in it," said Avis, picking up her banjo and striking a pretty attitude, "but all the same, I vote for the Dells."

So I wrote back : "Avis is here. We unanimously decide in favor of the Dells. We two, and Flossie, of course, will drive out to M. whenever you say."

The next day brought us a reply :

"That's all right. Avis is always a delightful addition, since she is not bad enough to be disreputable and not good enough to be disagreeable. Come on Wednesday, and bring the camera."

That was how we came to spend a few summer days at the Dells of the Wisconsin, though the getting there, delightful as it was, was not important. The main thing was that we reached our destina-

Photo by H. H. Bennett.　　　　LONE ROCK — LOWER DELLS.

tion one summer evening, just as the long shadows threw their purple lengths across the river. One glimpse of wonderland,—enough for the basis of a "Midsummer Night's Dream"; one swift selection,—"This green plot shall be our stage"; one correct conclusion,—that heads as fair as Titania's, and much more sedate than ours, had been turned by its bewildering beauty,—and then an impatient sleep, waiting for the morning.

"This is a beautiful place to be a little girl in," was Flossie's sedate morning remark. "I think it would have been nice to have been little when you were, mamma. Can't we move the house up here and stay?"

It *is* a "beautiful place to be a little girl in." Its braes and banks, its glens 'dripping with coolness,' its towering, wave-eaten rocks, its purple shadows, its golden bars, are not to be surpassed in beauty within the beautiful state of Wisconsin, and the traveler must trudge many a weary mile beyond its borders to find another spot where nature is so prodigal of her riches.

Standing on the deck of the little steamer, almost under the bridge that spans the Wisconsin, a troop of memories, as varied and active as Palmer Cox's brownies, fairly overwhelm me. Yonder

is the path by the river, and it is with a thrill of the horror with which one reads blood-curdling tales at midnight that I recall my careless, fearless stroll along that "cut-off" which led to the highway, and my sitting down to rest at the turn of the road across the Hurlbert Flat, where but a few hours later the "old man Gates" was mysteriously murdered by assassins who eluded the grip of the law and, for months after, darkened the lonely road with mysterious terrors.

Up the river a bit, where the saw-mill used to stand, I remember "once upon a time" to have taken another short cut to the landing, across the logs which lay between my boat and the shore. But things are not always what they seem, even on the Wisconsin, and one apparently robust log was nothing but the hollow bark, and down I went. I was saved to write this recollection by the agility of an Evanston theological student who had charge of the spiritual welfare of the Methodist flock in the village, and imparted to them his freshly-acquired knowledge what time he could spare from picnicking and boating. He is now a distinguished D. D., with a big church and a big salary, and I suspect would linger more graciously in my memory if he had come to the rescue sufficiently early to have saved my ap-

Photo by H. H. Bennett.   LOWER JAWS OF THE DELLS.

Photo by H. H. Bennett.   IRRITATED ROCK, LOWER DELLS.

pearance as well as my life. Having to parade the streets of that resorter-lined village with "garments clinging like cerements" was, to my girlish imagination, but one remove better than having to appear as the principal at a funeral.

But—*presto!* The scene changes! Under the mossy rocks the red blazing pine knots throw their long flashes across the river, and the rippling waves are a sheet of glistening ice. I hear again the song and laugh of the skaters and see the merry couples flying through the light and shadow. "All of which I saw, and part of which I was, O, years and years ago!" I tell Flossie: Yes, and there is one of the boys who used to share the frolics, looking rather dignified and portly, but with the same smile in his eyes!

But though the faces change; though some have left the quiet streets of the pretty village for the quieter and narrower ones up on the hill, where one can look miles away across the river and into the shadowy depths of glen and forest; though strangers meet one everywhere, the river, unchanged and unchanging, flows on and on. A spell is upon me as I sit in the prow of the boat, oblivious to the chatter of tourist and "resorter" in the rear. If Prue's castle-

building husband were beside me he might surely think he was on the way to Spain at last; but no—there is no need. He has already found the way!

The ripple of wave, the swiftly changing gleam of pine-clad cliff and cliff, the beds of fern, the trailing vines, the narrowed vision—as the rocks close in as if some mighty power were putting an imperious "thus far" upon the reckless spirit of the eddying stream—flit across the vision like the wonderful fancies of a midsummer dream, in which the passive mind accepts, without question, all the transformations wrought by a fairy charm. A tall, fair young man, wearing glasses and a distinguished air, walks up and down the deck, discoursing learnedly to whomsoever will listen—and there are people who are bent on improving their minds, even in vacations—of "Potsdam sandstone" and "quartzite ridges" and the "glacial period." I bestow upon him a glance of pity. Scientists are necessary, no doubt; but he is a superfluous man for whom the Dells is nothing but a geological specimen. As for us, desire for useful information was left behind along with all our earthly cares. One has no business even with memories; the best of them have an undertint of sadness; time mellows their bright colors into half-tones and neutral tints. Let the future, too, take care of itself. Its grim custodian will be standing at the front door ready to hand over the latch-key when the vacation is over; but over to-day he has no control. Life would soon lose its value if it were not for the rare days — or moments — when there is no past, no future, when the longing lips drink deep of the living present, and out of its fulness gather strength for the days that are to come, strength, also, for that harder thing to bear, — the memory of the days that shall come again no more forever. Even Heaven cannot give us those!

But through the absorption of my mood comes the sweet voice of our friend whom the tourists have discovered to be a "residenter." I listen in spite of myself, though the stories are the ones that

a child's vivid imagination tinted in colors that flash their realistic brilliancy through all the years between.

The Dell House, old, shattered, windowless, standing in the opening of a ravine with the towering rocks on one side and a bit of sandy beach on the other, dates back to 1837, and might reveal, if it would, the story of many a midnight revel, many an uncanny deed; might give the dark sequel to more than one mysterious disappearance, of the days when the Wisconsin was the highway between the pine forests of the north and the markets of the world.

The Dell House has served for the background of a number of imaginative stories, which would have lost nothing in picturesqueness or of thrilling interest if ·acts instead of fiction had served as the basis of the plot. I remember one which

"DELL QUEEN" RUNNING THE NARROWS.

appeared in one of the leading magazines a few years ago, which afforded the inhabitants of the pretty village below the Dells not a little amusement, albeit it was not a humorous tale. It was so evidently written by the man — or woman — who recognized the situation as good "material." The setting of the story was such as a clever person might easily have constructed in a few days' stay, — but the people! They might have been Tennesseans or Californians or Alaskans or Hawaiians for aught I know, but they were *not* inhabitants of the little village of Kilbourn. The atrocious dialect, attributed to the unfortunate "villagers" who were the victims of this particular story-teller, was very funny. I protest against my native state being utilized

as a field for the dialec-
tician, for, if we may be
pardoned a shortening of
the Italian "a" and an
occasional dropping of a
final "g" in common with
other Westerners, the
only dialect we hear is imported from foreign coun-
tries or New England!
There is nothing resem-
bling a native article.
Eastern writers, and western ones, too, ought to
know that in a state which
is a highway between the

Photo by H. H. Bennett.

THE OLD DELL HOUSE.

East and the West, and in which the
population is constantly changing, such
a thing is impossible. A dialect is a
growth of generations and flourishes only
where the conditions of life are fixed, and
the population changes only with the incoming of new generations.— But this is
a digression.

We are passing Black Hawk's Cave.
We peer into its gloom, thrilling with
the interest which a human life gives to
this grotto beyond the others. After all,
there is nothing in nature so rare, so
picturesque, so beautiful, that the hope,
the love, the hate, the despair of a human
soul cannot deepen its tints or intensify
the halo that surrounds it. One needs no
imagination to picture this stalwart figure
in Wisconsin's Indian warfare seeking
in the familiar haunts of his tribe a refuge
in the hour of his peril, when the determined foes of his race are hot upon his
track. But all the reserves of the imaginative faculty are called upon to picture
the leap of Black Hawk's Indian pony,
carrying its rider across the Narrows,
where the bare and slippery rocks would
scarcely afford footing for a squirrel.
But there are stories, like Putnam's ride
and the storming of Lookout Mountain,
which one can believe possible only because they are accomplished historical
facts, and Black Hawk's leap may find
a corner of refuge among them from
the ruthless hand of the searcher after
truth.

The bridge which spanned the Narrows
was built in 1848, and was the first which
was ever thrown across the Wisconsin.
People came many miles to cross it, and
paid their toll for the privilege. It was
swept away by the rushing torrent of the
spring of '66, when the echo of venturesome feet had scarcely died from its
trembling timbers.

As we passed a name cut in huge capitals, high above our heads, I heard the
gentle voice of our friend telling her interested audience that the high water
sometimes swept it out of sight. Of
course, at such times no baby steamer
wends its peaceful way between rocks
and shallows. The rocks are dwarfed to
one half their height, and there are no
shallows. If one chooses to follow the
foot-path beside the river, or takes the
carriage-road to the Dells, he will see a
whirling, tumbling, tempestuous stream,
a miniature Niagara Rapids, that tosses
its white spray over the sight-seer venturing near its slippery edge, and throws out
an unanswered challenge to the most
daring spirit.

It is still early in the season, and the
walks through the canyons — which have
to be rebuilt every spring — are not quite
in good repair. The high-water marks
in Witch's Gulch,— but a few days old,
— are high above our heads; and Flossie
gazes regretfully at her new tan boots, as
a venturesome climb results in a slide into
a muddy pool. The water dashes down

In sparkling falls under our very feet, and, if there were any disaster worse than wet shoes possible, the timid might hesitate to thread their way through the dark gorge. But O, the delicious coolness after the burning sun! It is a spot to dream of with the thermometer in the nineties,— overhanging cliffs shutting out the sunlight, green beds of moss and fern, pines towering straight up to the smiling sky,— it is enough! Let the world go by!

An arrow pointed to the Witch's Head, which gave the gulch its name, but some miscreant had shot off the old hag's nose disfiguring it for all time to come; but since she has perpetuated herself in the glen we can let her go. It needed some imagination to make out her profile in her palmiest days. Indeed, one little needs the assistance of that water-carved face to imagine, in some of the dark recesses, a blazing fire of pine knots, a witch's cauldron, and grotesque figures dancing about it in the fitful firelight. Witches and fairies and ghosts belong to the hill country and the forest. They do not inhabit the plains or the prairies where the eye takes a broad sweep to the far horizon. With nothing between one and the blue arch above, the vague mysteries that lurk in glen and grotto and in the shimmering depths of the forest are swept away; the imagination is dwarfed and life moves in a broader plane, guided by common sense and fortified by reason.

But as for me,— I prefer the glen and the forest. They have lost nothing of their charm since the days when I used to look in hollow stumps for pink-faced babies; when the white, ragged roots of the dead pines, from which the sand had drifted away, represented to me the ghosts of Indian warriors, straying back from the happy hunting-grounds; when the three lonely pines — which the sacrilegious hand of the woodman dared not touch — told to me, under each sunset sky, the romance of the first death in the new country, before God's acre had been set apart.

I have said that memories should have no place in the day's program; but in spite of the changing tints of rock and river, in spite of the sunny sky, the fragrant air and the life throbbing responsive to all of nature's varied moods, they come thronging back. "The woods are full of them," in a literal and not an applied sense. There is not a spot, up or down the river, but is alive with flitting forms. From the days when I gathered wintergreens along the rocks,

LOOKING OUT OF THE CAVE IN LONE ROCK.

and dug out the arbutus from under the late snows, when I waded in the shallows and gathered the dewberries under the bank, to the later time when at the Dell House. I confiscated an old boat, nearly as dilapidated as the house itself, and recklessly paddled across the river, while two equally reckless comrades industriously bailed out the boat to keep it afloat,—through all the golden days of girlhood the river is one panorama of my life. Yonder, at "Paradise," I camped with a party of students. Stand Rock is another monument to the memory of happy days. From the tunnel under "the Fill " I look down the river, where I have rowed and skated until every way-mark is as familiar as the walls of my own rooms ; and over one summer — the sum-

mer of summers — is thrown the glamour of my own little story, whose sequel will be found beyond the golden sunset gates.

So we lived for a few rare days,—close to nature's heart, under the spell of her subtle charm. There were no offices, no clients, no pending law-suits, no houses to keep, no clothes to mend, no books to read, no committees to shirk. The world went on its riotous way without us, with neither our sanction nor our disapproval. We were indifferent alike to its struggles and its triumphs.

But the end of our vacation came at last, O, far too soon !

"I think the hardest work
One ever does is not to shirk
On days that follow holidays,—
We love so well our laggard ways.
Alack, the holiday is o'er!"

THE RIFTING CLOUDS.

CLOUDS are God's master paintings in the sky,
In which the lights and shades in colors glare
Unceasingly, in combinations rare,
Across the firmament and do not die!
We look to-day and watch the colors vie,
And forms compete, to make a changing stair,
On which we'd mount, in fancy, through the air,
To realms of God, o'er mountains towering high.
And, as we try to climb up to God's home,
The steps are changed which lead up to its dome ;
The rifting clouds they break to shifting foam.
The color still remains, as does the shade,
And, in recurrent years, the dell and glade,
God paints the clouds in mists that never fade.

A. Milo Bennett.

A-FIELD—A SKETCH.

By Minnie Stichter.

With Illustrations by Alma G. White.

SOMETIME I expect to turn a sharp corner and come face to face with myself, according to the ancient maxim, "extremes meet." For, did I not vow to the Four Great Walls that had imprisoned me for nine months, that I would fly to the uttermost parts of the earth so soon as vacation should open the doors? And did I not spend almost my entire summer within sight of my home, and in a field of a few acres' dimensions?

The flat contradiction of romance by reality came about in this wise: In my romance I could "fly"; in reality I had no wings — no railroad ticket. Then it is only here at home that I can "turn the corner of the street and come face to face with an angel." And I feared homesickness.

"Come over," said my friend, "sometime, when you don't have the backache, or the side-ache, or the headache!" — from which invitation you may fancy the state of dilapidation I was in. I cared for nothing else than to report to myself the different miseries of each day. I was sunk so low that I did not care if I did not care for anything else! I determined to rouse myself by heroic measures.

"The Fairy Clover."

I had been reading an article by Sandow. "Now, here is a man who knows," I said. I will follow him and be strong. But when I read the injunction, "Walk," it was like being told to wash in the Jordan seven times! Had I not been walking in the school-room for full nine months?

But if I were to walk I might at least explode some of those fine theories about early morning walks, and the virtues of early rising, and so help exterminate from literature those nonsensical heroines who are always found in the garden in the early morning in dainty array despite the fact that the ball closed only two hours before, and the grass is dew-wet. Then, those fabled beings who tramp ten or a dozen miles "betimes," with never a thought of tramps! I might prove that they were not indigenous to this region.

Waking the first morning of my vacation, with my occupation gone and the feeling that there was nothing to get up for, I suddenly remembered my resolution to test the virtues of Sandow's recipe,—a recipe probably concocted before a cozy fireside. I grumbled while dressing in the early morning half-light.

I arrayed myself in rubber boots, an old short cloth skirt and waist and a brother's broad-brimmed hat, and sallied forth into the dawn. If I could have seen myself, I need not have been afraid of tramps. I hadn't selected my garb with any romantic story-book adventure in view.

Out of doors I hesitated, my courage almost failing. To follow the street north would lead through the town; west, into the cemetery; south, down the dusty highroad, past prosaic farms; east, to the fruit-fields and pastures. Nothing of much promise! Uninspired still, I turned eastward. The strawberry pickers were already in the fields, crouching beside the long dark rows of vines that alternated with rows of yellow straw, like devout Mohammedans on a striped prayer-rug of green and gold. Taking a box of their fruit, I hurried on. Their work had been too painfully familiar to me all the years of my childhood to seem attractive to me now.

The level meadows, the town's pasture, now stretched before me monotonously enough. Only a little narrow-gauge railway track, field and flower bordered, provided an egress. Its lariat length seemed trying to snare my feet into some happy way. I trusted to its promises and began to walk rapidly. Once upon the high grade I looked and, lo! the whole world lay at my feet — and so dwarfed that I was greater than it all! Why need I envy my neighbor his fine mansion, now, when by a few steps I could reduce its size to a doll-house! Why fear my enemy when he was no longer as large as a hair-pin! A new power was mine. I could cast a spell by which I could dwarf a whole town to the size of an ant-hill and cover a whole farm with my hand — so in miniature lay the landscape before me. Only the sky seemed vaster, more illimitable. The sun was beginning to push up a great, gray cloud — like a giant mole at work.

Just before me lay a great curve in the track. If I ventured beyond, I shut out completely the sight of the town and the feeling of its protection. I longed to know what new scene would greet me; but I had already come too far to satisfy my curiosity to-day. To-morrow I would do so. But that to-morrow never came! For, as I turned to go back, I caught sight of some flowers, just inside the barbed wire fencing the track, that were fairer than any I had yet gathered

" The wild crab-apple bloom."

for my vases. As the old song has it, "O, brighter the flowers on the other side seem!" No one saw me get under that six-stranded barbed-wire fence, and I am not going to tell how I did it. But when I got through I felt as well guarded as though attended by a retinue of soldiers. And I found myself in another world — a dream-world!

It was a large field rosy with red clover and waving with tall timothy. A single tree glistened and rustled invitingly. In its shade I rested, refreshing myself with the field sights and sounds and fragrances. It was delightful to be the center of so much beauty as circled round about me. Then I had only to rest on the rosy clover-carpet at the foot of the tree, and all things earthly were eclipsed by the tall grass save the tree, and the sky overhead, and the round mat of clover under the tree which the grass ringed about. I had often wished for Seigfried's magic cloak. Well, here was something quite as good, which, if it did not render me invisible to the world, made the world invisible to me. Who of you would not be glad to have the old world with its "everyday endeavors and desires," its folly, its pride and its tears, drop out of sight for a while, leaving you in a flowery zone of perfect quiet and beauty, hedged in by a wall of grass! It would be balm of Gilead for any, most of all for one who has commenced a battle with Fate that is not for a day nor a year, but until one shall overcome the other.

Prodded by hunger, which had been an almost forgotten sensation, I at last rose to go. But I must yet have greater handfuls of daisies and clover. If, as Emerson says, the true appreciation of flowers is the ability to enjoy and leave them where they are, I have it not. And I don't care if I haven't, when my great vases and pitchers and things are all filled with field-flowers, their pungent odors and sturdiness of stem suggesting the munificence, the *roughness*, of the Maker and Doer of them all.

The fainting fits of florists' flowers must be what appealed to Emerson's kind heart. Anyway, I came home with my arms full of blossoms. Sometimes afterward, I could coax a small boy, on his way home from pasturing his cow, to attend me. Then I loaded his arms, too.

There were many "afterwards." And the marvel of it all was that, for all I could do, the field retained its virgin splendor and kept the secret of my goings-in and comings-out most completely.

After the daisies, there came a season of nigger-heads or black-eyed susans, or whatever name you like best to call

" The bell rang out from the fields about a-downward time."

them. That was when the grasses were tallest and the feeling of mystery did most abound. I know I had been there many days before I discovered the myriads of wild roses near the crab-tree thicket— those fairies' flowers so exquisite in their pink frailty that mortal breath is rude. Only when I reached the hedge, bounding the remote side of the field, did I enter into my full inheritance. Along a barbed-wire fence had grown up sumac, elderberry, crab-trees and nameless brambles, while over all trailed the wild grape-vine bearing the most perfect miniature clusters, fit to be sculptured by Trentanove into immortal beauty. And this hedge was the source of ever increasing wonder the whole summer long. I depended on it alone for sensational denouements after the grass was cut for hay. When the field lay shorn, like other fields about it far and wide, I could not have been lured hitherward but for the hedge. There the hard green berries of a peculiar bramble ripened into wax-white pellet-sized drops clustered together on a woody stem by the most coral-pink pedicles ever designed by sea-sprites.

These clusters furnished a unique dining-room decoration when the Chief Musician came from the far East to be my guest, and friends were bidden to feast in her honor. So exquisite were the berry decorations that the Rich Lady who saw them gave me some of her jewels for a duplication of them in her stately home. There they were as much admired as though they were the product of enchantment, or brought from over seas.

This was the beginning of the demand for my decorations,—a demand that gave healthful employment for many hours of the summer and roused me from the lethargy that bound my brain with bands of iron in the beginning.

In their time the alderberry bloom, and its purple fruit; the garnet fruit of the sumach and its flaming foliage; the lengths of vines and their purple clusters,— all these and more also ministered to the delight of many.—"And the barrel of meal wasted not; neither did the cruise of oil fail, according to the word of the Lord."

I was not always alone in my enjoyment of the wide, free fields, the freshness of the morning, the splendor of the evening, the jewels of the meadow, the infinite beauty of the skies. Once, our "Martha, troubled about many things" was induced to go with me. She was loth to go and leave her serving, but much more loth to return to it. Out there she felt as never before her slavery to trivial possessions got by chance, and to the honeyed sweets that must her daily bread enhance.

Many times my Artist Friend, who tells you in picture what I tell you here with the pen, went with me and rejoiced with me in my new world—"that new world which is the old"—much as one rejoices over a child's first steps or its first syllables. My senses had hitherto been sealed to so much that was inexpressibly dear to her. When one has been blind and begins to see, is it not cause for rejoicing? I think she taught me to enjoy everything

"Field-broidery of amethyst"

in a landscape—except cows; and at a safe distance even they might fit in somewhere.

We are great friends—this artist, so unspoiled by the beginning of the world's recognition of her worth, and myself. Our real lives, and not those that pass for ours in the eyes of the children of men, are known to each other. And together we state many human problems and solve them, too,—for our own wise selves. We have untangled nearly all the snarls in the town beyond—to our own satisfaction. The indifferent husband has turned to his faithful wife; the heart of the cruel father has been softened toward his child; the patient man has been freed from the exactions of his unreasonable wife; and goodness knows how many children we have trained up in the way they should go! If only those "whom it may concern" would apply to us for wisdom, it might yet be well in the land.

But, seriously, we are both of us trying to learn from the experience of others so that God need not speak to us in the earthquake, nor the lightnings, nor the flood, nor the hail, nor the plague, but only in the "still, small voice."

About goldenrod time, the school-bell rang me in from the field, but I managed to take recesses long enough to behold the kaleidoscopic views brought before me by the turning of Nature's hand. The smooth velvety green of the field with its border of gold and lavender—great widths of thistle and goldenrod following the line of fence—was like the broidered mantle of some celestial Sir Walter Raleigh, spread for the queens of earth. I was no queen; but I did not envy royalty, since I doubted if it had any such cherished possessions as my field in its various phases.

One Sunday, when I had gone for a quiet walk, I found my pleasure-ground invaded by small boys. I marveled; for, beside the hay-makers and my guests there had been no signs of humanity before. I resented it as a personal intrusion. When I first saw them, they were fighting out bumble-bees, though that was only by the way; for soon they moved like an army of fell destroyers upon the tall stalks of the sun-flowers that stood in ranks by the hedge.

"Just like the red-handed murderers that boys are," I said to myself; then aloud, "Why are you breaking down the sun-flowers, boys?"

"Aint sun-flowers," they replied, "they're rosin-weeds."

At which I elected myself captain of the company and went on the rampage with them. Upon breaking the rosin-weed, a gum exudes which soon hardens. To my mind, nectar and ambrosia and milk and honey are to the taste not to be compared with this aromatic, cream-white stuff,—an excellent aid to digestion, too.

As we were "gumming" we saw a shower on the far-away hills, while we were in the bright sunlight. Then we heard the wind-blown rain advancing. Without ceremony the small boys scampered across the fields towards shelter. I panted after—but it was like a freight train after a fast mail. The rude shed, in which we waited for the shower to be over, was open, and so we had the vision of low skies laced to the earth by silver cords of rain.

In the November days, the brightness of the fields seemed to be inverted and to be seen in the opalescent tints of the sky. Then, the clearness of the atmosphere, the wider horizon, the less hidden homes and doings of men, had this message for the children of men: "If there is any secret in your life, leave it out."

Lingering by the hedge one evening with my Artist Friend, we saw the moonrise of the fields. It was the same moon that you saw, but it behaves differently out there,—with more sentiment and in

"The purple rim of the hill, beyond which only my fancy has ever gone."

" My pleasant ground cold and wind-swept."

wondrous harmony with the beauty of the fairy field surroundings. Nothing seemed too strange or too good to be true, in that place, at that time, with the moonlight over all. But nothing happened — except within our own souls.

When it is December and the fields are too snowy and wind-swept for pleasure-grounds, where the only bits of brightness are the embroideries of the scarlet pips of the wild-rose, it is good to nestle by the cosy fireside; and conjure it all up again, and nourish a feeling of expectancy for the spring and the summer that shall come. Again, the flowers and waving grass and drowsy warmth of the summer day; again, the songs of flitting birds, the scented sweets of the new-mown hay. Again the work of the fields goes on before me like a play in panto-mime! Again, with my eyes, I follow home the boys with their cows, to the purple rim of the hill beyond which only my fancy has ever gone. Again I quit work with the tired laborer. Again I dream of the open, free, unfettered song that Life might be if it were lived more simply, with less of artificiality. And again, for the sake of one patient toiler in the town, whose life-task admits of no holiday, I have the grace to return thither and begin where I left off, — the life common to you and to me, the life ordained for us from the beginning.

"I SHALL ONCE MORE SEE HER PASS."

ONCE more through the path that strays
   On the low field's tangled edge;
By murmurous water-ways,
   By blossoming thicket and hedge;
Once more with her flowy gown
   Bending the soft new grass,
Her radiant eyes cast down,
   I soon shall see her pass!

For to-day in the sweet spring wood —
·The silken-tasseled wood —
   In the sunlit wake of a shower
And fresh from the dewy mold,
   I saw her own loved flower —
   The tender, frail wind-flower —
Lifting beneath its hood
   A welcoming eye of gold.

And straight within my breast
   A slumbering gladness woke;
And the spell of a deep unrest,
   Of a lingering sadness, broke;
For although nor love nor bliss
   My heart hath found, alas!
Yet fate doth yield me this;—
   I shall once more see her pass!

CEDAR RAPIDS.

JULIA W. ALBRIGHT.

A NATURALIST'S VOYAGE DOWN THE MACKENZIE. III.

AN ARCTIC SUMMER — OUT INTO THE ARCTIC OCEAN — A CALL ON THE KAMCHATKANS.

By Frank Russell.

ON OUR way down the Mackenzie to Good Hope,* seven hundred miles from the starting point, we passed many picturesque stretches, where the noble river breaks through the easternmost chain of the Rockies. The Nahanni Mountains, Roche Carcajan, and Roche Trope à L'eau, all rose to a height of from one to two thousand feet.

Just above Good Hope the river narrows to a quarter of a mile, and flows between vertical limestone cliffs called the Ramparts. Three hundred feet of sounding line has been used here without reaching the bottom.

We arrived at Good Hope on the 12th of June, the "Wrigley" at once returning to the Great Slave Lake.

I started for Fort MacPherson, two hundred and eighty miles distant, on the 14th, crossing the Arctic Circle that afternoon. On the following day I traversed the Grand View. There the river is two to three miles in breadth, without a bend as far as the horizon extends, its width giving it more the appearance of a lake than a river. The Long Reach and many other long, straight stretches characterize this part of the Mackenzie, impressing one with its immense size and grandeur.

LOUCHEUX BOYS.

* See illustration in the July MIDLAND.

113

Owing to an ice jam at the lower Ramparts, the river had risen sixty feet above its ordinary level, making it difficult to find a dry camping place at night.

There were several camps of Loucheux along the river, who, when they saw that I was going past without stopping, would rush down to their canoes and follow me for a mile or two, begging for tea and tobacco. They were rather handsome fellows, with oblique, intelligent-looking eyes. Mackenzie, the first white man to visit them, called them Squint-Eyes. Their begging proved such a nuisance that I avoided them as much as possible. I was in haste to reach Peel River Fort as I had heard that a boat would be sent up from Herschel Island, which would afford me an opportunity to accompany the boat crew on their return. I would boil a kettle of tea and then push off and drift while eating my meals. As there is continuous light at this season in that far northern latitude, I could travel at any time.

On the fourth day I reached Point Separation, the head of the delta, so named by Franklin and Richardson when they parted there to explore the coast east and west of the river. Here I was nearly drowned by a sudden squall while crossing a channel a half-mile wide.

The following day I reached the last trading station of the Hudson's Bay Company,—Fort MacPherson,—situated on the Peel River, thirty miles south of the Mackenzie Delta. No boat had arrived from the whalers, but I was fortunate enough to find a French gentleman, Count de Sainville, about to start for the "Yankee ships." He was accompanied by Tothin and Vusso, two Loucheux who understood no English.

We left Fort MacPherson on the 25th of June, following the western channel of the "Big River." The country is low, wooded, and cut up into islands by a maze of channels, the delta being a hundred and fifty miles in length by fifty in breadth.

The sun shone all the time, its uninterrupted power being sufficient to melt the snows to a high altitude on the Rocky Mountains, along whose eastern base we were traveling. The banks were still muddy from the sediment deposited by the overflow of a few days before. Moose and grizzly bear tracks were frequently seen, while thousands of geese, ducks, loons, swans, cranes and other water-fowl swarmed on every hand.

On the evening of the third day, as we were drifting quietly around a short bend, we caught sight of a large grizzly bear walking down stream by the water's edge. As I had the only rifle in the party, I hastened to draw it from its case and prepare for trouble. The bear, without seeing us, entered the stream, with the evident intention of swimming across.

"Take care," said Tothin, "he is wicked. If you kill him, rush in and grab him or he will sink."

I was within fifty yards of the animal when he discovered our presence. He turned and raised his head well out of water to get a good look at us, at the same time giving vent to a roar of rage as he realized his disadvantage. I was in a little birch canoe, which was very cranky to shoot from. When I laid down the paddle to use the rifle the canoe veered around in the current. I did not relish the idea of "grabbing" a dying grizzly to save him from sinking. However, I paddled toward him to get a close shot, when he turned back to the shore. Just as he was gaining a foothold in the soft mud, in which he sank to the frost line, I fired. The bullet lodged in the neck, rendering him helpless, but not killing him.

"Shoot, shoot, shoot again!" cried the Indians, wild with excitement, as the huge beast rolled and floundered, covering himself with mud until scarcely recognizable. Another shot through the brain ended his career. We could not camp in the mud, and found it necessary to tow the bear across the river. The Count took the line in the large canoe. The carcass followed the bottom pretty closely, requiring all his strength to raise it to the surface in approaching the shore. It was three o'clock the next morning before I had the skin and skull cleaned and had turned in to get a little rest.

Continuing our journey, I worked pretty hard to keep up with the large canoe, which was made of pine, covered with painted canvas. We reached the mouth of the Mackenzie July 1st, having passed the timber line forty miles above. The larger lakes were covered with unbroken ice, but the sea was open to the horizon.

Crossing a shallow bay we came upon an Eskimo family encamped in a new toopick, or canvas tent, which they had obtained from the whalers. At our approach several salutes were fired from

COLLECTION OF ESKIMO PIPES.

their rifles. We were hospitably received by the head of the family, a tall, ferocious-looking fellow with a turquoise labret thrust through a hole in his lower lip, with an ivory disk, as large as a silver dollar, surrounding it. While he and the Indians talked with extravagant gestures in "Pidgeon Eskimo," the universal trade language of the coast, the "lady" of the toopick was busily engaged in mixing a large pan of stiff dough. This the younger members of the family proceeded to fry in a pan of seal oil on an open fire of driftwood.

They were all dressed in reindeer or seal skin garments. The woman wore an *itity* reaching to the knees. I thought at first that she was one-armed, but soon saw that she drew her arms inside occasionally and thrust them out again with a few circling flops of the empty sleeve.

By entering the tightly closed tent we succeeded in eating one meal without being tormented by the omnipresent and insatiable mosquitoes. We were treated to bread — a great luxury — and to coffee and syrup, articles quite unknown in the interior.

Pushing on again we soon reached a broad shoal, behind which we passed by wading and dragging our canoes for a mile. The temperature of both air and water was very near the freezing point, and our spirits away below zero before we reached deeper water. We were then exposed to the full sweep of the north wind across the Arctic Ocean. The swell increasing, we were compelled to put ashore and camp on the sandy battures about the mouth of a mountain torrent. There we remained for two days, trying in vain to keep warm by maintaining a huge fire of wet driftwood. This wood is brought down by the Mackenzie and strewn for hundreds of miles along the coast.

We continued on the night of the 3d.

The glorious Fourth was ushered in by the sun standing 1° and 43′ above the northern horizon at midnight.

South of us the lofty snow-crowned peaks of the Rockies formed a fitting background to one of the most beautiful scenes that I have ever witnessed. The gently rolling hills near the sea were literally covered with flowers. Along the northern horizon the ice floes were closely packed; near at hand they were piled high on the beach and floating about us, worn in an endless variety of grotesque forms by the action of the waves, and varying in hue from flashing white to indigo blue. Over all hung a faint roseate mist which suffused and softened the harsh details.

The immense volume of water carried down by the Mackenzie keeps the sea fresh and clear of ice for several miles beyond the mouth. As we passed Escape Reef,—the scene of Sir John Franklin's adventure with the Eskimo,— we entered

GROUP OF SIBERIAN VISITORS ON OUR STEAMER.

ANOTHER GROUP OF SIBERIANS.

the salt water and were soon threading our way through a narrow channel between the ice pack and perpendicular, frozen mud cliffs which rose to a height of one to two hundred feet.

Every few miles a small stream has cut through the hills, forming a lagoon enclosed by a barrier of sand projecting a mile or two from the line of the coast. On these low points we found the abandoned winter houses of the Eskimo. These habitations are made of driftwood covered with earth. The interior is a mass of ice and filth. Near by are conspicuous cones formed of drift-logs set up on end to keep from being buried in winter snows. Back of these deserted villages, on higher ground, are the graves, — not turf-covered mounds, but heaps of driftwood, designed to protect the bodies from the dogs.

We were now traveling whenever the wind and ice permitted, sometimes being delayed for forty-eight hours at a time by head winds. The waves were short and choppy in the shallow bays, making canoe navigation rather dangerous.

On the 7th of July, as we rounded a long point, we caught a glimpse of Herschel Island through the fog which hung over its rolling hills of frozen mud and clay, which rise to a height of five hundred feet. The unbroken ice of winter soon barred further progress. We were still twenty miles from the island, entirely out of provision, and the ice unsafe to travel upon. The ducks and loons, upon which we had been subsisting, were becoming scarce.

Soon after our tent was pitched a strong southerly breeze arose, which moved the whole ice-field fifteen or twenty yards from shore, enabling us to proceed by making a few short portages over jammed and broken ice.

The channel fortunately continued across to the point of Herschel Island, taking us within seven miles of the harbor. We could now reach the vessels overland, but were so exhausted from paddling and loss of sleep that we first tried to get a little rest. Vusso soon awakened us with the information that the ice was moving. The wind had changed to the westward and another narrow lane allowed us to approach within six hundred yards of the ships, which were held at their anchorage by large floes that filled the harbor. These were crossed at a hop, skip and jump, more than one of the party of sailors who came to our assistance getting a ducking before reaching the vessels again.

We were received on board the bark "Balæna" by her genial captain and the assembled officers of the fleet. We brought them news only five months old!

Two days later, the 11th of July, the whalers "bucked" their way out of the harbor and disappeared in the fogs and ice-field toward the eastward. There were seven vessels, all using steam to work through the ice or during calms, but at other times depending on their sails. The strong currents and the close proximity of the ice, which is driven ashore by every north wind, make the use of steam necessary. Three or four sailing vessels came in later in the season. One was wrecked by the ice driving her ashore.

The natives at the island were representatives of the Kosmollik tribe of Eskimos which inhabit the coast west of the Mackenzie as far as Alaska. Those east of the river differ materially in customs and language. The Kosmolliks have been in contact with the whalers for the last five years, so that they are now quite civilized. They play foot ball with the seamen and barter their last worldly possession for whisky, and have acquired a taste for civilized food. The women sing "Ta ra ra" when *molly kelly*—that is, when drunk, and even some of the children are "mised on the bottle," with condensed milk.

On the 30th of August I embarked on the steamer "Jeanette." We worked along the edge of the ice-pack toward the westward for several days. Near Point Barrow, the northernmost point of

Alaska, the ice always lies close along shore, during some seasons not allowing vessels to pass at all. East of that point the ice forms a month earlier than in the western Arctic. Each night a heavy coating of ice formed on the rigging. We were often working our way through the floes and in danger constantly, owing to the liability of being nipped by the ice in the strong currents which characterize these shallow waters. The fogs and snows greatly interfered with the search for whales, so that it was my fourth week on board before I saw a whale killed and cut in.

On the 5th of October we turned homeward, borne swiftly on the wings of a norther, which compelled us to heave to before reaching Behring Straits. On the 9th we touched at East Cape, Siberia, where a native settlement of hovels clings to the steep cliff like the nests of barn swallows.

October 11th we anchored at Indian Point, Siberia, where a large settlement of Tchuckches,—or, as they call themselves, Massinkers,—forms an important trading station. They came aboard in large numbers with fur, whalebone and ivory to trade, and with all sorts of human parasites to cause us to remember their visit for the remainder of the voyage.

Their chief, Gohara, has property amounting to $50,000, valued at San Francisco prices. This consists of whale boats, alcohol and reindeer.

We crossed Behring Sea in four days. The snow squalls obscured the Fox Islands until we were entering the pass of Unimak, when we caught a glimpse of the volcanoes on either hand.

We were soon upon the open Pacific, with a straight run of two thousand miles to the Golden Gate. The crow's nest, or lookout box, was taken down and the t'gal'nt and royal yards sent up in its place. Ten thousand pounds of whalebone was washed and bundled, when the weather permitted, but the North Pacific in October is anything but pacific. We were compelled to heave to five times and ride out as many gales.

On the 26th of October we threw our fur garments overboard and resumed the habiliments of civilized man. The whaler is a rough and often dissolute character, but he keeps a suit of "store clothes" in his "diddy box," which, creased and wrinkled though they are, will not betray his calling as he passes the San Francisco small boy, ever on the alert to shout, "There she blows!" at a reindeer-clad figure.

We raised the flash-light on the Farallone Islands, outside San Francisco Harbor, that night, but laid aback outside until daylight.

The morning sun rose from behind the eastern mountains upon a scene of beauty which, to our eyes, so long accustomed to snow, fog, and ice-fields, seemed like a glimpse of heaven.

On either side of the narrow entrance the rugged hills rose abruptly from the water's edge, where the heavy ground-swell broke in long lines of white against the dark cliffs. How different those green hillsides, dotted with trees, with the balmy air of a perfect day, from the barren, fog-enveloped and snow-covered mountains of the Aleutian Islands, which we had passed twelve days before!

What language can express the feelings of the exile as he nears his native land; of the sailor as he enters the harbor after the long voyage in Arctic seas!

Our hearts beat quickly with the thought of home, home, home again — thank God!

The journey of over eighteen thousand miles was ended. I had been absent two years and a half, and had made a collection of twenty-one large mammals of the North, six hundred birds, and hundreds of ethnological and other specimens. Nothing has been said of my outfit, because I had practically nothing except guns and ammunition. I was without companions or assistants, except Indians hired temporarily. Lack of means added greatly to the hardship. The collection could easily have been trebled could I have had a few dollars added to my letter of credit, — which additional sum the University was very willing but, at the time, wholly unable to supply.

THROUGH GRAND RIVER CANON AT NIGHT.

ON either side tower rocky heights that lean,
　　Threatening and close, above the narrow pass ;
　　Now gloomy walls, and now a glimmering mass
Of rich mosaic, red and white and green ;
Anon, wild pointed spires and turrets seen
　　Darkly against the lowering sky, and domes,
　　And castle battlements. Below them foams
The river, rushing wild and dark between.

Far up the heights upon an upland dim,
　　Twinkle pale lights and house-roofs glimmer faint ;
　　Not hermits' cells nor watch-fights of a saint,
But miners' cabins ; across the broken rim
　　Of yonder height dark shadows flit, and far
　　Above the summit hangs a single star.

SACRAMENTO, CALIF.   *Virna Woods.*

STARTING A CITY IN RANCHLAND.*

BY MRS. BARBARA R. GARVER.

THE terminal of the new railway had finally been located. This decided upon by the great corporation controlling the matter, the site of the new town which was to be the metropolis, the "future great" of the whole western country, the center of commerce for a vast territory, was reserved from the surrounding lands.

Streets were surveyed and laid out ; corner lots were staked off; depot grounds, stockyards and freight houses were all laid out on paper, fully three months before a lot could be bought or any im-provements made upon the grounds, even to the cutting of sage-brush or the digging of cacti.

All improvements and industries were to be held in abeyance until such time as the first puff of smoke could be seen, the first whistle and engine bell could be heard, as the train comes around the curve from among the hills ; then city lots were to be staked off on the grounds, and, the day after the arrival of the special coach bringing the directors of the "Great Interior Railroad," there would be a public auction, and happy would be the man who could secure a corner lot in the most desirable location.

The "Squatter City" which lay in all its pristine newness and uncouthness on the outskirts of the coming city was a medley of incongruous humanity, consisting of "all nationalities and conditions of men"—and women, too.

Every day, all summer long, especially during the two months preceding the auction, had brought its new supply of immigrants by wagon, by stage, by mule and by ox train. Tents and shanties abounded, and all were crowded to their utmost capacity. A mammoth tent did duty as a hotel, where the habitues fared sumptuously every day. Its rival, built of discarded telegraph poles, prided itself on its magnificence, with the added luxury of a dollar

* Prize Descriptive Paper in THE MIDLAND'S March 29th Competition.

MRS. BARBARA R. GARVER, OF DES MOINES.

more per day for its superior accommodations.

Fresh meats daily bought from hunters' wagons were delicacies indeed to many of us. These consisted of elk, antelope, venison and mountain sheep. Bear steaks, too, were plentiful, but a number of our party were a little squeamish about eating what a hungry dog will not touch, however nicely cooked or disguised in stews or roasts. Sage-hen and rabbit pie soon grew stale and palled upon the taste. The tidbit of all game is the tenderloin of a young antelope ; but even of that we tired, turning with gusto to a bit of ham or bacon.

Our near proximity to a river, which had its source in the eternal snows on the distant mountain tops, made fresh fish abundant on the tables, brought in by the idlers belonging to camp. Bakeries did a thriving business. Excellent bread and cake were to be had, baked in very primitive ovens. The oven generally consisted of a ground floor with an arch built about three feet high in the center and sloping down to the ground on each side, made of broken stone laid up without mortar or cement.

Canned goods and fresh fruits could be bought in any quantity at the tent groceries, while the ranch-wagons every day brought in a fresh supply of vegetables raised in the nooks and valleys among the hills with which we were surrounded. Larger and finer ones never grew in all our fruitful land than are raised along those irrigating ditches which cross, re-cross and check every valley in Ranchland like a huge chess-board.

One side of the railroad track in this squatter city was dubbed " Poverty Flat " by some one who had read Bret Harte's poem, and the name stuck there longer than the buildings. Saloons, faro-banks, chop-houses, cheap restaurants, second-rate drug stores and all kindred ills flourished here like a green bay tree.

On the opposite side of the track was "Puritan Hill," where the virtues were supposed to abide, in a corresponding manner, with the vices of the above-mentioned Flat. Here were the rival hotels, dry goods stores, the post-office and the tented homes of the better class of the inhabitants. Many large and commodious tents were ranged here in lines corresponding to streets, in which a thriving business was done in many trades and professions. Here were the banks, three in number, which held chattel mortgages on two-thirds of all the personal property in the city. In their immense safes was hidden a large part of all the watches and jewelry owned by the floating class that congregate on the outskirts of every new town, waiting for the good time coming when each particular owner would be a millionaire speculator in town lots, and when these valuables could be released.

Here also was another tent which for five days in the week did duty as a public school building, where a young lady taught thirty or more pupils in the rudiments of their native language. It could hardly be called a graded school, although there were several grades as regards culture, refinement, and cleanliness among the scholars. In this modern temple of Minerva there was no floor but the virgin soil of yellow sand; there were no seats but split telegraph poles upon which to rest during the six hours devoted to the service of the goddess. This tent was also a church, in which a precocious youth of eighteen summers broke the bread of life for the benefit of the multitude of reprobates who never attended, and for the few in different degrees of wickedness who sometimes did attend on Sunday evenings.

There was no morning service, as the youthful preacher would have spoken to empty benches. He put in his time novel-reading, hunting, fishing, or engaged in innocent games suitable to the leisure of a summer vacation. An old box melodeon — so small that it could be carried under one arm from one part of the tent to another — did duty as reading desk and altar, also as leader in the singing during church services, and as writing table and teacher's desk in school hours. The lithe and supple fingers of the young man drew from its rusty keys some discordant music which was supposed to rival the attractions of the many brass and string bands that were giving out sweet strains of seductive music in many places where

whisky was freely flowing and cards were manipulated with surprising dexterity.

Murders and accidental shootings were not uncommon, as firearms were the brilliant decorations of nearly every person old enough to know their use, — even of the women, — or else "laying handy by" for instant use if the temper of the owner so required, and giving many an item to the *Metropolitan Press* or blazoning forth in startling headlines in the *Ranchland Boomer*. The perpetrators sometimes met summary punishment without the formality of a trial. At other times they were handed over to the authorities to be dealt with according to law; the aggravation in the case decided the course to be pursued.

Chinese laundries were numerous, dotting every part of the city. John also kept a supply of native goods and curios to tempt the American dollar to his guardianship.

Hotel life brings about a great many incongruous friendships, especially when such a mixture of inharmonious humanity is thrown together as was found in that tented caravansary. My chosen friend was a young Jewess, wife of one of the most noted gamblers of the Flat. In the several months of our acquaintance she never alluded to her husband's business — except once, and then she was showing me her photograph album. Coming to his picture she said, —

"I ran away from home to marry him, because he loved me. My mother died when I was a child. My father soon married again, and love was left out of my home life. I grew to womanhood without any showing of affection, hardly knowing what the word meant until I met my husband. He is good and kind to me if he *is* a gambler, — which I did not know when we were married; but I doubt if it would not have been the same, had I known it, for I love him dearly as he does me, and in all the five years of our married life I have never for a moment regretted the step."

The time would have hung heavily on our hands had it not been for the long rides my friend and I enjoyed together over the smooth and winding roads, sometimes visiting the neighboring ranch homes, and at other times calling on the ladies in the camps of the graders engaged on the unfinished railroad. The contractor of the work and the foreman of the employé's had brought their families with them. Their wives proved to be delightful, cultured ladies who enjoyed their nomadic life during the summer months, but "went into camp" in good homes, in an Eastern city, in the winter time, where their children could have the best educational advantages, and where the money so quickly made and so carefully saved during the working season was then lavishly spent.

One morning a party was made up to visit a cattle-ranch and take breakfast with the owner, who was a friend of some of the gentlemen of our party. As we rode up to the door we saw one of the "hands" lying on a bench, with his hands tied beneath it. Standing near were the herders who had come in to their morning meal. As each man came near the bench he took off his big sombrero and gave the captive a half-dozen slaps with as much vim as his regard for his head-covering would allow.

"What has the man done to merit such punishment?" inquired I, indignantly.

"Nothing, nothing at all, ma'am; he only drew the booby prize and is taking it like a man," said the ranch owner.

Cards, with accompanying "chips," were the only amusement or pastime of these men, and even the work done on the ranch was settled by a game of cards. Before "turning in for the night" they played for hours to arrange the "business" for the coming day. The winner of the first prize was "boss," and if there were errands to be done in the village it was his privilege to go to town and attend to them. But woe betide the one who gets the booby! He must be fag for the others, and, should he be so unlucky as to draw it two nights in succession, he must submit to the ordeal of

"chapeauing" without a murmur before he can have his breakfast.

"We must have some fun," continued the man, "and must take it out of each other. Anything to break the horrid monotony of our lives."

One morning I stood by the "little table,"— the one reserved for ladies with their attendant husbands or brothers,— gazing listlessly from a hole in the tent, the flap having been rolled up and the opening doing duty as a window, through which the sweet mountain air drifted like a benison over the scene of disorder.

I was waiting for the great throng of unkempt laborers to be served their morning meal. These were they who worked by the hour and who credited time lost that was given to sleep or to satisfying hunger. It was jostle and push to be first seated at the long table which ran the entire length of the tent. It was rush and hurry, in swallowing scalding coffee and hot biscuit. With curses and slang they sought to hurry the waiters, who with deft hands placed huge dishes before these men, dishes which needed almost constant replenishing. The scene had been enacted so often before me that I had become calloused, and heard the tumult no more than the inhabitants of Niagara hear the roar and thunder of the great falls bellowing in their midst.

All at once I become conscious that the gambler's wife stood outside beckoning me to come to her. I knew from the expression on her face,— half sorrow and half horror,— that something terrible had happened.

"What is the trouble?" I asked.

"A girl was accidentally murdered this morning at Penny Pete's dance hall. Will you go with me to see that she is decently dressed for burial? I know so little about such things; our Jewish customs are so different from yours."

I hesitated a little, for I had been Pharisaical and had pulled my skirts aside when meeting this unfortunate class on the streets for fear of contamination. I looked up and saw great tears in the eyes confronting mine, and heard the quaver in the voice which added, "Remember, she is a sister woman, sinned against, perhaps; and who are we that never have been tempted, that we dare stand in judgment on her!"

Unable to withstand the eloquence of the pleading eyes, I consented. After a hasty breakfast we put on our bonnets and crossed to the next street, less than a block away, going to a huge barn-like structure, whose great double doors, wide enough for a carriage to pass through, stood open. A few men were standing idly around with half-smoked cigars in their fingers or between their teeth. They stared curiously at us as we entered the door, but did not remove their hats nor quit smoking. Facing the door at the opposite end of the room a platform about three feet high was built for the musicians. In one corner were wooden chairs, nail-kegs, soap and cracker boxes and a bench for the use of the smokers. The other corner had a small round table and a few chairs for those inclined to test their fortunes at cards. In the corner behind the great swinging doors was a bar fitted up with all sorts of drinks and

tobacco. In the other and corresponding corner was a free-lunch table for the use of the patrons of the establishment. Between the doors, on each side of the dancing hall, hung gaudy chromos of the cheapest and coarsest variety.

Standing there a moment we saw that the card-table had been pushed into the extreme corner of the room, and there lay the murdered girl on the rough, unplaned floor. A frowzy-headed girl, in a green broadcloth dress conspicuously decorated with coarsely-painted poppies around the bottom and over the front width of the skirt and on the collar and cuffs of the waist, sat on an inverted nail-keg, and with a palm-leaf fan kept the flies from the face of the dead girl. There was a set look, almost unemotional, on the face of the living one as she sat there waving the fan to and fro above the face of the dead.

Going to the bar we asked the man in attendance if there was anything that could be done to get the body ready for burial.

"No, they haint had the inquest yet; she's got to be left right where she is till after that. Pete's telegraphed for instructions to the Missus in Denver who owned

ON THEIR WAY TO THE SALE.

her. You'd better wait till the inquest is over and come again. As for me, I can't see any use havin' the coroner and crowd around; everybody knows it was an accident from outside gamin', without intent to kill; some cowboy fired his revolver 'cause he was too drunk to know what he was doin'."

We walked back to where the girl lay in a little pool of blood which was oozing from a temple wound. My companion, stooping down, with her own white hand picked up the soiled hands of the dead woman, covered with cheap rings, and tenderly crossed them on the pulseless breast, saying in a low tone,—"Poor little hands, with proper training what good you might have accomplished!" And, closing the staring eyes she added, "Pretty brown eyes, which should only have looked upon innocence and purity but have seen so much of sin!"

Then, going around the body, she straightened the bent knee, and placed the ragged-slippered feet close together, saying, "Feet, that have stumbled, there must somewhere be an avenger of innocence to plead your cause for you!" Then, arranging the soiled and tattered drapery about the slender form, we went and sat down on one of the long board seats arranged for the musicians.

"Shall we not go home now and wait until the inquest is over?" I asked.

"If you do not mind waiting, I prefer to stay here. The men who will hold this inquest—It's such a shame that it could not be women, educated medical women —these men will not see that death has cleansed the poor, stricken body of all defilement, and they will be rough in words and actions unless we stay here to protect her from unseemly exposure. Shall we stay?"

In a few minutes the physicians came. My friend, the Jewess, stood beside the dead girl, with a look on her face which Diana might have worn, so chaste and pure it was. Had the dead woman, lying there so prone, been one of earth's tenderly reared daughters she could not have been more respectfully or more carefully handled.

"Accidental shooting in the temple,— by party unknown,—shot coming in through a crack in the outer wall of the building," was the verdict brought in by the coroner and the two physicians.

As we stood there the proprietor, "Penny Pete," came along and said to one of the loungers:

"We might as well close up the business now; 'cause nobody'll have any luck till three's passed in their checks. Every girl here will run away before to-morrow night, thinkin' it'll be her turn next. It's the way with 'em. They're that scared now, they don't dare go out-doors,"

Just then a telegram was handed him which he opened and read aloud : " Send the body to "—here followed the address. " Write parents any fiction you like to account for death ; go with body to Omaha ; have it billed from there ; send all bills to me."

The telegram was signed by " the Missus in Denver," who, according to the barkeeper, "owned the girl."

When the inquest was over, my friend went to one of the many small doors and rapped. The girl we had first seen opened it and stood waiting, but did not stand aside so that we might enter. We asked her if there was any clothing belonging to the girl, fit to bury her in.

" No, she hasn't any, but Pete'll have to get some ; its rules."

Neither suggestions nor entreaties could induce my friend to leave the place until all preparations for the removal of the body to the depot were made. She took upon herself the responsibility of seeing that the remains were neatly dressed, and laid in the coffin. When the hour came for the body to be taken to the depot we went together to see the long deal box placed in the baggage-car. The Jewess had violated the long continued customs of her people, in being about the dead, as she had been that day; but she excused herself by saying, "These poor misguided girls, against whom everybody's hands are arrayed,— I feel so sorry for them! Certainly Jehovah will not count it sin that I have looked after one of his wayward children who had no friend."

———

" There is never so long a lane but has a turn," says the old adage, and the long weary waiting for the completion of the railroad was at an end.

For two days prior to the expected sale of lots there was a steady increase in the population. They came from every surrounding ranch, as well as from all parts of the country,— Boston, New York, San Francisco, and all intermediate points furnishing their quota. They came by every mode of transportation known on this continent. With the first locomotive, to which a few passenger coaches were attached, what an influx of speculating humanity! Every car was crowded to its fullest capacity ; even the flat-cars, which the "construction train" brought in, were one immense jam.

Then arose the query. "Where are all these people to sleep and wherewithal shall they be fed?" Every tent, shack or shanty was converted into an inn. Many beds were spread in the open air on piles of sage-brush, for which the occupants — two to each bed — paid one dollar each for their use for a single night. Standing near, in the morning, while some were paying their bills, I could not help hearing much that was said, and after their departure I remonstrated a little with our landlady on what I called extortion.

She withered me with a glance of her one good eye and with the sage remark, "We did not come West to keep hotel for our health."

The day of the sale was cold, rainy and dreary,—such a day as permeates one's whole being with a general uncomfortableness. But, according to printed handbills liberally strewn about, the masses gathered in front of the post-office where, headed by a full brass band playing lustily, they formed into line and marched to the grounds whereon was to stand the "Magic City."

A movable stand, to which were hitched twelve yoke of oxen, stood on a prominent corner. Here the auctioneer and band were stationed.

The Public Square, on which were to be built all city buildings, occupied the center of the grounds, and was donated for public use by the Great Interior Railroad Company. From the square radiated streets in every direction. The lots surrounding the square, and separated from it by a broad street, were the first to be sold and brought the highest prices ; then the less desirable ones, until every lot in the plat was sold, except the few reserved by the company, to be donated to the city for school buildings or to the church organization that would promise to immediately build thereon.

The auctioneer's stand was moved from point to point, or from corner to corner. It was followed by lunch stands on wheels, where hot coffee, sandwiches, doughnuts, and triangular pieces of pie were dealt out over the edge of the wagon-box to the hungry multitude.

Despite the dreary weather the bidding went on briskly, speculators buying by the whole block or square, expecting to realize a fortune in a few days from private sales. At 4 o'clock the sale was practically over, and in less than an hour, notwithstanding the cold and rain, Squatter City began its hegira to permanent quarters. Our landlady, who prided herself on the title of "one of the hustlers from Hustlerville," came in from the sale hungry, cold and wet. She never stopped for rest or refreshment, but accosted us with the information that several teams would soon be at the door, and she would move before supper.

"Ladies, you ken pack yer trunks immejit, fur we're goin' to move, an' we're goin' now. Y'cmum, we eats our next meal in the new town, an' I gives you fair warnin'. There's no time fur foolin'. Yer trunks ken go on the last load if you pays for 'em."

We obeyed orders and, while we were busy with our affairs, the bedding from the various box-like stalls was rolled together and tied up; the furniture was piled upon wagons, the tent-stakes were pulled out and the tent was folded up; but, unlike the tents of the Arabs, it was not folded in silence.

Our ubiquitous landlady saw to everything. There was a landlord, too, but, as she said, "he didn't count," being busy dealing out what she called "rail-fences in tum'lers" over one of the eighty-nine counters where drinks were sold in Poverty Flat. He did not appear, nor figure in our domains, except at breakfast,—his wife sending his other meals to him, "bein' to busy to come home."

Such a commotion as that woman could raise in a few moments! Her orders

were loud and imperative. The cooks and waiters hastily packed dishes, provisions, stoves and kitchen furniture promiscuously into boxes, tubs and barrels, and with their accoutrements about them took possession of the first wagon and started for the site of what in the future was to be one of the most commodious of hotels, could one believe the flaring advertisement in the evening edition of *The Boomer*.

For nearly two hours my friend, the Jewess, and I sat upon our saratogas under umbrellas, waiting for a place to which we might go. The last wagon was gathering up the remnants of the hotel belongings; then, with our baggage piled on top, it started; and in the growing dusk we took up our stations and meekly followed in its wake, over cactus beds and through wet sage-brush toward our new home. It was "road" anywhere; we had our choice of routes. Slowly we plodded along with only an occasional stop to pull from our shoes the long cactus spines which had penetrated both rubber and kid.

While we were impatiently waiting, the wagons had been carrying the furniture and bedding, and had dumped them in a heap; the sleeping tent for the boarders was erected over them as they were piled, and the general and her aids had brought something like order out of chaos. We arrived just as the last stake was being driven and the last rope was being pulled taut. We were thankful for the shelter and for the appetizing odor that came from the viands cooking in the open air and in the drizzling rain; the kitchen tent was not yet up.

When bedtime came, the curtains had all been hung from their accustomed hooks and the beds neatly made, and, though the clothing was damp and the roots of the sage-brush were uncomfortable to walk over, yet we gladly took possession and went to bed — and slept.

After a night of rain the sun came out gloriously. Early dawn found us astir, for the "noise of the whip and the noise of the rattling of wheels," besides a number of other noises that the prophet

POVERTY FLAT.

speaks not of, was more than we could endure. At this early hour, not yet 6 o'clock, hundreds of men were busy at work. In fact many a one had worked through all the long night hours in the darkness and rain, guided by the feeble glimmering of a lantern attached to the top of the ox-yoke, or dangling from the ring in the end of the wagon-tongue.

While we slept, the Squatter City had moved to its permanent home. The shacks, shanties and tents had all been brought over and placed upon the newly-purchased freehold. These were generally left upon the rear end of the lot and facing the alley, so that the substantial improvements could be built on the street, which was then given over to the graders who with plow and scraper had already begun work upon the great thoroughfares.

It was indeed a Magic City upon which we gazed from our windows,—said windows consisting of a small slit in the canvas. The "dwellers in tents," chophouses, restaurants and hotels, were busy with breakfast. The merchants were putting their wares in the most tempting forms on shelves in their tent stores. Teams were hauling water from the river, the drivers hawking it about from door to door, selling it by the gallon or barrel to suit the needs of customers. Other teams were hauling sand for mortar, or brick from the kilns, which had been burned during the months of waiting, and which now found ready

A RANCH NEAR RANCHLAND.

sale. Foundation rock from the neighboring hills was being heaped up in preparation for the mason's chisel, to be used in building the " mammoth " stores and hotels. Lumber, with other building material, was being unloaded from the many side-tracked cars.

A busy scene! And so it continued for many days. There was no eight or ten hour system of labor in force. Every man and team worked as many hours as human or brute nature could stand the strain,—sometimes as many as eighteen hours a day, with only occasional rests for drink or food. Wages were paid by the hour and the workman who could endure most was the richest on pay-day. Figuratively speaking, " there was no night there," nor Sabbath day, either, for all day long was " the sound of the hammer and saw in the land." The voice of the laborer crying "mort " or " brick," and the click of the mason's trowel made music continually.

Two weeks of push and laborious work brought the city to a very fair start. Great blocks and commodious hotels began to climb skyward. Then came the reaction. Workmen began to leave as fast as they could get their pay. The lots did not sell as readily as had been expected, and "millionaires of a day" found themselves in the predicament of Mark Twain — confronted by the inevitable tomorrow. The brick blocks and hotels left off a story or two ; family mansions omitted the bay windows, turrets and towers in the original plans. Before winter came the great city had dwindled into a village. The dance halls, the gambling dens, the faro banks, the wheels of fortune, all had gone to seek newer fields. The speculator, like a bursted bubble, was not to be found. The boom was over.

LOVE'S ROSARY.

" One, I love ; two, I love ; three,
  I love I say ;
Four, I love with all my heart, and
  five I cast away."
Thus the little maiden —maid of
  summers seven or eight —
Scans with earnest mien the simple
  horoscope of fate.

" Six, she loves,"— she bravely
  counts, and "seven he loves,"—
  she sighs,
"Eight, they both love" runs the
  rhyme,—she coyly droops her
  eyes.
Thus the little maid tells off the
  wheaten rosary beads,
And gayly treads the summer paths
  where golden fancy leads.

"Nine, he comes," she chants the
  song, and then comes "ten he
  tarries,"
"Eleven," she whispers soft, "he
  courts," and "twelve"— ah —
  " twelve he marries!"
And thus through childhood's passing quips, and simple, happy
  creed,
There run the golden threads that
  to mature ideals lead.

William Harrison Ellis.

VERGENNES.

By M. E. Hall.

RISING on the western slope of the Green Mountains and flowing north-westerly through the fertile Champlain Valley, until, after a meandering course of ninety miles among picturesque hills and teeming meadows, it empties into the lake that gives name to the valley, is a stream called Otter Creek. In any other country it would obtain the grander title of river. To the Indians it was known as Won-a-ka-ke-tuk, also as Pe-konk-tuk. Long before any settlements were made by the English in Vermont it was named by the French la Riviere aux Loutres, the River of Otters. Lake Champlain was named by its discoverer, Samuel Champlain, a French nobleman. It was called by the Iroquois Canideri Guarunte, signifying the door of the country; by the Abenaqui, who claimed its eastern shores, it was called Pet-a-wa-bou-que, meaning alternate land and water, in allusion to its numerous islands and projecting points.

It is doubtful if the world can show a more attractive sheet of water, where quiet beauties are so deftly blended with its grander features that the eye is constantly feasted without satiety. Especially is this true in glorious October, when the lake seems to flash back from its mirrored bosom reflections of sharper details and bolder outlines than are possessed by the objects themselves. The most delicately penciled shades and deepest coloring of the deciduous trees, in marvelous contrast to their somber background of evergreens; each filmy cloud-speck, each skimming swallow and gaudy insect, comes back with such glowing intensity that the gazer is fain to believe the limpid waters have purged them from all material grossness. Eight miles up from its mouth are the lower falls of Otter Creek. Here the stream is divided by two diminutive islands into three channels, whose

waters plunge with a leap and a roar over a limestone ledge to a pool forty feet below. At this point, located upon both banks, is Vergennes.* In rural quiet the city nestles in the center of the valley, the emerald of whose fields and woodlands shade with imperceptible gradations into the perennial verdure of the Green Mountains that mark its eastern limits, and to the west the turquoise of the lake is merged into the deeper blue of the more distant and loftier Adirondacks. The sun's first beams, touching with rosy fingers the tops of Mansfield, Camel's Hump and Potato Hill, greet the early villager and awaken the singing birds in the grove; its departing rays lighting up with mellow radiance the higher peaks of their western neighbors, Marcy, Whiteface and Old Raven.

The city was named after Count de Vergennes, a French nobleman and a friend of Lafayette. The first settlement was made in 1766 by Donald McIntosh, a Scotchman and veteran of the English service, who had fought at Culloden and had come to this country with General Wolfe during the French war. He died in 1803 at the age of eighty-four. His grave, marked by a modest stone, is in a sequestered spot on what is known as the Seymour farm. In 1761 the land about the falls was granted by New Hampshire to Isaac Peck, John Griswold and Daniel Barnes. In 1769 these pioneers entered upon their possessions and built a saw-mill. They were shortly afterward driven off by Colonel Reed, who "claimed" under a grant from New York. The Colonel put his tenants in possession and made further improvements. The next year Ethan Allen, with a party of Green Mountain boys, dispossessed these tenants, burned their houses and threw their mill-stones over the falls. In 1773, Reed

*Pronounced Ver-gens.

137

again renewed his claim and induced some Scotch emigrants to occupy the place. Ethan Allen, Remember Baker and Seth Warner, with about one hundred followers, dispersed the Scotchmen, destroying their property and ordering them not to return "on pain of suffering the displeasure of the Green Mountain boys." To prevent a recurrence of this, Allen and his companions built a small block-house at the falls and garrisoned it with a few men under Ebenezer Allen, which effectually protected it from further inroads of the New Yorkers.

What is now Vermont was then a "no-man's land" and the actual settlers, holding under grants from New Hampshire, were constantly harassed and oppressed by the greedy speculators from New York. Being an unorganized community of scattered settlements, the settlers, with grim humor, were wont to authenticate the decrees of their assemblies with the "beech seal" impressed upon the bare backs of offenders, and imposed such novel punishments as "to be chastised with the twigs of the wilderness."

During the Revolution a number of persons living about the falls were captured by the British or their Indian allies and were carried to Canada, where they were kept as prisoners until exchanged, or they managed to escape and, after tedious wanderings in the interminable forests, beset by dangers and privations, safely reached the American lines. The stories of these adventures are still related by their descendants living in the vicinity. Most of the remaining settlers abandoned their homes and did not return until after the close of the war.

Vergennes was incorporated with city privileges October 23, 1788, the third city in age in New England, Hartford and New Haven having earlier charters. The land on which it is located is hilly and is further broken by Otter Creek, and Potash Brook, which, flowing from the east, enters the creek at nearly right angles just below the falls. Some of its streets, winding about with a delightful uncertainty, encourage the belief that they were located by that primitive method of surveying, adopting the route taken by the early settlers to drive their cows afield. Others, at prim right angles, hint at the later citizens' efforts to make straight the paths of their feet. The names of several localities smack of the early settlers' habit, sacrificing euphony

RUINS OF FORT TICONDEROGA.

to terse description. "Over the Creek," "French Village," "Comfort Hill," and "Nigger Hill," are still retained.

Near the center of the town is a little space tastefully set out to native trees, once the village green where the noisy mirth of the village boys' evening sports was wont to be abruptly hushed as the bell from the neighboring church-tower pealed out the curfew hour of nine. Now it is "the Park," and the bell that used to proclaim the old fashioned ways and simple habits of the town is silent. While the city has some fine residences and its churches are quite creditable, the chief interest which one feels in them is because of a few specimens of colonial architecture, the associations which connect them with the past. For, though the oldest buildings were erected after the Revolution, there is, notwithstanding, a colonial flavor about them. The school-house and city hall are both frame buildings of ordinary type, though the latter has a façade supported by Doric columns, and serves to illustrate the prevailing

fashion of sixty or eighty years ago, when it was customary to adorn the fronts of both public and private buildings with a façade supported by either Doric or Corinthian columns. Throughout Western Vermont many examples of this affected taste yet remain. The spirit of progress, remodeling these to suit the taste of to-day, (whether more nearly correct or not I will not attempt to say,) is fast obliterating these evidences of our forefathers' attempts to imitate in wood the Greek idea of architectural beauty expressed in stone.

Aside from the natural beauties of the locality, there is much of historic interest to attract the curious. Until within a few years the old McIntosh house was standing on "Comfort Hill," on a gentle declivity shaded by two great locusts. Its front, covered by clapboards, gave the impression of a much later date than it actually represented, but in the rear it showed the immense pine logs nicely squared and fitted, yet bearing the marks of the hewer's axe. Thompson, in the

FALLS OF OTTER CREEK.

Arsenal Grounds in Background   Old Steamboat Landing   Comfort Hill.

BELOW THE FALLS.

"Green Mountain Boys," makes its capture from the New Yorkers one of the
incidents of the story.

Seven miles west of the city is a bay of
the lake, where Arnold, after a desperate
running fight from Valcour Island, ran
the "Congress" and three other vessels
ashore and, after landing his men, blew
them up to prevent their falling into the
hands of the enemy. The bay is still
known as Arnold's Bay, and in very low
water some of the timbers of the vessels
are yet to be seen. In December, 1813,
Commodore Macdonough with his flotilla
went into winter quarters at Vergennes
and, to strengthen his squadron so as to
be able to cope with the British on the
lake, there built the schooner "Ticonderoga," the brig "Eagle" and the ship
"Saratoga." It is said that ninety days
before these vessels went into action off
Cumberland Head, in September, 1814,
many of their timbers were growing trees
on the banks of Otter Creek. While the
fleet was being built at Vergennes, for its
protection a rude earthwork, called Fort

Cassin, was thrown up at the mouth of
Otter Creek, eight miles below the city.
Its garrison of one hundred ninety men
was composed of militia and sailors from
the fleet, commanded by Captain Thorn-
ton of the artillery and Lieutenant Cassin
of the navy. On the 14th of May, 1814,
the British, with five vessels and eight
row galleys, attacked it, hoping to silence
its guns, pass up the river and destroy
the fleet that was then being built. After
a sharp engagement they were compelled
to withdraw and proceed down the lake.
The mouth of the creek is yet called
Fort Cassin. The remains of the fortifications are still easily traced, and, until
within a few years, an elm tree was growing on the point bearing the scar of a
British cannon-ball.

In 1807, Robert Fulton made his first
successful experiment in steam navigation on the Hudson, and the next year a
steamboat was built at Burlington, on
Lake Champlain. In 1815, seven years
later, the first "Phœnix," a steamboat of
three hundred and thirty-six tons, with a

speed of eight miles an hour, was built at Vergennes. She was followed by the "Champlain," built in 1817; the "Congress," in 1818, the second "Phoenix," in 1820, and the "Water Witch" of one hundred and seven tons, built at Fort Cassin in 1832.

In those early days the steamboat men were the grandees of the community. The writer remembers one of the younger Captains Sherman, "Captain Richard," who was then past sixty and had retired. He was pointed out to the youth of that day as a veritable Chesterfield in manner and deportment. These early fresh-water sailors were accustomed to maintain a regular man-of-war discipline aboard their vessels, and to pride themselves on extending the utmost courtesy to their passengers, and making all their landings on schedule time in spite of weather or other obstacles.

In 1827 the general government bought a tract of twenty-eight acres of land a short distance below the falls, and on it established an arsenal for the safe keeping of arms and other ordnance stores, designated an arsenal of the third class. The post contained an arsenal, officers' quarters and a magazine, built of stone, a gun-house, armorer's shop, laboratory, blacksmith shop, stables and wharf. The grounds, which were nicely laid out and kept in excellent order, together with the uniform courtesy of the several commanding officers, made it a favorite resort and promenade of the citizens of the town. There were convenient seats for the aged and feeble, with pleasant walks and shady groves for the sentimental.

Just prior to the breaking out of the Rebellion, Secretary of War Floyd stripped it of its most serviceable arms and munitions, transferring them to southern posts that he might have them ready at hand to arm his co-conspirators. Shortly after the Rebellion it was abandoned as a post, and in 1876 was sold to the State of Vermont, and is now the site of the State Reform School. It is still a delightful spot to visit, located as it is upon wooded banks that slope gently down to the river, which they overlook.

The city is no stranger to war's alarms. Its hills reëchoed to Abercrombie's guns at "Old Ti" (Ticonderoga), in 1758; to Allen's victorious salute from Fort Frederick (Crown Point), in 1775; its handful of remaining settlers had been startled by the sullen growl of the guns of Arnold's retreating galleys, in 1776. In 1777 they had heard St. Clair's guns at "Old Ti" mutter defiance to Burgoyne's advance. The crash of Cassin's artillery at the point in 1814 had been answered later in the year by the deep rumblings of Macdonough's cannon off Cumberland Head.

It had its modest share of incident during the Rebellion, though from its distance from the scenes of operations nothing would seem more unlikely. One warm

BEND OF OTTER CREEK BELOW THE
CAPTAIN HALL DOCK.

afternoon late in the summer of 1864, this message was flashed over the wires to the astonished people : "The Rebels have made an incursion from Canada and are plundering and destroying St. Albans." The citizens of Vergennes at once collected on the Green and wired an offer of assistance to the Governor. Nearly all the able-bodied men being at the front, a body of about fifty boys, from fourteen to twenty years old, were collected and placed in charge of Captain C. E. Parker, of the Seventh Vermont, who happened to be at home, with the writer — who was absent from his battery on wounded furlough — as his lieutenant. A little later orders were received to remain at Vergennes until further orders. In the absence of news the wildest rumors were afloat. One was that the Rebels were likely to seize some vessel at St. Albans, thirty-five miles distant, and proceed up the lake to Vergennes and capture or destroy the arsenal with the military stores of arms and munitions kept there. About dark, Captain Parker, with the approval of the Mayor and Captain Ellsworth, the military store-keeper in charge of the arsenal, marched his men to the arsenal, where arms and ammunition were issued to them. He established his reserve at the gun-house and placed pickets at some distance down the river. Pickets were also posted well advanced on the Fort Cassin road. All approaches to the town from the north both by land and water were thus guarded, except the stage road, which was effectually covered by Burlington, twenty-one miles north. With morning came the news that the raiders were few in numbers, and that, after looting the banks and frightening the inhabitants of St. Albans, they had dispersed to make their way back to Canada as best they could with a troop of cavalry in pursuit. It is said that the line between genius and lunacy is difficult to define ; so, in this case, it is hard to determine whether the St. Albans raid came nearer a farce than a tragedy. Though the precaution was taken to remove the caps from the guns of all except those

actually on post, it is a wonder that the awkwardness of the men did not produce more casualties than could any enemy they were at all likely to encounter.

Like the aroma from the wine of some rare vintage that has aged in the musty gloom of its cellar prison, fragrant with suggestions of vine-clad hills, of sunny climes and dark-eyed maids, of tempestuous voyages and new-land wonders, of gay merry-makings and sad sorrowings, of joyful greetings and tearful partings, are the memories that float in the atmosphere of many a New England village. Of these memories Vergennes has its full share to beguile the summer lounger or comfort the long evenings of a northern winter. The rude camp of a family of St. Francis Indians which one may stumble upon on a sheltered hillside, serves to recall the distant past, when their ancestors with stealthy tread traced a way through the perplexing labyrinth of the mighty forest, either to elude or to pursue their hereditary foe, the Iroquois. One might easily imagine a Sharky's Bend on Otter Creek, — on which, according to my friend Rowland E. Robinson, in his "Along Three Rivers," once stood the humble dwelling of Alexandre Chartier, son of Pierre Chartier, who came to America with Lafayette at the time of the Revolution, — haunted by the ghosts of those venturesome Frenchmen. For they penetrated deep into this then unexplored wilderness, forgot their race, forsook their civilization and, mingling their blood with that of their savage hosts, left a progeny whose ancestry is only to be guessed at from the corrupt lingo they speak.

A mile or so below Sharky's Bend there lived a few years ago a person of this class. Ambrose, or Old Semineau, as he was styled, was a pure-blooded Frenchman, past eighty, whose years of service as trapper and voyageur for the Hudson Bay Company, had shrouded him with the mystery of an abundance of unrecounted adventures. He had wintered on the Mackenzie ; the shores of the Great Slave Lake had echoed the roar of his fusee ; the prow of his birch canoe had

FIRST BEND OF OTTER CREEK, BELOW STEAMBOAT LANDING.

cut the waters of the Lake of the Woods; his traps had been set along the headwaters of the Columbia, and Richardson speaks of him in his "Oregon Trail" as a trusted guide on the Upper Missouri.

Or, a locality may be associated with some ludicrous incident of its early history, as Nigger Hill, where tradition says there once lived a descendant of a colored hero of Macdonough's fleet. When the wife of this hero presented him with the first fruits of their mutual affection, a buxom lass of shining ebony, his generosity must needs saddle the damsel with the Christian name of his lieutenant, to whom he was devoted, and that of his wife, whom he loved, while his pride, to balance the load, perched his own name between them, compelling the girl to bear for nearly threescore years the euphonious name of Peter Joe Phœbe.

Among the many originals, whose sayings, doings and oddities crowd the memory, one only shall beguile a passing mention. "Uncle" Ben Allen, a descendant of the redoubtable Ethan, a man of uncommon size and a confirmed bachelor, kept a private school here for more than thirty years. The living remnant of his three thousand pupils will recognize their quondam teacher, even to the minutest detail, in Goldsmith's lines descriptive of his English prototype, far better than in any image other language can portray:—

"There in his noisy mansion, skill'd to rule
The village master taught his little school;
A man severe he was, and stern to view,
I knew him well and every truant knew;
Well had the boding tremblers learned to trace
The day's disaster in his morning face;
Full well they laughed with counterfeited glee
At all his jokes, for many a joke had he;
Full well the busy whisper, circling round,
Convey'd the dismal tidings when he frowned;
Yet he was kind, or if severe in aught,
The love he bore to learning was in fault."

To all who long to see nature's charms in all their unveiled loveliness, and, while gazing on her chaste beauties, would pass a drowsy summer's day in dreamy musing, let me commend Vergennes as the shrine to which to direct their pilgrimage.

"THE LAZY HAMMOCK SWINGS."

How soft the sunshine is,
   how quiet and how
   fair!
What peaceful happiness
   pervades the summer
   air!
The wind plays softly
   through the branches
   bending low;
The lazy hammock swings so
   slowly to and fro,—
While in my heart a voice does ever
   say:
     The world is gay,
     Life's naught but play,
And all our days are surely days of
   May!

Drawing by Mary A. Kirkup

The autumn air is soft and fair as day in June;
The hours are full of melody, more bright the moon;
Through branches, crimson tinted, sighs again the wind;
The hammock now swings empty; yet, amidst the grind
   Of ceaseless household mills, these words belong:
     The world is bright,
     True love is might,
   When labor sweetens every day with song!

FORT DODGE.
                                      Mary A. Kirkup.

MIDLAND WAR SKETCHES. X.

THE BATTLE OF MOBILE BAY.

By E. R. HUTCHINS.

FRIDAY, August 5, 1864, brought to the United States Navy the greatest naval battle of history. For months the West Gulf Squadron had lain at anchor off the Bay of Mobile, and the officers and sailors, weary with the monotony of blockade life, were eagerly enthusiastic for the long promised fight. The writer was the surgeon of the U. S. S. Port Royal, commanded by Lieutenant-Commander Bancroft Gherardi, now a retired rear-admiral. Two days before, we had been ordered to Pensacola for coal, and in the early dawn of the above date we caught an indistinct view of the fleet as we returned. Unusual activity was manifest. Upon reaching the Flag-ship Hartford — Admiral Farragut's vessel — we were ordered alongside the Richmond and lashed to her port side. Then came the order, "Prepare for battle."

The preparations are soon made. The anchors are weighed and the vessels are forming in line. As the Hartford passes us, with the intrepid chief, Farragut, on her deck, we give three rousing cheers, which are taken up by the entire fleet, and cheer after cheer rings in the air.

The following is the order of the vessels:

First, the Brooklyn, with the Octorara on her port side;

Second, the Hartford, with the Metacomet;

Third, the Richmond, with the Port Royal;

Fourth, the Lackawanna, with the Seminole;

Fifth, the Monongahela, with the Kennebec;

Sixth, the Ossipee, with the Itasca;

Seventh, the Oneida, with the Galena.

Inside, and over the bar our ironclads, the Tecumseh, the Manhattan and the Chickasaw, have taken their positions on the starboard side of the wooden ships, and are exposed to the fire of Fort Morgan, and to the first attack of the Rebel ironclad ram, Tennessee — the pride of the Confederate Navy. On our right, two miles away, on Mobile Point, is Fort Morgan, with her sixty guns. Upon our left, on Little Dauphin Island, is Fort Gaines, with thirty guns. West of this is Fort Powell, with ninety-eight guns. West of this, and as yet out of reach of harm, are

From his latest Photo.

ADMIRAL FARRAGUT.

fifteen hundred Union soldiers under General Gordon Granger.

Four bells have sounded six o'clock, and we are under way. Simultaneously, as if by magic, "Old Glory" streams from each mast's peak in the great fleet. Cautiously and slowly we are steaming into the jaws of danger. Three-quarters of an hour has passed, and the Tecumseh, commanded by the gallant Craven, fires the first shot. The fort is silent. The fleet steams proudly on, every flag unfurled, and with as brave men as ever a fleet possessed.

A few moments later the first shot comes from the fort — and falls short. The Brooklyn immediately answers with a shot from her starboard side.

At this moment the Rebel fleet, led by the ram Tennessee, followed by the gunboats Selma, Morgan and Gaines, steam slowly around the point and stop, as if waiting to meet us. The Tennessee is commanded by Admiral Buchanan, a classmate of Admiral Farragut when in the Naval Academy.

When within twelve hundred yards of the fort, the firing becomes general. The screech of shot and shell is indescribable. Shells shriek over our heads and through our rigging and plunge into the water. Those from our vessels fall on and into the fort by hundreds.

The Brooklyn and Tecumseh are still in the lead, closely followed by the Hartford. Suddenly the Brooklyn stops, and a tremendous upheaval of water is seen, and the Tecumseh, with her commander and one hundred and ten of her crew of one hundred and twenty, goes down in the sea, a torpedo placed in the channel by the enemy having exploded beneath her.

The cry is heard, "The Brooklyn is backing!" And so she is, but Farragut, having climbed part way up the rigging, is lashed to the mast. He gives the order "Starboard!" to the Hartford's wheel officer, and that vessel quickly steams by the Brooklyn, amid the cheers of the fleet.

Every gun in the fort is centered on the fleet. Every starboard and bow gun of

SURGEON E. S. BUTCHER, IN '64.

the fleet is sending its missiles of destruction on the fort. It is one sheet of fire and one awful boom of cannon.

> "How they leaped, the tongues of flame,
>   From the cannon's fiery lips!
> How the broadsides, deck and frame,
>   Shook the great ships!"

Up to this time the Rebel fleet have been silent, but now they commence a steady and annoying fire on our ships.

The huge, black monster, the Tennessee, now dashes at the Hartford.

Imagine those old sea-dogs, Farragut and Buchanan, — the best the navies had, — who from early boyhood had been intimate friends — the one fighting for and beneath the flag of his country, the other fighting against that flag !

Every eye possible seeks these commands, and when the Rebel monster fails to harm the Hartford, every heart thanks God. She now attempts to shove her ram into the Brooklyn and here, too, fails, and she makes the same attempt with every vessel on the starboard side, and, strange to say, fails in every trial, and her commander is compelled to content himself with broadside after broadside along the line. As she passes the Oneida, the last vessel in our fleet, she gives her a broadside, and a shell penetrates her boiler and bursts, scalding many, and shattering the arm of her gallant commander, Mulaney.

And now the fleet has passed and is in the bay, and the lashings which held ship to ship are severed. The Tennessee, like a sullen giant, goes under the fort as if to rest. She is followed by the gunboats Morgan and Gaines. The Selma has been struck by a shot from the Hartford and is fleeing up the bay towards Mobile. The Metacomet and our vessel pursue her, the former in her wake, while we attempt to cross her bow. Both vessels are constantly firing at the fleeing Rebel and slowly gaining on her. And when her capture is close at hand her flag is hauled down and she surrenders to the Metacomet. Her dying and dead are literally piled upon each other on her deck.

It was the writer's duty to go on board, and the suffering he witnessed was terrible. A pathetic scene is here recalled. A lad of sixteen was stretched on the deck, close to death's door. Our flag had been placed just above him and, looking towards it, he said with a sweet smile on his face: "I am happier now to die under that flag." His sufferings soon ceased and he passed away. The results of a battle are far more dreadful when confined to the narrow limit of a ship's deck than when strewn over a battle-field on land.

But now the Tennessee emerges from under the guns of the fort. Slowly and steadily she comes. She seems like a huge living monster eager for battle. She pours out her shot and shell as if with venom. The Monongahela rides down upon her twice, but she seems unharmed by the terrific force. The Lackawanna follows with similar results. The Hartford strikes her with full steam on, but only to receive the deadly fire from her guns. The monitor Chickasaw keeps up a furious fire on her stern, and the Manhattan hurls her fifteen-inch shot upon her with terrible precision. As the Tennessee is steered, so is the Chickasaw, following literally in her course, the heavy shot from her guns ceaselessly pounding her, carrying away her smokestack, breaking in her port shutters and shattering her steering gear. No vessel can hold out under such conditions, and after an hour's constant fighting the white flag is seen on the Tennessee; the firing ceases and Buchanan surrenders to Farragut.

"From the first of the iron shower
　Till we sent our parting shell,
'Twas just one savage hour
　Of the war and the rage of hell"

The victory was won. The greatest naval battle of history had been fought and the Union cause had triumphed.

Besides the one hundred and ten who were buried in their iron coffin, the Tecumseh, twenty-eight were killed on the Hartford and twenty-two on the other Union vessels. Altogether we had one hundred and sixty killed (including those on the Tecumseh) and two

DR. R. R. BUTCHINS, OF DES MOINES

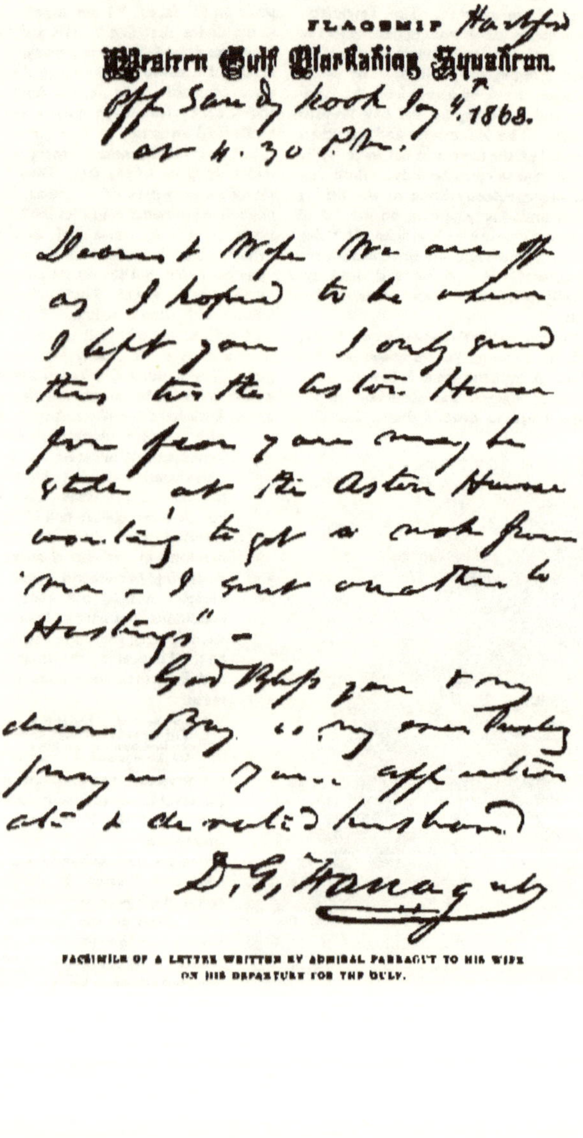

FLAGSHIP Hartford
Western Gulf Blockading Squadron.
Off Sandy Hook Jay 4th 1863.
at 4.30 P.M.

Dearest Wife We are off
as I hoped to be when
I left you   I only send
this to the Astor House
for fear you may be
still at the Astor House
wanting to get a note from
me — I sent one to the
Hastings" —
    God Bless you & my
dear Boy is my own hearty
prayer   Your affectionate
& devoted husband
    D. G. Farragut

FACSIMILE OF A LETTER WRITTEN BY ADMIRAL FARRAGUT TO HIS WIFE
ON HIS DEPARTURE FOR THE GULF.

hundred and fifty wounded. The enemy's loss was less than ours, but we took as prisoners two hundred and eighty, officers and men. Admiral Buchanan was seriously wounded in the leg. Our ships all came to anchor and, in the quiet hush of that summer night, with sorrowing yet grateful hearts, with appropriate services we buried the dead beneath the sea.

During the night Fort Powell was abandoned by the enemy, and in the early morning of the 6th we run up the starry flag over its deserted walls.

On Sunday divine services were held on board all the ships, and Admiral Farragut's congratulatory order was read. In the meantime the troops on Dauphin Island were slowly investing Fort Gaines and on the 10th that fort surrendered to the navy. When the news of this surrender reached us, every vessel's rigging was manned with the sailors and nine cheers were given for the victory. The surrender was made to the navy from choice of the enemy, they having the opportunity to choose between the army and navy. The surrender gave us thirty-seven officers and eight hundred and eighty-six men.

On the 9th the troops on shore moved eastward and a demand was made upon General Paige, the Rebel commandant of Fort Morgan, for its surrender. He was familiarly known as "Bombast Paige." He replied to the demand in this terse way: "No. I consider you all my prisoners."

The monitors and one or two of the larger wooden vessels commenced firing on the fort. This was kept up at irregular intervals until the 22d, when a general bombardment commenced and the firing was almost incessant. That night a fire was discovered in the fort, and on the 23d General "Bombast" Paige surrendered. He was too proud to give up his sword and it was afterwards found in a well within the fort. The enemy had thrown ninety thousand pounds of powder into the cisterns.

The Union victory was now complete. Old Glory was floating from Forts Morgan, Gaines and Powell, and while the gunboats, Gaines and Morgan, had escaped up the bay, the boast of the Confederacy — the Tennessee — lay at anchor near our fleet, and from it, also, our flag triumphantly waved.

TWO ROSES.

H E HAS brought me a royal hot-house rose,
    Unkissed by the wind or dew;
I pin it on with a smile and a jest,
    Yet thinking, the while, of you.

I dream of another red rose, dew-wet,
    You pinned at my throat, you know,
In the warm, sweet dusk of a summer eve —
    O summer so long ago!

To you it meant nothing — a sudden whim,
    But it meant the world to me!
I gave you a heart for that crimson rose,
    And the thorn I could not see.

Ah me! for the foolish heart of a girl,
    And the tender dreams it knew!
And he does not know, as I kiss his gift,
    I think of that rose and you!

HAMPTON.   *Florence A. Jones.*

A HISTORIC CASTLE AND FORTRESS.

THE EDITOR ABROAD. XVI.

IT WAS an ideal summer day, the temperature was at perfection point, leaving the mind free from all thought as to relative thickness or thinness of clothing. The sun shone brightly upon green and golden-yellow fields. The streams, swollen by recent rains, rushed madly through culverts and across low-lying meadows. There was no dust, no mud. So perfect are the roads in Germany that there is no room along the highway for water or mud, and almost no material for the wind to work up into dust.

A short ride by rail from Aix brought us to the smart little city of Düren, where a rich manufacturer — a relative of our friend — had his private carriage in waiting at the station and at our disposal. The driver ceremoniously placed himself at the service of our party of four and, as directed, drove us through the city and southward into the country.

We passed through a pretty village where everybody was either going to or coming from the little stone church seen through a long avenue of trees. It was a Catholic holiday and the villagers were in their "Sunday best."

Out into the country again. Almost before we knew it, our heavy carriage was rattling over the rough pavement of a village that looked as though it had stopped growing centuries ago. The men with their long pipes and their klumpen, or wooden shoes; the women in their short frocks, pink stockings and heavy slippers; the children chasing one another in sabots; the dogs, cows, pigs and chickens, — everything in the village that had life looked up at us amazed at the invasion of such an overwhelming equipage in such a modest and inoffensive community, and at the projection of so much noise upon such a narrow, quiet street!

From the carriage our driver could look into the projecting second-story windows of the little, old, bulging houses. He

THE WALLED TOWN OF NIDEGGEN.

could, but he wouldn't! Attired in a suit of green, "with buttons all over 'im," and with a shining silk hat upon his head, he had more dignity to sustain than the rest of us, and he looked neither to the right hand nor to the left. We did the looking.

We next rode through a village composed wholly of German Jews. The place swarmed with children. The houses were poor and uninteresting, but the synagogue was quite imposing.

On through another village and then again on and up, and soon the walls of Nideggen startle us with their nearness.

We look in vain for guards at the city's brown stone gate. This entrance is, as we learn, a modern reproduction of the ancient "thor," in defense of which the retainers of the historic Counts of Julich, in their time, lost many lives. We ride through the gate, admiring its grandeur —and, scarcely less, the dignity and conscious pride with which our stately driver passes under the arch, not deigning to notice the uplifted hats of the old men and young boys sitting and standing along our triumphal way to the hotel!

We make quite a commotion at the inn. After arranging for supper, for it is now about 3 o'clock, we climb the rustic stairs back of the hotel, which lead us to an elevated flower garden. Thence, with the turn of a big key we are let out into a narrow roadway and are directed to the castle. Passing under a genuine old arch, past a real Twelfth Century church that looks its age,— the carvings of saints and angels over the doorway having been worn almost smooth by the winds and storms of nearly eight hundred years,— we soon reached the ruined wall and the great gate of Nideggen's castle.

While waiting for the deliberate old woman to come with her big key and let us in, I will improve the time by making the original remark that there are castles and castles! Some are worth going miles to see, and some are not. Some are solemnly grand in their ruin. Others, covered with modern roofs and converted into places of restauration, would look quite fantastic in their assumption of youthfulness but for a settled air of melancholy from which they cannot escape.

The ruin before us is the largest and grandest we have yet seen, with the single exception of Heidelberg.

Handing the stout old woman a mark, we enter the castle grounds. The gate-

THE VALLEY OF THE ROER, WITH THE RUINS OF NIDEGGEN ON THE RIGHT.

keeper's pretty daughter accompanies us. Embedded in the wall of the castle is the "wappen" or escutcheon of the historic family of Julich, that once with a high hand lorded it over all this region, over whose claims the Thirty Years' War was fought,—or at least begun,—and before whose power the great and good and brave, as well as the servile, were made to bow. The "lion rampant" of the Julichs, once so terrible, now hardly attracts the visitor's attention.

We stand by the thick stone wall of the immense well from which the servants of the Julichs once laboriously drew water.— Bear in mind we are upon the topmost ledge of a great rock, more than five hundred feet above the valley of the Roer. The girl lights a bundle of straw and drops the blazing mass into the well, the pointed end down. As it winds downward it roars like an expiring animal. Soon the roar ceases to reach our ears, but we still see the blaze revolving in its descent. Suddenly the light goes out. The girl good-naturedly repeats the act, a strangely fascinating one to the beholder.

We look about us and proceed to explore. The castle walls, unlike any we have elsewhere seen, except at Heidelberg, are of a red sandstone. The general effect is grand, according in color-tone with the outcropping rocks, and affording a rich background to the bright green of the trees and grass. The older portion of the castle, what remains of it, has the tall, slender windows for the archers; the smaller windows, or holes, for the stone-throwers, and the small, grated windows for observation. The larger and grander new castle, adjoining the old on the west, and extending over to the very edge of the rock, is built upon a more generous plan and is more ornate. But the new castle is a ruin, along with the old. It is grand in ruin and must have been magnificent when, three hundred years or more ago, on festival occasions its halls were brightened with the spectacular gaieties of the time, and enlivened with brilliant balls and banquets.

The windows of the new castle were once double, but now the smaller, inner windows are gone, and the great high-arched openings, some broken and some intact, let in floods of light from the afternoon sun. These windows are ten feet wide and about sixteen feet high, and there are four of them on the exposed side of the castle. Above these windows are remains of four ornamental arches with pillars. Above these arches were once four smaller windows communicating with chambers overhead. Ruined inside walls show the ground plan of the building. The dimensions of the castle are about 70 by 140 feet.

The only room in the newer portion which still retains its top wall is the one labeled "Damen Erker," or Ladies' Balcony. There being no door, without even so much as "by your leave," we enter the once beautiful room in which medieval ladies were wont to sit and chat while their lords were banqueting or hunting or fighting. The walls are now bare, and a half-dislodged stone over the bay-window tells us that a few decades more of wind and rain and frost will complete the desolation here as elsewhere upon this height.

From this portico and from other points on the height we obtain rare views of the Roer Valley and of the distant hills. The little river, last seen by us at Montjoie, winds one way and another among the hills, as if uncertain as to its course. Below is a little village, the dwellings huddled along the stream on either side. Standing upon the bridge is a rude statue of Johannes Nepomuk, the saint who presides over bridges, and to whom the people who reside along streams are wont to pray for protection against drowning. A winding road leads over the hill to an ancient Trappist monastery, recently abandoned as such and converted into a distillery for the making of "schnapps." An acorn-top church spire stands out against the sky to the west. Woods and fields fill up the background with dark and light greens and yellows.

We turn from the view to explore the older and historically more interesting portion of the ruin. We enter the dreary old chapel. Here a rebellious Archbishop, long held a prisoner, was wont to worship. The rude relics of this gloomy worship, including the altar stone, can be seen by light which strays in from a small grated window. The walls of the tower are at least eight feet thick. The chapel opens into a dungeon in which the Archbishop was confined. Part of the time the prisoner was permitted the use of the better-lighted apartment overhead. A sacrilegious Count of Julich even went so far as to cause the Archbishop to be put into an iron cage, which was hung outside the castle wall for the further humiliation of the offender and the exasperation of his sympathizers. The cage is still preserved as a relic in the old village church we passed.

Let me tell the story of the House of Julich, a story verified by the Chronicles of Cologne. In the Thirteenth Century there was a rough and barbarous Count, named Wilhelm, lording it over the vast possessions of Julich, and living in state in this old castle of Nideggen. In those days an Archbishop had his castles and army of retainers. Archbishop Engelbert II, of Valkenbourg (or Fauquemont), deciding that Wilhelm needed disciplining, moved against Nideggen with an army. The Julichs were fighters from away back, and Wilhelm, true to the traditions of his family, refused to be disciplined. He called on Aix la Chapelle, Cologne and other cities roundabout, for support and prepared to give Engelbert a warm reception. The two armies met in battle in the woods near Nideggen. At first the Archbishop seemed likely to win; but the Julichs were stayers, and the stayers won. Wilhelm took prisoner both Engelbert and his ally, Conrad, Archbishop of Cologne. Conrad bought his freedom by promising his daughter to the Count's eldest son in marriage. Great pressure was brought to bear upon Wilhelm to procure the release of Engelbert, but to no avail. To a delegation of priests he said:

"I found, to my chagrin, a bird preying upon my land, and I caught him. I choose to confine him in a cage. No priest have I imprisoned; he is a robber, a base knight and a destroyer. Let him who would free him come and take him if he can."

The Chronicler relates that "they brought him to Nideggen, to the strong castle, shut him up in the tower, put upon him great and strong iron chains, and fastened him to the wall in a place so damp and foul that he nearly died in his chains."

But that was not enough. To further humiliate the Archbishop and exasperate his petitioners, he caused an iron cage to be made, as for a bird of prey, and directed it to be hung from a window in the wall, as one would hang a bird-cage, and there, dividing his time between chapel, dungeon and cage, during the long days, in heat and cold, in rain and shine, for three and a half years remained the poor humiliated Archbishop, the prisoner of the Count of Julich.

Relief finally came, in the shape of a papal ban. On the 10th day of August, 1270, the church bells rang out over the land, announcing that, because of the indignity put upon a servant of God, Wilhelm III, Count of Julich, was under the ban of the Pope, with all the prohibitions and isolation which such papal nunciature then implied. This was more than Wilhelm had anticipated. He let the Archbishop go.

The Chronicler, too indignant to stick closely to his text, ventures to add that the ghost of the wicked Count, unable to sleep nights, awakens, frightened from bad dreams, rolls from side to side in his tomb, gets up and goes down into the dungeon of the Archbishop and, as he was wont to do in life, rattles the chains to waken his prisoner, that he may not only rob him of his rest, but also put upon him some new indignity; and then said ghost takes up his weary walk about the grounds and rooms of the castle, doomed to nightly live over again this most shameful chapter in his shameless life.

We didn't wait to see the ghost, but were tempted to wait and watch the early moon steal into the ruin through those great windows, and to note the picturesque effects of the lengthening shadows projected by these crumbling walls.

We climbed the long spiral stairway until we reached the yet firm and strong east side of the old tower. The dust of decay and the wind's deposits had transformed the top walls into a flower garden, and delicate little yellow and blue flowers were everywhere springing from the moss between the stones. Long we sat upon the tower viewing the wall, the dungeon and the chapel of this historic castle. To the south was the valley. To the east stood the old church, with graves all about it. Beyond was the walled town, a vista through an open gateway revealing a row of queer old houses standing out upon the street; and on beyond, gently shading the clear blue of the sky with dark blue lines, rose the distant peaks of the Seven Mountains overlooking the Rhine above Cologne.

The scene from the ruined tower cannot be pictured, for it is all-sided; but the memory, within its appointed limitations, is all-seeing, and ever afterward, at the suggestion of Nideggen, or at the mention of the history-making Counts of Julich, that old tower with its dungeon and chapel, and that grand panoramic view from the tower, will flash upon the mental vision with the quickness of thought, recalling that summer afternoon.

We retrace our steps to town. We seat ourselves upon the bench in the street in front of the inn and watch the everlastingly knitting women and maidens, and the men and boys in wooden shoes, as they pass up and down the stone-paved street like "supers" in a spectacular play. After supper we take a walk through the town, then out by the old eastern gate, and to an opposite hill, from which we obtain a good view of the castle suffused with the crimson glory of the setting sun.

Drawing by Clara Hendricks.

"O PASSIONATE HEART OF THE SUMMER."

O passionate Heart of the Summer!
 You throb like the pulses of pain,—
The riotous, fevered vibrations
 That torture the sensitive brain!

You send out the life-giving current;
 It rushes through fiber and cell,—
The leaf and the bud and the blossom
 Respond to your mystical spell.

The lilies that sway in the meadows
 Are crowned with imperial bloom;
And, faint with delirium, trembles
 The corn with its shimmering plume.

Knee-deep stand the kine in the water,—
 The lazy bells tinkling less free,—
They drowse through the heat of the
 noontide,
 In the shade of the wide-spreading tree.

O, dear are the clouds and the sunshine,
 The thunder that bursts o'er the hills,
The drone of the bee in the clover,
 The echo of murmuring rills!

O passionate Heart of the Summer,
 Throb on in the mood you love best,
For the hopes of the on-coming harvest
 Are locked in your life-giving breast!

Barbara K. Garner.

A SUMMER IN SONOMA.

TROUT - FISHING IN SULPHUR CREEK — CAMPING IN THE FOOT-HILLS — A
DIGGER INDIAN BURIAL — A DEER HUNT.

By Edwin Preston.

WEARYING of the restless city of
the Golden Gate, I stepped aboard
a ferry-boat one morning, and was carried
across the finest harbor in the world toward the shore of dreamy Sonoma-land.
The water was merrily dancing and
sparkling and shimmering, giving forth a
combination of green and blue and white
such as no artist could even faintly portray, and no word-painter describe. Far
and near, above and around, sailed the
snowy-winged sea birds, uttering their
weird, wild cry.

The Golden Gate's portals were still
enveloped in the somber drapery of departing night. Faintly outlined amid the
dissolving mists, we could see the rugged
promontories that form this far-famed
place of entrance for the craft of all nations.

All too soon our boat reached her destination, and I boarded a
north-bound train, and
was soon speeding away
through canyon and
mountain and verdant
valley to Sonoma, whose
vine-clad hills vie with
those of sunny Italy or
castled Rhine.

Cloverdale, Sonoma
county, is a village of
about eight hundred in-
habitants. It is guarded
by mountains on all sides
but one, and on that side
the Russian River flows.
From this romantically-
situated town I took various excursions into the
surrounding country,—
climbing mountains,
camping, hunting, fishing
and sketching.

Usually, the rainy season here ends in
May, followed by bright skies and a long
procession of warm days, extending on
into November. A dreamy softness pervades the summer air and clothes mountain and foot-hill and valley with a dainty
drapery of charming colors.

The Coast Range has a bewitching
charm. It lacks the towering heights of
the Rockies, but equals, if it does not
surpass, the bonnie heather-clothed
Highlands of Scotland.

One morning before the cock crew, and
while the owl was still out hunting, and
the jack-rabbit was abroad in the land, I
gathered up fishing tackle and basket and
started for Sulphur Creek in quest of
trout. This stream comes rushing down
the mountain and empties into Russian

SQUAW ROCK.

149

River. The night wind was still sighing among the pines and hurrying whisperingly through the canyon.

On the way I passed an old deserted mill, gloomy and silent. In it the sleepy owl nods the day away. Among its timbers the spider spins the dainty drapery of its web, and the sad-voiced phœbe-bird makes its home. Through the broken windows the free and reckless breezes whistle a wild refrain, or moan and howl and shriek. After lingering a few minutes by the old mill, I scrambled on up the canyon, toward the trout-fishing place.

Climbing and sliding among great piles of water-worn boulders, and scaling great rocks that stood out in places so abruptly as to almost stop the flow of the water, which roared and foamed and dashed itself into a fury at the interruption, I finally succeeded in reaching the locality where the speckled beauties were supposed to abound. Nor did I "whip" the noisy water for many minutes before I had proven the fact that the trout were there, and also that they were in good appetite. The fly I offered was not the kind the fish were looking for, but notwithstanding that fact, they took it,—to their sorrow and to my delight! For some time this sport proceeded with varying success and interest, and then I built a fire of drift-wood among the rocks.

RUSSIAN RIVER RANCH.

The warmth from this fire served the double purpose of counteracting the chilling influence of the night wind that came howling through the canyon, and cooking a few of the trout for my supper.

There, in "the shadow of a great rock," with a boulder for my table and another for my chair, and the cheering firelight flickering around, I had a delightful repast.

Above the water's din I could hear the kingfisher's shrill cry and, at times, the little phœbe-bird's song.

For several weeks a jolly party of us were cozily camped in a sheltered glade near the western base of Iron Mountain, of the Coast Range. Wild grape vines clambered among the blooming buckeye bushes; the pines lifted their spikes and the ferns their feathery boughs toward the blue, and sighed and moaned when the wind wandered down the mountain or came roaring up the canyon from the restless river. The dark, moss-covered live-oak stretched its long, uneven boughs, greeting the passing breeze with the rustle of its small crisp leaves. Here and there bunches of pendent mistletoe were clinging.

The large-leaved, compact madroño, with its chocolate-colored bark, added its beauty to the place. The manzanita ("little apple") grew in thick bunches. The wild mahogany waved its feathery catkins. Wild flowers were blooming all around, smiling in sunny situations, sparkling in shady nooks. Like nuggets of gold, the California poppies gleamed in the open glades. Many other kinds of vegetation, majestic and lowly, graceful and abrupt, beautiful and homely, were strewn round about us with a prodigality characteristic of bounteous Nature.

From the shady glen came the sweet notes of the vireo. The soft, plaintive voice of the dove was heard. We were favored with choice medleys of the mocking bird's own composition. Among the thickets the crested quail called to his mate.

Sometimes at night we could hear the wild deer bounding through the glade. Cold springs of sparkling water came dashing down the mountain side. With all these delightful surroundings, he would have been unromantic indeed who had not become charmed with it all.

One morning, long before the sun had chased the mists away, we buckled on our lunch baskets and started on a mountain-climbing trip. Away we went, climbing over foot-hills, through rugged gulches and gloomy glades. We found a pure, cold stream dashing among the rocks, or resting in clear pools, inviting the thirsty to partake. As the day dawned in all its freshness, the wild birds awoke, and began twittering and caroling and calling from tree and rock. The fresh breezes were rambling far and free, gently swaying the crests of the trees. The feathery fern lifted its plumes among the crannies. The mountain jay answered its mate's harsh cry; and the road-runners began calling to each other among the chemese on the mountain side. This bird's cry is as strange and lonely as is its habitation. It might be compared to the noise produced by a distant kine-caller.

With many a slip, and numerous windings, we finally reached the top of the mountain.

Above the clouds ! Valley and mountain were at times hidden from view, and then, as the fleecy screen floated away, the grand panorama was revealed in all its rapturous beauty. The nearer heights were fresh in their emerald dress ; and, as range after range melted into the distance, an exquisite robe of purple and blue enveloped them. Away, and afar, the eye could feast on billows of mountains. As they lifted their heads toward

the heavens, one could almost imagine the snowy clouds that floated over and around them were crafts for ethereal fairies to float wherever the freshening winds might waft them !

The dreamy softness of the atmosphere made one wish to ponder on things above this mundane realm. So calm, so pure, so illimitable, and so impressive was the view that the passing of time was unheeded.

The setting sun informed us that we must return. The descent requires even more care than the upward climb, as a misstep might hurl one onto the rocks below, and give the watchful vultures employment. At last we reached the base in safety. As we hastened toward our camping place, the sun sank behind the mountains ; twilight lingered only for a little time, and soon all was secure under shelter of the night. Save the restless, dashing river, struggling among the rocks, or the distant barking of some mountaineer's dog, or the hooting of a lone, shadow-loving owl, telling its wisdom to the listening rocks and woods,—Nature seemed at rest.

The tribe of Indians known as "Diggers," live in this region. They are more like the negro, in color, than are any other American Indians. They are short in stature. When in their wild state, unannoyed by the encroachments of civilization, living on simple food, and unacquainted with the fearful effect of "fire water," these simple people were noted for longevity. It was a common thing to find among them individuals who had passed the century line. If, as is often asserted, fish is a brain food, these aborigines certainly ought to be exceedingly intellectual ; for they devour great quantities of the finny tribe. They weave nets of willow roots, and drive the fish into them. They also put some kind of herb into the water, which makes the fish drunk. While the fish are under the influence of it, the cunning fishermen fill their baskets. They also use a rude spear in procuring salmon. When bucks, squaws and children are engaged in fishing, the scene is very picturesque. They gather acorns and buckeyes, from which they make a kind of bread. They are skillful in the construction of baskets, many of which are decorated with a variety of colors in quite an artistic manner. In some places they live together in rancheros, and have a small church, in charge of a Spanish priest. This tribe is nominally Roman Catholic in religion, but the individual members are not religious to any serious extent. For the most part the Diggers are scattered along the river, living in miserable little shacks, except during the hot, dry summer months when they sleep in rude arbors, or utilize the cool shade of the live-oak.

An Indian funeral, which we witnessed, seemed to me so strange and weird that an account of it may be of interest.

The starter for the Happy Hunting Grounds was a maiden of some thirteen summers. She was liked and mourned by all. Before dawn, Indian runners had already started in different directions to carry the tidings to relatives and friends living in other valleys and canyons. As distant members of the tribe came sauntering in, it was plain to see that the heralds had done their errand well. Even before the girl died, a vociferous wail was kept up, and at each new arrival the wail

was increased in vehemence. The funeral proper generally begins about midday. The solemn march to the grave is begun amid the startling din of many voices. This tribe uses no drum or other "instrument" save the tongue. In fact they need no other.

The place of burial, to which this strange, irregular procession wended its way, is situated on the bank of Russian River. The winds seem to sing a requiem among the gloomy moss-draped boughs overhead. Many other weary sons of the forest are resting there. All that mark their graves are small stakes and a few pebbles.

The procession has reached the open grave, around which the chief mourners kneel. If the wailing was intense before, it is startling now. If there is any articulation at all, it sounds like our word "why." With their voices pitched in a very high key, they repeat the sound in rapid time. They keep this up until compelled from exhaustion to desist. Then an attendant dashes cold water on the wailer's head. After a few minutes he or she recovers and joins in the pandemonium with renewed vigor.

The mother of the deceased wailed, howled and screamed, and tore her hair, and scratched her face until the blood ran down. Meantime she destroyed her clothing for the most part.

IRON MOUNTAIN.

EVENING IN THE COAST RANGE.

You must remember that this performance is kept up for nearly four hours. It takes much water to run such a funeral.

Finally "Captain Jack," despite his years and stiff joints, went through a peculiar dance at the foot of the grave, moving his body from side to side, and uttering a strange, wild song the while. He kept this up for a half hour or so without stopping. Then a large, thick loaf of bread, made of acorn meal and baked on heated rocks after the loaf was well covered with madroño leaves and sand, was brought to the wailers. They ate it greedily until there was none left.

All the clothing, trinkets, etc., belonging to the deceased were also placed in the grave. At this stage of the obsequies the mother began a more intense lamentation. It required the earnest endeavors of several Indians to prevent her throwing herself into the open grave.

The shallow grave was then filled with gravel and sand. After that task was completed some of the mourners knelt around the mound, repeated the church service in Spanish, frequently crossed themselves, and removed the small stones and pebbles from the mound until you could not have found one as large as a pea.

This finished the ceremony and the mourners and beholders went their various ways. The former showed no signs of sorrow as they departed.

For several nights after an Indian burial a lone watchman stands guard at the grave. He is there not to keep coyotes or other prowlers away, but to ward off the evil spirits.

This tribe used to practice cremation. It was done in a very crude manner. It often required twenty cords of wood to complete the incineration of a deceased "Digger."

One of the most striking objects in this region is a high cliff which rises abruptly from the brink of the Russian River. It is called "Squaw Rock." An immense rock near the top of the precipice forms an unusually good profile. It takes no imagination whatever to see the effect.

There is the regulation legend connected with it. An Indian brave loved a dusky maid, but he changed his mind and deserted her for another. Her heart bowed down with weight of woe, Maiden Number One climbed that frowning pinnacle, leapt out into space and was dashed to pieces on the rocks below.

Early one morning, when a cool, fresh wind from the sea was drifting the low-hung clouds and fog across the valley and against the mountains, there was an unusual stir in our camp. The horses were all equipped and impatiently jangling their bridles; the hounds were struggling to be free and away to the wilderness; rifles were cleaned; breakfast was eaten, and we were off for a deer hunt. There were three of us, and, as we sped away on our sure-footed cayuses, our interest in the sport was intense.

The hounds are trained for the work. They know just how to bring the deer within rifle range. As we were ascending a gulch among the foot-hills one of the dogs started a buck. He was out of range, but made a fine run and was soon out of sight. The hounds were close on his trail, however, and it was not long before the noble animal came over the hill at a lively pace. It was still a good long shot, but a ball from one of our rifles reached the mark,—only wounding the buck, however. The dogs managed to work him around into range again, and another shot finished him. It was a fine antlered buck.

After hanging him under a madroño, we started on again, but had not proceeded far before the rough and steep nature of the ground precluded further progress on horseback. Dismounting, we got the dogs down among the chaparral. No deer were started there. So we separated, and began a steady climb, over very difficult ground.

It was not long before loud "baying" gave proof that our faithful servants had found more deer. Suddenus the speeding of an arrow one was dashing past me. I sent a bullet after it. It sprang into the air and fell crashing among the brush and rocks. It seemed like cruel work; but one does not stop to think much of that when in the thick of the hunt.

"Crack, crack !" went the other rifles. Somewhere, out of sight, there were more victims, no doubt. Away up the mountain side I saw a doe and a fawn fleeing for refuge.

Then under the cool, pure shade of a bay tree, with the pretty deer lying near, I rested awhile. Then, by prearranged signals, our trio came together again, and we clambered laboriously down to where our cayuses were grazing among the wild oats.

We only had two deer as a result of our morning hunt, but the excitement of it can be better imagined and felt by every hunter who reads my account than it can be described by at least one of the participants.

THE AID SOCIETY TEA AT JANE CRAIG'S.

BY MARY E. P. SMITH.

"YOU'RE cleaning house early, Jane." Jane Craig stood on the step-ladder. She was cleaning the top shelf in the sitting-room cupboard. She was tall and thin and wore a lilac calico dress that had faded in the washing. She turned her head slowly and carefully that she might not lose her balance.

"O, it's you, is it, Catherine ? Just take a chair and excuse me if I don't get down. I'm up here and I'd like to stay until I get through."

"O, I couldn't set down, anyway. I left bread in the oven. I want to get your mother's receipt for fruit-cake, Jane. All of Uncle John's folks are coming up from West Hampton next week, and I want to make some fruit-cake that will taste just like your mother's, if I can."

Mrs. Seeley stood within the door. The cat had followed her in and rubbed about her with a loud purr. She stooped to stroke it.

"Can't I get it without your getting down ?"

"I was trying to think where it is. I don't believe I've had mother's receipt book since she died. Look in the pigeon-hole in the secretary — in the one farthest to the east. It's a red-covered book — seems to me I've seen it there."

It was an old-fashioned secretary, with rows of black-bound books on its shelves —Josephus, Rollin's Ancient History, etc, and in the pigeon-hole to the east, as Jane had said, was the red-covered volume, full of recipes written out in a fine, painstaking hand.

"Did you find it, Catherine?"

"Yes, and if you don't care I'll take the book right along home with me and write off the receipt. I don't want to stop to find it now."

"Yes, take it right along. It's a book that mother set great store by. She'd been writing off some receipts in it the day she died. Someway I never felt like using it, and I never have, from that day to this."

"Well now, Jane, maybe you'd rather I didn't take it."

But Miss Craig assured her of her willingness, and Mrs. Seeley carried away the book.

Jane Craig went on with her cleaning. At last the top shelf was finished. It had been cleaned before, but she was satisfied now. She came down from the ladder very carefully. "Well, poor Nita, you want your dinner, don't you?" This to the big cat that lay in a patch of sunshine in front of the secretary. Miss Craig stooped to stroke her, and her glance fell on a folded yellow paper before her. "A receipt that dropped out of mother's book," she thought. "Jane" was traced on the outside in the same fine hand that had written the recipes in the book.

Jane was tired. She sat down in the rocker by the window to rest while she read. It was a red-cushioned rocker that ill became her lilac dress. She shivered a little. There was no fire in the sitting-room. She had had the stove taken down that morning.

"Dear Jane: I've been thinking that maybe I've been prejudiced against Philip Joy. You needn't keep that promise after I'm gone. Marry him, if you want to. You've been a good daughter to me, I want you to be happy."

No name was signed—what was meant for one was a wavering mark that trailed off to the edge of the page. Jane Craig leaned back against the red cushion. She looked pale and old. Nita's purring sounded like the roaring of the sea. She could remember it all,—how her mother sat in the rocking-chair and tried to sew, but the cramped fingers refused to make their wonted stitches; then she had asked for the red book and a pencil; and there they found her in a little while with the

book in her lap and the pencil on the floor,—and a peaceful smile on her face. The book had been laid away—twice a year to be taken out and dusted and put back again. For ten years it had held her freedom papers. Ten years—they passed before Jane's eyes like a procession of ghosts.

Ten years out of life is a good while. Her hair was brown when her mother died; now it was gray. At thirty she looked young enough for twenty-five; at forty she might have passed for fifty. For ten years she had been upon the altar a sacrifice to her mother's wishes and memory,—and the sacrifice had been useless! That was what hurt so. The children trooped past on their way to school. The sunshine moved across the floor. Nita resigned herself to go dinnerless and went to sleep.

"Miss Jane!"

With an effort Miss Craig opened her eyes. The minister stood before her, surprise and sympathy on his face.

"Pardon me, Miss Craig. I was afraid you might be ill."

Jane did not answer for a moment. She was bewildered. By degrees she took it all in—the room, neat as always, for disorder and Miss Craig knew not each other, even at house-cleaning time. But it was bare, and chilly now that the sun was getting low; and there was the minister standing before her, and there she sat in her old dress, her face wet with tears.

"No, I'm not sick," she said at last, slowly.

"Have you had bad news? Can I help you in any way, Miss Craig?"

"No, there can't anyone help me, unless it would help me to tell someone. I've sat here thinking it over and over all the afternoon."

She still spoke slowly. Mr. White was afraid that she had had a shock. He sat down uninvited and waited.

"You see, I've been going on for ten years thinking I was doing something I ought to do, and now I find that I have been all wrong. I needn't to have done it at all."

Mr. White didn't see. He could only look interested and wait.

"Perhaps you could tell better if you read this. Mother wouldn't care. I just found it in a book I hadn't opened since she died."

The minister read it. When he came to the name of Philip Joy, he repeated it aloud.

"Yes, that was the name. He went to California after that — when I wouldn't even see him, thinking mother wouldn't like it."

"Where did he go?"

Miss Craig thought nothing of the question. "It was one of those towns you hear so much about, where sick folks go — Los Angeles, I guess. But he's married now — dead, maybe. He wrote two or three times and I sent the letters back unopened, and then I didn't hear again. And I've lived a lonely life all these years for nothing."

There was a pathos in the words that thrilled the kind-hearted pastor. He saw it was the uselessness of the sacrifice that gave added bitterness to the hour. The door opened, and a bright-faced young girl came in.

"Why, Aunt Jane!"

"No wonder you say it, Jennie."

Jennie Craig's name was Jane, but she did not own it. She boarded with her Aunt Jane and went to school.

"Have you had bad news?"

"I don't know what to call it, good or bad. It took my strength away, but I'm over it now, I guess."

"You look so pale —"

"A cup of tea will do me good. Start up the kitchen fire, Jennie, and fry some of those potatoes and a slice of ham. I didn't have any dinner."

The minister rose to go.

"Stay to tea, won't you, Mr. White? Jennie will have it ready in a little while."

But the minister declined and went home straightway. And then he sat down at his study table and wrote a letter.

Dear old Philip, — Do you remember the glimpse of your heart's history you gave me last summer, in the rose garden there by the Tracy's? You called the

lady Jane. Was her name Jane Craig? Did she live at South Hampton? Did her mother die ten years ago? If so, she is living here still, sweet-faced and sweet-spirited, though grayer than when you knew her. I found her to-day almost broken-hearted because she had found a letter her mother had left when she died, releasing her from some promise in reference to marrying you. You will know what the promise was. The name mentioned in the letter was Philip Joy. It's not a common name, you know. Take it all around, I was struck by the coincidence. I have said my say now, Philip. If I have opened up another chapter of your romance, I can only say, God bless you. And may this story end in the only legitimate way, where the hero and heroine marry and are happy forever after.   Yours,   JOHN.

Miss Craig had finished cleaning house. She was ahead of her neighbors, but then she generally was. She had cleaned this spring with even more energy than usual. Nita had finally left the house last she be: scrubbed also. Jane had seemed tireless. But when night came she fell asleep as soon as she went to bed — a blessed thing when there are ghosts to rise up and haunt one if wakeful. She had even nodded at prayer-meeting, and had told Jennie when she came home that she was getting too old to go out evenings — she could not keep awake.

———

The Aid Society was to meet at Miss Jane's. The Aid Society at South Hampton met every other Wednesday and had tea, and this was Miss Jane's turn.

"Jennie, have you asked Mr. White to come to tea this afternoon?"

Miss Jane was counting her best napkins. Jennie sat by the window that looked out upon the street, across the little strip of grass and lilac bushes. She was feather-stitching her new red dress which she wanted to wear that afternoon.

"No, I didn't ask him, but he'll come anyway. Ministers always come to tea."

"You ought to be ashamed to talk so. Run right down now and ask him. I'd feel dreadful not to have him come."

Jennie would have made an excuse had she not lifted her head in time to give a nod to a young man who passed by; then she went with alacrity. Miss Jane counted the napkins, got out her best fringed table-cloth, and took from the shelves the rare old china that had been her grandmother's. She moved very carefully with it from the cupboard to the table, handling each piece as if she loved it. "It's almost a sin to use it," she thought, as she stood looking at it. "But somehow this seems a little extra. Mother used to use it when she had a tea-party. I don't believe she'd care.—Well, did you ask him?"

The door had opened for Jennie, pink-cheeked and bright-eyed. "Yes, I didn't have to go to the parsonage. I met him going to the train—'to meet a friend,' he said."

Everything was in readiness. Miss Jane was dressing in the bed-room. Jennie called from the kitchen, where she was washing the dinner dishes, "Put on your new dress, Aunt Jane."

"My gray one?"

"Yes."

"Why, I'd look too much dressed up. I was going to wear the black one."

"Do wear the gray one, Aunt Jane. You're always afraid of trying to look young and dressing up too much."

Miss Jane hesitated. She took the gray one from the closet and looked at it. "I might spill something on it."

"You can wear an apron. Now, Aunt Jane, fix up for once just to please me."

Miss Jane yielded. She put on the gray dress and confessed to herself that she did look young. Jennie added a velvet band around her neck, and braided her hair in a heavy coil at the top of her head. "I declare, Aunt Jane, I shouldn't have known you myself."

"Well, as like as not I'll spill something on my dress and be sorry I wore it."

Parlor and sitting-room were filled when the minister and his stranger friend arrived. The Aid Society was always well attended, and more than the usual number had gathered on this beautiful spring day. There was a hum of voices —some were sewing, some had laid aside their work, some were arranging the bright-colored squares of patch-work on the floor. Three or four white-aproned children were playing about. Tea was just ready.

"Leave me on the porch, John, and send her out here," said the stranger.

Mr. White came in alone. He shook hands with one and another as he passed through the room, then out in the dining-room he spoke in a low voice to Miss Jane, who was just setting the big salad bowl on the table.

"There's a gentleman out on the porch who would like to see you, Miss Jane."

"A gentleman? Can't he wait? I was just about to call them to tea."

"I'm afraid he can't wait very long."

Miss Jane sighed, but passed out on the porch. Mr. White talked his best in the parlor. The coffee boiled up again and Jennie set it back. The scalloped potatoes threatened to be done too much. Still Miss Jane did not come back. Jennie came to the parlor door. "Does anyone know where Aunt Jane is? The supper will be spoiled and she has disappeared."

"A gentleman wanted to see her at the door, Miss Jennie."

"Well, I shall give him a hint to go, no matter who he is."

Perhaps Mrs. McConnell can tell you best what happened next. "We were wondering what was the matter that tea wasn't ready. We always have tea at five, because some live in the country, and it was nearer six than five when in stepped Jane Craig and a man with her. He was a fine-looking man—you'd never have known him for Philip Joy that used to live here. As for Jane, her cheeks were pink and her eyes were bright. She tried to speak but her voice was all of a tremble. And then Mr. White stepped up and introduced him to us all—I guess he saw Jane couldn't—and then Mr. Joy said something in a low voice to the minister, and Mr. White turned to us and said: 'Friends, these two before us have been separated by circumstance for many years. It is their wish to be joined together in the presence of you all.' It was so sudden that it took our breath away, but it was awful solemn, and, as I said to Jane the other day, what a blessing she had on her gray dress."

HER WEEK IN CAMP.

By Lucy Burkhalter.

I RECENTLY called on a friend whom I had not seen since her return from camp. The fact that there were mysterious stories afloat about the camping expedition she had joined, and suddenly left, aroused my curiosity, and I determined to obtain the story from her direct. And, finally, having overcome her reluctance to going over it again in her own mind, she told the tale in about this fashion :

"Well, I received an invitation to go camping in the Lake Superior region. Some of our friends who were getting up the expedition asked me to make one of six or seven young people in the party whom the professor's wife was to chaperon.

"The professor went camping, not because he enjoyed fishing and hunting and outdoor exercise generally, but because his wife thought it good for his health. He had rarely been in the country before, and dreaded, as only people who have lived fifty years in a big city and enjoyed all the comforts it gives, can dread an outing in the wild woods, associated with harrowing tales of mosquitoes and snakes. His wife was the jolliest woman imaginable and seemed hardly severe enough to manage six young people on mischief bent. The professor's son was fond of hunting deer but had a great distaste for 'dears' ; his daughter was pretty but rather uninteresting, since she was engaged to her brother's college chum and spent most of her time keeping him amused so that he wouldn't be interested in anyone else. I can't say anything was remarkable about her *fiancé* excepting the fact of his having auburn hair verging on the red. His young lady cousin made one of the party, and her particular friend made another,— a jolly fellow, but not interested enough in the rest of us to make it worth his while to be entertaining. Last, but not least, of the campers was your humble servant, who unfortunately knew nothing of the facts just outlined till many trials and tribulations had brought her to a true knowledge thereof.

"Nothing could have been pleasanter than the first day of our travels. We took the steamer at Duluth, and a merry party of nine we were. Number nine was our cook, a stout, red-faced man of fifty who had acted in the capacity of *chef* on a Lake Superior steamer till his fondness for intoxicants had caused his dismissal. Learning that his culinary abilities were in no wise lessened by his fondness for grog we had hired him at no little expense, thinking that if we could keep him fifty miles from the nearest town he would be serviceable ; but how little did we know what a vast store of flat bottles could be packed into a small box ! He proved, however, very amusing in camp, with his stories of the logging regions in winter. He was a weather prophet, too, and knew just when to fasten our tents securely with stakes and when it would be wise to venture on the lake. When he said, 'Gentlemen, I think to-morrow we will have a snorter,' we knew a big storm would come.

"But I am anticipating. The whistle blew, the bell rang, and the gang-plank was hauled up. Soon the land was only a little line of hazy blue melting into sky in the distance. A fresh breeze blew strong from the north ; the gulls flew about the steamer, and, where we stopped now and then at the little logging stations along shore, a spicy odor came from the pine woods beyond, suggesting hemlocks, wintergreen and blueberries. All day we steamed along the south shore of Lake Superior, and toward evening we arrived at the place selected for the camp. It was certainly wild enough, reminding one of the forest primeval, where the 'murmuring pines and the hemlocks'—you know the rest,

"The boys soon got the tents up and our first supper was delicious. Broiled ham, potatoes, crackers and cheese never tasted so well; but by the end of the week this uniform diet, in which dried apple or peach pie and baked beans formed the only variety, waxed a little monotonous. Of course, we used condensed milk in our coffee and diluted it with water to form cream on the two occasions when we had oatmeal for breakfast. The butter, of which we secured fifteen pounds hoping it would last the month, seemed likely to last a much longer period, since it was rancid at the start. But then, we hardly thought it necessary to obtain any provisions at all, for we had been told the woods abounded in deer, the lake was filled with a great variety of fish, and blueberries grew in abundance along the shore.

"Our beds were soon constructed and were rather unique, consisting of hemlock branches piled high and covered with blankets. We dispensed with sheets and truly we all confessed the next morning that we had never slept better. To be sure, an unusually stout branch under me insisted in rearing itself upward and, as a result, I was somewhat lame. Then, too, the mosquitoes were so vicious that I appeared at breakfast with one eye swollen shut,

"Well, the next day the fun began,—fun for the rest. You see, as there were only eight in the party, we thought three row-boats would be sufficient, as all would not wish to be on the water at one time. I soon gathered from keen observation that of the five young people two were engaged, two more were on the interesting point of becoming so, and the one remaining gentleman — the professor's son — seemed to have a great distaste for female society. However, his heart being his own, he was the most feasible one to smile upon and encourage. Of course you know that in camping unless you have a right-hand man you are quite likely to be left alone sitting on the bank when

your companions are having a jolly time. It is well, therefore, to figuratively take the bull by the horns in the beginning. If you wish to enjoy life in camp. Now, it happened that for some reason or other I did not study the bull sufficiently before taking him by the horns, for my attempts at taming him were futile. Notwithstanding all my efforts to amuse the professor's son, he collected his guns, cartridges and other paraphernalia and soon after breakfast went hunting. The professor and his wife took a boat and went fishing, and the other two remaining boats were immediately preempted by the engaged couples, who likewise went fishing,— with spoon hooks. Thus it befell exactly as I had tried not to have it; I was left alone sitting on a log.—no, not alone, I was left to the tender mercies of the jovial cook.

"At noon the fishermen returned —with no fish, and our hunter — with no game; but all had had a pleasant time, while I,— I posed as the patron saint of industry; told how I had made the beds, had helped get dinner, and had written several letters. In the afternoon the program was repeated; they all went off in pairs — this time to read. I might have read, too, had not all the interesting books and magazines been carried off by those first on the field. Nothing remained but a dilapidated Shakspeare and a French Bible.

———

"By the third day these uniform proceedings grew monotonous; so, in order to relieve the tedium of affairs, I thought of organizing an extensive fishing expedition to one of the small trout streams in the vicinity. An old Scotchman, who held a claim of land three miles across the bay, had visited us the day before, and his logger's shack could be seen on a high bluff overlooking the lake. He laughed at us for not catching any fish, and told us of a beautiful trout stream where a party of four had caught seventy-three rainbow trout the day before. That sounded enticing. If four people could catch seventy-three fish, six people ought

to catch one hundred and nine and a half!
The Scotchman, at my suggestion, made
arrangements to meet us the next morning at 8 o'clock at his shack and show us
the way up the stream. Only four in the
party could be induced to accompany me
on the expedition, especially since rising
at 5 o'clock was part of the undertaking.
To encourage the lazy creatures, the cook
got ready an appetizing luncheon consisting of cold ham, blueberry pie and the
inevitable crackers and cheese. Our fishing tackle was all laid out — three trolling
hooks and five small hooks for trout.
After digging two hours for angleworms,
we decided that that species of 'articu-
lata' did not inhabit this portion of the
globe and gave up the search hoping, on
the way, to find frogs for bait.

"I was dressed by 6 o'clock and ready
to start, but not a camper put in an appearance till after 8, and by that time the
breakfast was stone cold. No wonder the
lazy people did not get up early ; they had
to have some sleep, since they had sat up
nearly all night making the night hideous.

"Most of the sleeping was done between 4 and 6 in the morning. The first
night they were all too tired to make
much noise, but the second evening they

sat around in hammocks till the cold night
dews drove them in, and then they had
another supper. When all the girls were
finally in our tent and were snugly tucked
in, they talked and told funny stories and
made idiotic puns till I was in a fury. Two
weeks of such proceedings would surely
drive a person crazy.

"Sleep is necessary, to me at least, and
that is one reason why I left the camp.—
But I am anticipating.

"By 9 o'clock we were through breakfast and it was nearly half past 9 before
we got through arguing whether to take
the blue boat or the green one. It finally
being decided in favour of the green, a new
point arose as to which of the girls was
the lightest and could sit in the bow. The
two were lifted in turn before it could be
determined. I was out of the discussion
since it was evident to the naked eye that
my weight was much greater than either
of the other two. By this time I was
angry enough to shed tears. I only re-
frained when I remembered how much
was still expected of me in getting the
expedition under way. When we finally
got out into the middle of the bay, the
wind, which blew a little when we started,
kept rising until by the time we got
around the second point of land the waves
were covered with white caps and dashed
over the bow of the boat. The only
thing to do was to turn around and make
for home. It was too exasperating. I said
nothing,. but my blood boiled and my
heart was moved with anger. If we had
started at 6 o'clock as we had planned,
we might have gotten to the stream before the wind came up. When we got
back to camp our noble efforts were
greeted with a roar of laughter. I was
so angry that, when all had landed, I
pushed off again with the boat containing
all the fishing tackle and blueberry pies,
hoping to accomplish what the others had
failed to do. It seemed an easy matter
to follow the shore around and reach the
logger's shack before noon.

"'Where going ?' was the query.

"'Going fishing,' said I, and my wrath
waxed hotter.

"'Ho, ho, you go fishing in such a wind?'

"They laughed; but I pulled the harder at the oars, determining to gain fame at a bound and have an adventure or die in the attempt. No one seemed in the least alarmed, supposing that of course I would turn around as soon as I discovered how rough the lake was. I rowed in a straight line for the logger's shack, which could be seen in the dim distance; but soon the boat pitched about in an alarming manner and several waves dashed over me. My hat blew off, pulling my hair down as it went. I feared that in order to escape being swamped I would have to turn around. How to accomplish the feat in this rough sea without getting in a trough of the waves was a question. After pulling on one oar with both hands I saw it was more dangerous to attempt turning about than to keep on in a straight course. Finally I grew tired of rowing with one oar and backing water with the other, and had to give up. The boat rocked about, threatening to upset me with every wave. I lay down in the bottom, on the blueberry pie and fishing tackle, and said a little prayer, expecting to 'shuffle off this mortal coil' at any moment. I thought, now those heartless men will feel sorry! They will say, 'Yes, we drove her to self-destruction, leaving her so much alone! It was a pity—so young, and intellectually so promising, too! Maybe she would have been interesting had we ever thought it worth our while to find out!'

"As the boat did not capsize but rode right over the waves, I got up and began rowing in earnest. In the course of an hour I reached the shack and found our Scotch friend standing on a rock to lend a helping hand. He was evidently very much excited. He had no boat to go to the rescue. Another man was with him. When my boat landed, he cried out, 'For heaven's sake, is every one shot at camp? Why did you brave the storm?' I said nothing was the matter, but I was going fishing as we had arranged the day before. He laughed a relieved and amused

sort of laugh and we started up the stream. He eyed the five fishing poles and the blueberry pies with satisfaction.

"'An enormous appetite you must have, Miss, to lay in such a supply! Be you agoin' to bait all your hooks at once?'

"Then I had to tell how the rest of the party had gone back. 'I hope you'll catch a fish' was his only response.—And thereby hangs a tale.

"We rowed two miles up the stream and drew our boat up on the bank, hiding our luncheon under the willows by the stream. Armed with poles we started briskly along the slippery bank, when I remembered we had no bait. We hunted for frogs, but not a frog deigned to show his head above the stream. Then the Scotchman suggested grasshoppers, and we walked half a mile to a meadow, where we heard them chirping. Then began an amusing chase. My Scotch friend was quite stout and slow in his movements, and I not at all an adept in the art of catching grasshoppers. By noon I had caught nine grasshoppers and in the absence of any other receptacle I pinned their slimy corpses in my pocket. It is amazing what vitality a grasshopper has! By the time we got back to the brook three of them had seemingly come to life again and crawled out of my pocket! I am sure I squeezed them well as all the legs were there as souvenirs. Why a grasshopper should want to go away without such necessary appendages as legs, I can't see. I adorned my hook with the largest head, which looked at me in a pathetic manner, as John the Baptist's might have looked at Salome from the charger, and dropped my hook in a deep hole where I saw a big trout flashing about. Do you know that impudent fish nibbled the bait right off my hook? I then produced the tail of my insect and held my breath while I curved the gummy thing around the hook, only to have it eaten off by the clever trout. After all six grasshoppers had been chewed off in like manner we gave up in despair, deciding that grasshoppers are not well put up for baiting hooks,—too

11

loosely put together and come apart too easily. We tried all the parts, even the hind leg—which, by the by, a fish will not even look at, as we found to our sorrow after holding it out temptingly for fifteen minutes. The Scotchman said he was hungry and suggested going back to the blueberry pies, and I was so crestfallen that even such a tame thing as eating seemed a pleasant diversion.

" After walking some distance through the deep underbrush we came to a swampy place where a corduroy bridge formed the only means of crossing. The logs seemed quite rotten, and weeds and pitcher-plants had grown up between them so that as we stepped upon the first log it sank into the green mud and we thought it best to walk around the marsh and not attempt crossing the bridge. After walking around the edge I discovered the woods were too thick to attempt making a way through them ; and, as we had found out the difficulty of wading up stream, the only thing to do was to cross the bridge. My friend the Scotchman, therefore, stepped upon a log first and, after testing its strength, he stretched out his hand and helped me over. We pursued this method till we came to a place where two logs were missing and we had to jump across. He jumped safely and held out a helping hand for me to grasp. In trying to reach the log my foot slipped, and I fell into the slimy mud, where I might have caught frogs had I been in a proper frame of mind ! My ! it was nasty, —all green from decaying vegetation. While he was attempting to pull me out, the log turned over and my guide fell in, too. It was real cheerful ! Fortunately no one saw us. When we had struggled out, we wended our weary way in silence, which was not broken till our lunch basket was reached. As it was nearly four o'clock we wasted no ceremony before beginning on the blueberry pie. Did I eat a whole pie ? Well, there were two pies when we began, and when we got through there were none. When the repast was finished, the melancholy fact stared us in the face that we had fished

all day and caught no fish. Therefore we decided to row about the mouth of the little river and troll for salmon trout. It seemed preordained that we were to catch no fish, so at 6 o'clock we wound up our trolling lines and decided to walk over to the next village and buy some fish. It happened unfortunately that the whole supply consisted of three salmon trout weighing four and one-half pounds in all. Unfortunately they had been caught two days before and, as the weather was rather warm, the old fisherman had cleaned and salted them. We gave the man a dollar and made the best of a bad bargain, for fish we must have,—if not fresh, then salted. As the wind still blew a gale we left our boat on the shore of the river and walked back to camp through the woods. We quite enjoyed the long walk for we calculated it would take us at least two hours to think up a big enough ' yarn ' to cover the unmistakable fact of our fish being salted. One thing after another was suggested and abandoned for fear the red-haired youth would discover some flaw and have base suspicions. The following statement of the case was decided upon :

" My companion was to say that we caught the three fish trolling up the river soon after my arrival. The die being cast, I was to put in the finishing strokes as to how we caught and landed each fish, and when our audience were sufficiently impressed, I was to go on and recount at length our adventures from the beginning. The *coup d' etat* would be when I displayed my muddy garments and shoes with holes worn through the bottoms, all in order to bring home these three paltry fish ! Then he was to corroborate my statement and add that we had hoped to arrive in time for supper and cook the fish ; so, while I was removing some of the mud from my garments in the brook, he had amused himself cleaning the fish to have them ready for the frying-pan as soon as we arrived. Then as the day was so warm and fish are so easily spoiled, we put them in a pail containing salt water to keep them fresh. Now this all sounded feasible enough, so we walked along chuckling with glee at the prospect of taking in so many smart people.

"It was 8 o'clock when we arrived at camp. The whole party had been alarmed as to my whereabouts all day, and the professor's son had walked around to the Scotchman's shack to learn if I had arrived there safely. Ascertaining that I had, he returned home greatly comforted; but when tea-time came without my appearing, the anxiety was renewed. When we finally appeared in triumph, carrying the fish, there was a shout loud enough to bring the fishes to life again if they had not been salted. A gun was fired notifying the hunters of my safe arrival, and our story was listened to open-mouthed, and evidently swallowed whole. The fish were cooked and heartily partaken of. There was much sympathy expressed, too, for my melancholy plight, evincing much hard labor on my part, so that when the story of the swamp was told, and how hard we had fished for brook trout, my torn boots and muddy skirts eloquently corroborated my story. For once I was a heroine. My tale was listened to with rapt attention, and I went to bed tired but happy, with pleasant dreams of the 'five loaves and little fishes,' only the five loaves melted into blueberry pies and the little fishes multiplied into millions of trout, with grasshopper heads, all laughing at me.

"Now I come to the conclusion of the whole matter,—but let me state right here a fact which everybody knows. No one ever believes fishermen's yarns. All sportsmen are magnificent liars. Lying has come to be a pleasurable pastime. A man who has not hunted or fished considerably can't lie without offending the intelligence of that part of his audience who have. Being inexperienced, we fell into a trap. Now, there were members of our audience who had gone through similar experiences and they read us correctly. One member, who had been a story-telling fisherman in by-gone days and so judged others by himself, next

morning kindly offered to go for our boat. I could not understand the motive of my red-haired friend, for I knew he must have a motive, and I doubted his sincerity. About noon he returned with the boat and with a smile upon his countenance that fairly illuminated the dark woods. I wondered at his joy and surmised he must have a letter from home containing a check. But alas! woe betide! his first remark told the whole story: 'Why were your fish salted?'

"'Why?' said I,—but the answer died on my lips, for I knew his vile suspicions had led him to enquire of the fisherman (where he learned a bedraggled-looking young lady had purchased for a dollar four and one-half pounds of salted fish). Oh, why did we not bribe that fisherman! Why, in our haste, did we forget so important a feature in the case!"

Miss Dodd here paused for breath. But I was not satisfied; there surely was more to tell, so I said: "We heard you went deer hunting. Did you shoot any deer?"

"No, I did not shoot any deer," said she.

"Why?" I enquired.

"Why?" said she, looking cross. "Are you trying to ask one of those needless questions illustrated in *Harper's!* I did not shoot any because they are such graceful little creatures it would have been enough to have broken my heart. Would you like the particulars?"

"Yes," was my quick response.

"You see, it happened in this way. Fishing was decidedly a failure; we hadn't tried hunting, and we thirsted for adventure. We knew the best methods of securing a deer, for the old Scotchman had fully instructed us the day before, and all we needed was practice. A deer is a shy creature and up in those northern woods the deer have been so hunted and persecuted that they keep far away from the haunts of man, and if it were not for the necessity of coming down to the lake to drink would never come out of their native forest. There are two little lakes about four miles back in the woods which were nearly dried up on account of the unusually dry season. From the tracks in the mud about the margin of the lakes it was easy to be seen that deer were in the habit of coming down to drink. Knowing the fondness of deer for salt, a handful was put in a hollow rock which contained water, and the next day it was evident a deer had drank up a portion of the salt water. It would be a simple matter to conceal oneself behind a tree shortly before sundown and shoot the deer as it comes to drink. Accordingly, about 5 o'clock, three of us,—the professor's son, my red-haired friend and myself,—set out for the deer lake. The two boys were armed with Winchesters and belts containing thirty-eight caliber cartridges. I carried the lantern, since we had not provided ourselves with the little lanterns usually fastened by hunters to the front of the cap. We hoped to shoot the deer before dark and not wait till night, as hunters usually do, for we did not consider ourselves good enough shots to fascinate the deer with the light of our lantern and trust to shooting him when only his two glowing eyes could be seen. Besides the lantern, I carried a knife which was intended to be used in skinning the deer and quartering him, to make it convenient in carrying the load home; also a rope to swing the larger portions over the strongest shoulder. We scrambled over fallen trees covered with lichens and through thick brush, picking our way by blazed trees. When we arrived at the place where two roads meet, our hunter declared that one would have to take one road and wait for the deer at the larger lake, while the other took the second road and located himself by the smaller lake. Now which road and which man would I take? I knew which I should prefer taking, but seemed to hesitate, and suggested deciding the matter by the method known as "heads or tails." Chance, however, decided it, so I took what the gods sent without a murmur. Soon we arrived at the lake, deposited ourselves on two separate logs and waited for the deer to materialize.

In order to while away the weary hours of waiting, my companion lit his pipe and puffed away with much complacency. Now, experience is a good thing in hunting, and all hunters know that deer recognize smoke as peculiar to their enemy, man. Our deer, therefore, went many miles back into the forest and in good season was shot by some other hunter. After smoking till nearly dark in silence, my companion said, ' Hang it ! where's that deer?'

" The deer seemed to answer, for hark! what was that ! A rustling of branches—a bounding sound. He grasped his gun and excitedly whispered, ' Hush '—bang! and a poor little stray calf from a neighboring loggers' camp skipped out from the bushes ! Fortunately he missed the calf.

" The occurrence proved rather dampening to our spirits, and, as the night dews were still more dampening to our bodies, we went in search of our lantern and knife; but, to our consternation, both were gone, and we had to grope about in the darkness to find the road home. Who could have taken our lantern? An unpleasant surmise caused by a dark night in the woods, and the terror which imaginative minds connect with it, made it seem probable that we were surrounded by a band of Indians, lying in wait to scalp us. We crept along, a step at a time, shuddering whenever a twig snapped. The trees fallen across our path, over which we had jumped on our way there, now loomed up like small mountains. We carefully crawled over them. When we came to swampy places we lit a match to avoid the deepest spots till the matches were all gone, and then we waded recklessly through the mud. Finally we saw a light coming toward us, which proved to be a lantern carried by the other member of our party. He had seen a deer and missed it and was coming to tell us. Seeing two motionless figures and the smoke curling up from a pipe, the humor of the situation got the better of him and he walked off with the lantern ; but when it grew so late he became worried and feared we had lost our way, so he brought it back. When we reached the camp and heard the laugh, we said nothing.

"This experience only increased my weariness of camp life and my longing for home. Fishing was a failure, hunting was a failure, I could not rely upon the company for amusement, nor could I sleep nights on account of the noise and the mosquitoes. Then, the table manners of the campers grew worse every day. Their uncouth way of eating with knives, throwing objects — whole slices of bread and chunks of cheese — at one another while seated at the table, was having a demoralizing effect upon my own table manners. Then, when the three hornets were rescued from a sticky grave in the syrup pitcher, and I saw the primitive manner in which our cook wiped the tin plates, — sometimes removing grease with a wedge of bread when the luke-warm dish-water did not prove effective, — my appetite waned to such an extent that I was in danger of starvation. Then, the camp slang was another drawback. If you asked a civil question, such as 'Where have you been?' the stupid answer was sure to be 'Oat-bin'; or, 'Where are you bound?'—'Snowbound'; or, 'Where did you go?'—'Cargo.' Then, one day they tried to teach me to smoke, 'to take the taste of prunes, prisms and preciseness out of my mouth,' they said. I was forced to smoke a nasty pipe while they shouted at my amateur proceedings. When I appeared in my bathing suit,— which *was* odd, I must confess, for it was one I had purchased the summer before at the sea-shore, and it had shrunk at the knees, and had been lengthened by means of ruffles, —they all laughed till the tears ran down their faces. I call that rude, don't you.

"When the third disaster befell, I packed my trunk and left by the next boat. The third event happened as follows : Some vicious animal seemed in the habit of visiting our kitchen supplies. The ham was gnawed, and the bread-box had been opened. The cook said it was a porcupine. One night we heard a sound in the ladies' tent. I awoke first and gave the alarm, and as the other girls were soon wide awake, we lit the lantern. There was a chattering sound, like the rattle of teeth when one has a chill, and in one corner of the tent a bristly porcupine was prancing about. We shrieked and threw shoes at him and, holding up a corner of the tent, invited him to walk out, which he did in a stately manner, but without throwing quills — a quill-throwing porcupine being a fiction invented by the author of the Swiss Family Robinson. We set a trap and the next evening we had another visit. Knowing how harmless he had been on the previous evening, we did not even light the lantern, but threw shoes to speed him on his way. It was a sad mistake, as we soon discovered, for the animal proved to be something totally different from our friendly porcupine and of a totally different species. Mephitis is the zoölogical name and his method of defense is very effective, I assure you. We dressed in haste and gave the alarm. The men came to the rescue and everything was taken out of the tent. The most odoriferous articles were burned; others were hung out for the sun and wind to do their part.

"That evening, when the boat came past, bound for Bayfield, I hailed it and my baggage was put on board. I followed."

THE WEST SHORE.

GREEN leagues of wood and red rose bowers
    With yellow sunshine sifting through;
Tall billows flinging white foam-flowers
    To kingly peaks in skies of blue.

TACOMA, WASHINGTON. *Herbert Bashford.*

OVERSHADOWED.

By Elizabeth D. Preston.

CHAPTER I.

"Her life had reached that radiant goal —
The trysting place of heart and soul —
Where youth and beauty grow complete
As womanhood and girlhood meet."

"ALL the beauty and fashion of the city," as the journals of the next day expressed it, were assembled in the concert room of Mrs. Eugene Serle, to listen to selections of classical music and to witness interesting tableaux by a company of amateurs, each individual member of which possessed both skill and courage for the undertaking.

Everything went on as usual until, suddenly, the brilliantly lighted room was darkened. The raising of a curtain displayed to expectant eyes the first "*tableau vivant.*" It was strikingly beautiful. A dark, fierce-looking slave-dealer stood behind a young Persian girl, from whose face and form he had just removed the thick, burdensome veil wherewith she had been covered, thereby revealing to the sensuous gaze of a voluptuous Turk, who was seated in true oriental style upon a pile of handsomely embroidered cushions, so rare an aggregation of charms that not only his eyes but those of the spectators were riveted upon her. The shrinking timidity of the girl, as she stood with each bare and rounded arm pressed closely to her side and her slender, white hands clasped gracefully before her, bespoke a true artist's comprehension of, and ability to personate, the rôle assigned her. Long lashes drooped over eyes of purest hazel, while from an exquisitely moulded head fell a wealth of golden hair that half hid a scarlet vest and nearly touched the heels of as dainty a pair of slippers, heavy with jewels, as ever peeped from beneath the white satin pantaloons of any queen of a harem.

For one moment only was seen this perfect picture. Then the curtain fell. The lights were turned on. All united in praising the flawless harmony and coloring of the scene. One voice was heard to inquire the name of the lovely girl. That voice belonged to Philip Gordon who had been away from Santa Illa for many years, and a girl of nineteen had had ample time to outgrow his recognition even had she been a playmate of "auld lang syne."

Turning to his father, Philip asked: "Who is the girl?" Doctor Gordon laughingly replied: "I thought you wouldn't know her, yet it seems a little strange that you shouldn't remember Helen,—your sister Helen, you know."

Surprise silenced the young man for a moment; then he lightly responded: "A little strange, yes; but you can't blame me for not recognizing my own relatives when I have so many new ones thrust upon me at once. Ye Gods! a mother and two sisters *are* a good many, are they not?"

The truth was that Philip was abroad, pursuing his medical studies preparatory to entering into partnership with his father, Dr. Maurice Gordon, when his father remarried.

When there had come to Philip a letter from his father announcing his intention to marry the widow of the late Doctor Kent and mother of two girls whom he indistinctly remembered, he had also read "between the lines" a desire for approval, a silent appeal for approbation. He remembered his mother's great love for her husband, her unfaltering efforts to promote his happiness, and he felt she would, and perhaps did, approve of this step whereby his father's declining years might be made happier. For himself he felt more glad than otherwise. He remembered Mrs. Kent as a sweet-voiced gentle-faced lady and he felt that were she other than wise and kind she would have failed to attract his father's fancy

166

or win his affection. So he wrote a dutiful, affectionate letter. He sent his kindest regards to his new mother to be; he made inquiries about the girls and urged that the marriage might not be postponed on account of his absence, for the date of his return home was not yet settled.

In a short time the wedding occurred, and within the year Philip arrived at Santa Illa after an absence of nearly ten years.

Few were the old-world lands that had escaped his observation. While at Cape Colony he had become interested in the work of the missionaries and had stayed and labored with them until a letter from his father bade him return and relieve him of a portion of his arduous duties. Business took him to China and thence he sailed for San Francisco. Another passenger upon the steamer was Dr. Ernest Gray, a fellow student for three years in Germany.

Doctor Gray was a man possessed of those noble qualities that endear, and with whom a friendship once cemented is never broken. Listening to his entreaties Philip consented to land with him at Honolulu and there remain a few weeks.

And now he was at home again. The time of the home-coming had been a little uncertain, so he had passed twenty-four hours beneath his father's roof and had not yet seen his two new sisters, Margaret and Helen. They had gone, three days before, to Mrs. Serle's, where, with others, they had been diligently practicing for this evening of evenings for Santa Illa.

An evening passed at Mrs. Serle's could not fail to be filled with the indescribable charm which that talented woman seemed to cast about all who came within the range of her influence. And, too, she had ever about her those whom one could both like and esteem. To-night, "for the benefit of the poor," was carried out the greatest social triumph of the season.

Again the curtain rises on an artistically represented tableau wherein Margaret's fair face, her golden-brown hair and eyes

"so deeply, darkly blue" are easily distinguished. The curtain once more rising, Helen again appears. This time she is a Guardian Angel and all the beauty and purity of a spotless soul shows in her angelic countenance, making true the lines "too sweet and good for human nature's daily food."

Within the hour Philip has met his "sister" Helen. How absurd the word already sounds to his ears! She will never be sister to him. He knows, even now, that there is but one place in his life which she can fill.

Ah! ye wiseacres! scorn this "love at first sight" if you will; but so long as the world stands, just so long will there be devout believers in it,—and those who can prove it, too.

CHAPTER II.

It was the week before Thanksgiving Day when Mrs. Serle gave her parlors, concert room, and her influence, for the benefit of those whom we have always with us; and the three months following have been filled with many gayeties.

The young people have become very well acquainted. Lately Helen has fancied that Margaret is not quite as light-hearted as formerly. After an evening's pleasure she is not so ready to sit for hours, perhaps, in dressing-gown and slippers, and review every item of the night's enjoyment, as she has formerly been. She sometimes complains of being tired, sometimes a headache will annoy her, but more often there is no excuse given. It would seem that from the gayest, merriest of girls she has suddenly become the quietest and most absent-minded.

Had an agreement been entered into between these two sisters they could not more absolutely have tabooed the name of Philip Gordon, save when it became positively necessary to make mention of him. Had either given the matter much thought she must have read the truth. Unhappy Margaret! Happy Helen!

At young Mrs. Pendleton's home a dancing party is at its height. It is the last of a very successful series, and upon that last adjective Mrs. Pendleton is plainly congratulating herself. The last waltz is being played and Philip and Helen are among the dancers. Helen realizes the divine ecstasy of the poetry of motion as Philip guides her lightly and easily, yet surely, amid the swaying couples on that crowded floor. His eyes magnetize her; his touch is both caressing and firm without seeming to be either. She feels the grateful submission which woman loves when the true monarch of her heart inspires it.

To Helen this new happiness seems almost insupportable. He is gazing at her with his soul in his eyes; she feels it, but, trembling, fears to read what she so longs to hear. At last, as though compelled by a stronger power than her own will, she slowly raises the heavily fringed lids that hide the tell-tale eyes, and the great love radiates from his to her very soul.

All too soon the waltz is ended and she suffers herself to be led to a conservatory, where, beneath a fronded palm, she listens to that sweetest story, the story of man's love.

What an old, old story it is! It was told in the days of Eden, and yet, somewhere on our great earth, it is retold with every passing moment! No doubt Philip used the expressions that have been used millions of times before, yet it seemed to these two young beings that the words were freshly coined for them. They had a new and strangely sweet sound. Love! love! love!

Other lovers, with similar stories to tell, perhaps, or with little jealous misunderstandings to rectify, disturbed them all too soon; but they left the shelter of the friendly palm an affianced couple, and there was for them—O, blessed thought!—a to-morrow. A to-morrow wherein again to meet, wherein again to say,—"I love you." "I love you" is the sweetest talisman ever given to weary mortals; has incited to nobler deeds, has cheered more burdened hearts, has conquered more battles fought with self than the world has ever dreamed of.

Laurance Cameron and Philip Gordon had been schoolmates in olden days, and, since the latter's return, the old-time friendship had been renewed and strengthened. Laurance's way home from the party lay beyond

MRS. ELIZABETH D. FRENTON, OF COLORADO SPRINGS, COLO.

the Gordon's, and he now accompanied them, walking by Margaret's side, and telling himself that never before had he seen her look so altogether charming and lovely as upon this occasion.

Philip knew that the greatest desire of Laurance's life was to win Margaret for his wife, and he heartily aided him where he could. Of this conspiracy Margaret, of course, was innocent. Having known Laurance for years, and never having had a brother, she had put him in such a position as to herself—placing little tasks upon him, deferring to his judgment in small matters and asking his advice in trifling affairs. Laurance was also the confidant of Philip and knew how ardently he desired to win Helen. It pleased them both to think of the possibilities the future held in store for them.

With but a tender pressure of the hand, which doubtless spoke much to the young girl, Philip left Helen at the steps of their home while he passed on with Laurance.

"I can read you like a book," said Laurance, after a moment of silence, in which the smoke from their cigars curled gracefully in the still night air. "You have put all to the test and won; is it not so? Shall I congratulate you, Philip?"

"You may," said Philip, "and, to express myself in the fewest words possible, I will say, you see before you the happiest man that walks this earth to-night. It may wear off, but I think not." So saying, he gave a happy, contented laugh.

Then Laurance confessed his fears as to the outcome of his own love affair. He felt that as yet Margaret had for him but a sister's affection; likewise, she was unaware of his love for her and he dared not break the spell of her ignorance of his passion, and, startling her, dash to destruction his own hopes. He realized that the time had not yet come when he might go to her and tell her how important an accessory she was to his happiness. No, not yet had the time come. Alas, would it ever come? "Thank God, I have no rival," he said earnestly. "That makes it some easier." And

Philip had answered, "There is no rival."

What blind, stupid beings we are—sometimes!

The two girls whose fate was so interwoven discussed the events of the evening as they sat before the glowing grate fire and combed and brushed their long hair upon which the firelight glistened.

Not until they had retired and the lights were turned out did Helen allude to her precious secret. Then, with one arm about her sister's neck, and thankful for the darkness which hid her burning blushes, she repeated all, or nearly all, that Philip had said to her, and told how great was her own happiness.

And Margaret? She too felt grateful for the blessed darkness that hid her tell-tale face from the glance of her sister's innocent eyes. For the time being, it was the mirror of her heart and faithfully portrayed all its anguish. By almost a superhuman effort she compelled her lips to meet those of Helen's and forced her palsied tongue to form phrases of love and of wishes for happiness. Little did she hear of the joyful plans that had already formed in her sister's mind. Long after Helen was dreaming of that first, rapturous lover's kiss, the pale moon was gazing pitifully through the dainty muslin curtains on a pale, pain-drawn face; and angels were carrying cries and prayers from a broken heart to the throne of heaven.

Why had she been so blind! Never for a moment had she thought that Philip cared for Helen in this way! O, would that there had been fuller confidence between them! and O, the shame of her position! She loved as such women love but once in a lifetime. Her pure young heart had gone from her keeping and was irrevocably given to the man who would soon claim her sister for his wife!

"How he would despise me were he to know!" she said. "What shame is mine to give my love where it is unsought and where it can never be welcome!"

Then came a great desire to die. The task of living, of daily meeting these two happy beings and keeping such constraint upon herself that they might not suspect her unhappy secret, seemed almost beyond her strength. But those earnest prayers of an hour before were already partially answered, and when morning came there were no traces of that hard-fought night battle, save cheeks a trifle paler than their wont and eyes a little dimmed, perhaps, by the scalding tears that had come to the relief of the over-burdened heart.

The next day Doctor and Mrs. Gordon were told of what had transpired on the previous evening, and, expressing nothing but approbation, confessed that it had been their dearest wish.

Then Philip, with the impatience of the average lover, at once took steps to "build," within "easy" distance from his father's home, in order that the girls might not be too much separated, and that the business intercourse between himself and father might not suffer. He felt that the sooner the house was ready, the sooner would come the day when he might truly call Helen his very own. But the house, complete in every part, handsomely furnished and lacking nothing, stood many months awaiting the presence of its sweet mistress.

It was now nearly March and the wedding day was set for September. With shopping, dress-making, and the thousand new duties that present themselves, clamoring for attention in the home where there is soon to be a wedding, the time passed swiftly until September was almost upon them.

Then, suddenly, Helen was stricken down with typhoid fever. None ever had more tender nursing, for no one have ever risen more piteous prayers to Heaven. For a time all seemed in vain. With life still remained hope, yet even as that life seemed held by an invisible thread, so hope was frail and almost left the watchers.

At this time Margaret learned lessons that she never forgot. She vowed that neither envy nor jealousy should ever

again be hers could she once more see her beloved sister restored to health.

For weeks the poor, pain-racked form tossed upon the bed, and when all danger from the fever was at last passed her convalescence was so slow that, again, much apprehension was felt.

It was nearly spring when Helen looked and felt quite her old self again. Her grief at having the wedding postponed was sincere. "I cannot help feeling superstitious about it," she said to Philip one evening.

He only laughed at what he termed her "sick fancies." Then, as if inspired by a sudden thought, he said: "Let's get married in May and defy the Fates. Indeed, dear, I cannot wait longer than that, and if not then it must be before."

At first Helen was shocked at the proposition. Did she not know of at least a dozen historical characters that had made May marriages and whose ends had been most miserable; yet, to be sure, did she know that these same marriages would not have terminated in the very same way had they been contracted in June?

Enough to say that the wedding day was appointed for the 12th of May, and Helen thought that by appointing "Wednesday, the best day of all," somewhat of evil might, perhaps, be averted; for, in spite of Philip's arguments, she still felt a little frightened at her own temerity in thus entering into a conspiracy to so tempt the Fates!

CHAPTER III.

"The pretty thing, the finger ring, was worn
    by slaves in token
That they for aye should well obey in servi-
    tude unbroken.
The wedding ring, that pretty thing, supposed
    of love a token,
Doth it not say 'I will alway obey' though no
    such vow be spoken?"

In spite of the superstitious whims regarding a postponed wedding or a May marriage, when "the horses of the sun brought round the long expected day" no fairer bride or happier groom could be found though one search the whole world over.

Someone has called the honeymoon a "wearisome institution." and cynically observed that "some sworn foe to matrimony, some vile misogamist, took to himself a wife in order to discover, by experience, the best mode of rendering married life a martyrdom. Enlightened by experience this miserable wretch said to himself, 'I will introduce a practice which, in the space of one short month, shall transform the doting bridegroom into the indifferent husband, the idolatrous lover into the miserable expiator of a wretched mistake. For one month, I, by my invisible agent, Fashion, will bind together bride and groom in dread imprisonment. Impalpable shall be their fetters, fair and luxurious shall be their prison, and in their bondage there shall be no worse chastisement than each other's society. They shall be forever plumbing each other's souls, and forever finding shallows; forever gauging each other's minds and forever being disappointed at the results. And not until they have learned to thoroughly detest each other shall the order of release be granted and the fiat be pronounced: Ye know each other's emptiness of heart and shallowness of mind; go forth and begin your new existence profoundly wretched in the knowledge that your miserable lives must be spent together!'"

Perhaps of some honeymoons this might be said, but every day of sweet companionship brought Helen and Philip nearer together. Instead of emptiness of heart and shallowness of mind, each discovered in the character of the other veins of true gold whose existence had before been all unsuspected. Few men are loved with such a love as Helen felt for her husband, and mingled with the adoration and passion he had felt for her came the almost reverential thought that she had been given him from the very jaws of death; that his great love and earnest prayers had drawn her back to life again, even from the very arms of the angels. Thus, the marriage seemed ideal and there was every reason to prognosticate happiness.

Bright, cheerful letters came to Margaret from Switzerland, from Italy and from the Holy Land; letters whose contents showed the writer's heart filled with love and faith and hope and contentment. Then Margaret was glad with exceeding joy that she had bravely kept her own secret and had not marred this perfect happiness by a syllable relative to her own heartache.

Lately this dreary sorrow had somewhat ceased. Since Philip's and Helen's departure Laurance Cameron had often called at Woodbine. To the young girl's heart had come as yet no thought that he held for her other than a brother's love. She felt that he was now more than usually kind in the effort to brighten her dark hours, for without Helen, from whom she had not before been separated for more than a week at a time since the latter's birth, it was very lonely. So with him she went for long walks. As the weather grew warmer they stayed more upon the shady and cool piazzas, and she listened to his manly voice as he read aloud, or with him she discussed the social and political events of the day.

Their favorite author was Heine, from whom Laurance read in the original tongue. If left to himself he would invariably open at that group of short poems called *Heimkehr*, and read here and there as fancy led him. Sometimes the poem chosen would be a love song, brief, passionate as the cry of a soul in anguish. Then he felt that he would give all might he but speak such words to her heart, and his voice, trembling with emotion, would almost betray him. Sternly he silenced the stifling cry of his soul, for he felt that it was not yet time to give its deep emotions words.

Sometimes the verses were bitter and cynical; sometimes full of tenderest sympathy, telling of childhood, youth and purity; sometimes dark, with hidden meanings, grim, awful, cold with a chilling breath from the tombs. Sometimes Margaret's heart beat a little faster as he read; but the sweet messages of love, the echo of a despairing swain's cry or the anguished wail over the bier of the dead, only spoke of Philip,—never of the man who read so well and felt so deeply.

Although Laurance felt, and a thousand times acknowledged to himself, that the heart of the young girl was not yet won, her gentleness in those long, beautiful days, her womanly sweetness, her kind sympathy and graceful tact, endeared her more than ever to his heart and inspired him with hope. The day at last came when he felt that he might with some degree of assurance speak of that which had so long been a part of his life.

It was the afternoon of a languorous June day; the sort of day when time slips away from us unnoted, and the minutes, from morn to even and from the gloaming to the nightfall, melt into one another until all seem one sweet, lengthened hour. The sun poured down upon Santa Illa. Except the hum of the industrious bees not a sound was heard: even the streamlet at the end of the long lawn was running sleepily, making sweet music, indeed, as it went, but so drowsily, so heavily, that it hardly reached the ear; and so, too, the lapping of the waves upon the shore below as the tide came and went. Not a breath of air disturbed the languid grandeur of the high elms that stood, like huge sentinels, guarding the hall door, and stared up into the sunny heavens, studded with little stationary clouds that lay like flecks of silver upon the pale blue sky. The birds that sat in the branches up above had hardly energy enough to flap their tiny wings.

Laurance Cameron, strolling with Margaret on the beach, determined not to let the afternoon wane without asking for the one gift on earth that had power to make him happy. They two sat down in the shelter of a huge rock. All around was glaring sunshine—so beautiful when looked upon from the shelter, so pitiless when there is no protection from its rays.

"Had I known the weather was so warm, I question whether I would have ventured out. How you do enjoy this walk along the beach!"

"Anything that brings me near to you and takes you away from the rest," laughed Laurance.

Startled eyes for a moment sought his, and the expression read there did little to reassure the woman's heart. "O, not this," thought Margaret; for although mortal man had never yet spoken to her words of love, instinct, woman's birthright, told her what this suppressed emotion meant. The deeper tone in his voice, the graver look within his eyes spoke volumes to the heart that had schooled itself to hide these same symbols of love.

Hastily rising she said: "Let us go on." He caught the hand that was about to raise the crimson sunshade, and for one short moment both were silent, bound by a spell that neither dared to break. At last the man spoke:

"Margaret, you know that I love you," he began in his low voice, tremulous with feeling. "No words that I can say to-day can tell you of my love more plainly than my heart has been telling you in every hour of these last few, happy months. I love you as I never hoped to love—fervently, completely. The perfectness of earthly bliss will be mine if I can but win you. Dearest, is there such sweet hope for me? Are you indeed mine as I am yours, heart and soul and mind and being until death?"

Margaret sat down; alas, she could no longer stand. She had grown pale and there was infinite distress and a frightened expression in the eyes that looked entreatingly into those of Laurance. Regardless of the intense heat a chill had settled about her heart and a shiver escaped her. She felt, however, the necessity for speech; yet as she turned her fair young face toward her passionate lover its expression could be read as clearly, could be understood as easily, as the most fluent speech. Not easily came the words: "Believe me, Laurance, I am your friend always; your wife I can never be. O, why have I—why have you—O, I am so sorry!"

The latter part of the exclamation was wrung from her at sight of the man's face from which the color had fled, and whose expression was one of intense disappointment.

Mechanically repeating her words, "Your wife I can never be," he asked, "Margaret, tell me why. Surely one so fair, so gifted, so womanly, cannot elect to walk alone alway! And rival I know I have none. I have spoken too soon; let me expiate my mistake, if need be, by years of waiting, but do not remove, I beseech you, dearest, the blessed boon of hope."

There was no answer. She could not tell him a falsehood; she could not tell him the truth. "Rival I have none." He had spoken confidently. She could not say, "You are mistaken; all the love my heart can ever give to mortal man has been given to my sister's husband. He did not ask for it, as you have done. He did not care for it as you do. Indeed, the knowledge that it is his would only make him miserable, while to you it might bring happiness. Yet, strange as it may seem, it is his alone. I have not power to take this unholy love from my heart and replace it with one that is holy. I have not even the inclination. I can but live happy in the knowledge that it brings no one unhappiness but myself. Alas, I can but pity myself; I cannot alter my wretched fate."

Bending over her, he suddenly possessed himself of both her hands and gazed into her face as though he would read all its secrets. It told him that hope was indeed dead. This was no piece of womanly coquetry, no attempt to further lead him on to warmer declarations.

Bitter as his disappointment necessarily was, he could not fail to read that Margaret was infinitely distressed, and fearing to add one further pang to her suffering he said: "Forgive me, Margaret, and for God's sake never forget to accord to me the friendship you have just promised. Without that I think I could not live. Let us be as we have been, and forget all that this afternoon has brought to us. I think better of myself for having loved you. A man privileged to meet you day after day, as I have been, and

who did not love you would not have been worthy the name of man. For the past I have only happy memories; for the future—ah, how can I bear it; how support the truth that my love is hopeless! But I must—I will. Almost before I was aware I found a craving in my heart which now I know all the world cannot satisfy. But do not grieve, dear one, we have both been blind."

"I shall go away," Laurance said later. "It is better so; but if ever you want a friend, if ever you can recall me for a sweeter reason, I will come to you proud and happy to have retained your trust."

Far into the night Margaret sat pondering, her elbows on her dresser, her head upon her hands, thinking, with a startled, suddenly awakened sense of sorrow. Indeed, she had been blind, and he, too. Each had misconstrued the friendly actions of the other.

Strange and sad it is that love should be given where it is not wanted, and must be withheld where it would bring so much of happiness! Without the slightest effort on his part Philip had at once gained a strange influence over her. From the first hour of their meeting he had attracted her unaccountably. His very unconsciousness of self, which gave such dignity to his manner, was to her irresistible. On the evening before Helen's betrothal it was borne in upon her that this feeling was love, and it was clearly revealed to her how heavenly it would be were her love returned. She had thought that she had conquered self, but hot tears fell—perhaps in pity for her own weakness.

CHAPTER IV.

"Under the gloom of the shivering pines,
That whisper when it blows,
Behind the creeper-covered wall,
In a garden that always grows.
The hand of man has made it.
The white stones stand in rows;
The tears of the world have watered it,
And the garden always grows."

Rain, rain everywhere. The light was dimmed; the winds sighed heavily; and "the hooded clouds, like friars, told their beads in drops of rain." A dull, leaden gray morning. The birds hopped about disconsolately, giving many a fluttering shake to rid themselves of the moisture. The landscape lay in a lethargic shadow, and time seemed to loiter somewhere, so long were the hours, so little did they change. In the afternoon the drops were redoubled on the roof, but later they grew fewer, and then sounded only the fitful patter from the foliage overhead. A stiff breeze arose, and with it came a chill that penetrated to the very marrow. Turbulent gusts arose that shook the doors and went screaming away into the early falling night. The gusts became fewer and fewer and, roving for a time among the garden bushes, were at last hushed and lulled to sleep amongst them. Then ensued a quiet, which, after the fitful winds, seemed almost uncanny. Not even the ashes crumbled in the wide chimney-place where they lay beneath the huge logs that fed the voracious flames.

The silence became oppressive, and Margaret found herself unconsciously listening, alert to catch and distinguish some sound that might break it. That of carriage wheels rolling rapidly up the graveled walk was the first to break the stillness, and knowing that they whom she had been expecting had arrived, Margaret went forth to meet them with emotions almost overpowering.

On this wild night in November, Philip and Helen Gordon returned from their long honeymoon. In July Helen's mother had died, and it was of her that they were thinking as they gazed at the empty chair that would never again enfold the beloved form.

Letters are uncertain things when one is traveling with indefinite plans. At Rome Helen knew that her mother was ill; at Cairo, two weeks after the dear one had done with earthly trials, she first knew that she was orphaned.

How kind Philip had been! How much he had done to keep her from dwelling upon her loss! Once she had said: "Our May marriage; O, Philip, do you suppose there *can* be anything in that superstition?"

He had not even looked grave, but at once pronounced it nonsense. "Never," said he emphatically, "shall I regret the day upon which you came into my life. May, June or December cannot matter. That day shall be of all my days the happiest, and the one for which I shall be most thankful when to me shall come the last day of all."

Slowly Helen went about the room, looking with love-lit eyes upon this and that; making trifling comments upon any article new to her; touching with reverent hand the little rocking-chair. At last, throwing herself upon the lounge, she said, "It is very nice to travel and see all the things one has read about, but it is far better to be at home again."

Then Doctor Gordon came in. He looked much worn and a great deal older than he had on the wedding day a short time before. His affection for his wife, lacking the fierce blaze of youthful love, had but burned the deeper, and the loss of the beloved object had reflected upon his face the grief felt in his heart. He plunged into conversation relative to his business; said Philip must not play truant again for many years; there had been much illness in Santa Illa and he had had incessant demands upon his services. He felt tired and old beyond his years. To a younger man these duties would not seem so arduous, and so upon Philip he was ready to put the greater portion of his work.

———

Margaret spent many hours in Helen's new home, while their father and Philip were in town. One evening as the two were sitting in the window, in that sweet hour before the lights were brought, Helen told Margaret how happy she was at the prospect of motherhood in the coming springtime.

Students of human nature, will you tell me why, when your love is irrevocably lost to you, there should come an additional pang when you hear that she is a mother or he a father? Margaret now felt that she was more alone than ever. She could not have described the sensation, nor would she have made any attempt to analyze it even to her own heart, but the feeling of more absolute loss than she had yet realized came to her and for a moment held her mute. Helen, having taken Margaret's hand, told her many things which she did not hear, but she was so happy in her own story that she did not note any lack of attention on her sister's part.

By the light of the moon that was rising, slowly wrapping the earth in its pale glory, Margaret gazed through a belt of trees, now nearly stripped of their coverings, to the limitless ocean lying in restless waiting in the bay below. Upon the water a sort of enforced tranquillity had fallen—a troubled calm—belied by the hoarse, sullen roar that arose, now and again from its depths, as if some larger death-wave had broken its bounds and, rushing inland, rolled with angry violence up the beach. Soft, white crests lay upon the great sea's bosom, tossing idly hither and thither, glinting and trembling beneath the moon's rays as though reluctantly subdued by its cold influence.

Ere Helen's talk was ended, Margaret had again gained mastery over herself, and, indeed, something of the joy and excitement that is natural to women in a case like this, came to her and made her interested and sympathetic with the new happiness in store for the two whom she loved best on earth.

In the long night watches Margaret had sometimes been tempted to recall Laurance Cameron, for whose exile she felt wholly responsible. She could not calmly think of his enduring the desolation of heart that she endured. Of Laurance's exile she was the unhappy cause and yet she dared not bid him return.

CHAPTER V.

"What will you find in the future years,
　Oh baby boy, Oh baby boy?
When the ship of your fate in port appears
And the bells of destiny ring in your ears,
What will they bring you, hopes or fears,
　Oh baby boy, Oh baby boy?"

When the spring came, with the return of birds and the budding of flowers, a new joy was given to Philip and Helen

Gordon. A new life had begun in their home,—a human life with all its joys and sorrows, with all its hopes and fears yet to be enjoyed or suffered. With what unutterable joy did each gaze upon this child; with what care and tenderness were its recurring needs supplied! Long and frequent were the debates over the baby's name. If only one might be coined for the purpose! A name once borne seemed hardly good enough to bestow upon this matchless boy. Most of the discussions had been between Margaret and Helen in "the watches of the day," for Margaret had, at last, found a resting place for her weary heart. The touch of the soft, clinging arms, the happy baby smile, the pretty dimpled cheeks, had all carried their messages of love to the bruised soul: her heart went out to the innocent child, and through Philip's son she had conquered the love given Helen's husband.

With the growth of the baby Helen grew more and more beautiful. The tender light in the hazel eyes, the tremulous smiles on the sweet lips, so illumined the fair face with its dawning of mother-love, that there were times when Philip, looking at her, felt something like awe at her wonderful loveliness, and surprise that such a beautiful creature should be his.

Little Arthur was a revelation to them both. The little, flower-like face, the rounded, dimpled limbs! Helen remembered the ecstacy of long ago, when her father had brought her a French doll that could walk and talk and go to sleep, and she again felt the same strange thrill that then pervaded her being, and longed to hear her baby say that which her doll had uttered,—the one word—"mamma."

How happy and well the child was! He laughed at his baby fancies and smiled at fairies that hovered, in his dreams, about his dainty pillow. The soft touch of the chubby arms inspired the father to added energy and nobler resolves.

One day a funeral procession passed the house. Between her and the water, through the great elms, Helen saw a white hearse, with snowy, nodding plumes, white horses, and within, a tiny white coffin. The casket of a baby, perhaps no older than hers. Somebody's loved one — perhaps her only one — was being carried out to sleep beneath the waving flowers and swaying grasses. As the cortege passed beyond the view of the young mother, her heart went out in sorrow to the weeping ones who were following the — to her — unknown child to its rest and sleep. Tears came to her own eyes as she thought of the mother's anguish, and she wondered how she could bear the loneliness of the empty house, listening in the stillness of the night for the baby voice that would never call again. Almost unconsciously she clasped her sleeping boy to her heart and a pleading prayer arose that not yet might her child's pathway be to the river-side where waits the boatman pale.

The baby thrives; there is no immediate need of concern. His father, being a physician, could he not detect the slightest touch of fever, an unnatural brilliancy of the eyes, or too great a drooping of the heavily fringed lids?

Yet to Philip, last of all, came the knowledge that his fair young wife, whose growing beauty he could discern, was not as well as before the baby came. It was Margaret who spoke to him, and with almost a curse at his own blindness, his criminal thoughtlessness, he realized that her beauty was not that of health. Her cheeks lacked their old-time luster; her lips were far too crimson; the brilliancy of the eyes exceeded that which nature gives; the slender form was too attenuated and the small, white hands were almost translucent.

Thoroughly alarmed at what before he could not even see, Philip went to San Francisco and brought back with him Doctor Floyds. The old physician expressed little anxiety; a warmer climate would, no doubt, restore Helen to her old-time health and strength. She was not strong when she married; she had traveled much, and the baby coming so soon had overtaxed her strength. Especially so as she had devoted herself so assiduously to the young autocrat. A climate with a more even temperature, where the chill of the fall and the damp spring with its dreary rains could not be felt, would, no doubt, restore her.

Philip at once thought of Hawaii; of the need of good physicians at Honolulu; of his friendship with Dr. Ernest Gray that would help to make the place more home-like, and decided that to no place could they better go than to this capital of the Hawaiian Islands.

To Helen it did not matter, and so a hurried departure was made from Santa Illa. Margaret wept many tears over the separation from her baby, as she called him. "I shall come, like a thief in the night," she said, "and carry him away."

Margaret's home was very quiet now. Philip and Helen and the baby were gone and Laurance had not been heard from for many months. Doctor Gordon's added labors kept him away from home nearly all the day and sometimes far into the night. So Margaret's life was lonely, and over Woodbine there seemed to have fallen a great shadow.

(Concluded in the September Midland.)

THE WATERS.

WHAT is it that aileth the waters — the river, the lake, the sea?
Forever a miserere they chant of a grief to be.
They have garnered the fear and terror from æons of pain and woe,
And from land to land go sobbing in minors weird and low.
Only the heart sore-stricken by sorrow's heavy hand
Can hear below the rhythm, interpret, and understand;
Only the soul grown hopeless can hear again and again
To earth's cry of baffled longing the water's sad "Amen!"

STOCKHOLM, WIS.

Ninette M. Lowater.

THE HEGIRA OF THE ELK.

By J. A. SMITH.

THE great stretches of prairie between the Mississippi River and the Missouri have, within the memory of people yet living, been the home of the highest types of wild animal life known to the North American continent — of the buffalo, the elk and the deer. The former, wilder by nature, fled faster when he learned that the skin-hunter yearned for his hide. The latter, more timid, yet less fearful, was the last to linger and may now be found in some of the most secluded nooks between the two great American rivers.

But it is to the elder class of the deer family, whose cast-off antlers may still be found, whitened by the snows of many winters and charred by the fires of many prairie burnings, that I desire briefly to call the reader's attention.

Until midsummer of 1871 a considerable drove of elk had found feeding grounds and comparative security for rearing their young in the then unsettled region of northwestern Iowa, where the trend of drainage is toward the Little Sioux and Rock Rivers and near their headwaters.

A colony of settlers, planted by Captain May in Lyon county in 1869, the railroad surveyors and advance guard of pioneers in Southwestern Minnesota in the same year and the influx of homesteaders into Dickinson, O'Brien, Clay and Sioux counties at that period, compelled this herd of elk to take refuge in the valley of the Ocheydan River, a tributary of the Little Sioux. There they remained undisturbed, except by an occasional band of hunters, until a memorable July morning in 1871 when the writer, at a distance of some two miles, saw them pass southwestward down the further border of a small stream that emptied its waters into the Ocheydan River.

His coign of vantage was a lone house on a homestead claim in the extreme southwestern corner of Dickinson county, miles away from any habitation to the east and many more miles away from any on the west. The herd passed down on the east bank of the stream, while the homesteader's cabin was on the west bank, with the wide valley between. To the northwest the view was unobstructed for a half-dozen miles, and it was from this quarter that the elk were moving from their violated jungle homes amid the tall rushes and willows of the Ocheydan valley.

Peering through the vista of pink and yellow shades of a rising summer sun, the first thought of the early-summoned dwellers in the cabin was that some emigrant's cattle had stampeded — a not unusual occurrence. A few minutes later and the use of a field-glass disclosed the identity of the swiftly galloping animals. Ere they reached the nearest point on the eastern range we were able to classify them as a drove of elk, consisting of four old bulls, ten full grown cows, twelve yearlings and ten calves. Judging by the peculiar articulate movements, which were plainly visible through the glass, the pace did not seem to be fast, but the conclusion arrived at, from the distance covered within a given time, led us to believe that it would be useless to try to intercept them without swift horses.

Some weeks later (for news traveled slowly in those days) we learned that the entire drove in its hegira was scattered and killed before reaching the Missouri river. They took refuge in the larger bodies of timber that skirt the lower waters of the Little Sioux River, and relays of hunters slew, to the very last one, this fleeing remnant of noble game.

An incident in this connection may not be uninteresting.

A member of Company I, Seventh Iowa cavalry, to whom the writer mentioned these circumstances, said: " In 1862 I was one of a squad detailed on a trip from Sioux City to Spirit Lake. One afternoon, as we were following the old St. Paul military road between Cherokee and Spirit Lake, we sighted what was first thought to be a band of Indians with ponies. Three of the squad who were well mounted volunteered to reconnoiter, and approached near enough to discover that the suspected enemies were a herd of about seventy-five elk, gathered in curiosity to watch our approach. Our skirmish line frightened them, and a report of the facts relieved us of some anxiety."

And this, in brief, is the story of the exodus from Iowa of the American elk — the Wapiti deer of the Encyclopedia Britannica, the half brother of the European elk (Cervus Alces), the morganatic son of the moose (Alces Malchis) and cousin of the reindeer (*Rangifer caribou* and *Tarando Groenlandicus*). The elk had no liking for the steppes that our earlier geographers designated as the Great American Desert. He may be found now among and beyond the Rocky Mountains; but there he is generic. It is quite probable that the remnant, the fate of which these pages record, was the last vestige of the American elk east of the great Rocky sierras and south of the unsalted seas.

AT THE SEASIDE.

THE reigning maiden of the ball
    Was born of purest Pilgrim stock ;
    Her fathers landed on the Rock —
And she herself is fair and tall.

I hear them whisper as we glide —
    "Who is that dancing with Miss May?
    She might have found a courteous way
To keep such stumbler from her side !"

She passed two years in Europe, though
    Her years all told reach not nineteen ;
    Ah well! I saw in Muscatine
Some forty Hawkeye blizzards blow !

O Iowa ! thy exile longs
    For boyhood years, for prairie town
    Where one small maid in school-girl gown
Ruled boundless realms of dreams and songs.

And maiden of the Mayflower strain,
    Thy frowning friends cause me no fret ;
    A lifetime, brief or lingering, yet,
The boy's first love yields not his reign !

          Selden L. Whitcomb.

HOME THEMES.

LOOK BEYOND.

"Whatever tends to render us ill contented with ourselves, and more earnest aspirants after perfect truth and goodness, is gold, though it come to us all molten and burning, and we know not our treasure until we have had long smarting."—George Eliot.

Happy is the spirit that can come up through fiery trials undimmed and shining; that can send out a ray of light to cheer the pathway of some other soul, struggling in the waves of adversity.

He who has climbed some dangerous ascent can easily locate the rock against which he was dashed; the pitfall into which he stumbled; the obstacle which arose to obscure the path, overcome only by the most indomitable courage and tenacity of purpose; the crystal spring where he slaked his fevered thirst; the tree by the wayside, beneath which he rested from the glaring heat of the noonday sun; the verdant mead through which he passed, where the breath of a thousand blooms filled the air with fragrance.

That the experiences of life help to mould the character is an immutable law. But it is hard to realize, when smarting under fiery trials, that just such an experience was necessary to bring out latent traits of character, which else might have lain dormant.

To touch hidden springs of sympathy in one's nature, springs that may burst forth a crystal fountain to refresh the thirsty and arid soul of many a way-worn traveler,—therein is the superiority of one over another made manifest.

The spirit in which one meets adversity is the supreme test of character. The man who seeks to learn just the right lesson from severe discipline, whose soul is lifted, rather than embittered, is the superior man.

But, if one should faint by the wayside? Are there limitations, hindrances, which cannot by the most superhuman efforts be overcome? It still were best not to be discouraged.

Progression is the word — is the law. He whose face is turned in the right direction will make some advancement.

Progression is not alone a law for this present life; it is for all eternity. How the very immensity of the thought startles one! A light from Heaven flashes into the heart and fires the soul!

Almost everyone has at some supreme moment been suddenly transfigured by a burst of music. Some familiar strain, that takes one back into bygone days, that brings up faces and scenes from out the past, that controls time, place, even the faculties, just for the moment.

Thus am I transfigured by a picture that rises before my mental vision, and takes me into the future, the Beyond, when I shall sit at the feet of some loved friend who has gone before, and learn of the ways of Heaven; and, perchance, speak of many things which happened while we journeyed here below. How like a term at school it will seem to us then!—for this life is indeed but a training school in which to prepare for eternity.

Then fret not, weary heart, though friends fail you, and those nearest and dearest prove false; though disappointments await on every hand; though clouds black as midnight arise! Keep your soul alight and your eyes lifted toward the lofty mountain peaks, and all the powers of Satan cannot rob you of your hope of Heaven. Naught but your own faltering can do that. Flowers perennial shall bloom at your feet. The longing and thirst of the heart *shall be satisfied*. Tenderest and truest friendships shall be yours in the bright beyond, "world without end."

Katherine Mansfield.
Burlington, Vermont.

DOG DAYS.

Hot and dusty,
House-wives crusty,
Victuals dusty,
Garments rusty,
House-flies lusty,
Dogs not trusty,
Villains scheming,
Lunatics raving,
Children screaming,
Tear-drops streaming,
Sun-light beaming,
Poets dreaming.

Dunlap. *Ernest Wylde.*

179

THE FARMER GIRL.

Sitting in the hammock,
  'Neath the willow's shade,
Wandering o'er the velvet turf
  In the flowery glade,
Treading on the new-mown hay
  In the meadows wide,
Gazing on the distant hills
  From the river side,
What a happy life to lead,—
  Free from care and strife;
Surely, does the farmer girl
  Have the happiest life.

Washing dishes late at night,
  Weather very warm,
Insects buzzing round her head,
  In a perfect swarm,
Milk-pails brought at half-past ten
  By the hired man,
Pails to wash and milk to strain
  Into crock and pan;
What a weary life is this,
  Free from care and toil;
Happier lot does not exist,
  O, daughter of the soil!

Alden.   *May Cunyes.*

SYMPATHY.

Of course we were not at all surprised,
it had been so long expected! And yet
it is none the less saddening simply because it was expected. The very fact
that it could not be averted,—that it must
be, that no skill, no love, no tenderness,
no care,—that nothing within human
power, could stay the march of that dark,
deep shadow,—made it all the more sad.
How our hearts ache when we know our
friends are weeping! How little of the
real human is in our nature if our tears
can never mingle with the tears that wash
the cheeks of those around us!

How sad, sad death is! But how utterly
without consolation would it be if this
were all! If, with the last view of that
cold form, the solemn words, the somber
garments, the rattling earth as it hides
away that which has been so much to us,
there were no thought of an after-life, no
hope born of Faith,—who would care to
live! Despair and Hope, twin sisters
born in each human soul! One brings
grief beyond measure, whispering to us
that life is a useless burden, tempting us
to break the brittle chain that holds us
here; the other bids us look upward and
beyond. The one covers our skies with
darkest storm-clouds; the other bends
her bright bow of promise across those
stormy wastes.

Hamilton, Ill.   *K. H. L.*

ORIGINALITY.

They said she was original,—the ones
who knew her best; but none can, in this
life and age, that title claim. The poet
finds within his mind a thought most
beautiful and gives it wings, but someone
else that thought before has spoken. 'Tis
truly said that no new thing exists beneath
the sun, and yet we find, each passing
hour, what we call new; but, like the
bee, from flower to flower we flit, collecting here a sweet and there a sweet to suit
our taste. We did not make the flower,
nor yet the sweets, but in the choice of
both lies our originality. If that be pla-
giarism, we all must stand condemned
before the world.

Des Moines.   *Lillian Barker.*

COMPENSATION.

If you think and say and do
What is right and just and true,
Then the graves you will traverse
Every day your journey through.

Cloudy days will then seem bright;
Dark will never be the night;
Light within will radiate,
Circling round your outward state.

For the thoughts within that burn
Will externalize in turn,
And your pathway surely strew
With the choicest flowers that grow.

Thoughts and words are real things,
And they fly as if with wings;
And whate'er you think or say
Will return to you, some day.

San Diego, Calif.   *Mrs. C. K. Smith.*

MOTHERHOOD.

One morning fair, my baby
  Climbed up into my bed,
And down upon my shoulder
  She laid her golden head.

She had her precious dolly
  Clasped in a close embrace;
She told me how she loved it,
  And kissed its battered face.

I asked her if she couldn't,
  For only one short day,
Give me her precious dolly
  To take with me away.

She slipped her arm around me,
  And tears came to her eye.
She battled with them bravely
  And sweetly said, "I'll try.

"But mama, while my dolly
  Is gone away from me,
Is there some other dolly
  Whose mama I can be?"

I wondered if in heaven
  My sorrow I could bear
If asked to give my darling
  Back to my Father's care.

Mason City.   *Lily E. Markley.*

EDITORIAL COMMENT.

It is interesting, if not amusing, to listen to the critics as they separately sit in judgment on a new book. Take Zangwill's "The Master," for example. Mr. Payne, the critic of *The Dial*, of Chicago, says it is "more than half paddling," abounding in "artistic 'shop' of the cheapest sort, its style nearly always unfinished, and often bad." According to *The Dial* critic, "overmuch Journalism has well-nigh wrecked in him [Zangwill] what might have been an admirable talent for description and characterization." *The Critic*, of New York, finds "'The Master' is far too much of a book to have been written, as the phrase goes, with a purpose." This critic finds that "Mr. Zangwill's purpose *sings*"; that his work has "the profundity of the flash," "the power which puts a chapter into a phrase." He tells us that "the great sad beauty that underlies the life of men and the life of art is the secret of a book that no one can read and be quite the same, and which, with all the brilliant cynics in it, leaves a long, soft whisper in our hearts." After being thus driven and tossed between two opinions, (not having read the book), we turn with fear and trembling to Boston's *Literary World* to find what it has said. The Boston editor, like his progenitor in the garden, puts upon a woman the responsibility of decision under the pressure of this new temptation. Katherine Tynan Hinkson, in her London letter to the *Literary World*, after reading "The Master," rises "with a profound conviction that in the author we have to reckon with one of the coming men." But, to those who have followed Messrs. Howells and James to the conclusion that Dickens is not artistic, judged by the best work of a later period, what a shock to read that the London critic finds Zangwill's book "in many ways reminds one of Dickens"! She finds Zangwill's success "like his master's [Dickens'] is in dealing with humble life." While *The Critic*, of New York, finds the many and various episodes "all very interesting and quite perfect in their way and very finished," the London critic "would fain blot out the whole episode of Eleanor Wynwood and her eccentric friend,"—And there you are!

* *

"THE LOUNGER" in the *Critic* says that "every one the book publisher knows has some friend or acquaintance who writes prose or poetry, and experience has told him that not once in a thousand times does the novice amount to anything." The remark, though too sweeping, suggests a few words crystalized from editorial experiences. The relation of author and publisher, or author and editor, is essentially direct. In that relation there is no room for the middleman. If a position of trust is to be filled an endorsement is serviceable. But if a manuscript is seeking publication, it matters not whether the editor's dearest friend, or his richest patron, or his bitterest enemy — or the postman — lays it upon the editorial table, the one only question with the editor is, or should be, "Is it what's wanted?" A MS. may be good — very good — and yet not be "what's wanted." That essential point is usually quite as hard for the interested friend to see as it is for the author himself. Some excellent people who haven't looked on all sides of the question of authors' opportunities and editors' rights, seem to regard the editor as they would a civil, or military, service examiner, as somehow bound to accept whatever comes to him of requisite weight, proportions, character and standing. But, even accepting this theory and for the moment barring out the supreme question of availability, shall the civil service examiner, or the recruiting officer, continue to accept all worthy and well-qualified candidates after the vacancies are all filled? Not long ago Captain Adams, U.

S. A., detailed as a recruiting officer at Des Moines, remarked to a friend : "I was obliged to turn off a splendid fellow to-day ; he came all the way from O—— on purpose to enlist ; but I had just received orders to temporarily suspend enlistments and so I had to send him home." Since the government service wisely suspends enlistments and appointments whenever there is a temporary cessation of the demand, why should an editor be charged with unfairness or arbitrariness when he refuses to load up with manuscripts for which he can see no immediate use !

* . *

PROF. GEORGE D. HERRON'S "Political Vision of Christ," published by Crowell, consists of six lectures delivered in various American cities, said to be the outgrowth of an address which Governor Crounse, of Nebraska, thought it necessary to protest against last summer, at the time of its delivery before the Nebraska Chautauqua. Doctor Herron reminds *The Literary World* of the Altruist, in Miss Hastings' clever story, who supposed he himself had discovered, or invented, the brotherhood of man, and thought himself called to interpret God and patronize man. Though we can but imperfectly judge of the man behind Doctor Herron's books from listening to a single fragment of his religio-social philosophy as given by him in a classroom lecture at Grinnell, our impression of him is that he is a thoroughly consecrated man, that he has a well-developed *ego* which is also thoroughly consecrated, and that his strength as a social reformer is weakness in that he seems to lack the element of trust in the "one unceasing purpose" running through the devious ways of men, and appears inclined to take upon himself the whole burden of the sins of the world. Dr. Herron has been thought by some to be insane on this one subject of individual accountability for things as they are. If so, his is a noble madness, for it would supplant selfishness with sympathy—would convert the egoist into the altruist. Madness is ordinarily

self-centered. Yet here is a man who, apparently lacking faith in the ultimate outcome of good from the present tangle of evil influences in our social state, takes upon his own insufficient shoulders the burden of society's shortcomings and sins. He reminds us of that other noble madman whom Browning has grandly pictured. May the outcome of his career be as satisfying ! The great-souled Paracelsus, who early found the seal of his "authentic mission" in his "fierce energy," in "the restless, irresistible force that works within," after all his strivings and burden-bearings found at last man's mission fulfilled in having performed his share of tasks awaiting his hand ; "the rest is God's concern." He came out into a clearer view of life. From the high plane attained at last, he comprehended the futility of his attempts to relieve God of the burden of the sins of the world. He came to see what he had blindly failed to see before,—

"A mind in evil, and a hope
In ill success : to sympathize, be proud
Of their [the world's] half-reasons, faint aspirings, dim
struggles for truth, their poorest fallacies,
Their prejudice and fears and cares and doubts ;
All with a touch of nobleness, despite
Their error, upward tending all though weak,
Like plants in mines which never saw the sun,
But dream of him, and guess where he may be,
And do their best to climb and get to him."

* . *

MISS KATE E. CORKHILL, of the faculty of Wesleyan University, Mount Pleasant, presents her views on the question of organizing a Society or Academy of Letters in Iowa, similar to the one which has proved so successful in Kansas. Indiana and Ohio have some such organizations, and their popularity commends them to other states. Postal card views from Iowa writers will be gladly received by the editor, and the substance of the same will be aggregated and reported in the September MIDLAND. The character and extent of the replies will indicate the degree of interest taken in the subject, and will determine the question, for the present at least.

THE comparative greatness of Napoleon, of which we hear so much of late, if measured by the test of time, as Historian Fay measures it in his "Three Germanys," dwindles to pitiable proportions. Says Doctor Fay: "The Empire of Charlemagne lasted ten centuries, that of Napoleon ten years." But, in fairness to the Corsican, it should be said that Charlemagne's ten-century empire was for the major portion of the time little more than a name.

* *

MISS BURKHALTER, in her clever sketch, "Her Week in Camp," speaks of "the quill-throwing porcupine" as "a fiction invented by the Swiss Family Robinson." We remember years ago to have seen this fiction of the quill-throwing porcupine gravely given as fact in Goldsmith's "Animated Nature." How much older the error is we cannot say; but the presumption is that Goldsmith simply embodied in his library-edited work the general impression of his time relative to the porcupine.

* *

AN English writer would abolish the honeymoon, insisting that it spoils many a promising marriage by wearying the young couple one of the other. There are not a few old couples left who would suggest an indefinite extension of the honeymoon rather than its abolition, having found that closer acquaintance opens up depths of affection undreamt of on the wedding journey. The subject recalls the reply of a homesick soldier to General Thomas. The General met the man's request for his second furlough in a single year with the remark that he himself hadn't been home in a year and a half. "That's all right for you, General," retorted the homesick man, "but me an' my wife aint that kind."

* *

WITH the recent death of Thomas H. Huxley, the great biologist, at the rounding out of the allotted three-score and ten, closed the earthly career of one of the noblest and most successful searchers after knowledge that ever dignified humanity, and verified the universal tradition of the divine in man.

* *

THE SECOND of THE MIDLAND'S "Types of Midland Beauty," in this month's magazine, is Miss Margaret Mahon, daughter of Major Mahon, an influential citizen of Ottumwa.

In this connection it may be well to outline our purpose in bringing out these types. A partial friend of Miss Grace Rawson, of Des Moines, with whose portrait the series last month began, asked why we did not print the name with the picture and give a sketch of the lady. The answer given covers the whole question. Our purpose is not to exploit the individual, but to present Types. The vulgar "write-up" of society ladies was farthest from our purpose in inaugurating the series. The presentation of Types is without the least sacrifice of modesty on the part of the subjects chosen, or of dignity on the part of the magazine. The portraits are obtained from the artistic photographers of the midland region, and are thus a healthful stimulus to artistic photography. The first knowledge the subject has of the use made of her picture comes through a request from the editor direct, or from the photographer at the editor's suggestion, that her consent be given. Thus the presentation of these Types is wholly free from individual objection and is a real contribution to the artistic side of our midland life. That the feature is well received is evident from the enthusiastic comments of the press of the country.

* *

THE overworked New Woman asks and is entitled to a vacation.

* *

"TO SIN against art is the unforgivable offense in a dramatist," says Dorothy Leighton, director of the Independent Theater, London. The theater directors who turn down really artistic dramas and play only the catch-shilling spectacular and the fast-set society dramas of the day are largely responsible for the fact that dramatists are sinners all.

And yet, why blame the theater directors? One might as well blame a caterer for making a specialty of lobster, or terrapin, when his best paying patrons are continually calling for those viands. If there is any unpardonable sin in the case, the public is "chiefest of sinners"—but the public, unlike Paul, isn't willing to admit it.

* *

An exchange tells us of an editor whose continued ill-health has compelled him to abandon his editorial work. It then significantly adds: "He anticipates entering the ministry." That editor must have in mind some "Church of the Heavenly Rest"—certainly not any one of the live, active, up-and-coming churches we see all about us, thoroughly organized for work all along the line, the pastor the *ex-officio* head and front of its every movement for the enlargement of its own usefulness and for the betterment of the world.

* *

The amazing ignorance of most Europeans relative to our country—its people and their achievements, tendencies and purposes, its resources, its scenery, and even its political geography—is the subject of frequent remark. But when an American abroad glances down the columns of the European press in hope of finding some telegraphic news from home, he comes to see how it is that to dwellers on the other side America is still an unknown world. The European press is not doing for its readers the cosmopolitan work which the American press is doing. Thanks to the press associations and the special correspondents, and, behind them, the world-embracing policy of American editors, we are able to keep the run of affairs in England, France, Germany, Russia, Turkey, and the uttermost parts of the earth. But take up, for instance, an English paper! Before us lies the Birmingham *Daily Gazette* of June 7. With a whole page devoted to markets, another page to sporting news, and nearly a page given up to editorial, with much city and country news and a few, a very few, columns of news by telegraph, the only cablegrams from this entire Western continent are four lines relating to the insurrection in Guayaquil, four lines from Louisville and three lines dated "Illinois," wherever that city or telegraph station may be!

* *

James Harlan the strong commonwealth builder, the great campaigner of other days, the swayer of political conventions, the orator and statesman, the confidant of Lincoln during the War and the adviser of his party's leaders ever since, the "Grand Old Man of Iowa" has a place in the hearts of our people and in the history of our country which no circumstance can in the least affect.

* *

The individuality of the voice is a trite subject of remark among telephone users. Though there are only nine perfect tones to the human voice, we are told that there are seventeen and a half trillions of different sounds.

* *

It is said that there is not a student paper in all England. How different in the United States! Here, in every college, in most normal schools and in many seminaries and high schools, there are two or more weeklies or monthlies, and in most of the great universities there are literary magazines and daily papers, conducted solely by students. It is barely possible that in a few of the higher institutions of learning the journalistic desire is developing into a craze; but the college paper as an institution has come to stay.

* *

An English physician, presumably bald, informs the world, through the *British Medical Journal*, that baldness is a sign of breeding and that hairiness and anarchism often go together. There are those who would gladly take the chances of moral degeneration and would even be willing to stand suspected of anarchism, if they could win back "the crowning glory of their boyhood days."

AMONG THE MAGAZINES.

The best thing we find in the July *English Illustrated Magazine* is a sketch of Bismarck, by "H. B." Without grudging the great statesman his fair share of praise for the creation of the German Empire, this writer's judgment is that "that end was due more to the spontaneous outburst of enthusiasm evoked by the great victory, in the heart of every German, than to any carefully planned scheme such as Bismarck claims to have originated years before the war, and to have brought to fruition by the exercise of his genius." A writer who comes out from anonymity so far as to give us his initials should give his full name.

While several of the newer magazines run to cover, the homely old face of Harper's looks well to those who are not satisfied with mere surface attractions.

American readers of English fiction who visit England look in vain for the smaller gentry of old English life. *Macmillan's Magazine* explains the void. It appears that at the close of the Seventeenth Century the "little squire" with his patrimony of two or three hundred pounds a year was still a familiar figure in English country life. A hundred years later he was practically extinct—absorbed by the larger land-holder.

In the July *Arena*, Helen M. Gardner continues her good fight for raising "the age of consent" to eighteen years. The discussion has drawn out hundreds of affirmative and but two negative responses from legislators. The two legislators who give themselves this "bad eminence" are Representatives C. H. Robinson of Iowa and A. C. Tompkins of Kentucky. To offset the injustice done these states, by these representatives, Mrs. Gardner introduces the eloquent appeal of Senator Rowen and Representative Gurley of Iowa, and Representatives Tompkins and Lyons of Kentucky, for the speedy inauguration of the reform.

"Political Heredity in the United States," by Henry King, leads all the rest in the July *Chautauquan*. This interesting paper naturally pays respects to the great and the small Adamses, Samuel, John, John Quincy, Charles Francis, and the four sons of Charles Francis, the last named eminently respectable but in no sense great. The other families mentioned are the Edwardses, the Lowells, the Winthrops, the Lees, the Henrys, the Rutledges, the Kings, the Hoars, the Randolphs, the Shermans, the Harrisons, the Choates, the Breckenridges, the Lincolns, the Sewards, the Camerons, the Greenes, the Grants, the Fields, etc. Mr. King shows that the law or custom of political heredity obtains in this country. While many rise to high place independently of ancestry, he finds "the fact remains that in many cases family prestige insures and transmits public rewards and official authority, and thus practically contradicts the cherished theory of uniform chances of success." The question arises is this as it should be in a republic that aims to go as far in the direction of pure democracy as it can safely go? In the language of the parodist on Whittier's "Of all sad words," we answer, "It is but it hadn't orto be."

The difficulties of the late Secretary Gresham, unpopular as he had become among republicans and distrusted as he was by democrats, are fairly stated by the *Review of Reviews*, and the man's patriotism and ability, his gifts and graces are generously recounted The opinion is moderately expressed that "he would have been wiser if he had not oscillated between the career of a jurist and that of a politician and statesman," a conclusion which compels almost general acceptance.

The State's Duty is another evidence of cerebral activity in this midland region. It is a monthly published in St. Louis, "devoted to consistent education, legislation and labor, for the elevation of dependent and homeless classes." It has thirty-two well filled pages of reading matter and its price is $1 a year.

The comparative value of wood engraving and half-tone engraving is considered by Edward L. Wilson, in *Wilson's Photographic Magazine*. The wood engraving admits of artistic changes but the half-tone is absolutely faithful in its report. Great advances have been made in half-tone work and many of the improvements which a wood engraver would make can be made in the photograph itself by a skilful artist. Blemishes can be covered, important features accentuated and many of the efforts of the wood engraver may be imitated. Says *The Writer* for July, "The great advantage of a half-tone landscape is its absolute fidelity to nature. In a travel article readers do not desire a pretty picture or an artistic picture so much as they do a truthful one."

A writer in the London *Saturday Review* finds women in literature more pessimistic than men. He wearies of stories of "unregenerate man and crushed woman," and concludes that they are written with "the sick air of the boudoir and irritability of overstrained emotion."

It is too true that about all most of us know of Buddha and the ism that operates in Buddha's name comes to us through that highly idealized picture drawn by Edwin Arnold in his "Light of Asia." Many a surface-reasoning reader of that poem has risen from the book with the question, "What is there wanting in Buddhism?" Nothing, as an idealization; nothing, as the basis for a pretty poem on living for others and dying without fear; but everything as the basis of a practical twentieth century religion or a practical twentieth century life. Buddhism's condemnation is to be found in the lax morality of the masses in countries where Buddhism is the prevalent religion, and in the deadness of the faith of its preachers and exemplars. This reflection is suggested by Mr. E. S. Irving's description[*] of a visit to the Buddhist and Tao-ist monasteries on the Lo Auu San, a six hours' journey by river steamer from Canton. This writer accounts for that puzzle of the nations, the Mongolian race, by remarking that the conscience of China is acted upon by four influences,—agnosticism, a folk lore, and the fossil remains of two religions, one Tao-ism, native born, and the other Buddhism, an importation from—somewhere, probably Japan. Agnosticism he finds embodied in Confucianism, the easily worn philosophy of the gentry and the literati. The masses hold to their belief in the traditions of their fathers. Buddhism and Tao-ism are characterized as fossils. Their fundamental doctrines have long since been unheeded and forgotten. Buddhist monks are called in to bury the dead and they are half credited with having power to regulate the rainfall. Their services for this last purpose are invoked as a reckless gamester invests in a losing game. This traveler found the Buddhist priests surprisingly ignorant of the doctrine of their order — ignorant and indifferent. He found the priesthood filled by men whose motives for entering the order were confessedly low. He found them past reasoning, past curiosity, past hope and fear, and absolutely careless, useless and opium-besotted. Their monasteries are supported by the contributions of tourists and the fees of shrewd seekers of eternal life insurance, who, while not caring for the doctrine, nor looking for the consolations of religion, invest in the mechanical prayers, the drum-beating and the gong-ringing of the priests as men in this country invest in wild-cat mining schemes on the theory that they can't lose much and they may win. These

[*] See Littell's Living Age for April 6.

priests idle away existence eating and smoking and saying prayers on demand, — and these are the exemplars of him who consecrated his life to the service of humanity. By its fruits is Buddhism condemned.

The mania for cheap picturing reaches absurdity in the *Nickel Magazine*, a picture periodical intended to undermine *Munsey's*. The publisher of the *Cosmopolitan*, in his absurd re-cheapening, might as well have made it the price of a Sunday paper and thus have done with it!

"Nurses of Great Men" is the *Sunday Magazine's* latest contribution to the satisfying of the public's inordinate desire to know more about the incidents of greatness rather than to grasp the real thing itself.

Among the new magazines are the following : *The Bachelor of Arts*, a beautifully printed, high class, four dollar monthly devoted to university interests and general literature, John Seymour Wood, editor ; published at 15 Wall Street, New York; also *The Wheelwoman*, devoted to the entertainment and the interests of women who ride the bicycle. It is published in Boston, and its price is $1. Just why women who ride a wheel should need a periodical exclusively for themselves is not apparent, even after reading the first number through.

GOSSIP ABOUT AUTHORS.

Robert W. Herrick, who has a story in the July *Scribner*, is a professor in the Chicago University.

Anne Katherine Green, the famous writer of detective stories, failed in the Bacheller Syndicate detective story competition which resulted in the award of the first prize to Mary E. Wilkins and the second to Brander Matthews. *The Editor* intimates that the contest was prejudged by the committee, and mentions a suspicious circumstance in connection with the competition ; but the high character of the judges would seem to preclude such a possibility.

William Cullen Bryant was satisfied with $2 for one of his poems ! Arthur Lawrence, in the July *Century*, says that a gentleman, once meeting him in New York, said, "I have just bought the earliest edition of your poems and paid $20 for it." "More by a long shot," replied Bryant, "than I received for writing the whole work."

John Addington Symonds, born in Bristol in 1840, died in Rome in 1893. He was the typical literary man of his century as distinct from the more robust man of the Eighteenth Century, and, let us hope, the Twentieth also. *The Critic* thus vividly portrays the type: " Feeble-bodied, weak in nerves, but strenuous in intellect, a self-tormentor more pronounced than the Terentian type, dyed through and through with the henna of insatiate melancholy, a Werther whose imaginary sorrows began generations ago with some abnormal paternity, a very Epicurus in the exquisitely attuned griefs to which he is addicted, and which he plays upon like an intellectual Pade-rewski, skilfully, eternally." It is hard to find good reason why Charles Scribner's Sons should contribute two volumes of Symonds' biography to the world's over-stock of pessimistic literature ; but possibly the pessimists are indulging in rather more cerebral activity than the optimists just at present. The large sale of Nor-dau's " Degeneracy " may have given the publishers a pointer.

John Davidson is another Scotchman who has come to the front in the London literary world. He is thirty-seven, and the son of a minister. A few years ago he couldn't find a publisher. Now everything goes — good, bad and indifferent — that bears the name John Davidson.

The persistency of error finds note-worthy example in the republication, in the April *Good Housekeeping*, of the poem, " There is no Death," over the name of Bulwer(Edward Bulwer Lytton), who in his lifetime scornfully denied having had anything to do with the verse. This immortal poem has time and again been traced directly to J. L. McCreery, formerly of Dubuque, now a resident of Washington, D. C., and yet here it comes again, credited to one who once sneeringly declared that he was " very glad to say " he never wrote it !

A similar instance recently occurred nearer home. One Sunday a daily paper contained an editorial article tracing the authorship of the pretty little poem "If You Want a Kiss, Why Take It!" to Major S. H. M. Byers, of Des Moines, author of "Sherman's March to the Sea." But it chanced that, in the very same issue, this identical poem — fresh from its long slumber on the " time-copy " hook — appeared over the name of Doctor Mary Walker !

James Payne, author of numerous Dickensy stories, says that while he has been exceptionally fortunate in receiving such small prizes as literature has to offer, the total income he has made with his pen has been but an average of £1,500 a year for thirty-five working years. There are many literary men of high degree in this country who would scarcely use the word "but" in connection with an income of $7,500.

Mrs. Ward received $15,000 for " Bessie Costrell," a 25,000 word novel. This is sixty cents a word—$150 for the MS. and $13,500 for the selling value which the novelist's well earned fame imparts to her work.

The Springfield, Massachusetts, *Republican* reviewed at considerable length Mrs. Reid's MIDLAND article on Julia C. R. Dorr and Some of her Poet Contemporaries, rather ungraciously conceding that Mrs. Reid gave some *few* incidents in respect to Mrs. Dorr which had not theretofore been presented.

Miss Julia Bracken has finished a bust of the late James W. Scott, which she will present to the public library of Galena. Miss Bracken was a pupil of Loredo Taft. She went from Galena to Chicago to study art eight years ago and now has a studio of her own. Her " Illinois Welcoming the Nations," which stood over the main entrance of the Illinois building at the World's Fair, is to be placed in the state capitol at Springfield.

James Payne, in *The Independent*, says that if Milton was ludicrously underpaid for " Paradise Lost," it is doubtful if he would get more for his work now. But such speculation is idle. Were Milton alive to-day he wouldn't be the Milton of " Paradise Lost." His eloquent plea for a free press gives us a clue to that other Milton, the pamphleteer who in this controversial age would have had his say and would have felt little inclination to dream.

Miss Bertha L. Patt, a former pupil of Professor Baldwin, of Des Moines, last October entered the Art Students' League of New York, and on the first of the following May stood first in *concours antique*, which honor enters her in the life classes — a high honor never before won by an Iowa student.

Major S. H. M. Byers, well known to MIDLAND readers, will read the poem at the September meeting of the Army of the Tennessee at Cincinnati.

Mr. James Knapp Reeve, of *The Editor*, Franklin, Ohio, has organized the American Fraternity of Writers, with headquarters in Cincinnati, and with his monthly as its organ. Mrs. E. C. Haire is vice-president ; Mr. S. S. Tibbals secretary and treasurer, and Mrs. Haire, Miss Belle K. Adams and Messrs. Reeve, C. D. Wilson and E. B. Fitzgerald, executive committee. Its principal object appears to be to compel publishers to do the right thing by authors.

Captain Charles King, whose stories of soldier life have made him famous, has recently been appointed Adjutant-General of Wisconsin. Captain King left Columbia College to enter the army as a drummer-boy in the regiment of his father, Colonel Rufus King. Later he took the West Point course, took part in the Apache, the Sioux and the Nez Perces campaigns. *Current Literature* says that in his love affair and marriage his life is no less interesting than are the stories he talks into a phonograph for publication.

A. J. Blethen, Jr., of the Minneapolis *Penny Press*, though yet a young man, has already achieved measurable success as a dramatist as well as literary editor. His plays, "Old Kansas," "Battle of Roses," "Doctor Hunter," etc., are full of promise.

Hon. R. F. Clayton, a MIDLAND contributor, has written an article on "American Wealth and Its True Sources," for the *North American Review*. It will appear soon.

"The Need of Sound Logic in Fiction" is a sensible paper by Frances Albert Doughty in *The Critic* of June 15. This writer reasons that the weakness of many of our ephemerally popular novels lies in the illogical turn given the story. The weakness of "Trilby" lies in the Svengali monstrosity; that of "The Heavenly Twins" in the unwomanly course pursued by the bride, on her wedding day and thereafter, in not accepting her husband's renunciation of his sin; that of "The Quick or the Dead" in the sentimental rejection of the lover, with which the book closes; and so on through the list. These stories are unwholesome because giving wrong impressions of duty and of life. The paper thus concludes : "Meanwhile, in considering the novel with reference to the young person, its chief patron at all times—one whose ignorance and inexperience may not detect the unsoundness in its logic, the divergence from real life—is it fair and friendly to put before that reader weakness for strength, morbidness for religion, folly for wisdom, and wrong for right, at a period of life when enticing voices and dazzling lights within and without are already dangerously bewildering?"

TALKS WITH CORRESPONDENTS.

A postal card comes all the way from Alabama which reads : "If you need any manuscripts I have three . . . Please let me hear from you as early as possi-

ble." Our friend mistakes the nature of the magazine-making industry. His notification is quite as if a planter were to write a manufacturer, "If you need any more cotton, let me know ; I can let you have three bales."

To W: We referred your inquiry and one of our own to Mr. Binner, of the Binner Engraving Company, of Chicago, and his general reply is as follows : "I appreciate the difficulty you encounter in having old photographic prints sent you to illustrate, and am aware that in a great many instances [notably war portraits] you cannot obtain better copies . . . When it *is* a matter of choice with you as to selecting copies, for half-tone reproduction, at all times avoid selecting a reddish tone photograph. Have your photograph more of a chocolate color, and you will get a black and white picture which will always make a good reproduction." We might add that photographs sent us for reproduction should be laid one on top of another with soft paper between, that they may not be rubbed or marred.

I write for much more prominent magazines than THE MIDLAND. But only being able, owing to ill-health, to write occasionally instead of regularly, I am not so well known as some. A magazine accepted an article of mine recently with the words, "All right; haven't read it, but your name is a guarantee." I feel quite proud.

You make a mistake in feeling proud of such a triumph as that. Whoever the editor may be, his theory of editing is pernicious and will in time prove fatal to even the best-founded periodical—that of accepting manuscripts without reading them; simply because he recognizes the name as that of an author who has before written something acceptable to him. One of the commonest experiences of an editor is that of rejecting manuscripts from authors who are known to him as having done good work. The flow of soul is fitful and uncertain, sometimes strong, sometimes weak, now clear as crystal, now muddy from contact with earth.

If my story is not accepted will you kindly return it?

Yes, but the next time, when you desire to have a MS. returned, will you kindly enclose either postage or a stamped envelope for that purpose?

Is [the story sent for editorial consideration] was a real Christmas episode and I hope may prove available.

If the story shall fail to make the episode seem real to the reader, then it makes no difference how closely you have conformed to the truth. The aim of the wise story-writer is not necessarily to be literally true, but always and in all respects to be artistically true.

CONTRIBUTORS' DEPARTMENT.

FROM RICHARD REALF'S LITERARY EXECUTOR, COLONEL HINTON.

The July MIDLAND publishes this:

Those interested in the John Brown movement, as well as students of American poetry, will be interested in the announcement that a subscription edition of the poems of the late colonel Richard Realf will be prepared in the fall. The widow of the poet lives in Pittsburgh. She holds a copyright on all her husband's works.

Let me make clear the facts: Mrs. Katherine "Realf" lives in Pittsburgh, that's true. The story of Richard Realf's sad suicide in 1879 links itself with that announcement, for it was the presence of the person referred to that caused my friend Richard Realf to seek "that bourne whence no traveler returns." Before he did so, he left an oleographic will or paper, requesting me, his friend and comrade of twenty-five years, to serve him as literary executor. He also, in severe language, directed that in no way or form should she be allowed to have aught to do with the collection and publication of his poems and writings. Before leaving San Francisco she sold to the proprietors of the *Argonaut*, for the sum of $100, which was paid, all right or title she might be possessed with in the literary work of Richard Realf.

Now, let me state a fact not publicly known. The late General John F. Miller, then United States Senator from California, was Realf's commander at Nashville, the poet serving on his staff there. In his distressed circumstances General Miller aided him in the sweetest of ways. It was General Miller who furnished the $100 to the *Argonaut* for the purchase aforesaid. When the mutilated scraps, excerpts and MSS., taken from Realf's trunk as he lay dying in Oakland, were transferred privately to General Miller, they were by him immediately turned over to me and are still in my possession. Within two years the Pittsburgh woman took out a copyright. That was in 1882. In 1885 I took out one also, for "Richard Realf's poems, with a memoir and other papers." No publication has yet been made on either copyright paper. But without further comment I desire to say, apart from the sale above referred to, that I have excellent and authentic reason for stating that the person resident in Pittsburgh has no copyright "on all" Richard Realf's works. She has not got them, and cannot obtain them, either. Several persons, to whom she has submitted for editing purposes such fragments as she

has retained from the sale, or collected since his death, have assured me that the scrap book fragments contain thirty-two poems,—such as have been widely published and so become public property, the little English printed volume of boy poems, with manuscripts of lectures entitled "Battle Flashes," "Shakespeare" and "John Brown." This is all, except some press reports. As a consequence, all such persons have declined to prepare for publication on so meager a basis.

As Richard Realf's selected editor, I am at last able to announce the progressive preparation of a volume of his poems. I have in my possession sixty-eight sonnets, seventy-three lyrics and other poems, the lectures above named, the boyhood book, and a mass of autographic letters and other material for biography and reference. Among these are over one hundred war letters of the most exquisite character. I have at this writing about two hundred fifteen subscribers at $2.50 per volume. The edition will be limited to five hundred — numbered,—the price as stated. I shall be glad to receive the names, etc., of any persons wishing to subscribe. Numbers will now commence at about two hundred twenty.

Yours,

RICHARD J. HINTON,
Author of "John Brown and His Men."
P. O. Box 21, Bay Ridge, N. Y.

A SOCIETY OR ACADEMY OF WRITERS SUGGESTED.

Since the establishment of THE MIDLAND has given a new impetus to literary pursuits in the Mississippi Valley, the idea suggests itself that perhaps we, who receive the benefit of this new effort, might and ought to do something to aid in the good work already begun,—to help ourselves somewhat, and by raising our standard both of appreciation and effort, render better service in literature, and establish a fixed name and place for ourselves in the intellectual life of our country. Iowa has won for herself an enviable position among her sister states. Every true-hearted Hawkeye is proud to be known as such. Our broad prairies, that just now are a living picture of green and gold, compare favorably in point of beauty with the landscape of any state, and their products promise to swell our purses to enviable proportions. Our educational system is equal to that of any state, and our per cent of illiteracy is among the lowest in all the states. There are some names in our nation's records that we are proud to point to as Iowans. Now, with such a good foundation laid, ought we to be content with mere "averageness"? If we rank among the first states in agricultural products and live stock, might we not also stand as well to the front in literary statistics? We certainly can if we will. We have the ability if we will but use it as wisely and with as much clear business sense as our agricultural brethren use their resources.

This new movement could be best inaugurated by the perfecting of a state organization, by means of which our efforts would be concentrated, and so made more effective. Much of what we admire and long for in the life of our literary centers, and some of their greatest movements, — revolutions, innovations, discoveries in the thought world, — are the result of concentration of ability and effort. We can have quite as good help and benefits as the literary centers afford, if we will but follow their examples and methods. We Westerners are too much inclined to take our opinions and ideas in literature at second or third hand. They come in, just as do our fashions, from the East. While a certain amount of this deferential spirit is good, more than that is a detriment, and dooms us to the life of intellectual automatons. We can be broad-minded, tolerant and receptive, and still have an activity and individuality of our own. Now, why not organize a State Society, or Academy, to which we could bring our work and ideas for comment and discussion? Kansas has such an organization that has maintained a healthy and interested existence for twelve years — the Kansas Academy of Language and Literature. Its object, as stated in its constitution, is to promote the love and study of literature, and to encourage investigation and original production therein. Why might not we have a similar organization?

From some opponent of this scheme there may come this objection: What need of multiplying organizations? Do not our colleges already do this work? Yes — they do — for their students. But there is no provision for encouraging and caring for the work and ambitions of students when once their school-days are ended. Farms, offices, counting-rooms open to them as the college closes its doors upon them; and all the love of study, with its best fruits which they had barely tasted in their college days, is all but crushed out in the multitude of business cares that rush in upon them. Then, too, there is that great class whom circumstances have deprived of a college education, and who are yet earnest students and fully imbued with the scholar spirit. An Academy of Letters might open to them a door which they had long been seeking, and they, from their outside experiences, might bring to those more fortunately situated many helpful hints and suggestions For these two classes — our scholarly busy people — an Academy would keep alive the love of letters already kindled, and might urge it on to a higher and broader life. It would give a new zest and impetus to their work whatever it might be, for there would go hand in hand with it, an interest in a work that is at once its own inspiration and reward.

To those who have chosen letters as their profession, a united effort, a comparing of notes and ideas with their fellow-workers, once a year, or oftener, would be a wonderful aid in suggesting new ideas or thoughts, in developing old ones, bringing them out in new phases, and clearing up shadowy or uncertain places. The mere talking over of any subject by persons interested in it is quickening and vivifying; but if this talking over could be changed to a systematic discussion, the vivifying influences would be doubly potent, and the participants might carry away with them not alone encouragement, but also hints and suggestions for improving and carrying out their plans, and so lead to the production of some work which shall be a source of pride and pleasure to themselves and of help and inspiration to their co-laborers. Our state has many individual clubs that have, for years, done meritorious work, and have kept alive a love for literature. Our State Academy should not be a federation of clubs, nor should it be in any sense a rival of such federation; but the clubs and its individual members could contribute much to the up-building and strengthening of the Academy, and so become strengthened themselves.

Suppose we were to form this Academy. It might be well to admit anyone to membership who would pay the annual fee, which could be fixed according to the pleasure of the members. This would insure a treasury, which is something. But, on the other hand, it might lead to an unduly large organization — so large indeed as to be useless and to prevent the attainment of the end for which it was formed. If there could be some plan devised by which membership could be restricted, and yet not shut out any who are really desirous to aid such an organization, and are willing to do their part to make it successful, it would seem better than a membership upon a purely financial basis.

The Academy should be officered as any other organization, but its chief official strength should be in its executive committee. This committee should consist of persons fully competent to carry on the work of the Academy. They should arrange all programs, and have the general management of the annual meetings. They should, of course, work in accordance with the wishes of the Academy; if it should seem desirable to consider any particular subject or line of study at any meeting, let the committee be instructed to prepare a program bearing upon it. Or if the Academy should wish to map out any work for general consideration before the next meeting, let them do so. But otherwise let the work of planning be left to the committee. It should be understood, however, that all parts of the program presented at the annual meetings — whether criticism, essay, poem, story, or whatever it may be — shall be original. One of the chief aims of the Academy should be to encourage original work, and this will be best accomplished by excluding from the hearing of the assembled Academy all copied or quoted material. There should be no "readings" or so-called "studies" of authors, however good. This does not exclude the study of an author for the purpose of discovering and setting forth his ideas and his methods. This is a necessary and legitimate part of criticism which is one part of Academy work. But it is meant to exclude the mere reading of the works of well-known authors, and so filling up the program with things which we could accomplish alone, and taking up time which should be given to the exchange and discussion of individual theories and work.

This is only a suggestion of what an Academy might be and do. It may never make us famous over seas, or even very widely known in our own country. But we are not seeking notoriety. An effort made with no higher aim had better never be made. But it will foster and keep alive a philosophical spirit, a commendable ambition and friendly rivalry, and will be a source of mutual helpfulness — a bringing out of one's best efforts which is the most important and abiding result. All this and more an Academy would do for us. Shall we have one?

Mt. Pleasant.   KATE CORKHILL.

THE MIDLAND BOOK TABLE.

An advantage attendant on literary fame is the certainty that the author's next book will not go begging for a publisher and will not lack readers. A disadvantage attending the success of a book is the insistence of the critics first, and after them the public, on judging subsequent books from the same author, not upon their own merits, but upon their merits relative to the author's previous work. Scott and Dickens, keenly appreciating the limitations of their own genius, shrewdly made the most of the advantages and bravely overcame the disadvantages consequent upon their fame. Tourgee and Bret Harte have not been able to even remain upon the heights they so suddenly attained. Barrie's latest work gives unwelcome evidence of limited powers. George Moore's early suggestion of strength proves to have been only a suggestion. George Meredith, on the contrary, evinces a degree of power at least equal to that displayed by him way back in the forties.

Putting Mrs. Humphrey Ward to the tests created by herself, namely, her "Marcella," "David Grieve," and "Robert Elsmere," the latest work of her pen, "The Story of Bessie Costrell," [b] is clearly not an ascent to higher ground. But, judging it as standing alone, the reader must see in it the promise of better things—the promise which lies in reserves of power. Mrs. Ward is too great to be measured by a book of 181 pages. The story we have just laid down is a tragedy, the motive of which is cupidity. The subject is a weak woman, fond of drink, resentful under the rigid discipline of an unloving and exacting but religiously conscientious husband. The scene is rural England — a community cursed with the beer-drinking habit. The story is, briefly, this: John Balderfield, an old laborer, completed his last harvest at home and went to a distant town to do one more piece of work before permanently quitting. He left the earnings of a lifetime with the husband of his niece Bessie Costrell, his faith in Isaac Costrell being greater than his faith in banks. Bessie finds she has a key that fits the cupboard containing the treasure. Her weakness for drink, for gay companionship and for dress does the rest. She would of course replace the money taken; she does not reflect on the impossibility of restoring it. One night while she is counting what remains of her uncle's gold, her husband's

[b] Published by Macmillan & Co., New York. Seventy-five cents.

son by the first wife, a vicious tramp, happens in. He attacks her and makes off with the gold, magnanimously leaving two sovereigns for the old man. Recovering from his brutal attack, Bessie goes shivering to bed. Her husband comes home from a church meeting and for the first time his heart is warmed toward his erring wife. He dresses her wound and gently chides her for going to the inn so often. Next day old Bilderfield comes back. A picture never to be forgotten is the old man's eager return to his well-earned rest only to find his treasure gone. The meeting of John and Bessie is intensely dramatic, only exceeded by the meeting of the brutally conscientious husband whose "righteous indignation" almost impels him to murder the woman who on her knees implores him to help her make good the loss. The almost divine compassion with which Mrs. Ward regards this miserable woman as she moves about her work half conscious of the tragic fate of her own weak choosing — that fate culminating in her mad leap into the well just outside the door of her home — evinces a power for future work in fiction which "Marcella" and "David Grieve" and "Robert Elsmere" have far from exhausted. The closing words of this realistic story are so full of suggestion that we cannot do better with the space at our command than republish them entire :

"No human life would be possible if there were not forces in and round man perpetually tending to repair the wounds and breaches that he himself makes. Misery provokes pity ; despair throws itself on a Divine tenderness. And for those who have the 'grace' of faith, in the broken and imperfect action of these healing powers upon this various world — in the love of the merciful for the unhappy, in the tremulous yet undying hope that pierces even sin and remorse with the vision of some ultimate salvation from the self that breeds them — in these powers there speaks the only voice which can make us patient under the tragedies of human fate, whether these tragedies be the falls of princes or such meaner, narrower pains as brought poor Bessie Costrell to her end."

"Daughters of the Revolution and Their Times,"* by Charles Carleton Coffin, is a profusely illustrated story designed to impress young readers with the manners and customs, thought and life of the interesting formation period of our Republic's history. Well has its author

* Houghton, Mifflin & Company, Boston. The Lathrop-Rhoads Company, Des Moines; $1.50.

carried out his purpose. The book opens with a vivid picture of Boston just before the War of the Revolution, of the great personages of that era—Adams, Hancock and the rest, of the family life of that period, the arrogance of British officers in society, the independent spirit of the maidens of revolutionary tendencies, etc. Then follow thick and fast the events of that memorable struggle for independence, making the events seem a part of the reader's own experience. This style of book has for long been almost out of fashion — for there are fashions in books as in everything else — but we are glad to see it in vogue again. Many of us, it closely questioned, would have to admit that our strongest impressions of historic characters and eras were obtained, way back when we were boys and girls, from historical novels and from history and biography treated in popular style by Abbott, Headley and the rest.

"Unknown Facts About Well Known People," by Frank Graham Moorhead, is a convenient and reliable biographical dictionary and directory containing sketches of over seven hundred living authors, artists, explorers, inventors, statesmen, soldiers, scientists, etc. The author of this work is a promising young autograph collector, of Keokuk, whose interesting paper in THE MIDLAND of April, '94, entitled, "Trials and Triumphs of an Autograph Fiend," made very interesting reading. His book is replete with transcripts of personal letters written by celebrities to the author, many of them throwing light upon the character behind the letter. In cloth, postage prepaid, $1.25. Address the author at Keokuk, Iowa.

OTHER BOOKS RECEIVED.

"The Naulahka," by Rudyard Kipling and Wolcott Balestier. Macmillan & Co., publishers, New York ; paper cover, 50 cents.

"Notes by the Way," by T. H. Macbride. Lee Brothers & Co., publishers, Iowa City.

"Selections from the Poetry of Robert Herrick," by Edward Everett Hale, Jr. Ginn & Company, Boston ; $1.00.

"An Introduction to French Authors, for Beginners," by Alphonse N. Van Doell. Ginn & Company ; $1.10.

"An Introduction to the French Language," by Alphonse N. Van Doell. Ginn & Company ; 91 cents.

"The Prodigal, a Poem," by Edward Arnold Lee. W. E. Ewing, publisher, Odessa, Missouri ; 10 cents.

"Sappho and Other Songs," by L. B. Pemberton, Los Angeles, California.

TYPES OF MIDLAND BEAUTY. III.

The MIDLAND MONTHLY.

VOLUME IV.   SEPTEMBER, 1895.   NUMBER 3.

GRANT AND GALENA.

By Leigh Leslie.

HIGH among rugged, picturesque hills, skirting a winding river spanned by red and black bridges, nestles the quaint, peaceful old town of Galena. Its streets are long, narrow and crooked; many of its shops are dingy, dusty and old-fashioned, and on its deserted levee, once the scene of the activities of a mighty commerce, are the crumbling walls of great warehouses. Occasionally the echoes are awakened in these rat-infested ruins by the hoarse bellow and the clanging bells of some packet bearing a party of gay young folk from one of the neighboring towns, or by the shriek of some wheezing stern-wheeler towing a barge freighted with wood. Nowadays the sleepy bridge-tender has little else to do than to smoke his clay pipe and nod in his arm-chair in the doorway of his little red house. Fifty years ago his office was not a sinecure. Time has wrought wonderful changes here in a half-century. The memory of the cheery, accommodating old drayman, who for nearly three-score years has been jolting about on his clumsy New Orleans cart, runneth back to a time when Galena was greater than Chicago, when fortunes were being made in these decaying buildings, and when it was no uncommon thing to see a dozen or more boats laden with heavy cargoes in the river side by side. This funny little man with white hair, wrinkled face, squinting eyes, horny hands, and an amusing habit of informing everybody he meets that "it's a fine day," whether it be fair or stormy, enjoys nothing else so much as to sit down at close of day with one of his aged cronies, or with one of a younger generation, and recall the years agone.

With the decadence of its commerce, Galena lost much of that energy and en-thusiasm which characterized it in the early Forties. Turmoil and strife have given place to tranquillity and good-fellowship. The people live a quiet, abundant life, undisturbed by the bitternesses and contentions of the outer world. Of a moonlight night pleasure craft ply on the river, and the willows that line the banks of the lazy stream sway gracefully in the breeze, casting fantastic shadows on the water, and affording romantic retreats for lovers out boating. In summer-time the ragged boulders on the hillsides glare under the scorching rays of the sun; the cozy cottages hidden in a wealth of foliage look cool and inviting; birds hop about merrily and sing sweetly in the tree-tops; happy, irreverent children romp amid the neglected graves in the old, ill-kept government cemetery, and ivy creeps tenderly over the stone walls of the little Gothic Episcopal Church, set snugly between great, jutting gray rocks, and peeps up over the moss-covered roof. In the cool of the morning the gabbling old German hucksters come in from the country-side, and gather in the market-place, where they are patronized liberally by the housewives of the town.

II.

Very sweet and precious to the good people of Galena is the memory of a simple, honest man who, about a year before the breaking out of the War of the Rebellion, came among them to clerk in a leather store. His patronymic was Grant; his dual Christian name, Ulysses Simpson. He lived in a plain two-story brick house on the great, frowning hill which looks down upon the shops, the market-place and the river, and up the steep, rocky side of which creep several flights of wooden stairs. The past had

GRANT'S HOME BEFORE THE WAR.
" He lived in a plain, two story brick house on the grass, sloping hill."

been fraught with adversity for him ; the future held out promise of little else. When the day's work was done — how irksome to him that work must have been ! — he would leave the store, his slouch hat pulled well over his grave thoughtful eyes, and climb the hill to his home, there to eat the frugal evening meal and try to forget his cares and perplexities in the companionship of his gracious wife and of his children.

This man read the newspapers diligently, and was profoundly sensible of the dangers which threatened the life of the Nation. As day by day the shadows lengthened and grew more ominous, he became more and more apprehensive. Long before the crisis actually came, and while others, less observant and far-seeing, still thought that it might be averted, he saw that war was inevitable. But that it was to last four long years, and entail so dreadful a sacrifice of blood and of

treasure, — that he did not foresee. Nor had he any prescience of his own great destiny. He had once held a captain's commission in the regular army, and he had enough confidence in himself to think he could command a regiment creditably ; further than that, his ambition did not go. And among all the other men of the town, — and there were men here possessed of keen powers of discernment, — there was not one who saw in him that genius which was so soon to make him famous.

On the Sabbath day he would go to the little Methodist Church in the shadow of the hill, to worship the God in whom he trusted through all the years of his life. When the good pastor, John H. Vincent, now honored as a bishop of the Methodist Episcopal Church, and as founder of Chautauqua and of the Chautauqua Circle, offered up earnest prayer to Him who ruleth the universe to stay the giant hand that was slowly rising in the South to smite the Nation, the worshiper in the pew, unconscious of the great responsibilities that were to be laid upon him, bowed his head reverently, and said a fervent amen.

Such was Grant, and such were his environments, when Sumpter was fired upon.

After Appomattox, who was it the people of Galena welcomed back to their hearts and to their homes? A strutting egotist? No! It was the same manly, modest man who, before the War, had dwelt and worked in the midst of them. To him they paid the tribute due to genius and he accepted it with that unaffected modesty which ever denotes the truly great. The plaudits of the civilized world had not destroyed the splendid simplicity of his character ; so pure and so valorous a nature was not thus to be spoiled.

III.

So much of myth has gathered about the name of Grant that it is well-nigh impossible to separate that which is historical respecting the man from what is purely fabulous. Writers for the press seem to have taken particular pains to misrepresent his life in Galena.

During Grant's brief residence here before the War he was strictly attentive to business, and rarely was he seen in the streets, except when he walked to and from his home. There were not a dozen men in the town who had social intercourse with him. He was poor and obscure. Yet, when he came into eminence, the public was regaled with a surprising number of stories about him from men who perhaps had never seen him, but who said they had been his intimate friends before the War. Some contented themselves with exploiting his virtues ; others recounted his alleged vices. Bar-room loafers affirmed that they had drunk gallons of whisky with him. One old barber, as if bent on outdoing all others in mendacity, solemnly averred that, in the early Forties, Grant used to call at his shop precisely at seven every

morning and go out with him to take a drink. In charity let it be presumed that the garrulous hair-cutter's addiction to a deplorable habit was responsible for his false utterances. The fact that Grant had never seen Galena at that time gave the barber no concern whatsoever. It is in evidence that Grant never drank a drop of intoxicating liquor while he lived here. He had only two conspicuous habits at that time : one was smoking his pipe and the other was attending to his own business. Occasionally he would meet with a few friends to play whist. Some of those friends are still living, and, being honest and truthful men, they will tell you that the story to the effect that he was a drunkard is utterly false.

Grant was a man of the highest virtue, reverencing all that was pure and sweet and noble. Though not a church member at the time, yet he was of a deeply religious nature. He was never heard to utter a profane or an unchaste word. There has been iterated and reiterated, until many people have come to credit it, a foundationless story to the effect that he used to sit in the leather store till late at night smoking his pipe, gambling, drinking whisky, and "cussing the damned niggers." All the time he could spare from his business was given to his wife and children. His devotion to them was beautiful in its tenderness. His home was almost severe in its plainness, yet it was very precious to him.

IV.

In 1841 Ulysses S. Grant's father, Jesse R. Grant, and E. A. Collins formed a copartnership to carry on the tannery business in Ohio established by the elder Grant. In the same year Mr. Collins came to Galena, then at the perihelion of its commercial glory, and the metropolis of the Northwest, to open a store for the purpose of buying hides and placing on the market the products of the Ohio tannery. In 1853 there was printed in the local paper a unique notice of the dissolution of the copartnership between Mr. Grant and Mr. Collins in the form of some

verse by Mr. Grant, wherein that somewhat eccentric old gentleman evinced
much good-nature and very little genius
for metrical composition. The partnership was dissolved for business reasons
only, and the *entente cordiale* between
the two men was not disturbed thereby.
Mr. Collins continued business at the old
stand, and Mr. Grant opened a store
farther down street, the management of
which he intrusted to his second son,
Simpson Grant, an honest, capable young
business man. In May, 1860, his eldest
son, the subject of this sketch, removed
from St. Louis to Galena to accept a
clerkship in the store. It was the intention of the elder Grant to soon sever his
own connection with the store and transfer the business to his three sons, in whom
he had the fullest confidence. But unfore-
seen circumstances arose to prevent the
consummation of his plans. Within a
year Ulysses S. Grant was in the service
of his country, and Simpson Grant was
lying on his death-bed. In the autumn
of 1861 the latter succumbed to that

THE OLD GRANT & PERKINS STORE.

insidious malady, tuberculosis. In the
beautiful cemetery in the western outskirts of the town is a grave marked
with a simple marble monument bearing
this inscription :

SAMUEL SIMPSON GRANT :
Born
Sept. 23, 1825.
Died
Sept. 13, 1861.

The elder Grant never lived in Galena.
While his sons were in the store here,
he was operating his tannery in Ohio.
Simpson Grant was compelled to retire
from active business life months before
his death. From the time of his removal
to Galena until Lincoln's first call for
troops, a period of eleven months, Ulysses
S. Grant had charge of the business. At
the breaking out of the War Orville Grant,
who had been assistant to his brothers,
became the head of the house. A few
years later he and C. R. Perkins formed
a copartnership, under the firm name of
Grant & Perkins, and bought the stock
of goods belonging to E. A. Collins, con-
solidating it with that of the Grant store.
After his retirement from business Mr.
Collins migrated to Iowa, of which commonwealth he became an honored and
useful citizen. He died several years ago
at his home in Shelby county. He was a
man of broad sympathies and of sterling
integrity.

It may here be said, parenthetically,
that Ulysses S. Grant first saw Galena in
1856, or in 1857, while on his way by boat
from St. Louis to St. Paul. The boat arrived late in the evening, and, in the short
time it was in port, he called on his old
friend Mr. Collins. He did not come
again until March, 1860, when he made
arrangements to move his family here.
"Now, Ulysses," said his father, "you've
made a failure of life so far as you've
gone ; I hope you'll do better in the store
than you have elsewhere. I am afraid
West Point didn't do you any good. You
must get down to business now."

Grant's first opportunity to vote for a
presidential candidate came in 1856, when
he was a citizen of St. Louis. At that

time he was nearly thirty-five years old. Since attaining his majority his sympathies had been with the Whig party. But that party had now ceased to exist. He believed that the election of the republican candidate for the presidency would precipitate the secession of every one of the slave states. He argued that the election of a democrat would leave no pretext for secession for four years at least. He hoped that the passions of the people would subside meantime. If the catastrophe could not be averted, he believed that the country would be better prepared to meet it four years later than it was then. He, therefore, voted for Buchanan. When the election took place in 1860 he had not resided in Illinois long enough to entitle him to vote. This was not a disappointment to him, for he would have been compelled by his pledges to vote for Douglas, whose defeat was inevitable. He desired, as between Breckenridge and Lincoln, to see Lincoln elected. The campaign was an exceedingly sharp one. The republicans of Galena organized a "Wide-Awake" club. Although he did not take an active part in the public demonstrations of either party, he occasionally met with the "Wide-Awakes" in their rooms to superintend their drill. It is said that he also frequently performed a similar service for the "Douglas Guards," a democratic campaign club. His sympathy with the republican party was well known to his friends, although he did not say much on the subject of politics. His wife was a Southern-bred woman, and at that time she owned two slaves in Missouri. Prior to the breaking out of the War, her sympathies were undoubtedly with the people in the midst of whom she was reared; but, when the crisis came, there was no woman in the land more loyal than she. Whatever may be said of the political affiliations of her husband before the War, no one who knew him could have had any doubt of his undying devotion to the Union. He was more of a patriot than a partisan at all times. "He was always in favor of the United States."

In the winter of 1860-61 he did considerable traveling through the Northwest. The leather house had customers in all the little towns in Southwestern Wisconsin, Southeastern Minnesota and Northwestern Iowa, and he called on them occasionally to get their orders for goods. When it came to be known that he had been an officer in the regular army he attracted attention everywhere he went. Of an evening the men about town would congregate in the hostelry at which he was staying to discuss with him the relations between the North and the South, and the probabilities of the future. He thought that a conflict was inevitable, but that "the War would be over in ninety days." He was an interesting conversationalist, and on those occasions he would talk with impressive earnestness on the subject that was uppermost in the public mind, the group of men about him listening eagerly to every word that fell from his lips. None dreamed, however, that the name of that unpresumptuous man was to go down in history with the names of Cæsar, Hannibal, Napoleon and Wellington.

V.

April, 11, 1861, "the shot that was heard round the world" was fired, and immediately thereafter came Lincoln's call for 75,000 volunteers. Intense excitement prevailed in Galena. A call was issued forthwith for a meeting of patriotic citizens at the court house. When the meeting was called to order Mayor Robert Brand, a Southern-bred democrat, was elected to preside. It was suspected by some that he sympathized with secession, and an effort was made to oust him from the chair, but it did not succeed. Subsequently another meeting was held, and Grant, doubtless by reason of his being an ex-officer in the regular army, was chosen chairman. He was much embarrassed, but he succeeded, with prompting, to announce the object of the meeting. The two principal speakers on that occasion were Postmaster Howard, who had voted for Breckinridge for president the fall before, and John A. Rawlins, a young lawyer who had been a candidate for elector on the Douglas ticket. Congressman Elihu B. Washburne came in after the meeting had been organized, and made a patriotic speech. After the speaking, volunteers were called for to form a company. Inasmuch as the quota of Illinois had been fixed at six regiments, it was thought that not more than one company would be accepted from Galena. Before the meeting adjourned the company was raised and the officers were elected. Grant was tendered the captaincy of the company, but he could not be induced to accept it. In a characteristic speech he explained the duties of a soldier, emphasizing the necessity of implicit, unquestioning obedience to com-

With Permission of Col. O. M. Fox, from his "History of Public Farmers."

GENERAL GRANT.

From a Photograph taken soon after his Return to Galena at the close of the War.

BIRDSEYE VIEW OF GALENA — LOOKING TO THE SOUTHWEST.

petent authority. He announced that he would be glad to assist the company to the extent of his ability, and finally evoked cheers by declaring that he intended to go into the service. His labors in the leather store ended with that meeting. The next day he wrote a letter to his father-in-law, predicting the uprising of the North, and the doom of slavery. Of all the other exalted intelligences of the time, none saw with clearer vision the course of events. From the viewpoint of an inconspicuous citizen he had watched the lowering of the fearful war clouds, and, far in advance of men high in public station, had foreseen the issue.

The ladies of Galena immediately set about the task of making uniforms for the company. Grant furnished them a description of the United States uniform for infantry, and they prosecuted their work with vigor and enthusiasm. Meantime Grant was drilling the company, and in a few days it was prepared to report for assignment. As the valorous soldier boys were marching briskly down the main street on their way to the station to take the train for Springfield, Grant, wearing an old army uniform, and carrying a grip-sack, "fell in" behind them, having made up his mind to go with the company to the State Capital.

Arriving there he was assigned to duty as clerk in the adjutant-general's office, where his army experience was of invaluable service to the State. He possessed little clerical capacity, but having been quartermaster, commissary and adjutant in the field, the army forms were familiar to him, and hence he could direct the work of the office. Meantime the legislature had authorized the governor to accept ten additional regiments, and Grant had charge of mustering these into the service. One of the regiments was organized in and about Belleville, twenty miles southeast of St. Louis. On his way there to muster it in, Grant visited his old Galena friends in the Twelfth Regiment, which was stationed at Caseyville.

While Grant was doing duty at Springfield, nearly all of the prominent public men of the State were assembled there. The only members of congress he knew were Washburne and Foulk, neither of whom paid much attention to him. He was acquainted with Governor Yates, and, by chance, he met Senator Stephen A. Douglas. General John Pope was stationed there as United States mustering officer. Grant and Pope had been classmates at West Point, and they had served together under Taylor in the Mexican War. One day Pope suggested to Grant that he enter the army. Grant said he intended to should the country need his services. Pope had a wide acquaintance with the public men of the State, and he offered to request them to indorse Grant for some acceptable position. But Grant was " unwilling to receive indorsement for permission to fight for his country." Later Grant wrote from Galena a letter to the adjutant-general of the army expressing confidence in his ability to command a regiment, and tendering his services to the government. That letter was never answered.

Subsequently the Twenty-first Regiment, which Grant had mustered into the State service, was threatened with mutiny, by reason of the incompetency of its colonel. Governor Yates promptly removed the cause of the trouble, and appointed Grant to the colonelcy. A few days later Grant had his men in camp, and when they had been reduced to discipline, he returned to Galena to procure a horse, and to order a uniform and a sword. He soon found a horse to suit him, but cash was demanded for it, and that he could not pay. Of a truth, the owner of that steed did not know whether Grant was honest or not ; he had never heard of him before. This only goes to show how obscure Grant was,—how limited was his acquaintance in the town. Finally he was told that if he would give his note with security he might take the animal. He requested Mr. Collins to go his security, and his friend cheerfully granted the favor.

VI.

Several persons have made claim to honors, the gratitude of the Nation, and the inevitable pension, on the ground of having been the first to suggest to President Lincoln the advantages of a campaign against the South by way of the Tennessee and the Cumberland rivers ; albeit such advantages must have suggested themselves to every school-boy familiar with the map of the Southern states. On the occasion of his visit to Galena immediately before he went to the front, Grant, in conversation with a few friends, pointed out the strategic advantages of the very campaign which, a few months later, he himself was conducting, and which resulted in the capture of Henry and of Donelson, the fall of Nashville, the battle of Shiloh, the fall of Corinth and of Memphis, and virtually the driving of the Confederate forces out of Tennessee.

A short time before he was appointed colonel of the Twenty-first Regiment, Grant had gone to Cincinnati to see General McClellan, then in command of the Military Department of West Virginia, hoping, through his good offices, to get a commission. But McClellan's headquarters was so closely guarded by armed sentinels, and the General himself was surrounded by such a retinue, that it was impossible for the unknown Galenian to get an audience with the little commander, and, thoroughly disgusted, he returned to Springfield.

VII.

The impression obtains that Grant owed all his successive advancements to the influence of Elihu B. Washburne. It is possible that this impression might be traced to its fountain-head in the person of a very astute politician. In truth, there is no foundation for it. While Grant was trying to obtain some position in which he could be of service to his country, Washburne tendered him no assistance whatsoever. The two men had never spoken to each other until they met at the " War meeting " immediately after the firing upon Fort Sumpter. It is in evidence that Washburne was displeased that Grant should have been elected to preside at that meeting. Grant was given a clerkship in the adjutant-general's office because he could make himself useful there. No man had to sacrifice himself on the altar of friendship to get that appointment for him. Indeed, Governor Yates personally requested him to accept it. Governor Yates soon learned that Grant was better qualified to discharge responsibilities than were many of those who were seeking and obtaining preferment, and he gave him a colonel's commission. No one had asked the Governor to make that appointment; Grant was indebted for it to no one but the governor. Then Grant was appointed a brigadier-general. It is true that Washburne recommended him to the President for that position, but so also did the other members of the Illinois delegation in Congress. He was now in the direct line of promotion, and for the opportunities that came to him later, he was indebted to the generous, sagacious Lincoln, more than to anybody or to anything else,—Providence excepted. Washburne's greatest solicitude for him was shown when he was beyond need of assistance from "the Commoner." It is difficult to assign motives; it is not the purpose of this article to attempt to assign those that prompted Washburne finally to so ardently espouse the cause of the great warrior. Whether or not they were tainted with self-interest is left for the reader to determine for himself.

"Words"—President Lincoln was tired of these; they were not putting down the Rebellion. "Action"—it was for this that he was praying. The plain, purposeful patriot who had gone out from the leather store in Galena came upon the scene. "Belmont"—it was not exactly a victory, but it showed that there was a man in the West who had a genius for doing,—who was not afraid to fight. The President took heart. Then Fort Henry fell. Then Fort Donelson, with its large garrison and all its stores, was captured,—the first substantial victory of the War. Grant, with the brave Western men under him, had done it; and he had

sent word to General Buckner that "no terms except an unconditional and immediate surrender can be accepted." To Lincoln there was much generalship in these words.

Almost immediately thereafter was issued Halleck's order relieving Grant of his command, and virtually placing him under arrest. The fatal illness of General J. F. Smith restored him to his rightful place too late to avert the disaster of the first day at Shiloh. But at daybreak on the morrow, the defeated army of the previous day was moving upon the enemy's position, and the last gleam of the setting sun shone on the victorious banners of the Union hosts, with Beauregard's legions in wild retreat. Here was another victory to the credit of Grant. To him war evidently meant fighting. Halleck again subjected him to unjust treatment. At the same time it was heralded throughout the North that Grant had been drunk at Shiloh. But Lincoln had been watching it all. "Tell me," he said, "what brand of whisky Grant drinks, and I'll send each of my generals a barrel of it." Then Halleck permitted the Confederates to get away from Corinth with all their stores and munitions of war. Would Grant have committed so stupid a blunder? Lincoln was not long answering this question. He called Halleck to Washington, and Grant, as the senior officer, succeeded to the command. History tells the rest.

VIII.

On March 18, 1864, Grant was presented by the people of his old home with a beautiful and costly sword as a "token of their appreciation of his inestimable services to the country in the suppression of the Rebellion, and particularly in opening to the people of the valley of the Mississippi their great pathway of commerce to the ocean." The sword was rich in design and elaborate in finish; the grasp and guard were ornamented with figures representing the heads of Jupiter, Mars, Mercury and Minerva; the grasp was inlaid with tortoise shell, held in place by gold studs, and the pommel was encircled with diamonds set in pure gold. Underneath the circle of diamonds was a shield bearing the motto, "*Sic Floret Respublique.*"

Men are judged by the means they employ to the attainment of their ends no less than by what they actually achieve. That Grant accomplished a stupendous purpose is no longer questioned; it is within the record. But what of a method of warfare which sacrificed thousands of precious human lives for immediate results? Was such a course sagacious in generalship or defensible from a humane point of view? This generation is far enough from the prejudices of the cruel civil strife to see what the country did not see then, — that a policy less aggressive would have been unwise in tactics and unmerciful to all engaged in the struggle. Supported and protected by Lincoln, whose faith in him never wavered, Grant followed the dictates of his own superior judgment, organized victory, crushed the Rebellion and restored peace.

The world requires a retrospect to take the correct measurement of men. Genius grows as it recedes from us. Full justice has not even yet been done the great, generous, heroic soul that, throttling treason, won for this Nation the right to live.

IX.

Back on the hill, scarcely a stone's throw from the house in which Grant lived, are two frame cottages, so near together and so much alike that sometimes the occupants, looking from the street, are doubtful which to enter. One of these, at the breaking out of the War, was occupied by John A. Rawlins; in the other lived William R. Rowley. Rawlins was a young lawyer; his opportunities for acquiring an education had been limited, but, being diligent and possessing a good mind, he had succeeded in building a practice at the bar. In the presidential canvass of 1860 he had been a pronounced Douglas partisan, and his speeches had attracted considerable attention. But when the integrity of the Union was threatened, no other man was more patriotic than he was. Rowley was clerk of the circuit court; he was amiable, valorous, and a strong Unionist. Grant had enjoyed the acquaintance of these men when he was a clerk in the leather store.

When Grant was appointed brigadier-general, he asked Rawlins to accept the position of assistant adjutant-general, with the rank of captain, on his staff. Rawlins was about to go into the service as major of a regiment then being organized from volunteers in and about Galena.

THE RAWLINS AND ROWLEY COTTAGES.
"Back on the hill, scarcely a stone's throw from the house in which Grant lived, are two frame cottages."

He considered the matter carefully, and finally made up his mind to go with Grant. He had had no military training or experience, but he possessed the qualities of a good soldier, and became a very useful officer, remaining with his chief to the close of the War. He rose to the rank of brigadier-general and chief of staff to the general of the army, — an office created for him. He was unselfish, loyal, brave and at times headstrong. Much that is untrue has been written about the relations he sustained to Grant during the War. Though his services were valuable, yet they were by no means of so great importance as some writers would have us believe. It has been maintained that he exercised a sort of censorship over Grant,—was virtually master of the situation. Those who knew Grant appreciate the absurdity of this. Grant had respect for and confidence in Rawlins, but he did not permit his subordinates to dictate what he should or should not do. Rawlins was in no sense a boaster. A high moral principle served as his rule of thought and action, both in public and in private life. He did not seek to create the impression that he was greater than Grant. He awarded credit to whom it was due. He acknowledged heartily and admired ardently the genius of the commander-in-chief. He asserted time and again that Grant was the most self-reliant general of the War; that his reserve powers were extraordinary, and that, as his responsibilities increased, his intellect became clearer and his power of action greater.

Rowley entered the service as lieutenant of Company D, Forty-fifth Regiment Illinois Volunteer Infantry, and was soon appointed to a position on Grant's staff. The services of this gallant officer on the memorable 6th of April, 1862, were of incalculable benefit to the Union cause. It was he who, as the curtain was about to be rung down on the first act of the bloody tragedy at Shiloh, brought General Lew Wallace's division on the field, thus assuring a turning of the tide of battle in favor of the Federal forces on the morrow. General Rowley was a man of remarkable equipoise and courage. He was compelled by failing health to retire from the army a short time before the close of hostilities. He died in 1886, after a painful illness. He enjoyed in fullest measure the respect of those who knew him. Grant was one of his warmest personal friends.

It is noteworthy that, besides Grant, Rawlins and Rowley, Galena gave to the Nation in the hour of its peril many

GENERAL M. E. ROWLEY.

others who attained high rank in the army. Among these may be mentioned Major-General John E. Smith, Brigadier-Generals J. A. Maltby, A. L. Chetlain, J. C. Smith and J. O. Duer, and Dr. E. D. Kittoe. Doctor Kittoe, who had gone out as surgeon of the Forty-fifth Regiment, was appointed surgeon on Grant's staff and medical director of the Army of the Tennessee. Subsequently he was promoted to the position of medical inspector of the Military Division of the Mississippi, commanded by General Sherman. Doctor Kittoe possessed many noble traits of character, and both Grant and Sherman loved and admired him. He died in 1887.

X.

Immediately after the close of the War Grant returned to Galena, where an enthusiastic public reception was tendered him. He was glad to be in the midst of his old neighbors again. The town was in brilliant apparel. Flags floated from every building, arches spanned the streets, and the name of the great soldier was displayed everywhere. On one occasion Grant had said that his highest political ambition was to become mayor of Galena. "There is no sidewalk leading to my house," he explained, "and I should try to induce the council to appropriate money to build one." The sidewalk had been built in his absence, and a conspicuous motto surmounting one of the arches proclaimed the fact to him when he came back.

Nothing gives a man greater popularity than do military victories. It was plain to the leaders of the republican party now that by the logic of events Grant was to be made the candidate of that party for the presidency. The signal services he later rendered the country in his contest with President Johnson still further popularized him. When the convention met he was nominated without formidable opposition. He was elected by a handsome majority. On his return from the War the people of Galena had presented him with a comfortable house, and he still considered this his home, although his official duties had kept him at Washington almost continually since the War.

DR. E. D. KITTOE.
From a Photograph taken shortly before his Death.

XI.

When the time came for him to select his cabinet President Grant gave Washburne the portfolio of State, and Rawlins was appointed Secretary of War. In regard to the premiership he afterwards said: "My first choice for the State department was James F. Wilson, of Iowa. I appointed Mr. Washburne under peculiar circumstances. Mr. Washburne knew he was going to France and wanted to go. I called on him one day when he was ill. I found him in a desponding mood. He said that before going to a country like France he would like to have the prestige of a cabinet office; that it would help his mission very much. He suggested the Treasury. I had already spoken to Mr. Stewart on the subject, and said I would make him [Washburne] Secretary of State. So came the appointment.

It has been stoutly denied that Grant offered Wilson a position in the cabinet. The following letter (hitherto unpublished), which was written by Grant's own hand, will serve to settle the question forever:

WASHINGTON, D. C., April 9, 1869.

HON. JAMES F. WILSON:

Dear Sir,—It is but an act of simple justice to you that I should state that I have seen, with pain, for the last few days, studied and persistent attacks upon you for a vote which it seems you gave, as a member of the judiciary committee in the last congress, upon the McGarrahan claim. I was not aware that you gave such a vote until I saw these attacks, and now have no knowledge or opinion upon the merits of the claim. My opinion of you, however, is such that I do not doubt but you cast your vote conscientiously, and according to the testimony advanced before the committee. The gossip, therefore, which says "that a distinguished member lost a seat in the cabinet, and a place in the confidence of his friends, through his connection with the case," is untrue. If it alludes to you, and it clearly does, it is refuted by the fact that I tendered you a place in my cabinet, and very much regretted that you felt constrained not to accept, for reasons entirely personal to yourself, and having no connection with any official act of yours.

With assurances that I still entertain the same high opinion of you that I did when tendering you a cabinet appointment, I remain, very truly,

Your obedient servant,
U. S. GRANT.

It was distinctly understood when Washburne was appointed Secretary of State that he was to resign within a few months and go as Minister to France, and that Wilson was to succeed him as premier. Wilson meantime was tendered another place in the cabinet, but he declined it. Once ensconced in the State Department, Washburne set diligently about the task of dispensing the patronage of the office, and so well did he accomplish his purpose that, when he resigned, all the offices at his disposal had been given to his own friends. Naturally enough Wilson was indignant at the turn affairs had taken, and, without regaling the public with an exploitation of the reasons that impelled him to do so, he dignifiedly declined the highest place in

THE WASHBURNE MONUMENT AT GALENA.

the president's council. He could see no other course open to him consistent with dignity and self-respect. He cherished, however, no resentment toward Grant. The latter had no better friend than he proved to be. The vicious spoils system nearly wrecked Grant's first administration. The successful soldier made a poor politician; he did not understand the arts of self-seekers and demagogues, and he was, therefore, easily imposed upon. To the unscrupulous place-hunters by whom he unsuspectingly surrounded himself were due the scandals that came so near destroying him. In the bitterness and the blindness of party rancor he was assailed most mercilessly for the acts of his betrayers.

Washburne was unquestionably able but inordinately ambitious. As Minister to France he performed distinguished services. At the breaking out of the Franco-Prussian war, Germany requested him to extend protection to German sub-

MAIN STREET, GALENA.

Decoration on the occasion of the Reception of General Grant on his return from the War. — "General, the sidewalk is built."

jects then in Paris and in other French cities. He exercised his influence very sagaciously in compliance with that request, enabling many Germans to communicate with their homes, and to pass thither in safety through the French lines. He returned to America in 1877, an aspirant for the presidency. He failed to attain the goal of his ambition, and died a disappointed man. His grave is in Greenwood Cemetery in Galena, a plain granite monument surmounting it.

XII.

When, in 1877, Grant retired from office, he had regained the respect and confidence of all the people. It was well understood then that he had had all the civic honors he desired.

On May 17th of that year, accompanied by his wife and his son, he sailed from Philadelphia on his famous tour around the world. He was received with marked favor by the sovereigns and the peoples of the Old World, and on his return he was greeted affectionately by his countrymen. The trip from San Francisco to Galena was a succession of ovations. A cheering multitude welcomed him home. Arrangements had been made for a brilliant public demonstration. Cannon boomed, bands played, and men marched through

GRANT TO WILSON.

(Facsimile of President Grant's Letter to Senator Wilson — now published for the first time, by permission.)

Washington, Ill.
Apl. 9th 1869.

Hon. J. F. Wilson
Dear Sir.

It is but an act of simple justice to you that I should state that I have seen, with pain for the last few days, abusive and personal attacks upon you for a vote which it seems you gave, as a member of the Judiciary Committee in the last Congress, upon the McGarrahan claim. I was not aware that you gave such a vote until I saw these attacks and now have no knowledge or opinion upon the merits of the claim. My opinion of you however so much that I have no doubt but you cast your vote conscientiously and according to the testimony adduced before the Committee. The paragraph therefore which says "that a distinguished member lost a seat in the Cabinet, and a place in the confidence of his friends, through his connection with the case" is untrue. If it alludes to you, and it clearly does, it is refuted by the fact that I tendered you a place in my Cabinet and very much regretted that you felt constrained not to accept; for reasons entirely personal to yourself, and having no connection with any official acts of yours.

With assurances that I still entertain the same high opinion of you that I did when tendering you a Cabinet appointment I remain

Very truly,

Yours obt. svt:

U. S. Grant

the streets and shouted themselves hoarse.
The streets were gorgeously decorated.
It was a notable expression of popular
homage to a great and good man. To
the formal address of welcome Grant
made a brief, prudent and practical response.

Grant was at home when the national
republican convention met in Chicago in
1880. The Western Union Telegraph
Company had offered to run a wire from
its central office to his house that he might
receive private bulletins there; but he
courteously declined the favor. His tour
around the world had fatigued him, and
he was now living a quiet, restful life.
Every morning immediately after breakfast he would seat himself at his desk and
go carefully over his voluminous correspondence. That task done, he would
light a fresh cigar, send his servant Yanada for his cane, and, accompanied by
the faithful Jap, walk to the office of
General Rowley to greet his old staff-

GENERAL ROWLEY'S OFFICE.
In which General Grant received Bulletins from the National Republican
Convention in 1880   Lewis A. Rowley at his desk.

officer, and to get the latest news from
the convention. Then he would stroll
leisurely up street, stopping frequently to
shake hands with old friends and acquaintances of ante-bellum days. At
Mr. B. F. Felt's grocery store there were
usually gathered a few old-time citizens
in eager anticipation of a morning call
from him, and it was rare that he disappointed them. He went among these
"plain people" now no less quietly and
modestly than in the years gone by.
Kings but a few months before had doffed
their crowns to him, yet to the people of
Galena he was the same gentle, retiring
man they had known before the War. That
extraordinary self-poise which had served
him to such good purpose during the
turbulent war period was strikingly manifest now. The people generally were
excited, but the principal figure in the
great political contest which was the pro-
vocative of their disquietude,—the man
whose name was upon the lips of millions,
—maintained throughout those
eleven feverishly exciting days the
utmost composure. He gave no
sign whatsoever of the solicitude
he must have felt respecting the
action of the convention; apparently he had less personal concern
therein than had the humblest laborer in the streets. It was his
habit to go to General Rowley's
office every evening; there he
would sit and smoke and listen to
the reading of the bulletins and
converse with friends till near midnight, when, with the devoted
Yanada at his side, he would climb
the hill to his home. His conversation was charming in its simplicity and directness, and he would
hold his auditors in delighted attention for hours at a time. His tour
around the world had appreciably
broadened and enriched his mind,
and he seemed never to tire of
talking about what he had seen in
Europe and in Asia. He was endowed with great powers of observation, he was an omnivorous reader

of the choicest literature, and his mind had become a veritable storehouse of useful information. His narrative was simple and graphic.

On one occasion an important bulletin came while he was telling one of his inimitable stories. Every one else in the room was anxious to hear the reading of the dispatch, but to him the story seemed to be of first importance. He went on talking, while the others moved uneasily in their chairs.

One morning, near the close of the convention, Louis, son of General Rowley, entered the office, much excited, and said: "General Grant, I have a very important piece of news for you." "All right, Mr. Rowley," said Grant with characteristic *sang froid*, "what is it?" "There is a rumor," said Mr. Rowley, "to the effect that Hamilton Fish's name will be sprung on the convention." Thereupon Grant turned to General Rowley, his face beaming with pleasure, and said: "Rowley, undignified as it might seem in me to do it, if the convention will agree to nominate Fish, I'll agree to stand on my head right here. Fish is one of the best men in this country; he is splendidly equipped for the presidency."

Early one morning the younger Rowley went to Grant's residence to deliver to the General a telegram from J. Russell Young, wherein the distinguished journalist conceded the defeat of Grant. Grant put on his spectacles and read the dispatch carefully. Thereupon he lighted a fresh cigar, looked out of the window thoughtfully for a moment, re-read the telegram, and, turning to his visitor, offered him a cigar. "Thank you, General Grant," said Rowley, "but I can't stand the cigars that you and father smoke; they're too strong." Grant smiled. There was nothing in his looks or in his actions to indicate disappointment. When the dispatch announcing the nomination of Garfield finally came, he said: "I can't say that I regret my own defeat. By it I shall escape four years of hard work and four years of

abuse. Now I hope the newspapers will let me and my family alone."

XIII.

For many years the relations between Grant and Washburne had been of the most cordial nature, but now friendly intercourse between the two men whose names were associated so intimately in the public mind ceased entirely. Grant could not escape the conviction that he had been betrayed by Washburne. It is affirmed that Washburne had early importuned Grant to become a candidate for a third term nomination, and that it was largely through Washburne's representations that Grant finally consented that his name should be presented to the convention. Grant was told that the people were clamoring for his renomination and his reëlection. That he was a victim of misplaced confidence there is little doubt. Before the delegates had assembled, his friends suspected that plans had been laid looking to the nomination of Washburne; and later developments served to confirm their suspicions. Grant was slow to suspect others of bad faith, and slower still to accuse them of it; but the day after the convention was called to order, he divined that a combination, to which some of his professed friends were parties, had been formed against him, and he predicted his own defeat. He accepted the issue philosophically. "The 306," under the leadership of the peerless Conkling and the gallant Logan, went down in honorable defeat.

Washburne passed quickly out of public notice, his ambition crushed, his prestige gone. It was sought afterwards, through the medium of friends, to arrange a meeting between him and Grant looking to the restoration of friendly relations, but all overtures to that end were unavailing. Grant and Washburne never spoke to each other again.

The true history of that memorable convention is yet to be written. That Washburne was guilty of any turpitude has been no less strenuously denied than affirmed, but the fact remains that

Grant himself believed that the old "Watch-dog of the Treasury" was culpable,—and Grant, of all men, was in position to know. It is believed by some who were near to the General that Washburne had carefully gone over the situation while Grant was abroad, and had come to the conclusion that, if Grant could be induced to enter the contest against Blaine, there would be a dead-lock; that a compromise candidate would finally have to be agreed upon, and that in all probability he, being so near to Grant and so well equipped for the office of chief magistrate of the Nation, would be nominated. The plan looked tantalizingly practicable, but it turned out badly for him who conceived it.

XIV.

In 1881 Grant purchased a house in New York City, where he took up his legal residence, spending a part of each summer, however, in his cottage at Long Branch. He retained the house here that his old friends and neighbors had given him; it is now a part of the Grant estate. It is a comfortable, old-fashioned brick structure on the brow of one of the heights skirting the east bank of the river. Grant had a very warm attach-ment for Galena, and it is believed that if no outside influences had been brought to bear upon him he would have passed the remainder of his days here. When he returned from the Old World he said he intended to make this his home. His Japanese servant accompanied him to his Eastern home, but he did not stay there long. Under date of November 26, 1881, Yanada wrote General Rowley a long and interesting letter. Among other things he said:

"Now I have a good chance to go with our minister in Washington, and I have to leave General Grant's house very soon. I am really sorry to miss my dear General Grant, as you know that I have been with him over two years; but he has been not a single day angry about me, and always so kind and familiar in his manner, that I will appreciate to his high stand, and I think that I have done my duty well while I was with him, and I shall remember that I had the honor of being with him so long."

General Grant wrote to General Rowley frequently. In one of his letters he extended a very cordial invitation to General and Mrs. Rowley to visit him and his family at Long Branch. Louis A. Rowley is in possession of all the letters written to General Rowley by General Grant after his removal to New York

THE HOUSE PRESENTED TO GENERAL GRANT BY THE CITIZENS OF GALENA.

City. I am indebted to Mr. Rowley for a copy of one of the most interesting of these:

LONG BRANCH, N. J., Aug. 8, 1884.
Dear Rowley.— As I told you, I am writing a few articles on the War of the Rebellion for the *Century Magazine.* "The Battle of Shiloh" and "The Vicksburg Campaign" are completed. I am now engaged on "The Wilderness Campaign." I have got up to the crossing of the Rapidan, and I have told the story of Swinton's eaves-dropping. But I am afraid I have not got it entirely correct. I know he was introduced by Washburne, with the assurance that he was a gentleman and was not a newspaper correspondent, but a literary man who proposed to write a history of the War after the War was over.

Will you write me the particulars of your detecting him listening; who were with me at the time; what you said to the man, and what action was taken. My recollection is that this occurred the first night after crossing the Rapidan — May 4, 1864 — and that my headquarters were in a tent not far south of the river. Badeau's history says that my headquarters were that night in a deserted house overlooking Germania Ford. Please state whether it was the first night after crossing, and if I occupied a tent; if neither, when and where it was.

You may remember that later — when we were at Cold Harbor, I think — Burnside found Swinton within his lines, arrested him, and ordered him to be shot before night. He had given Burnside offense by his publication a year or two before when I was in command. Meade reported this to me, and I ordered Swinton's release and expulsion from the lines, with a warning that he was not to be found within them again.

The *Century Magazine* has employed writers on every battle of the War. They are to appear in a series, commencing next January 7th. Shiloh, therefore, will not probably appear before next July, and the others much later. I intend, however, now that I have commenced it, to go on and finish my connection with the War of the Rebellion, whether I publish it or not. If it pleases me when completed, I probably will publish it.

Very truly yours,
U. S. GRANT.

XV.

Long and anxious were those months when the great warrior was battling with death. From every pulpit and from

HERMANN H. KOHLSAAT.

every fireside were offered up prayers that he might conquer his insidious foe; and from every heart went out to the sufferer love and tenderest sympathy. In that last desperate struggle, as in no other crisis of his life, was "Grant the hero" supremely revealed. But neither his own fortitude nor the prayers of mankind could save him.

When the news came to Galena that Grant was no more, the shadow of a deep affliction darkened many homes. Flags were floated at half-mast, bells were tolled, and a call was issued by the mayor for a meeting of citizens, that formal expression might be given to their sense of bereavement. These folk mourned not as the world mourned; to them it was not Grant the great resistless soldier who was dead, nor Grant the statesman; it was Grant the citizen,— Grant the gentle, gracious, sympathetic man. No other community had known him as they had known him; nowhere else was sorrow so profound.

Crowning a grassy knoll in a spacious park richly adorned with beautiful flowers, sparkling fountains and stately old trees is a heroic bronze statue of Ulysses

S. Grant,—a gift from Hermann H. Kohlsaat, editor and publisher of the Chicago *Times-Herald*, who was reared here, and who witnessed the General's return home in 1865. The sculptor, James Gelert, of Chicago, did his work with rare fidelity. The statue is remarkable in conception and perfect in modeling. The hero is represented as he was wont to appear here—a plain citizen. The figure stands upon a broad pedestal; it faces the west. The attitude is easy and characteristic. There are several bas-reliefs in bronze; one of these represents Lee's surrender to Grant. On the cornice are chiseled these words:

> **GRANT OUR CITIZEN.**

With pomp and circumstance this magnificent memorial was unveiled June 3, 1891, Chauncey M. Depew delivering a masterly address on the occasion.

THE GRANT STATUE AT GALENA.

On each recurring anniversary of his birth, Galena pays tender tribute to the memory of Grant. The Grant Birthday Association was organized two years ago, and every citizen of the town is a member of it. On these fete days many people journey hither, business is suspended, flags are unfurled, various societies march through the streets, and some distinguished public man pronounces a eulogy on the illustrious dead. The celebration this year was of exceptional interest, there being unveiled a great historical painting by Thomas Nast, reproducing with striking effect the momentous scene of the surrender at Appomattox, April 9, 1865. This picture is entitled "Peace in Union." It was presented to Galena by Mr. Kohlsaat. The canvas is nine by twelve feet. It hangs in the public library room in the government building. With clasped hands and earnest faces the protagonists of the mighty conflict are portrayed. Behind the Confederate chieftain stands Colonel Charles Marshall, one of his staff, and Colonel Orville E. Babcock, the Federal staff officer deputed by his commander to act as General Lee's personal escort to 'the place of meeting. Behind and beside General Grant stand Major-Generals Philip H. Sheridan, E. O. C. Ord and Seth Williams, Brevet Major-General Rufus Ingalls, Brigadier-General John A. Rawlins, chief of staff, and Colonels Horace Porter, Ely S. Parker, Theodore S. Bowers and Adam Badeau. The arrangement of the figures in the low-ceiled room of the McLean homestead brings into strong relief the two leaders, whose appearance bears out to the letter General Grant's own description of the event: '

"General Lee was dressed in a full uniform which was entirely new, and was wearing a sword of considerable value, very likely the sword which had been presented by the state of Virginia; at all events it was an entirely different sword from the one that would ordinarily be worn in the field. In my rough traveling suit, the uniform of a private with the straps of a lieutenant-general, I must have contrasted very strangely with a man so handsomely dressed, six feet high and of faultless form."

Thomas Nast did this great work in his studio at Morristown, New Jersey. Mr. Nast had enjoyed the friendship of Grant, and he traced with tender, loving brush the sturdy frame that for so many weary months was the chief support of the Nation. By those who are competent to judge, the painting is pronounced historically correct. The artist had the use of a contemporaneous portrait of Grant and of articles of clothing worn by the victor on the historic occasion. Colonel Frederick D. Grant, General Horace Porter and Colonels Ely S. Parker and Charles Marshall visited the studio frequently, and offered valuable suggestions. The picture was finished April 9, 1895, the thirtieth anniversary of the surrender.

The name of Galena is linked indissolubly with the name of Grant. It will abide, immortal, in the hearts of men. This is indeed sacred ground,—consecrated forevermore to the memory of one of the bravest, sweetest, choicest souls that ever fought for a great cause.

REINCARNATE.

A STRANGE, mysterious tenderness —
Not like the love that lovers know
Who dare to touch in fond caress
The sharers of their blessedness —
    Not this — ah, no! —

Fills all my soul when your sweet eyes
As blue as larkspurs drenched in dew —
Blue as the cloudless summer skies —
Meet mine in sudden, mute surprise
    When I tell you —

That long ago, in years gone by,
When life was young and love was near,
Those azure-tinted eyes of thine
Looked shyly, fondly into mine. —
    You doubt me, dear?

To solve the riddle, maiden fair,
One does not need a magic key;
She whom I loved with love so rare,
Whose beauty was beyond compare—
    Sweet memory!—

Was, little friend, your counterpart—
Your mother whom I used to know,
And who, although I won her heart,
From my life drifted far apart
    Long years ago!

DAYTON, OHIO.   *Eva Best.*

OLD MISSION CHURCH AND HARBOR BEACH.

THE ISLAND OF MACKINAC.[*]

BY EBEN E. REXFORD.

WHOEVER is fortunate enough, as I was, to see Mackinac Island for the first time at sunset, from the water, will never forget it. There will always thereafter be a beautiful picture hanging on memory's wall.

On the first part of our trip up Lake Michigan there had been a gale that would have done credit to the Atlantic, and some who felt sure, from the rolling and pitching of the steamer, that they were never to see land again, had sought the solitude of their cabins in the weariness of the reaction that comes after a day of seasickness and excitement. I was one of these. I had been asleep, and was just waking from a bit of restful dreaming when my friend put his head in at the cabin door to say:

"If you want to see something beautiful, come on deck."

I obeyed him. And I indeed saw "something beautiful."

Our boat had touched at Mackinaw City, a thriving town lying at the extreme northern point of the peninsula of Michigan, and was therefore headed due north for Mackinac Island. The west was bright with the beauty of a cloudless northern sunset, which is a blending of soft rose tints and palest amber in a color that has no name. Against this background stood out, with all the sharpness of a silhouette, the wooded crests of the island. At their feet, following the curve of the little harbor, lay the village with its strange mixture of the old and new. And just above it, on the brow of the crest, the white walls of Fort Mackinac showed against the green pines which cluster in its rear, and above the fort floated the stars and stripes, against the yellow-rose of the sunset sky.

[*] Awarded the prize for the "Best Descriptive Paper" in THE MIDLAND competition which closed June 30th. Its author is a resident of Shiocton, Wis.

THE GRAND HOTEL, MACKINAC.

It was like a dream, or a vision born of a dream. Its spell awed us into silence, under which the beating of the great engine alone was heard. Suddenly there was a boom that startled us like "thunder out of a clear sky," and above the ramparts of the old fort a puff of smoke curled lazily in the air. "Ah, the sunset gun!" we cried, remembering, then, that we had been told a gun was always fired at the sunset hour.

Such were my first impressions of Mackinac.

The island is situated in the Straits of Mackinac, at about their narrowest part. It contains two thousand two hundred and twenty-one acres, of which one thousand acres are in the National Park, which belongs to the United States ;* one hundred acres are in a military reservation, and the balance is made up of private claims.

The base of the island is limestone rock, identical with the lower division of the Helderberg series, while the higher parts of it contain fossiliferous matter

similar to that found in the Upper Helderberg system. The rocks prove undeniably to the geologist one of two things : that ages ago water either stood two hundred and fifty feet above the present level of the lakes, or this island occupies its present lofty position as the result of some tremendous upheaval of nature.

One of the principal objects of interest to the visitor is the old fort. There are two ways of reaching it from the village at its foot : by a road which winds about the bluff on which it is situated and which approaches the top by easy gradations, or a "short cut" up the steps which have been built into the side of the bluff. The climb is a long one, and you will be pretty well out of breath before you reach the level of the fort ; but there are seats here and there along the stairs, for one to rest in, and you will be wise if you take advantage of them, and make a leisurely ascent.

On reaching the fort, your attention will at once be drawn to the old block-house which was built in 1780-82, by British troops. Farther on, you come to the officers' quarters, built in 1876. There is another set of quarters, built in 1833, near another old block-house, whose up-

* Since this article was written, the United States government has decided to abandon the island as a station of defense, and that portion of it belonging to the government has been ceded to the State of Michigan. It will be held as a State Park.

per story is now occupied by a tank into which water is pumped from a spring near by. From this place water is taken by pipes to all the buildings in the fort.

On the right is an old building formerly used as a hospital, about which Indian ghosts are said to gather in the "dead hours of the night." Tradition has it that in times of peace, years ago, there was a surgeon of enterprising and inquiring mind who used his scapel with deadly effect on poor "Lo," for the gratification of his own curiosity and the advancement of science, and the spirits of the victims of his ambitious research still haunt the scene of their untimely taking-off.

The barracks were built in 1859. They are two stories in height. A company of soldiers occupies each floor, with mess-room and other necessary conveniences of army life, which are kept in a condition of neatness that would do credit to any housewife. Grouped about here and there are the guard-house, the office and store-house of the commissary of sub-sistence, the office of the commanding officer and adjutant, and the quarter-master's office. Next to the latter is a bath-house, which the soldiers are required to make use of with religious regularity.

From the gun-platform,—where cannon keep constant guard over, and watch of, the peaceful straits,—one gets a magnificent view of the town and the waters between the island and the mainland. Immediately below us, at the foot of the bluff, are located the government stables, blacksmith shops, and granary. Beyond them are the garrison gardens. Looking out across the straits to the south, we see the hazy shores of Michigan in the distance, with here and there a little island dotting the blue expanse of water. You can hardly look in any direction, at any time, without seeing the smoke of vessels headed for the island, or leaving it, or those engaged in through lake traffic, which do not touch at this point as they go through the straits. The boats that stop here are generally the large steamers carrying passengers, and freight

of the perishable class, which demands expeditious delivery. To the left, four or five miles away, the smoke of the mills and manufactories at St. Ignace darken the horizon. St. Ignace is on the mainland of Northern Michigan, and from this point communication can be had with the outside world by a railroad running south and west through Michigan and Wisconsin, and north to Sault St. Marie. If more direct communication is desired, one can cross to Mackinaw City, thirteen miles to the south. This place is the northern terminus of several roads running through the vast lumber regions of the upper portion of the Michigan peninsula. St. Ignace is a town of considerable importance, being on the mainland and a railroad point. In winter an ice-boat, capable of cutting its way through ice several feet in thickness, makes regular trips between it and Mackinaw City. This boat is large enough to take on loaded cars, which are transferred to the various roads terminating at Mackinaw City. Mackinac Island is dependent on St. Ignace to a great extent in winter for all the necessaries of life, but in summer it asks no odds of its less picturesque neighbor, which seems dull and insignificant compared with the life and gaiety which make Mackinac Island one of the most delightful of our northern resorts. If you visit this place, be sure to take a trip to St. Ignace, to see the beautiful monument erected to Père Marquette, who is buried there.

The village, as looked down upon from the fort, shows a line of ancient and modern houses built mostly on one side of a street that closely hugs the shore line of the harbor. The Grand Hotel, with its hundreds of rooms and "all modern conveniences" contrasts sharply with the old, weather-beaten, tumble-down houses only a stone's throw away. This is the most pretentious public building on the island. Here wealth and fashion reign supreme during the brief season of summer pleasure. It is magnificently furnished, and makes a brave show, but it lacks the quiet, homelike atmosphere which characterizes some of the other hostelries of the place, where people congregate who have come hither in search of rest. One of the most delightful places for the rest-seeking pilgrim to "put up at" is the Old Mission House. There is a charm about its time-stained walls and lichened roof which suggests a bit of old-world life, where everything is peaceful and quiet, and removed from the bustle and rush and "style" which characterize the great hotel at the other end of the town. In it you feel you are part of the life of a by-gone day. You wander through its old garden and at every turn you fancy you are going to meet some adventurer who sought this out-of-the-way place years before you were born, or, perhaps, some pale-faced priest who came hither to tell the Indian of the Christ. It is a place to dream in, as well as to rest in. But if you come for gaiety and fashionable pleasures, go to the Grand Hotel, with its electric lights, its elevators, its velvet carpets and elaborate furniture, its excellent cuisine, its "celebrated orchestra" which discourses sweet music every afternoon and evening in the pavilion on the lawn, —which is itself a glimpse of fairyland

Everything about the fort is a model of neatness and cleanliness. It would seem as if, in times of peace, there was little for the garrison to do but "tidy things up," but the show of war goes on in mimic fashion. Every day you see the blue-clad soldiers out on drill or parade ; every day you hear the sound of fife and drum ; and day and night the sentry paces up and down the ramparts, with his gun upon his shoulder, polished to the last degree of brightness. During the greater part of the season you will hear the sharp crack of rifles from somewhere beyond the fort and, if you are imaginative, you can fancy the enemy has begun an attack. But a little investigation

will show you that the war-like sounds originate in harmless rifle-practice on the target-range. Soldiers are frequently sent here in summer, from other points, for rifle-practice, and occasionally the officers of the fort give a grand ball, at which visiting soldiers and visiting civilians meet, to the mutual pleasure of each class. A garrison ball is a great event in Mackinac Island life. The soldiers, weary of the routine of their life in peaceful times, welcome any change as a relief. The young lady visitor to the island has a romantic idea of military life, and sees in every trim young soldier a possible hero.

But the interest of the visitor to Mackinac Island will not be confined to the fort and its inmates. The scenery of the place is grand and beautiful, and varied in character.

If you go up the beach from the eastern end of town, one of the first points of in-

ROBERTSON'S FOLLY, MACKINAC ISLAND.

terest you will come to is "Robertson's Folly." This is a mighty projection of rock thrusting itself out through great masses of evergreen growth, from the higher level of the island. The place gets its name from a story which the old residents of Mackinac will tell you, and vouch for as true.

Robertson was an officer of the fort at the time of its occupancy by the British. One day, while strolling along the bluff beyond the fort, he saw before him a beautiful woman. He approached her. She turned and ran, looking back over her shoulder at the gallant captain, more in coquetry than in fear. He came quite near her, but all at once she vanished, near the edge of the cliff. He was bewildered by her sudden and mysterious disappearance. Where could she have gone? Long he sought, but could find no trace of her. He went back to the fort and told his story, and made diligent inquiries about the women of the island. No one knew of any who answered his description. There were but few, and these were

ARCH ROCK MACKINAC.

known to all the members of the garrison. No strange woman could be among them, for no boat had touched there for weeks. Next day he saw the beautiful mystery again. He spoke to her, and again she disappeared as mysteriously as before. Day after day the strange appearance and disappearance was repeated. He could think and talk of nothing else. He was laughed at by his companions for being in love with a creature of his own fancy. "The captain isn't just right in the upper story," some of them said. But he declared he had imagined nothing. One day he vowed to solve the mystery if it cost him his life. Tradition has it that that day he met her and implored her to speak to him. She retreated toward the edge of the bluff, smiling back upon the captain, who followed her. She seemed to pause upon the very verge of the abyss. He gave a great cry of fright, thinking she did not realize her dangerous position, and sprang to seize her and draw her back. She flung her arms about him, and with a wild, shrill laugh of triumph that can be heard even yet on stormy nights, if one takes the trouble to visit the spot, she plunged over the bluff, and her victim was hurled down to destruction on the rocks below. Next day they found his mangled body, but no trace could be found of the mysterious creature who had lured him to his death. Some persons who are utterly lacking in reverence for the romantic will tell you that the captain's delusion grew out of too great indulgence in strong old French brandy, but you are under no obligation to believe such a story.

Fairy Arch is a great mass of stone through which wind or wave, or both, have worn an opening of considerable size, high up in the cliff. Maiden Arch is somewhat similar, but more accessible. It affords the geologist an excellent opportunity for studying the formation of rock which prevails here. Arch Rock is a wonderful piece of nature's handiwork. Looking through it, from the bluff of which it is part, one sees the blue waters

MACKINAC ISLAND — BRITISH LANDING.

of the straits flashing in the sun from a point above the tops of the highest trees. If you creep out on the arch and peer over, you shiver at the dizzy prospect below. Lover's Leap is something like Robertson's Folly, only on a grander scale. It takes its name from an old Indian legend which has the merit of being poetical if not truthful.

On the northern point of the island is Early's Farm, one of the most quiet and peaceful spots imaginable to-day, but here, in 1814, a battle was fought between the forces of the United States and Great Britain. Near by is British Landing, where the troops of the king gained entrance to the island the day before the bloody encounter took place.

In those days the present fort was not the chief defense of the island. On the highest ground were rudely constructed breastworks and wood-and-earth defenses known as Fort Holmes. Here may still be seen the pits and embankments of that long-ago time, overgrown with grass and bushes, but still clearly outlined in the space from which all trees were cut away when the fort was built, and which is like an open field to-day. Here is a "look-out" from which a view of the entire island can be obtained.

One of the most striking objects to be seen on the island is Sugar-Loaf Rock. This is a gigantic formation of limestone on nearly the highest portion of the island. About it is the great forest, like a sea, and above the green billows of the towering trees it lifts its mighty crest like a great rock in mid-ocean. Standing at its base and looking up at it, one does not fully comprehend its great magnitude. But climb the look-out on old Fort Holmes and look down upon the forest below; through it the rock rises far above the tall maples and beeches. It has a dignity and grandeur that makes the sight of it in the midst of a forest one of sublimity and impressiveness that can never be forgotten. It lifts its head so far above the trees that they shrink into insignificance and seem but shrubs at its feet. It has been crumbling away for ages. Its base is a mound of *debris* fallen from its sides, gathered there until the ground all about it is covered to an unknown depth. Majestic as it now is, it must have been a vastly more impressive object centuries ago, before ruthless Time had begun to destroy it.

Other interesting points to visit are Scott's Cave, Ruggles' Pillar, Devil's Kitchen, Donan's Obelisk, Chimney

Rock, Skull Cave and Pontiac's Lookout. The National Park is threaded in all directions with roads which it is a delight to drive and ride over, and all points of interest are easily reached from them. In the village comfortable and stylish turnouts can be procured, with careful and intelligent drivers, that can be engaged by the hour, or the day, at a reasonable price.

Near old Fort Holmes is the Military Cemetery, and just across the road from it is the Catholic cemetery where French soldiers and Indian converts to the Catholic faith are buried side by side. A short distance west of the village, near Pontiac's Lookout, is the old Indian burying-ground, with its strange mounds which examination has shown to be each a common grave for those who are supposed to have met death from battle or disease in such numbers, and so suddenly, that general burial was made necessary.

Boating is one of the principal amusements of the summer visitor. Sail-boats of all kinds, skiffs, canoes and row-boats

SUGAR-LOAF ROCK. MACKINAC.

are everywhere seen. Steam yachts and trim little steamers are always making excursions to St. Ignace, Mackinaw City, or some of the out-lying islands. One of the favorite ways of spending the day is to charter one of these boats and visit Round or Bois Blanc Islands, for fishing or for a picnic dinner. The lover of piscatorial sport will find himself in fisherman's paradise here, for the waters abound with lake herring, lake trout, white-fish, muskallonge, pike, rock bass, white bass, yellow perch, and the great lake sturgeon. Bathing is not indulged in to any great extent because the water is too cold for comfort. The average temperature of the water during July is 56° Farenheit; during August, 60°. The middle of the day is warm and summer-like, but after 3 o'clock one finds an over-coat or shawl very comfortable when out of doors. The yearly average of temperature for July and August is about 75° from 10 to 3 o'clock.

The mean surface of the water in the Straits of Mackinac is 581 feet above mean tide at New York. There is a variation of about five feet in the height of water in the straits. The greatest depth of water on the bar between Mackinac and Round Island is forty feet; between Round and Bois Blanc Islands, sixteen feet; between Bois Blanc Islands and the Michigan Peninsula, eighty-four feet; between Mackinac Island and St. Ignace, two hundred and ten feet. The greatest depth of water in the straits is at a point between St. Ignace and Mackinaw City, where it is two hundred and fifty-two feet.

The following table gives the height of places of interest mentioned above the mean surface of the water in the straits:

Fort Mackinac, parade-ground........133 feet
Fort Mackinac, highest gun-platform...181 feet
Fort Holmes, lookout ....338 feet
Top of Sugar-Loaf Rock.............296 feet
Top of Chimney Rock................238 feet
Hubertson's Folly..................129 feet
Arch Rock.......... ....138 feet
Lover's Leap .. ..145 feet
Upper plateau of island ....385 feet

One of the most interesting things to see in the village is an old house which is

said to have been built by those connected with the Great Northwest Fur
Company, when it first occupied the
island as a winter trading-post. It is a
venerable-looking building, now fast falling into decay. In one of the village
stores they will show you John Jacob
Astor's "safe," in which the funds of the
Fur Company were kept. It bears little
likeness to the safe of to-day, being simply a great iron box, with a padlocked
door. In the days when it was in use,
professional burglars must have been unknown. Our modern knight of the jimmy
would think it beneath his dignity to waste
time on such a "strong box" as this.

Mackinac Island has of late years become a favorite summer home for wealthy
residents of Chicago, Cleveland, Detroit,
Milwaukee and other western cities. The
government has not sold building sites to
anyone, but it has leased them at nominal
rates for a term of years. The bluffs
overlooking the town, east and west from
the fort, are now thickly dotted with
houses, some of them very ornate and
expensive, others built more for comfort
than for style.

There are over seventy of these delightful summer homes built along the bluff,
and the social atmosphere that prevails

in this locality is enjoyable. Many families bring with them a full complement
of servants, and "keep house" exactly
as in their city home. Others bring but
two or three servants, and take their
meals at a club-house. There are several
houses of this kind on the bluffs, conducted in a style to suit the most exacting
taste and appetite.

From 3 o'clock to sundown everyone is out of doors. The one street of
the village is gay with promenaders,
among whom one sees everywhere the
blue uniforms of soldiers from the fort
on the hill. The drive along the bluff is
alive with turnouts. The wharves are
crowded with people, for boats arrive
about this time of day from Cleveland,
Detroit, and Chicago. All is bustle and
excitement at this hour.

One day we heard that a soldier who
had been given an honorable discharge
from the army was going away by the
afternoon boat, and they told us we ought
to see the parting of the man with his old
comrades. We went down to the wharf
at an early hour, and waited. By and by
we heard the sound of fife and drum
from the fort on the hill, and presently
we saw the soldiers marching out in
squads, the afternoon sun flashing on

PONTIAC'S LOOKOUT, MACKINAC.

their guns and the bright trimmings of their uniforms. They came down the steep road to the village street and on to the wharf, while the fife shrilled out some patriotic air and the drum beat the time for marching feet. Their old comrade marched with them, but he seemed no longer of them. When they reached the wharf, arms were stacked, and then good-byes were said. The poor fellow who was leaving army life forever seemed to feel as if he were about to lose his last friend. His eyes would fill with tears as his comrades gave the parting hand-shake, and he could not speak. When the steamer's whistle gave notice of departure, the soldiers suddenly formed in two lines and, as their old comrade passed through, each one gave a parting salute. The man walked by faith rather than sight, for tears blinded him. He turned as soon as he reached the deck of the boat and faced his comrades, and I fancied from the look in his face that at the last moment he would willingly have given up his plans for the future and come back to the old life, which he had doubt-less been eager to leave. The bell rang, the steamer was let loose from its moorings, and then, at a signal from the officer in command, the soldiers raised their guns and fired a volley in honor of their departing comrade. The man upon the deck dropped his head and hid his face in his hands, and then the boat swung away from us and we saw him no more.

If you are tired of the fashionable "watering-place" and the stereotyped modern "resort" and want to find a place that is unique, picturesque, health-ful and altogether delightful, visit the Is-land of Mackinac.

THE BOATS.

TO and fro
The white-caps go—
    Sea-gulls are a-flying—
From across the water low
    Come the breakers, crying;
And the waves that ebb and flow,—
    Sighing, sighing, sighing.

Up the bay,
And through the gray
    Mist the storm is bringing,
One by one they make their way,
    Like swift sea-birds, winging;
And their crews debark to-day,
    Singing, singing, singing.

Frank H. Sweet.

"When frostfus Autumn came."

SONGS IN SEASON.

WITH the first breath of Spring,
  With the first blue-bird's wing,
Delight, in Life's employ,
Sang loud a song of joy.

When Summer, crowned with flowers,   When fruitful Autumn came
Reigned through glad days and hours,   Fulfilling Summer's aim,
  Rapture sang thrilling song,   Amid her garlands, lent,
  Nor deemed the time too long.   Ease sang of sweet content.

      And when wild Winter rose,
    Hope, struggling through the snows,
      Paused on a southern slope
      And sang a song of hope.

CHICAGO.   WILLIAM FRANCIS BARNARD.

MIDLAND WAR SKETCHES.

XI. THE BATTLE OF CHICKAMAUGA.

By General R. W. Johnson, U. S. A.
Commanding a Division at Chickamauga.

NO ONE can write the history of this battle from personal knowledge, for no one saw any considerable portion of the field during the engagement, nor witnessed the movements of many of the organizations in that bloody contest. The battle was fought in the woods, and the heavy foliage and dense undergrowth made it impossible for regimental commanders to see both flanks of their regiments. A division commander could have no personal knowledge of the operations of his command, and had to rely upon the reports of his subordinate commanders, which were often not wholly reliable, because of the difficulty of ascertaining the exact truth. All that can be

expected is a report of the individual observations of the several commanders, and then these reports cannot be reconciled and woven into a connected and correct historical account.

A well-written article in the April number of the *Cosmopolitan*, by Judge Albion W. Tourgée, who, in the battle of Chickamauga was a member of Reynolds' division, is undoubtedly correct from his point of view, but to my certain knowledge some inaccuracies have been embodied in his narrative, and some of these I hope to point out before I close.

The Confederate General Bragg evacuated Chattanooga because he could not hold it against an enemy in possession of the commanding hills on the north side of the Tennessee River. When he withdrew, the Union General Rosecrans seemed to believe that the withdrawal was, in effect, as substantial a success for him and his army as a victory gained by battle; that the Confederates would retreat far to the southward before hazarding another stand, and that to gather and secure the fruits of his successful manœuvers it was his duty to cross his army to the south bank of the Tennessee River and order the various parts to move out in all directions, like the spokes of a wheel, and in this way rapidly cover the abandoned territory.

This movement was ordered and continued till General McCook's corps, in which I commanded a division, reached Alpine, Georgia, when the extreme right and left flanks of our army were fully forty miles apart. Surely, had Bragg known the scattered condition of the Federal forces, he, with an army well in hand, would have attacked and defeated them in detail, and thus destroyed our magnificent army.

Finally it dawned upon Rosecrans that Bragg, reinforced by Longstreet's corps from Virginia, did not propose to abandon the country without giving battle. To encounter him successfully it was necessary for Rosecrans to concentrate his army.

Accordingly, McCook was ordered to close to the left with all possible dispatch. This movement began at once, and on the night of September 18, 1863, the corps encamped some fifteen miles from Crawfish Springs. At 1 o'clock on the morning of the 19th, the march was resumed with my division, consisting of three brigades, 4,200 strong, in advance.

On my arrival at the Springs, about 8 A. M., I met General Rosecrans. He ordered me to detach my division and move as rapidly as possible and report to General Thomas. At that time the battle was on, and the roar of artillery and rattle of musketry told plainly that Thomas was heavily pressed. When I reached him he said: "Your arrival is opportune; form your line here and move forward." I deployed the brigades of Willich and Baldwin, and held Dodge's in reserve. As soon as the line was formed, knapsacks and other encumbrances were laid aside and the movement to the front began. Soon we came to some troops lying on the ground. On inquiry I found them to belong to Hazen's brigade, and that they were out of ammunition. A short distance in front of these we encountered the enemy in force, and a desperate battle ensued. The Confederate line was driven back about a mile, with great loss in killed, wounded and prisoners. We also captured seven pieces of artillery. Darkness came on and all was quiet for a short time, but we were not allowed to remain so long.

The enemy under General Pat Cleburne rallied his shattered forces for a final charge. I do not remember to have passed through a more stubborn or deadly conflict than this one, precipitated after dark, when it was impossible to recognize friend from foe. The firing was so heavy that General Baird, whose

GENERAL ABSOLAM BAIRD.

division was not far away, came to my assistance with two of his brigades, and soon thereafter the enemy was repulsed. Judge Tourgée refers to this engagement in these words: "After dark there came from away upon the left the most terrible outburst of musketry, cut now and then with the roar of cannon, we had ever heard. We could only see the flashes as they lighted up the clouds above, but it seemed a thousand times worse than a fight by day, as we sat in the murky darkness and wondered how it fared with friend and foe. This night battle raged for more than an hour, and then ceased as suddenly as it began." The enemy having been driven from the field, quiet was once more restored.

Among the many who were killed in this night fight was that gallant soldier, Colonel P. P. Baldwin, of the Sixth Indiana Volunteer Infantry, one of the brigade commanders, and he was succeeded by Colonel W. W. Berry, of the Fifth Kentucky Volunteer Infantry, a tried and true soldier. A short time after the repulse of Cleburne's command, General Thomas ordered me to fall back and take up a position on a line selected by him from which to operate on the following day. In this line, so far as known to me, the formation of divisions were: Baird's on my left, Palmer's on my right, and Reynolds' on his right. I formed my front line with Dodge's and Berry's brigades, and held Willich's in reserve. Here, without food or water, the tired, jaded men lay on their arms during the night.

As soon as it was light enough to see, on the morning of the 20th, Dodge and Berry fortified their fronts by felling trees and using such materials as were at hand. We confidently expected to be attacked at daylight, but General Polk, who was in our front, very considerately waited till about 10 o'clock, and by that hour we were prepared to give his troops a warm reception. Repeatedly he massed his columns, and hurled them against the Federal line, only to reel, stagger, and fall back, leaving their killed and wounded.

On the afternoon of the 20th, heavy firing was heard on our right and rear, on what was known as Snodgrass Hill. Palmer, recognizing the fact that if Thomas, who was there in person, was defeated, we would have the enemy both

COLONEL W. W. BERRY,
Fifth Kentucky Volunteer Infantry.

in front and rear, proposed that we should send our reserve brigades to that point. To this I readily assented and ordered Willich to proceed with his brigade and report to Thomas. Thomas told me subsequently that the timely arrival of those two brigades contributed largely to the defeat and dispersion of the enemy.

About 4 o'clock I received an order from General Thomas to fall back to Rossville. The movement was to begin at 5 o'clock, with Reynolds; Palmer was to follow; I was to follow Palmer, and Baird was to follow me. When I received the order my division was resisting a determined assault, and I directed the staff officer to return to General Thomas and explain to him that a retreat under the circumstances would prove most disastrous. In a short time he returned with a message from the General authorizing me to exercise my own discretion in the matter. Unfortunately the divisions on my right were not ordered to remain. Just how and when they withdrew I have never known. They could have been gone only a short time before I discovered a line of the enemy, perpendicular to my own, crossing the field in my rear. I was on the south side of the field, and on foot, having but a short time before sent a wounded officer to the rear on my horse. I sent staff officers at once to order the division to move by the left flank and remain in the timber till they had passed around the field and reached the northeast corner thereof. When I reached the timber on the east side of the field, I secured another horse. Here I met General Thomas, who was dismounted, feeding his horse on corn obtained from a neighboring field. I told him of the near approach of the enemy, and he was not long in changing the location of his headquarters.

Owing to the suddenness of the withdrawal of my division from the line it had held for twenty hours, there was some confusion, but before reaching Rossville order had been restored, and we entered town in good shape, about 10 o'clock P. M.

Willich, who had been ordered to Snodgrass Hill, was ordered by Thomas to coöperate with Reynolds in bringing up the rear, and he claims in his report that his brigade constituted the rear guard of all the troops that fell back on that line.

Judge Tourgée was a member of Reynolds' division, and when he asserts that it fought on Snodgrass Hill, I cannot dispute it, but for more than thirty years I have rested in the belief that he was in the line on the right of Palmer. In his admirable article Judge Tourgée says: "The woods in rear of our line were full of moving columns; regiments and brigades, going they knew not where, by roads it was almost impossible to follow. Sheridan and Davis, Johnson and Van Cleve, Negley and Crittenden, marched and countermarched through the baffling umbrage, following now a fancied path, now misled by the trend of a hill, going to the left with no knowledge of where the left was, rushing to the right with only the roar of battle for guide."

Now, if this reference was to me alone, I would let it pass; but I owe it to the memory of the gallant men who laid down their lives on that bloody field, and I owe it to those who survived the fearful struggle, to enter my protest.

Johnson's division did no aimless marching or countermarching, and if any portion of his command was in the rear of Reynolds' division it was Willich's brigade on the retreat to Rossville.[*]

Johnson's division held the position assigned to it by General Thomas on Saturday night till it withdrew Sunday evening at 5 o'clock, in compliance with his order.[†]

I regret that such a well-prepared article as that of Judge Tourgée should be marred by the great injustice done unintentionally to the brave troops I had the honor to command on that occasion.

The reports of the Federal and Confederate commanders, in my opinion, show that the battle of Chickamauga was fought without a plan on either side, and whatever success we may have achieved was due to the gallantry of the various divisions, brigades and regiments acting

[*] Reference is made to the reports of Thomas and Willich, to be found in Rebellion Records, Series I, Volume XXX, Part I; the former on page 254, the latter on page 541.

[†] See Baird's report in the same volume at page 278.

GENERAL J. J. REYNOLDS.

independently. When General Thomas succeeded to the command of the whole, our lines had been broken at many points and many of the troops were fleeing in all directions. The Twentieth and Twenty-first corps had been broken up by detaching divisions to various places on the field to support other commands or to operate independently. That General Thomas was able to accomplish what he did was due to his iron will and the confidence the men had in his courage and ability. Well may he be called "The Rock of Chickamauga."

It may be a matter of interest to some persons to know how this battle was precipitated. Colonel Dan McCook reported to General Thomas that there was a Confederate brigade on the west side of Chickamauga Creek; that the bridges had all been destroyed so that it could not join the main army, neither could it be reinforced.

Thomas sent Brannan with two brigades to capture it. It was but a short time before he called for reinforcements. Brigade after brigade was sent to him, till not only Thomas' corps, but all of Rosecrans' army was engaged. What McCook took for an abandoned brigade was Forest's division of cavalry holding the right of Bragg's army.

There is an interesting incident connected with this battle-field. Before the removal of the Cherokee Indians to the Indian Territory, many of them were encamped on the ground upon which this battle was fought. The cholera broke out among them and many died from the fearful scourge. After its disappearance the Indians named the stream Chickamauga, which signifies "The River of Death." Again it became the River of Death,—to over 12,000 Federals and as many Confederates,—on the 19th and 20th days of September, thirty-two years ago.

A SOUTHERN BATTLE-FIELD.

FAIR is the landscape from this lofty hill;
   So calm it is, so tranquil and serene.
   No sign appears that this was once the scene
Of deadly strife. Yet many, living still,
Have seen the burning tide of battle thrill
   These peaceful slopes. On yonder hillsides green.
   And in the grassy vale that lies between,
Vast armies struggled with heroic will.

But kindly Time upon the scene has spread
   A mantle all-concealing. Naught I see
   That tells of strife. This spot, where armies bled,
Rejoices now in sweet tranquillity.
War's deluge passed, its fierce, ensanguined waves
Have left no scars—save yonder unknown graves.

GRUNDY CENTER.   *Walter Hall Jewett.*

REMINISCENCES OF JOHN BROWN.

By Narcissa Macy Smith.

THE deeds that men and women do, the principles for which they stand, the truths they utter, and the songs they sing, make for them a place in the hearts of the people.

When John Brown and his followers entered the quiet little village of Springdale, in the fall of '57, for a season of waiting, it was the voice of sympathy welling up from the hearts of her people, in the great cause of human liberty which bade them welcome. There never was a prophet or leader who believed himself divinely called, but had his garden into which he went for a deeper baptism of power and broader conception of the work before him. John Brown's Gethsemane was Springdale, and as he walked calmly in and out among her people, his great sympathetic heart was bearing the burden of the shackles of four million of slaves, as though bound with them, and whoever may have questioned his judgment, or the wisdom of his methods, none doubted but that he believed he was raised up by God to strike the death blow to human slavery.

That John Brown felt at home on reaching Springdale is evidenced by the immediate preparation he made for the restful sojourn. Even the gentle admonition of the plain, quiet Quaker folk, "Thou art welcome to tarry among us, but we have no use for thy guns," did not in the least disturb him, for with their words of loyal testimony came the sweet smile of benediction ; and although they would beat his swords into plowshares and his spears into pruning-hooks, he well knew they would take every peaceble precaution that nothing should molest him.

John Brown's character was irreproachable. Many living witnesses testify to the fact that he was a total abstainer from all intoxicating liquors. He did not use tobacco in any form, and his language on all occasions was pure and chaste, making his life a beautiful exemplification of the Scripture text, "As a man thinketh so is he." Henry D. Thoreau, an intimate friend of John Brown, in one of his published books says : "I have heard John Brown say that in his camp he permitted no profanity. No man of loose morals was suffered to remain there, unless, indeed, as a prisoner of war. I would rather have the small-pox, yellow-fever and cholera, all together, in my camp, than a man without principle." Thoreau further says : "John Brown went to the great university of the West, where he pursued the study of Liberty ; and after taking many degrees he finally began the public practice of Humanity, in Kansas. Such were his humanities, and not any study of grammar ; for he would have left a Greek accent slanting the wrong way, and righted up a falling man."

Springdale at that time represented Old and New England, Canada, New York, Ohio, Indiana, and other states, sections and countries ; and the harmonious blending of character, through years of pioneer life, had brought forth a citizenship which, for intelligence and high moral standing was far in advance of the ordinary prairie village. With the mental activity and literary attainments of Brown's men, Realf, Kagi, Cook and Coppuck,* added to the large array of home talent, both men and women, it is no wonder that in the forum of debate that winter passed into local history as a memorable period.

The writer has in her possession the secretary's book of the Mock Legislature held during that sojourn, and it reads like a veritable Congressional or Legislative Record. That the public may see the range of thought and the varied questions

---

* Commonly spelled "Coppoc."

JOHN BROWN'S SONS AT HOME.

which occupied their attention, I have taken the following from the minutes:

December 1, 1857.

The Governor — Emmor Rood — was informed that the House was ready to receive his message. Among his recommendations was one to build a turn-pike from Iowa City to Davenport through the capital of the State of Springdale.

Bill No. 1: To render operative the inalienable right of women to the elective franchise.

Realf gave notice of a bill to render null and void the Dred Scott decision in all the courts and jurisdiction of the State of Springdale.

Cook introduced a bill to make null and void the Fugitive Slave law of this State.

Resolved, That the repeal of the Missouri Compromise was in accordance with the true principles of our national government.

Bill No. 13: Relating to the banking system of the United States.

JOHN BROWN'S SONS AND A CABIN ON BROWN'S TRAIL.

Winn gave notice of his intention of offering a bill relative to the conduct of Commodore Paulding in the arrest of Walker.

The question of prohibition was discussed and it was decided that a prohibitory liquor law was both wise and practical.

A bill [introduced] for the establishment of a manual labor school.

Realf gave notice of his intention of speaking on the constitutionality of the Fugitive Slave law at next meeting.

A bill for the establishment of a college for classical, physiological and political education of women.

Resolved, That the law for the organization of the grand jury be and hereby is repealed.

Resolved, That John Brown is more justly entitled to the sympathy and honor of this nation than George Washington.

The political atmosphere at that time was not all serenity, in proof of which we give the following bit of unpublished

From Photo loaned by Edna M. Smalley.

THE HOME IN WHICH JOHN BROWN WINTERED HIS MEN, IN SPRINGDALE, IOWA.

Kagi gave notice of a bill to establish a militia and harmonial college in the State of Springdale.

Resolved, That we look with regret upon the position which the *New York Tribune* has taken in regard to the reëlection of Stephen A. Douglas to the United States Senate.

A bill to appropriate 50,000 acres of land, to be divided into small farms for the benefit of fugitives from slavery.

history from the pen of Hon. William P. Wolf:

Tipton, Iowa, April 10, 1895.

Respected Friend,—In answer to your request, I gladly add to your reminiscences an incident which came under my personal notice. It is the account of the effort at Iowa City to raise a force to go out to Springdale and capture John Brown, Kagi, Stephens and Coppock, together with about twelve or thirteen negroes, whom they were conveying to Canada and all of whom were stopping with the people at Springdale. In the spring of '59 I had been getting law books to read from a certain firm in Iowa City, whose junior member was quite a rising young lawyer and republican politician, and who was extremely solicitous lest the sentiments and doings of John Brown should be charged up to the republican party, thereby convicting it of being composed of abolitionists; so that when I arrived at his office that morning, he seemed very much excited, and said he thought it the duty of the republican party to have Brown and his men arrested and punished, and the negroes sent back to their masters. He went out of the office with the apparent determination to see that this was done, and in the afternoon I learned that a squad was gathering at a saloon on the east side of the street, near the corner of University Square. I also learned from Craft Coast that Jerome and Duncan, editors of the Iowa City *Republican*, might want to see me, as I lived three miles northwest of Springdale and could carry a message for them. I went to their office and they stated that they were in communication with the officials of the C., R. I. & P. R'y at Davenport, in regard to getting a car for the purpose of transporting Brown's people to Chicago, and that they were awaiting an answer and desired me to wait till they received it, and carry it to Brown at Springdale. I waited until late in the afternoon, when they received an answer granting a certain box-car at West Liberty, which was to be loaded at night, without being billed, and pulled out under the direction of the officers at headquarters, as the agent at West Liberty was an intense pro-slavery man. Jerome and Duncan's office was in a building near the southeast corner of University Square, and they told me to inform John Brown that they would provide him with a room in the same building, where he could spend the night. I learned from Craft Coast that by telling the saloon crowd blood-curdling stories of how they would be waylaid in the woods, on their way to Springdale, he had so worked upon their fears that the uncertain courage they had imbibed soon slipped away, and they at the same time slipped out the back door, some saying they would return after attending to certain domestic labors. It is unnecessary to state that they did not return. I then took the permit of the Rock Island officials and started for Springdale. It was stated in the city that the opposition had sent a scout out on horseback to Springdale in the morning. When about two miles out, in the timber, I saw a horseman approaching at the other end

of a patch of brush that divided the wagon track, and who seemed desirous not to meet on the same track. When opposite, I crossed to his side, and in answer to my questions, he made evasive statements, the import of which I understood, and I said to him that I had an important communication that I must deliver that night, and that if he was a friend of John Brown's he would not deceive me. He asked if I had a letter. I replied that I had, and also something more important. He then said, "I guess you are all right. I am a friend of John Brown's. My name is Kagi, and John Brown has just passed by us." I then turned back with him and overtook Brown riding with a rag peddler in his wagon. He had a blanket over his head and shoulders, concealing his face, the rain then falling being a sufficient excuse therefor. I delivered the permit to him and told him of the efforts made in Iowa City to accomplish his arrest. He simply smiled and said "Ah!" I told him of the room prepared for him where he could overlook the saloon rendezvous. He replied that he and Kagi would occupy it and observe any further proceedings. My brother has a little book by Richmond in which it was stated that Realf and Kagi walked to Iowa City to get the permit, so you will see that mistake is herein corrected.

Yours truly,

WM. P. WOLF.[*]

John Brown's kindliness of heart and strict integrity were shown in all the incidents of his daily life.

When he first arrived at Springdale, a gentleman seeing that his shoes were badly worn, purchased a new pair and gave them to him. He thanked the gentleman, and said, "My shoes are all right and if you are willing I will be glad to give them to one of my negroes who has none at all."

One day John Painter, an old resident and successful farmer, met John Brown and said to him, "I understand you wish to sell your mules, and I want to purchase one of them." Brown replied, "Yes, they are for sale, and I want to ask you how much you think they are worth." Painter said, "I think they ought to bring one hundred and twenty-five dollars apiece." Brown replied, "The mules

[*] District Judge, Eighteenth district of Iowa.

are all right only for one thing, and that is they have the habit of occasionally kicking, and I don't think they are worth but one hundred dollars each." "Very well," said John Painter, "I will give you one hundred dollars for the one I want, and donate twenty-five dollars to the cause in which you are engaged."

It is refreshing after the lapse of years to give to the public this golden rule method of settlement of a business transaction between two honest men.

Although Springdale, strictly speaking, is a prairie village, hard by is the beautiful Cedar River with its clear crystal water, pebbly bottom and rocky banks lined on either side with a heavy growth of trees of great variety, with here and there a little stretch of scenery such as an artist would be glad to gaze upon and transfer to canvas. Nestled among the trees close to the by-road, leading to the timber, in a quiet sequestered spot stood the home of William Maxson, where John Brown and his men were welcome guests during their stay at Springdale. In this peaceful abode, the voices of friends, the birds in the trees, and the very air he breathed, betokened rest for the weary body, while his active, fertile brain was busy perfecting plans for the great deliverance.

In the spring of '59, when the time of departure came, having no further use for his mules and wagons, they were purchased by residents of Springdale. The wagon was the one made especially for his use by the Massachusetts Aid Society and sent to him at Iowa City in care of Doctor Bowen, the bill of lading for which is now in the Historical Society at that place. Moses Butler bought it of John Brown and soon after sold it to Gilbert P. Smith for seventy-five dollars in gold. It remained in use on the Smith farm for twenty years and was known as the John Brown wagon. At a general sale, in 1882, H. S. Fairall, of the Iowa City *Republican*, bought the wagon. He still retains it in his possession, though overtures from Massachusetts and Kansas have been made for its purchase.

When the day came for John Brown to take his final leave of Springdale, he rode on horseback from house to house —the deep mud making it impassable for a vehicle. He bade a tender farewell to friends whose kindness, sympathy and love had given him courage and strength, and, when in tenderness of spirit, grave fears were expressed for his future personal safety, he replied, "God will take care of me, and of the cause for which I am ready to die."

Methinks the heart of our immortal Lincoln beat with stronger pulsations, and his hand held with firmer grasp and guided with surer stroke the pen which traced the words of the Proclamation of Emancipation, because of the human sacrifice on Freedom's holy altar, at Harper's Ferry!

Iowa guarded well the lives of John Brown and his followers while their feet trod her soil, and she has sought on all possible occasions to do honor to the sons for their own sake, and as a tribute to the memory of their father.

———

The mountain home of John Brown's sons at Pasadena, California, situated on one of the foot-hills of the Sierra Madre range, two thousand feet above sea level, is the Mecca of tourists from all parts of our land, and no one has completed the round of places of special interest until this pilgrimage is made. Many readers of THE MIDLAND will remember with pleasure the kindly greeting of the elder brother, Owen Brown, who strikingly resembled his father, and who as host gave glad welcome to all who climbed the steeps to this cabin home, until he himself, putting aside the shackles of mortality, went higher still, through the gates ajar, into everlasting freedom.

The writer recalls with recurring delight, during the winter of '87 and '88, an interesting journey to the Brown sons' cabin. A narrow wagon road is cut winding up the mountain side, which to our right reaches almost perpendicular, high in air, while to our left we gaze into the abyss five hundred feet below, and across the chasm, to range after range beyond. On and on we climb, our gentle horse seeming to know that danger lurks on either side. With steady, careful tread he slowly makes the ascent. Suddenly the road turns round a ledge in the mountain we have been circling, and we find ourselves on the crest of Brown's Peak. A party of tourists are just leaving in the opposite direction, down the foot trail to the valley below, where their teams are in waiting. We pass through the little garden and dooryard, noting the rude implements of husbandry, the out-door oven, and a few goats grazing near, when Owen Brown, who has just waved the party good-bye, turns to give us a friendly hand-shake and bids us enter the cabin. When he finds our old home was Springdale, he clasps our hands again, speaking tender words of appreciation for the kindness shown his father by her loyal citizens.

Looking about the room, the humble bed in one corner, piles of boxes in another, and everything showing the absence of woman's hands, I turned and said:

"Owen Brown, I see that thee has made one great mistake in thy life."

With a beaming smile he asked, "What is it, my friend?"

I replied, "Thee has never taken unto thyself a wife."

"Ah," said he, "true, true, true, my sister, and the sad thing about it is the mistake is irreparable."

We tarried a little while upon this pinnacle, breathing the pure air of heaven, with the mountains in the background towering high above, as if keeping watch over this humble home. Far below lay beautiful Pasadena, the crown of San Gabriel Valley, stretching away through orange groves and vineyards to the sea, where ships lay at anchor. I was awed with the grandeur of the scene before me, and the majesty of the power above me, and thrilled with tender memories of the past, and with the homage shown this spot by the multitude. Turning again to take a last look at the gray-bearded old man before me, I said in my heart, no people on the face of the globe pay higher tribute to true manhood and womanhood than do those of our own America.

SIERRA MADRE.

ENROBED in kingly purple thou dost stand
    A snow-crowned monarch; at thy feet the land
Stretches afar to meet the slumb'rous sea.
About thy whitened summits, flying free,
Are clouds that, 'gainst the blue of heaven displayed,
Like pennants float; the mist-enwreathed cascade
Leaps from thy heights, its pure drops flinging wide,
And falling, mingles with the streams that glide
Through fruited groves and vineyards far below.
No whiter is thine own eternal snow
Than the sweet, drifted orange bloom that gleams
Upon the trees fed by thy mountain streams.
That granite breast of thine withstands the shocks
Of earthquakes, yet among thy piled rocks
Are tender flow'rs, that lend a blooming grace
To the stern grandeur of thy rugged face.

LOS ANGELES, CALIF.   J. Torrey Connor.

FATHER OF WATERS.

" Thy hills
Give back the murmurs of the stream and plain."

SMOKE of the wigwam, slk and soft-eyed deer,
    Far in the North look down upon the rille
Which, gathering for their mighty sweep, ring clear
And soft the unfathamable Pool. Then trills
The woodbird to his mate, and then the mills —
Grim city builders of the West — profane
The wood with jangled harsh discord; the hills
Give back the murmurs of the stream and plain.

More populous grow thy shores. King Traffic's fame
Falls rude upon the ear — like fretting rain —
And more thy pence with trailing foam and farms.
Then bronzed sea-traffickers, where strange craft float,
Catch up the ribbant accents of thy name
And bear it on to silent shores remote.

" King Traffic's fame
Falls rude upon the ear — like fretting rain —
And more thy pence with trailing foam and farms."

BURLINGTON.   W. C. KENYON.

IN AND ABOUT MEXICO.

A VISIT TO PRESIDENT DIAZ.

By Ida Charlotte Roberts.

A VISIT to the chief executive of our own land is so easily accomplished and of such common occurrence that it is scarcely worth mentioning. All can see our President if they wish. Hence, we do not readily comprehend that in other republics the presidents are more exclusive than ours, and it is often with great difficulty that an interview is obtained.

A short time ago it was my good fortune to be in the City of Mexico. We had the usual offers from guides and interpreters to show us about the city, and after due consideration we decided to employ as our "Moses" to guide us through the wilderness of sights, a man who purported to be the son of the successor to the illustrious Santa Anna, and who said that he was Diaz's first interpreter, and also General Geronimo's. He showed us his father's picture among those of other presidents, and

asked me if I saw any resemblance. Truth compelled me to say that the picture was so small I could not see the "family likeness." We felt it our duty, as we were paying for information, to believe everything he told us. Occasionally, while listening to his story of some miraculous thing that had happened, we were inclined to doubt, but we usually thought better of it and went on believing.

He promised to take us to call on President Diaz, who comes in from his Chapultepec residence on certain days and receives visitors for a short time at the National Palace.

Just after noon on a certain Friday we went to the palace and sent in our cards, and were asked by the servant if we had come on business, or, if not, then for what purpose, what titles we bore, etc. We had to confess that we were only private citizens. We were told to return at

SCENE IN THE CITY OF MEXICO — ZOCALO Y CATHEDRAL IN BACKGROUND.

A HOLIDAY SCENE.
The 1894 Celebration of the Anniversary of Mexican Independence, September 16, 1894.

4 o'clock. As we left the palace we met Colonel Priscillamo M. Banibez, one of the President's staff, who told us if we would come at 5, he would be there and attend to us personally.

Like children who are invited to a party and are afraid they may be late, we arrived before the appointed time. We were shown into a long, narrow room, on the floor of which was a light Brussels carpet of a greenish color, and which was seated with immense, leather-covered chairs and sofas. I was informed that these, with the ones in the next room, were purchased in Chicago last year.

In this room were about thirty other people, all bent on the same errand. We sat there very demurely, looking at each other and wondering who would be chosen first to enter the august presence. After what seemed to be a long time — only about fifteen minutes — an attendant came to the door, from an inner apartment, and called the names of twelve or fifteen people, who, as they were named, filed into the next room. I never thought my name was specially euphonious, but

coming from the lips of the attendant and sounding through the spacious apartment, it had a highly pleasing sound that I had never noted before. The fact that the majority of those present waited in vain to hear their names gave us an indescribable feeling of superiority. The second degree was much like the first, only all of those in the room were congressmen or generals, excepting ourselves. Among them was Benito Juarez, son of the illustrious and much-loved President Juarez, whose monument is in a little plaza in the city, and for whom the city of Juarez was named. We were introduced to him and he conversed very pleasantly with us, speaking English fluently.

After a long wait our party was summoned by the attendant into another room to take the third degree. In this room was the Colonel, dressed in full uniform. He wrote on a card, giving the card to the guide for me, stating that Col. Priscillamo M. Banibez kissed the feet of Miss Roberts and had the honor to be at her service. This was a little surprising, but I learned that "kissing the feet" was equivalent to our "presents compliments" and is so commonly used that only the abbreviation b. l. p. is necessary. Our conversation with the Colonel was very limited, as he knew no English and our Spanish was not of the conversational sort, being only suitable for making purchases, giving orders, etc. But we smiled sweetly and profusely, which probably counted for quite as much as words.

I removed my right glove as the guide directed and we sat there, not with bated breath, but wishing the ordeal were over as our dinner hour was fast approaching.

Black is the proper color in which to call on the President and this was fortunate for me, as the only dress I had there was black. Bright colors are worn but little by the *elite* or, indeed, by any one in Mexico. After the clock had struck six and when we were beginning to wonder if the person who was with the President would never leave, the door softly opened behind us, and we three were ushered into that presence, admission to which so many seek in vain.

There, to one side, amid the shadows of the darkened room, stood the stately, handsome Porfirio Diaz, in his plain, dark business suit, with his hand outstretched toward us, and his face wearing a charming smile. After giving us hearty handshakes, he beckoned us to seats and he himself took a seat near us. The other member did most of the talking, which our guide interpreted. President Diaz understands a good deal of English, but will not attempt to speak it. He assured us that he was always glad to see any of our people and thought that, as we were such near neighbors, we ought to be brothers and sisters.

I think we remained fully three minutes and then made our adieus. We marched out through the waiting-rooms and looked with compassion on the weary ones who were still waiting. Some, however, having given up in disgust or despair, had gone away.

We went down stairs and back to the Iturbide hotel, and among our friends made quite a little of our visit, but until we had met Minister Gray and Consul-General Crittenden and other people from the United States, we did not appreciate how greatly we had been honored in being given an audience by the chief

CASTLE OF CHAPULTEPEC.

executive. Messrs. Gray and Crittenden both assured us that we were fortunate, indeed, and the latter said that it was only a chance in a hundred that one could see the President, and that he had gone more than once before being able to do so.

The National Palace is a two-story stone building, stuccoed, occupying the east side of the Zocalo or Plaza de Armas, one of the two important plazas in the city. On the north side of this plaza is the Great Cathedral, on the site of the old Aztec temple, in which cathedral President Diaz was married. Immediately after the church ceremony, he and his wife went out and had the civil ceremony performed. This is necessary as no church marriage is legal. Mrs. Diaz is a very devout Catholic, but her husband is not.

The National Palace contains the ambassadors' hall, a very long and comparatively narrow room with a plain floor of wood, uncovered, at each end of which is a chair, one the chair used by the President, the other, made by the Mexican women, and given to Mrs. Diaz. It will be remembered as occupying a place on the second floor of the Woman's Building at the Columbian Exposition. Many wondered why it should be there. It was to show the work—the fine embroidery—of the Mexican women. I was urged to sit in both these chairs, and the attendant addressed me as "Senorita Presidente," which he seemed to think very complimentary and deserving of remuneration on my part. Paintings of ex-presidents and other historical personages adorn the walls, and we were happy to see among the number the benign face of our Washington looking down upon us. There are many rooms interesting to visit, one having the walls covered with red silk in which are woven designs of crowns, and a design of Maximilian's coat of arms. This was done during Maximilian's time of power. The President has a handsome private room where he can make his toilet, and is shaved while his advisers and men of influence sit near him

and converse. There are the cabinet rooms, Senate chamber, etc., and the building corresponds in its uses to our Capitol at Washington. The palace was built in 1693, and has been occupied by twenty viceroys and by Maximilian.

On another day we visited Chapultepec, the Mexican "White House," about three miles west of the city. From it one of the grandest and most picturesque views imaginable can be obtained. The city, the beautiful valley and the encircling mountains with grand old Popocatapetl to the southeast, all combine to make the scene one never to be forgotten. It is what the Mexicans call a "buena vista."

Chapultepec, the "Hill of the Grasshopper," is several hundred feet higher than the city, and is readily seen at different points in the valley. Here was Montezuma's favorite park, and as we wander or drive about among the stately trees and thick shrubbery we almost expect to see his dusky visage peer out from the thicket. The bath he used to delight in is now used by the city water-works department. Here are some of the most magnificent trees in existence. One cypress we saw was one hundred and seventy feet high and the trunk forty-six feet in circumference.

On one side of the hill in the lower part is a cave through which there is said to be an opening into the castle above. Iron bars prevented us from making an investigation.

The Mexican "White House" makes a much more commanding appearance than ours, being situated on an eminence. It is grayish in color and is surrounded by broad verandas, and the interior is handsomely appointed. A large military and naval school is at the rear of the castle, and is apparently perfect in its arrangements and courses of study. The castle was built by Viceroy Galves and was at one time occupied by Maximilian, since which time it has been somewhat remodeled.

The Governor of the National Palace, General Juan Villegas, was at Chapultepec the morning we were there. He

Is a charming man. He insisted on our making him quite a visit and made many suggestions in regard to our sight-seeing in Mexico. One of his first questions was, "How long were you prisoners in the Pullman coming to the city?"

To the young military student who was detailed to show us over the school, and who could speak a very few English sentences, but was anxious to learn more, I remarked, "When I come again perhaps you will be a general or hold some other office." He said," Das is me aspiration." Mexican boys are ambitious, as well as our own, and I was glad to find it out, as they have a reputation for slowness, procrastination and don't-care-ism.

The Paseo, one of the famous drives of the world, leads from the city to Chapul-tepec, and every morning early, and every afternoon, the fashionable world of the city may be seen driving here. Statues line part of it and it is the intention to have the entire drive lined with them, which will add much to its already great beauty.

We could not help thinking, while visiting the National Palace and Chapultepec, of the many interesting events that have transpired in these historic places. Our admiration for Mexico's brave men was measurably increased. Not the least of these is Porfirio Diaz,—now occupying the president's chair for his fourth term, the third consecutive one. His aims and aspirations and hopes are evidently all for the good of the republic, for which he has already done so much. "Viva Presidente Diaz!"

VOICES OF WANING SUMMER.

SWEET PEAS.

CAMEO tinted, and sunset hued,
    Even the softest winds seem rude,
As they fall against thy delicate sprays.
A tendril entwined and intricate maze
Of pale sea green, and pink and white,—
The fairiest colors of woven light.
And there they lie on my lady's dress,
And their perfume comes like a soft caress,
From the beautiful gardens of long ago,
Where dead love lies, as white as snow.

THE SUNFLOWER.

THE sun has photographed upon the fields
    A myriad golden pictures of his face,
A myriad lesser suns, that wheel and watch
    His glowing course throughout the azure space.

THE KNIGHTED CORN.

AS sultry Summer aged grows,
    Along the rows of corn she goes,
And knights each subject standing there,
And gives each one a plume to wear,
And straps below each coat of green
A golden sword, all bright and clean,
With which to fight the warrior Want
When he shall come the bed to haunt
Of th' aged, weary, dying year,
Fast falling on his wintry bier.

SOUTH OMAHA, NEB.

W. Reed Dunroy.

MIDLAND WAR SKETCHES.

XII. SEALING THE FATE OF THE CONFEDERACY—SCENES AND INCIDENTS OF THE BATTLE OF CHICKAMAUGA.

By Colonel A. G. Hatry.

IT IS now thirty years since the close of the War of the Rebellion, and it seems to me that, as the years roll by, the lessons taught by this severe struggle for national existence become more interesting. The government is now wisely taking possession of the greatest battle-fields and laying them out in National Parks, for two objects: one to preserve them as resorts of pleasure and interest, and the other as studies for our army and its officers and soldiers. The greatest of these is the park now about to be finished at Chattanooga, reaching from that city eight miles to Chickamauga, including the whole of that famous battle-field. Much contention has existed between officers and soldiers of the late War, as well as historians and civilians, as to what battle or event did more to crush the Rebellion than any other. Many contend that it was the Battle of Gettysburg; but history and events, as well as the admissions of many of our most prominent generals on both sides, now place that battle merely as one of the great battles of the War and a fatal experiment on the part of the Confederacy. The battle was a great loss to them in numbers, but it left the situation the same. Lee abandoned Pennsylvania and retreated to his old base in Virginia, and the situation remained *in statu quo.* I therefore contend that the capture of Chattanooga and the Battle of Chickamauga broke the backbone of the Rebellion and, as one of the greatest Confederate generals remarked, sealed the fate of the Southern Confederacy. He says, "they fought stubbornly to the last, but, after Chickamauga, with sullenness and despair and without the enthusiasm of hope." The following reminiscences and sketch will, to some extent at least, substantiate my assertions.

The army to which I had the honor to belong was the Army of the Cumberland, and operated in the Southwest. During the summer of 1863 this army was marching on its way under the leadership of those two great strategists, Generals W. S. Rosecrans and George H. Thomas, against the enemy's great stronghold, the city of Chattanooga. This campaign was directed against a city which was the very key to the interior of the Confederacy, the crossing point of its greatest lines of railroads from all directions, the citadel of Georgia and the whole interior South. So long as Chattanooga remained in Confederate hands their power was practically unbroken, the great Slave Empire was untouched. In an interview with a prominent Confederate general regarding this movement, he said: "When General Rosecrans commenced his forward move-

ment for the capture of Chattanooga, we laughed him to scorn; we believed that the black brow of Lookout Mountain would frown him out of existence, that he would dash himself to pieces against the many and vast natural barriers that rise around Chattanooga, and that then the Northern people and the government at Washington would perceive how hopeless were their efforts when they came to attack the real South." How sadly were they mistaken!

General Bragg was in command of the Confederate army and had erected strong fortifications at Tallahoma, but at our approach, after a slight skirmish, evacuated the place and retreated to his stronghold, Chattanooga. Jefferson Davis, the Confederate President, became alarmed and sent two of the great Confederate generals to his assistance, Longstreet and Hill, with their invincible fighting Virginians. These troops openly boasted that they intended to show those Western Yankees how they had whipped the Yankees in the East. We toiled over hills and mountains toward the Tennessee River; the country between Tallahoma and this river is almost a barren waste of unproductive timber and woods. How well I remember our march, day after day, over this barren country, where even water was scarce, and how we rejoiced as we reached the Sequatchie Valley at the foot of the mountains, with its abundance of good water and its green fields teeming with vegetation,— the garden spot of Tennessee. How good the roasting ears tasted! How comfortably we rested!

After a few days we again started and soon stood upon the banks of the Tennessee in sight of Chattanooga, which, strange to say, General Bragg evacuated. On our approach he retreated to the Chickamauga Valley, south of Chattanooga, there to await our coming to give us battle. Crittenden's division occupied Chattanooga, while the rest of the army were again obliged to cross two vast mountain ranges, Raccoon and Lookout. This was accomplished with great labor and fatigue. To do this the army was

obliged to march by different routes, and the divisions were often separated many miles. General Bragg occupied the gaps and defiles on the opposite side and expected to capture us in detail. In this, however, he was mistaken, for we so outwitted him by feints and strategic movements, that September 17th found our army well in hand at the head of Chickamauga Valley, and by the 18th we had concentrated at Crawfish Springs. Our brigade came down the mountain into Pound Gap and we marched all night through thick dust, and reached the Springs at daylight on the 19th. As the morning dawned we heard our advance troops firing, which increased every moment. It now became evident that a battle was about to be fought. We were told to have our coffee made as quickly as possible, as we were soon to go forward. During the cooking we heard the cannons boom.

It would be difficult to describe a soldier's feelings in a time like this. There is little said, everybody is thinking, some try to be cheerful and joke, but the effort is not appreciated by the majority. We get through, slow away what we can in our haversacks, the order is "forward, double quick," and almost before we know it, we are in sight of the Rebels and the Battle of Chickamauga is begun.

Our troops were worn out by constant marching for weeks, while the Confederates had been resting and were fresh and eager for the fight, and, with the advantage of good condition, they were also one-third in excess of our number.

After the first day's fighting the victory was on the Union side. The battle was fought in a dense wooded wilderness. Facing north, the battle-field is bounded on the east by Chickamauga Creek, west and north by Missionary Ridge and gaps leading to Chattanooga, and south by Lafayette and Lee & Gordon's Mills. The day was very sultry and water was scarce. On our extreme right near the Widow Glenn house — an old log cabin — was a pond of fresh water to which our men went for supply. It was right between the lines and the Rebels planted a battery to cover this spot, which opened on our men whenever opportunity offered, until so many were killed that the water turned into blood. It still goes by the name of Bloody Pond.

Night ends the first day's fighting of Chickamauga and we rest in the woods, everyone thinking "what will be done to-morrow?"

I commanded a company, but was unfortunate in being detailed to go on picket duty for the night, a duty extremely hazardous on such an occasion. I shall never-forget that night. Through all the long hours the Confederate troops were constantly moving and new troops and reinforcements arriving. Our army was at work fortifying certain positions, and particularly the road leading to Rossville, and I knew that the next day the battle would be renewed with redoubled energy, and so it proved.

It was Sunday morning, and at the first dawn of day the Rebel pickets opened on us and with the greatest difficulty I got my men back to our lines, but not without leaving a number killed and wounded behind, and shortly after 9 o'clock the battle opened in all its fury and swayed from left to right and center. Our division was the center. We had a barricade of logs thrown up during the night and were ordered to hold the road at all hazards, and upon this, first General Buckner's, then Stewart and Cleburne's divisions made desperate charges, only to be repulsed with heavy losses.

I remember a captain, slightly wounded, came into our line to surrender, and as he went to the rear I asked him where he came from. He said he belonged to Buckner's Confederate Kentucky troops and served with Longstreet's corps from the Army of North Virginia. He claimed he had been in the Eastern army all through the War, but had never seen such fighting; he said he much preferred fighting the Army of the Potomac to fighting us Western Hoosiers.

About noon, through some misunderstanding of orders, a division on the right of the center was withdrawn to support the line further to the left, where the fighting was very severe, thus leaving a gap in our line. Longstreet, perceiving this, pushed in eight brigades, and thus getting in our rear, caused our lines to waver, and somewhat demoralized the right. All would have been lost had not General Thomas come to the rescue, rallying the broken line and falling back a short distance to Snodgrass Hill, where he made his stand, and thus connected this position with the center and left where our division lay behind the logs. In this position we repulsed all their attacks.

General Thomas well deserves the name of the "Rock of Chickamauga." He was always in the right place at the right time. Thus, the battle waged until nearly sundown, when, finding that we could not maintain our position any longer, General Thomas concluded to withdraw to Rossville Gap. He was not a moment too soon, for the Rebel General Lidell had worked his division of fresh troops to our rear and across the road leading to the gap, and was opposing our way with several batteries of artillery and a strong line of infantry. We were now really surrounded, — Confederates on every side. The situation looked indeed desperate.

I well remember that General Thomas approached General Turchin, our commander, and said to him, "General, you will have to clear the road; give them the bayonet and don't stop until you drive them beyond the woods."

Where they were stationed was the famous Kelly field, for whose possession four charges had already been made during the afternoon, and this was to be the fifth and last. This field was a half-mile long and a quarter of a mile wide, and there stood a wall of cannon and muskets at its end.

The charge is sounded and off we start across this field, the Confederates opening on us with shell and cannister. General Turchin on his gray horse leads the charge, the shells bursting in our lines, plow great furrows through them, but they close up and on we go. One big shell bursts in my company, kills and wounds eight of my men. The explosion stuns us all but we recover quickly. There is no time to look after our poor comrades. A shell kills General Turchin's horse and he falls to the ground, but rises, quickly disengages himself and turns to the men shouting "Forward! Forward!"—and on we go. As we near the enemy's lines the infantry opens on us and we meet a rain of lead, but we close up more determined than ever, and thus we strike their line, and hand to hand we drive them from their guns, which we disable. Their line is broken and they give way and run; we drive them beyond the woods, and the road to Rossville is ours, and Chattanooga is safe!

General Thomas, in his report to the War Department, says of this charge: "I ordered General Turchin to file to the left and, after changing front, ordered him to charge the Rebel lines. This he did, faced to the front while moving at a double quick and darted at a run into the faces of the enemy." It was one of the bravest, most brilliant, most important and effective charges of the day, the fifth and last over these Kelly fields, thus ending the most sanguinary and bloodiest battle of our Civil War, and the greatest of any War in the history of the world. The following few statistics will substantiate this fact:

The Army of the Cumberland, under General Rosecrans, went into this fight with 58,000 men all told. General Bragg on the first day had 76,219, and on Sunday, with his reinforcements, had 81,219, nearly one-third more than the Union forces. Our total loss was 16,179, while the Confederate loss was 17,804. Thus the loss of each army was nearly 30 per cent of the entire force engaged, and on Sunday the losses averaged 36 per cent. The losses of regiments and brigades were often as high as 45 per cent to 75 per cent. Helms' Confederate brigade lost 75 per cent, while in many of our own regiments, mine included, the loss was 50 per cent.

Let us compare this with the battles of European nations:

Waterloo was one of the most desperate and bloody fields chronicled in European history, and yet Wellington's casualties were less than 12 per cent. His losses of killed and wounded were 11,960 out of 90,000 men. At the great battle of Wagram, Napoleon lost but 5 per cent. At Contras, Henry of Navarre was reported as cut to pieces, yet his loss was less than 10 per cent. At the great battles of Marengo and Austerlitz, sanguinary as they were, Napoleon lost an average of less than 14½ per cent. In the Franco-Prussian War in 1870, at Werth-Specran, Mars La Tour, Gravelotte and Sedan the average was 12 per cent. The losses of other battles in our own War seldom averaged over 25 per cent.

The loss of Chattanooga was a great blow to the Southern Confederacy and one from which it never recovered. Fate seemed to be against it. The failure of the Confederates to recover Chattanooga after desperate efforts in the battles of Missionary Ridge and Lookout Mountain, and the failure of the Atlanta campaign and loss of that city, with Sherman's march to the sea, were all events that followed thick and fast. Their cause was lost. Their failures in Tennessee and beyond the Mississippi River and in Virginia were but as the night that follows the day. Their last ditch was in sight.

HOME THEMES.

I HAVE been thinking a good deal lately about the cultivation of manners in the home. There are no schools where we can learn manners, at least none that are accessible to the most of us, even if we were not already through with lessons, save those learned in the school of life. So it seems to me the best we can do is to fit ourselves for teaching,—we mothers, I mean,—and start private schools in our own homes.

I remember reading once a little anecdote of an olden-time lady who, when reproved by a Puritan father for wearing scarlet bows on her shoes, replied that she wanted her little son to remember her as having worn scarlet ribbons. There is a beautiful thought beneath the words. To be remembered by our children as having been possessed of peculiar charms and graces, as having been different from this girl's mother, or that boy's mother, though by only the wearing of a scarlet ribbon, it seems to me, were worth living for. And then the dainty bows of scarlet signified something more. A nameless charm was tied in their folds that pervaded the whole attire, the walk, the voice, the conversation of her who wore them ; at least, I like to fancy it so.

This brings me to my starting point ; namely, the manners in the home — fine manners, the charm by which our children shall remember us. We have Miss Parloa, with her recipes and her cooking-schools, and Jenness Miller, the picturesque advocate of dress reform ; we have Emily Willard and her temperance reform ; why cannot some one start a Home Manners crusade and make it popular? It would give the world a strong push onward toward the millennium,—indeed it would. I cannot imagine very many coming from homes where the perfection of fine manners pervades the very atmosphere and joining the ranks that move downward. Courtesy shown by parent to parent, and by child to child, and by child to parent and by parent to child — company manners used every day, and not put away with the best china or hidden carefully in the folds of the fine table linen ; no loud tones, no rudeness, no cutting speeches, no petty selfishnesses — O, what a delightful place this old world would be to live in ! I suppose we mothers might start this crusade, this " Home Manners" reform, right in our own homes. There is full scope there for all our powers. Husband, children, man-servant, maid-servant, stranger within our gates, will all unconsciously be our pupils. And so, not by the scarlet ribbon, but by the golden rule written on our foreheads, will our children remember us.

Grundy Center. —*Mary E. P. Smith.*

PASS IT ON.

Pass it on !—
The little deed
That was done you in your need —
Pass it on !
Do not think to pay back double
For a kindness done in trouble,
Pass it on !

Pass it on !—
The ray of light
That has made your day more bright —
Pass it on !
If the word so sweetly spoken
Seemed to you a kindly token,
Pass it on !

Pass it on !—
The bit of gladness
That has driven off your sadness —
Pass it on !
It perchance may cheer another
Weary, struggling, tired, brother,
Pass it on !

Peoria, Iowa. —*Josie Haynes Canaday.*

THE VICTOR.*

ONE *Spring,—the time of birds, of flowers, of mirth,—*
Fate took a prisoner from the glad, green earth
And shut him in a dungeon, cold and gray,
Dim with the twilight of a bygone day.
"Here will I nourish thee with bitter bread
Of sorrow and the cup of tears," he said,
"And here each night a hopeless head thou'lt lay,
Pillowed on mocking dreams of yesterday.
No brighter morrow comes; but, lest too soon,
I'ining, my victim 'scape me, ask one boon."
"My loom"—the wretched prisoner plead—" whereon
I labored in the happy days agone.
Happy my hand—for here naught else may strive—
Shall keep its cunning, and my soul alive."
Fate grimly nodded. And new life upsprang
Within the prisoner as he worked and sang;
Yea, sang! For think you that the dungeon's blight
Fell on his web? Nay, rather, by his might
And magic art did birds of wondrous hue
Flutter across it; flowers budding grew
Upon its meshes; all things strange and rare
That flourish in a brighter, purer air.
Though round about him chattering bats did dart,
A god's creative joy possessed his heart.
Thus wrought he many years within his tomb,
Weaving a web of beauty and of bloom
For after ages.— Then Death's solemn tone
Rang on his ears. "O Angel, now I own
Blest was my lot and happy my estate;
Though mortal, heaven-taught, I conquered Fate!"

BERWYN, ILLS.   ELIZABETH M. BLANDEN.

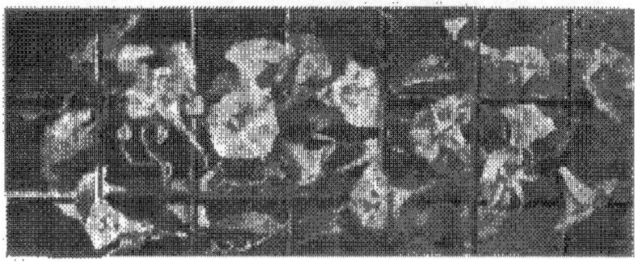

Drawings by Mary A. Bishop
*Awarded the prize for the Best Original Poem in the June 30th Competition.

WHEN THE HOT WINDS BLOW.

By George William Gerwig,
Author of "The Return," in The Midland of December, 1894.

TOWARD the end of a growing day in July, the air full of that swishing sound and that sugary odor so characteristic of a corn-field—warm, damp, oppressive, in spite of the breeze that blew across the prairies. A single team plodded backward and forward between the corn rows, the plowman whistling softly to himself, oblivious to the stifling heat, because it seemed an earnest of a bounteous harvest,—a harvest that meant so much to him. Nothing distinguished him especially from any other young man except his eyes, so large, brown and sympathetic.

His mother used to say that she could always tell the mood he was in — and he was a creature of moods — if she could either see his eyes or hear his whistle. It was no ordinary whistle, for it had the velvety softness and sympathetic range of a 'cello. Just now it happened to be Mendelssohn's "Spring Song" that he was whistling,—one of the treasures his memory had brought from his earlier life in old York State.

And as he whistled he thought; thought of all he was missing out on the plains, in music and in art. He longed, as he had so often done before, for the full notes of an organ, for a Thomas concert, or a Spring Art Exhibition. There is one thing on the plains however that almost makes up for the absence of many other delights,—the sunset. He grudged the time it took him to plow the eastward row, though the interval made his appreciation keener when he again faced the glowing west. On and on into the deepening twilight he plowed, building and rebuilding his air-castles. If things would turn out as he hoped! His thoughts were back at the university. Perhaps — who

knows! — if the corn only yielded well enough he might be able to take a year in Germany after graduating; or if they could have one of the phenomenal crops everybody talked about he might even take the coveted doctorate at Berlin.

With a start, as if suddenly awakening from a dream, he noticed that his team showed signs of weariness. He stopped instantly, just where he was, and going to the heads of the horses, patted and stroked them, soothing them with pet names before beginning to unhitch. After providing for them all the comfort that the shed of a stable would furnish, he neared the house. It was only a dug-out, the conventional first home of the sturdy pioneers who take up claims on the virgin prairies. But a dug-out, or a sod house, in spite of its homely appearance, often gathers about itself in the passing years as sacred memories as did the old log houses in the uncleared forests of Pennsylvania and Ohio, when *they* were "west."

His mother was in the doorway smiling a welcome.,

"You are tired, aren't you?" she said.

"No, mother, not very; the horses were, though, so I stopped. If this weather only holds we'll have a glorious crop, and then —— "

They both smiled in anticipation of all that a good year meant to them. While he was getting ready for supper his mother told him of her little visit,—for even the seven miles she had to walk had not kept the neighborly Mrs. Duncan from seeing Bartley's new baby, and visiting the Swede family, beyond, in which there was sickness. She told him of her long walk across the prairies; how cool and fresh it seemed at first; how she rested here and there beside the ominous piles of whitened bones that marked the old California trail; how weary the way at length became as the sun rose higher, until she almost wished she had listened to his plea to take one of the horses, even from the plowing. She told him of the wonderful baby, of the father's almost frantic delight, and of Mrs. Bartley's gratitude for the little bouquet of old-fashioned flowers.

"Mr. Bartley says he's going to get that boy the finest baby-carriage this side the Mississippi,—if the corn only comes out all right!"

Then she told him of the Jansens; how much her home remedies seemed to help the sick Swede, how fearful Mrs. Jansen was lest her husband's illness should prevent them from paying the mortgage; how hard it would be if after all their efforts they should lose their little farm.

Then Jack got his books, lit the student lamp, and settled down for an evening's study. But it was an ordeal to keep awake, for tired nature would assert herself, in spite of his most rigid determination. Every evening he fought the same battle. His mother always sat near him with her sewing, giving him the moral support of her presence. He had asked her, time and again, to arouse him when she saw that he was becoming drowsy. But as she watched him nodding over his studies, then catching himself with a start and trying again, only to nod once more, she had not the heart to deprive him of the much needed rest.

"My boy, I think you need the rest more than you do the study," she would say, in reply to his protests at not being wakened. There was always a struggle for an hour or so. Then the sleepiness would be conquered by sheer force of will, and he would pore over his books intently until the time he and his mother had agreed upon as a compromise hour for quitting.

"I must keep up my work or fall behind my class," he said, in answer to all protests. She was as ambitious for him as he was for himself, so this plea usually

won. As the son studied, the mother rocked and knit; and as she rocked she kept thinking of a question Mrs. Jansen had asked her:

"Mees Duncan," she interrupted suddenly, "what for you come live way out here?"

"The settlers" on the western edge of our prairie country have all come from somewhere else. It is only a question of how long ago and for what reason. The reasons have almost always some of the tragedy of life about them. They tell of shattered fortune, shattered health, and sometimes, too, of shattered reputation, and of that pathetic yearning for another chance, a new trial. They tell, often, of revolt against the hard conditions and hopeless grind of foreign lands, and of flight to that golden America of which so many fables have reached them,—to find, alas, that the golden rewards come only as a result of persistent endeavor, of relentless activity, of suffering and heartache. · They sometimes tell of a breaking away from the class distinctions and complications of an effete civilization, in a wild, uncontrollable hope for an independent, self-reliant manhood and womanhood that asks nothing more than to stand or fall on its own merit.

She thought of her early married life in New York State, of Jack's birth, of their journey to the Middle West, of her husband's death, and the troubles that followed compelling Jack to leave the university at the end of his sophomore year and to come with her to this frontier claim,—the only thing remaining for them. They both consoled themselves with the reflection that as soon as the corn crop was in, the real hard part of the struggle would be over, and he could get back to the university and to an equal chance with the other fellows.

Time passed, each week bringing nearer the hope of a bountiful harvest. There was a thrill of joy in the air; Jack whistled now. Three weeks more of the right kind of weather and all would be well. There had been no rain for ten days, but the ground was still in good condition. He gave it an extra plowing making the most of the moisture from the dew. Two weeks passed, but still there came no rain. The freshness was gone from the prairie and everything began to show the effects of dry weather. Mother and son, each trying to keep up the courage of the other, prophesied in turn that rain must come soon and that the crop was all right *yet*. It was the "Miserere" from "Il Trovatore" that Jack whistled most now. It seemed to express, better than anything else, the vague but powerful yearning that had taken possession of him.

> "Ah! I have sighed to rest me
> Deep in the quiet grave."

These were the words of that divine plaint, but the notes, as he caressed them, expressed his meaning without need of the words. He remembered the vivid description of a desert by Pierre Loti, and that wonderful "Passion in a Desert" of Balzac's. By a rare fatuity his mind was filled with all the drought and desert lore he had ever read, and he wondered apprehensively whether this claim of his, in which he had come to take so deep an interest, was to be burnt back to that brown barrenness and desolation.

Another week passed, a week of torment. The bodily suffering it brought was all but unbearable. Added to that was the mental torture. They were powerless; there was absolutely nothing they could do except wait, and pray for rain. The heat during the day was blinding, but the nights and early mornings were still fresh and cool, seeming to taunt them with the beauty of relentless Nature. The sunsets were superb; but what heart had they for beautiful sunsets! The starlight was clear and magnificent; but there was no sign of rain.

They had become so heartsore that they stopped talking about it, and only exchanged a silent sympathy, or tried in vain to introduce new subjects of conversation to distract their minds. The strain was terrible. Jack had not looked at his books for a week. It was absolutely impossible.

"How much more can the fields stand?" asked Mrs. Duncan one morning.

"The edges of the corn-blades are beginning to wrinkle now. Another week without rain, or two days of the hot winds, and the crop will be a complete failure. But," he added, hoping almost against hope, "if we get a rain, even now, we'll be all right."

It was the first time either of them had mentioned the hot winds, though it was the fear of them that had been uppermost in their minds all along. They had heard much of that fierce hot blast that comes from the south, superheated, toward the end of a drought, as withering as if direct from the mouth of a furnace. The hot winds do not blow often, but when they get fairly started all hope is gone. In a single day, in one fiery breath, they shrivel up miles of cornfields, until what has been green and full of life in the morning, at night is brown and dead, until the hopes of the year are blasted. The dread of the hot winds was even too terrible to talk about.

Two more weary days! Still the sunshine laughed at them; still the stars taunted them with twinkling coolness; still the sunsets tormented them with the vision of unattainable gold. Jack spent his time in the fields, watching the effect of the drought on the corn, frantic almost at his utter helplessness. When he could stand it no longer, he walked out on the open prairie. But the heat there was intolerable, and he went to the house. It was cooler there, for the thick sod walls were a protection. The strain was telling on mother and son.

The next morning dawned more sultry than ever. The wind was from the south. There was none of the prairie vigor in it. Each tried to conceal from the other the apprehension felt; each stole furtive glances toward the south. Jack left for the corn-fields as soon as breakfast was over. All morning the mother watched. The breeze strengthened. It would bring either rain or destruction,— no one could tell which. Toward noon it became hotter and fiercer. Jack came home looking years older, his teeth set and a haunted look in his eyes. His mother knew now why it was that she had not heard his whistle all the morning.

"It's coming!" was all he said, as he sank into a chair.

"My poor boy," she sighed, as she stroked his hair from his feverish forehead. And so they sat through the long stifling afternoon, waiting and watching for all their possessions to wither before their eyes.

"And the poor Jansens!"

"And the Hartleys, too!"

The hot winds usually blow three days. They were unconsciously saving their strength for the other two days. Toward 4 o'clock the wind became blistering. Metal was too hot to touch, and even the wood, what little there was about the house, burned the naked hand.

Near dusk it grew cooler, and Jack went listlessly to the fields to see the amount of the damage. His mother went with him. All along the southern edges, where the corn had been exposed to the full force of the blast, the stocks were dried up completely, as dead as in December. Then for the next ten yards into the fields the tops were yellow; but beyond that apparently little damage had been done, although the blades were withered along the edges, and hung limp,

like the leaves of long neglected hothouse plants. They were devoutly thankful for the wonderful ability of the prairie to resist long continued drought.

That evening the two were sitting in the doorway, much in the spirit of the condemned awaiting execution. Suddenly Jack started and stared at the horizon. Was he dreaming, or losing his mind?

A cloud!

How eagerly they watched it. They remembered the "cloud the size of a man's hand." But this was larger. Though it grew, they scarcely dared hope, for often during that trying drought clouds had gathered and given every promise of rain,—but not a drop had fallen. A different breeze had come up. It was fresh and almost cold! The clouds were dense and black now, advancing, like an army, in straight, battalion-like lines. Something was bound to come of it. But perhaps it would be a cyclone. The hope that had arisen in their breasts was chilled for an instant. Then they watched for the outcome with bated breath.

As the first drops fell, the light of a new hope came into the eyes of mother and son. The tears of relief fell with the rain of heaven. The drought was at an end.

- - - - - - - - - -

TYPES.

A little nymph, with cheek that glows
Like petal of a damask rose,—
Herself the sweetest flower that grows
    In east or west.

A maiden in a snowy dress,
Vision of radiant loveliness,—
Who would not at her feet confess
    "Here ends love's quest!"

In filmy laces pale and rare,
A jewel flashing in her hair,
My lady with imperial air,—
    Divine the rest!

Each of these types, by love's decree,
Might win a kiss on knightly knee,
Yet who will tell which of the three
    Were loveliest?

CINCINNATI.   *Wilbur Dubois.*

JANET.

By Zoe Norris.

JANET sat listlessly in her saddle, and looked out on the prairie.

The sunshine had toned down her color until she might have passed for a study in sepia, so still she sat on her sturdy pony, with the sky for a background. Her rough dress and cow-boy hat had faded to warm yellow. Her sunburned face was touched with carmine at the cheeks and lips. Her hands were bronzed, and her yellow hair had taken on the tawny shade of her pony's mane. It was not strange, since she had lived in the sunshine all day long, tending the herd.

To-day, used as she was to the heat of the Kansas midsummers, the sunshine scorched her. Her eyeballs hurt with the glare. The hot winds struck her cheek like the blast from a furnace. Yonder, at the horizon, billows of heat palpitated like the waves of the sea, then rolled across the prairie, scorching the grass and burning the corn in the distant fields, the tassels hanging disconsolate, as if begging for rain.

The songs of the birds were hushed. The bees droned almost inaudibly as they hung over the parched prairie flowers; and the herd stood close together, crunching the burnt grass.

Janet, alighting from her pony, scanned the brazen sky for a cloud. Not one was visible. Nevertheless —

"There will be a cyclone before night," she said aloud.

"Better be saying your prayers then, little girl," cried a merry voice behind her. "That is, if you are a true weather-witch."

She turned and smiled up at him, and forgot the heat of the day. The molten lead of the sky ceased to glare in the light of his blue eyes.

"Janet—" Her name was plain Jane, but he had softened it thus. Children born in sod houses are rarely given fanciful names. "Janet," he said, moving between her and the sun so that she, wee thing that she was, stood in his shadow, "is this the place for you, here in this miserable simoon, unprotected in the heat of such a day? Where are your father and brothers that they leave work like this to you?—a man's work! You poor little thing! You know what I wish. Must I ask you again to leave all this misery and come with me?"

Janet rested her arm on her pony's neck and her head on her arm, thus shutting out together the glare of the sunshine and the fascination of his eyes. She wanted to think. Many times he had begged her to go with him, bringing to bear upon her all the charm of his manly strength and beauty, but she had laughed him away for very pride. How would it

MRS. JOE NORRIS, WICHITA, KANSAS.

look for a grand Englishman to marry a girl who tended the herd?—"a cow-girl" as she styled herself, derisively.

It is true, her father scoffed at the English settlement at Runnymede. "English noblemen! swells indeed!" he cried in fine scorn. "Rather, younger sons, who have committed some petty crime, whose people have sent them to this Kansas wilderness in order to save the good old name from disgrace. So they come for the shooting, do they? Better tell the truth and say they were forced to come."

Then would this prominent member of the great populist movement, at its height at that time, launch out in a tirade against noblemen, monopolists, money-holders, and swells in general, until he was obliged to stop from very hoarseness and exhaustion.

"The populist movement!" It was this that had so changed Janet's life.

It seemed a fine thing at first, the farmers going into town with flags flying and banners waving and bands playing, the common people running everything; sending their men to congress to make great and good laws for Kansas; laws that would do away with the grasshoppers and the chinch bugs, the hot winds and the drouth; laws that might provide some farming implement that would cultivate the land without the aid of a guiding hand while the farmers lounge about the streets of the small towns and talk politics, and grumble about monopolies and trusts and hard times, with the whole country going to the dogs! It came to be a chronic thing—this going into town; for these men they had sent to Congress failed to distinguish themselves except in the way of forming a collection of Kansas curios for the laughing stock of the world, and something must be done about it. In any event, if nothing could be done, they must talk it over. While they talked it over, the women did the work of the farm, trying to save the wheat and the corn from the terrible hot winds, from the chinch-bug and other destroying insects.

Janet's poor old mother, overworked and tired always! Her sisters with brawny hands, always busy about the house! Her own lot was best, she thought,—out under the blue sky, in the springtime, listening to the bob-white calling and the field-lark's low, sweet note; drenched now and then by a shower; not minding that at all, rather laughing at the fun of it. But oh! the heat of this particular summer! The sweltering dog-days,—this blazing day of all others! It had taken the heart out of her.

The voice of her sweetheart was like the voice of an angel, promising the glories of the Golden Gates and the Great White Throne. She longed for shadowy meadows and cooling breezes. He had promised her these. There, in his English home were hawthorn hedges, and primrose paths, and tall, wide-spreading oaks, standing like sentinels through the centuries. To-day, in the hopeless heat of the burning prairie, the thought of those oaks came like cooling water. She looked down at her coarse dress. He had said she should walk "in silk attire" —in that glorious future when she was to be his wife. He had caressed her little brown hand and promised that it should be white and soft. She had laughed at that,—her hand white and soft! Then, his eyes had grown sad at her mocking, and he had vowed to care for her tenderly through life; for was she not his love, his darling, his pet lamb that he would shield from all harm?

O yes, she loved him; she would go with him. She was ready to leave everything and be his wife. She had little enough to leave, but she would let him plead a little longer. His voice was sweeter than music in her ears.

"Janet," he whispered, bending down under her big hat until his lips almost touched her brown cheek, "are you listening? Will you come with me? You shall want for nothing. You shall be my queen, my little queen—come, will you?"

She lifted her head at last and looked at him; then past him, with a scared look in her eyes.

What change had come over the blazing day! A lurid light, like the light of Judgment Day, enveloped them. It was as if they looked at the earth and sky through a piece of bright red stained glass. In the southern sky clouds were piled up, black and threatening. They heard a rushing sound of wind,—wailing, moaning, thrashing, roaring in the distance.

On it came, the darkness growing until they stood in the blackness of night, with the horrible fear of the unknown upon them,—this awful roaring, rushing, whirling, murderous thing that was coming to crush them! Something swept past them with a great noise, distinguishable above the roar. It was the herd, stampeding, running with the wind and bellowing with fear.

Oh! that awful darkness! The terrible fear of sudden death, of being crushed and mangled, of dying by inches maybe beneath some heavy weight. Then, great sheets of water, as if the sky had opened and emptied itself upon them, and—a vivid flash of lightning.

Janet saw it coming in that flash,—a horrible thing like something alive, black, funnel-shaped, awful! She threw herself upon her lover's breast. He felt her arms about his neck in the darkness,—then a blow, as if a great hand out of the darkness had struck him, felling him to the ground. During the next few moments of inky blackness, of terror, of flying missiles armed with death, he was unconscious. When he opened his eyes, a calm twilight spread over the track of the cyclone; and Janet lay still on his breast — too still!

Close beside them was a great bough.

It was the hand that had struck them in the darkness. She had seen it coming in that vivid lightning flash, and, throwing herself upon him, had herself received the blow.

He laid her upon the wet grass and chafed her hands. They were cold and limp. The half-shut eyes filled him with terror; and the lips — lips that had smiled back at him when he told her to say her prayers, only a short half-hour ago — were painfully drawn across the little white teeth.

She had no need of prayers now.

She had only fainted, he thought. She could not be dead, the poor little girl who had never known what it was to live! He took her hands again, and rubbed them, calling her loving names.

Then he grew wild with anxiety and — with remorse. He began talking to her earnestly, over and over, explaining to her something that was on his mind. He wanted her to know "the straight of it."

"Little one," as if she could hear, "listen to me. I never meant you harm. Your poor life was hard. I would have given you care and happiness and love. I would have made your life one long summer day. No more watching of the herd under the burning sun; no more work; but rest, and cool paths, and sheltered ways. It is I — do you hear? I, who would have led you in these sheltered ways,— I, who love you. And all along, I have meant you no harm. I really meant to make you my wife. Do you hear, Janet? I meant to make you my own little wife!"

But the lover's words fell upon deaf ears. Without help from him, Janet had found the "sheltered ways."

OVERSHADOWED.

PART SECOND.

By Elizabeth D. Preston.

Chapter VI.

"Sing it mother, sing it low;
Dearn it not an idle lay;
In his heart 'twill ebb and flow
All the life-long way.
Sing it mother, love is strong;
When the tears of manhood fall,
Echoes of thy cradle-song
Shall its peace recall."

THREE thousand miles from her old home, in picturesque Honolulu, Helen at last found rest. Latitude and longitude were nothing to one whose entire interests were centered in the two loved ones that were with her.

She did not realize that she was ill, yet she faithfully obeyed Philip's entreaties that she should almost live out of doors. She would take little Arthur away from his nurse and for hours would sit beneath the shade of the fragrant acacia trees listening to the murmur of the bees among the dainty blossoms, and watching the efforts, most of them futile, of the child to catch the gaudy-colored butterflies, or pluck the flowers whose stems resisted his baby strength.

Health and strength and ambition gradually came back to the young mother, and when Arthur was three years old she was, to all appearances, the same bright, winning girl whom Philip had married. No more children came to them, and so a love approaching adoration was lavished upon their son.

"We might return to Santa Illa, Philip," said Helen one day. "I am quite my old self again, and doubtless the schools and all that sort of thing will be better there for Arthur."

Philip laughed. "'Schools and all that sort of thing' we are in no hurry for," he said, "and you had better stay here until the summer."

So they waited, and fall and winter and spring passed away. Through the influence of Doctor Gray, who was over-worked, and his own skill and untiring efforts, Philip had come into a good practice. Thus, time passed rapidly for him,—a habit time has always revealed to his faithful servants.

These two married lovers asked not, cared not, to look into the future. They were happy, having no thought of the possible dangers awaiting them.

Dinner-time had long since passed, but Philip had not come. Midnight came and morning dawned, but Philip came not.

As Helen passed down the stairs in the morning she saw a note addressed to her lying upon the table. Her name was written in Philip's handwriting. As innocent looking as the calling cards beside it,—how could she know that, having read the contents, she would cease to live! She would exist; she would breathe and walk and talk; yes, she would even smile again, but the great joy of living, that feeling expressed in the words, "I am glad I am alive," would never again be hers. Smilingly she raised the letter from its resting place, marveling at its thickness. Tenderly she carried it to her lips. The act brought the color to her cheeks. These two married people, how dearly they loved each other! He had been detained and sent her this message,—possibly last night. Why had she not been possessed of it at once? Such carelessness was inexcusable in a servant; she would read the letter first and afterward ascertain who had been so negligent.

The first few lines drove all thought of servants and their shortcomings from her mind.

She read along, dazed, uncomprehending. A patter of tiny feet recalled her wandering mind to the present. She turned and swiftly passed back up the stairs to her room. Then, once more she opened the letter, and read:

My Darling Wife ; my Beautiful Helen, —Alas, what wickedness have I done that I am condemned no more to gaze upon your fair face, or to hear the voice that has been as sweetest music to my ears! In the bitterness of my heart I can almost "curse God and die."

I am bewildering you, and so, with the hand that should have been severed from the arm ere I ever lived to write such a terrible message for your eyes to rest upon, I will tell you what you must know at once.

Do you remember a case on lower Heurfano Street (that alley of filth and vice), that I mentioned to you as being a peculiar skin disease,—something quite new to me? The trouble did not yield to the usual treatment for similar difficulties and I was forced to turn the case over to Doctor Templeton, the dermal specialist. Burdened with other duties I never, until yesterday, spoke to Doctor T. about this case. Since then, my attention has been repeatedly called to that most horrible, loathsome disease, leprosy, which is, I find, very common in these islands.

Now to my story. Yesterday, after leaving home and kissing your dear lips —for the last time without knowing it— I noticed in the center of the palm of my left hand a tiny spot no larger than the head of a pencil. It was that deadly white tint that made my heart stand still with fear. I tried to wash it away; the effort was useless. I applied both creams and salves; they had not the slightest effect.

I spent four hours in my office, and no man ever suffered more, mentally, than I did in that brief space of time. As a flash came to my memory the haggard face of the young man whose disease I did not know. I, Philip Gordon, who have studied and traveled as few men of my age are privileged to do, did not know the signs of leprosy, and carelessly exposed myself to a living death.

At 2 o'clock I telephoned Doctor Encke to attend to such of my patients as I felt must have immediate attention.

At 4 o'clock I went to Doctor Templeton's office and mentioned the case of a year ago. Since then I have given the man many a similar case, that has yielded to his treatment. That is, I, until now, had supposed them to be similar cases. It was some time before I could bring to his mind the case I desired to recall to him: but, as it was burned as a picture of fire upon my memory, I at last succeeded in bringing it before his mental vision.

"Oh, yes ; that man had leprosy," said the doctor lightly ; "we sent him to the colony at Molokai."

With simulated calmness I held out my hand, saying. "What is that spot?" Before one word had been said in answer, I read from the look of horror that swept over his face, what I already knew to be the truth.

"I see you have your suspicions," said the doctor gravely; "they are correct ; it would be unkind to keep you in suspense."

My beloved, can you imagine my misery? For one moment I think I was insane. Had there been a murderous instrument at hand I feel I would, in very despair, have taken the wretched life that from now can be but a curse to me.

Helen, no doubt you have read and heard of this leper colony in Molokai. It is the Hawaiian law that all lepers must be banished to it, and as there is absolutely no cure known to science for this dreaded disease, this horrible affliction, they must there end their miserable lives deprived of all they love, deprived of all the joys of life, as if, indeed, they were the veriest criminals that ever walked the earth.

From a scientific standpoint, from the standpoint of the value of human life, we could not complain of so necessary a decree. I could return to you to-night if I would. I am under no restraint, yet I could not endure to expose you to what might be a similar calamity. Up to now I have not known. Now I know, and I could never again touch your dear hand. I will believe that you are still unscathed; I think you are ; your health is perfect and my affliction is, as yet, in such a mild form.

I will force myself to be content with this wretched explanation of circumstances; I will not recklessly tempt fate by coming to you again. You see where all this leads to, do you not, my sweetheart? I leave to-night for Molokai; I do not wait for the authorities to send me. I must never again see all that I hold most dear to me,—my darling wife, my beautiful boy! How can I bear it! To know that you are living and that I may not come to you ; that you need me, and that my son needs me, and I may not aid you!

My father's home can never again be visited by me. An alien land must be my home,—my interests only those to be found in the wretched colony at Kalaupapa. Worse than Job am I afflicted. When God removed from him his sons and daughters, his lands and stock, he left to him the wife of his youth, the woman with whom he had chosen to spend his days.

Although you will ever think of me with tender pity and love, you cannot but remember that each year will make me more loathsome.

My dear Helen, I am miserable at causing you such bitter pain. Believe me, if I only were to suffer this bitter curse it would not be so hard to bear. Where my manhood gives way is at the thought of you and the boy. Now there is one last request to make: I wish my going to Molokai kept a secret. Tell the people at Honolulu that I have been suddenly called back to America. Take Arthur to Santa Illa and let our little world think I have died.

Send by the steamer that next carries provisions to Kalaupapa my books, papers and clothes, and enclose photographs of yourself and Arthur. I am not quite sure, but fancy that the blessed privilege of correspondence will be allowed to us as long as I can hold a pen, and mind and memory remain unimpaired. I think the officials have a system of fumigation, as I have taken the precaution to fumigate this.

By my will, which has been made some time, you will have enough to live on, beside the fortune that is your own.

Let even my own father think I am sleeping the calm sleep from which there is no waking, and, O! I pray that it may soon be a blessed reality. As a request from the dead might be honored, so now I beg of you to give no such painful thoughts to our son as the truth would bring. Cloud not his young life with such dreary shadows. I am dead.

Dear Helen, good-bye! You have Arthur to live for. There is but one thing that can make my exile more miserable, and that is to know that you have allowed this calamity to crush you.

You may write to me at the post-office of Kalayo.

With thousands of kisses for those sweet lips that can never again meet mine; with a heart almost breaking with its heaviness, I am, in life, in sickness and in death,

Your devoted lover,
PHILIP GORDON.

CHAPTER VII.

"And when the step you long for comes,
And all the world is full of light,
O women, safe in happy homes,
Pray for all lonesome souls to-night!"

How long she sat there with that death-dealing letter in her hands I cannot say. The maid had come to the door and told

her that breakfast awaited. She had aroused herself sufficiently to say she was ill and needed nothing. Later the nurse had brought little Arthur, who had pounded upon the door with his tiny fists, but to no effect. It was barred to all.

At 1 o'clock, with a supreme effort, she dragged her weary limbs down to the dining-room and forced herself to eat. In those morning hours her mind had been made up to a great undertaking.

After luncheon she gathered together all of Philip's books and, putting her own with them, she wrapped them in papers and placed them side by side in a large packing box. Next, she took down her husband's clothing and packed it in a trunk and most of her own she placed in another. In another box she placed such mementoes of a happy life as she felt she must retain, and she smiled as she thought of what Philip's sensations must be when he unpacked those trunks. The books would not startle him; he would think she had sent them as a part of herself. But what but the truth could he believe when he saw her clothing? Ah, what but the truth!

This, then, was the meaning,— she was going to him. Of her own free will she was about to give up all that had been forced from Philip. O, her baby! How could she leave him! But her husband —did he not need her more? What of her vow, uttered from the depths of her heart, "until death us do part"? And was not there a special clause in reference to sickness? Were such vows to be overlooked when the test came? Was she to say, "My child is dearer than my husband"? Again, could not she give up her child into the tender hands of her sister with an easier struggle than she could give into alien hands the care of her husband? Indeed, if such great love can bear the test of analysis, did she not better love her husband, the lover of her youth, the father of her child, than she did her only son? Ah, may few of us be compelled to make similar decision!

It was hard to choose between the two she loved best on earth. She did not put herself in the balances. So free from selfishness was she that her life seemed a thing apart and not to be considered. It held no charms for her now. Life for her was dead even as Philip was dead, and she had made up her mind.

Like a dream came to her the time when Philip had laughingly accused her of robbing him of his rights in lavishing such affection on her baby; and she had replied: "I hope I may never be obliged to choose between you, but if ever such a time does come I shall unhesitatingly go to him who most needs me."

The one who most needed her—the words came back to her in a double meaning. The one who most needed her, —that must be Philip. None other could comfort and love as she could. Heavy henceforth must be their hearts, but they need not add the anguish of separation.

As for Arthur, Margaret would take him and care for him as tenderly as she herself could; perhaps she could not love him quite as much, but perhaps for that very reason the love would have a happier ending. Yes, Margaret should know all, and to her should be given the custody of this one precious jewel from her casket.

She could not take him where she was about to go. She could not condemn that spotless young life to premature and loathsome death. For herself she could endure all things; but she had no right, no inclination to take her precious child with her.

As the last garment was folded and hidden from sight, the overburdened heart found its first relief in a torrent of tears. Ah, happy, reason-saving tears! Great, relentless sobs shook the slender form, and hot, scalding tears burned their way down the white cheeks. But, alas, she felt that for grief there was little time. She had much to do, and with a mighty effort she arose from her knees. She had been kneeling, but she had not tried to pray. Her innocent prayers had always been said,—never prayed. Mechanically had they been uttered because no great grief had ever come to her.

Only once, the day she saw the small white coffin, had the possibility of grief been felt; so, only once had a genuine prayer welled from her heart to Heaven.

"Through chastening are we ennobled, through suffering, purified." This sentence came to her mind, and that night as she lay down to sleep,—sleep broken with horrible dreams,—she prayed as only they can pray who have felt the cruel hand of death.

There was much to do. First she had a long journey to make in order to place her child in Margaret's care. She lost no time, but it was, necessarily, many days before she found herself again in her Hawaiian home.

To Margaret she had laid her heart bare; without reserve she had told her all the particulars. Margaret, knowing well what she, under similar circumstances, would have done, made no useless plea for the abandonment of the plans formed.

At first it was to be understood that Arthur was but a temporary inmate of his aunt's home; that Philip had been suddenly called to China; that Helen, desiring to accompany him, had left her son in charge of Margaret. Then, when the time should come when Philip and Helen might have reached the Orient, a letter would be received by Margaret which she would mention to their old friends; then a silence would fall until such time as some fearful ocean wreck occurred and then it would be announced that Philip and Helen had perished with the fated steamer.

The world is credulous where it is not particularly interested, and unbelieving where its interests are at stake. In this case, when the time came and the story was told, none doubted its truth,—none save Doctor Gordon, who insisted on disbelieving the story; and Margaret, fearing he would discover the truth, told him all. Already aged beyond his years, overworked and half ill, the sad news so affected the poor man that, with hardly an effort to resist, he laid himself down upon his bed, from which he never rose.

Childhood is incapable of sorrowing for long (O blessed thought!) and gradually Arthur began to feel for "Aunt Marjet" an affection like to that which he had given his mother.

In all the wide world there was nothing left to Margaret but little Arthur; so, unto him was given all the care and attention, the love and the devotion that even the best of mothers give to their own.

CHAPTER VIII.

"Were God to strike me blind until the day
My lids unclose to show my trembling soul
Beneath His gaze – beloved, I would say,
'I was content to stumble to the goal
Through darkened years; once having seen
    a face'
That glowed - a lamp eternal – at the end
Of Life's dark corridor.'"

Great was the consternation of Philip when Helen appeared on the Island of Molokai. Schooling himself to hardest self-denial, he went to the officials and begged that they would have her removed. He trembled lest it were already too late. It seemed to him that even the air they breathed was impure, although it came from the broad Pacific. Helen would not go. Instead, she ran to Philip, and closely linking her arms about his neck she kissed him over and over again; then exclaimed, hysterically, "Now I am polluted; now I may stay; ah, Philip, you cannot send me away!"

What could he do! At the sacrifice of his own life he would have forbidden this reckless throwing away of hers, but the deed was done; she gloried in it, and she was so inexpressibly dear to him, her presence was so strangely sweet, that he held her to his wildly-beating heart and thanked God for giving him, thus against his will, this one more taste of earthly bliss.

The books and clothes had not yet arrived, and the pitying letters had been so non-committal that Philip had had no intimation of this great sacrifice.

So began another life. The old life, with all its pleasures, all its pains, was to be forgotten. There, shut in by a precipitous mountain wall on the one side and the great sea on the other, in the desolate yet beautiful Kalaupapa, were these two self-exiled until released by death.

In itself the place was filled with grandeur. To the south was the mountain wall toward which one insensibly gazed when he thought of all he had left behind — the world and its pleasures, its hopes, joys and happiness. On the north lay the great Pacific.

The mountain ranges reflected every tender phase of purest color and by infinite distances challenged the capacities of farthest vision. They contained softest pastoral suggestions of cove and slope. The primeval wilderness and stern and rugged solemnities of crags were disturbed by phantasmal chutes of flying mountain torrents. Cataracts danced like jewels endowed with flashing life. Far up the heights were many noble trees bearing their pristine richness of foliage, and some that towered into the air, dead, white and unsightly, so characteristic of the lepers themselves — dead, yet still standing.

In one of the detached cottages, provided for the harborage of these unfortunate people, Philip and Helen Gordon commenced a new life, a life so vastly different from the old one that at times they almost doubted their own identity. Doubtless Philip would die long before Helen, yet there lay before them, or so they presumed, many years of life, — many years before either would lose the power to think and act and work.

It was a long time before Helen could accustom her eyes to the strange sights about her. There were creatures — she saw them sitting before the little houses that had been provided at government expense — who bore scarcely the semblance of human form. They were unable to speak or move; they were lifted from place to place by those who were yet able to do for others, and perhaps still loved them.

These were the worst cases, — those who were nearly free from earthly thralldom. Then there were those who had been afflicted for perhaps six or eight years, with eyes still bright but complexions darkened, whose lips were parched and voices shrilled by some affection of the throat caused by the malady.

There were others whose faces, hands and necks indicated all too plainly the whole condition of the body,—a mass of ash-colored scales, hands rigid, a stiffness in walking showing that the tissues and cartilages had begun the process of hardening.

"O Philip, can we ever be as loathsome as this!" Helen wailed. "Please God we have some terrible accident—even fall from yonder dizzy height in some one of our pilgrimages, rather than endure such misery as we see about us!"

But when she saw the anguish in Philip's face and felt that he would suffer more to see her ill than from anything he might himself endure, she repented her impetuous words and never after broke forth into lamentations, but bravely set herself to endure, and to help Philip.

At the beginning of their sojourn upon this island they absented themselves, selfishly perhaps, from the rest of the inhabitants. There were fully a thousand lepers on the island. The greater portion of each day they spent upon the mountain side, within the fragrant forest or upon the beach. A portion of the day was devoted to the care of their little garden. They also had a flower garden, to which they had transplanted from the mountain-side many rare, exotic plants. Wonderful to them were the tree-like proportions to which the ferns attained. One who has never visited a tropical forest can form little idea of the surprises which awaited these two flower-lovers. Gracefully entwined, or standing firmly by themselves, were masses of beautiful plants with many-colored blooms, while cocoanut and palm and pine trees whispered one to another or stood like sentinels guarding the hillsides and coast. The graceful pampas grass swayed in the passing wind and the perfume from the acacia sweetened the air.

It had been their custom to go to the mountains before the sun was intensely warm, and there, beneath the shade of a huge boulder, or under a friendly tree or fronded palm, they would write or read or talk, as their fancy led them to do. Philip was engaged upon some scientific work that might yet live if he could not. Already had there been many strangers to this island on scientific knowledge bent—mostly medical men—and Philip had held converse with them. Such moments were sweet to him. Sometimes they had left their addresses and had begged him to write certain articles for them, and afterwards these articles would be sent back, in printed form, upon the leaves of some well-known magazine.

One day, as Philip and Helen sat beneath the shelter of a rock and watched the trickling, babbling water coming in thread-like, silvery streams down the hillside on the one hand, and on the other a foaming cascade dashing down some fifty feet into a deep, dark pool beneath, Philip took the little hand of his wife and searched for the sign that would tell that she, too, must suffer as others were suffering.

Helen understood the gaze perfectly although there was no word spoken. "There is a spot just beneath my ear, Philip; I have known it for some time and have rejoiced over it, for I was about to believe that I was fated to outlive you by many years. Now, may its work be speedily accomplished!"

After this they mingled more with the other unfortunate people, and thereby made some pleasant acquaintances. Probably three-fourths of these miserable exiles were those who, in the world, had little to recommend them.

Doctor Gordon again resumed his title and both he and Helen felt that they were doing much to alleviate distress. Cure was impossible, but a mitigation of suffering lay in their power. The disease until eight years old or longer, is painless; simply a wasting away of physical and sometimes mental powers. So it is that those last to come to the island can be of much service to those who have been there for years, and, consequently, few missionaries are called for.

Yet missionaries there are also; brave, noble men and women; people who have given their lives to the service of Christ and make no provision as to how He shall use them.

Doctor Gordon found that the bark of the acacia tree, when steeped, made a powerful tonic. As appetite was almost a lost factor with many of these poor people, Helen made herself greatly beloved by preparing this beverage in large quantities, and distributing it among them. From the pods she made a strong extract, which being allowed to ferment made a pleasant drink, a kind of beer.

So the years passed. Instead of living for themselves, as at first, they lived for others.

They had reached the point where the hair and eyebrows were white. Had it not been so coarse it would have only enhanced the beauty of their faces. By the constant application of those salves and creams, which Doctor Gordon knew so well how to prepare, the disease had been held in check.

One day Dr. Ernest Gray came to the island. There is no harbor at Kalaupapa, but by means of the open inroad his ship landed. He came on scientific purposes intent, and the great surprise with which he beheld his old-time friends nearly overcame him. He had long believed them dead.

Earnestly he listened to their sad story, and agreed with them that it were better to remain as dead to the world. Philip said,—"You know how the Talmud has it: 'These four are dead: the blind, the poor, the childless and the leper.'"

By the next ship sent by the government loaded with provisions, medicine, etc., came a box containing the latest scientific works for Philip, and handsome volumes of poems, new to the world, for Helen, together with an expression of the undying friendship of Doctor Gray.

CHAPTER IX.

"But if there be a blissful sphere
Where homesick souls, divided here,
And wandering wide in useless quest,
Shall find that longed-for haven of rest —
If in that higher, happier birth
We meet the joys we missed on earth,
All will be well, for I shall be
At last, dear loving heart, with thee."

So passed the years. There came to them added discomforts, although they were more in the nature of wasting strength than infirmities of the body.

Once in every three months since their exile they had heard from Margaret,— long, loving letters; but rarely, indeed, had they been answered. It was deemed better so, lest by some unhappy accident Arthur should through them discover his weighty inheritance. They had wept over the letters received in praise of their boy; each letter had been re-read many times. This tie to the world yet remained to them. Unmindful of their own unhappiness they kept up a certain spirit by dreaming and talking of him.

One morning Philip said: "To-day Arthur is twenty; we have been here sixteen years!" Later in the same day came a letter from Margaret saying that Arthur was going to Germany in pursuance of his medical studies.

During the evening after Philip was asleep—he slept so much of late—Helen wrote to Margaret as one despairing woman will write to another woman whom she loves. She knew that Philip was dying. Of course he had been dying all of these long, dreary, yet not altogether unhappy years; but now the end was near, and Oh, her great sorrow was best told in the words, "I shall yet live." Perhaps years must pass before freedom would come to her and how could she live without Philip? How wearily would drag the days upon this lonely island without one loving soul near her; to die attended by strangers, to be borne to her grave by alien hands and wept for by none of her kin! Of this would she in her young days have dared to dream? It was too hard.

Of Arthur she spoke as only a mother can speak. She blessed Margaret for her tender, thoughtful care of one who had been more than motherless. Freely she spoke of her life at Molokai, and ended the letter with the wish that the next word Margaret should receive from Kalaupapa would be written in a stranger's hand.

This letter she addressed to Woodbine, believing that Arthur was in foreign lands. Her letters had formerly been sent both to a distant post-office and to an assumed name. In all previous letters she had mentioned Philip as "my husband" and signed her name as Nellie, by which name she had never been called since a little girl.

When this letter came to Woodbine Arthur Gordon lay in the delirium of fever, and his aunt Margaret, careless of all save the restoration of her beloved nephew's health, placed it with others, in the desk that had formerly been Helen's but was then used jointly by Margaret and Arthur.

During the days of convalescence Arthur did everything to occupy his time ; among other things he arranged and sorted the papers in this desk. It was then that he discovered and read the letter which had not been written for his eyes to rest upon.

It is night ; the birds are asleep in their nests ; the wind has died away. There is nothing to break the exquisite stillness save the monotonous beating of the waves against the rocks and the faint, rippling murmur of the streamlet falling from the heights above. The moon has risen, hanging over a dip in the mountains far away. The stars are out, and the clouds are all gone ; the rain of the afternoon has ceased.

The mists are barely visible hovering above the dark ravines ; the shadows are long ; the dank breath of the herbage sodden with rain comes to the window raised to let in more of Heaven's air to the sick chamber.

Philip Gordon is dying. Blessed relief to him,—the depths of despair for Helen.

Two days later, a funeral cortege passes

through the streets of Kalaupapa to the hillside burying-ground. All that was mortal of Philip Gordon is laid away to rest.

CHAPTER X.

"In sorrow and disappointment,
  When our eyes are filled with tears,
We cannot start a new song
  With the old one still in our ears ;
But when shadows gather around us,
  And still watching the night be filled ;
When tired wives fade as the stars die out,
  And the voices we loved are stilled ;
We can keep a little silence
  And whisper a prayer in the calm ;
And perhaps for the song we were singing
  There may rise to our lips a psalm."

All day the clouds seemed mustering. The leaves hung still ; a breathless, sultry pause bated the pulses of humanity. At night the long monotony was broken by a gradual darkening and presently rain was gently falling. The clouds were rolling down the mountain sides. They came in fleecy ranks along the dark purple indentations which marked the ravines, suggesting a vanguard with broken flanks. Then rose the wind ; the batten shutters shook and the great outer door rattled, and, though tightly fastened, let in great gusts of wind that made the lights tremble and flicker and almost go out. A sudden silence, and then a blast that shook the house to its foundation. Away into the darkness it went, shrieking with a voice so dolorous and wild that Helen put down her book and looked up, agitated, as if she realized in the sound, the utterance of the dreary grief that rent her heart. A sudden stillness, in which, with ears alert, she seemed to hear the wild beating of her own heart, and longed with an intense yearning for some sound to break the awful silence ; and again, that wild, relentless, screaming wind ! A cricket shrilled and shrilled in a distant corner of the room, and at last, growing weary, became mute. Again raged the storm, accompanied by thunder that rolled and crashed, echoing and re-echoing among the rocky ravines. Tiny rivulets were everywhere hastening to join the wrathful ocean. Flashes of vivid lightning were followed by noise of falling timber in the distant forest. The rain drove in sheets against the sides of the house, and the thunder of the rising tide filled the silence like the constant discharge of artillery. The clouds were black as Erebus.

Silence once more! For a long time no sound had broken the stillness of the night. Helen arose and, drawing aside the curtains, saw that the moon had risen. A glorious moon in all its beauty stood in "Heaven's wide, pathless way" as though unconscious of its grandeur, yet sad for the sorrow of the seething earth below.

Finally came peace to the weary heart and sleep to the tired eyes, but the time had come when sleep tarried not long. When the mists still lingeringly kissed the distant hilltops, Helen witnessed the morning's glory. The birds slowly wakened; first a faint peep was heard which was as faintly answered; then a sudden twitter and the whole air was full of bird voices. Bees buzzed about the sweet acacia trees and dipped into the red and white clovers. The dainty morning glories, refreshed by their night's slumber and morning shower-bath, lifted their faces to the light.

Helen, too, felt refreshed and her anguish weighed less heavily upon her. Somehow in those weary watches she had felt that Philip was very near to her. Was it an omen? Was her time to be but a little longer? Would the blessed liberation come soon?

For three months Philip had lain dead. Three months ago she had written that letter to Margaret, and had heard in reply that Arthur had not yet gone to Germany but lay ill of a fever. Ill,—perhaps he was dead now! Perhaps,—and the mother's heart beat for one moment in supreme though selfish joy at the thought, perhaps these two would come together to meet her at Heaven's gate which she was each day nearing.

So strong is the force of habit that this woman, so delicately reared, so tenderly shielded, had grown not merely to speak composedly of her disease but to behold its ravages as a matter of course. The

care she had given herself, the physical exercise she had persistently taken, her healthy constitution — all, united to check in her the transformation she observed going on all about her. For nearly seventeen years she had lived at Kalaupapa, and yet she was beautiful. True, her eyebrows, lashes and hair were white, her complexion dark that once had been so fair; but her eyes still retained their brilliancy, the deep hollows in the cheeks were partially hidden by the hectic flush with which they were always surmounted. The change that had taken place internally was more severe.

The lungs and throat were seriously affected; the voice was shrilled, and had a strange, uncanny sound. Appetite was gone; she ate no more of solid foods. She took no more long walks upon the distant hillsides. Strength was slowly leaving the weary body; patiently could she wait for the end, happy in knowing that each hour of living was but an hour of dying — happily in her case a painless dying.

She would no longer repine. Weak though she was she yet had more strength than many of those about her who had been there not half as long. She would not sit in idleness while those about her might be made more comfortable by even her wasting strength. So long as she had the power to minister she would work. She would be brave. In all humility and with a cheerful heart would she accept all that was meted out to her. God was nearer to her in those days than He had ever been before.

CHAPTER XI.

"There I have seen a sunset's crimson glory
Burn as if earth were one great altar blaze;
Or, like the closing of a pious story,
Light up the misty world with dying rays."

At Kalayo, in the presence of the governor and the physician of the small domain of Kalaupapa, stood a young man whose pale countenance showed sickness and perhaps nearness to death. Within his hand he held an open letter. "My aunt would tell me nothing," he said. "'Her promise was as given to the dead,' she would but say. However, this letter tells me all,—'Sister Margaret.' My aunt had but one sister, my mother.—'Philip is dying.' Philip was my father's name. —'My darling son, Arthur.' That is my name. Oh, there can be no mistake. I stopped at Honolulu and saw Doctor Gray; he had pity on my distress and told me that my father was dead, but that my mother still lives—here. Gentlemen, in exchange for a few years of mother-love, for the blessed privilege of being with her until her dying day, I offer you my services as other missionaries have done who had no such excuse as mine. From this day I shall never leave Molokai."

He was not strong, poor boy! Too soon had he left the faithful care of his adoring aunt. Too soon, to the mind weakened by fever ravages, had come this terrible revelation — that he was not an orphan; but O, how much worse than orphaned! The dreamed-of meeting, the longed-for reunion, was, he felt, near at hand; yet suddenly he seemed bereft of all physical power. His head swam dizzily; he swayed, tottered and would have fallen had they not caught him. Hurriedly they carried him to the small boat that waited at the landing. He was transported away from the island whose every breath was poison. In the hospital at Honolulu he lay for many weeks, frightening his nurses by his terrible cries, "Unclean! Unclean!" Deliriously he raved. Lovingly he called to his mother and promised to remain with her forever. Then he seemed to be kneeling at the side of the grave that held his father, and curses deep and loud were given one he called a "selfish coward" for allowing his sweet mother to so exile herself; then his voice would change and a glorious light would come into his eyes as he told how pure and exalted a character it was, how grand a nature, that one so pure, so fastidiously reared as his mother had been, would deem the whole world well lost for his sake, in exchange for his father's companionship.

With returning strength came again the desire to visit Molokai. To his physician

he told a part of his sad story, but it was met with little sympathy. So little consideration is felt for this poor class of unfortunates, so few sympathetic words did he hear in their behalf, that more than ever was he determined to return to Kalaupapa and spend his life in the amelioration of the sufferings of the lepers.

That he had not yet obtained a certificate as a doctor of medicine was of little importance. There was always a physician in charge upon the island, and in his own quiet way, and with the aid of the fortune that had come to him years ago, at the time of the supposed death of both his father and his mother, he would be enabled to relieve the pain and misery, in part, that was then endured in the hospital and in many of the cottages. Now fully understanding the true value of health, he visited on the other islands until he felt he was completely restored; then, in the full possession of all his youthful vigor, he again set sail for Molokai.

This time, as before, he went directly to the governor, who, reading that the young man's determination was not to be altered, went with him to his mother's cottage.

At the end of the walk the governor withdrew. In a moment the young man had entered the low building and stood before his mother, with feelings that even he could not express. For so many years she had been but a dream to him, a vision of white with an angelic face and a low, sweet voice, a memory of childhood songs and fairy tales mingled with melodious laughter. Before him sat a woman whose age it would be hard to tell; her face bespoke much suffering, mingled with perfect resignation.

Mothers, explain to me the mystery that revealed to Helen the identity of the stranger! Why should she rise with one glad cry and stand before the young man with a wealth of mother-love in her face, though he had not yet spoken?

She had not been told of his previous attempt to see her; the governor had relied upon his powers of persuasion to force the young man to forego this attempted suicide. She had not heard from Margaret. The mother's intuition gave to her the knowledge that before her stood her child, her Arthur.

While yet with arms extended to embrace him, she bethought of the terrible consequences, and, in a voice filled with deepest emotion, she cried, "Go back; I beseech you to go back; know you not what folly you are committing? It is not yet too late. Ah, you know not what you do. Listen to me; life is too great a gift to throw it thus recklessly away."

Tears checked further utterance. Of what was she thinking? Did she at that late day repent of her early sacrifice?

Arthur stepped boldly forward and caught the slender, almost fainting figure in his arms. He pressed her to his heart. "Dear mother," he said, "I have thought it all over a thousand times. Your sacrifice has so impressed me with its beauty that I, too, have had something of your strength given me. While you live you shall be my only thought; your joys, your sorrows, your hopes and fears shall be mine at last. When you are gone, until my time shall come, I will labor on for the many others who will need me. In the hospitals and cottages will my heart and hands be employed carrying on the work that you and my father have begun."

The mother listened with mingled pride and love, joy and sorrow,—too late to reason with him, too late to convince him that his idea was, possibly, quixotic. Perhaps it was better so; how could she know!

For four years the constant companionship of mother and son was beautiful to behold. Back to the drooping spirits came new life, to the wasted form fresh strength. Then gave she to the world that pathetic story whose giving had been dreamed of long before, and she thanked heaven that it had had a happy ending.

Husband and son seemed united in the son. Philip younger grown, her baby Arthur older grown — which was it? The love given to the one seemed to have a new lease of life, and the love given to the other so long ago and for so long denied her, came in overwhelming torrents.

In four years it ended. As Arthur knelt beside the graves that held so grand a tragedy, no thought of regret came to him. Sweet had been the sacrifice he had made. Patiently, uncomplainingly, he took up the work that was now left for him, and although none lived to say to the great outside world, "He did so much for me!" still, it was reported in Heaven, and to his account there stands, waiting for his coming, this glorious sentence: "He loved much."

EYES OF BROWN.

TWO eyes of brown, long years ago,
    Held my young life in fee,
And as they looked, or gay or sad,
    So went the world with me.

Though many other eyes since then
    Have led my heart away,
Those eyes so brown, so bright and true,
    Delight my dreams to-day.

They taught me this: naught else can bring
    A joy more deep and pure
Than when upon a woman's love
    A woman rests secure.

GRAND RAPIDS, MICH.   *Clara J. Denton.*

MOTHER'S JOE.

I. SKETCHES FROM LIFE IN LABOR'S WORLD.

By Adrian Rosecrans.

Author of "When the Mine Whistle Blows" in The Midland for July, 1894.

A HAZY, dreamy, Indian summer afternoon. An old-fashioned cottage nestled among the trees. A sweet-faced elderly woman dozes quietly in her rocker. The soft summer wind gently rustles the leaves on the vine about the window, and caresses her silvery hair with gentle touch. Outside, the flowers nod sleepily in the summer wind. A robin, perched among the branches of a leafy oak down by the old rustic gate, gives two sleepy chirps and then relapses into a dreamy quiet. All is sunshine and peace.

As the old clock in the cottage chimes the hour of four, a rosy-cheeked lass, lying on the grass at the foot of the old oak, lazily rises to a sitting posture and, rubbing her sleepy eyes, gazes dreamily down the lane leading from the cottage to the main road. As she gazes she becomes more attentive. Then suddenly she springs to her feet, takes another hasty glance down the road and scampers toward the house.

"Mother! Mother!" she cries, "wake up! There's someone coming up our lane and he's riding very fast! He has a blue uniform and cap on and he looks like a soldier!"

The startled old lady opens her eyes and, hastily adjusting her spectacles, looks out of the window. Sure enough! There is a horseman dismounting at the gate. He has, however, none of the accoutrements of a soldier and, in fact, is but a boy.

"O, I know what he is now," says the girl, "he's a telegraph messenger, and he has something in his hand that looks like a letter. I wonder if it's a message for us?"

The youth has by this time reached the door. "Is this where Mrs. Rebecca Allison lives?" he asks.

"Yes sir," answers the old lady turning pale and grasping a chair for support. "Have you a message for me?"

"Yes ma'am," replies the youth, "here it is, all charges paid. Then he turns away.

Mrs. Allison takes the telegram and hands it to the girl. "What does it say, May? Open it, I can't." And she sinks into a chair. The girl hastily tears open the envelope and this is the message enclosed:

> RED CLIFF, 12.
> Your son was hurt last night in a collision near Jackson Siding. Come at once.
> J. BURLEY, Sup't.

"Wait May—wait dear—let me rest a moment — let me think a moment!" exclaims the distracted mother. "My son hurt? my boy — my big, brave, handsome Joe? It can't be! Why, his letter yesterday said he'd soon be home. But that was written last week, and he was hurt last night. It must be true. I am going to him."

She totters feebly to her feet, but her trembling limbs scarcely support her. "Help me, May," she says, while the tears course down her cheeks, "help me to go to Joe!"

———

"Here's the order, old man. — 'Meet Anderson, fast fruit, at Jackson's Siding.' The dispatcher says to hurry, as we'll hold 'em ten or fifteen minutes, the best we can do." And the conductor climbed on the engine and handed the order to the engineer. "Go back to the way car, Jim," he said to the head brakeman, "you're worn out: go back and take a sleep. I'll ride here the rest of the way in." As he spoke he swung his lantern high in air in answer to the rear brakeman's signal to "go ahead."

Away they went down through the yard, around the curve, and out along the river bottom, whirling away into the night.

"Say, Barney," said the conductor as he climbed on the seat box beside the fireman, and watched the sparks fly from the smoke-stack and fade away into the darkness, "they the diamonds into her lively to-night; its my last trip with you and you ought to give me a ride."

"Your last trip, Joe?"—said the fireman—"Why, how is that?"

"Well, I'm going to quit railroading for good," returned Joe, "and yet I rather like it. But I've got an old mother back East, who wants me to come home, so I'm going to quit and go. Its five years now since I saw 'er, God bless 'er! Five years of wild life over the world—but the other boys, my brothers I mean, are all married now, and mother's growin' old; so I'm goin' home to take care of her." He paused, took a puff at his cigar and looked out into the night.

"Joe," said the engineer, "who was that duck you give the dollar to and told to climb into a box-car back there at Long Pine?"

"O, that's a poor devil that was up in Spokane and 'went broke' in a card game. They robbed him, but he took the law in his own hands—cleaned out the place—and then he had to take to the woods. He hadn't had a bite to eat for two days. I'm a fool I s'pose, but I can't see a poor devil go hungry."

For a time only the throbbing of the engine and the rattle of the train broke the silence of the night. On they flew, now panting up a stiff grade, now darting down an incline, around curves and over bridges,—on and ever on. Here a light in a farm-house flashes by; now they thunder down a steep grade and into a long belt of woods.

"Well Joe," said the fireman, "here we are in Dead Man's Hollow; forty-

three minutes comin' over; guess you've had a ride so far, eh?"

Joe roused himself from a reverie and shuddered. "I always feel a chill come over me in this place," he said. "I don't know why, but s'pose it is on account of poor Jack bein' killed here. Just about here was where it happened, too." As he spoke he turned again and looked ahead out of the cab window, then suddenly sprang to his feet with a cry. The glare of a headlight coming around a curve not two hundred yards away shone full in his eyes!

"Jump Bill—Barney—jump for your lives!" he cried. "Anderson has run by the siding and is into us! Jump, for God's sake! I'll warn the boys!" and he pulled the whistle valve and sounded a piercing blast.

Out at either side went the fireman and engineer and Joe turned to follow.—but too late.—A crash! a mighty roar of bursting boilers and escaping steam, and the heavy freight trains, like grim monsters of death grappling each other, had come together!

The uninjured found no one missing except Joe. For a long half-hour they searched through the wreckage and darkness, aided by the light of the burning cars, retarded by the smoke and heat. They toiled on, hoping to find that he had escaped, yet trembling lest he should be found buried beneath the burning timbers.

A strange man was seen in the midst of the wreck, surrounded by smoke and flame, one arm dangling broken and useless at his side, blood dripping down over his face from a wound in the head—sobbing like a child, as with his uninjured arm he tore and pulled at the heavy beams and irons underneath which some one was buried. The man, bruised and battered, but working heroically, was Joe's tramp, and the man buried beneath the wreck was the missing conductor.

They moved the heavy timbers and, tenderly lifting poor Joe, they bore him out of reach of flame and smoke. On a rough bed made of their coats they laid him while they waited for the relief train with doctors. Pale and motionless as the dead he lay, and only by the feeble fluttering of his heart could they discern that life remained.

After two seemingly interminable hours the whistle of the relief train gladdened the ears of the waiting men, and in another half-hour Joe was stretched on a cot in the city hospital, where the company's old gray-haired doctor examined him, while the men anxiously awaited his verdict. After a careful examination the old man sadly shook his head. "Poor Joe!" he said, "he has quit railroading forever."

Just then Joe turned slightly, opened his eyes and muttered, "Going out on 19 — full train of fruit!" No one moved, and he was quiet for a moment. Then he spoke again, "Look out for the switch, Jim; we meet No. 2 here." Then he was quiet again.

"He thinks he's out on the road," said a brakeman, tears blinding his eyes. "Poor Joe! Poor Joe!"

All day long and all that night he tossed and raved in delirium; but in the afternoon of the second day he suddenly grew calm.

An express wagon with a jingling bell passed down the street, and Joe, half turning his head as if to listen, smiled and whispered, "There they are, mother, I hear the bell now." Then the breeze wafted a scent of flowers to him through the open window. "Let me get this flower for you, mother, then I'll bring the flock back. Hear the bell? They are gettin' farther away now, but — why, where are you, mother?"

Just then the door opened softly and a voice, choked with tears, said: "Here I am, Joe; I've come to you — come to take you home!" And the hot, delirious head was pillowed on the mother's breast.

Silently the watchers slipped out of the room and left the gray-haired mother and her boy together. Half an hour afterward a sweet-faced Sister of Mercy paused at the door and, hearing no sound, noiselessly opened it. The old mother still knelt beside the cot. Her silvery hair, stirred gently by the wind, mingled with the brown, tangled locks on the pillow. So still were they, both seemed to be sleeping. The wondering Sister drew nearer — then knelt in prayer.

Stealing softly through the window a ray of sunshine rested for an instant on the two heads, crowning them with a halo of gold. Then the sunlight faded behind the hills; the vesper bells rang out sweetly on the evening air. Mother and Joe had both gone home.

INK-PA-DU-TAH'S REVENGE.

By Harvey Ingham.

AN IMPRESSION prevails that the Spirit Lake Massacre of 1857, so graphically described by Governor Carpenter in THE MIDLAND for July, was a wholly unprovoked assault on the part of the Indians. Irving B. Richman, in his "Tragedy of Minnewaukon," briefly hints at the facts, but the only connected story of the troubles which preceded the attack at the lakes appears in Judge Fulton's "Red Men of Iowa," and this work unfortunately is no longer procurable on account of the limited edition originally published. Major Williams, who commanded the relief expedition from Fort Dodge and Webster City, in 1864 contributed to the *Iowa Northwest* a very complete and authoritative statement, upon which Judge Fulton undoubtedly relied. The story as gathered from these sources and from the recollections of pioneers still living may not prove an uninteresting appendix to the chapters already given in THE MIDLAND.

The retirement of the Sac and Fox Indians from Iowa in 1845 was followed by

CHE-TON-MAGA, AGED 71 YEARS,
Reticent of Abigail Gardner Sharp, Present at the Dedication of the Spirit Lake Massacre, July 26, 1895.

an influx of rough border characters, lawless, half civilized, often criminal. Among them was Henry Lott. He is first found at Red Rock, in Marion county, the year the Indians moved. The following year, 1846, he was at Pea's Point, in Boone county. His chief business seems to have been selling bad whisky to the Indians, horse stealing being a diversion. He did not remain long at Pea's Point and in 1846 was found at the mouth of the Boone River, in Webster county, being forced north into Sioux country by the soldiers who followed the retiring Sacs and Foxes. Two years later, in 1848, the Sioux traced stolen horses to his cabin and notified him to

leave. This he refused to do, and after shooting his horses and cattle and robbing his bee-hives the Indians drove him and his stepson away, threatening his family. Si-dom-i-na-do-tah, Lott always insisted, was the leader of the band.

The only event in Lott's career to occasion feeling of sympathy for him or his occurred at this time. His little son, twelve years of age, attempted to follow his father and half-brother after they had gone, and, losing his way, was frozen to death near where Boonesboro now stands. Lott went to his old haunt at Pea's Point and here met Chemeuse, or Johnnie Green, leader of the Sac and Fox stragglers who have since had a home in

Tama county, and persuaded him to lead his band in pursuit of the Sioux. They came to the invaded home in Webster county and, finding the remainder of the family safe and the hidden barrel of whisky untouched, no further progress was made. The Indians, taking the whisky, returned to the south. Lott applied to the government for $3,000 indemnity, but all decent citizens denounced him. He returned to Webster county, where his wife died, the first white woman to die in that county. Here the troops stationed at Fort Dodge watched him until their removal in 1853.

Lott was cherishing all this time a plan for revenge against the Sioux. In 1853 he moved to Humboldt county to be nearer "the old head devil," as he called Si-dom-i-na-do-tah, and located at the mouth of the creek since called by his name. Major Williams, who suspected him, cautioned him against taking whisky with him, but he claimed that it would assist him in getting into favor with the Indians.

On the creek below Lott's Creek, now called Bloody Run in memory of the events which followed, Si-dom-i-na-do-tah was living with his aged mother, his wife and two children, a boy and girl, and a younger squaw who also had two children. He was in winter quarters. Lott, by pretending friendship, had gained the confidence of Si-dom-i-na-do-tah, and in January, 1854, after having loaded his valuables, he went south to the Indian tepees and persuaded the aged chief to join him in hunting buffalo on the high ground beyond. Once out of hearing he shot the Indian. Returning to the camp with his stepson, both disguised as Indians in order to convey the impression that the crime had been committed by Winnebagoes, or Musquakies, they murdered the helpless women and children, two only escaping, a girl and boy, children of Si-dom-i-na-do-tah. The boy was left for dead with a scalp wound, and the girl lay unnoticed in the tall grass. Lott burned his cabin and journeyed south. The news of the murder soon

reached Fort Dodge, and Major Williams organized a troop for pursuit. But Lott escaped into Missouri and thence to the plains, and there, later, he was killed while trying to mislead and murder a party of emigrants.

The connection of these events with the Spirit Lake Massacre is intimate. Ink-pa-du-tah, who so fiendishly murdered the helpless settlers about the lakes, was a brother of Si-dom-i-na-do-tah, and it was his aged mother who was chased in the snow and killed by Lott at Bloody Run. He was then in command of an outlaw Sioux band not recognized by the Sioux leaders. He is described by Mrs. Abbie Gardner Sharp, in her valuable book narrating the Spirit Lake Massacre, as six feet in height, of powerful frame, marked with small-pox, desperately bold and revengeful. He was so deeply affected by the death of his mother and brother that the settlers spared no pains to secure and punish Lott. Failing in this, they attempted to pacify Ink-pa-du-tah by the forms of an inquest held at Homer, then county seat of Hamilton county; but the Indian could see no point to legal proceedings which did not lead to the capture and punishment of the murderer. His enmity was still more inflamed by a report that some mischievous settler had taken Si-dom-i-na-do-tah's head and nailed it up to public view on the Homer court-house. He retired in a bitter frame of mind towards the whites.

The trouble anticipated began in June and July of that year at Clear Lake, when the Sioux made their last invasion into the Winnebago reservation. Here they annoyed Hewitt and Hickinson, pioneers dating back to 1851, until the latter, enraged at the breaking of his grindstone by a young brave, seized a fragment and sent the Indian sprawling. This incident has been given as the cause of the disturbance which ensued, called in local history "the Grindstone War." It was only by the payment of money and household goods that the Indians were bought off until sufficient aid arrived from Mason City, when a determined stand was taken, the money and goods were demanded and returned, and the Indians were driven back without bloodshed. After they had gone, terror seized the settlers and a general retreat occurred to the Shell Rock River, near where Nora Springs is located, and a fortified camp was established.

The Sioux were reported to be in pursuit with a band of five thousand. They did make a camp with rifle pits in Hancock county, but evidently never pursued the settlers, who soon returned to their homes.

It was during this trouble that Asa C. and Ambrose A. Call passed through Fort Dodge to make the first settlement on either branch of the Des Moines above the forks. They located at Algona while the Sioux were still east, their cabin fortunately escaping notice on the westward retreat. This was the beginning of the tide of immigration which in 1855 and 1856 poured into both valleys and overawed the savages. Major Williams expresses the opinion that but for this rapid influx of settlers an attack would have been made on Fort Dodge in 1855. As it was, Ink-pa-du-tah and his followers contented themselves with stripping trappers and surveyors, stealing horses and foraging upon the scattered settlers, always maintaining a hostile and threatening attitude. Many pages of THE MIDLAND would be required for a brief enumeration of the petty annoyances, pilferings, and more serious assaults which occurred. At Dakota City, in Humboldt county, the cabin of E. McNight was rifled in the spring of 1855. Farther north, within a few miles of Algona, the cabin of Malachi Clark was entered and the settlers gathered in great alarm to drive out the Indians — a band of eighty braves led by Ink-pa-du tah in person. Still farther north, near where Bancroft stands, W. H. Ingham was captured by Um-pa-sho-tah, a leader under Ink-pa-du-tah in the massacre, and was held a prisoner for three days. The summer of 1856 was comparatively free from trouble and the Des

Moines valleys filled rapidly with settlers, the hardy but ill-fated band which met disaster the following spring pushing west of the valley line and breaking the solitude about the lakes.

The winter of 1856-7 was bitterly cold. The Indians suffered extreme privation in their Dakota winter quarters and returned in the spring prepared for any crime. Their course from the Missouri river east was marked by hostile attacks upon the settlers. They wreaked their full revenge at Okoboji and Spirit Lake.

It is entirely possible that this massacre would have occurred without further provocation than that naturally arising from intrusion into the favorite hunting-grounds of the savages. Ink-pa-du-tah and his followers were fully equal to an unprovoked assault. But it is not at all certain that without the previous massacre at Bloody Run any serious attack would have been made. The openly hostile attitude of the Sioux dates from that occurrence, and no settler on the unprotected frontier felt any safety after that time with Indians in his neighborhood. There is reason to believe that in this, as in nearly every case of serious misunderstanding with the Indians, the trouble dated back to bad whisky and bad faith both liberally dispensed by the border ruffians who, to escape the clutches of the law, kept well in the vanguard of civilization in its westward march.

The pioneers who came to northern Iowa in good faith were able to maintain friendly relations with even the Sioux. It was such men as Lott who made the term "Wasecha"— bad white— common in Indian speech. In any event the massacre at the lakes should always be associated with the massacre at Bloody Run, and when the story of the former is told it should be accompanied by the scarcely less terrible story of the latter. If there is no excuse for the atrocities perpetrated by Ink-pa-du-tah, there is equally none for those of which Lott was guilty. "Never," says Major Williams, "was a more brutal murder committed than that of these poor helpless squaws and their children."

SIGHT-SEEING IN COLOGNE.

AMONG WORKS OF ART—THE GREAT CATHEDRAL—THE CITY—THE VIEW FROM THE CATHEDRAL TOWER—A PLACE OF SKULLS.

THE EDITOR ABROAD. XVII.

IT WAS an unpromising morning. At 6:10 we started from Aix la Chapelle by rail, and at 7:30 we were breakfasting with friends in Cologne. Our breakfast was served in a cozy little room back of the neatest and prettiest of business houses. The room looks out upon a court such as one might expect to see in an Italian palace, but would scarcely look for in the rear of even such attractive shops as are to be found along Hoch-strasse.

After a brief rest we set out for the Wallraff-Richartz museum, a capacious and imposing stone structure in the English-Gothic style. It was completed thirty-two years ago. The museum takes

its joint name from the liberality of two public-spirited citizens of Cologne. Herr Richartz, a wealthy merchant, gave over $150,000 toward its erection. Professor Wallraff gave the collection of paintings and antiquities which suggested the erection of a suitable building in which to house them.

Passing up the long stone stairway, surrendering our tickets and umbrellas at the left-hand window, hastily glancing at a formidable array of casts of famous sculpture such as confront the visitor at the Corcoran Gallery in Washington and the Metropolitan Museum of Art in New York, hurrying past innumerable interesting antiquities lest they put a spell upon

THE CATHEDRAL OF COLOGNE.

us and compel us to spend the day with them, we reluctantly quit the cloisters all and ascend a second stone stairway, and are soon in the midst of the principal paintings upon the upper floor.

The staircase claims passing attention, being adorned with frescoes by Steinle, illustrating the history of ancient and modern art and progress. The most interesting of these frescoes is the representation of Charlemagne enthroned, his retinue about him including our friend Eginhard, private secretary and son-in-law of the king, also Alcuin, the greatest scholar of his time, whom Charlemagne enticed from England, and other ancient worthies, not to speak of unworthies.

Turning to the left, we see a group of pictures illustrating the early school of German art. To our untutored vision it is a sorry collection of un-Christlike Christs, and unmotherly Madonnas. The most interesting feature of these relics of early German art is the mute testimony they give to the supremacy of religious thought in mediæval life.

But the rooms on the right amply repay us for the visit. Among the paintings which stand out in memory are, first of all, the large, full-length portrait of Queen Louisa of Prussia, by Gustav Richter, painted in 1879, and since reproduced in numberless engravings. It is a face of rare beauty, and the commanding figure, clothed in white, is grace embodied. The queen is descending a stairway. The light shines upon her yellow hair and makes it golden. The picture is instinct with life. The folds of the dress and the swaying of a filmy scarf about the neck and the poise of the white-slippered foot between the stairs, all suggest the poetry of motion.

Grand old Bismarck, by Lenbach; the famous "Camphausen"; "King William at Sedan"; Defreggar's "Wrestling Match," a strong facial study; Piloty's "Galileo in Prison," as fascinating as it is severe; Böttcher's "Summer-night on the Rhine," in which candle-light and moonlight are presented with rare skill, a painting well embodying the grandeur of the Rhine scenery and the holiday spirit of the German people; the popular genre sketch by Gautier, "The Funeral Feast"; Kray's "Undine"; Gunther's amusing sketch, "Theologians Disputing," and a host of other paintings rivet the attention.

———

We betake ourselves to the great cathedral. Our German friends here join us, and, thus reinforced, we are prepared for what may come. I speak feelingly of "what may come," for only those who have traveled in a strange land, where months of language study avail little in the presence of some slight unanticipated complication, can quite appreciate the sense of relief from care which comes over one who, after "going it alone," finds himself once more with those who are to the manner and the language born.

Do not imagine we have been in the city four full hours without coming under the influence of the great cathedral which more than anything else gives Cologne its fame abroad. Before we arrived we were on the lookout for it. It passed before our vision like a panoramic view and then disappeared. On leaving the station we gave quick glances at the scenes about us, and then turned again to the cathedral. With umbrellas turned aside and the rain beating in our faces, we stopped in front of the tower, to gaze up that great height and wonder at its marvel of beauty and symmetry.

Many lives have been spent in the building of this remarkable edifice. Millions of marks have been expended upon it and millions more will go toward renewing and perfecting it. The grandest thought of Thirteenth Century Germany was embodied in its noble plan. The deeply religious feeling of many succeeding centuries was concentrated there as its solemn arches and floriate spires took shape and form. Instead of the long guide-book description, let me give the reader a few of the facts and the principal impressions that stay by me. The principal fact is that the Cathedral of Cologne is the grandest specimen of Gothic architecture in the world. It was conceived by Archbishop Engelbert and was founded by his successor, Conrad. Its corner stone was laid with great solemnity August 14, 1248. It was planned by Mehster Gerard. Its spire was not completed until our time—in 1880. It wore out several architects and builders, and cost no end of money. It has in its time looked down upon millions of saints and sinners. It has witnessed solemn consecrations of souls and treasure. It has witnessed quite dissimilar scenes, for instance: in 1796 the sacrilegious French turned the cathedral into a hay magazine, and the chapels around the central place of worship were used as stalls for horses. Even the lead of the roof was ripped off to make a fresh supply of bullets for French muskets.

The cathedral is cruciform in shape. Its length is 148 yards; breadth, 67 yards; height of roof, 201 feet; height of towers, 512 feet — the loftiest church towers in Europe. This enormous mass of masonry is enlivened by a profusion of flying buttresses, turrets, gargoyles, galleries, cornices, foliage, etc., the whole presenting an exterior the grandeur and beauty of which is said to be unsurpassed by any architecture in the world — that of Milan's Cathedral excepted.

Standing there in the rain, looking up that grand height and thence down to the broad and apparently everlasting foundations, impressed with the rich gray blackness of that immense mass of stone now polished by the rain, our attention was directed to a family group seated upon a projecting row of massive stone at the base of the building, eating their early dinner and chattering as merrily as were the birds upon the solemn gargoyles far above their heads. They were hucksters from the country, who had sought shelter from the shower. With the confidence which the humblest devotee feels in the all-protecting power of the Church, they had sought shelter here, quite as free from man's interference as were their voluble neighbors overhead.

When we came into this solemn presence the second time, later in the day,

the cathedral towers were resplendent with the glory of the midday sun, and every shadow intensified the brightness of its glory.

A massive door opens and the interior presents itself to our wondering gaze. In figures, here is an area of 7,399 square yards. Its arches are supported by fifty-six massive pillars.

The stained glass windows tell their several stories of the mysterious union of the Human and the Divine. Their colors seem to have deepened and become more clear with age, like the old wines of Burgundy and the Rhine.

The carved stalls are marvels of the curious workmanship of the Fifteenth Century.

The choir chapels are of themselves a special study. Many of them have carvings and altar-pieces which separately might well command the day's attention.

The chapel of St. John contains the tomb of Archbishop Conrad, the founder of the cathedral. In this chapel under glass is seen the original sketch of the west façade of the building, with the two great towers. Part of this sketch was found in Darmstadt in 1814, and the rest of it in Paris in 1816. It shows the great skill of the draftsmen of other days. We purchase an entrance to the treasury and a handsome young sacristan in black tells us, in English and in German, his well-learned story as he points out the rare jewels and vestments here collected. The golden Reliquary of the Magi, a fine and costly specimen of Romanesque workmanship, is thought to be over eighth hundred years old. Ivory carvings and mosaics, immense rubies and emeralds in old and gray settings, gold and red vestments each with a history,— such are the treasures here carefully guarded.

As we resume our walk from chapel to chapel, and our ancient guide talks on and on of saints and sinners long gone by, clouds gather and darken the interior, and as the guide emerges from one chapel and another and dodges from behind one and another tomb a professional smile plays, or rather works, upon his pale, sallow face; his black, bead-like eyes twinkle; his humped shoulders seem to bend more and more. His general mummified appearance and mechanical voice belong to the place. I fancy him sleeping among the tombs, himself a part of the past concerning which he glibly talks. With our friends about us we really didn't need a guide, but we did well to engage this ghost of the Twelfth Century. Our visit to the Cologne Cathedral would not have been complete without him — or it!

———

After dinner we take a carriage and drive about the city. First, we are given a ride through old " Köln " with its narrow streets, and then we make the circuit of the city via the famous boulevard, " Ring-strasse." Its connecting streets stand upon the old ramparts, for Cologne was once a walled town and one of the strongest fortresses of the middle ages. New Cologne blossoms out in fountains and statues and spacious homes and business houses; and yet it is proudest of its old stone towers and gates. This close union of the old and the new gives to the city a picturesqueness charming to American eyes.

Our drive ends at Holzmarket where we take our first good look at the Rhine. The scenery immediately about Cologne is not especially impressive. The beauty of the Rhine of which so much is written and sung is farther up the river.

The *Schiffbrucke*, or Bridge of Boats, is the most interesting object to an American, much more than the costly *Feste Brucke* with its immense piers and abutments, a short distance farther on. It vividly brings to mind mediæval times when the *schiffbrucke* was the only bridge, and when men fought single-handed and in groups to defend these passes over the otherwise impassable stream. At any time during the day hundreds of people may be seen crossing upon these boats. When a steamer would pass up or down the river, a boat or two is slipped out of its place, thus making a channel through which it may pass.

We take another day for a visit to the church of St. Ursula and for the climb to the top of the Cathedral Tower.

It is a strange curiosity that leads the visitor to the quaint old Thirteenth Century St. Ursula, with its skulls and crossbones, grim reminders of the inevitableness of death. The structure was dedicated to the memory of the English princess Ursula who, with her eleven thousand maiden attendants, was murdered by the Huns at Cologne on her way back from a pilgrimage to Rome. The legend dates back to the Ninth Century, and four centuries later found permanent embodiment in the *schatzkammer*, or treasure vault, of this church. The bones of St. Ursula are here enshrined in a beautiful casket. The bones of the eleven thousand maidens who followed her to death are arranged in all sorts of rosettes, crosses, initial letters, and other devices, and are fastened to the walls. Skulls of these martyrs grin at the visitor from shelves, niches, and windowed holes in the wall. The spaces between the inner and outer walls are packed with human bones. The reader should see the bland smile and hear the sweet inflections of the sacristan as he remarks, "This is the skull of another saint "; or, "That is a lock of Saint Ursula's hair," etc.

———

Passing reluctantly through the solemn aisles of the great Cathedral of Cologne, we present ourselves to the keeper of the towers, and are soon making the ascent. We pass through dark winding stairways and passage-ways, on and up, on and up, stopping to rest at one and another balcony from which we obtain gratifying views of the somber interior, lighted by the afternoon sun, its rays filtered through the beautiful stained glass windows. We stand under the enormous bell which is rung at Christmas time and on other great days, the ringing of it requiring the combined pull of twenty-eight men, as we are solemnly informed. The relatively smaller bells do service on ordinary occasions. But they are far from ordinary bells. The big bell, the Kaiserglocke, was cast only twenty-one years ago, and was made of metal obtained from French guns captured in battle. It weighs 50,000 pounds. The next in size is 448 years old and weighs 72,000 pounds. Its tones which we are permitted to hear are of marvelous richness and strength. As they resound through the upper corridors and hallways the effect is deafening.

We pass up the three lower stories of the south tower, and then proceed on up the octagonal section, upon which rests the magnificent open spire which, with its companion spire, from the ground looks very light and lace-like, but which, viewed from its base, seems to have been built to last forever. We have ascended 365 steps, our guide informs us, and we are not inclined to question the correctness of the count. The hard climb has its compensation. The view from the south tower of Cologne's cathedral is not as grand as other views which I have attempted to describe. But no view from such a great height is uninteresting. To look down upon the cathedral itself is a rare privilege. The foliage cut in stone, the gargoyles, the turrets, cornices, flying buttresses, which seemed so small from the street, now stand out startlingly

prominent, their great size quite overwhelming us. The city below is interesting with its ancient town hall and churches, its narrow old streets, its broad avenues extending along the line of the ancient city walls, its picturesque bridge of boats, thronged with pedestrians who look like mere insects moving in two intermingling currents, the costly railroad bridge beautifully arched and ornamented with equestrian statues — all these sights fascinate the beholder. And then, when the eye is wearied with looking at the hive of humanity below, it ranges off over the low level valley of the lower Rhine, through which the river takes a winding, reluctant way to the sea. We turn our gaze up the river to obtain, if we may, some suggestion of the famous scenery of the Rhine, which we anticipate seeing on the morrow. We are not disappointed, for there to the southeast, beyond the university town of Bonn, beyond Godesberg with its ruined tower, loom the famous *Siebengebirge*, or Seven Mountains, guarding the passage up the river, and far up on the heights is a faint outline of the ruins of Drachenfels — first of the ruined castles which look down upon the Rhine. The river view is a restful one and one which we find full of promise, the fulfilment of which promise will be my next theme.

IS CYCLING A FAD?

By G. F. Rinehart.

THE popular appetite for the bicycle is no less remarkable than the popular bicycle appetite. There is a sort of David and Jonathan affinity between the two. The old question of priority, waged in the interests of the oak and the hen, as against the acorn and the egg, seems to arise here. This question of antecedence might be carried yet further to determine whether the "new woman" preceded the popularity of the wheel, or whether the wheel craze is responsible for the

"new woman." Public sentiment seems to be about equally divided. The wheel, like Barkis, is "willin'" to assume the responsibility for its offspring. It *is* evolving a new woman,—sensible, vigorous and lovable as of old. She is no less modest and no less womanly than the daughters, sisters, mothers and sweethearts of bygone years. Only a few people are alarmed at what they presume to call the "innovation." They are fearful lest "bloomer picnics" become as popu-

C. B. MCGREER,
Manager Bicycle Department Mayo & Spalding Co.,
Sioux City, Iowa.

lar as "Trilby teas," and the garb of the
bathing beach be utilized inland. This
fear is ill-founded. Woman will still be
woman, though a little bicycle sense and
common sense do make a wondrous
change. She will be nearer nature, perhaps, less waspish in figure, and her vital
organs will not be forced to pose as the
ejected tenants of their wonted habitations. People who wonder at the new
costumes will sometime die, and their
grandchildren will look through the back
numbers of the fashion monthlies and
wonder why their foremothers wore those
funny long street dresses which they had
to hoist so high when it rained.

After all, a sound constitution is not a
crime, and it is better to amend a bad
one than to let it remain a prey to the
ninety-nine diseases so encouragingly

portrayed in the almanac. This is the
mission of the wheel, — man's "best
friend." A vigorous woman, with enough
vigor to rear children and maintain her
independence, is not an element of danger to anyone but a narrow-souled husband. Medical authority has been cited
by well meaning but mistaken people to
discourage cycling. They say the anatomy and the hygiene of the coming race
will be deplorable if we perversely persist in much riding. "The bicycle face"
is the latest nightmare following some
doctor's impaired digestion. This scared
physician evidently needs the professional
attention of some broad-minded brother.
The heroic treatment of ozone imbibed
through the medium of a country bicycle
ride would do him good. When his hallucination is thoroughly removed, and he
resumes his normal mentality, he will,
perhaps, recall the fact that in his budding
infancy he was obliged to learn to walk;
that ever since that time he has been
expending nerve force, unconsciously
though it be, to maintain an equilibrium.
He will then arrive at the conclusion, by
easy stages, that if the "bicycle face" is
caused by nervous exhaustion, due to
sustaining a balance on the wheel, his
own walking, standing and running must
have given him an equally frightful face.
If his theory were correct, nothing but a
hobby horse could stand alone without
serious waste of nerve force.

The large percentage of sallow faces

W. W. ORCUTT,
of Orcutt & Orcutt Co., Sioux City, Iowa.

W. W. BOWERS.

W. M. ORCUTT,
of Orcutt & Orcutt Co., Sioux City, Iowa.

F. D. THRALL,
(Winners, Iowa, Chairman Racing Board,
Iowa Div. L. A. W.

RALPH E. McCURDY,
Oskaloosa's Famous "First."

W. W. ANDERSON,
President Jefferson Wheel Club,
Jefferson, Iowa.

and pinched features that furnished the doctor with his favorite chimera have taken to the wheel for the express purpose of removing these marks and brands of physical indisposition. To expect every cyclist to exhibit a round face and a rosy complexion is as unreasonable as to hope that all of this great physician's patients will avoid an epitaph. The learned dissertations of the whole school of theoretical generalizationists could not convince the wheelman that his inflated lungs, capital digestion and superb muscular development are indications of speedy dissolution. His clear reasoning faculties, due to a vigorous circulation, point to long life and a '96 wheel.

Some people who do not ride have characterized the present popularity of the wheel as a mere "fad," and argue, with what is perhaps slanderously called a woman's reason, that the cycling spirit will wane simply *because it will.* On the other hand, the enthusiast sees in the constantly growing interest anything but a momentary inspiration. He views the sport as even yet in its infancy, and looks forward with prophetic eye to a future of surprising revelations. The wheel has already practically revolutionized modern methods of locomotion. It has furnished inspiriting recreation to the thousands whose struggles for existence heretofore precluded the possibility of an outing. It has turned inventive genius into an avenue of great possibilities, and we can confidently expect extraordinary develop-

ments in the years to come. Even now progressive France has taken the initiative and has startled the conservative world with a trial test of horseless carriages for eight hundred miles over ordinary roads at an average speed of fifteen miles per hour. This remarkable accomplishment is but an incident of the new outdoor sport, born of the cycling movement, diverted to the broader field of general locomotion.

The invention of the pneumatic tire was a great step in the direction of the ideal vehicle. By reducing the discomforting jar of travel to a minimum it was possible to make lighter mounts and construct a staunch frame on the artistic lines

GEO. MIERSTEIN,
A Promising Young Cyclist.

that the up-to-date wheel presents. It was this tire that made cycling popular and the development of man-power a source of wonder. The mile record has come down from the three-minute mark by slow gradations to the time of one minute, thirty-five and two-fifths seconds, made by the champion athlete of the world, John S. Johnson. Now we hear of a reckless rider who proposes to ride at the marvelous speed of a mile a minute, paced by an engine! This feat, incredible as it may seem, is wholly pos-

sible and will, no doubt, be accomplished.

The love of sport is inherent in mankind, and its outward manifestations can be diverted but never wholly restrained. Cycling is the only real sport that forms a working partnership with utility. It is a panacea for lassitude, and one of the most agreeable medicines to take. It is the very poetry of motion and comes as near to flying as some people are, presumably, likely to come, either *ante* or *post mortem.* As to appetite — there is no law yet enacted that prohibits one from

SOME RACING MEN WHO RIDE THE RELAY.
T. B Ashley.
J. R. Morrow
W. J. Ashley.
C. W. Ashley.
W. M. Enright

A GROUP OF CYCLING ENTHUSIASTS.

O. L. Su... C. R. Po... F. C. Mer...
N. T. Moore. A. A. Herring, C. D. Hale.
President Lakes Quaker W. C., Sioux City.

eating as much as he wants if he liquidates his bill.

The old idea that one cannot ride a wheel without the sacrifice of necessary dignity is, happily, exploded. The dignity that would suffer under such circumstances is better vaporized. When the proper position is maintained, cycling is the embodiment of grace. It gives symmetry to the frame and elasticity to the muscles, the vigor of health to the body and pure outdoor air to the lungs, and is, withal, the sworn foe of "that tired feeling" we read about in the patent medicine advertisements.

A contest of science, skill and muscle, with all brutality removed, ought to be the ideal sport of cultured people. It does not require recourse to the imagination to predict that the time will come when bicycle racing will be the crowning sport of the world. It affords all the latitude of other sports with the added element of speed. What can be more thrilling to the lover of outdoor sports than to witness, for example, the "Minneapolis Wonder," John S. Johnson, speeding straight away at a rate surpassing that of the fleetest running horse the world ever produced? What can be more inspiriting than to see the phenomenal Arthur A. Zimmerman pedalling like a hero in the contest where only honest blood and brain and brawn excels? No wonder that such events attract more people than the English Derby, and that the assembled thousands applaud the victors and welcome the advent of the manly sport that sounds the death knell of bestial contests!

Will cycle racing supersede horse racing? As certainly as the vestibuled train

KNAPP & SPALDING'S IMPERIAL RACING TEAM, SIOUX CITY, IOWA.
W. R. Hitch.   A. L. Leggett.   A. J. Hopkins.

has taken the place of the stage coach. The necessity which first gave an impetus to horse racing, and which has subsequently sustained it, is now and forever removed. In its time it made horse breeding a science, but it no longer pays to rear fast horses for a dead market. The "silent steed of steel" has given the roadster a rest. It has shouldered his burdens, cheapened his production and left him a relic for museums of the future.

Railroad corporations are worrying over the problem of the wheel. Several companies are absurdly inconsistent enough to charge the cyclist for his twenty-pound wheel while carrying the one hundred and fifty pound trunk of his fellow passenger for nothing. Others condescend to check a wheel after the owner has signed a document releasing the railroad companies from all responsibility in case of breakage. This admirable provision leaves the wheelman in mortal agony for fear the baggage smasher is deliberately demolishing his hundred dollar wheel out of pure antipathy and irresponsibility. Some roads will not check a wheel at all, but leave the whole question with the baggageman, who never fails to remark, "Here comes a quarter," when he sees a wheelman pushing his mount toward the train. A few companies, however, are obliging and consistent enough to regard bicycles as baggage and check them accordingly.

The growing popularity of bicycle racing has led to the great national organization of the League of American Wheelmen, which superintends all races, whether professional or amateur. The line of prejudice between these two divisions is no longer drawn, and it is at last possible for open courtesy between them. After all, it matters little whether one races for money direct, or by some freak of propriety is forced to take various articles as prizes, which he invariably discounts if he can.

It is difficult at this time to calculate the effect of the bicycle on the oats market. The "hungerless horse" no doubt affects it, but even this is not without its compensatory advantages, for cheap oats make cheap oatmeal and the hotel and boarding house managers find oatmeal, as the landlady recently remarked, "so fillin' and so cheap!"

The pneumatic-tired bicycle of the period is a peaceable revolutionist, making life worth infinitely more to the housed-up classes, to whom the horse, with its costly keeping, is an impossibility. Among the benefactors of these end-of-the-century days, place the little group of personally unknown inventors who have mounted the world on wheels.

EDITORIAL COMMENT.

THE letter of President Grant to Senator Wilson, for the first time published, in this number of THE MIDLAND, must forever silence the charge of the Senator's enemies that the vote cast in favor of allowing the McGarrahan claim cost him a seat in the President's Cabinet. The President twice tendered the Iowa senator a place in his Cabinet — the second time as Secretary of State; but, Mr. Washburne having held the office longer than was anticipated, and having called about him in the Department of State his own personal and political friends, Mr. Wilson felt it would be ungracious to remove these gentlemen and might prove an embarrassment to retain them in his political family. This consideration, coupled with his desire at the time to return to his Fairfield home, led him to decline the premiership in President Grant's cabinet. The letter is gratifying reading to friends of the Senator as to admirers of our Soldier President. It is a strong proof of the President's confidence in his friend and another pleasing instance of his personal loyalty.

* *

THE godlike ego of Victor Hugo in his old age was a narrow escape from the ridiculous. It was thought to be incomparable. But, now comes the Hungarian poet, novelist, editor and patriot, Maurus Jókai, claiming, with Hugo, the right to a prominent seat in Parnassian councils. Scarcely less interesting than the story of his life, as told by himself in the August *Forum*, is the sublime yet childlike complacency with which Jókai tells it. He begins his life-sketch with an exhibition of the Old World pride of birth. He says: "I spring from a noble family." He tells us he invariably took rank in his class as "*premier eminent.*" He terms his wife "the most sublime figure in Hungarian dramatic art." Explaining his phenomenal work — phenomenal in quality as in extent — he says: "More than any other mortal, perhaps, I have been loved and hated." In recounting the varied nature of his literary subjects and of his attainments, he incidentally remarks: "My library is the most valuable in the possession of a private individual." Of his own works he modestly says: "There is on earth no valley wherever hidden, nor country, nor vegetation, of which these books do not treat.....I undertook the profound and complete study of the history of my people as well as that of the universe. ....I know all the vegetable kingdom by name and I have a magnificent collection of conchifera." Here he gives away the whole art of novel-writing as he understands it: "I reveal the secret which the world may imitate" — a secret the world has at least guessed at already — "the careful germination of a leading idea, the careful evolution of the character and scenes from the actual rather than the fanciful." But who has a better right to enjoy himself! Here is a man of three score and ten who has fought his fight and nearly completed his work and yet lives to enjoy his crown while here on earth. On attaining his seventieth year, and the fiftieth year of his literary career, two hundred villages elected him to honorary citizenship and scores of societies gave him honorary degrees. His literary labors are chiefly included in three hundred and fifty bound volumes and his most popular works have been translated into fourteen different languages.

* *

BEFORE dismissing this remarkable man let us make a guess at the real secret of his power. Not in his erudition, but in his right conception of what constitutes the fiction that men, women and children feel to be true to life. The crisis in his literary career came in 1848 when deep feeling for the first time permeated his writing. He well says: "Abandoning the fantastic creations of a sick brain and its accompanying style of warped obscurity, I forced myself to discover the

283

characters having an actual existence in life, and to write in a language comprehensible to the people. The proof of my success is shown in the comment of a peasant who cried out after reading one of my stories, ' It is not bad to write like that ; I could do as well myself.' "

* *

To BRING into striking contrast with this the natural story-telling method, turn to a fair sample of the opposite method—the art of picturing people who may have lived and incidents that might have occurred in some other age or country than that with which the author has an acquaintance from actual heart touch or knowledge. Take, for instance, Conan Doyle's novel, " The White Company." Given a degree of brutality enough to load down a half-dozen of Scott's novels ; given a distant approach to historical fact ; given a touch of youth and beauty and love and mystery, and a genuine talent for description ; add to this a liberal use of old-time oaths, such as " by my hilt "; vary this with " by St. Paul," or, " by St. George," " by our lady," " by my soul "; and when these seem a trifle wearisome introduce " by St. Martin of Tours," " by the three kings," or, " by God's coif." Then, with the aid of an old English dictionary, and a few English and French classics, fill in liberally with even the most commonplace dialogue, with worn-out words and forms of expression, such as " methinks," " sooth," " fair sir," " my liege," " quotha," " anon," " bide," " get thee hence," " scath," " scathless," " beholden," " I pray you," " prithee," etc., etc., and with more smashing of heads and slashing of bodies and carrying off of women than was at first thought necessary for the delectation of the reader,—you have a story of " The White Company" sort, and you may then complacently conclude,— as does Conan Doyle, in his preface,— that you have done a virtuous thing in " dignifying our English past," and incidentally written a book which is, borrowing a phrase from the newsdealers, " a good seller."

SOLOMON was a wise man in his day ; but—have you heard of that Missouri magistrate's shrewd sentence? An illiterate man was remanded to jail until such time as he could demonstrate that he had learned to read. Another offender, an educated man, was sentenced to keep the illiterate man company until such time as he could demonstrate that he had taught the man to read. In three weeks' time both men were discharged from custody.

* *

AN English reader of THE MIDLAND thinks it hardly fair to name a Birmingham journal as illustrative of the lack of English journalistic enterprise in the matter of reporting American news. He tells us we should look to the great journals of London for news from the outside world. And so we looked through the first London newspaper that came to hand, *The Standard*, of July 27,— but only to find in that great blanket-sheet of a newspaper just eleven lines of telegraphic news from North America and not a line from South America. The eleven lines reported some occurrence on the island of Newfoundland.

* *

THE *Century* terms the year preceding a national campaign " the season of timidity in presidential candidates." But is " timidity " the word? This is, certainly, an excellent time for a show of modesty from presidential possibilities.

* *

JAMES WHITCOMB RILEY attempts Irish-English verse in the August *Century*, and does pretty well with it, we are sorry to say. Why is it—tell me ye winged winds — why is it that a man rather be called versatile than great?

* *

AFTER reading Commander McGiffin's vivid description of the battle of the Yalu, in which engagement the author—an American ex-officer— had charge of the Chinese battle-ship, *Chen Yuen*, the question will rise, what kind of a man must he be who voluntarily quits his country's service to enter the Chinese navy? Mr. Foster refused an enormous sum of money and unusual honors, rather than longer remain in the diplomatic service of the Chinese Empire as counsellor to the emperor. We can see how Mr. Foster could honorably accept the position urged upon him, one which opened a thousand opportunities "to serve the present age," his "calling to fulfill." But the only possible justification of the trade of war is patriotism. When a man rents himself out, as Commander McGiffin does, to a foreign government — and a heathen nation — as a professional fighter of its battles, how much better is he than the hireling butchers whom decadent Rome used to maintain her power !

* * *

WE ARE threatened with another attempt at spelling reform ! Funk & Wagnells threaten to introduce into their publications a series of new spellings, such as "beutiful," "glimps," "skul," and "yern," "provided a reasonable number of other periodicals, and writers, and literary men will adopt the same so as to help break the force of the criticism that they may oppose." We intimately know an editor who once set out to reform the world's bad spelling and, after a six weeks' daily trial of it, came to the conclusion that the world needed several other reforms more than it needed a spelling reform, and that changes in spelling, as in pronunciation, are not the result of a formal movement, but are, rather, the product of a natural growth.

* * *

THE young lady selected for the third Type of Midland Beauty, in the present number, is Miss Minnie Myers, of Belle Plaine, Iowa. The excellent portrait from which it was engraved was taken by Mr. O. E. Pearson, the well-known Des Moines photographer. Miss Myers is a graduate of the Drake University School of Oratory, of which department Professor Ott is the successful head. Her picture represents her as "Lady Teazle," in Sheridan's "School for Scandal."

* * *

TRAGIC as was the recent death of Thomas Hovenden, whose painting,

"Breaking Home Ties," is to thousands a vivid memory of the World's Fair, yet there is a sad satisfaction in the thought that one to whom home and loved ones were evidently so dear should have lost his life in a brave attempt to restore a child to her mother. Death came to him in one of his most exalted moments when self was lost in sympathy. The last thought registered upon his mind was wholly outside of self. What more fitting time for the transfer of the artist's soul from time to eternity ! And yet it was pitiful.

* * *

"THE reader is obtuse who is free from the impulse to read the last three cantos of the 'Paradise' on his knees." Thus saith Miss Vida D. Scudder in her "Creed of the English Poets." Miss Scudder must feel that she has happened in on a very obtuse and irreverent age. She should have been on earth centuries ago, contemporaneous with Dante, when men and women did most of their reading on their knees.

* * *

IN THE recent death of Frank E. Pixley, the Pacific Slope lost one of its most luminous writers and eloquent orators. What would we not give could we but hear from this departed Argonaut a report of that far away country, not down in our geographies, which we confusedly term the Beyond !

* * *

MRS. ABIGAIL GARDNER SHARP corrects THE MIDLAND's statement under its picture of the Spirit Lake Massacre Monument, in substance that the spot where her father fell is marked by the pile of stones in the foreground of the picture. Mr. Gardner was shot and killed in his own house, as Mrs. Sharp relates on page 34 of the July MIDLAND.

* * *

WE carelessly omitted last month to acknowledge our indebtedness to Mr. A. E. Woullett, Ottumwa's artistic photographer, for the fine portrait of Miss Mahon, THE MIDLAND's second "Type of Midland Beauty."

CONTRIBUTORS' DEPARTMENT.

JUDGE FLANDREAU AND THE RESCUE OF ABIGAIL GARDNER, NOW MRS. SHARP.

Ex-Governor Carpenter cheerfully consents to the publication of the following letter from Judge Flandreau, relative to an unintentional departure from historical accuracy in his able and valuable paper, "The Spirit Lake Massacre," in the July MIDLAND. All who know Mr. Carpenter's high sense of honor will agree with Judge Flandreau in that injustice to anyone was furthest from his thought and purpose:

ST. PAUL, July 13, '95.
HON. CYRUS C. CARPENTER, *ex-Governor of Iowa*, Des Moines [Ft. Dodge], Iowa:

My Dear Sir,—I have just read with much interest your article in THE MIDLAND MONTHLY for July, on the "Spirit Lake Massacre." The facts as stated therein are generally very accurate, and it will be a valuable contribution to the history of your State and the Northwest. I feel confident that you will be pleased to make any corrections that I may convince you should be made, in the cause of history. On pages 30 and 31 of your article, after telling of the delivery to me of Mrs. Marble, you speak of my efforts in connection with Governor Medary, Missionaries Riggs and Williamson and Colonel Alexander to rescue the rest of the captives, and use this language:

"It required weeks of negotiation to secure the proper Indians for the mission, and to supply them with the articles which would be likely to secure the ransom, and one of the results of a delay which could not be avoided was the fact that but a few days before its consummation, a son of Inkpaduteh, because he had not been obeyed in some demand upon Mrs. Noble, who was a most spirited and high-minded woman, had beaten her brains out with a club."

The mistake in this statement is that no delay at all occurred in fitting out the expedition to rescue the remaining women. Mrs. Marble was delivered to me on May 21st, and on May 23rd, less than two days after, my expedition started from the Yellow Medicine River, all well equipped for its mission. I send you herewith an article on the subject that I read before the Minnesota Historical Society on the 8th day of December, 1879. On pages 9 to 12 you will find a full history of this incident, with the dates and all the minutiæ. On page 11 you will see what I thought of the necessity of expedition, and how I hurried matters up. There I say: "I had no public fund that could be devoted to such purposes, but I had confidence in the generosity of the people, *especially if I succeeded*, and as every moment might be worth a life, I determined to assume the responsibility of anything that was necessary," etc.

You will see by Mrs. Sharp's article in the same magazine with yours that my party arrived in their camp on the 30th day of May, just seven days after they started (see page 39) and from what I infer from her account of the killing of Mrs. Noble, that it must have occurred before Mrs. Marble was delivered to me on the 21st of May. So my delay could not have had anything to do with it.

It was sufficiently distressing to me to know that Mrs. Noble was killed; but to have it intimated, from so distinguished a source as yourself on Iowa history, that it occurred in consequence of the dilatoriness of myself, is the occasion of this letter. Of course I do not intimate that you had any intention in the matter, but you will readily see that it is of sufficient importance to me to call for explanation.

I hope to be present at the dedication of the monument at Okoboji on the 26th inst., where it will afford me pleasure to meet you and become better acquainted.

Sincerely yours,
CHARLES E. FLANDREAU.

CONCERNING THE PROPOSED ACADEMY OR SOCIETY OF WRITERS.

Does it not seem a little too ambitious for a society of unknown western writers to call itself after the most renowned literary institution in the modern world? Does not the name, Academy of Literature, lack the element of modesty which all young things should have?

I am very much in favor of an organization of writers and think such a society would be both entertaining and profitable; but let us start as becomes youth; let us take a humble seat at first, and then be called up higher. Why not have a society of western writers; call it the Midland Contributors' Club; limit it to accepted contributors in some magazine of good standing, if such a limit is thought wise; organize with an initiation fee of (say) two dollars; have our first meeting at Des Moines (say) this fall? Then let it grow into an academy of learning and literature if it can!

Fort Dodge. MARY A. KIRKUP.

Have just read Miss Corkhill's article and your suggestions. It seems to me that even the mere touch of minds in such association justifies it if no more is accomplished. I would like a place in it—one near the door.

Boone.　　JOHN M. BRAINARD.

The suggestions made by Kate Corkhill in the August MIDLAND should be productive of practical results. An Iowa Academy of Letters might be made very helpful to our young writers, and exceedingly interesting to those who are older in the work. I would gladly become a member of such an organization.

Dunlap.　　ERNESTE WILDE.

GOSSIP WITH CORRESPONDENTS.

If not too great a demand upon your time would you kindly pass your opinion as to whether or not I have any journalistic ability.

You write well; but journalistic ability means more than mere ability to write well. Not knowing anything about the degree of readiness with which you write, the range of your knowledge, both practical and theoretical, the interest you feel in public affairs and measures, the degree of physical health you enjoy, the amount of tact you possess, the relative quickness and correctness of your judgment as to what is news, and what are the most pressing themes for comment, and how far a particular item of news or subject of comment should be carried, etc., it is impossible to pass intelligently upon the question you raise. Study your own present capabilities and your capacity for growth. Feel your way along until you are able to answer the question yourself.

If you consider it "trash" you will do me a personal favor to say so.

The editor of a periodical goes out of his way when he passes on any question, relative to a manuscript, beyond the one question of availability for his own future use. Gil Blas' experience with the Archbishop is the common experience of the critic who accepts an invitation to let the author know the worst.

Are photographs or drawings obligatory with the Original Descriptive Papers, entered for the $10 prize?

No, but they are given their due weight in the judgment as to relative availability.

May I send the same stories I send you to any other periodical at the same time?

No; one periodical at a time. If we hold your MS. too long, say six weeks, send us a postal of inquiry. Constantly in receipt of MSS., there is sometimes a longer delay than there should be;

though we aim to report on all MSS. sent us within thirty days of receipt of same.

In arranging work for the year beginning September 1st, 1895, I would be pleased to contribute one piece to your magazine. No material for inspection. No contracts made after that date. Price of story, 1 500 to 5,000 words, $50; price of poem, $100. Please let me hear from you.

Your terms and conditions were evidently sent to the wrong magazine.

As I can scarcely hope to win a prize on one poem when another [one previously submitted and returned] is not even available for publication at any price, etc.

This writer's inference is unwarrantable. (1) An author's mental and moral height, unlike the physical stature, varies continually. At one time, the mind is a pigmy, incapable of high thinking; at another time it towers giant-like. (2) A poem not available at one time may be available at another time, *e. g.*: Suppose an editor to have accepted all the Easter poems he can possibly use, and along come several more Easter poems. In justice to all parties, he should promptly return the last ones sent him, however acceptable they would otherwise be. (3) A poem not available for publication in one periodical may be acceptable in another, *e. g.*: A poem returned by *The Cosmopolitan* was accepted by THE MIDLAND; and another poem, by the same author, returned by THE MIDLAND was accepted by *The Cosmopolitan*.

GOSSIP ABOUT AUTHORS AND THEIR WORKS.

Max Nordau is writing a novel. It may turn out to be an illustration of his own position as to the decadence of literature.

Union College, Schenectady, N. Y., gains and Iowa's State University loses Edward Everett Hale, Jr., professor of English, and author of various works on subjects relative to English literature.

Enrique Parmer has a spirited paper in the August-October number of *The Hesperian*, of St. Louis, on "Emancipation of Western Literature." While various ones are doing good service writing about it, THE MIDLAND is steadily and surely doing good service in effecting it.

Hamlin Garland's "An Evangel in Cyene" in the August *Harper's* is one of that author's most virile short stories.

Mrs. Madeline Yale Wynne, author of "The Little Room" in August *Harper's*, is a western writer of promise.

Beatrice Harraden's next will be a story of California life. She is not looking for a publisher now.

MIDLAND BOOK TABLE.

Col. Dorus M. Fox, whose able paper on Capital Punishment in the March MIDLAND was the subject of much comment, has just published a book of rare interest to many, one which he has long been at work on, entitled, "History of Political Parties, National Reminiscences and the Tippecanoe Movement."[*] The book includes 541 pages and is well printed, profusely and handsomely engraved and substantially bound. The work includes "elaborate accounts of the Federal and Republican parties of the olden time," of "their passing away, the organization and historic acts of the Whig, Republican and Democratic parties, with brief allusion to the other political bodies of ephemeral existence, together with an appendix containing a variety of useful tables," etc. The book is dedicated to the Republican party and to the volunteer soldiers of the country. Its author, president of the Des Moines Tippecanoe Club, was one of the most influential originators of the Tippecanoe Club movement which played an effective part in the memorable Harrison campaign of 1888. He is a fine specimen of the mental and physical vigor typical of the western pioneers who, in 1840, made the woods and the prairies ring with "Tippecanoe and Tyler, too."

To many, the most interesting chapters of Colonel Fox's work are those which relate to the Tippecanoe campaign of fifty-five years ago, and its far-reaching echo seven years ago, part of which its author was and much of which he saw. The vivid picture of the log cabin and hard cider campaign (beginning on page 133 is one to be read with enthusiasm by old-time participants in that campaign and with keen interest by those whose memory runs not back to that era. There are several other able contributors to chapters of this work, notably Henry Sayers, president of the Old Tippecanoe Club, of Chicago, Joel P. Davis, a member of the Veteran Tippecanoe Club, of Chicago; Rev. Dr. Hanson, formerly of Chicago, now of Pasadena; Congressman Lacy, Hon. Charles Mackenzie, of Des Moines, Hon. James S. Clarkson, author of the sketch of Father Clarkson the personal friend of the elder Harrison and Colonel Gatch, a delegate to the first Republican national convention. The numerous illustrations include most of the public men prominently named in the book and many active members of the Tippecanoe organization of the West.

———

The increasing popularity of Robert Herrick is an interesting subject of inquiry. Here was a man who wrote hundreds of poems without regard for their effect and with little regard for their chronological order and arrangement, and with extreme carelessness as to his own fame; a poet concerning whose life very little is known, whose verse attracted little attention in his own time, a single edition sufficing for nearly two hundred years. And yet now, in the latest tribute to his fame, by Professor Hale, five pages are given to simply a list of the several editions of Herrick's poems and of other works relating thereto! After an interval of silence covering 162 years, thirteen exhaustive editions of Herrick have appeared, with hundreds of Herrick brochures, reviews, etc. This poet has somehow commanded the profound study of such men as Hazlett, Grosart, Palgrave, Dobson, Morley, Swinburne, Saintsbury and Hale. The latest study of the subject is "Selections from the Poetry of Robert Herrick,"[*] edited by Edward Everett Hale, Jr., late professor of English in the State University of Iowa. These selections include all that the general reader need have of the poetry of Herrick. The book is made doubly valuable by the editor's introduction, which covers the life of the poet, a careful analysis of the two parts of Herrick's verse, "The Hesperides" and "The Noble Numbers," and much other matter pertaining to Herrick's poems, altogether a valuable contribution to the subject. Much of that which finds place in even a book of selections from Herrick is surprisingly free from suggestion of genius; but the rest is so fresh with the dew on the grass along country roads and with the pink on the cheeks of rural maidens, so redolent of the fields and lanes of rural England, so suggestive of rural sports, of "pageantry and plays," of "eves and holidays" and of "Maypoles, too, with garlands graced," that one can see why it is that men deep in the literature of all ages and peoples go back to the simple lays of Herrick with increasing rest as the years increase which separate them from their youth.

*D. M. Fox, author and publisher, Des Moines, Iowa. $1.00.

*Ginn & Co., Boston, publishers.

TYPES OF MIDLAND BEAUTY. IV.

THE MIDLAND MONTHLY.

VOLUME IV.   OCTOBER, 1895.   NUMBER 4.

By HORACE THOMPSON CARPENTER.
With Drawings by the Author.

I.

THERE are still to be seen in New York carrier-pigeon cotes, which within the memory of many were not unimportant factors in the beginning and development of the present vast system of collecting news by The Associated Press.

Perhaps in no better way can the uninitiated understand and appreciate the present system than by first glancing at the methods of gathering news in vogue some fifty or sixty years ago.

When the Whigs were in the heyday of their exuberant youth; when Webster, Clay, Calhoun and their associates were making history — and the people only half understanding it — and when the cool and prudent General Zachary Taylor was in Corpus Christi making preparations for the famous victories that followed; and, too, when the now half-forgotten Dr. Anson Jones was occupying the presidential chair of the thriving Republic of Texas, then it was that newspaper men began to fret and chafe at the limit of their horizon. The course of empire was spreading westward; our shipping was in the ascendency — well in the lead of the world's maritime procession; the vast resources of the Republic were daily becoming more apparent; the pulse of American life was beginning to beat faster and faster. While the nation and its affairs were developing, business of every description increasing, opportunities of boundless magnitude presenting themselves, the newspaper world found the problem of securing quick and reliable information of the world's doings daily growing more complicated and the necessity and importance of united action and combined effort more and more apparent. Electricity had not yet been bridled and tamed; steam was yet in its infancy and an unfeared rival of horse or sail power. Therefore, what more natural than to try

"Then it was that the newspaper men began to feel and chafe at the limit of their horizon."

and utilize — as in the days of old — the carrier-pigeon! The thought was acted upon and this fleet little carrier bore a useful and interesting part in transmitting messages within certain limits. So the pigeon cotes that received and sheltered this unique flock still stand as eloquent reminders of one of the characteristic traits of Americans, that of adapting and utilizing the means at hand. The swift carriers of Persian kings and Turkish sultans were trained for this special service of message-bearing. This was the embryo of the present Associated Press.

The expense of the service was jointly borne by a number of leading New York journals of the time that had banded together for mutual benefit and in the interest of the public.

But news was at first received through comparatively slow channels. Stages, canal packet-boats, steamboats and, only too often, sailing vessels were the media relied upon. Travelers were interviewed then as now. The first question, however, would not be as to personal opinion upon a country and inhabitants that had been observed only from the vessel's deck. But the traveler who had not something of interest to impart in those days was a rare exception. The blasé globe-trotter was not then known. He is a product of later day civilization, whose reason for being has not yet been satisfactorily determined upon.

Somewhere about this time, the elder Bennett, with his small tugs and steamers, established a system of going out to meet all incoming vessels for first news.

The Pony Express was also one of the important media in receiving and dispatching news, and was widely used until the introduction of telegraphy. Prior to these rather crude though energetic efforts news-gathering was largely a matter of individual effort. While dispatches of importance were still being rushed through from town to town, across wild and half-broken country; while swift but tough and shaggy, mud-bespattered ponies, with equally mud-soiled riders, were daily received and dispatched; while stages with their promiscuous and adventuresome occupants — with haughty or loquacious

" The elder Bennett, with his small tugs and steamers, established a system of going out to meet all incoming vessels for first news."

driver, as the case might be, well-braced amid great mail-pouches — were eagerly watched for and welcomed, the great forerunner of our present civilization was emerging from its embryonic state, stretching out its web-like strands across the hills and valleys of New York and Pennsylvania, westward bound.

The year 1846 found this marvelous piece of mechanism actually penetrating as far into the "wilds" as Pittsburgh, Pennsylvania. Here it rested for a time. The messages received over the wires were once more handed over to fleet couriers and were carried as far west as Cincinnati and neighboring towns. The less fortunate papers still farther west relied upon the less rapid method of stage and boat.

On the advent of telegraphy, the press, as a matter of course, was the first institution to show the marked change and benefit. Thence on, the world — at least the part of it that represented progress and civilization — was to enter a new era.

If the press was the first to adapt itself to these new conditions, and show its powerful and civilizing influence, and to be itself lifted out of ruts, yet never for a moment did it shirk its duty in fulfilling the exacting requirements of these new conditions.

Individual direction has erred from time to time, as it doubtless will err in all time; but the press as a whole has not only moved forward with the times but, for the most part, has proven the forerunner of progress.

II.

That various associations for the gathering and disseminating of news should, under the circumstances, spring up and strive for existence and wide recognition, stands to reason. No less in reason that out of the efforts of many to reach perfection some one in particular should, by virtue of the same logic, reach that perfection, or at least supremacy.

In thoroughness, in reliability, in the extent of field covered and in the number of its representatives, it can be said without exaggeration that no news association has ever equaled The Associated Press.

" So oft had tough and shaggy, good-tempered ponies, with equally good-natured riders."

Its 20,000 miles and more of leased wire in the United States alone and its connections abroad, covering every country where civilization has penetrated, well attest its preëminent facilities.

This leased wire mileage, enormous in extent as it is, in reality represents but one branch of the field controlled by and available to the Association. Special agents are located everywhere. Special facilities, either with wire or carriers, are utilized and established under certain conditions. For instance, leased wires are run directly to the scenes of national conventions, and full reports of proceedings sent out without a moment's delay. In any event of special interest to the public, no pains or expense is spared to have complete and immediate reports made. In Chicago, upon the execution of Prendergast, the murderer of Mayor Harrison, wires were run into the jail, and both the reporters and operators of the Association made immediate reports of everything pertaining to the execution. At the time of the notorious prize fight in Jacksonville, Florida, between Corbett and Jackson, seven mounted couriers on fleet racers carried the dispatches containing reports of the progress of the much discussed fight to the nearest telegraph wire a mile and a half distant. The energy shown and brilliant work done upon this occasion by the Association's representatives, under countless and aggravating difficulties, elicited the admiration of the newspaper world both at home and abroad. Something like 50,000 words on this event were filed between daylight and dusk.

In this connection it should not be overlooked that The Associated Press, in its dealings with the world and as a gatherer and a distributor of news, must of necessity be not only impartial in its handling of news,—so long as it is legitimate and sought after,—but, as a coöperative institution, must be absolutely non-partisan, non-sectarian and broad, that its clientage of newspapers of every shade of opinion may be satisfied. So, whether it is dealing with a national convention, a great temperance reform movement, a hanging or a prize fight, its province is only that of a news gatherer in presenting to the public prompt and accurate reports of what occurs.

Not that it should be inferred that opportunity never occurs when its mighty power can be used for the purest, noblest and highest principles. But it can well be understood that with its varied clientage, and greater sub-clientage in the legion of readers who hold views of every known character, sect and ism, strict-moraled and lax-moraled, it requires a nicety of judgment and discernment to know when and where to tighten the line, which is not often vouchsafed to any one individual. Yet that this very thing has been done by the present management with admirable effect will not be gainsayed by anyone familiar with the facts.

One instance in point, which came under the writer's personal observation. During the recent great strike and subsequent railroad riots, when good government for the moment seemed almost paralyzed, and lawlessness seemed let loose the country over, a series of communications and addresses were widely published throughout the country that unquestionably did incalculable good in restoring order and respect for our local and national government. It was the good Archbishop Ireland from whom these emanated, and it was the present manager of The Associated Press, with whom the Archbishop was so frequently closeted, that made it possible for the widespread good to be accomplished.

III.

The membership of The Associated Press consists, with only few exceptions, of the leading and most influential journals of the country. The papers that are not members are out of the Association either on account of their having been refused admittance through the action of local boards — the mission of which will be explained further on — or perhaps from some strong personal feeling of pride toward propping up a declining pet hobby.

I believe the first news-gathering association of which there is any record was called the New York Associated Press, though never incorporated. Their clientage was large. It was under the management of D. H. Craig, who was succeeded by Mr. Symonton. Horace White, now editor of the New York *Evening Post* and first vice-president of the Associated Press, was the first agent of the New York Associated Press appointed in Chicago. Marvin Hughitt, now president of the Chicago & Northwestern Railroad, it is

simply clients. Coördinate agents were the New England Associated Press, the New York City Press and the Philadelphia Associated Press (including Philadelphia and Baltimore papers). Another was the Western Associated Press already mentioned, then the Northwestern Associated Press. The Southern Associated Press was afterward formed and served the South, and Washington and Philadelphia

" But the New York Associated Press was immovable in its short sighted policy "

interesting to note, was then one of the telegraph operators under Mr. White. Wilbur F. Storey, editor of the Chicago *Times*, was afterward their Chicago agent.

About 1865 the Western Associated Press was established, under the laws of Michigan, with headquarters at Cleveland. It bought its news from the New York Association, which comprised seven papers, the *Tribune*, the *Herald*, the *World*, the *Times*, the *Sun*, the *Journal of Commerce* and the *Express*, afterward the *Mail*. The other papers were

papers. The papers of the far West were clients only.

With the unpleasant theory (at least to " the under-dog ") that might is right constantly and unceasingly exemplified, the New York Press Association began in the early sixties to make itself somewhat obnoxious to its western clients. This theory was shown in many ways, not only in the arbitrary stand made by the New York Association in not allowing the western members a voice in the management, but also by endeavoring to

Drawing by Hunter Thompson Carpenter.

MR. MELVILLE E. STONE, GENERAL MANAGER OF THE ASSOCIATED PRESS, AND HIS
PRIVATE SECRETARY, MR. P. H. EISET.

saddle all the expenses of the entire association on the western constituency. In other words, taxation without representation.

But the New York Associated Press was immovable in its short-sighted policy. Discontent grew stronger and stronger, yet, fearing the consequences of a break with the older organization, definite action was deferred by the Western Association.

However, in 1882, an arrangement was finally effected that brought these two great news organizations of America together, under the management of a committee composed of proprietors of three New York and two western newspapers.

William Henry Smith, who had been general agent of the Western Associated Press, was appointed general manager of the combined associations. The consolidation or working arrangement was entered into for a period of ten years, and while the two associations retained their respective titles, they were generally known from this time on as "The Associated Press."

In England, where only the New York

and the two associations prepared to separate. The Western Association in 1892 obtained a new charter under the title of "The Associated Press," while the New York Associated Press disappeared, having fallen under the control of another press agency called "The United Press."

Between the latter and the new Associated Press a working arrangement was entered into, in some respects similar to that with the New York Associated Press, but which was made more to the advantage of The Associated Press.

THE MESSENGER BOY.

" At times he seems to be largely responsible for his reputation."

Associated Press was known, the title was changed to "The Associated Press," which the letter-heads and similar documents showed represented the Western as well as the New York. The latter association under the new management had an equal voice with New York in controlling the cable news sent to America.

When the agreement of 1882 neared a termination, proposals were made to form a National Association under a single charter, but no agreement was reached

In this contract, as well as in all the negotiation which preceded and followed it, the United Press admitted and recognized the right of the organized company to the title "The Associated Press."

For some months—from December, 1892—the United Press and The Associated Press exchanged news as the New York and the Western had done; but finally, in August, 1893, all relations between the two agencies ceased The immediate cause indeed of the dissolution of the working arrangement was the fact of the United Press encroaching upon the territory of The Associated Press.

The news of the Reuter, Havas and Wolff agencies had always formed the basis of a successful foreign news service for America, and a draft contract had been drawn between these agencies on the one part and The Associated Press and the United Press on the other. Owing to the attitude of the United Press towards The Associated Press, however, and to certain secret proposals which were made by the manager of the United Press to Reuter's agency, in which the United Press endeavored to induce Reuter to execute the contract in the name of the International Telegram Company (a concern owned entirely by three or four members of the United Press), Reuter and his allies refused to enter into any arrangement with the United Press alone. The latter, in August, 1893, reopened its London office and resumed its functions of gathering and sending news to America.

The Associated Press has, since its revival, become gradually well known to newspapers in England, and it has been steadily growing in importance. It has established relations with the London *Times* and other newspapers and has formed many connections of great value to it as a news agency.

IV.

So many false and apparently malicious statements regarding The Associated Press have been circulated, so many petty slanders have been set afloat touching the *personnel* of the organization, that the quiet and dignified but forceful policy which has unceasingly been pursued compels our respect and admiration. The magnitude of success that has crowned the labor of those who have brought it to its present complete condition must be a matter of congratulation alike to its management, its members and the public.

The Associated Press as an organization has never pretended a philanthropic origin or existence further than is sug-

gested in its coöperative and mutual features. The stand is well expressed in the legend adopted, "One for all and all for one." And the organization is true to this, its strongest principle. Nor is there any thought or possibility of turning it into a money-making institution, but its aim is to do business at cost. Membership is on a basis of equalization; each assessment is made in proportion to the character of the news report taken. The mutual and coöperative features cannot be too strongly presented. Indeed, its very existence as an organization is dependent upon this position. As no one newspaper could alone stand the enormous expense entailed in gathering the news of the world, it was but the logical sequence of events in the progress and development of our modern wants and necessities that a number of leading journals should combine and bear their proportion of the expense of purchasing news in bulk as their needs should direct.

One of the most important as well as heaviest items of expense is the ocean cable service. For the younger generation it is a difficult matter to imagine a time when such service must not have been a necessity, but there are few men who have reached middle age that do not recall the excitement of the first experiments in laying the ocean cable. It was in 1858 that Cyrus W. Field sent the first message to The Associated Press announcing the successful laying of the cable; but disheartening failures to continue the service were encountered before the wonderful achievement became a permanent realization for all time.

That time finally came in 1866, when the universal rejoicing was commensurate with a great victory. The uniting of the Eastern and Western Hemispheres, with a strand so slight that it seemed hardly more than a good-sized hawser, might not in itself seem such a marvelous achievement,—though certainly it was such merely as an engineering feat,—yet what could it not portend!

It is only necessary to look back through the files of newspapers of that time to appreciate the incredulity, ridicule and opposition which the projectors of the cable encountered. But this has been the history of all great accomplishments. Who can measure the effect produced by that little group of wires since the first message was sent under the ocean—a telegram of congratulation from President Johnson to Queen Victoria—in broadening and civilizing the world and increasing the world's material prosperity, comfort, happiness and knowledge! The incredulity and skepticism, which had everywhere greeted the project of an ocean cable service, was challenged in a manner that brought fortune and fame to those interested, and a successful solution of the problem of rapid communication beyond all hope and expectation. It is perhaps superfluous to add that of all enterprises or organizations The Associated Press of necessity must have been most benefited by the Atlantic Cable, because of its position as a gatherer and distributor of news.

In all great and revolutionizing changes, inventions and adaptations, the pioneers of progress and improvement have had obstacles thrown in the way of success from every conceivable quarter. Nowhere was this narrow and bigoted spirit and unresponsive attitude shown in a more discouraging and aggravating manner than when Professor Morse struggled and waited in vain for recognition and action from Congress to enable him to prove to the world that he had discovered a means of fairly starting civilization upon a new era.

With indefatigable courage the inventor had braved the ridicule, skepticism and opposition that everywhere met his efforts to induce public trial of his invention, and it is surely a part of the history of a news-gathering association to refer to this, the most important branch of such an organization.

It was on a bright day in May, 1844, that messages were first actually exchanged between Baltimore and Washington, and thence until the present time each day has seemed to bring forth new evidence of the magnitude and importance of the invention that enables the press and the world to control the swiftest and most subtle of all mediums, Electricity.

The reports of the recent yearly contest between Oxford and Cambridge is a good illustration of the rapidity with which a world-wide matter of interest travels nowadays.

Last April when the race was rowed, the operators for thousands of miles of cable and wire were prepared to receive the name of the winner, as has been the usual custom for several years. But, to show the extraordinary quickness of telegraphy, it took only two minutes by actual calculation for the name of the winning college to reach Denver from the finishing point on the Thames, and four minutes to reach San Francisco. Of course, as above stated, every operator for thousands of miles was prepared for it, but even so the fact is not less wonderful.

Take another instance—and one even more extraordinary—the assassination of President Carnot. It was of course known by news managers and the public generally that Carnot was to be at Lyons on that day and to take part in a demonstration, but no one feared such a catastrophe as did happen. When the murderer committed his dastardly act, the news was at once flashed to London by The Associated Press agent, who was in close proximity to the scene of the tragedy, and the news reached London fully five minutes before it was even known at the rear end of the procession which the carriage of the President was leading. But, more wonderful still, it almost simultaneously reached New York, and fifteen minutes later the New York *World*, a member of The Associated Press, had an "extra" on the street containing a quarter of a column of the news in regard to it.

V.

The Associated Press has a membership of two hundred and eighty affiliated members and one hundred and fifty stockholders. The clientage served through minor agencies includes about seventeen hundred newspapers—something over rather than under.[1] The members are scattered from the Atlantic to the Pacific, and, though seldom brought together, the principle of self-governing is so strongly imbedded in the management that, with the *esprit de corps* and enthusiastic loyalty everywhere shown, it is bringing results which the most sanguine and hopeful could hardly have anticipated.

Each of the members engages by contract to contribute the news of his immediate vicinage to The Associated Press and to no other association. This mutual feature, each newspaper constantly on the alert for news and transmitting immediately anything of importance within its field which is of interest to the world at large—such as ruinous floods, devastating fires, unusual crimes—to the nearest accredited division agent, has developed a vigilant, exhaustless and admirably equipped corps of news-gatherers, the equal of which could in no other way be maintained. As every news member expects to be impartially and reliably served by fellow members through the general offices of the Association, so each in his turn strives to outdo his rival as to dispatch and accuracy. As might be expected, under such a system, little of interest escapes the Association's agents, for an agent each member practically constitutes himself.

The Associated Press system in the United States is divided into divisions. The Eastern Division has its headquarters at New York, in charge of Mr. Frank W. Mack. Col. Charles S. Diehl, Assistant General Manager, has also his headquarters here. The Southern Division has headquarters at Washington D. C., with Charles A. Boynton in charge. The Central Division is at Chicago, with Addison C. Thomas superintendent. The general offices are located in Chicago, Melville E. Stone, its General Manager. The Western Division headquarters are at San Francisco, John P. Dunning in charge.

In these divisions at certain central points agents are appointed who are held responsible for the Association's work within their prescribed limits, and to whom reports are submitted by the various newspaper members for transmission, and to whom the latter, in their turn, look for such reports, for which they have respectively contracted.

As a necessary and vital check in the protection of the privileges of The Associated Press members throughout the country, and to preserve the salient and coöperative features of the Association, a plan was adopted for forming local boards. The members of the local boards have by right of priority the privilege to decide upon the admission of any newspaper applicant. It is provided in the by-laws of the Association that in every city where there is more than one member holding membership certificate, entitled Series A, a local board, acting under a charter issued by the Board of Directors of the Association, shall be formed with proper officers,—president, secretary, etc.,—and that it will require the unanimous consent in writing of such members for admission. When there is only one member in a city holding this certificate, Series A, that member can exercise all the power and privilege of a local board. This power tends not only to keep out all undesirable applicants that might use the privilege for speculative or ulterior purposes, but also serves to keep in proper balance the value of the franchise itself.

The extent of the leased wire system of The Associated Press as it now exists is indicative of the Association's magnitude. These wires stretch out a great network across the American continent from St. Johns to Seattle and San Diego ; from Duluth to Jacksonville, New Orleans, Galveston and San Antonio, with a total of over twenty thousand miles—day and night wires.

Take this grand total, and then try and grasp the fact that not a hamlet so small, not a section of the country so remote but that when it has something to report which the world wants to know, it becomes for the time being an important feeder to this great system.

A very recent extension of the leased wire system is of universal interest, inasmuch as it now places the City of Mexico in direct communication with all parts of the world touched by The Associated Press. Strange as it may seem, this is the first time in the history of the two republics that direct telegraphic news connection has been an actual fact. The connection has been made through San Antonio and Laredo, Texas. At Laredo, on the border of Mexico, connection is made with the Mexican National Railway Company, that runs direct from that point to the City of Mexico. The full report is now being transmitted to Laredo, and there placed on the wires of the Mexican National and transmitted direct to the City of Mexico for publication in the *Herald*.

While the bare statement of this fact perhaps furnishes an ordinary item of news for general publication, yet any one familiar with methods of obtaining news in this near "far-away" country will realize and appreciate the real significance of it, for in truth this is the first time that Mexico has received the press dispatches fresh.

Heretofore it has been largely the custom to clip from Galveston and El Paso papers the news that had been published in those cities and sent as best they could over government wires and otherwise, to such papers as might wish news in the way of briefest form. In one way and another the news that has been sent, when finally published, has been so garbled and unreliable that a great deal of misconception has resulted on both sides, and it not only retarded national friendship but has been of incalculable harm in diverting trade and preventing business relations.

Now the capital of the Mexican Republic is enabled to receive the authentic news of the world as quickly and reliably as Denver or San Francisco. The night the service was started, the news was actually transmitted from Chicago to the City of Mexico within ten minutes.

Did space permit, it would be interesting to here note the strong words of approval expressed by such men as President Cleveland, President Diaz, and President Raoul, of the Mexican National, as to the importance of this difficult and enterprising move of The Associated Press; but one and all agree as to the beneficial results that will surely follow.

The European agent, Mr. Walter Neef, through his London office, receives news from the European centers all fed by a system hardly less vast and infinitely more complicated than our own. Many companies in the Old World give their aid and facilities toward a complete foreign service. Far-reaching and comprehensive contracts with the largest and most important news-gathering associations of Europe give to The Associated Press unlimited facilities. Try and conceive what all this means,—the enormous expense involved, the unceasing and untiring vigilance of the Association's allies, and you may the better understand the reason that the words are well chosen which ascribe to the Association a system of magnitude unparalleled in the history of news gathering.

Apropos of expenses incurred and the unique character of the system, the writer, while in the general office of The Associated Press recently, had his attention drawn to a little bunch of manifold matter that lay on the top of a desk at his side. This bunch of manifold probably did not exceed in size eighteen inches square. It represented the net result of The Associated Press for the month of April, 1895. It was type-written as a matter of course. Upon inquiring how many words it contained, the information was given that it consisted of a million and a half of words and represented a cost of over $100,000. Few readers of the daily newspapers' realize the tremendous outlay and what little there is to show for it at the end of the month or year.

The same is true of every large metropolitan journal. At the end of the year they simply have their files containing copies of their paper of every day during the year ; yet the news contained therein has cost the Press of which the paper is a member about a million and a half dollars, with nothing to show for it except a little roll of manifold and a small file of newspapers.

VI.

To touch upon one of the details of this great system, though by no means the least, the admirably arranged and perfected system of pneumatic tubes for transmitting messages, etc., to the various editorial rooms of the members, must not be overlooked.

Endless trouble, aggravating and annoying beyond endurance, had been experienced for years in getting matter delivered quickly and promptly from both Associated and City Press to their clients' rooms. In Chicago the long-suffering victims seemed to have endured unwonted hardship in this direction.

The messenger boy is doubtless a much-abused, slandered and generally scoffed-at creature. At times he seems to be largely responsible for his reputation,—the obliquity cast upon his gentle and restful profession. But, responsible or not responsible, maligned or rightfully "jumped upon," manifold copy, reporters' copy, important and non-important matter, were all alike delayed.

To remedy this world-wide condition the country was ransacked for a Pied-Piper of Hamelin, as it were. He was found in the person of Addison C. Thomas, of Chicago, the present superintendent of the Central Division of The Associated Press. The choice was wisely made. Having surveyed the group of messenger boys, Mr. Thomas concluded he could improve upon the article, and though the temptation to play upon words should be resisted, yet as a recorder of history the writer feels bound to say the group, like our little friends of Hamelin, were literally piped away, and to-day the most complete system of pneumatic tubes that has ever been devised connects the Press Association with the newspapers.

Though it was a serious problem to solve, Mr. Thomas was given full leeway so far as expense was concerned. After extensive and thorough research and study, familiarizing himself with all that had been done with pneumatic tubes both at home and abroad, the present system was planned and put into practical operation, and to-day stands without a superior. The careful and intelligent manner in which all of the details of this complicated undertaking are watched, the difficulties and obstacles successfully overcome, not only redounds to the credit of Mr. Thomas, but is proof of the progressive and modern character of the press organization.

In Chicago the tubes are laid under some of the principal streets, running from the Association's rooms in the Western Union Building at Clark and Jackson streets, diverging at intersecting streets to the various points of destination.

While the scientific and technical points of this system are varied and interesting to the expert, it will perhaps be sufficient to say here, for general information that, with the aid of these transmitting tubes, news-matter that is received in the telegraph operating rooms of The Associated Press is, upon receipt, instantly transferred to the various newspaper offices that are members of the Association.

For instance, a great calamity occurs—say a Mississippi steamer destroyed by fire, the occurrence accompanied by great loss of life. Either a division or local agent is immediately dispatched to the scene of disaster or the nearest point where reliable information can be obtained. As quickly as an intelligent and accurate understanding of the occurrence can be secured, a condensed report is hurried to the nearest telegraph office, received by the Association's own operators at the general office, and manifold copies written out on typewriters directly from the wire. These sheets are without delay put into pneumatic tubes leading to the transferring room below, and thence thrust quickly into a little tube box called a carrier. This carrier is made of flexible leather with an inner spiral frame to keep it in proper form that it may readily travel around the curves. Each end has a band of soft fur or wool to make it fit snugly. Not infrequently in sending reports of this nature, or indeed of any important event, members of the Association actually have the first sheets from the reporter's or correspondent's report that have gone through the operators' hands, the general office of The Associated Press and pneumatic tubes, all without delay or hitch, while the account is rapidly being written wherever the representative may have found a convenient place to use his pencil.

It may be that a point or two about telegraphy, its capabilities and possibilities, could be discovered that Mr. Thomas and his keen and able assistant, Mr. Baughan,—in charge of the telegraph department,—are not familiar with, but it is to be doubted. Certainly no institution in existence has greater need of expert and able men in the operation of the various departments ; and the staff in charge at the general offices in Chicago is but a criterion of the service at all points.

VII.

Perhaps the most interesting features of almost any successful enterprise of magnitude are the men who by their ability, integrity, and indefatigability have made possible such success.

The Associated Press as it stands today is permeated through and through with the brilliant and forceful character of its general manager, Melville E. Stone. Mr. Stone's accession to the managership, his able and masterly generalship in the building up of this great Association, his rare insight into broad and national questions of the day, his keen discernment of that which should be given to the world and that which should not, his unusual executive powers, have all tended to make him one of the noted and interesting characters of our time. Not yet forty-six years old, Mr. Stone's record has been one that any man at the end of a long life might well feel proud of ; but, having come in contact with his strong personality, one

may well believe Mr. Stone's own thoughts upon the matter would show that he regarded his career hardly more than begun.

The pretty little town of Hudson, Illinois, near Bloomington, claims Mr. Stone by right of birth, but early boyhood found him in the schools of Chicago, his father, a minister of the gospel, having been called to a church in that city about 1860. The Great Fire of 1871 illustrated the old adage, " It's an ill wind that blows nobody good," for, although Melville Stone not only lost his all, along with thousands of others in that terrible conflagration, but found himself badly in debt, yet the world at least was the gainer by securing a leader in the newspaper world instead of an iron-founder — the business Mr. Stone had embarked in upon graduation.

Starting anew, he became reporter on the old *Republican* and then city editor of the *Inter Ocean*, a paper that soon succeeded the *Republican*. His editorial connection with the *Mail* and the *Post*, and his subsequent withdrawal to undertake the important field in Washington as special correspondent for several papers, were but steps toward the control and ownership of the *Daily News* in conjunction with Victor F. Lawson, now President of The Associated Press. The success of this venture enabled Mr. Stone in a few years to withdraw with a large fortune. After traveling abroad for two years, his active brain rebelled at longer cessation from business. Returning to Chicago he organized the Globe National Bank, of which institution he was long vice-president, and is now president.

The Associated Press in the interval had been assailed right and left by its enemies. The independent stand it had taken, its refusal to submit to the uncalled-for and humiliating attitude taken by its eastern associates, its insistence that it should have a voice in the management and direction of what was as vital to its own life and usefulness, its refusal to submit tamely to having the greater part of the taxation burden thrust upon its shoulders without adequate represenlation, and its objection to having only such news for its western clientage and members as should be the pleasure of certain members of the East to allot, all combined to make a state of affairs exist that required a genius in ability, and executive power and cool and clear-headed judgment. In the opinion of those in control of the most influential papers in

passed upon by his colleagues, bears an enviable record for all that is most modern and progressive in the realm of newspapers. His business sagacity, foresight and staunch character lend an element of strength to the Association that would be hard to find elsewhere. The close friendship and business relations that have for many years held Mr. Lawson and Mr.

the land, the man who had shown he possessed all of these qualities in a high degree was Melville E. Stone, and he was induced to accept the management. How true and sagacious their judgment was, the splendid record of the Association, with its stable condition to-day, fully attests.

The President of The Associated Press, Victor F. Lawson, whose fitness for the presidency has twice been unanimously

Stone together, make their connection with The Associated Press a peculiarly fitting and appropriate one, and whose combined efforts are thoroughly appreciated as evidenced in the last election of officers for the ensuing year.

Eleven members compose the board of directors, and are now as follows: S. S. Carvalho, New York *World;* Charles W. Knapp, St. Louis *Republic;* M. H. de Young, San Francisco *Chronicle;* Clay ton McMichael, Philadelphia *North American;* Frederick Driscoll, St Paul *Pioneer Press;* Albert J. Barr, Pittsburgh *Post;* F. B. Noyes, Washington *Star;* James E. Scripps, Detroit *News,* Detroit *Tribune;* E. H. Perdue, Cleveland *Leader;* Victor F. Lawson, Chicago *Daily News,* Chicago *Record;* Thos. G. Rapier, New Orleans *Picayune.*

They are all men of influential journals, men who are everywhere recognized as representing the most liberal, broad-minded and progressive element in our national life.

When Mr. Stone took hold of affairs it did not take him long to recognize the important part the Pacific Coast must play in any national organization of this kind; nor did he overlook the fact that it would take a man of not only rare executive ability but of the utmost discernment and tact to reconcile disturbing factors already at work in the news field there, so as to bring them in working harmony with its eastern adherents, and a man as well who was familiar with the utmost detail in practical newspaper work.

Perhaps it was one of the pleasant

surprises in store for Mr. Stone that he found just such a man in charge of the Coast service, and who now, under the present changing conditions of

the Association, could better than anyone else bring it to its desired state of perfection, and whose pioneer work had already made it a possibility. Certainly it attests Mr. Stone's judgment of character and fitness that he continued Col. Charles S. Diehl there in charge until his ability and energy were needed elsewhere.

The loyal and enthusiastic support that is now a conspicuous feature of the Pacific Slope members and clients attests not only to good management, but the sensible and desirable features of the Association itself. The Associated Press is doubtless to-day the best perfected example of mutual coöperation in existence, and the newspapers of the far Western States, as well as others, once understanding this, have become its strongest adherents.

Colonel Diehl having shown so conspiciously his capacity for large as well as small affairs, soon found himself a needed factor in the Eastern world, and is now sharing with Mr. Stone the responsibilities and honor of directing affairs as Assistant General Manager. The Eastern Division, with headquarters at New York, is directly under Colonel Diehl's supervision, and the growth of the Association's membership there is proof that his capacity has not been found wanting. Personally Colonel Diehl is a delightful man, his frank open face and genial though always dignified manner inspiring trust and respect at first glance.

Not unlike Colonel Diehl in some respects, Walter Neef, General European Agent, with headquarters at London, England, has also been an exemplification of the sound judgment shown in appointments by Mr. Stone. Like Colonel Diehl, with a comparatively small number of years to his credit, time does not seem to have been wasted. The important negotiations that have so successfully cemented all the large European agencies together, so far as their coöperation and exchange of news with The Associated Press is concerned, has been largely due to the efforts of Mr. Neef.

The post of any agent of The Associated Press may, by force of circumstances, become at any moment a field of the utmost consequence, and one to be filled by capable, loyal, enthusiastic and tireless newspaper men. The agent in almost or quite every case has been an editor and proprietor and is thoroughly experienced in all departments of newspaper work. He must be broad-minded and able to do not only a reporter's duty, but sift the chaff from the wheat in the reports that come in from the legion of correspondents. With such men is the discipline and usefulness of the world's greatest news organization kept intact.

Unscrupulous individuals and combinations have intrigued and sought to undermine the very foundations of the organization, that their own pecuniary gain might be the more secure. But the reconstruction has been under the generalship of a man of courageous spirit and marked ability,—a man whose genial and attractive personality shines out as happily amid almost unsurmountable difficulties as do the traits that originally pointed to him as the needed leader. And to-day, both at home and abroad, the reading and thinking world is infinitely the gainer by such an organization as The Associated Press.

THE RHINE JOURNEY.

THE affection of the Germans for the River Rhine surpasses any other localized sentiment I have ever found. We Americans are proud of our Hudson and contend that in natural beauties it surpasses the Rhine. We speak with pride of the Mississippi, the Missouri, the Ohio, the Columbia. But these rivers are so completely and unquestionably ours that we are not so aroused at the mention of their names. Quite different in degree are the emotions stirred in the German soul when the River Rhine is named. Said a German gentleman to me on the journey up that historic river, " You cannot fully understand how we feel whenever the Rhine is mentioned in connection with possible political complications. I was opposed to the Military Bill; but if I had believed there was danger of a renewal of the old attempt of the French to make the Rhine the boundary line between France and Germany, the bill would have had no warmer supporter than myself. Whenever the French attempt to carry out their ancient purpose, then you will find us all one, as our fathers were when Blücher and Gneisenau drove the Corsican back, and as we ourselves were when Von Moltke cut short the ambitious dream of Louis Napoleon."

To this people, the desire of the French for an extension of their boundaries beyond the Vosges Mountains to the Rhine is but a repetition of the old Bible story of Ahab's desire for Naboth's vineyard, except that the modern Ahab would take the coveted property by conquest, not obtain it by purchase. The emphatic response of the German Naboth is :

"The Lord forbid it me that I should give the inheritance of my fathers unto thee."

But let us be fair with the Frenchman. He makes quite a case of ancient right. Both Cæsar and Tacitus tell us that the Rhine separated Gaul from Germany before the Christian era. Richelieu shrewdly made out an apparently clear title vested in the King of France as successor to the empire of Charlemagne, created eight centuries before. Under Louis Philippe the authorized school book of geography designated Rhenish Prussia as part of the region which properly belonged to France. It declared that "the natural boundaries of our country are the Rhine from its source to its mouth."

Napoleon I. found his fate when he met the brave defenders of the Rhine. Napoleon III. was defeated not so much by the superiority of Germany's needle-gun as by the new unity of a people before divided, and their band of union was the Rhine, "a German river and not a boundary line."

The German army which won the battle of Sedan was an army of singers. They sang themselves to sleep in camp. They sang themselves into the victory-compelling mood before going into battle. Their most stirring battle songs were, "*Sie Sollen ihn Nicht Haben,*" "*Am Rhein, am Rhein,*" and "*Die Wacht am Rhein.*" The first named thus vigorously closes:

"No, not the sons of Hermann
Will hold their own dear Rhine,
Until the last true German
Lies buried 'neath the Rhine!"

It would be hard for any invading army, however well led, to make headway against an army of home defenders who, with every draught of their Rhine wine, swear anew the old oath of allegiance with which "Am Rhein" concludes:

"—The German shall thy green
Our own, our German Rhine!"

With "The Watch on the Rhine" Americans are more familiar. Its stirring music set to such soul-stirring words as—

"Dear Fatherland, no fear be thine,
True hearts watch, we guard the Rhine!"

is enough to make a hero out of a very commonplace sort of a man.

We take an early evening train from Cologne to Bonn. Thence we proceed

WHERE BEETHOVEN WAS BORN.
The House and Room in Bonn in which the great Composer first saw the light.

FORTRESS OF EHRENBREITSTEIN.
Bridge of Boats connecting Coblenz and Ehrenbreitstein.

by motor to Godesberg, a few miles farther up the river. A climb to the hill above the town gives us a charming moonlight view from a ruined castle on the height,—including villas and flower gardens, the narrowing valley of the Rhine, the Seven Mountains across and farther up the river towering far

THE CASTLE OF STOLZENFELS AND THE VILLAGE OF CAPELLEN.

above the plain, twinkling lights from homes everywhere about us and the halo above the distant city of Cologne. The sound of many voices lifted in song comes to us from a garden party just below, and farther distant an orchestra is holding a rehearsal, its exquisite music completing the harmony of sound and color which makes the time and place memorable to us.

We waken early the next morning. There is a confusion of tongues in the small windows. Standing on tiptoe in the third-story room, where the greatest of musical composers was born, my head easily touches the ceiling. The house contains the poet's violins, and his grand piano, with each string quadrupled to overcome the player's deafness; the trumpets he used in conversation; the desk upon which his immortal symphonies were composed, with its four sides for the four parts of musical composition; the life mask and the death

DEED IN THE RIVER NEAR BOPPARD.
Der Vierwersplatz in the Center — Boppard on the Right.

market-place in front of the hotel. Looking out our hotel window, we see the plaza literally swarming with men and women, chiefly women. The pavement is strewn with baskets of vegetables, fruits and flowers, and buyers and sellers are posing in picturesque groups for our benefit.

After breakfast, we walk to the home of the great, the only, Beethoven. Answering our loud ring at the gate, the occupant of the house shows us through the place, now a Beethoven museum. It is a pleasant old house with low roof and mask and the various original portraits of the master; specimens of his correspondence and musical composition, and a hundred other objects of interest.

At 11:40 A. M. we are seated on the deck of the "Wilhelm" and are moving rapidly up the Rhine. We who have all our lives read and heard and dreamt of the Rhine find it hard to realize that this is indeed the famous river. It is easier now first, however, for on the right is the ruined tower of Godesberg; and high above our heads upon the rugged peak of the last of the Seven Mountains is outlined in blue the ruined Twelfth Century castle of Drachenfels, a relic of the destructive Thirty Years' War; and there, half-way up the height is the cavern among the vineyards where the Siegfried of fable slew the dragon and became invincible by drinking his blood.

Then passes before us the Island of Nonnenwerth with its very old nunnery modernized. Rolandseck next comes in

CASTLE RHEINSTEIN.

sight, upon the west bank. Five hundred feet up the height above the town is a ruined arch, all that remains of the Ninth Century castle of the brave Roland, whose death by treachery in Charlemagne's War in Spain is the subject of the famous old Tenth Century poem, "Rolandslied." The sad story of Roland's long vigil over the convent of Nonnenwerth, where his sweetheart was long buried in life and found burial in

death, adds romantic interest to the mournful ruin.

Looking back on Drachenfels and the mountains beyond, on the east, and upon Rolandseck with its background of hill and sky, and the Island of Nonnenwerth, with the river losing itself in the lapping of the mountains below, we then begin to realize how beautiful and picturesque it all is.

But we soon enter a region of quarries and mines and the scenery for several miles is disappointingly tame. We dine in the cabin, satisfied from glimpses through the windows that we are missing little.

The river course veers to the left, and old Andernach directly confronts us. Our interest revives. This beautiful old town, with its queer houses under the hill and its famous tower, and its legend of a helpful Christ who nightly performs hard tasks to relieve the poor, is of itself an interesting relic of mediæval life.

Neuweid, with its palace and its schools and its Moravian Brothers, after whom our band of Amana colonists are said to have measurably patterned, attracts our attention on the east side.

Several islands now beautify the river. On the Island of Niederwerth is a gloomy convent church built in 1500.

We now pass the base of Ehrenbreitstein's bristling fortress on the left. [On our right we see the Moselle River and its beautifully arched bridge.

At the junction of the two rivers stands Coblenz, the capital of Rhenish Prussia. Few cities of Germany have passed through as much history as Coblenz, and few show as little the effects of war and time. Five years ago, her citizens removed the old walls which had been besieged by the Swedes and the French, respectively. Remains of an old Roman bridge tell of the town's importance way back before German history began. It

THE RUINED CASTLE AND FORTRESS OF RHEINFELS.

THE LORELEI.
Ich glaube, die Wellen verschlingen
Am Ende Schiffer und Kahn ;
Und das hat mit ihrem Singen
*Die Lorelei gethan.—*HEINE.

"WALLED BACHARACH."

is a busy, bustling town, full of soldiers and yet not given up to militarism. The fortress of Ehrenbreitstein, across the river, is a magnificent rock structure of the era now passing away—that of the small guns which did the artillery work of the first half of the century. The earth works of Cologne and Antwerp are

"PICTURESQUE BINGEN."
The National Monument in the distance on the left.

not as picturesque, but they are a much better protection.

Our steamer makes its first landing at Coblenz. We are soon on our way again. We pass through the bridge of boats, under the high railroad bridge and on past the Island of Oberwerth on the right, the mouth of the Lahn River on the left, and are soon in the midst of a region of enchanting beauty.

The little village of Capellen, with its one row of houses facing us, lies at the foot of a high hill, upon which stands a pretty chateau owned by the present Kaiser. Upon the rock above stands the Gothic castle of Stolzenfels, with its high tower. It was destroyed by the French, but has been restored with considerable regard to beauty and fitness.

Farther up the river on the left looms the castle of Lahneck, over seven hundred years old. This, too, was destroyed by the French, but has been restored.

In fact, underneath nearly all the pictures of ruined castles in Rhenish Prussia might truthfully be written the words, "Destroyed by the French."

Passing slightly Marksburg on the left, we note that this is the only old castle on the Rhine which has escaped war's devastation.

The river now makes a long turn to the right, and then a shorter turn to the left. The scenery at these turns, as all along the way, is beautiful with terraced vineyards, wooded hills and castellated rocks.

Boppard is in sight on the left bank — no, it proves to be on the right. The bends in the river are confusing. The general effect is that of a series of lakes. This historic town charmingly combines the new with the old. Beautiful villas and quaint old checkered houses, an old nunnery, a well preserved castle and general beauty of situation, commend Boppard to the tourist.

Knights Templars will be interested to recall the historical fact that here at Boppard, as at St. Goar and Bacharach, farther up the river, the Knights Templars of the Crusades located lodges, fragments of which, with round-arched windows, are yet to be seen. The Boppard knights were at the Crusader's siege of Ptolemais in 1191.

Just beyond, on the other side, rise the twin castles of Sterrenberg and Liebenstein, connected by a rocky path. There is in this connection a long and pretty legend of two brothers and only one Hildegarde, of generosity on the one side and selfishness on the other, of heartbreak and a nunnery.

Up from Welmich is the "Maus" castle of the Fourteenth Century, derisively so called because a larger one up the river was called "The Cat."

We are now in sight of St. Goar on the right, and St. Goarshausen on the left.

A thunderstorm is gathering. The air is full of electricity and we feel the rumble of the thunder. Anchors are thrown out and we await the passing of the storm. Looking up at the castle of Rheinfels, which stands upon the height back of St. Goar, we find ourselves in the presence of the grandest ruin on the Rhine. Its lofty walls and towers, broken arches and columns, and ivy-covered approaches look down at us with a solemnity which the now fast-falling rain augments. From 1245 to 1843 these walls withstood assaults and sieges, burnings and explosions, plague, pestilence and famine. As the lightning flashes above the castle and the thunder reverberates through its deserted halls, it is not hard to realize the storm and stress through which Rheinfels has passed. Soon the setting sun comes out and bathes its walls with a flood of yellow light, crowning its ruined tower with an aureole of glory. It is a grand moment. We are thankful for the timely thunderstorm that has given us this half-hour's delay and a lasting impression of St. Goar and its noble ruin.

We sail on past "The Cat," above referred to, at the foot of which castle flows the River Kaats, one of scores of cascaded streams tributary to the Rhine.

Another bend in the river, another island long and narrow, and the famous "Lorelei" (or Lurlei) of Heine's verse and of Wagner's "Niebelungenlied."

stands out before us, compelling attention. It is a rocky promontory projecting far into the river and rising 430 feet above the water (so says the guide-book), the forehead of the profile decidedly retreating. It is scarcely more striking in appearance than the promontory a little farther up the river on the opposite side, but it has the legend and the other has not. The familiar Lorelei legend may be condensed into a single sentence. A nymph possessed of rare charms dwelt upon the cliff, without any visible means of support, and her only occupation was the luring of fishermen and sailors into the deadly rapids below. With all the German love of legends, the practical executive arm of the Empire not many years ago drilled a hole through this promontory, and trains of cars now shoot through the tunnel, without even so much as a "pardong" to the siren!

On our right, above Oberwesel, rises the magnificent chateau of Schönberg, recently built upon a Twelfth Century castle foundation. These modern homes seem obtrusive in the midst of so many reminders of mediæval life. They suggest that pretentious newness so offensive to those who love to linger in the past, and to whom honorable descent is more than honorable ascent. The irrepressible conflict between the chateau life of the newly rich and the traditions of ancient greatness which hover about these ruined castles is nowhere so vividly pictured as in Auerbach's "Villa on the Rhine."

The village of Kaub next presents itself on our left, in a region somewhat defaced by the prosaic quarryman. But above the quarries rises, in solemn protest against the desecration, the castle of Gutenfels with its lofty pinnacled tower.

Near Kaub, on a rock in the river, stands the Pfalz, or Pfalzgrafenstein, a hexagonal fortress with a pentagonal tower. Its one small entrance is reached by a

drawbridge. As we sail past it we turn our glass on the lion of the Palatinate over the entrance, that we may the better see the once famous escutcheon of the ancient lords of the castle. New Year's day, 1814, was a red-letter day for this locality. Here it was the brave Blücher forced the passage of the Rhine over the stubborn resistance of the French. A small monument on the west bank commemorates the event.

Walled Bacharach presents itself on the right, with the castle of Stahleck and, at its foot, the picturesque ruin of St. Werner's church. On beyond looms the noble ruin of Fürstenberg, with more of history than could be related in this entire magazine. The strength of these castles and the audacity of their occupants in mediæval times is well illustrated by a single incident in Fürsten-

berg's history. Six hundred years ago, Adolph of Nassau proudly rode down the river to his coronation at Aix la Chapelle. All went well until he neared Bacharach. The garrison of Fürstenberg took to the river and forcibly detained the king until he paid the toll demanded.

Quaint old Lorch on the opposite side next wheels into line for our inspection, with its one street along the river bank. Its old ivy-covered Gothic church attracts our attention. In the heart of the village may be seen the dignified Renaissance structure in which once dwelt one Lorch, who distinguished himself against the Turks and the French in the first half of the Sixteenth Century.

The river narrows and its banks grow more precipitous. We soon behold Rheinstein, that most beautiful of all the castles in all this region of castles, this very home of mediæval romance. It

stands on the west side, 260 feet above the Rhine. With a history dating back at least six hundred years, its present condition dates back to 1829, when Prince Frederick of Prussia caused the castle to be restored after mediæval designs, with the pinnacled towers of that period. The body of the prince was interred in the ivy-covered chapel south of the castle.

The river again broadens, making a far-extending curve to the east. Soon we see picturesque Bingen, the town facing the north, extending southward from the river front and climbing far up the hill. Across the river to the north is the Niederwald. On the edge of the forest stands the *Nationaldenkmal*, or National Monument, which spot was recently the scene of a memorable reunion of the veterans of the Franco-Prussian War. Farther up the river on the north is the town of Rüdesheim, famous for its

PORT KLOPP, OVERLOOKING BINGEN AND THE RHINE.

high-grade wines. Opening before us is the Rheingau, a low stretch of rich valley land, in general appearance quite as much in contrast with the romantic region through which we have just passed as is the tamely beautiful upper Hudson unlike the enchanted region about West Point, or as the Mississippi River from Keokuk to St. Louis is unlike the rock-bound Mississippi from Lake Pepin to Dubuque.

We land at Bingen, and, after establishing ourselves at the Victoria, we go out for an early evening walk. Bingen is a delightful old town. Looking down upon it is Castle Klopp. This structure was also "destroyed by the French." The deed was done in 1689; but the restorer has done his work well, and there are few evidences of ruin or of newness.

Darkness comes on as we ramble up and down the narrow streets of the town, and in the gathering gloom we catch many a pleasing glimpse of the simple home life of the inhabitants. Children are chasing one another over the rough pavement, the clatter of their sabots echoing along up and down the narrow streets. Grandmothers, crowned with the regulation white cap, and mothers with children in arms sit in the doorway chatting of the events of the day, all the while with mild solicitude half watching the girls and boys at their rough play. The men sit in groups upon benches in front of the houses, smoking the pipe of peace and calmly thinking aloud between puffs. Try as hard as we may to shut out the romantic influence of that poem which so powerfully appealed to the imagination in our childhood, every mother we see, every pair of lovers, every maiden all forlorn, brings back the old time-worn story of love and war, which has done more to interest English-reading people in Bingen-on-the-Rhine than all the histories have done, from the Roman occupation down to the present time.

That was a blustering night we passed in Bingen — not cold but blustering. The wind whistled and howled like demons through the cordage of the sailing vessels and steamers at the landing just below. Long into the night we sat looking out over the Rhine, along the vine-covered heights beyond, and up at the great banks of clouds which every now and then eclipsed the moon, only to make the brightness of that orb more bright when the clouds had rolled away. Great flitting shadows darkened the surface of the river far to the left, and as the northwest wind rose and fell, the creaking of the boats and the whistling of the wind through the rigging made note of its changes. To our tired and confused minds it seemed as if all the fabled demons of the Rhine had followed us up the river and were loth to let us go.

JOHN BROWN AND HIS CAUSE.

BY J. L. COPPOC.

With Portraits from Old Pictures in the Possession of the Coppoc Family.

I.

"Shall tongues be mute when deeds are wrought
Which well might shame extremest Hell?
Shall freemen lock th' indignant thought?
Shall pity's tongue cease to swell?
Shall honor bleed? Shall truth succumb?
Shall men and press and soul be dumb?
No! By each spot of haunted ground,
Where Freedom weeps her children's fall;
By Plymouth Rock, by Bunker's mound,
By Griswold's stained and shattered wall,
By all above, around, below,
Be ours the indignant answer — No!"

JOHN BROWN and his followers accepted this sentiment, but they were not willing to stop here; they would translate the indignant "No" into vigorous action. As the Herods were called great, while the Savior was nailed to the tree, so now, the man whose "treasures of gold are dim with the blood of the hearts he has sold" is honored and courted, while he who "considers the oppressed as bound in the chains with them" is sent to the gibbet. As in the former case "the Scribes stood and vehemently accused him," so John Brown was accused of "many things" of which he was not guilty. Chief among these was that it was his intention to subvert

REV. J. L. COPPOC, OF CHAMBERS NEB.

the government of the United States and substitute for the Constitution thereof one which he himself had formulated.

That there was a provisional constitution found in John Brown's valise on the Kennedy farm, and introduced as evidence at his trial, is true ; but it was not a provisional Constitution of the United States, as many seemed to believe. It was that of the League of Freedom, an institution organized at Chatham, Canada, for the purpose of furthering the cause of the abolition of slavery. Blake, in his " History of Slavery," says in regard to this :

Among the documents found was what purported to be a regular plan of organization for a provisional government. Subsequent developments showed that this plan was matured at Chatham, Canada, some time before the outbreak..... The purpose seemed to be to take such steps as the case required to liberate the slaves.

This does not make the matter clear as to the design of the document. It would

MAX COPPOC.
Mother of Edwin, Barclay and J. L. Coppoc

leave the impression that it was intended as a substitute for the Constitution of the United States, which was entirely untrue.

Von Holst, an able German historical writer, says, " It was entirely rational to form and create a strong organization " and " sensible to appoint a Supreme Commander," though absurd to suppose " that a little band....without influence, should secretly put their heads together, ...to give a constitution to the United States." " This latter," says Mr. Hinton, " being, with all due deference to Von Holst, exactly what they did not intend or mean to attempt doing."

A motion was made at the Chatham convention to strike out the forty-sixth article of the provisional constitution, which was discussed at length and was finally lost, receiving only the vote of the mover. John Brown, Kagi and others made speeches strongly favoring its retention. It reads :

The foregoing articles shall not be construed so as in any way to encourage the overthrow of any State government, or of the general government of the United States, and look to no dissolution of the Union, but simply to amendment and repeal, and our flag shall be the same that our fathers fought under in the Revolution.

The hero of Harper's Ferry did not come to destroy the time-honored institutions of our nation, but to save. There was a state of things existing in the slaveholding states which was not understood and could not be appreciated in the North. G. B. Gill, secretary of the treasury under the provisional constitution, in a paper furnished Col. R. J. Hinton for use in his excellent book on " John Brown and His Men,"—to which work I am greatly indebted,—wrote :

" My object in wishing to see Mr. Reynolds, who was a colored man (very little colored, however), was in regard to a military organization which I had understood was in existence among the colored people. He assured me that such was the fact and that its ramifications extended through most or nearly all of the slave states. He himself, I think, had been through many of the Slave States inciting and organizing. He referred me to many references in the Southern papers telling of this and that favorite slave being killed or found dead. These, he asserted, must be taken care of, being the most dangerous element they had to contend with."

Two days before the outbreak, Watson Brown wrote to his wife, "There was another murder committed near our place the other day, making in all five murders and one suicide within five miles ...since we have lived here. They were all slaves, too."

"We knew that the slaves of that region," says Mrs. Doctor North, of Springville, Iowa, who lived, at the time of the raid, twelve miles from the Ferry, "were being armed, but it was not through John Brown that they secured their arms."

And so the Slave Power had been sowing to the wind and was now about to reap the whirlwind of wrath. The storm-cloud was gathering and was ready to burst in all its fury, and one of the objects of the provisional government was to organize, control, restrain, and utilize its forces. The preamble to this instrument reads thus :

WHEREAS, Slavery, throughout its entire existence in the United States, is none other than a most barbarous, unprovoked and unjustifiable war of one portion of its citizens upon another portion, the only conditions of which are perpetual imprisonment and hopeless servitude or absolute extermination in utter disregard and violation of those eternal and self-evident truths set forth in the Declaration of Independence : and therefore,—

We, citizens of the United States, and the oppressed people who by a recent decision of the Supreme Court are declared to have no rights which the white man is bound to respect ; together with all other people degraded by the laws thereof, do for the time being ordain and establish ourselves the following constitution and ordinances the better to protect our persons, property, lives and liberties, *and to govern our actions.*

CAPTAIN AVID OF HARPER'S FERRY.
John Brown's Captain and John.

Article 1 reads as follows :

All persons of mature age, whether proscribed, oppressed and enslaved citizens or of the proscribed and oppressed races of the United States, who shall agree to sustain and enforce the provisional constitution and ordinance *of this organization,* together with all minor children of such persons, shall be held to be fully entitled to protection under the same.

Articles 32, 35, 40, 41 and 42 are plainly intended to promote morality and restrain the evil passions engendered by the long years of oppression to which this people had been subjected. They provide that prisoners must be treated "with every degree of kindness and respect the nature of the circumstances will permit of"; they prevent the needless destruction of property and immoral behavior of any kind ; punish the violation of any female prisoner with death, and enjoin the keeping of the Sabbath. Provisions are also made for the establishment of schools and

THE LATE JOHN BROWN, JR.

churches and the reunion of separated families.

The more one studies this instrument in connection with the circumstances and conditions then
existing, the more profound is his
respect for the man from whose
mind it emanated.

II.

If John Brown's aim was not to
subvert the government, then *what
was it?*

When my eldest brother, Edwin
Coppoc, was asked if he had anything to say why sentence should
not be passed upon him, he said :

"The charges that have been
made against me are not true. I
never committed any treason
against the State of Virginia. I
never made war upon it. I never
conspired with anybody to induce
your slaves to rebel, and I never

even exchanged a word with any of
your servants. What I came here
for I have always told you. It was
to run off slaves into a free state."

In a letter written by Edwin Coppoc to his friends in Springdale,
under date of November 22, 1859, he
wrote : "Cook and Tidd had left
the Ferry early in the morning, by
the order of the Captain, to cross
the river for the purpose of taking
some prisoners and to convey the
arms to a school-house about a
mile and a half from the Ferry,
there to guard them until the Captain came."

This shows that the object in
capturing the arsenal was to secure
the arms, and it was then the intention to fall back across the river
and into the mountains.

One of John Brown's daughters,
Mrs. Adams, says : "It was father's

EDWIN COPPOC,
[One who gave his life in the Raid on Harper's Ferry.]

EDWIN COPPOC.

The answer was, "We came to free the slaves—and only that."

Again, in answer to a question, he said: "I want you to understand, gentlemen, that I respect the rights of the poorest and weakest of the colored people oppressed by the slave system just as much as I do those of the most wealthy and powerful. That is the idea that has moved me, and that alone.... *The cry of distress of the oppressed is my reason and the only thing that prompted me to come here.*"

In his speech, when asked if he had anything to say before sentence was pronounced upon him, he said: "In the first place, I deny everything but what I have all along admitted—the design on my part to free the slaves. I intended certainly to have made a clear thing of that matter, as I did last winter when I went into Missouri and there took slaves without the snapping of a gun on either side, moved them through the country and finally left them in Canada. I

original plan, as we used to call it, to take Harper's Ferry at the outset, to secure firearms to arm the slaves, and to strike terror into the hearts of the slave-holders; then to immediately start for the plantations, gather up the negroes and retreat to the mountains, send out armed squads from there to gather more and eventually to spread out his forces until the slaves would come to them or the slaveholders would surrender them to gain peace. He expected....that if they had intelligent white leaders that they would be prevailed on to rise and secure their freedom without revenging their wrongs and with very little bloodshed."

After Brown was captured, while lying upon the hard floor of the Harper's Ferry engine-house and "his enemies compassed him about like bees," Senator Mason asked him: "What was your object in coming?"

BARCLAY COPPOC.

21

designed to have done the same thing again on a larger scale. That was all I intended."

The "Subterranean Passway" was but the enlargement of the "Underground Railroad."

It was true that Brown aimed finally at the total extinction of slavery, and the Harper's Ferry affair was only a part of the general plan. He believed that the end desired could be reached by making the institution unprofitable and dangerous. It is a well-known fact that, previous to the invention of the cotton-gin by Whitney, leading Virginians, among whom was Senator Mason, were devising plans for the gradual abolition of slavery because of the unprofitableness thereof; but from that time the "peculiar institution" took a new lease of life.

John Brown believed that by making incursions into the Slave States at different points, and establishing "underground railroads" on a large scale on the borders of and extending into the slave territory, and effecting a thorough organization of the discontented elements among the slaves to assist in running the trains on these roads, that it would render slave property valueless and the holding of slaves hazardous, and thus secure freedom for the oppressed.

Mr. Alcot, one of Brown's confidential friends, wrote, " I infer it is his intention to run off as many slaves as he can and so render that property insecure to the master."

A trusty and observant man had been sent down into the Indian Territory and Texas with instructions, if it appeared necessary, to carry his researches as far as Louisiana, with a view of establishing routes and stations on the western frontier. The Appalachian range of mountains was to be utilized, and much information had been obtained by members of the little army of liberators by explorations, and from other sources, chiefly through Harriet Tubman, a fugitive slave who, after securing her own liberty, was successful in liberating several thousand of her race in the course of some twenty years, using the fastnesses of the mountains as hiding places.

III.

That no mistake was made as to the result of this kind of warfare was proven in Missouri, Kansas and Virginia. John Brown's raid into Missouri from Southern Kansas started an exodus from that region so formidable that slaves sold for from one-half to two-thirds their former price. Not long after this the Fighting Preacher, Captain Stewart, under whom the writer was initiated into the mysteries of border warfare, did in Northern Kansas what Brown had done in Southern Kansas, and every slave was cleared out of the territory.

In the East the very thought of what might occur, coupled with what had been, "frightened old Virginia till she trembled through and through." Excited imaginations transformed an innocent cow into a piece of artillery, and a burning stack into an invading army. Business was suspended and the militia was ordered out or directed to be in a state of readiness. The Southern papers published fearful accounts of the condition of their chattels, thus casting added fuel to the already too fiercely burning fire of anxious fear.

"The inhabitants," says a report published in one of these papers, "are not by any means easy in their minds as to the temper of the slaves and free negroes among them. Colonel Washington, who was one of old Brown's hostages, does not spend his nights at home; and we are assured that many other wealthy slaveowners whose residences lie at a distance from those of their neighbors also regard it prudent to lodge elsewhere for the present.... On Sunday evening before the attack, a gentleman on the way to the Ferry was stopped in a lonely place three or four miles distant, by a white man carrying a rifle and two negroes armed with axes, who told him there was something going on at the Ferry and he must turn back. He did so and they remained standing until he was out of sight."

Under these conditions it is not surprising that slave property depreciated in value to an alarming extent. "The loss from this source has been estimated at $10,000,000 in Virginia alone. For a considerable period thereafter some of John Brown's friends kept a record, as far as newspaper information permitted, of the enforced movement southward of slaves from the border states. It was very rapid, and extended from Virginia to Missouri."

Had Brown's plan not miscarried at Harper's Ferry, and had the mountains of Virginia and Maryland been peopled with little bands of liberators, the indications are that slavery must soon have been a thing of the past.

IV.

"But," says a critic, "why did this man assume to take property which did not belong to him and appropriate it to his own use?"

So far as the property of the slaveholder was concerned, he believed that a man justly owns what his labor creates, and that the slaveholder was a robber in that he had unjustly deprived the slave of this right.

Edwin Coppoc won Governor Wise's respect by calling his attention to the strength of this position. The incident, so far as I know, has never before appeared in print. While on the train conveying the prisoners from Harper's Ferry to Charleston, Governor Wise approached my brother and, after eyeing him a moment, said to him, "You look like too honest a man to be found with a band of robbers."

"But, Governor," he replied, "we look upon you as the robbers."

The candor and fearlessness and, too, the suggestiveness, of this reply won the Governor's favor, and thenceforth he exerted all his influence for the mitigation of his penalty.

This position accepted, the course of the old hero was simply the restoration of property to its rightful owners.

"But," continues the critic, "suppose we admit the correctness of this reasoning, that does not palliate the crime of

forcibly taking property belonging to the government."

Mr. Brown believed that "slavery throughout its entire existence in the United States is no other than a most barbarous, unprovoked and unjustifiable war of one portion of its citizens upon another portion .... *in utter disregard and violation of those eternal and self-evident truths set forth in our Declaration of Independence.*" He maintained that the administration had taken sides in this unequal war against justice, against the Declaration of Independence, against the Constitution (a fundamental principle of this document being that no person shall be deprived of life, liberty, or property without due process of law). He also maintained that the government was using this property to uphold the robbers.

It is interesting to note that the same people, who held up their hands in holy horror at this act of "robbery," did not hesitate within two years from that time to capture and hold—so long as they had the power—many millions of dollars' worth of property belonging to the government, and thought, or appeared to think, they were only defending their rights.

V.

Why was John Brown defeated? Let me answer that question by asking another. Can it be said with truth that the man who accomplishes his purpose is defeated?

"I came here," said Brown, "to free the slaves"; and again, "If it is necessary that my life should be sacrificed to this cause, I am content."

In a letter to Reverend Mr. North, a minister who visited Edwin Coppoc in jail, Mother wrote as follows relative to her own sons: "Every son of America whom you send to the North with the prints of the accursed halter upon his neck and whose funeral is attended by assembled thousands has a tendency to kindle the fires of indignant hatred against the common cause [slavery] which is at the bottom of all this."

Our mother's meaning can be better comprehended by the light of the following quotation, from a letter in regard to the funeral at New Garden, Ohio, showing the spirit of the time:

"Words are inadequate to convey an idea of the deep feeling and the tender sympathy felt for this victim of Virginia cruelty.... Yes, Virginia, a sister republic, has done that deed and Ohio stands aghast.... A large family assembled to weep over a murdered brother whose actions were worthy a better recompense than a Southern gibbet and a halter, the traces of which he bore upon his manly person deep-furrowed in the flesh."

Here is an extract from the Salem, Ohio, *Republican*, of January 7, 1860, concerning Edwin Coppoc's burial:

On Friday of last week, according to previous arrangement, the body of Edwin Coppoc, which had been removed from its first resting place, was reinterred in the cemetery in Salem. The wooden coffin, furnished by Virginia, was replaced by a metallic burial case, from which the youthful martyr preached such an anti-slavery sermon as has rarely before been preached; for, though the body was dead, yet by it, and through it, the spirit which had dwelt there spoke "high words of truth for freedom and for God." The noble lesson of self-sacrifice there taught, of heroic devotion to the principles of liberty, of a faith strong in death and triumphant over death, went down into the hearts of many whose sympathies had never before been thus moved.... At 12 o'clock the body was taken to the town hall so that all who wished to look upon it might have the opportunity. Every seat was speedily filled and for more than three hours a continuous stream of citizens and strangers passed into the hall pausing a moment to look on the body.

In the South every effort was made to "fire the Southern heart," and the agitators succeeded — succeeded in plunging the country into that fearful struggle by which negro slavery was forever abolished.

Robert E. Lee was victor at Harper's Ferry in order that the Institution which he represented might be ground to powder at Appomattox.

VI.

The defeat which ended in victory was caused chiefly by making the attack on the 16th instead of the 24th of October as was the original plan, thus disarranging the plans of many who would have been on hand to render assistance on that date. This precipitate action was made necessary by the fact that one who was familiar with Brown's plans had exposed them. When I say this I have no reference to Forbes, who had not been heard of in opposition to Brown for nearly a year. Nor do I have reference to the letter written to the Secretary of War in regard to the matter,—a letter written not by Mr. Babb as Colonel Hinton supposes,[*] but by a man from Springdale, Iowa, who sent it to Cincinnati to be remailed.

It is with great reluctance that I answer the question as to who the betrayer was. So far as I know, all the histories of these events have for some reason veiled his name in silence, and I would do the same but for one reason. "It is a thing well understood," as Redpath says, "the chief reason for the precipitate movement was that there was a Judas in the camp."

Perhaps the fact that this man did service for the Union in the late war and so expiated his offense has led the later historians to veil his betrayal in oblivion; but, to clear the noble men who fought at Harper's Ferry from any suspicion, it becomes necessary in this connection to mention the name of *Richard Realf*. Soon after the Chatham convention, Realf was sent to England, where his mother resided, to solicit aid for the "Subterranean Passway." He also visited France during his absence from this country and doubtless secured more or less money.

My brother, Barclay Coppoc, after his return from Canada and Harper's Ferry, told me that Richard Realf on his return from England and France had gone to New Orleans, joined the Catholic Church and made a confession in which he implicated John Brown, expos-

[*] Colonel Hinton's valuable work, "John Brown and His Men," page 253.

ing his designs, and that this was the cause of the premature movement. This explains the whereabouts of this man who was supposed by some to be dead. Redpath, in his "Life of Captain John Brown" (p. 168), states that he (Realf) "died on his passage from England." In the same work (p. 243): "One of the men who fought at Harper's Ferry gave me as the chief reason for the precipitate movement that they *suspected that there was a Judas in their company.*" This statement could not have referred to Colonel Forbes, as he was not "in their company" and had not been for over two years, — and then only for about two months, — and it could not have applied to any one else as no one of the other members of the company has ever been suspected. The whereabouts of Gill, Moffett, Lenhart, and all the others was known and the reasons for their not being on hand were well understood, and this statement of Barclay Coppoc removes suspicion from the innocent and places the guilt where it belongs. Some have supposed that Colonel Hugh Forbes was the Judas, but R. J. Hinton sets that matter at rest. On page 151 Colonel Hinton says: "There is not a particle of evidence to prove that Colonel Forbes went over to the enemy.....He did not send the warning letter to Mr. Floyd, Buchanan's Secretary of War." Mr. Forbes did cause delay after the Chatham convention by his letters to Senator Wilson and others, as Brown intended to strike the blow during the summer following that event. But soon after these letters were written "he dropped wholly from our vision until October, 1859, and later [the date of the outbreak at Harper's Ferry and the treachery of the "Judas"] when he was reported in command of a fortress under Garibaldi."

Barclay Coppoc's statement is sustained by the following quotation from the Austin (Texas) *Intelligencer*, as quoted by the *Anti-Slavery Bugle*, of January 7, 1860:

Seeing the foregoing article [concerning a lecture delivered by Mr. Realf to a Bible Society] on Saturday last, we sent for Mr. Realf and called his attention to it. He at once frankly avowed his identity and remarked that he had mentioned frequently that he had been connected with the affairs of Brown in Kansas..... He says that as soon as he learned Brown's purposes he renounced all notions of participation.....

Mr. Realf assures us that his renunciation of abolitionism is sincere, and that he has told his acquaintances here that should he remain out of the pulpit he intended to make speeches, giving his notions of the horrors of abolition in the North during the next presidential election.....

We will add that we yesterday suggested to the friends of Mr. Realf the propriety of his placing himself unconditionally at the disposition of the President of the United States. We are glad to say that he has done so, and has also offered to surrender himself to Governor Wise, and has notified these authorities that he will remain here until their wishes are known.

The second circumstance which led on to the defeat of the liberators was the holding of the Ferry too long. Mr. Brown explains the whole matter in his reply to a question by Mr. Valandigham. "I am here a prisoner, and wounded, because I foolishly allowed myself to be so. You overrate your strength when you suppose I could have been taken if I had not allowed it. I was too tardy, after commencing the open attack, in delaying my movements through Monday night, and up to the time I was attacked by the government troops. It was all occasioned by my desire to spare the feelings of my prisoners and their families, and the community at large." Had he, after accomplishing his purpose at the Ferry, immediately fallen back to the mountains, different results would have followed.

But why talk of what might have been, when we know that that which was was planned by the Omniscient Mind by whose wisdom ever the truth comes uppermost and ever is justice done! A just judgment is based upon what men aim to do rather than upon what they do, — not so much the deed as the motive, and, judged by this standard, where can we find a nobler type of Christian manhood than the hero of Harper's Ferry?

THE OLD MILL STREAM.

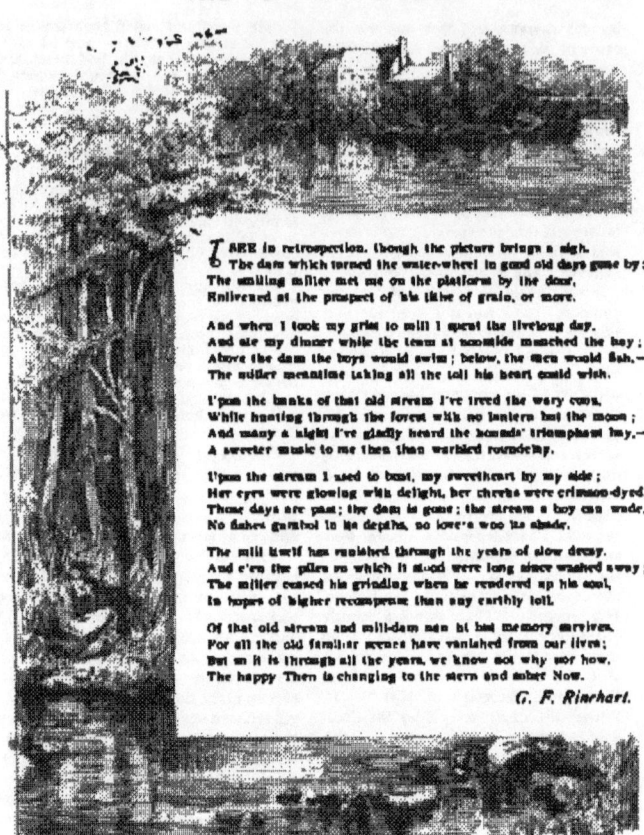

I SEE in retrospection, though the picture brings a sigh,
The dam which turned the water-wheel in good old days gone by;
The smiling miller met me on the platform by the door,
Enlivened at the prospect of his tithe of grain, or more.

And when I took my grist to mill I spent the livelong day,
And ate my dinner while the team at noonside munched the hay;
Above the dam the boys would swim; below, the men would fish,—
The miller meantime taking all the toll his heart could wish.

Upon the banks of that old stream I've treed the wary coon,
While hunting through the forest with no lantern but the moon;
And many a night I've gladly heard the hounds' triumphant bay,—
A sweeter music to me then than warbled roundelay.

Upon the stream I used to boat, my sweetheart by my side;
Her eyes were glowing with delight, her cheeks were crimson-dyed.
Those days are past; thy dam is gone; the stream a boy can wade,
No fishes gambol in its depths, no love's woo its shade.

The mill itself has vanished through the years of slow decay,
And e'en the piles on which it stood were long since washed away;
The miller ceased his grinding when he rendered up his soul,
In hopes of higher recompense than any earthly toll.

Of that old stream and mill-dam nau ht but memory survives,
For all the old familiar scenes have vanished from our lives;
But so it is through all the years, we know not why nor how,
The happy Then is changing to the stern and sober Now.

G. F. Rinehart.

LINCOLN AS A LAWYER.

HIS CAREER IN THE SUPREME COURT OF ILLINOIS — HIS FIRST CASE IN THAT COURT — HOW HE MEASURED UP WITH TRUMBULL, LOGAN AND OTHERS.

By George Beardsley.

FIFTY years ago the convening of the supreme court in Illinois was an annual occasion of much wider interest than attaches to the more frequent sessions of that body at present. There was but one meeting each year — in December — and, as most of the lawyers were also politicians, the event was of only less import to them than the meeting of the legislature. Party leaders met at the supreme court as they met at conventions and, — we are told by Senator Washburne,[*] — laid the wires of state politics.

A robust, holiday air invests the mental picture one conjures up of those pioneer lawyers journeying to the capital on horseback, over winter roads and against shivering prairie winds; the meeting at the tavern in Springfield; the genial salutations and mutual exchange of experiences on the road. Writers tell of the good-fellowship gatherings in the evenings, after the hard work among the books or before the court, where the seriousness of the profession was put aside and warmth and sociability were given sway. These were the men who were identifying their names with state and national history: Abraham Lincoln, Lyman Trumbull, Sidney Breese, Stephen A. Douglas, David Davis and a long list. These men in their early manhood and in their formative period, just getting a foothold upon political influence and power, — a genuine, hardy ambition moving them all, but yet all unconscious of Destiny's unequal hand upon their foreheads, — how one lingers in their presence! Oh, the eternal attractiveness of the unpresageful associations and atmosphere of historic figures and events!

[*] "Lincoln in Illinois," N. Am. R., vol. 141, page 307.

Greatness in its unaffected childhood, before realization and self-consciousness have arrived! In the manners practiced and the letters written after a great man has assured for himself a place in history one often fancies a note of affectation — "grand-stand playing." But before the great achievement we are sure of naturalness. Of course, one implicitly trusts Lincoln throughout, and rightly so. Still, how charming is this scene that has him, not yet thirty-two years of age, rough-riding it down to Springfield, his tall, large-boned figure wrapped in the shawl of those days, his easy-going, homely, but fetching presentation of his law case, and then at night, in the genial company of lawyers round the fire, he the best fellow of them all, telling his stories and tilting back in his chair!

When the four judges assumed their seats upon the supreme bench at Springfield to convene their honorable court for the December term, 1840, their dignified glance fell upon several men destined to be remembered in the annals of State and Nation. Stephen A. Douglas, John D. Caton, Sidney Breese and Thomas Ford were there, and they were later to find places upon the bench of that distinguished court. Ford was also to become governor, and Douglas a senator and presidential candidate. David J. Baker had already served in the United States Senate, and James Semple, O. H. Browning, J. A. McDougall and Sidney Breese were to be senators. Browning was also to be Secretary of the Interior. Stephen T. Logan was present, and he was winning for himself a place in Illinois history as one of the State's ablest jurists.

Eight or ten younger men, practitioners of less than five years' standing in the

Supreme Court, had cases to that term. Among them were James Shields, afterwards United States Senator, and Norman H. Purple, who was to lead a long career at that bar and afterwards occupy a seat on the State Supreme Bench. David Davis, with a distinguished life before him as lawyer, senator, judge of the Federal Supreme Court and nominee for President, was one of the young men who had business at that term. Lyman Trumbull had appeared the year preceding. It was probably among these younger men, in December, 1840, that another young man, with a single small case to look after, and that his first in the Supreme Court, was an inconspicuous companion. He was not unknown, to be sure, for he had already served three terms in the legislature, but he was a new man in that court. This was Abraham Lincoln, of Sangamon county.

By no means all the cases to that term involved large amounts. Many were begun in the justice of the peace court, and were brought up on points of statutory interpretation. (Those were the days of enactment, when the State was young.) Mr. Lincoln's business was to argue such a case, and, incidentally, to inaugurate a legal career — a career which has been too little studied and dwelt upon by the historian, yet which in extent and successfulness has hardly been equaled before or since in that court.

This first case of Mr. Lincoln's in the Supreme Court of Illinois is an interesting example of the proverbial small beginnings of great things. It was the suit of Scammon *versus* Cline,[*] and could not have involved a sum exceeding two hundred dollars, since it was begun in the justice court, and two hundred dollars is the limit of the justice's jurisdiction. Scammon sued Cline before Justice Alexander Neely, in Boone county. While we have no proof that Lincoln represented the defendant in the justice, and later in the circuit, court, yet it is no great risk to assume that he did. He took a change of venue — that first learned

stratagem of every young barrister — and won. The plaintiff appealed to the circuit court and upon a technicality Lincoln got the appeal struck from the docket. But the plaintiff, not to be discouraged, carried his appeal to the Supreme Court and was thus the instrument of introducing Lincoln into the highest tribunal of the Illinois judiciary. And when the little case was heard, Chief Justice Wilson, for the court, in a paragraph or two declared that the appeal had been improperly dismissed by "the Honorable Dan Stone," of the circuit, and Mr. "A. Lincoln" (with his associate, J. L. Loop), who had thus far staved off a judgment against his client, was sent back to the lower court. The final outcome of this case, if it was ever tried again, may only be learned by reference to the records of Boone county.

So the great lawyer lost his first case in the Supreme Court; but it is a way great lawyers have of starting. Melville W. Fuller, too, lost his first case in that court twenty years later; and so did Emery A. Storrs. Nor would it be safe to prophesy a lawyer's career on the basis of such a defeat, or upon the losing of any case. It is the appealing lawyer, if either, who assumes the main responsibility for the final decision. We are safe in assuming that one of Mr. Lincoln's objects in Scammon *versus* Cline was to gain time, in which he succeeded; and it may well be doubted if he expected his somewhat wily achievements below to be sustained in the higher court.

But Lincoln lost his second case also,[*] —this time to an opposing counsel whose name was destined to attract a large measure of that glory which the eventful succeeding years were to vouchsafe to public men worthy of high fame. Lyman Trumbull won the suit. Here was a trial that is interesting to posterity, not because it settled some struggling principle of law — for it has not become a "leading case"—but because the lawyers who tried it were two men who would later enunciate a higher than legal doctrine,

[*] 2 Scammon, 84.   [*] 1 Gillman. 163.

With Permission of D. McFee.

THE LINCOLN PORTRAIT.

Sent by Robert T. Lincoln, in response to request, for reproduction to Colonel Fox's " History of Political Parties.

namely, a practical principle of human liberty, and thus imprint their names upon the Nation's history. One was to wield the pen which should draw up the Thirteenth Amendment, and the other was to proclaim the emancipation of a race. Like a flash the mind recalls that it was Lyman Trumbull, too, who fourteen years later defeated the same antagonist (though perhaps not without the latter's assistance in the end) in a contest for a United States senatorship.

Just in this connection one may allude to a suggestive fact which comes out during such a study as the present. In his opinions from the bench Judge Douglas seems invariably to have overruled Lincoln, and, when the court sustained the latter, Douglas dissented. These opinions were very few, of course,—to be accurate, three in all,[*]—but they are interesting in view of the afterwards world-famous contest of the men.

[*] 3 Ne. Illinois, 349; 4 Ne., 650; 4 Ne., 70.

His third case Mr. Lincoln won.[*] Here associated with him was Stephen T. Logan, a personage in that generation only less picturesque than one who came after him of the same surname and known popularly as "the Black Eagle of Illinois." Logan was recognized as the foremost lawyer at the bar, and, with Lincoln as junior partner from 1841 to to 1843, "Logan & Lincoln" was a team of which Elihu B. Washburne says, "There was never a stronger law firm in the State."

Lincoln's fifth case was the first which he himself appealed,[†] and with it is begun a record of decisions in his favor which should assist to impress upon our minds, for a fitting background to his position as statesman, his preëminent ability as a lawyer.

A careful examination of the Illinois Supreme Court Reports reveals the fact that "A. Lincoln" appeared as counsel in 158 cases. He won eighty-two of these, or nearly 52 per cent of the whole number. The cases in which Lincoln or his law firm appeared for the appellant number 82. Of these he won 45, or nearly 55 per cent.

One who has never considered the point may wonder that I draw from these figures authority for declaring Mr. Lincoln an unusually successful lawyer. But I suppose the chances of opposing sides are about even, or that the average lawyer will win say fifty per cent of his cases. That is, if ability on both sides were equal, the lawyer's work, by reason of its peculiar nature, would hold out to him as about the highest possible reach of his success 50 per cent of the cases he might try. And since it is a fact that poor lawyers, as a rule, will meet poor lawyers, and good lawyers will be pitted against good lawyers,—somewhat after the manner in which water finds its level,—not only the best but the poorest legal talent may be expected to yield a harvest approaching one-half. Nevertheless, although it would argue nothing as to a

lawyer's standing among *all* lawyers merely to point out the percentage of cases won, yet it is a different and perfectly logical proposition that the balance of cases won may be a measure of comparative ability among one's contemporaries. In this way some conclusions may be drawn by which to judge Mr. Lincoln upon his own record and the records of his associates and professional opponents, some of whom I have mentioned. Before proceeding further, let it be said that it is not a man of straw I am setting up and knocking over in this exposition of Mr. Lincoln's Supreme Court record. I bear well in mind that no one has ever belittled his juridical attainments ; I write only to fortify with a few figures his recognized position as a lawyer.

There was only one other man who tried as many appealed suits as did Mr. Lincoln in the twenty years between 1840 and 1860. That was Stephen T. Logan. He tried the same number as Lincoln, but he held comparatively close to his profession, while Lincoln was always in politics.

I find that Logan won 85 suits, which is 55 per cent.

Browning tried 139, and won 51 per cent of that number.

Purple tried 147 and won 48 per cent. Onslow Peters, who tried 124 cases, won only 39 per cent of them.

Judge Trumbull, however, seems to have been successful above all the others in percentage of decisions in his favor, but he tried during that period fewer cases than the others. Of 87 cases he won 50, or 57 per cent.

As for other practitioners, few if any of whom approached the amount of work done by these men during the period mentioned, it could easily be shown that the percentage of cases won was as a rule smaller than that of cases lost.

Of course, legal ability cannot be calculated by arithmetic, but figures are a valuable aid in any study. It has seemed to my mind that Mr. Lincoln's real eminence as a lawyer has not been duly emphasized, the greatness of his public

[*] I. Gillman, 172.
[†] I. Gillman, 225.

service having overshadowed this minor consideration. Yet it is surely well to get a historically accurate conception of his extended career at the bar. Indeed, such an estimate is necessary before one may obtain the most adequate understanding of this mighty Nineteenth Century character, which developed, if one may in any degree define its development, along legal lines.

It will be worth while, in passing, to notice a fact which most readers will be unprepared to learn, that had Lincoln lived and practiced law in the present day he would have had to be classed with the corporation attorneys. He appears several times in the reports as attorney for railroad companies, representing, among others, the Illinois Central. The thirteenth volume of the Illinois reports, by reason of its size, is an object lesson of the stimulating effect exercised by the then new development of railroads upon the business of the courts. This volume contains the first cases in Illinois involving railroad corporations as parties, and in one of them Mr. Lincoln was counsel for the Alta & Sangamon Railroad Company.[*] But that was in 1851, when the railroad was a young and cherished growth, fostered and petted by the people, and to represent it in the court-room was probably looked upon as a good office done the commonwealth (and, after all, is it not?) as well as a recognition of a high order of legal ability. Let it be added, however, that Lincoln appeared also against railroad companies in a few cases, although in such he seems to have been less successful than when battling for the rights of that youthful enterprise.

The most interesting part of volume thirty-seven of these reports is that pertaining to the proceedings of the supreme court *in memoriam* the martyred President, at the April term, 1865. The remarks there made may be received as a candid statement of the estimate placed upon his legal attainments by his contemporaries in the profession.

Said Judge Caton (recently deceased): "From a very early period he assumed a high position at this bar. Without the advantage of that mental culture which is afforded by a classical education, he learned the law as a science ... His deductions were rarely wrong from any given state of facts. So he applied the principles of law to the transactions of men with great clearness and precision. He was a close reasoner. He reasoned by analogy and usually enforced his views by apt illustrations.... If he discovered a weak point in his case he frankly admitted it, and thereby prepared the mind to accept the more readily his mode of avoiding it. *Not deeply read in his profession*, Mr. Lincoln was never found deficient in all the knowledge requisite to present the strong points of his case to the best advantage, and by his searching analysis to make clear the most intricate controversy....For myself, I have for a quarter of a century regarded Mr. Lincoln as the fairest lawyer I ever knew."

Judge Caton then speaks of Mr. Lincoln's career at the bar as a brilliant one and one of "unsullied purity." The lay mind is apt to catch upon the emphasis here laid as in all eulogies of Lincoln, on the loftiness of his personal character, and seizing such statements as the one I have italicized, take home an insufficient, if not unfair, impression of Lincoln the lawyer. Whereas, a careful and comparative study of his record forces the very important conclusion not only that he was a good lawyer among good lawyers, but that he tried more cases in the supreme court (with the exception already noted) than the other good lawyers of his time, and maintained an average of success exceptionally high among them.

---

[*] 13 Illinois, 504.

JACK.

BY UNA B. NIXSON.

WE MADE a great mistake. By we I mean my aged father, who had met with reverses and come West in hope of regaining his fortune; myself, a "girl bachelor," having escaped the mortifying appellation of old maid by being a *fin de siecle* product; and our hired man, a "greaser" with an unpronounceable name, whom, for the sake of brevity, we called Friday.

I had been busy all day making preparations for Sunday, and father and Friday had gone to Lancaster, our nearest trading point, for provisions. When I heard them coming home I went to the door as usual to take the packages, but instead of stopping at the cabin,—it could not exactly be called a house,—they drove straight to the barn, put up the horses, and came in to supper, looking very much amused.

"Where are the groceries?" I asked.

"We didn't get any," was the prompt reply.

"But why not?" I persisted.

"Why, because it's Sunday," my father answered facetiously, just as if he had known it all the time.

The uninterrupted sunshine of Southern California and the absence of any event to break the monotony of the days in the desert had conduced to mix our wits, but this was an unprecedented mistake. The stores were usually open in Lancaster on Sunday, however; but on this particular day the merchants, three in all, had gone on a rabbit hunt.

The following morning the men decided that they must go to cutting the alfalfa. Here and there a purple blossom was already tentatively showing its head, and in a few days, at most, the whole field would burst into bloom, thus destroying to a great extent the strength of the roots.

So I was elected to go for the mail, and for the purchase of such small necessaries as my saddle-bag would accommodate. For, though we lived in a wilderness, thanks to the railroad and the press we were able to keep in touch with the outer world.

I was detained in Lancaster by the lateness of the Frisco mail, and by the time I was ready to start for home, my broncho — Sage-Brush Jim, or Sandy for short — and my dog were very impatient. A cool breeze sighed restlessly through the sage-brush with every wind-lap from the mountain pass; frightened birds flew to their nests on the ground; and evening primroses — pale-faced children of the desert—were beginning to open their sleepy eyes, as we hurried along the road, enveloped in a cloud of hot dust. Now and then the dog started a jack-rabbit or mourning dove, and the appearance of either was a signal for the horse and dog to take a short run. On we hurried toward home, never looking back to see whether the grotesque yuccas were running after us with their deformed legs or beckoning to us with their prickly arms.

When within a mile of the cabin, I let Sandy take his own gait, which was a run. As we neared the corral he stopped so suddenly I was nearly thrown off, in spite of my presumed ability to "stick on" under all ordinary circumstances. Regaining my equanimity, I looked about for the cause of this arrested motion of my animal. He had become frightened at the heads of two solemn-faced burros protruding over the top of his corral. I was as much surprised as he to see his sanctum thus invaded. To be sure, we had visitors occasionally, but they came from neighboring ranches, distant many miles, consequently never on such slow means of locomotion as burros.

I dismounted, tied Sandy to a post, and turned to go toward the cabin. Simultaneously some bright colors on the clothes-line attracted my attention,—a blue flannel shirt, three red bandannas and a pair of socks. These were signals that the intruder was of the masculine gender. I began to grow nervous. Father and Friday had not yet come, and the sun would soon sink into the sea. But visitors of all sorts are expected on the frontier, and if the owner of an establishment is absent, a stranger may take possession as long as he likes, or until the owner returns, and yet adhere strictly to the rules of frontier etiquette. I had several times discovered on my return from the town that neighbors or cowboys had stopped at our cabin, cooked and eaten a meal and left again during my absence. I was wondering as to the advisability of entering the cabin, when the door opened, and there stood the climax of my astonishment.

A man at least six feet tall stood before me. His shoulders were too broad for the door provided in shack architecture, so that he turned them sidewise, while he looked straight ahead, giving him the ap-

pearance of being out of drawing. His eyes were very black and had a fixed expression, which made them look more like big black blots than like eyes. A moustache partly covered a firm mouth, and his unkempt hair pointed toward all the points of the compass, like our desert shirt and buckskin trousers, and supported a brace of revolvers.

I tried to say something ; but, discovering that my tongue was at that moment entertaining an affinity for the roof of my mouth, I remained silent. But my uninvited guest relieved me of any embarrassment by beginning the conversation.

"Waal ! I'll be darned — be you woman or devil ? — one's bad as t'other tho'—ridin' like mad, a foot of a side Sombrero ! and them flyers, too ! Them's what gits me !" The latter satirical reference was to my bifurcated skirt.

Anger quickly came to my aid, loosening my tongue, and I replied unflinchingly :

"I am a woman and live on this ranch, sir. Who are you, and what is your business here ? "

"I'm Jack," he answered doggedly.

"Jack who?"

"Just Jack; t'other's no biz o' yourn, and I'll git if this 'ere shack's run by a —— woman."

It was difficult to decide whether the situation was serious or ludicrous. But the men were in sight now. I could see them following along the irrigation ditch toward the wind-mill, and I knew that a few moments more would bring them in. I sat down on a pile of grease-wood where I could look into the cabin. The stranger turned around and began picking up his things, which were thrown about in disorderly confusion, at the same time talking to himself ostensibly, but veritably to me.

"I might 'a' knowed so!—things right peert 'bout here—ponies, too! I just 'lowed my old pard had sold out, seein' garden sass 'round and so many fixin's; reckoned a d——, no, a pig-tail China-man was 'round. That 'ud be bad 'nough, but a woman—ugh! I 'lowed I'd turn in here—thought I'd hand in my checks if I staid in the diggin's."

"Are you sick?" I ventured, ignoring the decidedly pessimistic view he was taking of my sex. He did not answer, and I went on. "The men will be here in a few moments—there they are now, this side the pointed butte," pointing in that direction.

"I aint goin' to waste no time packin' my traps, if they be. I'll be —— if I'll have any —— women in mine!" Then he shambled out of the door, toward the clothes-line. As he came out I saw he looked very pale. When he went back in with his washing, he laid the pieces on the sack he had just packed and settled down in a chair, and really looked alarmingly ill.

"Wouldn't you rather stay until the men come?" I asked, undaunted. He roused up and exclaimed furiously:

"None o' your greased tongue for me; I've seen 'nough o' 'em," and he looked as white as death.

Father and Friday appeared just then, and I drew a breath of relief.

Friday had worked for the man whose claim father bought, so he knew Jack well, as he had at one time been a frequent visitor.

Jack rallied at the sight of a familiar face, and was finally persuaded to remain over night. They helped him into the adobe harness-room where Friday slept, and the next morning he was in a raging fever. There was no physician in the community, the only one that had ever attempted living there had been "starved out"; but we used all of the home remedies of which we were cognizant to allay the fever, and he gradually grew better. Whenever I went into the room he turned his face to the wall. Occasionally I took in magazines and papers and laid them on his bed, but he never touched them while I was present. But several times, when I reappeared unexpectedly, I found him eagerly devouring the contents of my home paper, the ——, New York, *News*, and I suspected there was some reason for the preference.

At the end of a fortnight Jack was so much improved he was able to sit up. I had his chair placed so that he could look out on the snow-capped Sierra Madres in the distance, or watch the strange antics of the atmosphere in producing some wonderful mirage effects. Such revelations of beauty come to the inhabitants of the desert-land—a recompense of nature for the sacrificed privileges of civilization. Frequently, in the early morning, one can see a perfect facsimile of some little desert town, suspended high in the heavens, with a like one, inverted, beneath it; perhaps watch the formation of beautiful bridges between mountain passes, and then see them blow away like smoke; or, follow the outlines of giant cacti, reflected in apparent lakes, where there is nothing but a barren waste of sand, until one grows breathless and doubts his own sanity.

I went in one morning when Jack was sitting by the window, and he looked so contented I said, "Jack, are you anxious to get away?"

He looked me full in the face for the

first time, and answered : "I'd jest like to kick myself fer bein' so mean, and I'm sorry I've made ye so much trouble and been so techy."

"Well, if you are really sorry," I said, "tell me about your home and your mother—she is a woman. Didn't you live in New York some place?"

He roused up, and then fell back again, letting his head rest against the wall, with his eyes closed, as he had done on that first day.

I started to leave the room, but he opened his eyes and called out : "Come back, and I'll tell ye all 'bout mother and the old home, but never mind if I git to rantin', fer I feel like shootin' when I git to thinkin' 'bout it."

"Perhaps you had better not tell me, then," I said, but he ignored my remark.

"My mother was a good little woman," he said. "I hope she's livin'. It's near twelve years since I left her, and her beggin' me to stay! My sister died the year afore, and my father had been on t'other side goin' on eight years. Mother an' I lived in a little house all our own, so contented and happy like. I worked hard, but I didn't succeed in much of a strike, and I knew that it 'ud be some time afore I 'ud git 'nough o' a pile to git married to Suze—Suze Stevens."

Here he began to get excited. His face flushed, and the strong arm, resting on the arm of the chair, trembled perceptibly. Then he grew quieter and went on :

"Suze liked fine fixins, so I jest 'lowed I'd go to Leadville, with a lot goin' out to the mines from our town, and see if I couldn't strike it rich. So I went, and I worked hard—tended to my own biz— didn't drink nor gamble a bit, and most o' my chums was regular bunco-steerer, thimble-rigged, three card-monte men.

"After 'while I got homesick and was thinkin' o' givin' up, when I struck up with an old prospector. He said he'd grub-stake me, so I started out, and I tell ye I made a find that time. I got half o' it ; but I sold my interest to an Englishman ; then I went back to Leadville, got into some fine logs and started for home

and Suze. You can jest bet I was glad to leave that shanty town under the mountain. I was the happiest man on this big footstool—three years was a coon's age to me !

"When I got home my mother was that happy she laughed and cried t' once; then she put her arms 'round my neck and laid her head on my shoulder, lookin' at me like I was a babe in 'er arms, an' then she said softly : 'Jack. I've bad news fer ye.' All of a sudden I felt sick-like, for I knew 'twas 'bout Suze she was goin' to say somethin'. I remembered it 'ud been a year since I'd heard from her; but I was so fur from the post-office, and we never had wrote so very often—though we'd taken an oath to be true to one 'nother. I spunked up my courage, after chokin' a bit, and I said, 'Mother—she aint—she aint dead—is she ?'

"'No,' said mother, gently, 'she's married.'

"First I was dazed, then my head went 'round like one o' them merry-go-rounds, then I was tearin'! I rushed out o' the house and over to where they told me Suze lived. I seen her at the window and I rushed in and caught her by the arm and I said, 'You lied to me, you miserable hussy !' She jest said, 'Oh, my Henry !'

"'No Henry o' yourn,' I said. 'Where's your d—— husband ?' Then she begun cryin'—

"'Oh, take me away—I'm neglected —and—my husband—beats me when he comes home drunk !'

"'It's good 'nough for ye,' said I. 'I come to build you and me a fine house, and this is the way ye've treated me '

"I started to go, but she held on to me with a grip like death, cryin'—

"'Don't go—don't leave me—I didn't hear from ye, and I thought ye must be dead, and my husband he said you'd found somebody you cared more 'bout 'an me.'

"I was gittin' madder and madder, and I said, 'Didn't I tell ye I'd come and git ye, and haven't I always kept my word ?'

"Then I made out o' that house, and for days I blowed my money and jest

raised cane —till at last my mother foun'
me and tuk me home, and kept me till I
was myself agin — no, not myself —
couldn't ever be the same agin — I jest
hated the sight o' a petticoat, and was
crazy to git where I'd never see 'nuther.
I give most o' my dust to my mother,
then I come out this side o' the Rockies
—nigh twelve years ago —and I haven't
seen but durned few females sence.

"When I seen ye flyin' up to that cabin
I was more skeered thnn if I'd see a
grizzly flyin' at me —'nough sight!"

He paused, looked out of the window,
and went on, meditatively : "I'm kind
o' glad now; fer ef I hadn't had to be
tuk care of by a woman, maybe I
wouldn't 'a' got to thinkin' 'bout my
mother, an' how she used to nurse me
when I was sick. Peers like the harder
a body hates a thing in this 'ere world,
the surer that thing is to bring him good
in some way or 'nuther — heapin' coals o'
fire on his head, you might say. When I
was layin' there so sick, seemin' to know
nothin', I was a thinkin' mighty hard,
now I tell ye! I guess the Lord sent me
here jest to set me to thinkin', and made
me sick so's I'd have plenty o' time to
think it out in. And I've done it, you
kin bet. I can see it all now — jest how
mean and cussed I've been, neglectin'
my poor old mother and hatin' all the
women jest cause one o' them lied to me.
Seems like good many folks git punished
in this world fer the things they've got
nuthin' to do 'bout. But ef the Lord'll
give me a show now, I'm with 'im !" —
and his fist came down on the arm of the
chair with a peremptory thud that shook
the adobe like an earthquake.

A few days later Jack was able to be
out. He busied himself about the ranch,
and my "garden sass"— which had
evoked his wrath a few weeks previous—
now grew and flourished under his care.
He went about quietly and did not say
much. But one evening he came in with
a handful of desert flowers, and seemed
inclined to talk. As there was really no
common ground for conversation, I expressed some interest in mining, which he

referred to frequently, and asked him if
he had any specimens of quartz-carrying
gold. I had seen several pieces of quartz
among his few belongings.

He brightened up and exclaimed with
enthusiasm, "You bet, do you want to
see 'em?"

I said that I did, and he went into the
adobe and brought out a number of large
pieces of quartz.

"That come from a claim I've had covered up in the mountains fer a long time,"
he said, handing me one of the pieces.
"I'm goin' down to Dagget to work in
the silver mines till I can raise 'nough to
work it, ef I can't git somebody to grub-
stake me, fer there 's 'nough in that hole
to make me rich agin."

"Why haven't you tried to open this
mine before, if its such a good thing ?" I
asked.

"Waal, I didn't care 'bout it much, but
now I do," and a new light came into
his eyes.

"How much money would it take,
Jack, to open the mine, and keep you
until the mine would bring returns?" I
asked. He named the sum, adding :

"It'll take some hard knocks to git
that, but I'll git there, don't you forgit ;
then I'm goin' home to see my mother."

That night I did not sleep much. The
idea had suggested itself that I might
furnish Jack the money from my hard-
earned savings from teaching school. I
turned the matter over and over in my
mind and tried to decide as to the advisability of such a step. I believed firmly
in Jack's honesty now ; but what if he
were deceived about the mine ! He had
told me that the mine was near a railroad,
and that, certainly, was in its favor. Then
came visions of my father reinstated in
the old homestead, free from care and
work, surrounded again by old friends
and associations. The temptation was
too great.

The next morning I surprised them all
by telling them I was going to Los
Angeles. A little shopping was my excuse. And none of them knew that the
real cause of this unexpected departure

was a small piece of quartz, carefully concealed in my hand-bag.

A hundred miles had never seemed so long before. But when I did arrive in the city, I lost no time in finding an assayer, and the certificate of assay, which I received later, showed that "The Find"—Jack's name for the mine—was worth mining.

When I found myself in the Lancaster station again, Jack was there to meet me. On the way home he told me that he had heard of a sure job in Dagget, during my absence, and that he would set out on the morrow. I didn't exactly know how to get at what I wanted to say, but I finally mustered up courage to venture casually,—

"Jack, would you like to have enough money to begin work on your own mine, and not go to Dagget?" He looked surprised and answered:

"I'd be the happiest man on the whole job."

When I told him that I had decided to furnish him the money, he was overcome with gratitude.

———

The money had been provided, the burros were packed and Jack was about to say good-bye.

"Jack, wont you tell us your real name now?" I asked. I had never mentioned it before.

"That's not much to ask when you're doin' so much fer me," he said; "but jest call me Jack till I come back, then I'll tell ye my name. I've taken the stakes, and I'll give ye half 'The Find' —here's my hand on it—I never lied to man, nor woman nuther—good-bye."

He was off. I watched him until he disappeared in the sea of sage-brush.

I ask you: Have I lost, or won?

———

THE WHISTLING BUOY.

By Edward Carpenter.

THE mouth of the river is very narrow, but that is only where it rushes through the thin line of sand dunes that guard this part of the New England coast. Behind them it forms a large, shallow bay bounded by great stretches of salt marsh.

The town lies at the head of the bay, —a quaint old place, its streets bordered by fine old elms, and its water-front by abandoned wharves. The town is not what it used to be in the days of the trade with India.

In the gray of the morning, one day in early summer, two fishermen are rowing out to the ledges that lie two or three miles off shore. One of the men is dark, almost as dark as a Spaniard; the other is fair, for a man who from his boyhood has followed the sea. The one last mentioned is very happy this morning — happy, thankful and proud. For after years of such pinching and economizing as none knew but himself, he has saved enough to buy a little cottage that stands, away from the main road, at the head of a quiet lane. Two great elms at the side overshadow and protect it, moss roses grow in the sunny dooryard, the wooden posts of the broad porch are covered from bottom to top with a mass of honeysuckle, which has been led from one to the other until a succession of green arches has been formed. The half-acre of land at the back is an old apple orchard, where the grass grows long and thick between the gnarled trunks of the trees. This is the home to which he is going to take the woman he loves. All these long years he has been working and saving with this for his goal. As he rows he sees picture after picture in the gray mist that hangs over the water astern, and he smiles as he watches them, for he sees always a sweet woman's face and a little vine-covered cottage in the foreground.

The face of the second man is hard and drawn, and his eyes are fixed on the broad, muscular back that rises and falls in front of him as it keeps time to the stroke. He needs money. He must have it, and at once. He knows that the man who is with him has the savings of years in his belt. If he should take them no one need ever know. That long, sharp knife used for cutting up bait would answer for a weapon. A single stroke in the right place and it would all be over. Then it would be an easy matter to weight the body with one of the several pieces of railroad iron carried for ballast, drop it over the side, and say that during the heavy blow, that was coming up, he had fallen overboard, had been struck by the plunging boat and had sunk before he could be rescued. They would never suspect him, for his life as far as was known had always

EDWARD CARPENTER, OF PHILADELPHIA.

been a straightforward one. It was not known by anyone who would hear of the accident that he was in need of money. And this man had been his closest friend from boyhood. But then he thought of all his partner had gone through, all the hardships he had endured without a murmur that he might add to his savings; how he had talked by the hour of the woman he loved, while they were fishing alone out there on the ledges. He thought, too, of the great happiness that had shone in his face as the day for which he had labored so long drew near.

And so, each absorbed in his own thoughts, they pulled steadily out to sea, past the sand dunes, with the Life-Saving Station nestled among them, a pistol-shot distant from the river's mouth, past the long granite breakwaters, past the dangerous bar that blocks the harbor entrance, a whistling buoy marking its seaward end, and so on straight out into the broad Atlantic. When the ledges were reached they anchored and began to fish. At first their luck was good, but the breeze which had been "pickling up" all the morning soon blew half a gale and they were forced to stop. They had intended to make a port twenty miles farther south where, owing to the greater demand, they could realize more on their catch; and it was for this reason that the fair-haired man had brought his money with him, the owner of the cottage living there. It looked so threatening to seaward, however, and there was such a sea running, that they stepped their reefed sprit-sail and ran for the mouth of the river.

The tide was ebbing and the northeast blow had raised a tremendous sea on the bar, where the combers broke all the way across. They rounded to in the lea of the whistling buoy and, making fast to it, waited for the tide to turn, when the sea on the bar would go down and they might run in with safety. The great iron buoy rose and fell on the waves every few seconds, giving forth its weird "wh-o-o, who-o-o-o," sometimes short, sometimes long drawn out, —

awful at any time, most terrible and awe-
inspiring as the accompaniment to a
gale of wind on a black winter's night.

In the course of a couple of hours, the
tide having turned, it was calm enough
to cross the bar. One of the men turned
towards the bow to cast off from the
buoy, which was thrashing heavily in the
rising waves. As he did so his hand
touched the long knife stuck between a
thwart and the combing. He turned his
head slowly and looked at his companion who was leaning over the stern,
shipping the rudder, the belt containing
his money showing plainly. He stood
for a moment looking fixedly at him;
then, in two steps, he was beside the
unsuspecting man.

"She jumps so, Jack, I can't——"

There was a flash, a blow, a sigh and
it was all over. The rudder floated
quickly astern, the hands trailed in the
water and the head drooped until the
still-smiling face touched the waves.

With shaking hands the murderer un-
did the belt, took out the notes and
strapped it in place again. He bound
two of the heavy pieces of iron firmly to
the feet, and, trying not to see its face,
slid the body over the stern. As it disappeared feet foremost in the dark
waters, he muttered, "No one will ever
know who did it," and turned with a
start as the buoy behind him moaned in
its deep voice, "Who-o-o?"

He looked in all directions, but no one
was in sight. The only house for miles
on this lonely shore was the Life-Saving
Station, and it was deserted during the
summer by all but the keeper. Quickly
hiding the money in his coat, and slipping an oar over to leeward in place of
the lost rudder, he cast off from the
buoy and headed for home, but all the
way the dreadful, questioning "who-o?
who-o-o?" followed him.

He reached his landing safely and reported the accident. There were few
questions asked. A sailor's life is an
uncertain one at best, and many a good
man had been lost before from the same
port. This one had no relations, few

intimate friends. There was a heart-
broken woman, one more tablet on the
wall of the village church, and a little
vine-covered cottage still for rent.

That was all,—except for a restless
man who roamed all day through the
fields and woods and at night shut himself up alone in his house. "He will
never fish on the ledges again," they
said, "how the poor fellow grieves for
his friend!" And the man wondered if
they knew how far back in the country
one could hear that fearful buoy.

The summer passed and then the autumn; at last winter arrived with its bitter cold winds and ice and snow. The
Life-Saving Station was all activity then,
the small colony of seven men and the
keeper being the only human beings for
miles along the coast. An extra man,
the December man, allowed them by the
government for this month of the year
only, had just arrived and taken up his
duties. He had been roaming about the
country for half a year, trying to get beyond the reach of the voice of the whistling buoy that marks the harbor bar.
Finally he had returned and was seeking
the other extreme by accepting a position that would keep him, all night and
all day, within sound of its eternal questioning. Seldom had there been so great
a change in a man. His shoulders were
bowed, his face was drawn and thin,
while his deep-set, flighty eyes gleamed
with a fire that was not natural.

The daily routine of the Station remained undisturbed by any unusual event
until, with the afternoon of the twelfth of
that month, there commenced a northeast
gale which will long be kept in mind on
that iron-bound coast by the bones of the
good vessels cast away during the three
days it was at its height. The barometer
in the dining room had been steadily falling during the past forty-eight hours, and
by 9 o'clock that evening the roar of
the wind and surf was so terrible that the
men, gathered around the stove, had to
shout to be heard. The house shook and
rocked on its foundations, and the entire
surface of the sea was one boiling, seeth-

ing mass of foam. Two men were put on the night-beats, as it was feared that a single patrolman would get bewildered and wander helplessly through the deserted sand-hills until, overcome by the cold, he would fall to the ground.

It was the second night of the hurricane, which was now at its height. All the night before and all that day the surf had broken with the noise of heavy artillery on the beach in front of the Station, and through it all, above the roar of the winds, the buoy out on the bar had screamed and shrieked "Who-o! who-o-o!" as it had never cried before.

The second night-watch of two men was being sent out, and one of them was the extra December man. Together they fought their way along, thankful that it was low tide and that they could walk on the hard sand beyond the reach of the waves. When about two miles from the Station they noted what appeared to be the bows of a small schooner standing out black against the foam of the surf, one moment thrown high in the air, the next almost covered by a following sea. They worked as close to the edge of the breakers as they dared and stood peering to windward, their eyes sheltered by their hands from the driving salt spray. Suddenly a giant wave reared the object on its crest and hurled it with a crash in the shoal water at their very feet, while at the same moment it gave a fairly human shriek. With a cry to Heaven one of the men started on a run for the Station. The other remained. And there they found him several hours later, when the search party arrived, squatting on his heels in the foam and spume, his gaunt face fixed in a horrid grin, while before him lay the shattered frame of the great iron buoy, a long length of parted chain-cable telling its story,—but nothing telling his.

MY NUT-BROWN INDIAN MAID.

ALONG the sun-kissed hillside
　　The sumac torches beam,
And bright in foggy fallows
　　The yellowed poplars gleam ;
The maples in the woodland
　　Their crimson flags unfurl,—
All earth is glad to greet you,
　　My nut-brown Indian girl !

Soft purple hazes drape the sky,—
　　Smoke-wreaths from camp-fires blown,—
The oak leaves rustle, rustle by,
　　The stream sings on alone ;
The bright-eyed asters wait with me
　　To greet you in the glade,—
October, decked in colors rare,
　　My nut-brown Indian maid !

Maude Morrison.

"THE TRAGIC TREES."

A TALE OF MOB LAW.*

I.

BY MARGUERITE CHAMBERS KELLAR.

WHEN the wheel of fortune turned Miss Ruth Hunter from the cheerful life of New Orleans into the village of Bourbonville, she rebelled, in a miserable, helpless manner common only among women. She was forty years old ; yet no society belle ever missed her triumphs more than Miss Ruth missed the opera, the play, and the other odds and ends of city life. And she was too old to find new friends or create new plans.

Nevertheless there was not the slightest use in beating against the bars. It was one of those tyrannical bits of life, called force of circumstances, which changed her surroundings as thoroughly as if she had been transported to another planet.

Her old-maid life was inseparable from that of her old-bachelor brother. They had been constant companions in childhood, they had shared each other's love dreams in early youth, and had taken to heart each other's broken hopes, afterwards. So, when he went to Bourbonville, she went too; he with his cold, self-contained nature; she, with sympathetic instincts alive to all the world. In fact, Miss Ruth had, on one memorable occasion, been called "meddler." This was done, however, by naughty boys, whom history had not taught that meddlers are often reformers. To the tortured kitten, rescued from their cruel hands, "meddler" had certainly meant benefactor.

In Boston atmosphere, Miss Ruth would have been a woman of "views," for, in her opinion, a great many things needed making over ; but the languorous air of the South had left her unable to do more than utter little protests, in private. She recognized the gap between her will and her strength, and might have appropriately said :

"The time is out of joint : Oh, cursed spite,
That ever I was born to set it right!"

It was probably some weakness in her character, some undeveloped attribute which robbed her life of success. As she said, pathetically, "I was too late, even to save the kitten." She had made faint little snatches at fame through her pen ;

MRS. MARGUERITE CHAMBERS KELLAR.
Hot Springs, South Dakota

*Awarded the Prize for the Best Original Story in THE MIDLAND'S March 31st Competition.

347

and, during the first loneliness in Bourbonsville, her brother advised her to write up the people.

"Use the material about you," he said.

"Use the material, indeed!" she answered. "There's no material to use; nothing can happen here. Gabriel's trumpet would not stir this place to life."

This lack of perception in her emphasized the truth, that "they only find, who know where to look."

She was not, even in a modest way, a satirist; and the quaint humor, the infinite pathos, which animates the pen of genius, had no existence for her, except through the medium of that pen. She could not fancy a thousand little conceits in the characters around her; nor see, in the uneventful tenor of their ways, material for the "Russet-coated Epics" of a George Eliot. Least of all would she have expected to find tragical elements in a spot so dull and lifeless.

So it happened, naturally, that she buried herself in books written by others, and let herself drift into this story, left for another to write.

Bourbonsville was in a healthy locality and rejoiced in being the oldest town in the state. It was a quaint, sleepy hollow of a spot, which Irving might have selected for the scene of his famous legend, and, having selected, would doubtless have doubled Rip Van Winkle's sleep. The men walked leisurely about, and the women strolled along on occasional shopping expeditions; or, to use a local expression, they sometimes "went down the street." One bank and six churches caused a stranger to wonder who filled the latter, and supported the former.

Among the churches was the Old School Presbyterian, in which services were held once a year, and sometimes not oftener than once in two years. A religious town!

Recreation consisted in attending church on Sunday and calling at the post-office every evening. Another custom, not to be lightly mentioned, was the social gathering at the dingy old depot, when one of the youths and maidens started on a trip to a neighboring village. On occasions of this sort, every acquaintance considered it a duty to be on hand and say good-bye.

Bourbonsville was a pretty, proper, prohibition town, with not even a beer bottle in sight; an orthodox village, where one felt as if the sun shone and the rain fell by rule. The houses were old and sturdy and looked as if they had been built for a population which expected to stay in them forever.

"No chance for any excitement here," said Miss Ruth, disconsolately; for, though well on in years, she had lost none of her relish for active life. Even in a picture, she preferred a storm scene at sea, or the tossing of forest trees, or motion in some form. From the days of her active gaieties, long passed away, there still remained the spirit, which refused to be in sympathy with a sluggish village, where existence was but a "death in life," yet where, to her continual wonder, the people seemed entirely satisfied.

Miss Ruth thought them an extremely patriotic community, for they possessed that loud-voiced patriotism common in some circles before the War — and again, just after. They shamed her somewhat, in their devotion to the South, and especially to their State. On one occasion, when she modestly expressed her opinion that "Uncle Tom's Cabin" was an impartial picture of Southern life, bright, amiable little Mrs. Mathes looked at her askance, and said, "I thought you were a Southerner!"

When she condemned the doctrine of secession, and, to describe it, used a woman's pet adjective, "abominable," Mr. Mathes came to his wife's assistance and with a lofty superiority, said, "You must have been born in Massachusetts instead of Mississippi."

The Matheses were Miss Ruth's next door neighbors, but, from the day of her unlucky speech, she lost caste.

Twenty years before, Miss Ruth's brothers had belonged to Lee's picked sharpshooters. They were among those who went first and staid longest. Her young lover had been a brave and faithful soldier in all the campaigns of the "Army of the Tennessee," never missing a battle; had lain at death's door, on hard hospital beds; had marched in summer heat and winter cold; and, after the battle of Murfreesboro, was buried, with other beardless boys, in a common ditch. Miss Ruth had been one of the young girls who knitted socks and sewed flannel shirts for Southern soldiers during the four dreadful years, considering herself miserable when Sunday interrupted the work. Her old father, too, full-handed and bighearted, had given the whole of his vast fortune to the "lost cause." But that record was worthless in Bourbonsville. A woman who endorsed "Uncle Tom's Cabin" did not love the South, and that ended the argument.

This pretty, curious old town, with its self-satisfied inhabitants, lay snugly in a basin, with high hills on every side. Describing it in one of her letters home, Miss Ruth said, "The hills shut in the old ideas and exclude the new." Whether the hills were responsible for the lack of progress, or not, they made a very pretty picture.

On the outskirts of the village stood three large sugar-maple trees, said to be a hundred years old. They formed with the spreading branches deep green in summer, gold in autumn,—a mass of grateful shade or of glowing warmth. Their arms grew low, as if in good will to mankind. No doubt innocent children for three generations had played in their shadows, and afterwards, as men and women, whispered tenderly to one another under the close, caressing boughs. The three trees made shade sufficient for a good-sized picnic. The view from them was fair and enticing. On one side were the hills overlooking the town; on the other, meadows and fields stretched away to what seemed an illimitable distance. On this spot Miss Ruth first found balm for homesickness. There the poetry and enthusiasm of youth enveloped her, and her whole being responded generously to the delightful charm of nature. The view

was hers; the trees were especially hers, for there no human being intruded. The birds in the boughs overhead sang a lullaby to her thoughts; and the mild-eyed Jersey cows had grown to be an essential part of the scene. The people of the village were altogether indifferent to the beauties of the spot: but Miss Ruth had no difficulty in explaining this according to the rule that every-day blessings are neglected. That the rule held good in this instance was a source of great satisfaction to her. Every hour she spent there held its distinct charm, impossible had chattering tongues intruded.

She had gone there at dawn of day, when the sun loitered behind the hills. The clear sweet air was sweeter and clearer then, as she waited and watched with a song in her heart, "while the still morn went out with sandals gray."

Even at midday, when desperately weary of the hot, dingy-looking houses, she braved the sun in order to find rest under the maple trees. But evening was the day's poem. The outlook then was most soft and touching, when the sun, like a great crimson ball, slowly disappeared, leaving a softly tinted sky: when the birds' songs were hushed and the spot was enveloped in a silence so entrancing and so satisfying that it seemed, not silence only, but some subtle essence, possessing myriads of sweet, tender, appealing voices, unheard except by a listening soul.

It was on such an evening as this that Miss Ruth sat on a large gray stone which lay at the root of her favorite tree, and which formed her usual seat. Spring and summer had come and gone, and the winds of the last October day had stripped the trees, and the leaves lay a golden carpet on the ground. Miss Ruth was touched by the loneliness about her, as by an infinite Presence. It was good to live; and Bourbonsville was not so bad after all. While she sat reading and dreaming, with the glories of earth and heaven closer to her than usual, a ragged boy came walking slowly toward her, swinging a small basket, half-full of withered vegetables. When he came near, he stopped and looked intently at her, and half-curiously, too; then, according to the local custom of greeting strangers, he said "Good-evenin'."

The next moment he was gazing up into the branches above her head. He was the first human being who had invaded her retreat. Others had passed by, but, intent on business or pleasure, had been satisfied to glance and go on.

"That's whar they hang folks," he next said, still gazing up into the trees.

"What?" asked Miss Ruth, as she looked at him half dreamily. The spell of the hour was upon her senses, and the boy and his words were vague and distant.

"Three men hung there jist befo' you come," he announced, tritely.

"Why, what do you mean?" a swift thought of his insanity possessing her.

"Mean jist that," he answered, as he idly swung his basket to and fro. "They hung three men thar one night, and one befo' that," and he stared up in the trees with a speculative air, altogether out of keeping with the subject.

"You are a wicked, wicked boy," said Miss Ruth, severely, "and you are telling me a falsehood."

"No'm I aint," grinning like a malevolent imp. "I seen 'em hangin' nex' day —two niggers and one white. The niggers say the ghosts come every night, an' mean ter kill the trees I reckon they know. I wouldn't set thar."

And she did not. The poor, ignorant boy had truth in his face. Before the close of his last sentence she was out from under the trees and standing by his side.

"Yes'm," he continued, in the tone of one discussing a chicken fight, "yes'm, they taken them from the jail, at night. I reckon them trees wus made fur the bizness. They does fust rate, anyhow. The limbs is low an' handy."

"Hush!" Miss Ruth's voice was harsh and angry. The boy started as from a blow.

Her heart was throbbing in her throat; her fingers were cold: the gray light of the dying day was hurrying on, and the mists were already rising between the hills down in the valleys. The woman and the tattered, insentient vagabond stood close together, the only living beings present.

To Miss Ruth's strained senses the trees began to take the form of grim specters; she gazed into the mysterious depths of the bare, black branches, and fancied moving forms. Shaking from head to foot, her books dropped from her hands with a loud noise.

"It's gittin' late, ma'm," said the boy, "I'll tote yer things fur yer. Air yer afeard? Thought yer knowed 'bout the trees, though," and he looked in her face appealingly. "Nobody ever sets under 'em but you."

Miss Ruth gathered her wits together. This talkative imp must not mistake horror for fear; so, controlling the tremor in her voice, she said, "You may bring the books; I am cold."

He hurriedly gathered up the books and followed, as Miss Ruth walked rapidly towards home. His tongue seemed hung on a hinge, and he chatted on.

"I live in 'Possum Range, three miles from town; my name is Lige,—Lige Gage." He continued reflectively, "Folks out thar call you brave,—ther 'brave woman.' They 'lowed you knowed 'bout ther hangin'; but is I They're might'ly out of it!"

"Will you hush," said poor Miss Ruth, desperately.

"I 'lowed you'd wanter hear," he continued placidly. "Them town folks wont notice us 'Possum Rangers 'less they want help to do some night work: *then* they buys masks and things, and all go in ther racket together."

By this time the gate of Miss Ruth's little yard was reached. She took the books from him and, without a word, walked quickly into the house. She found her brother in the sitting room, enjoying the warmth of the early fire, and she burst out like a volcano, giving him the story fresh from the 'Possum Ranger's lips.

Charles Hunter listened attentively, but, to her disgust, he betrayed neither indignation nor surprise, as he calmly answered, "My dear sister, let this matter alone, and don't make yourself unpopular. Remember this is a mob-law state."

"You, a man, and take it so calmly!" she retorted.

"My dear, experience teaches men the folly of useless opposition. Remember the fate of the frail broom against the sea waves. Take my advice: Live in your books. In them alone lie your safety and happiness."

"Did you know about those trees?" She glanced at him suspiciously.

"Certainly."

"And never told me? And let me go there!"

"Why, my dear, that is the finest scene in the whole country."

"But the horror of it!" she answered.

"Yes, it is horrible," he said seriously, "look at it in any light you choose; but, when I found you had learned to love the spot, I had not the heart to tell you; and I did not suppose anyone would be so brutal. You have seemed so much better contented of late,—almost happy." And he sighed, for her moods mattered much to him. Presently he resumed, more earnestly, "It is wiser to dwell as little as possible on evils you cannot remove."

"But," she continued, insistently, "to think and talk and act will mend matters."

"True. If you can act; but we are strangers here, and shall probably not remain long enough for me to vote."

"Vote? Who cares to vote! We want civilization."

He laughed a little maliciously, and said, "I advise you not to repeat that here."

"They are all barbarians," she answered, recklessly.

"Not individually, only collectively," he answered, still half smiling.

"Enough to be a disgrace," she returned, adding aggressively, "and you are getting to be as bad as any of them, for you defend them."

"No, I merely recognize my inability to change an evil, while you torture your heart in useless effort. I cannot endorse the theory that to be born here guarantees special beauty to women or bravery and honor to men. Yet that is the pleasant illusion hereabouts. It is possible for aliens like you and me to remember, not only the great men produced by this State, but also the notorious outlaws. In the face of these unlawful deeds, it is matter for surprise that egotism grows to its present proportions. It is certainly rank enough." And he knocked the ashes from his cigar.

"Cannot the civil officers curb the outrages?" asked Miss Ruth, somewhat more tranquil, seeing her brother was not the monster of indifference he had seemed.

"The officers partake of the nature of the people," he replied briefly, "and the people are responsible for these midnight deeds."

"Then what becomes of the political proverb, 'The voice of the people is the voice of God,'" she inquired, scornfully. "Does anyone believe God's voice was in the hanging of those poor wretches, without a trial?"

"I presume the truth of the proverb depends pretty much on the type of people," answered Mr. Hunter. "In this case I should unhesitatingly declare the voice of the people to be that of the devil."

"Oh, that we had power to change these customs!" exclaimed Miss Ruth, impatiently.

"But since we cannot hope to have that power, we shall allow this community to attend to its own affairs, in its own way."

"Even to committing murder in the most horrible of all ways, I suppose," she said, hopelessly.

"It amounts to that, yes," replied Mr. Hunter, in his irritating, imperturbable manner. "But," he continued, "if my opinions will add to your comfort, here they are in full: This evil ought to be uprooted; lawlessness has become notorious and has fixed a crime upon the

State; but the difficulty lies in the fact that the people are blind to their shame. 'Kings can do no wrong' is converted into 'my State can do no wrong.' Since the revelation of this local peculiarity, I have concluded that state pride in excess is an unfortunate trait, leading to blind egotism,—always a barrier to progress or to the highest civilization."

Miss Ruth, half awed by her brother's unexpected support and sympathy, said, "To express such sentiments would injure you, if you were in politics."

"And if I were, state lines would not be boundaries for my views Besides, I shall never touch the outer circle of the legerdemain of politicians."

He seemed about to dismiss the subject when she abruptly asked, "If you had reformatory power, how would you use it?"

Mr. Hunter answered earnestly, almost solemnly, "Andrew Johnson once said, 'Massachusetts and South Carolina ought to be lashed together on some rock, in mid-ocean, to be washed by the waves and cooled by the winds.' I should form a trio, by adding another state. And yet," he continued, after a pause, "social and political sins do not depend upon locality, or on any particular type of human nature; but rather in permitting conceit and unwholesome customs to obtain an abnormal development. Hence, communities, like individuals, should be continually alert.

"Puritan New England's vain assumption of superiority developed into witchburning. Slavery in the South became a cherished institution, until custom destroyed our sense of its enormity. Nor, do we forget the beautiful Roman women who, with thumbs turned down, smiled at the dying gladiators in the arena.

"Bourbonsville only needs the touch of elbows to the outside world as an eyeopener. So be patient, and now go to bed; I've said my last word on the subject."

The next morning the sound of Mrs. Mathes' voice at the hall door, enquiring for Miss Hunter, gave the latter more than ordinary pleasure. The experience of the previous evening had set her nerves in disorder, and Mr. Hunter's patient talk had not entirely restored her.

From Mrs. Mathes, who had been born and reared in Bourbonsville, and who, for that reason, understood its customs, Miss Ruth expected sympathy. For, incredible as it may seem, she meant to agitate the subject and attempt a reformation. "A very small pebble," she argued, "dropped in the sea will make a ripple."

Miss Ruth's pebble was diminutive, but it was real. She was sure of help from this woman, who occupied the foremost place in every charitable undertaking.

Mrs. Mathes was not only "good" in a conventional, orthodox way, but she aspired to intellectual superiority. She belonged to that class created by nature to do the correct thing, and who follow the beaten path, even in dispensing charities. She was an enthusiastic "church woman," an outward follower of Him whose gentle spirit rebuked all bloodshed. Her husband, being the most prominent man in the community, was understood to have political aspirations.

Viewed in the light of Miss Ruth's philanthropical plans, her pleasure at seeing Mrs. Mathes was natural.

"You look sick," exclaimed the latter, coming into the room, her voice alive with sympathy.

"I *feel* sick," answered Miss Ruth, simply.

"What is the matter? You are white, with dark rings about your eyes."

"I did not sleep well last night," replied Miss Ruth, wearily.

"Did you see ghosts?" inquired Mrs. Mathes, smilingly.

"Yes," and Miss Ruth's solemn eyes emphasized her answer. "Yes, I saw ghosts,—the ghosts of a murdered civilization."

Mrs. Mathes looked at her searchingly, saying, "Dear Miss Hunter, you are certainly sick; you are feverish; send for the doctor."

"No, no; you are the physician I need; you can tell me the truth. Yesterday evening a vagabond white boy came upon me, at those maple trees, and told me a horrible tale; but it cannot be true; I went over it all, last night "

"You mean about the men being hanged?" asked Mrs. Mathes, quietly.

"It is true then?"

"Oh, yes, it is indeed."

"Horrible!" exclaimed Miss Ruth, her face growing, if possible, more wan than ever.

"Yes," said Mrs. Mathes, "a great pity to desecrate those trees; they were the pride of the country."

"But," continued Miss Ruth, eagerly, "it is not the trees, it is the men. I hoped the tale was not true."

"True? Why, yes; the mob often takes prisoners from jail and hangs them."

"Where is your law?" and the indignant blood swept the pallor from Miss Ruth's face.

"Oh," said Mrs. Mathes, with a smile, "they don't wait for law."

"You do not defend the practice, I hope," said Miss Ruth, stifling her horror and beginning to cast in her pebbles.

"Oh, of course it's wrong, but they will do it."

"But your husband has influence; can he do nothing?"

"Miss Hunter," answered Mrs. Mathes, evasively, "the men deserved their fate."

"But that was murder; it was cowardly, and a disgrace to the people," Miss Ruth said, in consternation.

"Allow me to remind you, my friend," answered Mrs. Mathes, politely but with some heat, "it is not so easy to disgrace our State; her record for courage is past dispute, and we are proud of it."

"Then," said Miss Ruth, losing all semblance of self-control, "I rejoice in being a native of a State distinguished for nothing except the repudiation of her debts. Thank God for giving us no peg on which to hang self-approval. We may be steeped in sin, but we bear it with becoming modesty."

Her heart failed. That men were brutal was not so shocking as the amiable acceptance of brutality by a refined woman.

Mrs. Mathes had disposed of the subject in an airy, graceful manner, colored with the local conceit, which was simply appalling to one who went to the core in search of right and wrong. As Miss Ruth sickened with that pang of hopelessness which comes to every earnest nature at the sudden check of a high purpose, the conversation drifted to other channels, and she smiled and added that useful monosyllable demanded by courtesy from the most silent listener.

That Mrs. Mathes was not shocked and grieved, as she had expected, was, in itself, disappointing; but that she went beyond, even to the extent of approving the crime, was exasperating.

Afterwards, when reflecting on the interview, Miss Ruth concluded that as "one swallow does not make a summer," neither does one woman, or for that matter, any women, count where vital affairs are to be regulated.

Straightway she contradicted the latter conclusion by continuing to put her own little finger into this enormous pie. For the next few weeks she might have been called a most uncomfortable person. Like a politician who buttonholes every man he meets, she let no one escape. She carried out practically her theory that thinking, talking and acting bring about reformation.

"You ought to be abated as a nuisance," said her brother once, after he had listened to a warm discussion between his sister and the Baptist minister.

She saw the approving gleam in his eyes, and answered, "You agreed with me."

"Yes, and endorsed you."

"And kept silent," she said in a tone of reproach.

"You did not need my help, for the advantage was yours; and I believe in fair play."

The Rev. Hiram Ellis had been preaching a series of missionary sermons, and that morning had imposed upon himself

the duty of seeing Miss Ruth in person,
in order to solicit alms for the Chinese.

It must be confessed that very few of
Miss Ruth's dimes went to China. So
Mr. Ellis had scarcely opened his business when she informed him she had no
money for that purpose, while the heathen
were swarming at home.

Whereupon, he said, stiffly, "Ah, I
have heard of your views I presume
you allude to those occasions upon which
the citizens were compelled to dispense
justice in a summary manner."

"Not at all," she quickly answered.
"I allude to the acts of murder and outrage committed by the people on helpless
prisoners."

"Ah," he repeated with additional formality, stroking his chin, "you are mis-
informed ; or, to be candid, your judgment is over-severe. This is a religious
community, a religious people,"— with a
solemn emphasis on "religious."

"And is night lawlessness a part of
their piety ?" asked Miss Ruth.

"That is outside my province," he
answered, with a wave of his hand. "I
preach the Gospel, only."

"But how can you preach the Gospel
and ignore the question of decent morality?" Then, as the theme asserted
anew its power, she said earnestly, even
beseechingly, "Oh, try to preach a different spirit into the people!"

"I never mix politics and religion," he
answered, drawing a double mantle of
dignity over himself.

"But if you can do good ; and this is
not partisan politics," she argued de-
spairingly, "and how can you pass it by
unnoticed?"

"By preaching within my text," he answered coolly.

"Very well," she said, "whenever you
have preached the stain of barbarism
from Bourbonsville, come to me for missionary money."

Whereupon, Mr. Ellis, with solemn
leave-taking, went away to other women
of less pronounced opinions, who also
understood the meekness and humility
due a minister.

Notwithstanding Mr. Hunter's bantering tone, he was very glad his sister had
found an object on which to spend her
energies. He slyly encouraged her,
knowing that something must take the
place of the opera, the literary club, and
home. This curious missionary work,
into which she entered so heartily, was
innocent employment, and, he concluded
cynically, "useless as any other."

It was several days before her opportunity came with John Hogan, the sheriff
of the county. He passed her door every
day to and from his office, and one evening he stepped in to see Mr. Hunter on
business. He was a genial young fellow,
whose black eyes hinted at a reserved
power necessary for one in his business.
That he was courageous, no one could
doubt ; and he looked merciful.

Hogan was a pleasant, good-natured
adversary, whose present aim was to
make a start,—and find a wife.

He met Miss Ruth's hobby with the
careless assertion, "They will do it."

"What are you about, that you don't
stop it?" she asked.

"I never get there in time," and his
keen eyes snapped.

"Then arrest them afterwards," was
her rather naive suggestion.

"Can't find out who they are," he
smilingly answered.

"But," continued she, persistently,
"granting their purpose a just one, they
might, by a dreadful mistake, hang an
innocent man."

"No danger of that," he answered
confidently, "they know."

"Well, I do not believe in mob law,"
she exclaimed, with intense disgust.

"But the boys do." And he laughed
as if he rather admired the boys.

Not to be turned from her purpose by
his smiling answers, she said pointedly,
"Sir, it is your duty to stop these unlawful acts."

"Can't do it, Miss Hunter." And he
laughed again, as if mobs and ropes were
the most cheerful subjects on earth.

After a moment's pause, he added
more thoughtfully. "I am sorry you heard

about this, since it seems to worry you. I reckon you are not used to it, but we are."

"Used to it! Certainly not. The South has always been called hot-blooded, but I was born and reared among magnolia blooms, and I never saw a mob-tree, nor heard of its horrors. No, indeed, I am not used to it."

"You were born in the South?" he asked.

"Yes," in southern Mississippi; and have lived half my life in New Orleans. I must go back," she said, suddenly. And into her eyes crept the tender longing, born only of a homesick soul. The magnolia and orange blossoms of her youth, the scent of the olive, were hers once more.

From that moment her enthusiasm ebbed. Her pebble had barely made a ripple. She lost courage and grew morbid, her strength not being equal to her task.

When a sworn officer, a gentle Christian woman, and a minister of the Gospel discuss bloody deeds so lightly, it argues the entire community guilty. Her brother had stated the truth, in homely Saxon: "It is a mob-law State." The politics and piety of Bourbonsville were strong enough to bear the weight of grewsome, midnight deeds, undaunted.

Hitherto, Miss Ruth had supposed the border states less liable to acts of violence than her own beloved, hot-blooded South; but her views changed, and after making what her brother called a private stump speech, she concluded to follow his advice and let the world take care of itself.

"It will require a good many elbow touches to help these people," was her secret conclusion as she drew within her shell, and began anew her work of study and health-getting, avoiding walks or drives that led in the direction of the maple trees.

She thus found a scant measure of content; but occasionally, as if in warning, came the words, "We first endure, then pity, then embrace." And once, taking herself to task solemnly, she said, "I am getting like them."

There seemed no probability that the community would ever arouse itself enough to do either good or evil. The day of crime was evidently passed. A law-abiding spirit seemed brooding over the town, and it was formal, proper and staid as the hills around it. In fact, the Hunters had known it in no other light, and they imagined the evil had spent its force. They began to be contented, in a way. They made the most of life, as people do at their ages, who are fond of books and music and pictures.

But a day came when all this was changed.

OCTOBER.

I AM not saddened when I see
   These yellow leaves that fall in showers,
   Nor do I mourn the withered flowers,
Nor sigh beneath the barest tree.

I rather mourn the leaves that die
   In summer, when the boisterous wrath
   Of rough winds strew them in the path,
Where like untimely dead they lie.

I care not that life's lease be long;
   But I could wish my heart to beat
   Until my work is all complete,
And I have sung my richest song.

                      Ellis Parker Butler.

MISS WILSON'S OUTING.

By Marguerite Lee.

I.

AT FOUR o'clock on a warm afternoon in May, the bell rang for the dismissal of the Mayfield public schools, and, a moment later, Miss Wilson stood at the door of one of the grammar rooms watching her pupils file out.

Miss Wilson was not herself that afternoon and the pupils knew it. When Jimmie Smith pricked Tommy Davis with a pin — walking close behind his victim with a look of solemn, exaggerated innocence — the wriggle and squeal which followed failed to bring forth the expected reproof. Miss Wilson's scornful indifference to the whole affair rather took the bloom off Jimmie's enjoyment.

After the last boy had passed out of sight with clatter and yell, Miss Wilson returned to her desk and took from the drawer her class-book and writing materials ; for what purpose it did not at once appear, for after ten or fifteen minutes of silence, broken only by the ticking of the eight-day clock, her only accomplishment was a series of meaningless crosses and scrolls upon a piece of blank paper.

How long her meditations would have lasted it is difficult to say, had not the janitor entered and, with a suggestive rattle of brooms and sprinkling-cans, brought Miss Wilson back to earth so successfully that she immediately arose, replaced her writing materials and, retreating to the wardrobe, donned hat and gloves and left the building.

It was Miss Wilson's twenty-ninth birthday. She had awakened to the fact with a shock that morning. The shock had been sharpened by a dream she had had during the night. She had dreamed that instead of being twenty-nine she was nineteen, and that she had a lover. In this dream she was not troubled about her father's rheumatism nor the threadbare parlor carpet. It had nothing to do with the price of fuel nor with "made-over" dresses. There was none of the pathetic struggle, the pitiful, never-ending self-denials which attach themselves to genteel poverty. There was youth, hope, a lover, and therefore happiness. In the dream this lover took the form of a youth whom Miss Wilson had known years before, when both were school-children.

In those days she had not looked upon him as a lover, even in a childish way ; indeed he had not given her reason for doing so. He was only one of the Mayfield boys who went to school with Frances Wilson, and who thought of her in no other way than as a school-mate ; but as Miss Wilson saw him through the mists of sleep, he became invested with a dignity of manhood and with many a charm which had not belonged to him in actual life. He had left Mayfield fully ten years before the night Miss Wilson saw him in her dream. In all that time it is not probable that she had given him one hour of thought.

She awakened with all the details of the dream quite clear in her mind. She could feel his arms about her and his lips upon hers so plainly that she blushed furiously in the privacy of her own bed-chamber.

On going down to breakfast she had an almost uncontrollable desire to learn, if possible, his whereabouts ; to at least speak of him to her mother and father ; but she could not. She felt herself tongue-tied with the sort of embarrassment which might have taken possession of a maiden with a newly acquired fiancé.

The dream clung to her most persistently all day long. She could not rid herself of it. It influenced everything she did. It was with her when she left the school-building and walked slowly home in the still May sunshine.

All along the quiet street, clumps of plum-trees in the gardens were shrouded in the delicate white mist of their own blossoms. The air was heavy with their perfume and drowsy with the hum of bees. The dainty, frail little leaves of the maples cast fitful, uncertain shadows upon the sidewalks, and there was an odor of fresh earth, for the people had begun to "make garden."

Miss Wilson had not walked many blocks before she noted, just before her, one of the high-school girls, loitering homeward with her jacket swinging in her hand; beside her a youth, who carried her books, and who gave her many an admiring glance as they gaily chattered nonsense. For perhaps the first time in her life Miss Wilson felt that she could sympathize with a pair of lovers. How handsome the boy was, the childish color still glowing in his cheeks! And when his hearty laugh rang out from behind two rows of even white teeth, Miss Wilson found herself smiling in sympathy.

It was only when the pair turned a corner and passed out of sight that she came out of her fool's paradise, and remembered that her own lover existed only in dreams, and that she was twenty-nine years old that day. A faint blush of something like shame crept up into her pale face as she realized how surprised, and probably amused, the two school-children would be could they have known her thoughts. They no doubt looked upon a woman of twenty-nine as having long before passed the age of lovers. They could not have realized how they themselves could ever reach the same stage in life's journey. It was so very far away,—so remote indeed that it was not worth considering.

She went to her room immediately after supper that evening. "Be you sick, Fanny?" her mother inquired as she took up her lamp.

"No," she answered, "only tired."

At the top of the stairs she stopped to look out of the open window on the little landing. The air outside was soft and humid, with an odor of smoke in it from distant bonfires. From out the dusky stillness there arose the sound of children's voices shouting at their play. It served to remind her vividly of her own childhood and youth, which was so far spent, and which had contained so little that was bright and so much that was monotonous and colorless.

On reaching her chamber she placed the light upon the old-fashioned bureau, in front of the mirror, and, standing before it, looked long and carefully at the reflection. She saw a face which was somewhat thin, the expression telling of physical weariness,—a face which was not particularly striking in any way. The hair was a medium shade of brown. The gray eyes were good, but dark circles beneath told of weary hours in the school-room. The shoulders had a pathetic droop and the figure was too slight to be beautiful.

"No," thought Miss Wilson, as she gazed critically at the woman in the glass, "if I were a man I should not be attracted by such a face. I am commonplace in every way. Oh! why couldn't I have had something?" she asked herself. "If not wealth, then talent or beauty?"

She set her teeth angrily, as she saw the tears fill her eyes and roll down her pale cheeks. Her heart ached with self-pity as she turned impatiently away from the picture in the glass and went to bed. Not to sleep, however, for long before daylight she had made her plans. She would give herself, as far as possible, the opportunity which had been denied her all her life. The shabby little old house should go unpainted for another year—or more if need be. The fence with its many missing pickets should remain as it was; and the parlor carpet might be patched. The barren little farm just out of town would suffice to keep her parents from want, for they were not ambitious people. All the ambition which John Wilson and his wife had ever possessed had been ground down and worn out by long days of toil, while paying for the little patch of earth which, in their old age, brought them so ungrateful a return.

These obstacles disposed of, Miss Wilson arranged her affairs with hurried, joyful excitement.

Weeks before she had heard her fellow teachers and their superintendent discussing the meeting of an educational body which was to occur in London during the following summer months. A "Teachers' Excursion" was announced for that time, and the superintendent and his wife were going. Day after day she had heard the other teachers clamorously wishing they might go. She had heard ways and means discussed, but had taken no part in the conversation. She had not even dared to wish to go; but now, as she lay in her dark bed-room, with sleepless, wide-open eyes, she wondered, almost tremblingly, how she could have thought of allowing such an opportunity to escape her. She tried to recall all she had heard of steamers, sailing days, fares and hotel-bills, and made her plans accordingly. She felt sure Professor Morris and his wife would gladly offer her their protection, when she told them of her determination to take this pleasure trip. A pleasure trip! Her thoughts dwelt upon the expression, it was so new, so full of excitement for her.

All her wages so carefully hoarded in view of the needed repairs should be spent upon herself, and spent lavishly—extravagantly! She would for once in her life have becoming dresses, becomingly made. She would have dainty little trappings which other ladies wear, and which cost so much more than apparently they should. She promised herself that she would take her six weeks of pleasure recklessly. She would not listen to anything an over-tender conscience might have to say. And after this—she insisted on believing she would return and again take up with the routine of school life. But away down in Miss Wilson's heart there lurked a tiny, formless idea, a mere shadowy, frightened hope, which dared not show itself even

to her, that she should meet someone, who, never having seen her shabby and worried and tired, and who, seeing her for the first time possessed of the ease and grace which contentment and good clothes bestow, would admire her—would fall in love with her.

The day following was Saturday, and she was at liberty for the day. She came down to breakfast with her mind filled with her plans.

"Mother," she began, "I've been thinking I should like to go away somewhere this summer."

Mrs. Wilson stopped pouring coffee and looked up in such surprise that her daughter blushed slightly, and hesitated in an embarrassed way, as though she had proposed something wrong.

"I've never taken any real vacation, and I should like to go over to London on the teachers' excursion, with Professor and Mrs. Morris; and if you think the house could go unpainted another year ——"

"Oh," answered her mother, "don't let that stop you; I want you should use your own money as you please. Me and father'll get along, but I'm afraid, Fanny, it will cost an awful lot o' money."

"Yes, I know it will, mother; but I shall only be gone five or six weeks. I have never indulged in anything of the kind, and I should like to know for once what it is to gratify oneself."

"Well, Fanny, if you think you would enjoy spending your money that way ——" She hesitated and shook her head dubiously, and Fanny detected a disapproving ring in her voice, but for once her wishes did not immediately fall in with her mother's. She was determined to indulge in this bit of wild extravagance which had been suggested to her by a dream.

Immediately after breakfast she dressed to go out and, as she passed through the room where her mother was, she stopped in answer to an inquiring look and said, "If I go away this summer I shall need some new dresses; I am going to see Miss Spink about them."

"Miss Spink! why, Frances, don't you know she's the most expensive dressmaker in town?"

Miss Wilson blushed again. "But she does the best work, mother."

"Well, maybe she does, but seems t' me them Smith girls that do plain sewin' would be likely to work cheaper."

"Perhaps so, but I intend to have my work done well, for once, let it cost what it may." And Miss Wilson stepped out with a determined air quite new to her.

Mrs. Wilson looked after her daughter in surprise. "Well, upon my word!" she thought, "I never see Fanny so set in her way in all her life before. 'Taint like her to be so wasteful, neither."

Upon arriving at Miss Spink's dressmaking rooms, Miss Wilson was obliged to introduce herself to that most important person; for heretofore Mayfield's fashionable dressmaker had not had occasion to know Frances Wilson, the school-teacher. During the morning samples were inspected; styles, lengths and breadths were discussed, and materials chosen with a luxurious abandon as to prices which charmed Miss Spink.

The next few weeks were busy ones for Miss Wilson. The Morrises were pleased to learn that she was to accompany them, though they failed to conceal their surprise when she made known her plans. When the last day of the school year arrived, she unconsciously bade farewell to the familiar room with its long rows of brown desks and little chairs. She was possessed of a vague, unacknowledged feeling that her reign in that place was over, and when her fellow teachers talked together of their return at the end of the vacation, she found herself uninterested and unable to take any part in the conversation.

At last there came a day early in June when Miss Wilson and her friends were ready to to start.

The new dresses had been packed and sent to the depot; and Frances Wilson herself stood upon the smooth, hard path between the door and the gate, bidding her

mother good-bye. Seeing her about to depart, her father came round the house from the beds of radishes and lettuce he had been weeding,—a stooped, pathetic little figure, upon which the shabby old clothes hung loosely. Just below the knee the faded trowsers showed an awkward bulge, which marked the termination of the stiff, clumsy boot-leg. His hands were rough and warped with toil and he walked in a heavy, laborious way, which gave him the appearance of continuously crossing plowed fields. As his eyes fell upon the stylishly dressed woman before him, a smile of satisfied admiration crossed his features.

"Goin', be yuh, Fan?" he asked. "Well, you wont find no fashionabler dressed girl over in London 'n you be yourself, now mind yuh, I tell yuh." He walked around her and viewed the pretty traveling dress with critical eyes.

"I'll betch'uh now 'at that dress cost more'n all my clo's hes for three year." He chuckled with wonder and admiration at his daughter's bold extravagance; but the remark rankled in Miss Wilson's mind afterwards. "Hedn't I better go with yuh and buy your railroad ticket fer yuh, Fan?" he asked with sudden seriousness, as if the difficulty of the transaction had but just occurred to him.

"Oh, no, thank you, father, not unless you wish to go; I think I can manage it myself."

"Well, I d'know, Fan; you see you haint traveled as much's I have." His assumption of importance, so strangely at variance with his actual, simple ignorance of the world and its ways, was pitifully funny. "An' be careful 'bout gettin' your trunk checked," he called after her with tender solicitude as she walked away down the quiet light and shadow flecked street. Now and then a friend or neighbor called "good-bye" to her as she passed the open doors.

Some half-hour later she found herself, with Professor Morris and his wife, seated upon the hard-stuffed cushions of the railway coach, gazing through the open window at the flying landscape.

The following evening the three arrived in New York City in time for a night's rest before sailing.

As Miss Wilson stood at her window and looked out upon the endless roofs, chimneys and brick walls, upon miles of streets and thousands of twinkling lights, she experienced a brief pang of home-sickness. It did not reappear, however, the next day when all was bustle and excitement in the city streets, and she and her companions stood in the great bare room in the docks looking on at the frantic hurry of the sailors as they made ready for leaving at the appointed hour.

II.

A few days later the great steamer was far out upon the Atlantic. It was a somber, gray day,—indeed all the world seemed gray. There was a rough sea and, as far as the eye could reach, the water rose into innumerable billows which swelled and burst, and the spiteful wind switched their tops into spray and dashed it off contemptuously. A few ladies, wrapped in rugs and shawls, sat on deck under the canvas awning. Most of them were cold and miserable, but dreaded the warm, oily odor which greeted their fastidious nostrils upon going below.

Mrs. Morris sat in a steamer chair, absently watching the "weary waste of waters" alternately rise and disappear over the swaying line of the vessel's side. Her husband lounged beside her, carelessly figuring up the runs the steamer had made each day, and calculating how many more days it would probably take her to sight land. He cheerfully announced the result to his wife, failing, however, to impart to her any of his light-heartedness, for she looked at him in amazement, and answered dolefully, "O! surely it can't be so long,—try again."

"Our friends over there don't find the trip wearisome," said Morris, nodding toward a couple who stood in the shelter of one of the small boats. His wife's glance followed his and rested thoughtfully upon the forms of Frances Wilson and a handsome, well-dressed man of thirty. She was standing with her folded arms resting upon the side of the vessel. He stood with his back toward the water, leaning upon his elbows thrust out behind him. As he talked to her he seemed to compel her to look up at him occasionally, and he looked down at her with an expression which Morris, as he calmly studied them from a distance, described to himself as "affectionate."

"She has been interested in him from the first moment she saw him," began Mrs. Morris. "She says she had a dream about an old playmate of hers sometime before we left home,—she did not say what it was,—but it made a deep impression upon her, and this man so strongly resembles her friend of the dream that he claimed her attention on that account."

"I rather think he claims it upon his own, now," answered her husband, dryly.

"Well, he is certainly attractive. The first time we saw him was the evening we came on deck, after those first two awful days. A group of the passengers sat together singing, and he stood at a little distance from them, smoking and looking on with an air which was part interest and part indifference. He was purely unconscious, and he was certainly—well picturesque."

"Probably she never had an admirer before."

"Oh, John!" said Mrs. Morris, looking at him reproachfully, as if he were ruthlessly trying to deprive Miss Wilson of fond and raiment.

"Well, she is not striking. She's a nice girl and all that, but she's—she's—commonplace," he concluded, unconsciously describing Miss Wilson exactly as she had described herself.

The weather grew more chilly and disagreeable as twilight drew on, and no one returned to the deck after tea. Miss Wilson went to her berth at bedtime strangely happy. She did not question herself in regard to it. Many of the passengers experienced a depression of spirits, as they caught hurried glimpses through the ports of the black and cheerless twilight descending upon the lonesome, endless reach of waters. But she was in better spirits than she had ever been. She felt that she had never in all her life been so happy. She and Hartwell had spent the evening together in the saloon. She had brought out a paper which she and Mrs. Morris had drawn up together. It contained a list of places and objects of interest which they intended to see together, while Mr. Morris was busy attending his educational meetings. They had allotted a certain length of time to each place and opposite was the date. Hartwell had taken out his note-book and playfully copied the list. This act on his part Miss Wilson would have found to be the reason of her mysterious happiness had she sifted the sensation down to find its cause. It gave her reason to believe that he intended to make their plans his own.

The second day after this there was a hurried and early rising on the part of many of the passengers, more particularly the younger ones. Some one more wakeful than the others had set abroad the report that the coast of Ireland was in sight and there was a scramble to see it, as if it might be in the habit of floating away at sunrise. The older ones followed more slowly; and for some hours a swarm of passengers, young and old, pressed eagerly against the ship's side, watching the bare, bleak coast, the furze-clad hills, the tiny Irish villages, and the barren farms cut up into fields so small that they looked from a distance like patch-work quilts. As the steamer entered the bay at Queenstown an officious little steam tug rushed out to meet her, and, during the transferring of the Irish passengers, glasses were leveled at the quaint, hilly old town clustering about its beautiful cathedral,—and in an hour the steamer was again on her way up the channel.

All day long Hartwell was at Miss Wilson's side, pointing out and remarking upon the queer foreign-looking coast guards, the frequent soldiers' camps, and now and then a deserted-looking old castle belonging probably to some English-

man who dared not so much as inquire into its condition—let alone live in it.

The following morning the steamer was lying in the Liverpool docks, and the passengers were crowded in the custom-house waiting for their baggage to be examined. The Morrises, Miss Wilson and Hartwell were among the first to get away, and were in time to take an early train out of Liverpool. All through the tedious crush in the waiting-room, the scramble into the baggage-room when the doors were opened, and during the hurried emptying and re-strapping of trunks, Hartwell, tactfully, and I may say tenderly, took charge of Miss Wilson. It was both novel and beautiful to her to be thus cared for. She had enjoyed a very small amount of such treatment since she could remember, and of late years she had assumed the burden of "managing" for her parents, as well as that of supporting herself and "keeping up appearances."

Hartwell bade his friends a cheerful farewell as they entered the carriage for London. He had taken down their London address, and his last words were to the effect that after he had attended to a little business which called him to Manchester, he would "be around." "Probably Wednesday," he added, as they moved away, leaving him standing on the platform, smiling after them.

III.

The Morrises and Miss Wilson arrived in London Saturday evening. Sunday and Monday were devoted to rest, and early in the day on Tuesday Mrs. Morris and Miss Wilson found their way to the famous old Abbey. The visit to Westminster on Tuesday was according to their written plans, and Miss Wilson could not help hoping that Hartwell might have been able to transact his business in Manchester in less time than he had anticipated, and though she dared not allow herself to expect to see him there, she could not help scanning the long line of sightseers, mostly Americans, who, guide-book in hand, entered the doors just before them. The newly-married were there in full force, also the American college students taking their vacation.

It was past noon before Miss Wilson and Mrs. Morris found themselves as far away from the entrance as the south transept, where the usual crowd of admiring Americans surrounded the busts of Shakspeare, Milton, Thackeray, and the gray slab in the floor which marks the resting place of Charles Dickens. Not far away they found the bust of Longfellow, and beneath the marble lapel of the coat some wandering countryman had thrust a tiny silken banner—the "Stars and Stripes." The bit of color, resting amid the surrounding coldness of stone and marble, caught the eyes of every American who sauntered past.

It was toward the middle of the afternoon before Mrs. Morris remarked to Miss Wilson upon her sudden realization of weariness and hunger. As they emerged into the bold glare and clattering hurry of the street both had a curious sense of having just awakened from a kaleidoscopic dream in which such characters as Mary Queen of Scots, Elizabeth, Henry VII, and Edward the Confessor, figured in a vague and confused manner. The never-ceasing tramp of pedestrians and rattle of omnibuses across Trafalgar Square broke upon them rudely.

The following day was Wednesday,—the day Miss Wilson had looked forward to ever since she had smiled a farewell to Hartwell at the Liverpool station. She glanced wistfully about the long sitting room as she entered it to wait for Mr. and Mrs. Morris to come down to breakfast. Though her reason told her it was foolish to expect him so early, she could not help her longing to see him. He had not appeared when she and Mrs. Morris stood upon the pavement, scanning the passing omnibuses for the one which should take them to the "Tower." It was comforting to recall Hartwell's playful copying of the program she had shown him. She could not shake off her longing to see him even when the Tower was reached. She professed, and indeed

felt, an interest in the sad old place, but could not bring herself to take an active part in Mrs. Morris' extravagant delight at every fresh discovery.

"Here! Frances, here!" cried Mrs. Morris, catching Miss Wilson by the arm and hastening her forward toward a tiny brick-paved square near the center of the "Tower Hill." "Here is the very spot where Lady Jane Grey was beheaded, and Anne Boleyn, also," she continued, reading aloud from the guide-book. "'Also Queen Katherine Howard, fifth wife of Henry VIII.' Think of it, Frances Wilson! No doubt we are at this moment standing on the very spot where they actually stood a few moments before the execution. Poor Anne Boleyn," she added softly, her eyes filling with tears. She glanced up at her companion in search of sympathy, but found her carefully scanning a group of young men, apparently tourists.

"You—you don't seem to be interested," she said in reproachful surprise.

"Oh, indeed! Mrs. Morris, I am," answered Miss Wilson, transferring her attention to Mrs. Morris in guilty haste. "I have always thought Lady Jane Grey and Anne Boleyn among the most pathetic characters in history, but I—I—thought one of those gentlemen looked familiar to me. I was mistaken, however. They are strangers."

For some time after this she took care to make her interest apparent, and even shared her friend's raptures over the gorgeous display in the jewel room. But it was in the "armory" where Miss Wilson was most willing to linger. She acknowledged to herself that it was there most of all that she believed she would meet Hartwell. She thought that the guns, swords, and implements of warfare generally, would be most apt to attract a man. But her spirits sank when they left it half an hour later without having seen him.

That evening as the two ladies and Professor Morris sat at tea, the professor happened to remember for the first time what Miss Wilson had been thinking of all day. "Why! to-day is the day Hart-

well ought to be with us." He looked
up and discharged the remark at them
with an eager generosity, as though he
had a right to lay claim to this discovery
but was willing to share it with them.

But a mere glance at Miss Wilson's
face told him that the thought was not a
new one to her. A faint, unreasonable
flush crept into her face as she heard
Hartwell's name mentioned.

Mrs. Morris, leaning back in her chair,
slowly conveying to her mouth little
crumbs of potted beef upon her fork,
lazily remarked, " It *is* Wednesday, isn't
it ! "

Miss Wilson felt a little thrill of anger
at Mrs. Morris' apparent lack of interest.
It seemed to her impossible that, having
once known that this was the day he was
to come, they could have lost sight of the
fact for a moment.

The following day the ladies spent in
the British Museum, and among the shops
in search of little gifts for friends at home.
In their turn came the Kensington Museum, the Greenwich Hospital, the National Gallery, Regent's Park and the
animals, and other objects which are year
after year regularly and religiously visited
by the American tourist.

One afternoon they spent in Hyde Park,
having been told that the Prince of Wales
would drive there that day. While they
waited for the appearance of the royal
carriage they wandered up and down the
Serpentine Drive, looked at the gorgeous,
conventional flower-beds, and occasionally rested upon the benches.

As the time drew near for the Prince
and Princess to appear, the drives were
filled with handsome equipages and magnificent, high-stepping horses. Men and
women of all classes crowded the seats
and walks. At last an uneasy movement
and a gentle surging of the crowd toward
the edge of the drive told the ladies that
the expected party was approaching, and
Mrs. Morris excitedly hurried Miss Wilson to a good position.

The profile of the Prince, with his carefully trimmed gray beard, was familiar to
many of those who looked upon him that
day, as was also the sweet face of the
gentle and much-loved Princess ; but the
sight was a novel one to the Americans.
Mrs. Morris gazed silently until she could
no longer see, and then turned away with
a gentle sigh of satisfaction.

As the crowd surged and swayed from
side to side in its effort to disentangle
itself after the first few moments of intense
stillness while the royal carriage was
passing, the two ladies became separated.
When they caught sight of each other
again Mrs. Morris showed signs of excitement. "Did you see him ? " she cried,
while she was still some distance away.

"Who ? the Prince ? Why, of course."

"No, no, I mean Mr. Hartwell. He
was on the other side of the walk, just
opposite us. I waved my umbrella, but
he didn't see me. You must have seen
him."

"No, I didn't see him "

Mrs. Morris glanced at her in surprise
at the indifferent answer. How could
she know of the sudden, tumultuous
beating of the heart, the wild desire to
run after him, the agony of having been
so near him without having looked into
his eyes or heard his voice. She wanted
to demand of Mrs. Morris why she had
not succeeded in attracting him in some
way — no matter how. But instead, she
only walked silently beside her, trying
not to show that she was trembling. At
last she made a hurried, desperate attempt to frame a commonplace remark ;
to speak of him as she would of an ordinary acquaintance. The old childish
bashfulness had taken possession of her,
and she turned her burning face away
from Mrs. Morris and gazed intently and
unseeingly into a shop window as she began, " Do you think he — Mr. Hartwell —
he will no doubt call upon us at the
hotel."

" I suppose so.—What *are* you looking
at ? " For the first time Miss Wilson
realized that she was gazing at a window
full of men's hats and caps. "There !
isn't *that* lovely ? " added Mrs. Morris, as
they moved on to the next shop window,
— this time a display of gloves and fans.

The following day—their last in London—dawned gray and sullen. While Miss Wilson was still in her room, a few heavy, elongated drops flung themselves in slant lines against the window, and by the time she joined Professor and Mrs. Morris in the dining-room it was raining steadily. During breakfast the three tried to arrive at a satisfactory conclusion in regard to attending a morning service at St. Paul's. Mr. Morris thought it wise to remain indoors, and his wife declared she positively would not return to America without being able to say she had attended a service at St. Paul's.

"I know I should entertain a supreme contempt for anyone who could visit London and leave without attending at least a week-day service there," she insisted.

"That settles it,—we go," announced the Professor, solemnly. A hansom was called, and the three crushed into it and were jolted up to the great cathedral. The service had not begun and they proceeded to the gallery and were "whispered to," after which Mrs. Morris again expressed an aversion to returning to her native land without having done those things which she ought to have done, and insisted upon being taken up into the ball on the spire.

While she and her husband were attending to this important matter, Miss Wilson descended alone to the audience-room and found the service just beginning. She sank into one of the seats apart from the kneeling congregation, and listened to the chants and responses of the beautiful, solemn service. She listened at first with a quiet interest, and later with a vague sadness and depression of spirits. At last the low hum of voices faded into a dreamy murmur, and she realized nothing but a strange wonder at her own presence there. She was perfectly frank with herself for the first time since the morning of her twenty-ninth birthday, when she had awakened from her dream in which her old schoolmate had figured so prominently. She acknowledged that she had been so deeply under the spell of this dream that through

its influence she had come thousands of miles from home; had spent extravagantly—it was extravagant for her, poor girl—her hard-earned savings, and had ended by falling in love with a man who was not in love with her, it seemed, since he was in the same locality and had not sought her presence.

For the first time she realized that she had confused the two men—the one of whom she had dreamed and the one in actual life. Even now she could scarcely separate them. It seemed to her that she had been living in this dream for months; that, indeed, she was but now awaking from it. Suddenly there arose in her all her old protecting love for her simple, unambitious parents, all her old affection for her home, shabby though it was, for sleepy old Mayfield. She could see it now. The grass on the sides of the streets was white with the summer's dust. Elderly men, prosperous and contented, swung in hammocks and read the papers, or played at gardening. Companies of happy, squabbling boys passed down the street on their way to the ball-grounds. A tender, slumbrous stillness rested over everything. The whirr of a lawn-mower could be heard blocks away. Her mother sat sewing in the little shadowy sitting-room; beneath the open window grew great clumps of four-o'clocks and mignonette. The sweet south wind drifted in, heavy with their exquisite, languorous odor. Beyond the town the clover-blossoms lay thick upon the meadows, and along the roadsides the goldenrod hung "heavy with sunshine."

While she was in the midst of this strange reverie, this cruel self-examination, the choir began an anthem. Gradually the organ filled all the space with harmony, and out of the hush which followed there arose one exquisite voice— a boy's voice, pathetic and tender. And then without a jar, almost without a beginning, the whole choir was singing, too; a great and glorious sound which at the end melted into silence,—drifted away out of hearing among the arches and vaulted ceilings.

When the people rose from their seats and began moving about, she rose also in a sort of bewilderment. It seemed to her that for the first time in many weeks she was herself. She experienced a strange desire to live the last few weeks over again; to see once more what she had seen, this time with her own eyes.

IV.

It was more than two weeks later. Professor Morris and his wife and Miss Wilson had left behind them London, with its smoke and noise and conglomeration of poverty and wealth. They were making their way slowly back to Liverpool. One day they had driven out from the village of Kenilworth to the ruins of the castle. They had faithfully studied their guide-books and found, as therein described, the "Cæsar Tower," the "Banquet Hall," the "Tilting Yard," etc. Mrs. Morris had gathered a bunch of daisies and had carefully labeled it "From Kenilworth Castle," in order to distinguish it from the bunch "From Windsor Castle."

The sun was low in the west, and the beautiful stillness of approaching evening rested upon the ivy-covered walls and daisy-dotted fields. Miss Wilson had left her companions below and, as she ascended the narrow, winding, much-worn steps leading to the Myrvin Tower, a carriage full of American tourists drove up to the gate of the castle grounds and discharged its occupants. They were of that sort who make a business of "doing" Europe, and evidently they considered the old castle worthy of but a short space of time, since but a few hours of daylight remained to them.

Miss Wilson heard them come up from the gate, chattering and laughing. A little later she heard a sudden exclamation from Mrs. Morris, who stood with her husband in the yard below. It was followed by a clatter of greetings, and she easily recognized Hartwell's voice. In the silence which followed she heard him introduce "my wife" and "my wife's mother," and one or two friends. She heard him proceed to explain that his

wife and her mother had been traveling in Europe for some months, and that he had met them in Manchester on the day after reaching Liverpool, and the wedding had taken place a few days later. She heard Morris chaff him about his "business in Manchester," of which he had spoken at the Liverpool station. Miss Wilson listened with a feeling which was mostly indifference, as though it were a matter which could not greatly concern her. At the same time she was conscious of a thankfulness that the little incident which was unimportant to her now had not occurred before her awakening. She went down among them soon, and was also presented to the new Mrs. Hartwell. She listened to her as she explained to her new acquaintances that her party had "gotten through with" so much more than they had expected, and how fortunate they should consider themselves if they could only "finish" the castle before dark that evening.

After their return to the inn in the village that evening, Miss Wilson was able to discuss the late wedding and the bride with a coolness bordering on indifference. She could not help feeling the surprise which her friends tried not to show. She knew that they made it a matter of conversation in private, as indeed they did,—Mrs. Morris insisting that the little school-teacher loved Hartwell desperately, but was hiding a breaking heart beneath a cold exterior; and her more practical husband arguing that this was not the case, since so ordinary a woman could not be so good an actress.

V.

It was toward the last of September when the three reached home,—just in time for the opening of school. They arrived in Mayfield very early in the morning. The sun was scarcely risen. Miss Wilson gave her checks to an expressman and walked home through the quiet, familiar streets, glad to breathe the sweet, clear air. The spider-webs upon the lawns were wet with dew, and the sun dropped his first slant rays upon them and turned them into bits of silver lace. Most of the stores and shops looked queer and lonesome with their blinds drawn down and doors closed. In a few of them, boys were whistling loudly and sweeping out piles of empty boxes and bits of paper. A dapper clerk in a ready-made-clothing store was "opening up." A row of dressed-up wire dummies stood just inside the door, where they had been deposited hurriedly the night before. They had very pink faces, very black mustaches and big, surprised eyes. The clerk grasped them rudely by the necks, as if he had some grudge against them, and jerked and tumbled them out upon the sidewalk, to stand all day and show themselves and stare vacantly at the passers-by.

Looking up and down the streets Miss Wilson could see the meadows lying close to town. They were draped in a faint pearly mist, which the sun was rapidly dispelling. From a few kitchen chimneys the lazy smoke curled upward. It looked white and clean in the rising sun. A wagon coming early into town had an empty, hollow-sounding rumble. The beautiful melancholy of autumn, which so swiftly follows the perfection of summer, had begun, and little piles of yellow leaves had drifted under the edges of the sidewalks and against the picket fences.

As Miss Wilson passed the school, she remembered that a few short months before she had believed, had almost wished, she might never enter those familiar doors again. It gave her a faint sensation of homesickness now only to think of it.

At last she came in sight of her own home. It was not so well kept as its neighbors. The grass in front of the house was long and tangled, and looked untidy beside the closely-mown lawns on either side. The house, once white, was faded and rain-bleached, and one could easily imagine how forlorn a little habitation it might become upon a somber day. However, upon this bright morning it had almost a cheerful look. At least it presented to Miss Wilson an aspect which made it seem very dear to her. She caught a glimpse of her mother stirring about the kitchen, and the faint clatter of the breakfast dishes drifted out to her. As she turned in at the gate she began to calculate how soon her wages would allow her to paint the house and replace the fence with a new one.

AUTUMN.

NOW stands the rich Year in a fair array,
   And with a free, an overflowing, hand
   Lavishes blessings on the happy land,—
Fruitage of many a former arduous day.
Her springtime changeful garb of green and gray,
   Seedtime's accoutrements, the summer band
   That delved unceasingly at her command,—
All these, all effort has she put away.
By day, a mellow sun, soft-breathing airs,
   A silence like sweet music in a swoon,
     And ripened fruit hung o'er the orchard wall;
By night, the calm majestic harvest moon,
And joyous voices echoing unawares,—
     All these proclaim the timely festival.

              William Francis Barnard.

LIFE AMONG THE ALASKANS.

THE ALASKAN INDIANS AND THEIR CANOES — CANOE LIFE — ALASKAN CARV-INGS IN STONE.

By John H. Keatley.[*]

THE Alaska canoe is a unique means of navigation, unlike any other structure for the purpose in the world. There are two kinds of these canoes, one used in the far west of Alaska, called by the natives the *badarki*, and the other in the waters of the southeastern part of the territory, and made by excavating the craft from great cedar trees that grow in some parts of that country. The badarki is a skin boat in peculiar use among the Aleuts and Eskimo. It is made as follows: The northwestern coast of North America is strewn with driftwood; whence it comes no one knows. Much of this is wholly unfit for any use, but the natives find a good deal of it that can be utilized in making the frame-work of their badarkis, or skin boats. In addition to making the frames of wood thus secured, they frequently employ the larger bones of the various marine animals in that quarter for the same purpose. The boats are made of various lengths, depending upon the number of persons they are intended to carry. Some of them, the smaller ones, have only one hole in the covering or deck ; while the largest have three holes, in which the navigators or passengers can sit. A three-holed bidarki is about thirty feet long, fourteen inches deep in the hold, and twenty-four inches wide. The wooden or bone frame-work is skillfully lashed together with the sinews of animals, and the covering generally made of the un-tanned skin of the sea-lion, and other great sea animals of Bering Sea and the North Pacific coast. Formerly seal-skins were largely used for this purpose, but they are far too valuable now, as an article of commerce, to be used in that way. These skin boats of the greatest length have a capacity of several tons besides the crew, and will live in quite boisterous seas. The natives have been known to

*Colonel Keatley, now of the St. Paul *Dispatch*, late United States Judge of Alaska, began a series of four illustrated papers on Alaska in The Midland of June, 1864.

TREADWELL MILL, CHLORINATION WORKS, DOUGLAS ISLAND, ALASKA.

go several hundred miles to sea in these apparently frail craft; and much of the trading along the coast and in the great rivers of Alaska is carried on in this kind of craft.

The navigators and their vessel when at sea are practically one. The men, when in their boats, wear shirts made of various kinds of sea animals, which are entirely water-proof. The navigator rests on his knees in the bottom of the boat, the arms and upper part of the body appearing above the skin deck. The shirt, when the man is thus seated or kneeling, is closely gathered around the orifice in the deck and there fastened so as to prevent any rain or water from passing into the body of the craft. As it rains a great part of the time in that region, this is an important consideration to prevent rain or seawater from entering the bidarki and causing it to become water-logged and unnavigable. The shirt also protects the Aleut mariner from inclement weather. He also wears a rimmed hat made of the same materials as the shirt, which bears the strongest possible resemblance to the the ordinary sailor's "sou'-wester'." Paddles, and not oars, are used for both propelling and steering the vessel. In capturing the sea-otter and other valuable sea animals for their fur, the natives use the badarki because of the swiftness with which they skim over the water. Formerly, sea-otters and all such marine animals were killed with the spear, which was thrown a great distance with the utmost skill, but since firearms have been introduced among otter hunters, the animals have become correspondingly timid and scarce.

The manner in which North America was originally peopled has been an interesting study for many years. It has been objected to the theory that the original inhabitants came from the east coast of Asia, that the aborigines possessed no craft that would live in the intervening seas. Anyone acquainted with the capability of one of these Aleut skin boats to endure rough weather at sea would soon dismiss this objection. It is not an un-usual thing for Indian seal hunters, when intercepting the herds of fur seal when on their way to the seal islands in Bering Sea, to drift hundreds of miles out into the ocean, and afterward be picked up by passing steamships, or by whalers passing to and from the Arctic Ocean. Captain James Carroll, who was formerly the master of a Pacific Mail steamer between San Francisco and the Sandwich Islands, now the captain of one of the Pacific Coast Steamship's vessels plying between Puget Sound and Sitka, told me of having picked up two Aleuts, in their skin boat, who had drifted from their seal hunting grounds a distance of nearly five hundred miles west of San Francisco. Their food supply of seal meat had been exhausted for days, and their supply of fresh water was nearly gone; and though they had passed through several severe Pacific tempests, their vessel had received no appreciable injury.

I have already stated that the water craft used by the natives in Southeastern Alaska are totally different in structure from that used by the Eskimo, and by the Aleuts farther north and west; that they are constructed from large yellow cedar trees, formerly more abundant and more accessible near the coast than now. It is highly interesting to watch the making of one of these long, wide "dug-out" canoes. The Alaska natives, like all other savage people, take little note of the passage or value of time. Hence, it is of little moment to them whether it takes days, weeks or months to accomplish any definite purpose. Their patience, when engaged on one of their canoes, is incomparable. Before the advent of the Russians, the British and the American traders on the northwest coast, the natives were compelled to employ stone or obsidian tools to shape their canoes and point their weapons of war and of the chase. These have been discarded for the more desirable iron and steel implements which they readily procure, though the implements used in making their canoes are of the simplest character. They only use the ax for felling the large cedar tree from which they propose to finally shape the canoe. This is then rolled from the side of the steep mountain, with great labor, through the dense underbrush and over many rocks, into the water of the adjoining inlet or strait, and is then towed, often many miles, to the village by the water-side, where it is proposed to complete the canoe. It frequently takes a month to fell the tree and get it to its proper place on the beach in front of the village. Frequently, too, after considerable work has been expended upon it, the tree is found so defective, in the interior, by rottenness, which could not be discovered earlier, that it has to be discarded for that purpose. When such a discovery is made, the native does not give vent to any expression of disappointment, much and keenly as he may feel it. He has no other choice than to begin his task all over again. After the log, about forty feet long, has been put in place ready to begin work, the native begins the shaping of its exterior with a small steel adze not much larger than a man's extended hand. He uses no lines, marks or tracings to show the points to which he desires to cut, directing his operations entirely by the eye and the deftness of his hand, and securing almost perfect accuracy in outline. After the exterior of the proposed canoe is finally dressed off, with this simple implement, the inside next engages his attention, the sides by these patient processes being generally reduced to a thickness of an inch and a quarter from stem to stern. The final touches in this delicate hewing are thus given the canoe, but it has not yet received its beautifully and symmetrically curved shape which they all present when finished. This is finally done by a curious and primitive process. The hollowed-out part of the new canoe is filled with water to the gunwales; the cavity is then carefully covered over with hemlock bark, or with old sail-cloth or blankets if they can be procured, and red-hot stones are cast into the water. This becoming hot softens the wood in the sides of the new canoe,

and they are steadily pressed outward, and in perfect outline, until at the middle or waist the vessel has a width of several feet more than the diameter of the original log from which it was shaped.

Curious figures, in the shape of griffins and other grotesque representations, are generally placed at the prow and in the stern, according to the taste and superstition of the owner. These are generally the totems of the village to which the canoe belongs, and are painted in bright colors, in contrast with that of the body of the canoe, which is invariably black.

Alaska canoes are divided into two general classes : the war canoe, which is much larger and more powerful than any other, and that used for ordinary purposes. War canoes are becoming more rare every year, not only on account of the difficulty of getting the largest sized trees from which to make them, but because of the general peace which has prevailed among the people of all the villages along the coast. Some of these war canoes, made from a single yellow cedar log, are capable of transporting from thirty to forty armed warriors, and are from sixty to eighty feet in length. A war canoe of the Haidah village, eighty feet long and about eight feet wide at the waist or middle, was among the Alaska exhibits at the Columbian Exposition. Another great war canoe sixty-four feet long, brought from the northwestern part of British Columbia, contiguous to our Alaskan boundary, is a part of the exhibit in the great museum of natural history near Central Park in New York City. It is weirdly embellished with all the ancient heraldry of the Indians of the North Pacific coast.

The best trees for this kind of canoe building in Alaska are found at Prince William's Island, north of Prince William's Sound, in the southern part of the Alexandrian Archipelago. The natives of that island pursue canoe building as quite a regular industry, finding a sale for their work among the Indians among the islands farther up the coast. A staunch canoe thirty or forty feet long will bring

ALASKAN WOMEN — MAKING BASKETS.

in the neighborhood of three or four hundred dollars.

Princess Tom, an Indian woman of the Sitka Indian village, who possesses considerable wealth in silver dollars, had a Prince William's Island canoe of great beauty, strength and swiftness, for which she paid over five hundred dollars. Formerly the dug-out canoe was propelled and steered wholly with broad paddles, but the natives in that quarter are becoming expert oarsmen, and are generally discarding the paddle for the oar in rowing, but still adhere to the paddle for steering purposes.

Beside making canoes for sale, the natives of Prince William and adjoining islands are engaged in a new and different industry. In many places in those islands a very black, smooth slate is found, that is soft and yielding as soapstone when first taken out. Formerly they used wood entirely in making totem and other carvings, and many of these were made with uncommon skill. Since the discovery of this pliable slate they have turned their attention to stone carving, and enjoy quite a good trade in curios made from it, which find their way into the hands of the Alaska tourists.

I have in my possession a large piece of this slate from the center of which stands out in repoussé the figure of a native Indian. Facing him on each side are two enormous bears, threatening him, while at the extreme ends are two forms having the shape of griffins, evidently his totems attempting to rescue him from the clutches of the wild beast. This sample of native carving has certainly more elements of beauty and proportion in it than can be found in many of the remains of ancient Egyptian and Assyrian workmanship of a similar kind.

They also produce from the same stone many specimens of pottery that are marvels of grace and smoothness. While they have little sense of the value of time, they have learned from one source and another the approximate value of their efforts, and refuse to let anything go unless they are paid what an American would regard more than its full actual value. It is also so with the baskets they make for sale to tourists, or with the furs they gather for the general trade. In fact fur traders in that quarter are frequently compelled to pay far more to those Indians for furs than they are worth under the most favorable circumstances in San Francisco or any of the other markets below.

THE NEWS GATHERER.

By G. F. Rinehart.

WHEN the *Morning Tonic* is served with our breakfast and the *Evening Sedative* with our tea, we are in too much of a receptive mood to speculate on the probable expenditure of mental and physical energy required to cater to our demands so promptly and so well.

This is preëminently a reading and thinking age. People read to think and think to read and they find suggestions in passing events which set the complicated machinery of thought in motion. It has become a pleasure rather than a task for people to do their own thinking. They no longer feel the need of a mental pilot when they find that no two of these lucid and lucent individuals point out the same course. The tendency of the times, in a newspaper way, is illustrated by a newspaper joke.

It is said that the shortest editorial ever run in an American daily was that which appeared in a publication employing six public thinking machines to grind out six columns of editorial every day. The editorial was laconic and expressive. On July Fourth the publisher was thrilled by the commemorative fire-cracker and platform dance, and, desiring to place himself *en rapport* with the general exhilaration of the multitude, he wandered into the open doorway of a saloon. His six editorial athletes were drawn up in line at the bar. Indignant at the prospect, the publisher persisted in calling up the drinks in rapid succession, insinuating that a declination on the part of his men to respond would necessitate six temporary vacancies in his establishment. The result of the matter was summed up in an editorial next morning, by the only one of the six who was able to answer the call of the foreman for copy, in the simple statement, "Yesterday was the Fourth of July." The public, which had long suffered the stupidity of the editorial

page, complimented the publisher on his change of policy; and, being bright enough to grasp a suggestion and enterprising enough to use it, he made six good news men out of six poor editors, and is now spending his summers at Long Branch.

The day of the long, dry editorial is happily past. The public is clamorous for news. It is not so much interested in the learned dissertation on the Influence of the Chinese-Japanese War on Public Morals as in having the news of yesterday's and to-day's actual happenings. It wants the news in allopathic doses. When kept awake too long by the interesting narrative of the news man, it may hunt up an editorial as an effective soporific. As a result of this growing demand for news, the big-brained thought moulder has gravitated to the metropolitan daily.

HARRY B. LEASON,
City Editor of the *Courier*, Ottumwa, and President of the Association of the City Editors of Iowa.

R. B. ARMSTRONG,
City Editor of the Evening News, Des Moines.

The news man may be small of stature but he is a large portion of the anatomy of a newspaper. If his work is well done, the remainder of the force has an easy task. Editorial can be abridged or wholly omitted and the public will take no notice of the fact ; but when the news features are ignored, the whole constituency of readers are unanimous in protest. The prosperous and successful daily of to-day is the one which makes a specialty of news. Lucidity is necessary. Point and pith are virtues. Life is too brief to dissipate on an editorial or news article that goes from New York to San Francisco by way of Cape Horn.

With news valued at par, the news gatherer should be equally prized. A good news man should be more than a mere interrogation point juggling through newspaperdom in search of a temporary lodging place. He should extend his sphere of usefulness with his acquaintance and be able to incur the sacred responsibility of rearing a family without the Banquo's ghost of want making life a burden. Uncertainty is now the bane

of his existence. He cannot drop a dollar into the contribution box to-day for fear of needing it to-morrow. Publishers have a penchant for swapping horses. They want imported talent. As a result, a new face is often seen where an old one ought to be.

The news editor of the country daily must be familiar with local situations and conditions. He must know what news is, where and how to get it and how to serve it when he has it. He must be a man of breadth and judgment and yet the alert rider of a single hobby—news. As Frank Hatton is quoted as saying, " He must get the news,—get it honestly if be can, but—get the news."

Readers would be more charitable in their criticisms could they know the ingenuity and oftentimes intense labor required in securing news. The city editor or reporter starts out with the determination to secure the news at all hazards, and he usually succeeds. There is hardly any physical pain, any test of endurance, any mental strain or nervous tension that the news man would not undergo to se-

DAVID BRANT,
City Editor of the Evening Gazette, Cedar Rapids.

FRED S. WILCOX,
City Editor of the Galesburg Democrat.

cure an important item. I have known
him to lie in cramped positions, breathe
stifling air, suffer with intolerable heat,
endure scorching thirst and submit to a
nervous strain where a sigh would be
fatal to his object, when engaged in securing news of interest to the public.

I remember an aldermanic caucus in
which public interest centered. People
and reporters were forbidden. Doors,
windows, transoms, keyholes and all recesses were completely obstructed, and
jocose remarks were made that the blank
reporters were at last outwitted. As an
additional precaution, the members were
sworn to secrecy. A stormy session followed. Members lost their tempers,
made insinuations, called names, and
when they at last adjourned there was an
additional reason for keeping their proceedings secret — it was a disgraceful
assembly. The morning paper gave a
minute account of the meeting, names
were given, remarks quoted and the hot
words exchanged were given in detail.
It was done by an ingenious reporter;
but to this day every alderman secretly

suspects some other alderman of having
betrayed the oath.

A "scoop" to the news man is his
nectar and ambrosia. It is a delicious
morsel to remove the bad taste of routine
monotony. Every reporter has a legitimate ambition to get all the scoops he
can on his contemporary and prevent the
latter from getting scoops on him.

Every veteran news man has a history.
Some of these private sketches are as
thrilling as a realistic romance.

I recall an incident where a murder had
been committed at a little station twenty
miles from a city with two morning dailies
between which a news rivalry was maintained at white heat. After dark the
information of the fact reached both
offices simultaneously. Both city editors
detailed their best reporters on the
assignment. The *Record* man caught a
train. The *Tribune* reporter was delayed
and was compelled to employ a livery
team. When he arrived at the scene of
the crime the *Record* man was just leaving to catch the return train. His task
was completed. He glanced at the *Tri-*

C. D. SHIMBER,
City Editor of the Daily Citizen, Crawerville

H. M. KENDRICK,
City Editor of the Gate City, Keokuk

bune man in a supercilious way that implied, "You are too late; I have been
there." It was a little exasperating to

B. F. CRAIG,
City Editor of the Daily Constitution-Democrat, Keokuk.

the late arrival, but, while tying his team
in a clump of bushes near the house he
stumbled over something out of the ordinary. He felt of it. It was a dead man!
Here was a surprise. In the house a
murdered woman, in the bushes a dead
man, and the *Record* man gone! Nervous
to the highest degree, the prospect of a
great scoop made him cautious. He entered the house, completed his notes,
secured from the assembled neighbors a
description of the murderer and repaired
to the bushes. Striking a match over the
dead features, he found them to be those
of the murderer. A ghastly hole in the
temple, powder-burned, revolver in hand!

KIRK WATKINS,
City Editor of the Evening Journal, Burlington

Murder and suicide! Double scare head
for the *Tribune*, and but one for the
Record!

Driving rapidly back to the city, his
duty to the authorities formulated itself.
Turning his team over to the liveryman,
he looked at his watch. Three o'clock,
and the last editions of both dailies must
be on at five! The central telephone
office was near and he hurried thither.
Calling up the *Tribune* night editor he
told him to hold off the forms at all
events until he arrived. A half-hour was
spent in searching for the coroner. Under
promise of secrecy until morning, full
details of his discovery were given that
official. At four o'clock he was dashing

off copy, sheet after sheet, which the night editor was excitedly running over after him and rushing in to the waiting slugs. At five o'clock the forms for the last edition were on the press. At 5:15 the *Record* news room was rung up by the *Tribune* — once, twice, three times. No answer. The night force had retired and victory was won!

———

To give the position of the city editor a little more than a make-shift significance, an association of the city editors of Iowa was formed. Mr. Harry Lesan, of Ottumwa, was the originator, and is now president of the organization. Many city editors, knowing their tenure of position was merely a wager as to whether or not they would make a blunder in a given time, felt their way timidly into the organization. A few declined altogether to join it. It has, however, a membership of thirty, and, from an educational and social standpoint, has held two very successful meetings.

Similar associations are under consideration in neighboring states. Editors and publishers who are far-sighted enough to see beyond their own locality, welcome an organization which healthfully stimulates the ambition, broadens the mind and levels the judgment of the men into whose hands they are compelled to place their one most important interest — that of getting and telling the news.

———

MIDLAND WAR SKETCHES.

XIII. THE BATTLE OF ALLATOONA DESCRIBED BY ONE WHO WAS WOUNDED IN THE FIRST CHARGE.

By J. F. GRAWE,
Of the Ninety-third Illinois Infantry.

"I AM short a cheek bone and one ear, but we can lick all hell yet."

This more expressive than elegant message of sixteen monosylabic words was signaled from General Corse at Allatoona Pass to General Sherman at Kenesaw Mountain, thirty-one years ago. Chattanooga, Tunnel Hill, Snake Creek Gap, Buzzard's Roost, Allatoona, Kenesaw, Atlanta, and the mountains and valleys of North Georgia were in the possession of "Sherman's Bummers." The great march from Atlanta to the Sea had been planned. The gallant armies of the Cumberland and the Tennessee were in the vicinity of Atlanta, with the exception of garrisons along the railroad. Preparations for that sweeping march through Georgia were in progress all along the line.

Allatoona Pass is situated on the railroad between Chattanooga and Atlanta — about eighty miles south of the former and thirty-five miles north of the latter. Two elevations rise higher than the rest of the mountain, and the railroad passes through a deep cut between these two points.

Being a station that could be easily guarded, Sherman chose Allatoona as a depot for storing supplies for the march that was destined to startle the world. After the Union flag waved in triumph over Atlanta, the Sixth Wisconsin Battery, the Eighteenth Wisconsin Infantry, the Fourth Minnesota Infantry and the Ninety-third Illinois Infantry were detailed as a garrison for Allatoona, and the storing of hard-tack and "sow-belly" was commenced, and by the first of October, 1864, there were stored there two million rations, guarded by 890 men.

Up to this time, for about six weeks, we had a royal good time. But a threatening cloud was gathering for our little company. It was whispered that Hood had commenced what afterwards proved to be his fatal northward march.

On the 4th of October, French's division of the Confederate army had possession of the railroad north of Kenesaw and was going for the millions of rations at Allatoona. "Things was working, sure 'nough."

Gen. John M. Corse, who was stationed at Rome, was ordered to reinforce the threatened post. Corse, with the Thirty-ninth Iowa, and some companies of the Twelfth, the Fifty-seventh and the Seventh Illinois, and a few detachments from other regiments, reached Allatoona by rail at about 1 o'clock on the morning of October 5th. Another train-load of troops, which had left Rome a few minutes later, did not reach Allatoona, because the track was torn up by the Confederates, who had surrounded the garrison. The total defense now was 1,944 men. A few hours after Corse's arrival, French's troops were in line and opened a skirmish fire. By daylight

Loaned by Hon. Chas. Aldrich, Curator Historical Department of Iowa.
THE HERO OF ALLATOONA.

every man of the garrison realized that the post was surrounded by the Confederate army.

After some skirmishing and cannonading of about two hours' duration, French sent a note to General Corse, under a flag of truce, stating that he would give the garrison five minutes to surrender in order to save unnecessary effusion of blood. Without hesitating, the gallant Corse replied that he was ready for that unnecessary effusion as soon as his assailant chose to begin it. And soon there was music in the air!

Sherman was at Kenesaw and comprehended what was transpiring at his depot. The distance was too great to offer any hope of being able to render assistance before the struggle should be decided. From Kenesaw to Allatoona the signal flags, spelling their message in quiet defiance of hostile forces, waved from Sherman to Corse the words, few and simple but of thrilling import, which exhorted the garrison to hold out to the last. Quickly Corse's flags gave the brave reply, assuring Sherman that here was a garrison that would fight to the death for Allatoona.

———

In the charge by the Confederates on our skirmish line I was shot and fell into their hands. They took me back a few rods and laid me behind a fallen tree, where I was comparatively safe. I supposed our assailants had continued their charge and had taken our works, but when I raised my head and looked towards the fort I felt greatly relieved, because I saw that our flag was there.

The Confederates fell back a short distance, formed their line of battle, and with a yell, in which there was no music to my ears, they started on another charge. They got along famously until they reached the open space in front of our works, when our boys with their sixteen-shooters arose and greeted the line of gray with such a shower of minie balls that their enthusiasm was all taken out of them, and those who didn't bite the dust came to the rear in a manner

that was more satisfactory to me than the way they had gone to the front.

The firing had ceased, and I again ventured to raise my head and look towards the fort. I sank back with a satisfaction which language cannot describe, because I saw that our flag was still there.

But again and again during the day the Confederate lines surged madly up the hill, only to be as often hurled back by the intrepid garrison, standing as grim and immovable as the mountain itself.

Their last effort was the fiercest. They declared with oaths that this time they would "get the Yanks or die in the attempt."

"The rebel yell" came from a thousand throats. The cannonading and musketry made the mountain tremble. The unearthly, weird whiz-z of the minnie balls, mingled with the shrieks of the wounded and the groans of the dying, was painful and sickening.

The firing again ceased. The shattered remnants of French's proud command rushed wildly to the rear. It was evident that the battle was over. And when the smoke of burning powder had cleared away, I raised my head, my weary eyes looked toward the fort, and I thanked God that, although rent and riddled in the storm of battle until nothing remained but a few ragged streamers, *our flag was still there!*

Sherman was pacing to and fro in front of his headquarters on Kenesaw. His staff officers were using their field-glasses trying to make out whether the Union flag or the Confederate flag was waving over Allatoona. Some said it was the rebel flag; others thought it was the stars and stripes. To settle the question, Sherman signaled to Corse, asking:

"How is it with you now?"

Corse replied: "I am short a cheek bone and one ear, but we can lick all hell yet."

In this determined defense against overwhelming odds, the garrison, numbering less than 2,000, lost 707 men. The number in killed, wounded and missing on the Confederate side was equal to our

Hd.Qrs. 4th Div. 15th A.C.
Allatoona Oct 5th 1864
8 am.

To Officer Commanding
Confederate Forces —

I have the honor to acknowledge
receipt of your communication demanding
of my forces to avoid the needless
effusion of blood &c. to surrender &c.
Please to respectfully reply that we are prepared
for the "needless effusion of blood" whenever it
is agreeable to you — Very respectfully Jno. M. Corse
Comdg 4th Div 15 Corps U.S.A.

force when the "unnecessary effusion of blood" commenced, besides 800 muskets were left by the enemy upon the field.

When history shall have recorded facts impartially, it will be made to appear that for gallant, stubborn, brave, determined and deliberate fighting, that done by the garrison at Allatoona Pass on the 5th day of October, 1864, stands the peer of any. Others have done as well, but none have ever done better. The work on that day has linked Allatoona with one of the most stirring gospel lyrics of the English language. Early in the day Sherman signaled to Corse : "Hold the fort ; I am coming. Don't give up Allatoona." * From this message and the attendant thrilling circumstances has come the song which has been sung wherever the English language is spoken:

> " Ho! my comrades, see the signal
>   Waving in the sky!
> Reinforcements now appearing,
>   Victory is nigh.
> Hold the fort for I am coming," etc.

* New Midland War Sketch II., November, 1864.

HOME THEMES.

THE FINAL SLUMBER-SONG.

Up on the hill where soft winds blow,
  Under the bending skies,
Cometh faint whispers of long ago
And by-gone lullabies.
  Sweet and low, sweet and low,
  Softly the winds are sighing,
  Sweet and low, sweet and low,
  Where mother and babe are lying.

Summer sunshine and winter snows
  Cover their lowly bed;
While farther away the days past goes,
And quietly sleep the dead.
  Home and love, home and love,
  Rest, fond mother, dear ;
  Constant the stars shine from above,
  And baby lieth near.

Over thy mound Love bendeth low,
  With tribute of tears and flowers;
Yours is a bliss we cannot know,
But memory dear is ours.
  Soft and clear, soft and clear,
  Memory's ever singing;
  Sweet to hear, low and near,
  Comfort and solace bringing.

Day and night are the same to thee,
  Years into ages creep,
Still will thy home and thy haven be
A long, sweet, dreamless sleep.
  Sleep and rest, sleep and rest;
  Why should the heart be weeping?
  Over darling baby and mother, blest,
  Heaven her watch is keeping.

Harriet M. Talmadge.

OLD TIME LOVES AND LOVERS.

A beautiful story has drifted down to us of Governor Carver and his wife Katherine, and of their last days in the wilds of New England. After giving due praise to the fine, manly character of the Governor, the old record briefly states that "His wife, who was also a gracious woman, lived not six weeks after him ; she being overcome with excessive grief for the loss of so gracious a husband, likewise died." A whole volume of poetry and romance is wrapped up in these simple lines. How infinitely touching are some of these old records with their brief stories of devotion and self-sacrifice ! They honor human nature.

The quaint old love letters of Governor Winthrop show how large a niche love occupied in the lives of our serious old Puritan forefathers and foremothers. Under their somber garb hearts throbbed and thrilled with the tenderest human affections. Perhaps indeed, it was this earnest, serious element in them which made their loves and beliefs strike such deep root. These records of bygone times are like some sweet, old-fashioned garden full of myrtle and Star of Bethlehem and Life-Everlasting.

Ah! It does not require a great age of steam and invention and material progress to develop the highest products of human nature. The divine instincts of the soul burst into immortal bloom and beauty in the dreariest place, under the hardest and most adverse conditions, like the little flower that sprang up between the chinks of the stone pavement in Picciola's prison. *Mrs. Lillian Monk.*

A THOUGHT'S MISSION.

The Poet's pen a bright thought dropped. It sparkled like the dew. It sank into a human soul and. flashing forth again, its beauty caught the Poet's eye. He, wondering, knew it not.
Lillian Barker.

EDITORIAL COMMENT.

THE public has got in the way of expecting anything and everything from Gladstone, and had about settled down to the conclusion that the ex-premier would have no successor in all-aroundness of knowledge and power, when along came a young man named Balfour who, after distinguishing himself in statesmanship, gave evidence that he, too, had drank deeply from the Pierian spring in which the older philosopher perennially renews his youth. Strong as the Right Honorable Arthur James Balfour was known to be, the world's reading people were not prepared to find this man, yet in the forties, assume the leadership of the agnostic thought of the day along the devious ways of theology. Hence it is that this man's new work, "The Foundations of Belief," is the book of the period with thoughtful men who incline to unbiased speculation on theology. The degree of importance accorded the work may be inferred from the fact that the *Quarterly Review* gives nearly twenty-two pages* to a review of it. The wonder is not only that Balfour could write a book so erudite and commanding, but also that he should want to apply himself to a task which, beginning somewhere, must inevitably end nowhere! Who among our Christian statesmen would not turn with relief from "the Foundations of Theology" to the simple trust and faith of a Whittier that—

> " What to ther is shadow, to Him is day,
>   And the end He knoweth.
> And not on a blind and aimless way
>   The spirit goeth."

The thought is accentuated as one turns to the last page of this long review to find the conclusion of the whole matter. Here it is: "It would be difficult to express better the sense with which the reader arises from the perusal of this work, of the painful and even exaggerated sensitiveness of its

*Twenty-two pages are copied in *Luttell's Living Age* of June 15.

author to the limitations of human knowledge, to the shadowy and relative character of all we *can* grasp, to the darkness which shrouds the vast truth which exists somewhere to be known if ever the limitations of our present condition can be cast aside, than by recalling the words in which a great Christian thinker of our own time directed that his death should be described on his grave : ' *Ex umbris et imaginibus in veritatem.* ' "

* * *

THAT noble order, the Knights of Pythias, does well to keep alive the ancient Pythian legend of brotherliness and unselfish sacrifice. Every child should be made familiar with the grand old story of Damon and Pythias. The Pythian spirit is not, however, confined to Old World legends, nor to our Caucasian race. Rev. Dr. J. L. Pickard closes his valuable paper in the *Annals of Iowa* on "Indian Tribes in Iowa Before 1846" with this remarkable incident—remarkable as showing the depth of a brother's love, the strength of family and tribal pride, and the magnanimity and high appreciation of bravery and self sacrifice by a tribe that knew nothing of Old World ideals. Writes Doctor Pickard : "When the Ioway was treacherously murdered by a Sauk, Black Hawk found the criminal and was about to surrender him to the Ioways for punishment. Finding him too ill to go, a brother who offered himself as a substitute was accepted. In sight of the Ioway village Black Hawk dared go no farther, but the victim went on alone and surrendered himself. The Ioways were so struck with the magnanimity of the young brave, who was ready for the death which his brother had earned, that they released him and sent him back to his brother with a present of a pony."

* * *

THE Deep Waterway movement has aroused many far-seeing and deep-thinking men of affairs. It has millions in it

374

for the interior. Its success will mean nothing less than the commercial independence of the Middle-West.

* *

THE sketch of Linnie Haguewood, by Bernard Murphy, in the July number of this magazine, acquainted many with the sad story of the shut-in life of a young woman bereft of the sense of hearing and the sense of sight, and with the efforts then making to provide for the further education of her singularly gifted mind. We are happy to state that, through Mr. Murphy's disinterested aid the sum of money necessary to provide Miss Haguewood with special instruction has been raised, and her immediate future is, therefore, assured.

* *

A COMMON fault of young writers is likewise a very prevalent fault of young conversationists—the use of overworn and worn-out phrases. Let us make the point clear by a few everyday illustrations. Why always speak of the South as "the sunny South," or the West as "the wild West"? When you refer to your early choice of the West as your home, is it necessary to introduce the subject with the original remark, "I took Horace Greeley's advice"? When, after much exertion, a friend finally obtains a foothold on the street car, why should you make him doubly tired by the remark that "There's always room for one more"? When you find your neighbor running a lawn-mower, or pulling weeds, why not surprise him by saying something besides, "That's good for you"? When about to tell some off-color story, don't introduce it with the remark that you are "not going to spoil a good story for relation's sake." Tell some other story that doesn't call for an apology.

* *

ALBERT GALLATIN RIDDLE, in his "Reminiscences of Men and Events in Washington, 1860-1865," says: "No man has ever served through three Congresses and returned healthfully to take up his old life and pursuits No matter how innocent and regular may be a man's life and habits in Washington, his mind does not escape the kind of dissipation that in a way unfits it for the ordinary pursuits of life." While this strong statement may be founded upon fact, the fact makes a very unstable foundation for a statement so sweeping. There are thousands of three-term ex-members of Congress now serving their day and generation in our country's community life quite unconscious of the demoralization to which Mr. Riddle alludes.

* *

THE Type of Midland Beauty presented in this number of THE MIDLAND is Mrs. William H. Hubbard, of Chicago, formerly Miss Susan C. Weare, daughter of the late John Weare, of Cedar Rapids.

* *

THE latest attempt to create that long desired common gender pronoun is by Professor Henry G. Williams in his "Outings of Psychology." His pronoun is "thon." He says: "Every student should acquaint thonself with some method by which thon can positively correlate the facts of thon's knowledge." With all due deference to Professor Williams, we prefer to go on correlating in the old awkward way.

* *

"AFTER Christianity, What?" is the subject of a paper in the *Free Thought Magazine*, of Chicago, by Mr. E. W. Skinner, of Sioux City. Give us more real, live, all day and every day Christianity, and there will be no more question as to what may come after Christianity.

* *

H. C. BUNNER says colleges do much to foster disrespect of public judgment, and he proceeds to scold the colleges therefor. Mr. Bunner should begin at the other end and scold the public for the non-self-respecting variableness of its judgment.

* *

THE *American Newsman*, of New York, notes that "the increase of circulating libraries in the South and West is most marked, while no increase is noted in the East." What does this mean?

RIDER HAGGARD was treated better than he now realizes by the constituency that was asked to send him to parliament. Now that he has been retired from politics we may expect from him something better than "She" and the rest.

AMONG THE PERIODICALS.

The Macmillans announce that *The American Historical Review* will appear October 1st and quarterly thereafter—at $3 a year, or $1 a number. Its distinguished board of editors is made up of Professors Adams of Yale, Hart of Harvard, Judson of Chicago, McMaster of Pennsylvania, Sloane of Princeton, and Stephens of Cornell.

The most original paper in the August *Lippincott* is Annie Steger Winston's "Pleasures of Bad Taste." It is delightfully audacious and heterodox, for instance: "Bad taste, as we call it, is often but the manifestation of a strong individuality and an artless nature." And, again: "The people of bad taste are people who know what they like, which is a gift emphatically rare among those who only sin against beauty *en masse* and and with the sanction of authority. For them there are joys in every art, in every department of life, of which their contemners know nothing. The anxious effort to be correct, to follow precedent, is fatal to any real enjoyment."

Hawaii is getting ambitious literarily. It now has its magazine, *The Hawaiian.*

Mr. Page's resignation left the editorship of *The Forum* vacant. The temporary vacancy is filled by Mr. Rice, one of the founders of that great thought distributor.

The Writer for August says compensation for short stories, as distinct from novelettes or novels, varies all the way from the *Century's* or *Harper's* $150 to the *Waverly's* year's subscription receipt, and most writers begin with trying the former and gradually work downward toward the latter.

George Beardsley, of Chicago, whose new contribution to the yet unwritten complete life of Lincoln appears in the present number, has an able paper in the last Quarterly *Journal of Economics* (published by Harvard University) entitled, "The Effect of an Eight Hours' Day on Wages and the Unemployed." Mr. Beardsley argues that the general adoption of the eight-hour day would be a general blessing, increasing the number of the employed and not proportionately decreasing the daily wage. But there's the rub—that word "general." With an eight-hour day in the United States and a twelve-hour day in Europe, we would be compelled to rear the tariff wall higher than it has yet been raised in order to protect the product of our eight-hour labor from the output of their twelve-hour labor. As with proposed measures for revising our monetary system, so with this proposition to alter the standard of the day's work: two courses are open to us, one full of danger, the other inviting us to long and vexatious delay and no certainty at the end of our waiting. We may shut ourselves in and "go it alone" and take the consequences of our isolated policy; or we may from time to time renew our invitations to Old World powers to confer with us, and then resume our waiting for the troubling of the waters on the other side. The argument for an eight-hour day is, in theory, unanswerable; but, when we approach the question of practical application, we are beset with difficulties from which the wisest and best friends of the measure draw back in fear. The theorists with their great expectations, their noble enthusiasm and their missionary zeal may, however, ultimately succeed in opening the way now beset with seemingly insuperable obstacles.

A writer in the *Atlantic* pleads for the restoration of the word "lady," with all it once implied. The distinction this writer makes is well reinforced by this quotation from Dante: "Those who are gentle and are not women merely."

The most significant showing of progress made in the September *Review of Reviews* is relative to the growth of sentiment and of laws for the repression of the excessive use of intoxicating liquors. In France, Germany and Russia and in the Southern States of our own country the traffic in intoxicants has been greatly circumscribed in response to an aroused public sentiment.

The frankness of the Rev. William Hayes Ward, editor of Mr. Bowen's *Independent,* is refreshing—if not decidedly cooling. In *The Writer* for September, Mr. Ward says: "One of my principal duties as superintending editor of the *Independent* is to prevent the publication of articles in its columns. I do not prevent people from writing to the *Independent.* [How could he!] I am glad to have them do it. [He must be!] But I never encourage those whose literary position is not assured to write us." Further on, Mr. Ward admits that he does "once in a year or two find that

some new writer shows real genius."
Compare this clammily cold comfort with
the warm-hearted words of sympathy and
helpful words of counsel which Howells
utters in the *Youth's Companion* of September 5, and rejoice in the steadily en-
larging influence of the Howellses, and
the fast waning influence of the Wards,
as factors in the developing and shaping
of American literature.

While certain (and uncertain) monthlies have of late been falling over one
another in their mad rush to get down to
the *Nursery* price level, at least one periodical has dared face the discovery that
it has been selling too cheap, and has announced an advance of 50 cents in its
subscription price — namely, *The Editor*,
of Franklin, Ohio.

The *Ladies' Home Journal* for September contains a paper on "Cultivating the
Lily," by Eben E. Rexford, author of the
August MIDLAND paper on Mackinac.
Its editor, Mr. Bok, has a "Handful of
Laconics," which bear very remote comparison with Lacon; for instance, "To
be a good listener is to possess as great
an art as to be a good talker." Another
"laconic" is to the effect that "the
sweetheart does not always survive the
wife." The September number comes
folded flat, not round as before. The
unwieldy folio size of the *Journal* is causing much trouble. Folded flat it creases
and cracks; rolled, the paper retains its
tendency to roll. The August number
vaguely hints at a change of form, but the
publisher shrinks from the increased expense of the magazine form.

Mary Hallock Foote is even a greater
artist with her pen than with her brush.
Her story, "The Cup of Trembling," in
the September *Century*, is a tragedy that

thrills. It is also a picture of winter in
the mountains of Idaho which can be distinctly recalled a year hence — and that is
saying much for the picture.

The kindest and most helpful of talks
with young authors, by the one above all
others best fitted by nature and experience to give counsel, appears in the
Youth's Companion of September 5. "An
Editor's Relations with Young Authors,"
by William Dean Howells, is a paper
which ought to be in the hands of every
young aspirant for place in literature. It
is written in the philosopher's inimitable
style, familiar, good-natured, generous.
It embodies the wisdom which comes
with experience — in this case an experience covering the whole range of literary
activities. No young writer can lay down
this paper without feeling a sense of gratitude to the large-souled man for his half-
hour's talk with them. Send five cents
in postage stamps to the *Youth's Companion*, Boston, Mass., for a copy of the
September 5 number. This suggestion
is not an advertisement; it is intended as
a kindness to young writers — and out of
consideration for much misunderstood
editors.

Julia Magruder hasn't strengthened her
hold upon the public by her "Princess
Sonia," concluded in the September
Century. She tells the heart story of a
woman who dishonestly chose to remain
in the temporarily rôle of a Russian princess, and deliberately chose to leave a
true and devoted husband whom she herself loved, and, when the heart encounter
came, deliberately lied to her husband,
declaring she did not love him. There
are such women in the world, but why
should they be heroine ized?

CONTRIBUTORS' DEPARTMENT.

THE CHICKAMAUGA DEATH-RATE FUR-
THER CONSIDERED AND
COMPARED.

I have read with interest Colonel Hatry's article on the Battle of Chickamauga
in the September MIDLAND, and, while I
think his account is in the main correct,
I feel confident that, in his comparison
between our losses at Chickamauga and
the losses sustained in some of the great
battles of the Napoleonic era, he has
fallen into serious error. For instance:
He states that "Wellington lost in killed
and wounded at Waterloo, 11,960, or a
little less than 13 per cent (?) of his 90,000
men."

Now, Creasy, the historian, in his "Fifteen Decisive Battles of the World," tells
a different story. He says Wellington's
force at Waterloo was 67,655, or over
22,000 less than stated by Colonel Hatry;
also, that Wellington's loss in killed and
wounded was nearly 15,100, or about 22
per cent instead of 13. Again, in the account of this battle, as given in one of
our best encyclopædias, which is claimed
to be the *official report* of the battle,
Wellington's force is given as 69,884, and
his killed and wounded at 16,185, or about
23 per cent of his force. The English
historian, Green, agrees practically with
the authorities cited when he states that
Wellington's force at Waterloo was a

little less than 70,000 men. We may also as well remember that the battle of Chickamauga occupied two days, while Waterloo only began at 11:30 A. M. and was about over at dark the same day.

Comrade Hatry states that Napoleon's loss at Wagram was but 5 per cent, but history declares his force at that great conflict to have been 180,000 men, and his loss 25,000, or about 14 per cent. While Napoleon's loss at Austerlitz may not have been over 14 per cent, why, in discussing losses in battle, should we limit our investigations to only one of the contending armies? We shall find that at Austerlitz, as at many of Napoleon's battles, his loss was far less, proportionately, than that of his enemy, and that of the 164,000 men engaged, the loss was 42,000, or 26 per cent. It is no doubt true, that the losses in the battles of our late War, at least those of individual organizations, have not been exceeded in modern warfare. A few well-authenticated instances: At Antietam, the First Texas had engaged 226 men; killed and wounded, 186, or 82 per cent. On the Union side, at the battle of Cold Harbor, the Twenty-fifth Massachusetts had 215 killed and wounded out of 302 engaged, or 71 per cent. Tennyson has immortalized the *awful slaughter* sustained by the Light Brigade at the Battle of Balaklava in the Crimean War some forty years ago. Yet, what was the loss to that organization in killed and wounded in that historic charge? Not quite 37 per cent, or, in fact, scarcely one-half as great, according to numbers engaged, as was sustained by many organizations, both Union and Confederate, during our late Civil War.

It will be plain to the reader that this article has not been written for the purpose of belittling the achievements of our soldiery, for well I know that never, on the world's most famous and historic fields, was there witnessed greater valor, more heroic sacrifice. Never, from Marathon to Sedan, were there ever seen bloodier or more desperately contested fields than those of Chickamauga, Gettysburg, Shiloh and others equally famous in our War history.

Rockford, Ia.   L. BROWN, M. D.

TALKS WITH CORRESPONDENTS.

If you find my MS. not available, kindly inform me and I will send stamps for its return.

Where did this form of words originate? Why is it so persistently used? Look at it! A single mail this morning brought us forty-nine letters, all of which requiring some measure of our time. Why further multiply correspondence?

Why should we be expected to first write a letter informing the author that his MS. is not available; then store the MS. for safe keeping; then on receipt of stamps turn to our big book of listed MSS. to find out when this particular MS. was received and where it is stored; then search for it, then enclose it, then address the envelope, then stamp it and commit it to the mails—when all this time would have been saved had the MS. in question been accompanied at the first by a stamped and addressed envelope? We are not scolding—we are simply impressing upon the contributor's mind the aphorism that "time is money," and that the best way is the simplest and most direct.

If it is not too much trouble will you please publish my sketch "————————" over my own name instead of "————————" as signed.

At least six writers of accepted papers and poems have within the past six weeks written the editor to the same effect,—and they are sensible. Life is too short for the struggle to win literary fame for one name only to have that fame in the end transferred to another name. We venture to say, without knowing, that could Alice French, or Mary N. Murfree, or Marian Evans, live her literary life over again, she would not use a pseudonym. There may be some special reason why a person would live and die, as lived and died the author of the Letters of Junius, his personal identity unknown; but, in most instances of pseudonym the secret thought of the heart is alternating fear lest the first steps fail and anticipation of the future glad surprise of the author's world of friends on learning that they have so long been on intimate terms with genius and not known it. There really need be no fear of the first step, if that step is taken in THE MIDLAND, or any other distinctively literary magazine; for the magazine editor can't afford to be so cruelly clever as to admit anything into his columns that is not up to standard. He is compelled even to return so much good literary matter that his acceptance means that, so far as his interested judgment goes, the accepted manuscript is extra-available. Assuming that his is a fair average judgment, sharpened by interest and quickened by constant exercise, it is reasonably safe to say that any MS. good enough to find place in his magazine will be a credit, not a discredit, to its author.

Being only—years old, can't I lay claim to being your youngest contributor?

Yes, if you choose; but not in THE MIDLAND. The age of a writer has nothing to do with the MS. In literature there should be no "infant prodigies."

THE MIDLAND BOOK TABLE.

BLANCHE FEARING AND HER WORK.

Contributed.

The center of population has been steadily moving westward during the last century at an average rate of five miles annually. Westward, too, the literary center has advanced.—in late years at an accelerated pace. The strong and sturdy West, which has on more than one occasion astonished the world by her vast resources and achievements, has conclusively shown that the pen in the hands of her sons and daughters is at once an artistic and powerful instrument. The spirit of energy and enthusiasm characteristic of the region pervades its literary work. That work is strong, pure and wholesome, while ofttimes in æsthetic construction it does not suffer by comparison with the classics. The extent to which the western slope of the upper Mississippi valley has assisted in raising American literature to its present standard of excellence was never so fully appreciated as to-day, and to the timely sketches in THE MIDLAND MONTHLY a not inconsiderable proportion of this public recognition is due.

The recent appearance of "Roberta"* brings again into ascendency one who has been on more than one occasion a bright light in this literary firmament. For though now a resident of Chicago, Blanche Fearing is proud to claim Iowa as the State of her nativity. There her early education was received; there her poetic inspiration was born and nurtured; there, on the banks of her loved Mississippi, her first volume of poems was written; and there, in one of nature's charming retreats, readily located by some of my readers, she finds temporary refuge and relief for the grief-stricken Roberta.

Her taste for literature was manifested at any early age, and when only eight years old she wrote her first poem, "Happy Children." It was published in a home paper, and not only showed the child-poet's clear conception of rhyme and meter, but reflected her sunny disposition. Other poems rapidly followed until, at the age of twelve years, she had written enough to fill a good-sized volume and had taken two literary prizes in competition with adults. Many of these earlier poems were published in various papers and magazines, and some were copied,—for their merits alone, the author's extreme youth being unknown to the editor. In this way her verses found a place among the poetic "gems" of the Boston *Transcript*,—one of the most fastidious of journals—before she was ten years old. Her writings of this period were aglow with vivid and beautiful imagery, and displayed a depth of thought and feeling quite beyond the comprehension, much less the composition, of the average child of her age.

Her first published volume, "The Sleeping World and Other Poems," contains twenty-seven poems of varying length and meter, while the wide range of subjects reveals the versatility of the author. It met with a cordial reception in her native city and from the press in general. Of it William Morton Payne has written in a magazine article: "Its contents are essentially lyrical and subjective. The Tennysonian influence is very marked, but the poems are far from being merely imitative, A note of song stronger and more sustained has hardly been sounded by any other American woman." Especially gratifying must it have been to the young writer that this initial volume should bring personal letters of praise and encouragement from such masters in the art as Joaquin Miller, Edmund Clarence Stedman, Oliver Wendell Holmes and John G. Whittier.

A head less evenly balanced might have been rendered unsteady by so much commendation. Yet the showers of praise lavished upon her never, even in childhood, fostered any parasitic seeds of vanity and conceit, but only stimulated healthy growth. In "Praise," a poem included in this first volume, it is apparent that, while by no means indifferent regarding the opinions of others, her thoughts soared beyond earth for final approbation. The closing stanzas of the selection serve as illustrative of this point:

Though stars of human power should rise,
Should blaze, should burst, should sink unseen,

Though storms of change across the skies
Should sweep their fiery skirts,—serene
My soul could stand, could stand and clear.
Like God's own bugle-blast, could hear
Above the deep, tumultuous clash
All mortals judging mortal things,
Above the wondrous sliver crash
Of angel pinions swept by wings,
One grand note of approval run
Through all, above all,—God's "Well done!"

Several of these poems abound in philosophy and are couched in terms reveal-

*Chas. H. Kerr & Co., Chicago: $1.00.

ing rare depth of feeling and broadness of human sympathy. Yet, while quotations gleam like stray jewels taken from a rich mosaic, they cannot but suffer by detachment. These poems are too strong, too rich in depth of feeling to be broken into fragments. There is in them a power which not only holds the reader, but raises him to purer and nobler thoughts and aspirations. The following sonnet, entitled "The Snow," will be read with pleasure, not only for the exquisite beauty of poetic thought, but also because it is one of the author's favorite productions:

Between thy frozen eyelids, in swift grace,
Touched with the form and splendor of the spheres,
As white as angel's thoughts, thy gelid tears,
O mourning nature down thy bosom trace
Their way, and fold thee in a white embrace.
Oh, soft as footsteps of retreating years
That vibrate only in the soul's quick ears;
Oh, pure as kisses on an infant's face!
Thus may my days full white, and pure, and still—
Upon the world's cold forehead, tending so
More grace to her bleak brows which throb and thrill
With inward fevers, noiseless as the snow.
Oh, white and noiseless, may they drift, and fold
Dark spaces of the earth with grace untold!

Soon after the publication of her first volume, Miss Fearing went to Chicago and entered Union College as a student of law. Within the past few years many avenues previously barred, or at least seriously obstructed to women, have been

MISS BLANCHE FEARING, OF CHICAGO.

opened; and while she was not the first of her sex to enter the legal profession, the path she entered was, to say the least, not a well beaten one. If her fellow students looked a little askance at the slight young girl so presumptuous as to strive to enter their ranks as an equal, this feeling was soon replaced by astonishment not unmingled with admiration. The situation in the midwinter following her matriculation is thus described in one of the city papers:

"The students of the college of law simply hold their breaths when Miss Blanche Fearing arises to speak or answer a question.....A law point which she thoroughly understands she never forgets, and a student of the school told a *News* reporter that since she entered the law class last September she has accomplished the amazing and unprecedented feat of answering correctly every question put to her.....She is said to possess a power of expression and eloquence that promises a marvelous future."

She graduated the following year, taking a prize for scholarship, and demonstrating conclusively that even a woman's brain is capable of mastering the intricacies of the law !

Miss Fearing at once entered upon the practice of her profession in Chicago and has achieved success. Further, she finds the broad experience in and knowledge of human affairs and human character, which she acquires in this practice, a rich and constant source from which to draw for her literary work, and realizes that one can learn more from men and women than from books.

This is forcibly illustrated by her second volume, "In the City by the Lake," consisting of two blank verse narratives, the latter the complement and in a certain sense the sequel of the former. These combine the fine poetic qualities which marked her former work, with the broader and more practical applications which result from actual contact with real life in its manifold phases. The paramount interest in the stories, tender and pathetic in themselves, rests in the fact that the heroines are types of victims of our social wrongs. "Aside from beauty and perfection of construction," writes Frances E. Willard in the *Union Signal*, "the book is replete with profound truths, touching with unswerving directness and inherent delicacy upon some of the gravest social questions that are before the thinkers of the day." Of it Octave Thanet says: "There are lines in the volume that any of our poets might be glad to have written, and Magia is a heroine that any of our novelists might be glad to claim. I am mistaken if the lines before the title shall not come to be more and more on the tongues and pens of your countrymen as the fullest and truest description, in brief, of Chicago." The lines referred to are as follows :

Here in this splendid city by the lake,
I dream that man has a majestic hope.
Because all elements of life and thought
Enrich her blood and stimulate her brain.
Here is the world epitomized, for here
Are pulses out of every nation's heart,
And men may study mankind at their
      hearths.
This is to be a favorite battle-ground
For truth and error. Here, as time moves on,
Great causes will be marshaled. Times have
      been
Already, when the stirring trumpet blast
Of an approaching conflict shook the world.
Out of its dream of safety. Oh, then reach
All capable of bearing the bright arms
Of reason, fearless, independent thought!
If you would lead men safely admonish,
Teach them to think, not what to think,
      but how.

Memory gems abound ; in fact, there is scarcely a page without one or more passages worthy of special notice. How beautifully is the sunshine in the soul of the child Magla described :

      "There is something in me inside."
It was the ecstasy of perfect life.
That like an angel leaped and clapped its
      wings
With sudden of rhythmic sweetness in the
      soul,
And silver bursts of laughter from the lips
That rippled unrestrainedly;

Here we have defined the highest type of art :

            Men and women.
Who set us palpitating with the thrill
Of something loftier than we yet have
      dreamed,
Are God's sublimest poems.

How the general adoption of these lines as a motto would hasten the millenium :

      Let our chiefest mission be
To make ourselves the noblest that we may;
And second, to ennoble other men;
Because the great Christ-passion to redeem
Burns in our hearts, and life is but half lived,
Unless we feel that men have touched our
      robes.
And virtue has gone out from us.

Miss Fearing's enthusiasm for the great waters is evinced by frequent figures in her earlier poems. Perhaps this love was instilled by the "bird's eye glimpses of the vast river that the Iowans love," so quaintly described by Octave Thanet; for "the steel-blue glint of the water" and "the three bridges tying three towns to the island arsenal" were ever visible from the home of her childhood. But if she loved the Mississippi, how much more the great Lake Michigan, with its ever-changing colors and songs of many keys! Many of the most beautiful pen pictures in her later writings represent its magic sheet in the distance, and in not a

few is it brought so near that we can hear "those infinite voices that have a special meaning for every listening ear."

In "Roberta," Miss Fearing's latest work and first novel, we have depicted a transition from childhood to maturity, in which the evils of our social system weave their dark meshes over a pure life, obscuring but never totally extinguishing the angelic light in the soul ; and finally the emergence of an outcast, a criminal in the eyes of the world, into a true, womanly woman ; one who seeks power solely for the good of humanity ; who finds greatest contentment in saving a soul from despair. The story is a vivid one, and the panorama of life in the Western metropolis, as here displayed, arouses the most serious thought and contemplation. Here, too, the professional experience of the writer is of inestimable value ; of it the realistic court scenes and exposition of the workings of judicial machinery are a direct product.

Miss Fearing proves herself an astute and accurate analyst of human character. Her characters, eccentric though some of them are, become to the reader real personages.

There are many striking passages in "Roberta," in which those who best know her behold a revelation of the author's own remarkable personality. That the book is not weak, the opening lines are evidence :

The law of gravity which disposes the physical universe into planetary systems, constellations, spheres and firmaments, has its archtype in the universe of mind. All thought and action revolve about certain great centers. If there is a recording angel who keeps the ponderous records of eternity, he uses certain mighty pivotal transpirings about which to industry an eternity of lesser things. History is crowded with star events about which centuries revolve. Lo, here the birth of a Jesus, or there the flight of a Mohammed, and half a world has found a great, central, controlling power about which to revolve, from which to reckon, forward and backward. Nations have their revolutions and their restorations, their plagues and their famines. Cities have their great festivals, their fires and their floods from which to reckon. The lives of individuals have along a few controlling events, without which life would be a chaotic, disorganized rebato of happenings.

Chicagoans date all events from the fire of 1871. "And well they may, for out of it was the city born anew. All that it is to-day it might have been some day without the assistance of the regenerating flames, but its development would doubtless have been protracted through a much longer period. The gods seem sometimes to grow impatient of the slow processes of evolution, and send forth the ruthless angel of disaster with a blazing conflagra-

tion in his eyes, a whirlwind in his breath, or a social cataclysm in his bosom, to crowd the work of a century into one decade.....Happy were the individual soul if the great fires of grief and misfortune that sometimes sweep over it would consume its past and leave it clean for the building of a new life. But the soul, alas! can never burn away its ruins. It may build over them, but it is ever conscious of their presence." In this paragraph we catch a glimpse of the source of some of the author's inspirations, behold a revelation of her aims—a mirror of her soul:
"It is the unfolding consciousness of life that opens the deeps of both sorrow and joy. The less we know of life, the shallower are our griefs and our pleasures. But it is a blessed thing to have a long childhood, for childhood is the time of rapid and unconscious growth, during which the soul is preparing for blossoming and fruitage. After the blossoming and fruitage begin, the growth goes on more slowly, but the soul grows conscious of itself and what it is doing and becoming. A long childhood is a blessed thing to remember. I pity him who has had no childhood to live over in his dreams, and to wander in like a beautiful garden through which memory leads him, and where he may gather up the lovely flowers which he threw away by the handful when he wandered there as a child; flowers which he may press and analyze and keep their fragrance to sweeten his winter time. I pity him who cannot recall a time when he did not feel the great responsibilities of life weighing upon him, who cannot remember a time when he did not carry burdens, not such as are fitted to the shoulders of childhood, but burdens fashioned for the shoulders of men and women, burdens that crush the weak and make the strong stagger. Alas! for him who cannot remember the time when he proudly laid aside the careless joys of childhood, and stood up, strong, eager, fearless, stretching out his arms to life, crying:
"'I am ready for the burden: lay it upon me.'"

                                    BESSIE L. PUTNAM.

Harmonsburg, Pa.

———

Mr. Crawford has written many novels since his "Mr. Isaacs"* made him famous, some of them rare works of art, others continually suggesting that his publisher must pay him by the page. But that prolific author has not yet surpassed "Mr. Isaacs" in strength of plot and in sus-

*Macmillan & Company, publishers, New York; 50 cents.

tained interest. That portion of the public that couldn't afford to buy the high-priced first edition of this novel will rejoice to learn that Macmillan has included it in the popular "Novelists' Library" series. Unlike most paper-covered novels, the novels in this series are printed with beautiful typography and on good paper.

Another of this series is "Grania,"* by "the Hon." Emily Lawless, a tragic story of the Arran Isles in Galway Bay. It is thoroughly Gaelic in conception and execution and therefore sad. It is the old story of loving not wisely but too well, but with new and romantic stage settings. Grania loved a lazy, worthless youth and with the inevitable evil consequences. The story of Grania's drowning is a fine piece of description, recalling the tragic picture of the flood in "Mill on the Floss,"—recalling it by reason of its strength, and not because of any similarity of treatment.

So much has been said in the press about "doctoring" history for Southern schools, that when we opened the new "History of our Country, a Text-book for Schools,"† by an ex-superintendent of public instruction for the State of Texas, and two other Texas instructors,‡ we confess it was with a lurking suspicion that the book might prove to be sectional. But a careful investigation discloses a gratifying breadth and depth of the author's patriotism, and a well-grounded confidence in the supremacy of the Federal Union. As a text book it is attractive and well arranged, leading the learner on from strength to strength.

"Hamlet up to Date" is such a book as only a young man would conceive — and he a student. There is a keen relish of bookish humor which belongs to the young student and no one else — an inclination to turn Hamlet's velvet coat inside out, to guy the First Gravedigger, to tear the masks from the faces of the players and start a laugh at the critical moment when the killing should begin. O, glorious, good-feeling, irreverent, iconoclastic youth! You shall have even our "Hamlet," if you must have it, to amuse you when off duty! Nothing's too good for you — we fear. "Hamlet up to Date"§ is by C. Morton Sciple and Charles Coleman Stoddard, and these young men want it distinctly understood, for the benefit of posterity, that Lord Bacon had nothing

*Macmillan & Company, publishers, New York; 30 cents.
†Ginn & Company, Boston; $1.15.
‡Professors Oscar H. Cooper, Harry F. Estill and Leonard Lemmon.
§The Eschenbach Printing House, Easton, Pennsylvania.

to do with their play. They do, however, admit the collaboration of William Shakspeare! The work is not all good, but it abounds in good hits, catchy songs and rollicking dialogue.

"Iowa and the Nation,"* by George Chandler, superintendent of city schools, Osage, Iowa, was written, as the author declares in his preface, to answer a demand for a single text on state and national government. One of the best signs of the times is the increasing interest in civil government,—municipal, state and national, and it is well to utilize this hopeful condition by strengthening the department of civil government in our public schools. This book seems to cover the whole field of inquiry relative to Iowa and the general government. It is well indexed, the indices showing the completeness of the work. With such helps to the acquisition of knowledge the future graduates of our public schools will be better equipped than their fathers were—and, surely, they ought to be.

"Hours at Home"† has an original touch that we like. We can even overlook "lay" for "lie" in "Among the Peaks," and "I" for "me" in "Sheltered," in the joy of discovery on finding such real pictures as—

> My camp-fire leaps to greet the night,
> And paints the craggy cliffs
> With fitful, torn of flming light,
> That chase the windy whiffs.

Why the poet, Iowa born, happened to to be a citizen of Cripple Creek, Colorado, may be inferred from the last stanza of "Dissatisfied":

> Across the snow
> No buffalo
> Trails out his way with streaming breast.
> No, not a charm
> In this old farm!
> I must go West! I must go West!

"Simplified Elocution,"† by Edwin Gordon Lawrence, director of the Lawrence School of Acting, New York, appears to be the kind of a book a student of elocution ought to carry around with him. Instead of teaching the strained and painfully artificial method of rendering selections, it instructs the pupil to conceal art with naturalness. From Shakspeare's time down to date, the stagey manner, the strained pronunciation and the mere mouthings of ill-taught readers of noble lines, has been an abomination. We welcome any teacher who is trying to offset the false teaching and

bad example of the mouthers and ranters who take the name of elocution in vain.

Continuing the Macmillan series of old English authors, the next republication to claim our attention is "Jacob Faithful," by Captain Marryat.* What a windfall a volume of Captain Marryat was to the boys of other days! With "The King's Own," "The Poacher" or any one of the least of that author's novels, bed-time came all too soon, and sleep was full of dreams of boy and man adventures, of fortunes gained and love well won. The highest compliment that amiable cynic, Thackeray, ever paid others of his craft was in "Roundabout Papers." Speaking of the delights of fever and ague, he said : "In one or two of these fits, I have read novels with the most frightful contentment of mind. Once on the Mississippi it was my beloved 'Jacob Faithful'; once at Frankfort-on-the-Main the delightful '*Vingt ans aprés*' of Monsieur Dumas ; once at Tunbridge Wells the thrilling 'Woman in White,' and these books gave me amusement from morning till sunset. I remember those ague fits with a great deal of pleasure and gratitude." The ague test is surely one of the severest to which any book could be subjected. Jacob Faithful is a clever boy who after many downs and ups finally reaches success and with it "the sweets of leisure, an honored home." The story is bright, at times jolly, never of doubtful ending like the realistic novel of our time. It is light reading—entertaining, diverting, aguedispelling. One of the best things said by Mr. David Hannay in his introduction is this, relative to the Marryat style of novel: "The fashion for these things is gone and nobody wants to bring it back. It was better in its time, and will wear better, than the smart cackle, cynical humor at second-hand from America, 'cruelty' at second-hand from France, and gabble about social 'problems' which are the fashion of to-day." The book is pleasingly and profusely illustrated by Henry M. Brock.

Alphonse Van Daell, professor in the Massachusetts Institute of Technology, has done a service to students of the French language by putting into his "Introduction to French Authors"† and his "Introduction to the French Language"† a simple, logical, practical method of getting at the language and the thought of the French, a method developed by long experience as an instructor. The first part of the "Introduction to the

*A. Flanagan, publisher, Chicago.
*Published by the Author, Cripple Creek, Colo.; 75 cents.
‡Published by the Author, 108 West Forty-second Street, New York.

* Macmillan & Company, New York; $1.25.
*Ginn & Company, publishers, Boston.

French Language " is made up of practical lessons —variously arranged to meet
the principal difficulties of the student ;
the second part is a plain exposition of
the essentials of French grammar, this
part to be continually referred to, not
studied.   The   "Introduction to the
French Authors" consists chiefly of
short, easy stories, acquainting the student with the best French authors and
with a variety of styles and of material.
A second part, devoted to the history of
France and other information relative to
the people whose literature is under consideration, and a vocabulary, all together
make this little work a very valuable one
to the student who would go directly
into the heart of French literature.

"Sappho and Other Songs" (chiefly
Sappho) is a little book copyrighted by
its author, L. B. Pemberton, of Los
Angeles. Here is a born poet, who pictures "the Land of Love and Youth and
Harmony " as though he were a dweller
in that land ; a man who might do much
to make that summerland in which he
actually dwells, namely, Southern California, a dream of delight to others less
favored ; but instead of living up to his
opportunities, he has deliberately gone
back to the mythical Sappho of Lesbos,
six hundred years or more before Christ,
and rewritten and retouched the old
Greek story of Sappho and Phaon. A
sonnet on Sappho now and then is well,
continuing the flow of old Greek verse —
but a whole book ! When one acquires a taste for Greek poetry and the
myths which constitute its better part,
it's like an acquired taste for olives, or
for lobsters, it becomes a minor sort of
passion. This is shown by the concluding words of Mr. Pemberton's preface, in
which he says he launched his bark, his
poem, "on a sea as cold, unfathomable
and uncertain, perhaps, as that one on
which the divine Sappho desperately
threw herself more than twenty-five centuries ago."—thus showing that he built
his bark because he loved to build it —
and not because he thought it would
make a good sailor.

And, too, there is Edward Arnold Lee,
of Odessa, Missouri, a man with a head
full of poetry, but beset with the old idea
that one must dutifully thresh the old
straw over again. He has chosen to write
a little poem entitled "The Prodigal."
It is a rhymeful, rhythmical version of the
old biblical story. Turning to the simple,
narrative style in which the story was originally told—a style admirably retained
in the translations — one cannot keep
back the question : Why should anyone
attempt to better this ? Far from being
discouraged at this reception of his little
book, Mr. Lee should count his work
done on "The Prodigal" as so much
mechanical preparation for future more
soulful work.

This is the period for the chronicling of
local history — while the pioneers of the
midland region are yet with us. We hail
with satisfaction every contribution to the
general fund of truthful story and sketch
which makes us more familiar with the
heroic period of our development. One
of the most interesting books of this
nature is "Pioneer Life in and around
Cedar Rapids, from 1839 to 1849"* by
Rev. George R. Carroll, of Cedar Rapids, himself a pioneer from the far-away
period of which he interestingly writes.
One rises from this truthful narrative
more than ever impressed with the moral
courage of the pioneers and the debt we
owe the brave men and women who
founded our commonwealth.

OTHER BOOKS RECEIVED.

"Light Out of Darkness," by Mrs.
George P. Goldie. Goldie Bros., publishers, Sioux City. Fifty cents.

"The Whittier Year Book." Houghton, Mifflin & Co., Boston ; $1.

"The Flower of England's Face,"
Sketches of English Travel, by Julia C.
R. Dorr. Macmillan & Co., New York ;
75 cents.

"Ormond," a tale, by Marie Edge-
worth. Macmillan & Co., New York;
$1.25.

---

*George R. Carroll, publisher, Cedar Rap-
ids; $1.

Press Photo by F. W. Weaver, Des Moines

TYPES OF MIDLAND BEAUTY. V.

THE MIDLAND MONTHLY.

VOLUME IV.   NOVEMBER, 1895.   NUMBER 5.

NEWSPAPER ILLUSTRATING.

WITH SKETCHES BY THE AUTHOR.

BY CHARLES A. GRAY.

IN SOME respects the illustrating of a newspaper is similar to the illustrating of any other kind of publication ; in others it is very different.

The subjects illustrated in newspapers are matters of current interest considerably more localized than in magazines and other periodicals of a more general circulation ; and in newspapers the literary features are subordinated to the mere matter of news.

As a rule, the illustrations are not as carefully edited as the reading matter, so far as the writer knows only one paper in the country — the New York *Herald* — ever having had an "art editor."

The managing editor selects the pictures to be run in the paper. As a rule he has not had any education or special training in art matters, consequently expediency is his usual guide. Therefore,

HORACE TAYLOR,
Artist, Chicago Times-Herald.

it is not to be wondered at that a great deal gets into the papers in the way of illustration that is not very picturesque. It may be said, however, that it is not always possible to have the material to select from that might be desired. As is very often the case, the more important the news the less the chance for selection — although great change might be accomplished under the guidance of an able art editor, in not only the selection of subject but the selection of space according to quality, and instead of taking up half a page with a very poor subject, and reducing an exceptionally good one to a column, the order might be reversed.

There are really only three reasons why any paper, that prints pictures at all, should print poor ones : First, a lack of means ; second, a lack of knowledge about such things, and lastly, a belief that the public does not know, and cannot tell, the difference between the good and the bad.

Mechanical difficulties to overcome in the engraving and printing of cuts in newspapers make it necessary that the drawing be more open than work for magazines and the like that are printed on plate paper, with fine ink, and run through the press slowly. For that reason the best drawings for newspapers are made in what is known as "half-shade," only the darkest and half-shadows being used, leaving out all the finer tints. For instance, if a face be lighted from behind so that the greater part of the face is in shadow, it makes a very poor subject for reproduction, although in the photograph it may be very beautiful.

Therefore, for the proper editing of the illustrations there should be an "art editor" who is thoroughly familiar with the details of pictures and can tell at a glance their possibilities.

Then comes the selection of the artist to make the drawing. As no two artists work precisely alike, for every subject that comes, someone can be found who will do that particular work better than any other can do it.

The gentleman who was at one time the art editor of the New York *Herald* told the writer that during his administration he had a carefully prepared list of one hundred thirty-five artists, who were divided according to their qualifications, —some being better on portraits, some on figures, some on landscapes, some on marine views, some on animals, and so on through the list. Whenever he decided on a subject for illustration, he sent the order for a drawing to the artist whom he considered best in that particular line, and in that way the illustrations were brought up to the highest standard possible.

Drawings for newspapers should be bold and strong, and yet have the appearance of being finely finished, and for that reason there are very few artists who can do good newspaper work.

A great deal of the work printed is very poor. Either it is only a bare outline, or, if an attempt is made to put in the shadows, it is done so stiffly and ruled off with such machine-like accuracy that it is very monotonous. Much of it, commendable in other ways, is, for the use intended, flat and expressionless.

HAROLD R. HEATON,
Artist, Chicago Tribune.

The engraving of newspaper cuts is done by what is known as the "zinc etching" process, which is a process of transferring a drawing to a sheet of zinc by photography, and afterwards eating away the zinc from between the lines with acid, leaving a relief plate the same as though cut with a graver. This process requires for copy a drawing with pen and India ink on white paper, which is usually about four times the size the print in the paper is to be.

The growth and improvement of newspaper illustrating has been wonderful. Ten years ago scarcely enough was done to merit the name. To-day all dailies of any importance in the large cities, and a great many in the smaller ones, print pictures more or less, the more prominent ones having fully equipped plants, with everything necessary to do the entire work of making engravings from start to finish in the shortest possible time. On a properly equipped newspaper, a picture may be drawn, photographed, etched, stereotyped and printed within the space of two hours.

If the results are satisfactory, every person who has anything to do with the art department must be an expert in his line. The editor who selects the subject,

CHARLES F. BACHELLER,
Artist, Chicago Daily News.

FRED. KEMELBERGER.   WM. SCHMEDTGEN.

almost anything in that line that comes along.

The people, however, find out, some way, the papers that are worthless, and, as political ties were never less binding than at present, more attention is paid to the literary and artistic features than ever before.

In many ways pictures are of much value to a newspaper. In articles of a personal nature, where the interest is very great, a portrait is almost a necessity, as no written description of a face will convey an idea of the individuality as even a passable newspaper sketch will. Again, a good cartoon will carry and fix an idea in the mind better oftentimes than a page of reading matter would—

the artist who makes the drawing, the photographer, the etcher, the stereotyper and the pressman much each do his work well, as any single failure makes a failure of all.

The number of persons required in the art department of the average illustrated daily newspaper is eleven — six artists, two photographers and three etchers.

The expense of illustrating a newspaper depends more upon the quality of the work than the quantity. Some papers are filled with pictures at an expense of $300 or $400 a week, while upon others are expended from $1,200 to $1,500 a week for illustrations.

Illustrating has proven profitable to the papers, although the great bulk of it has been very poorly done. The great American public, if not very discriminating, is surely a lover of pictures, and will buy

which is also true of improvements, scenes of passing or general interest, accidents, etc.

There is probably no one thing that will make friends for a paper any more rapidly than plenty of good portraits. The love of notoriety is so inherent in the American people, of both sexes, that

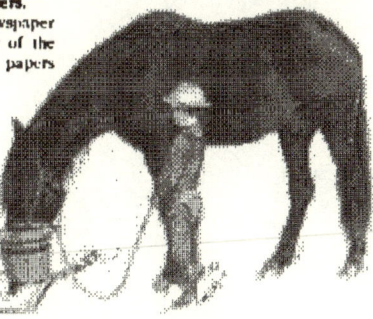

DOING THE "CHORES."

nothing pleases a person, or his or her friends, more than to have his or her portrait printed in a great paper, especially if the portrait be a satisfactory one. And nothing is of more interest to the public than keen, sarcastic, vigorous cartoons.

As the writer has been asked a great many times what compensation members of the art department of a paper receive, it may be of interest to say that there is probably no class of wage-earners whose salaries vary so much. Different artists have been known to receive all the way from nothing to ten thousand dollars a year, and in the photographing and etching rooms from five to fifty dollars a week. Much depends on circumstances, as well as ability. Some of the best newspaper artists in the country, who have grown up with certain papers, are still working for about the same amount per week that they commenced on,

while others have stepped into the ranks from the outside at two or three times the salary.

The natural disposition of the publisher also has considerable to do with the salary question. Some with penurious instincts never increase wages, although the net income of the paper may be a quarter of a million per year, while others are generous almost to a fault. The late James W. Scott was of the latter kind and known to all as one of the most liberal and kind-hearted of publishers, and no newspaper man was ever more sincerely liked through life or more generally mourned in death.

As a class, however, the art department has the easiest time and best pay on the paper, six hours being a usual day's work.

Much interest is now centering about the Sunday editions of the daily papers, some ministers going so far as to maintain that the literary and artistic features of the Sunday papers are such as to claim the attention of the purchaser during the day to the detriment of the church, which may be true to some, but to no great extent, as the excellence of the papers in question has not reached such a stage as to be likely to hold a person from doing anything else usually desired. However, in a city like Chicago, where no magazines or similar publications of any importance are published, the public would very naturally take kindly to the Sunday edition of the daily papers.

The question is often asked, "Where do all the pictures come from? Who gets them and who thinks them up?" The answer is, that all depends on circumstances. Some newspapers keep a cabinet of carefully arranged pictures of persons and occasionally of places,

AMONG THE SUNFLOWERS.

which, being increased by the addition of new subjects daily, in time becomes a storehouse of great value. Then there are private firms who deal exclusively in photographs of celebrities, from the best of which a paper can at any time get a photograph of almost any person of prominence in the world.

In illustrating local events and scenes an artist is usually sent out to make sketches. In cartoons, caricature sketches and other original work the artist usually evolves his own ideas, although he is often aided by suggestions from the editor. In articles on foreign matters the pictures are sometimes copied from the foreign magazines and periodicals.

The sun is just rising on the broad field of newspaper illustrating and its future promises to be bright. Artists of world-wide fame, including such men as C. D. Gibson, Charles Howard Johnson, George Wharton Edwards, Valerian Gribayedoff, and many others equally well known, are not ashamed to come to the aid of the illustrated dailies, and their work often appears in those journals.

Two prominent reasons why artists like to do newspaper work is that the work is given all the space necessary and is printed at once, while in the magazines the life is often all taken out of a bold and free drawing by being reduced to a miniature cut, and even that may not be printed for years after it has been accepted.

A great deal of jealousy exists between papers, even among the greatest, and if an employé of one paper should do a piece of work for another he would stand a good chance of being discharged. There is also an agreement among certain papers which prevents any member from employing a man who is employed by another. Some very large papers occasionally do some *very small* things, even going so low as to cut the artist's name from his work, if he happens to be doing work for another at the time the drawing is printed.

The old adage that "anything worth doing at all is worth doing well" is coming to be recognized, and the difference between the salaries paid poor workmen and good ones is much more than made up in the increased circulation of the paper.

Some papers have attempted to print in colors, and some to use "half-tones"; but unless they can be done better than the bulk of the work which has been turned out, they

ON THE "MIDWAY."

AN OLD TIMER.

RT. HON. WILLIAM E. GLADSTONE.
From his latest Photograph.

will not appeal very strongly to the educated mind.

A great newspaper artist is often better known to the readers of the paper for which he works than any other person on the staff. The public come to know his work at a glance and, as there is to the ordinary mind something of mystery about the work of an artist that is absent in the reading matter, they always take the deeper interest in it; and, although they cannot tell the name of the editor, they will talk of the artist as though they had been personally acquainted with him all their lives.

Some foundation for this intimate acquaintance, however, is attributable to the fact that the artist usually signs his name to his work, while the editor seldom or never does.

MIDLAND WOMEN IN CALIFORNIA.

By Clara Spalding Brown.

THE great State whose entire western boundary is washed by the Pacific Ocean has a cosmopolitan population emanating from every other state in the Union and from most of the foreign countries.

It is interesting to note, at even a small gathering in California, the birthplace of the individuals present. From east, north and south,—if not from the west,—from varying climes and conditions, the persons now uniting in common cause, with the bond of good fellowship, have journeyed to "the Land of Sunshine." They are an intelligent and thrifty class of people,—these persons who have had the courage to forsake old associations and seek their fortunes in an untried field. With their enterprise and breadth of thought, they have wrought such rapid transformation in the civilization of "the new Eldorado" that all the world marvels.

It is not alone the masculine sex which is conspicuous in the work of improvement. Valiantly toiling by the side of the men are the wives and the mothers, the daughters and the sisters. The West, more readily than the East, grants women opportunities, and in California there are many bright women who are stimulated to their best efforts by the generous amount of oxygen which they daily inhale. This intellectual activity manifests itself in the strong interest with which women inform themselves on local matters; in village improvement societies, Ebell, Chautauqua, suffrage, art, musical and literary clubs; and in a tendency to add to the literature of the day, which is so pronounced as to be notable.

A large proportion of these energetic women are from the Midland States; in fact, there are so many that it would be a futile task to endeavor to mention all who are prominent in even one line of work—

that of writing for publication. But enough can be said to show that the great midland country has contributed generously toward the fund of brain-power now being used by women for the advancement of the State of California.

———

The Pacific Coast Women's Press Association, whose active members are found from Washington to Mexico, has for its president a native of Versailles, Kentucky,—Mrs. Ada Van Pelt. In her are admirably combined a fine executive ability with a sweet dignity of carriage and nobility of character which inspire respect and affection. She resided in Kentucky until her marriage to Captain C. E. Van Pelt, in 1864. She then removed to Lincoln, Nebraska, remaining there until 1889, when she came to California. For twenty years she has been engaged

MRS. ADA VAN PELT.
President Pacific Coast Women's Press Association.

393

in newspaper work, and for five years past has edited the *Pacific Ensign*, an eight-page weekly owned entirely by women, which is the organ of the State W. C. T. U. It has the largest circulation of any publication edited by a woman on the Pacific coast, and Mrs. Van Pelt does all the work upon it except setting the type. She has published a book called "Life During the War." Living in the contested district, with members of her family fighting on both sides, her descriptions are vivid and true to life. She has a good deal of mechanical inventiveness, having taken out four patents,—two on combination locks and two on letter-boxes for use on house doors or in offices. Her husband, now deceased, was at one time postmaster at Oakland, and his difficulty in procuring satisfactory locks for the boxes led her to invent one about the size of a quarter-dollar which will admit of 3,000 combinations. All of the apertures in her letter-boxes are self-closing, yet no springs are used, gravity doing the work ; water and dust are excluded; a signal that may be set when the box contains letters for the postman to get drops out of sight when the letters are removed. Mrs. Van Pelt was made vice-president at large of the Woman's Congress Association, and labored earnestly for the success of those remarkable conventions of women at San Francisco, both in 1894 and 1895.

ROSE HARTWICK THORPE.

Michigan still claims Mrs. Rose Hartwick Thorpe, though her residence has been in California since 1887, and she was born at Mishawaka, Indiana. Her childhood days were spent in Litchfield, Michigan, and it was from that quiet village that she sent the first draft of her famous poem,

"Curfew Shall Not Ring To-Night," to the Detroit *Commercial Advertiser.*

It attracted widespread attention and made her reputation, though it never brought her much financial return. Her pretty home in Grand Rapids, however, was bought with the proceeds of her pen, —other poems, short stories and serials, meeting with ready sale. Here she lived quietly and contentedly with her husband and daughter until Mr. Thorpe's delicate health rendered a change of climate advisable.

It was the writer's good fortune to visit Mrs. Thorpe recently in her new home by the sea, "Rosemere," a fitting environment for a poet and romancist. The house, with its broad verandas, stands on high ground, about five miles from the city of San Diego, and within sound of the breakers on Pacific Beach.

There are few lovelier views in the world than that seen from the wide windows. The gently sloping land is tilled like a garden and set with a variety of fruit trees to the stretch of sandy beach where the waves dash in long lines of foam. False Bay, with several new settlements clustering around it, indents the coast; and beyond extends the bold promontory of Point Loma, which protects the harbor of San Diego. From the elevation of the house, the blue waters of the harbor can be discerned on the other side of the Point, and on its farther shore lies the city with its background of purple-veiled mountains. Around the house are orange, lemon, and deciduous trees, and a profusion of roses and clinging vines. The banner made by the women of Michigan, at an expense of over $300, and exhibited at the World's Fair, adorns the parlor wall. It is composed of silk and velvet, upon which is embroidered with gold bullion a part of the Curfew poem. In the center is a portrait of the author done in oils.

Mrs. Thorpe is a tall, slender woman with large, melancholy eyes that denote a poetic nature. She has been a contributor to many first-class publications, furnishing over a dozen serials to *Golden Days* alone; and has published several books for young people, besides volumes of poems. Recently she sold to a publisher a history of Oregon.

Many honors have been conferred upon the author of "Curfew" in England and America,—the latest her election as poet of the Alpha Kappa Phi and German Sodales societies of Hillsdale College, Michigan, for the reunion which occurred in June of this year.

———

Ina D. Coolbrith, generally acknowledged to rank the highest as a poet of any writer on the Pacific Coast, was born in Illinois and removed in early life to Southern California. The educational advantages of that section were very meager in those days and books were scarce, but Miss Coolbrith's intellectual desires were abundantly gratified in later years, for she became the librarian of the Oakland public library and retained her position for almost two decades. She has contributed poems of a high order to the leading newspapers of the Coast and to the *Overland Monthly;* the most important of these, showing a widely varied style, have been collected in a volume. Her work is characterized by great delicacy and refinement of feeling, and comprises dainty love songs, verses of deep religious feeling, stately odes written for special occasions, and charming bits of description. Her lyrical quality has been likened to that of Aldrich. Certainly no more idealistic singer ever adopted California for her home.

A sonnet entitled "March," which appeared in the *Overland,* conveys an accurate idea of that month in the "Golden State," besides exhibiting the beauty of her composition:

Hark, from the budding boughs that burst
   of song:
And where the leagues of emerald stretch
   away,
Out rings the meadow lark's erratic lay,
While the green hills the liquid notes prolong.
The slender callas shine: a saintly throng,
From their broad leaves, and her slim stem
   upon
The royal rose unfolds her to the sun.
O gentle March! O turbulent and strong!
The dove, the tiger, in thy changing mood,
For while the larks sing, and the linnets
   brood,

Lo! sullen storm-clouds sweep the smiling
  dome ;
And roar of winds, and the mad tempest-
  wrath,
Rests on the blossomed plain, the forest
  path,
And the vast ocean smites to seething foam.

Miss Coulbrith visited New England, the birthplace of her parents, a year or two ago, and was treated as a distinguished guest by the *literati* of Boston and vicinity. She is a life member of the P. C. W. P. A.

———

Another life member of the Association, Anna Morrison Reed, is one of the most widely known women of the Pacific Coast, admired for her keen intelligence and varied talents. Born in Dubuque, Iowa, she is a cousin of Gen. Wm. R. Morrison, the soldier and statesman of Illinois, and of the late Chief Justice Morrison of California. Her parents removed to the mining regions of this State when she was a child, and the young girl attended school but little. A taste for writing early displayed itself, and she dearly loved the few books she could obtain. The eldest of the children, she realized the necessity for action when, through illness and reverses, the family became utterly without resources, and she went upon the lecture platform at the age of fifteen.

Her discourses were on such themes as the proper sphere of woman and the temperance question. Throughout the northern part of the State people flocked to hear the precocious girl who was striving to maintain her family. Her success was phenomenal. Within three years she earned $6,000 by lecturing and writing for the press, and had the proud satisfaction of buying a comfortable home for her parents.

She published a volume of poems in 1880 and another in 1891, contributing all the while to the San Francisco and Sacramento papers. Her versification is graceful and her sentiments are tender, often patriotic. The following lines are taken from the collection published in 1891:

HER KING.

A little maiden planned her life -
How, when she was her hero's wife,
He should be royal among men,
And worthy of a diadem.
Through all the devious ways of earth
She sought her king ;
The snows of winter fell before—
She walked o'er flowers of vanished
  spring
Into the summer's fragrant heat ;
She beat her quest, with rapid feet,
Then saddened ! still she journeyed
  down
The autumn hillsides, bare and brown,
Through shadowy eves and golden
  morns ;
And lo! she found him — crowned
  with thorns.

As a lecturer Mrs. Reed is brilliant. She has several times been engaged to deliver the opening address at the State agricultural and district fairs, and her Fourth of July orations have been heard with enthusiasm by thousands. She had so long been known as an earnest worker for the advancement of California that it occasioned no surprise when she was appointed Commissioner for the World's Fair from her district and lecturer and

INA D. COOLBRITH.

ANNA MORRISON REED.

organizer for the whole State. She traveled over the length and breadth of the country, arousing public interest, presenting tax-payers' petitions, securing appropriations, and forming clubs auxiliary to each county association. Her many wise suggestions had much to do with the ultimate success of the exhibit made at Chicago by the women of California. She was also appointed Commissioner from Mendocino County for the recent Midwinter Fair in San Francisco.

Mrs. Reed is by no means one of the gaunt, wild-eyed "shriekers" whom the cartoonists like to label "The New Woman." Her personal appearance is very attractive, and her domestic life is as great a success as her public career.

A young author, with a strong, new voice, which she daringly uplifts in exposition of existing wrongs in modern society, is Miss Virna Woods. She was born at Wilmington, Ohio, and resided for seventeen years in Zanesville, graduating from the High and Normal schools of that place. Since 1883 her home has been in Sacramento. She has given spe-

cial attention to the study of the languages and literature of different nations, being familiar with French, German, Italian, Spanish, Greek and Latin. Her first literary reputation was gained in the field of descriptive verse. Since 1886 she has written for the MIDLAND, the *Chautauquan*, the *Youth's Companion*, *Chambers' Journal*, the *Overland*, and other periodicals. She won the first prize for a sonnet on "Life" offered by the *Magazine of Poetry*. In 1891 she published a lyrical drama entitled "The Amazons," of which Gladstone wrote, "I admire both its poetic force and its Hellenic spirit." Edmund C. Stedman, the New York critic, said, "No one can deny that the author has a very fine ear for rhythm, plenty of classical feeling and color, and a mastery of her special technique."

The following extract will show the nobility of her lines :

What's left the heart when love and hope
    are flown?
To live when all that makes life dear is dead ;
To walk with men, but be with them no more
In thought and feeling than the shadowy
    forms
That wander like the phantoms of a dream
In the dim twilight of the under world.

VIRNA WOODS.

To view familiar scenes with alien eyes,
To watch unmoved the splendors of the dawn,
Nor see in it a symbol of great deeds
That shed their glory over wondering worlds;
To note, without a thrill, the mountains lie
Among the flickering shadows of the brakes,
Or touch with silver softness craggy heights
That round the valley stand like sentinels;
To call the gods how fares the world below;
To hear without a heart-throb all the winds
Making æolian music to the night,
While lying far billows underneath the stars
Pallid with passion on the white-faced moon,
To breathe without delight the perfume
borne
From fragrant haunts of faun and woodland
nymph,
To blind my brow with garlands while the cup
Of Bacchus brims no pleasure; to lie down
On rose-strewn couches knowing but the
thorns ;
To feel unaltered the sweeping of the wings
Whose flight is life ; and hear the lapsing
of seas
That sinks its waters in the ocean flood ;
To wait for death as men who wait for sleep,
Through weary hours of sufferance and toil,
To drop at last into the great abyss,
Without regret or longing for the world.
This, this is life, the best gift of the gods.
What's left the heart when love and hope are
flown ?

Thus the plaint of Achilles, to whom a
chorus of Amazons respond :

To share the burdens of a hapless world.
To pour the healing oil of sympathy
On grievous wounds and aching scars of life;
To warm the soul that wanders in the cold,
To light the feet that stumble in the dark ;
To offer holy prayers to all the gods,
And rise, renewed, from purifying fires
Of sacrifices given to worthy deeds.

Not content with this strong poetic
work, Miss Woods in 1894 published the
realistic novel, "A Modern Magdalene."
Of this book *Boston Ideas* said :—" It is
a quietly but powerfully eloquent protest
against prevailing conditions of so-called
moral society."

" A Modern Magdalene " lays hold of
the darkest side of social life with a firm
and unsparing, yet delicate, hand. The
story follows the lives of two erring women who would have returned to virtue
but for the scorn and ostracism of their
acquaintances. Finally they are obliged
to choose between starvation and the lowest degradation, their brave struggles to
lead an honest existence having been in
vain. One of the unhappy young mothers
decides to summarily end her life in preference to either alternative, and the chapter describing the suicide is a powerful
piece of writing.

Mrs. Flora Haines Loughead, of Santa
Barbara, is one of the best story-writers

on the Coast, besides being a thorough
journalist. She is an indefatigable worker,
seldom mingling in society, but devoting
herself to her family and her literary tasks.
She is of New England descent, but is a
native of Milwaukee, and received her
education in the public schools of Wisconsin, afterward taking a classical course
in a co-educational college in central
Illinois. Her first experience as a journalist was on the Chicago *Inter-Ocean* in
1873, after which she was actively engaged
on the Denver and San Francisco dailies.
Nearly all the leading newspapers in the
United States, besides several first-class
magazines, have printed her short stories.
As a book publisher she has won considerable fame. Among her volumes are,
"The Libraries of California," "Hand-
book of Natural Science," "The Man
from Nowhere," "A Crown of Thorns,"
"The Man Who Was Guilty," and "The
Abandoned Claim." She was admitted
to the London Society of Authors on the
strength of her tale, "The Man Who Was
Guilty," which had a run in England.

Mrs. Loughead has a pleasant face,
dreamy gray eyes, a broad brow and pure
complexion. She has many times refused to give her portrait to the public,
and has not even been before the camera
for years.

We now turn to the consideration of
that true poet, Lillian Hinman Shuey.
She has resided in California nearly all
her life, but was born in Toulon, Illinois.
Her ancestors were of Puritan descent,
and it is a matter of family pride that
there were thirteen Hinmans serving at
one time as officers in the Revolution.
Anson Burlingame, the Senator from
Massachusetts, was her uncle.

The daughter of a Methodist minister,
she saw much of the varied scenery of
California, and, feeling a great love for
nature, began to write verse that she
might express that love. She also wrote
sketches of outdoor life for the *Overland*,
Outing, and other publications, which
brought her into favorable notice. While
living on a farm in Contra Costa County,

she composed a collection of poems which
was printed in 1889 under the caption of
"California Sunshine." In them she
painted the charm of country life in this
sunny land, reproducing many of the peculiarities of climate and scenery in
smooth, graceful versification and real
poetic sentiment. The lines, "September
Days," will serve as a specimen :

I like these low, calm days,
These far, pale reaches, and the autumn haze,
That o'er the distant fields comes low and
    near
To shield the fading glories of the year.

The river's tide is low ;
No tender grasses by the high banks grow.
The birds are silent in the shadows deep,
And all the flowers have hid away in sleep.

But there are forces still ;
The dusty whirlwind mounts the yellow hill;
Uncertain gusts of wind sweep here and there,
While misty powers rule the upper air.

We well may wait and rest,
The seed of life but slumbers in the breast ;
Strength will return, and shining hope im-
    part
A force and courage to the weakened heart.

She has long been a favorite contributor to the *Overland*, her sonnets for that
magazine being particularly commended.

Early in 1894 her first novel, "David of
Juniper Gulch," was published. It is an

MRS. M. BURTON WILLIAMSON,
President Southern California Woman's Press Club.

interesting narrative of life among the
placer mines. The strong character of
the heroine, and the descriptions of scenery, are worthy of special praise. Another novel, "Don Louis' Wife; A Romance of the West Indies," is ready for
the press.

Of a scientific turn of mind is Mrs. M.
Burton Williamson, president of the
Southern California Woman's Press Club.
She was the first lady to become a member of the American Association of Con-
chologists, and is General Secretary of
the Isaac Lea Chapter of the Agassiz
Association, which is devoted to con-
chology. Her collection of shells from
many lands numbers about 5,000. She
prepared an annotated list of the shells of
San Pedro Bay which was printed by the
Smithsonian Institution. As she is an
authority on Pacific Coast shells, she is
frequently called upon to lecture before
various clubs and societies upon this
topic, and the Chautauqua summer
schools of Southern California usually
include a class under Mrs. Williamson's
direction. She is a valued officer of the

LILLIAN BIRMAN SWEET.

Historical and Science Associations in Los Angeles, also of the Friday Morning Club, which is composed of three hundred of the representative women of the city. She is possessed of gentle and refined manners, an unswerving sense of justice and considerable parliamentary knowledge.

She is not a novice in literary work. When she was a resident of Terre Haute, Indiana, she wrote under the *nom de plume* of "Virginia Burton," contributing for years to the local papers and those of Kansas City and St. Louis. A prize offered for the best essay on the subject, "Do the Teachings of St. Paul Oppose Woman Suffrage," was awarded to her, and the essay was printed in pamphlet form for distribution by thousands. She has conducted conchological departments in several scientific journals. A good specimen of her work is found in the *American Naturalist* for October, 1894, where she discourses learnedly on "The Abalone or Haliotis Shells of the Californian Coast."

Margaret Collier Graham, another prominent member of the Friday Morning Club, occupies a high place in the literature of the Coast, having written some strong short stories which were published in the *Atlantic* and the *Century* and have recently been reprinted in book form under the title of "Stories of the Foothills." If Mrs. Graham had been spurred by necessity, no doubt she would have developed her talent more abundantly, but she is occupied with the care of her beautiful twenty-acre fruit farm in South Pasadena, and has other large interests to look after.

"What I have done," says this gifted and now well-known author, "is largely due to the encouragement of the magazine editors, who have been as considerate of an unknown author as the most exacting could require."

She writes in a clever, entertaining way, delineating the every-day lives of simple people with the magic touch which lends interest to every paragraph. Her book has been more highly commended by the leading Eastern critics than anything else in fiction that has been published by a California writer for a long time.

Mrs. Graham was born in Van Buren County, Iowa, and lived in Keokuk until her marriage, after which she spent some years in Bloomington, Illinois, coming to California in 1876 on account of her husband's

By Permission of the Critic, New York.
MARGARET COLLIER GRAHAM.

failing health. The efficacy of this climate manifested itself in his case, as his life was prolonged until 1890.

Pasadena is the home of another Midland woman, who is winning fame as a writer,—Mrs. Elizabeth A. Vore. She was born at West Branch, Iowa, and is the daughter of a Quaker minister. A part of her girlhood was spent in the mountains of North Carolina, where her father did missionary work among the negroes and uneducated whites. Afterward she was a student at Ames College, Iowa. Her experience in the South provided her with material for dialect stories and poems which have appeared in *Demorest's Magazine*, *Leslie's Weekly*, *Peterson's*, *Golden Days*, and other publications.

The cause of all who have their way to make in the world is very near her heart, and for some time she was a leading contributor to *Far and Near*, the organ of working girls' clubs in New York. She has set one or two of James Whitcomb Riley's poems to music, and among her prized possessions is a volume of his

MRS. ELLA M. SEXTON.

poems which was a New Year's gift from him to her.

Mrs. Vore is a frail young woman with warm and sympathetic feelings and the highest ideals. She has endeared herself to the writers of the Coast by her unselfishness and her cheery ways, undaunted by delicate health and arduous domestic cares, for she has four little children to whom she is so devoted that her time for literary work is very limited.

Mrs. Ella M. Sexton, of San Francisco, librarian of the P. C. W. P. A., is a popular writer of sketches and poems for the *Overland* and the leading Coast dailies and weeklies. She was born in Illinois and spent her girlhood days in St. Louis.

Her first verses were published by the Harpers when she was sixteen years old. California's scenery and climate have inspired her best work and her forte is in portraying nature. The following beautiful poem, written for the San Francisco *Traveler*, speaks for itself:

HALCYON DAYS.

"December!" says the year; but rose and lily,
And meadow-lark with trills of sweetest tune,
   Say, "No, 'tis June!"
Warm, black and white, the calendar's decree,
Yet we who read, bewildered, turn to see
Wide intervals of tenderest green, and thrill
To fire of southern sun caressing still
          December's noon.

MRS. ELIZABETH A. VORE.

The late dawns flush with mingled gold and
   rose,
And slowly brighten till the perfect day
   Smiles hours away
Under a cloudless, turquoise arch. Then
   shows
The pearly bubble of the moon, that grows
To luminous whiteness as the low sun wanes;
While, as the planets burn, December feigns
   June's mellow ray.

Unchanged the spires of cypress, and the
   sweep
Of crowding boats of gum trees up the hill,
   Where summer still,
With gold of vagrant poppies, flecks the
   steep;
Yet winter violets bloom with fragrance
   deep,
Perplexed, entranced, we are but sure this
   seems
The "land of afternoon," and lotus-dreams
   Our senses thrill.

Mrs. Sexton has three handsome "native sons," and she writes, "They seem
more creditable and precious to me than
all the literary results of years."

A sadder note is struck by Grace Hibbard, who is a native of Massachusetts,
but has spent much of her life in Colorado and is now residing in San Francisco. Since the death of her husband
and only son, she has been alone, for she
is without parents, brother or sister.
Her plaintive comment, "There's no one
to be glad if I should succeed," will be

MAUDE M. PEASLEE.

sympathized with by all who have parted
with the joys of life. A neat white and
gold volume of lyrics and sonnets by
Mrs. Hibbard was issued in 1893. It is
dedicated to the Military Order of the
Loyal Legion of the United States, and
contains some sweet and tender verse.

Residents of Colorado will perceive the
accuracy of this description of "Snow on
the Plains" :

Last night across the glory of the sky
   purple clouds lay;
The gray-brown, arid plains wandered away
   and met the sunset bright.
Like rusted blades the lush grass rustled in
   the balmy air.
The sage-brush in the gloaming seemed like
   timid deer in flight.
Or Indians, with feathers twined in their long
   floating hair,
Thus, through the sunset's golden gates,
   went out the autumn day.

Lo! in the night, the miracle of snow was
   wrought anew.
The gray-brown, arid plains were changed
   to marble pavements white;
Each rusty, rustling blade like frosted, fret-
   ted silver shone;
Each bush was turned to sculptured Indian,
   or deer in flight.
Autumn had vanished, and cold, ice-crowned
   Winter reigned alone;
And over all was spread a canopy of deepest
   blue.

A pretty souvenir composed of California wild flowers pressed and arranged
by Miss E. C. Alexander, is accompanied
by appropriate verses for each flower
written by Mrs. Hibbard and Miss Coolbrith, and is greatly fancied by tourists.

Up among the Sierras, acting as principal of the grammar school at Sierra-
ville, is a bright woman who retains interest in several of the Midland States,
for she was born in St. Louis and educated at Blackburn University, Illinois,
and the Indianapolis High School. Since
coming to California, Mrs. Maude M. Peaslee has taught ten years in the public
schools of Nevada and Placer Counties;
also in the kindergartens of San Francisco. In the fall of 1894 she was nominated for superintendent of schools in
Nevada County by the People's Party,
and would easily have won the position,
owing to her popularity with all parties,
had not her legal residence been questioned, causing her to withdraw from the
contest. She is frequently called upon

to address teachers' institutes on educational themes, and has always been active in progressive movements wherever she has lived. Mrs. Peaslee has written much for publication both in verse and prose. She is particularly successful in short stories of California life. While in San Francisco she was a valued worker in the ranks of the P. C. W. P. A., acting as a member of the press committee. She is now at work upon a book which discusses one of the social topics of the day.

Mrs. Mary M. Bowman, a Los Angeles journalist, spent nearly all her life in Iowa and Kansas. Her father served as a major in one of the Iowa regiments during the War of the Rebellion, and she was educated at Mount Pleasant. For six years she acted as librarian of the Creston, Iowa, public library. After removing to Kansas, in 1879, she engaged in active newspaper work, conducting the Abilene *Chronicle*, a weekly Republican paper. This was the only newspaper in the state at that time which was managed in all its departments by a woman, and the utterances of its editor showed not only a clear, intellectual mind, but an undeviating uprightness that is rare when combined with aggressive political principles, for Mrs. Bowman did not hesitate to deal sturdy blows in the cause of her party. A well-known Kansas literary critic said of her paper, that it was edited in such a way as to induce a man to read every word of it once and much of it twice for the sake of the manner of the writing, regardless of the matter.

A fair sample of this pleasing style chronicles the opening of the rainy season in Southern California, and may interest Eastern readers:

Monday evening about six o'clock a gentle rain began to patter down on the shingles, tinkle in the tin roof gutters, and raise little clouds as it sank in deep brown dust. It fell for about two hours, scarcely moistening the earth, and though there has not been a drop of rain since the 6th of last May no one wanted it, nobody was ready for it, and few were pleased to see it come. Those who were glad to sniff its refreshing breath were afraid to say so, for fear the bean crops would be injured and the raisins meet with a similar fate. It is a peculiar trait of California life

MRS. ALICE MOORE M'COMAS.

that people never get quite ready for rain. There was no damage done, however, by the moisture. The air was crisp and fresh on Tuesday morning, the sun shone brightly, and the white, fleecy clouds floated across the blue sky and cast deep shadows on the rugged mountains. The pepper trees swung their graceful, drooping plumes in the breeze and the bunches of bright red berries that hung from the branches took on a deeper shade in the warm sunlight. The birds twittered and sang in the feathery tree tops, and the rose bushes that have been resting in the later summer, burst out into new and greater profusion of bloom in the cooler atmosphere.

Mrs. Bowman was for some years associate editor and part owner of the Santa Paula *Chronicle*, in Ventura County. She is recording secretary of the Southern California Woman's Press Club, also of the Los Angeles Woman's Suffrage Association.

The president of this suffrage association, Mrs. Alice M. McComas, is a native of Illinois, the daughter of Gen. Jesse H. Moore, of Decatur, who represented his district in Congress for four terms and died while serving as United States Consul in Peru. After completing her education in the Convent of St. Mary's, at Terre Haute, Indiana, she was married to C. C. McComas, a young lawyer, who rose to the dignity of a judge. Her fair and interesting young daughters refute the assertion that a wife cannot concern herself with public affairs unless she neglects her maternal duties.

While Mrs. McComas has been a writer for years and is a member of both the women's press clubs of the Coast, she is specially renowned for her labors in the cause of universal suffrage. Besides standing at the head of the local suffrage club, she is organizer for Los Angeles County, State superintendent of the department of W. C. T. U. devoted to franchise work, corresponding secretary of the United Woman Suffrage Council of California, and a member of the executive board of the State Suffrage and Educational Association.

Being an effective platform speaker, she is often called upon to lecture in her chosen field; and she was given a place upon the program of the Woman's Congress in San Francisco both this year and last, speaking in May on "The Influence of Politics in the Family." She has given much thought to the subject of intelligent

motherhood, and believes that it should be made a part of the training of every young girl. Strangers have been surprised to learn that the author of such strong and fearless sentiments is a small, delicate woman whose physical strength seems entirely inadequate for the tasks she assumes. Her time during the next eighteen months will be largely devoted to arousing public interest in the vote to be taken by the State on a constitutional amendment granting suffrage to women. She has recently been engaged as Southern California correspondent of the Toledo *Blade*.

Dr. Dorothea Lummis, a resident of Los Angeles now taking a special course of medical study in New York and living in one of the notable college settlements, is an uncommonly brilliant woman who was born in Chillicothe, Ohio. Her literary work is taken up only as a recreation from professional duties, yet she has gained the *entree* to such publications as the *Century, St. Nicholas, Scribner's* and others. She has a keen, often cynical, wit, and her expression is always clear and fine; as, for instance:

Feel for others, but think for yourself.
It is the man who never speaks that best deserves to be heard.
There are certain duties one's friends never neglect: to refer to one's increasing infirmities, or to the follies of one's children.

The following little poem appeared in the *Century*:

THE AWAKENING.

A woman cried: "O soul of mine,
O heart, from love be free!
O body, be a vestal shrine!
Let thought be all of me!"

A woman wept, as eve was low,
Such tears as women may.
"How could I dream, how could I know,
'Twas life I threw away?"

There is in Los Angeles a modest little woman — Mrs. Mary Ives Todd, born in Eddyville, Iowa — who has published one book, "The New Adam and Eve," and is at work upon another. It deals with phases of life attendant upon the decree, "Thus saith the Lord," spoken by Joseph Smith, the Mormon prophet. She writes clever short stories and frequently takes up the pen in the interest of reform

MARY IVES TODD.

movements, being an advocate of social-
istic doctrines.

Two daughters of Ellen S. Tupper, the
famous "bee queen" of Iowa, now live
in California. One, Rev. Eliza Tupper
Wilkes, is assistant pastor of the Church
of the Unity at Oakland; and the other,
Mrs. Kate Tupper Galpin, is a conductor
of women's classes in Los Angeles and
principal of the academic work in Froebel
Institute. She is a small, energetic woman
with an uncommonly full brow, a clear,
sympathetic voice and magnetic presence.
Last autumn, when the need of taking
the management of the public schools
out of a political ring was manifest in Los
Angeles, the leading women of the county
rose up and named Mrs. Galpin as their
choice for the superintendency of public
instruction. With her integrity and decision of character, added to an educational career of twenty years in Iowa,
Colorado, Wisconsin, Oregon and Nevada, she was eminently fitted for the
position. Her nomination was requested
of each party convention, by an association of representative women, who required that their candidate should not be
committed to any partisan principles.

The Populist and Republican parties,
though they have woman suffrage planks
in their platforms, gave the male candidates a majority of their votes; but the
Democrats placed Mrs. Galpin upon their
ticket with much enthusiasm. It is not
the dominating party in Los Angeles,
however, and to that fact alone Mrs.
Galpin owed her defeat. She made a
decided hit at the World's Fair, speaking
before three congresses. *The New Cycle*
said of one of her lectures in Chicago,
"If any club wants to hear the best lecture and entertainment it ever heard, it
had better send for Mrs. Kate Tupper
Galpin and hear it." Reporters wondered, with admiring awe, "what that
little woman with the good voice and the
bright face could not say." She conducts
a class for the discussion of parliamentary
rules, also a Shakspeare Club, which is
studying the points of each play critically.

KATE TUPPER GALPIN.

At the close of the lesson Mrs. Galpin
delivers a lecture on the ethics of the
play, to which she devotes the best
powers of her broad and cultured mind.

Another member of this talented family, Rev. Mila Tupper Maynard, who
graduated from Cornell University in
1889, is a Unitarian minister located at
Reno, Nevada. She is identified with
the women of San Francisco in their notable Congress work, being one of their
most highly valued speakers.

Miss Tessa Kelso, for six years the efficient librarian of the Los Angeles public
library, was a well-known Ohio newspaper woman prior to her coming to the
Pacific Coast. She was born in Dayton,
and lived in Cincinnati from 1876 until
1886. She edited a department of "Books
and Music" in the Cincinnati *Illustrated
Graphic*, besides contributing to the
dailies and furnishing a syndicate of
Southern papers with special reports of
musical matters in the large Eastern
cities. When she took charge of the Los
Angeles library, it was a heterogeneous

collection of about 6,000 volumes. Now it comprises over 40,000 well-chosen books classified under the Dewey decimal system, and is equipped with modern appliances for the convenience of students. Miss Kelso is an honored member of the American Library Association, and during the Exposition at Chicago she read a paper before the Association, also before the World's Congress of Librarians. An article from her pen is occasionally seen in the magazines. She is paying special attention now to sociological questions. Thoroughly a "self-made woman," for she was early thrown upon her own resources, she impresses all who meet her with her remarkably strong physique and equally virile mentality.

A cultured lady in San Diego — Mrs. Evelyn Mosse Ludlum — met with her first terrestrial experiences in the State of Illinois, though for years San Francisco was her home. She occupies the chair of literature and history in the Southwest Institute, and conducts adult classes in her leisure hours. In 1877 she began writing stories of California in early days

MRS. THEODOSIA B. SHEPHERD.

for the San Francisco *Call*, *Argonaut* and *Overland*. She has the faculty of creating life-like characters and describing their surroundings in a truthful and vivid way. Mrs. Ludlum is a charter member of both the P. C. W. P. A. and the Southern California Woman's Press Club.

Up the coast, in the pretty town of Ventura, the daughter of one of Iowa's pioneer lawyers leads a busy, healthful life amid a wealth of the choicest flowers. The name of Mrs. Theodosia B. Shepherd is known far and wide as that of the most successful woman florist on the Pacific Coast, if not in the United States. She was born in Keosauqua, Iowa; after attending school in New York, she lived in Nebraska until her father's death. In 1866 she was married to W. E. Shepherd of Oskaloosa, Iowa, who is now engaged in the practice of law at Ventura.

A glance at the growth of Mrs. Shepherd's business reveals the possibilities that exist for the person who has ingenuity, courage and unflagging determination. A dozen or more years ago, she began collecting the mountain and beach treasures near her home, at first for the adornment of her new house, later for the Christmas souvenir trade, then for Eastern custom, arranging them so artistically that many orders resulted.

Prompted by her success, she next offered calla lily bulbs to distant florists in exchange for plants. Peter Henderson alone sent for one thousand bulbs, and Mrs. Shepherd was obliged to draw upon the stock of all her lady friends, providing them with plants in return. Then she built a conservatory at an expense of $2.50, and started out as a florist! Soon a much better conservatory became a necessity, and every inch of space in their home grounds was devoted to her business. Two acres of land close by were purchased, and little by little it was equipped with everything requisite for the seed and bulb trade on a large scale. The business now amounts to about $5,000 a year. Mrs. Shepherd has established connections with all the leading seedsmen in the country, and fills so many orders from the East, Canada and several parts of Europe, that she is obliged to lease a dozen acres more, in plats here and there about the town, upon which to cultivate her plants. She has a hedge of heliotrope four hundred feet long and many other notable specimens of floral perfection in this sunny climate. Assisted by her daughters, she attends to all the details of what she considers the most enjoyable occupation to which a woman can devote herself. It has renewed her health, besides bringing her an independent income, for when she began her out-door employment she was weak and delicate with incipient lung trouble.

Mrs. Shepherd finds time to write special articles which are recognized as authority in the floricultural matters of which she treats.

Her sister, Mrs. Ella Hall Enderlein, lives in Los Angeles, and has been a member of the editorial staff of the *Evening Express* for two years. She was educated in the Burlington, Iowa, High School and the Baptist University,

ENA FOSTER HABERKORN.

also at Monmouth College in Illinois, and taught in Iowa before coming to California in 1874. A few years later she was married. She was left a widow in 1882. For ten years she was a teacher in the public schools of Los Angeles. Her work on the *Express* includes that of the "all-around newspaper woman." She also contributes special articles to other journals. Ever since the inception of the Friday Morning Club, of which she was for a long time the secretary, Mrs. Enderlein has been an active and popular executive member. Both Mrs. Enderlein and Mrs. Shepherd are on the list of the Southern California Woman's Press Club.

ELLA HALL ENDERLEIN.

The librarian of the Club, Mrs. Ena Foster Haberkorn, was last year the professor of French and German at the University of Southern California. She is one of the daintiest, most girlish little professors imaginable, so youthful that life's mysteries would seem to be all before her; yet she is widowed and has an infant son dependent upon her care. Mrs. Haberkorn was born in St. Louis and, until she was twelve years old, lived in that city and in Springfield, Illinois,— her father, Mr. M. H. Smith, being superintendent of the rolling mills in both places. Her education was obtained at private schools in Illinois and New Jersey. After her graduation she spent two years in Europe, perfecting herself in French and German.

Having a strong taste for journalistic work, she became connected with several Pennsylvania papers after her return to America, and was sent to Alabama by the Pittsburgh *Dispatch* to study the lives of the negroes, a task which she accomplished with much success. After wedding Mr. Emil Haberkorn, a well-known musician, she came to Los Angeles as so many others have come, hoping that the loved one might be restored to health, but she was called upon to bear the final parting one year ago. Mrs. Haberkorn is full of energy and has turned her talents to the best possible use. She is a regular correspondent of Eastern journals, and her translations and original stories find a ready market. With it all, she manages to "coach" youths who intend to enter the University.

MISS GWENDOLEN OVERTON.

Quite a different life is led by the youngest member of the Club — Miss Gwendolen Overton — one which only an end-of-the-century girl would be likely to adopt; for her time is divided between the functions of polite society and the intellectual pleasures of literary creation. Miss Overton is the daughter of Captain Gilbert Overton of the Sixth Cavalry, U. S. A., and was born at Fort Hayes, Kansas. Although her name is frequently seen among the guests at luncheons, teas, receptions, etc., given by the society people of Los Angeles, she finds time and inclination for the writing of bright army stories which appear in the *Argonaut*, and are extensively copied. She also contributes to *St. Nicholas* and the Washington *Post* and *Star*.

Mrs. Laura Lyon White, of San Francisco, a member of the P. C. W. P. A., spent most of her life before marriage in Des Moines, Iowa, and gained her education at Oberlin College. She began to write when a young girl, but never made a serious occupation of it, having "spells of liking composition." She was an early contributor to the *Overland*, has corresponded for several Iowa papers and for the San Francisco dailies while sojourning in Washington. Some of the Eastern magazines have accepted her translations.

A valuable member of the Pacific Coast Women's Press Association from the date of its organization until recently was Mrs. Alice Carey Waterman, a native of Springfield, Illinois. Energetic, buoyant, unsparing of her time and abilities, she won many friends during her residence in San Francisco. Her specialty is descriptive writing for advertising purposes; she has a piquant, "taking" style which never fails to interest the reader. From 1880 to 1885 she traveled in the West as correspondent of the *Mining Review*, and, preliminary to her engagement, took lessons in assaying and map-drawing in surveys. In 1885 she published *The Messenger* in Chicago, where much of her life has been spent. She is now in Galesburg, Illinois,

ALICE GARRY WATERMAN.

where her parents reside, recuperating from a long illness, and is planning a book and other active work to be taken up as soon as her strength will permit.

Mrs. J. Torrey Connor, who modestly thinks she has done nothing to entitle her to a place among Midland writers, belongs by birth to Michigan. She has been a correspondent for the Kalamazoo *Telegram*, and is a charming writer of miscellaneous articles for several Eastern publications. Her residence has lately been changed from San Francisco to Los Angeles, where her brother, Eugene Torrey, a well-known artist, is engaged in his profession.

A native of Rochelle, Illinois, is distinguishing herself as one of the most wide-awake newspaper women of San Francisco, and has also been admitted to the practice of law before the supreme court of California. Miss Mabel Clare Craft was in the first class of babies gathered together for kindergarten training by the now famous Kate Douglas Wiggin, then

Miss Smith. To this experience she attributes all the imagination she possesses. She was encouraged, at the age of five, to invent fairy stories, which were written down by her teacher, as the child had not acquired the art of penmanship. She was graduated from the Oakland High School in 1888 as the valedictorian of her class, and from the State University in 1892, ranking second in a class of sixty. She then entered the Hastings College of Law, completing the course in June, 1895. Nevertheless, she will adopt the profession of journalism instead of the law. Three years ago she took up special newspaper work, showing such marked adaptability for it that she secured important positions, first on the *Examiner*, afterward on the *Chronicle*, where she now has full charge of the society and church departments. She has also written considerably for *Frank Leslie's Weekly* and other publications.

Miss Craft is a good specimen of the *fin de siecle* girl — healthy, happy, alert and cultured, making an honorable and useful career for herself, yet doting upon dancing, theatre-going and bicycle riding.

MABEL CLARE CRAFT.

Everyone is familiar with the *nom de plume*, "Annie Laurie," so often seen in the columns of that wide-awake journal, the San Francisco *Examiner;* but everyone does not know that its talented possessor is a sister of Mrs. Ada C. Sweet, of Chicago, and is known in private life as Mrs. Orrin Black, her husband being one of the editors of the *Examiner.* This Midland newspaper woman has many admirers. Although she wields a *fin de siecle* pen, she has quick sympathies and is ever ready to help along a worthy cause or expose an ignoble one.

My pen falters and my head is bowed in sadness as the thought comes that one who was an important factor in the literary life of the Pacific Coast has passed from earth. I cannot close this record without a tribute to Miss Louise A. Off. She was born in Newville, Wisconsin, and was educated at Fond du Lac and Plymouth. For some years she was known to the cultivated persons in the vicinity of Los Angeles, and elsewhere, as editor of the *New Californian*, a magazine devoted to theosophy, philosophy, and other subjects of interest to deep thinkers. Frail in body, gentle in manner, lofty in idea, wonderfully gifted with metaphysical powers, although young in years, she was held in reverent esteem by all. Every line of her composing in the *New Californian* gave food for thought; her mental grasp of the most refined themes was remarkable. A brilliant and useful career seemed to be in store for her; but the constitutional tendency which a residence of nine years in California had restrained became unconquerable, and consumption ended her life in January, 1895. The following little poem is a specimen of her dainty verse and recalls her beautiful character, for her soul was, in truth, "too pure to die."

THE NEOPHYTE.

Within the temple door, immaculate,
She stoops a fairy lily cup to kiss;
The rosy dawn bathes her with glows of heat's
She feels the pulsing of a wondrous bliss,
The pearly dewdrops, morn'ring breath of waking earth,
The fragrance of the verdure and pillars gleaming white.
Each for her heart some fleet caressing message holds,
That thrills her with a new, immeasurable delight.
Her eyes are crystal-blue, o'erflowing with serenity,
Unconscious mirrors of a tender sunlit sky;
In regal steps she wends her way through iris-hues of life,
While nature, hushed, adores the soul too pure to die.

PHILOSOPHY IMPOTENT.

REVEAL the fine celestial art
By which the sky's chill grays
Are warmed to trembling rose which glows
With passion's quivering blaze;

With lines and arcs explain a flower,
Its pulsing perfumes weigh;
In syllogisms prove to me
The witchery of May;

Then I can teach you Love's sweet speech,
Its overtones translate;
Then can I paraphrase a kiss,
A sigh's rare meanings state.

Bertha May Booth.

BELGIUM'S CAPITAL AND HER SEASIDE RESORT.

FROM AIX LA CHAPELLE TO OSTEND — ACROSS THE KINGDOM FROM EAST TO WEST.

THE EDITOR ABROAD. XIX.

THE ride from Aix la Chapelle to Ostend by way of Brussels takes one through the very heart of Belgium.

As we pass over the line separating the little kingdom from Germany, the custom house forms give us time to look about busy Verviers, with its numerous cloth factories. We give a passing thought to Napoleon III., that most remarkable adventurer in all history — excepting only his Corsican uncle. Here, in yonder hotel, Louis Napoleon, no longer Emperor of the French, spent an uneasy night of it on his way to Wilhelmshöhe, a prisoner of war, an even quarter-century ago.

Soon we are looking down upon Liege, with its 150,000 people and its great factories for turning out war guns, and, infinitely better, engines for the winning of victories over nature's reluctant forces.

A fast short ride and Brussels is ours. A four-wheeler takes us about the city, revealing to us, little by little, the wealth of our new possession.

Rue Royale, parked in the center and open on our left as we ascend the hill, affords a series of not very satisfying views of the older part of the city.

Palais Royal covers much ground and, aside from its large dimensions, is not exteriorly interesting. It is really two buildings joined in one. The long colonnade of Corinthian columns between the main portions is the most attractive feature. Above the palace the Belgian flag floats, informing us of the King's presence.

PALAIS DE LA NATION.
"Seen through a charming vista of noble trees."

Palais de la Nation, on the north side of the park, is seen through a charming vista of noble trees so tall that the statuary about the grounds seems dwarfed. Here the Conservative Senate and Chamber of Deputies are in session devising ways and means to quiet the bread riots —without making bread any easier to get by the men who want work.

In the same Rue de la Loi, which bounds the north side of the park, is the magnificent Colonne du Congrès, or Congress Column, erected to commemorate the founding of the government as it is now constituted, with a constitutional King and with two coördinate legislative bodies. This event occurred sixty-four years ago. As will be seen in the accompanying engraving, the column is Doric in style. It is 147 feet high and is surmounted by a statue of Leopold of Saxe-Coburg, Belgium's first constitutional king. The figures immediately below the statue represent the nine provinces of

THE CATHEDRAL OF BRUSSELS.

the kingdom. The figures near the base are designed to typify a free press, free education, free associations and free public worship. A spiral staircase leads to the top of the column, where a grand view of "Little Paris" is obtained. After looking down upon old German towns, with their narrow, winding streets and their quaint architecture, the conventional beauty of Brussels evokes a qualified admiration. Viewing its smart, pretty, made-to-order streets and parks, we strongly suspect that we are not yet wholly out from under the spell of German mediævalism, and conclude we must see the Belgians' capital city again, when the Twentieth Century spirit has fuller possession of us.

As we drive along Rue Royale we look down a narrow street and see the beautiful old Gothic Cathedral of Brussels. Drawing nearer, we find it stands in the center of Place St. Gudule, dignifiedly overlooking the lower part of the city.

We are again in the presence of the Past. This cathedral, though it has undergone many alterations and partial restorations, is in part — in the retro-choir — the identical structure erected in the first half of the Eleventh Century. It was then built upon the site of an earlier church. Other portions of the cathedral have been added all the way along through the centuries. The interior, grand and solemn, as are all pure Gothic interiors, is particularly interesting because of the beauty, costliness and historic associations of the stained-glass windows. Among the donors of these windows were Emperor Charles V. of Spain, and various members of his family, and other sovereigns of his time with their pious relatives. The pulpit is a rare piece of wood-carving by Verbruggen. It is about three hundred years old. It will be observed in the accompanying engraving that the canopy above the pulpit is surmounted by a Virgin with the Child.

The Virgin is crushing the head of the serpent with the Cross. Underneath the pulpit is a representation of Adam and Eve driven by the Angel from Paradise. The interior of the Brussels cathedral fills all the requirements of the imagination, to which Gothic architecture so strongly appeals.

I am not attempting to "do" Brussels, and shall therefore not detain the reader with a long account of the treasures this edifice contains, nor with detailed descriptions of other buildings for which the city is famous. But a visit to Brussels that should not include the new Palais de Justice would be incomplete indeed. The structure is immense, occupying more ground than St. Peter's at Rome. Its architecture is modernized from Egyptian and Assyrian models and is a magnificent tribute to the forgotten architects of ancient Egypt and Assyria, and, too, the great builders of Greece and Rome.

INTERIOR VIEW OF THE CATHEDRAL.

These massive columns and walls, grandly simple in detail and yet, as a whole, ornate, reveal the gratifying fact that the modern architect may lay claim to originality without despising the wisdom

PALAIS DE JUSTICE.

of the ancients — in other words, modern architecture is not driven to either monstrosities or absurdities in order to produce new effects. The genius of the modern architect lies chiefly in the skill with which old forms are made to yield new and beautiful combinations.

We stand awed in the presence of this greatest architectural work of our century, almost loth to enter the palace, lest the pleasurable impression be dispelled. But the interior is also grand, simple, substantial. Coming directly from a Gothic cathedral with its many arches, we are here impressed with the total absence of curved lines and the simple dignity and massive strength suggested by right-angles, pile upon pile. The vestibule is enriched with heroic-sized statuary. A feeling of reverence comes over one standing in the silent presence of the history-makers of every age and time thus housed in a splendor undreamt of in their respective lives. The interior is divided off into

COLONNE DI CONGRESSA.
(Congress Column.)

eight open courts, twenty-seven large court-rooms and two hundred and forty-five other apartments.

One more building compels our passing notice. A drive through a narrow street brings us to Hôtel de Ville, a venerable building of singular beauty and great historic interest. Its façade, in Gothic style, is wonderfully well preserved. It does not look its five hundred and fifty odd years! We glory in the eccentricity, or rather originality, of the Dutch architect, van Thienen, in that the beautiful tower, which rises 370 feet in height above the foundation of the main entrance, was placed, not in the center but a few feet to one side of the center, thus defying the predilection of his guild—for equal measurements one side with another. The irregular quadrangular form of the building is to us one of its chief charms. The façade has the somber beauty and unpretending dignity which age imparts. The modern-looking busts which fill the niches in the façade seem to obtrude upon us the pretensions of the unknown dukes of Brabant, whom they are supposed to have rescued from oblivion. The gilded Archangel Michael that whirls about with the wind from the top of the tall tower looks like a small bird with spread wings, but the reliable guide-book says it is sixteen feet in height.

Hôtel de Ville — not a hotel at all in the English sense of the term — is a depository of paintings, sculpture, tapestries and historical treasures, all together embodying in forms, as permanent as art can make them, much of the tragic history of the Belgians.

Readers of Motley's "Dutch Republic" cannot pass the monument to the memory of Egmont and Hoorn without recalling the sad story of their trial and execution. Motley gives this vivid picture of the scene of the execution:* "The

*Vol. 2, p. 302.

HOTEL DE VILLE AND THE ANCIENT PALACES OF THE GUILDS.

great square of Brussels had always a striking and theatrical aspect. Its architectural effects, suggesting in some degree the meretricious union between Oriental and a corrupt Grecian art, accomplished in the mediæval midnight, have amazed the eyes of many generations. The splendid Hotel de Ville, with its daring spire and elaborate front, ornamented one side of the place; directly opposite was the graceful but incoherent façade of the Brood-huis, now the last earthly resting place of the two distinguished victims; while grouped around these principal buildings rose the fantastic palaces of the Archers, Mariners and of other guilds, with their festooned walls and toppling gables bedizened profusely with emblems, statues and quaint decorations. The place had been alike the scene of many a brilliant tournament and of many a bloody execution. Gallant knights had contended within its precincts, while bright eyes reigned influence from all those picturesque balconies and decorated windows. Martyrs to religious and to political liberty had, upon the same spot, endured agonies which might have roused every stone of its pavement to mutiny or softened them to pity. Here Egmont himself, in happier days, had often borne away the prize of skill or of valor, the cynosure of every eye; and hence, almost in the noon of a life illustrated by many brilliant actions, he was to be sent, by the hand of tyranny, to his great account."

The street cars in the heart of Brussels run, as do our carettes, rattling over the stone pavements and weaving to right and left, accommodating themselves to the ins and outs of the thoroughfares, recalling Byron's familiar description of Belgium's capital on the night before the Battle of Waterloo. Every schoolboy can repeat the line, "And the car rattling o'er the stony street." "Did ye not hear it?"—as though one could escape hearing it!

We are off for Ostend, our sailing point for Dover, England. The train flies from town to town, deigning only to stop at a few of the larger cities on the way.

THE BEACH AT OSTEND — THE KURSAAL IN THE BACKGROUND.

The quaint old houses with neatly plastered fronts, the pretty flower gardens, the carefully tilled vegetable gardens and miniature strips of grain, the odd groups of people at the stations and the rapidity with which the people all talk at once, in vigorous French,—these are some of the impressions retained.

We stop at Bruges, where Longfellow found inspiration for "The Belfry of Bruges." It is hard to realize that this city of nearly 50,000 people,—mostly poor and helplessly so,—was six centuries ago one of the richest and most important cities in the world, vying with Venice and Genoa in wealth and splendor. Here the Counts of Flanders long lorded it. This was the great port of entry for goods from Venice and the Orient, in the era when the Hanseatic League ruled the commercial world. But now, aside from a few historic buildings, notably the cathedral with its historic treasures, how dull and uninviting!

We reach Ostend at 2 P. M. on a perfect summer day. After dinner, we proceed to see for ourselves what there is here to draw thousands of rich, gay and fashionable people season after season.

Our first impression of continental Europe's great seaside resort is not good. Cheap hotels and boarding houses; sidewalks monopolized by chairs and tables for beer-drinkers, fishing vessels by the hundred along the wharf and everywhere a smell of fish in the air.

But when we arrive at the terraced beach and enter upon the splendid promenade which seems to end with a large and attractive building in oriental style, we suspend judgment. When, on reaching this building, the Cursaal, we find that the seeming end of the promenade is only the beginning, that the most which makes Ostend attractive is still on beyond, we surrender at sight. Attractive as are our American seaside resorts, they are so unlike Ostend that the summer visitor from our side the ocean may well select the Ostend route to or from England.

The town lies about on a level with the sea; but between the town and the sea an immense dyke, or dique, has been thrown up. Upon this dyke are rows of elegant hotels and dwellings. These form an unbroken line from street to street. They face the ocean, commanding a view of the sunset at sea, of the black sails which hover everywhere along the coast, of incoming and outgoing steamers and of the animated scene along the beach.

These buildings, elegant and costly in design, are so arranged that in warm weather they are thrown wide open. Nothing but railing stands between the pretty porticoed parlors and the promenade below. The railings are beautified by trailing vines and flowers. Upon the portico of one residence sit a family quietly sipping their tea. In the elegantly furnished living room of another a tea or dinner party is in progress and all are sipping champagne to a toast which is evidently much enjoyed. Upon a balcony just beyond, two lovers stand looking unutterable things. The little lady, in pale blue silk and much lace, is substituting a delicate bouquet of her own making for a loud one of his own choosing, and he is blushing at the indirect judgment against his taste.

The hotels present an interesting sight. Their dining saloons are at the front, quite out upon the walk. One could almost reach in and help himself to the viands upon the outer row of tables. Every table is filled. The array of beauty, and of ostentatious wealth without beauty, make one wonder, as millions before have wondered, at the over-abundance of some who seem to deserve little and the pinching want of others whose heroic life-struggles against poverty entitle them to crowns of martyrdom.

The famous "beach at Ostend" stands below the dyke, the water's edge being more than thirty feet below. Several rods of sand intervene between the dyke and the sea. The sand is literally alive with humanity and horses, the latter for use in connection with what are oddly styled bathing machines.

A bathing machine is nothing more than a small bath-house on two wheels. The bather first buys a ticket which entitles him to a bath suit and the privileges of the beach and a cart. He passes on to a woman who hands him out a suit with the English words, "Anything you like, please," the same spoken in any language you like, their meaning being that, though entitled to nothing, she wouldn't scorn a fee. Men sitting sidewise upon harnessed horses await the new-comers. On call, one of them fastens his horse to a machine, or' house-on-wheels. The bather enters. A tap of the whip-handle tells him to sit down. The house is wheeled out into the ocean. Another tap on the door means the driver's fee. The bather dons his suit, descends the back stairs of his house and takes his swim in the salt waves. When he gets enough of it, he signals a driver, takes a seat in his house and is pulled ashore. Another rap of the whip and another fee is handed out the window. The "patient" dresses at his leisure and is allowed to escape without any more fees!

The charges and the fees expected here, as elsewhere on the continent, are all together not large; but to Americans in Europe the wonder is that people who have to live with all this service in public places can have the patience to continually keep up the petty business of feeing. But far from being annoyed by it, Europeans seem to enjoy the role of almoner even in these small ways. You rarely find a German or Frenchman without just the expected fee for every service.

In Holland's chief seaside resort, the men and women bathe separately, but the free and easy Belgians, male and female, bathe together as do the Americans. The few whose bathing suits and manners attract special attention are apparently strangers who, with all their elegant and numerous belongings, have forgotten to bring modesty along with them — or else, with all their gettings, have no such article among their possessions.

On beyond the bathing machines, along the shore line, there is a half-mile course

for running horses, also a roadway in the sand for donkeys. A running race is on and there is much excitement. At the finish there is of course a dispute — one jockey claiming a foul, and the crowd take sides in vehement French.

We walk on to the southward, beyond the hotels and mansions, to the very end of the mile promenade, much of the way over terra-cotta brick, or tiling. On our left, upon an eminence, is the Palais de Roi, a royal villa, at present not occupied by the royal family. Beyond is Fort Wellington, and beyond that is Hippodrome Wellington. On beyond is a lighthouse, the Estacade. Two long piers stretch far out to sea on the northeast, and hundreds of visitors occupy the seats provided for them and are watching the gorgeous sunset.

It is now early evening, and many elegantly attired ladies and gentlemen are entering the Cursaal to listen to the concert and to take part in the ball. As it is not an exclusively full-dress affair, let us enter just as we are, in plain traveling suits. Three francs apiece admit us to everything. Under the great dome of the Cursaal, in a vast and brilliantly lighted enclosure, an orchestra of perhaps a hundred pieces is playing, led by a venerable man with long gray hair. The music is delightful. Seated about small tea-stands around the orchestra are perhaps a thousand ladies and gentlemen, sipping tea and coffee, and chatting volubly, chiefly in French. After lunch in an elegant restaurant off from the rotunda, we visit the reading room and find only a few sorry-looking people reading and writing. We next step into the gaming room and find it thronged. Three roulette tables are in active operation, and silver and gold change hands with confusing rapidity. At the tables sit several elderly ladies, putting their money into the keeper's collection box, or taking their winnings, without any show of emotion. Old men and youths, matrons and maidens, sit side by side, watching the roll of the balls with subdued intensity. It is to us a strange, sad sight. Why men and women will thus eagerly confront the certainty of gain to "the house," and follow up their losses with more and still more, cannot be fully explained by the fact that at rare intervals some one quits ahead.

We look into the dancing saloon. The mad whirl is on — literally a mad whirl, for they waltz round and round, whirling like dervishes. When they can't whirl any longer, the gentlemen lead the way backwards a few steps — never reversing — and then the whirl begins again.

A little of this suffices. A long walk brings us to the wharf, where, after personally seeing that our "hand luggage" is on board, we find a comfortable corner on deck and await the custom-house examiners and our departure.

About 11 o'clock we move out of the harbor and beyond the piers. It is a pleasant night and we fall asleep in our chairs on deck, while watching the long row of lights along the dyke and the palace of light which only an hour before we had left.—And thus while we sleep the continent of Europe drifts away from us.

SERGEANT FLOYD'S GRAVE.

A CHAPTER FROM THE EARLY HISTORY OF THE MISSOURI VALLEY.

By Mary Elizabeth Brooks.

THOMAS JEFFERSON was always deeply interested in the great and then unexplored West, and the achievement that most marked his presidency was the Lewis and Clark Expedition. It is the generally accepted belief that this was the first expedition planned for that purpose, but this is an erroneous impression.

While Mr. Jefferson was residing in Paris, one John Ledyard, whose home was in Connecticut, went to Paris for the purpose of organizing a company to engage in the fur trade on our western coast, which object, however, failed. Mr. Jefferson then proposed that he should go to Kamtschatka by land, cross to Nootka Sound in a Russian boat, fall down into the latitude of the Missouri, and thence penetrate to and through that region to the United States. Such a trip was exactly to Ledyard's liking, who was of a roving disposition, always in search of adventure; but even with the aid of Mr. Jefferson, Baron de Grimm, then minister plenipotentiary of Saxe-Gotha, and M. de Simoulin, minister plenipotentiary of the Empress at Paris, it was some time before the consent of the Empress was received, together with assurance of protection while passing through her terri-

tory. Ledyard then proceeded on his journey. When within about two hundred miles of Kamtschatka, he was obliged to go into quarters for the winter. In the spring he was preparing to continue his journey when an officer of the Empress, who had by this time changed her mind, arrested him and conveyed him in a closed carriage to Poland, where he was unceremoniously put down and left alone. Defeat thus marked the first attempt at exploration of the far West.

In 1792, Mr. Jefferson proposed to the American Philosophical Society that a subscription be circulated to engage some one to explore the region of the Missouri River and the Rockies, and learn the shortest water-route to the Pacific Ocean. At that time, Captain Meriwether Lewis was in the recruiting service, stationed at Charlottesville, and solicited President Jefferson's aid in obtaining for him the direction of the party. Nor was his desire quenched when informed by Mr. Jefferson that whoever undertook the work should be attended by one companion only, in order that the Indians might not be alarmed. André Michaux, a professed botanist in the employ of the French government, proffered his services and was accepted as a companion for Captain Lewis. He had proceeded as far as Kentucky, when he was recalled by the French minister, who was at that time in Philadelphia, and ordered to proceed elsewhere upon his botanical investigations. It is said that this recall was effected by Mr. Jefferson who, after the outset of the expedition, discovered indications which led him to believe Michaux a French spy. And thus defeat marked the second attempt at exploration of the far West.

These two defeats, however, did not smother Mr. Jefferson's desire to have the West explored, but rather added fuel to the flame. On January 18, 1803, the act which provided for the establishment of Indian trading-places being about to expire, he sent a private message to Congress, in which he recommended certain modifications of the act, and an extension of its limitations, that it might include the tribes along the Missouri River, and suggested that the way be prepared for this by sending an exploring party "to trace the Missouri to its source, to cross the Highlands, and to follow the best water-communication which offered itself from thence to the Pacific Ocean." This suggestion was approved by Congress, who voted a sum of money for its execution. Captain Lewis, who, since early in 1801, had been President Jefferson's private secretary, at this juncture again applied to the President to secure for him the leadership of the proposed exploration party, and his wish was gratified. He at once placed himself under accomplished tutors in Philadelphia for the purpose of studying the natural sciences and astronomy. He also proposed that William Clark should be associated with him in the direction of the party, that the expedition might not be without a leader in case of accident to himself. This proposition was also approved, and Clark received his commission as captain.

A draught of his instructions was sent to Captain Lewis in April of 1803, and these instructions were signed June 20th of that year. They related entirely to his mission, its object, the course he should take, the observations he should make, the keeping of journals by himself and men, with instructions as to preserv-

THE SCENE OF FLOYD'S GRAVE BEFORE THE RECENT REMOVAL OF THE REMAINS.

ing, and forwarding as often as possible, the information thus collected, his conduct on arriving at the Pacific Coast, in regard to drawing upon the government for funds, to meet which, President Jefferson pledged the credit of the United States, his return route, etc., etc. By treaties signed at Paris on April 30, 1803, ratified July 31, 1803, all that territory comprised in the Louisiana Purchase, which had been ceded by Spain to France, was transferred to the United States, and the route of the expedition would therefore be entirely through its own possessions. This fact greatly increased the interest taken in the expedition by the people of the United States.

Captain Lewis left Washington for Pittsburgh on the 5th of July, the intention being to pick his men from the Ohio military stations. He was joined at Louisville, Kentucky, by Captain Clark, and they arrived at St. Louis in December. The winter was spent at the mouth of the Wood River, on the east bank of the Mississippi, in making preparations for an early start the following spring. The entire party comprised Captains Meriwether Lewis and William Clark, George Drewyer, a hunter and interpreter, fourteen United States soldiers who had volunteered their services, nine young men from Kentucky, two French-Canadian boatmen named Labiche and Cruzatte, and Captain Clark's negro servant, York. Out of this number the captains appointed three sergeants : John Ordway, Nathaniel Pryor and Charles Floyd. Beside these, there were a corporal, six soldiers and nine boatmen, who were to go only so far as the Mandan Nation, making a total of forty-five men. In addition to the necessary provisions, they carried with them a large quantity of beads, knives, flags, mirrors, handkerchiefs, etc., as presents for the Indians.

The start was made from the mouth of the Wood River (or Dubois River) opposite the mouth of the Missouri, at 3 o'clock P. M., Monday, May 14th, 1804, under command of Captain Clark, as Cap-

tain Lewis was detained a few days. They set out in a shower, and owing to the late start made only about six miles the first day. They arrived at St. Charles at 2 P. M., May 16th, where they waited for Captain Lewis, who joined them on the 19th, and they left at 4 P. M. Monday, May 21, making but three miles on account of wind and rain.

During this expedition journals were kept by Captains Lewis and Clark and by seven of the men, but the only ones that have come to light so far are those of the Captains, Patrick Gass and Sergeant Charles Floyd, which last was discovered on February 3, 1893, among the manuscript collections of the Wisconsin Historical Society at Madison. It is worth noting that those in charge of the expedition seemed to have no scruples against acceding to the urgent requests of the Indians for liquor, whenever they met them ; for instance, Captain Lewis records in his journal, under date of May 22d, that some Kickapoos brought them four deer, and in return were given two quarts of whisky.

Thus they proceeded up the river, going each day as far as their strength and the condition of the weather would permit, which was anywhere from three to twenty-eight miles, making friends with the Indians by giving them presents, sending hunters out through the land to procure game for food, keeping minute accounts of the weather, vegetation, soil, animals, condition of the river as to depth, width, current and bottom, the names, character and life of the different tribes of Indians en route, etc., naming rivers and creeks that had no name, and reaching, on the Fourth of July, the present site of Atchison, Kansas, on either side of which is a creek, which they named Fourth of July and Independence creeks, respectively. They observed the nation's holiday by the firing of their air-gun. This air-gun greatly astonished the Indians, for whose delectation it was exhibited and fired whenever they met.

On July 29th they sent an invitation to the Otoes to meet them on up the river, and proceeded to the present site of Council Bluffs, where they waited for the Indians. The land in this region was then covered with grass from five to eight feet high, the mosquitoes were abundant, and hence camping there was not especially pleasurable. At sunset on August 2d the Indians arrived, and on the morning of the 3d a council was held under an awning formed by a sail taken from their boat, which led them to name the place Council Bluffs. In the afternoon they pursued their journey. One of their men, Liberté, who had been sent to see why the Indians did not come, when they were waiting for them at the Council Bluffs camp, was never again seen by any of the party. Another of the men, Moses B. Reed, pretending that he had left his knife behind at the camp and wished to get it, deserted.

On August 13th they camped nearly opposite the present site of Omadi, Nebraska, and Sergeant Ordway and four of the men were sent to induce the Indians to hold a council with them. On the afternoon of the 18th the Indians arrived, bringing with them Reed, the deserter. They had also captured Liberté, but he had escaped them. The day was wound up with a very exciting dance. At 10 o'clock the next day the council was held. Presents and whisky were distributed freely to the Indians, who then departed, and the journey was again taken up to within a mile of what is now called Floyd River, where Sergeant Floyd died. The men were often sick along the way, and Floyd records in his journal the fact that at one time they were all sick. In another place he writes that his hand is "very painful," probably because of a boil. Under date of July 31, he says he has been very sick for some time but has recovered his health. These oft-recurring illnesses to which the men were subject were no doubt due, in part at least, to sleeping on the damp ground on the river bank, and to the conditions favorable to malaria which always exist in such places.

In three weeks from the time of the last-mentioned record in Sergeant Floyd's journal, just ninety-nine days from the time they started, he was dead. His death occurred a short distance southeast of the present site of Sioux City. He was the youngest member of the party, a relative of Captain Clark, and had gone with the party for the benefit of his health, as his constitution was not strong. His home was on Mill Creek at Pond Settlement, Jefferson County, Kentucky, a few miles from Louisville. On the evening of the 18th, when the Indians were assembled with them, Floyd became overheated at the dance. It was his turn to stand guard that night, and throwing himself upon a sand-bar, he was soon seized with a cramp colic, or bilious colic, as Captain Clark calls it. He grew worse, and nothing could be kept on his stomach. They gave him every attention, but were able to do nothing to relieve him ; his pulse continued to grow weaker and his strength failed him rapidly. He died bravely and with much composure late in the day on August 20, 1804, saying to Captain Clark a little while before his death, "I am going to leave you," adding, as he grew weaker, "I want you to write me a letter." Such was the death of the first United States soldier who died on the Louisiana Purchase.

He was mourned by the entire party, for he had proven himself to be brave and honorable and anxious to serve his country. They carried him to a bluff just beyond, and buried him on its summit with all the honors of war. This bluff they called Floyd's Bluff, which name it still bears. Another point of the same bluff a little farther down was given the name of Sergeant Bluff, which name it still retains, and a town at the foot of this bluff is called Sergeant Bluffs.

The place of his interment was marked with a cedar post inscribed : —

> "SERGT. C. FLOYD
> died here 20th
> of August, 1804."

They then proceeded to a small river about a mile farther on, where they camped for the night. This river still bears the name they gave it, Floyd River, and runs through the eastern portion of Sioux City, emptying into the Missouri close to the stock-yards as at present located. Patrick Gass was promoted to the position of Sergeant to fill Floyd's place. The following day they proceeded up the river, passing what are now known as Perry Creek and Prospect Hill, midway between which a large draw-bridge is now being built across the Missouri River.

They arrived at the point where the Columbia River empties into the Pacific Ocean, on November 14, 1805, where they established winter quarters, intending to remain until the first of April; but scarcity of food compelled them to abandon their camp at an earlier date, and they started at 1 o'clock P.M., March 23, 1806, upon the return trip.

In the fall of 1805, at about the place where the Columbia River first begins to be navigable, the tomahawk which had belonged to Sergeant Floyd was missing, but they had not then the time to stop and search for it. Upon reaching this place upon the return trip, about June 2d, however, they made inquiries concerning it, and heard that it, together with another tomahawk stolen from them at a different time, were in the possession of Indians on the south side of the Kooskooskee River. They were very anxious to return Floyd's tomahawk to his father,—who long survived the sergeant, at his home on Mill Creek,—that he might have some memento of his brave son whose death was so untimely. They therefore sent George Drewyer to secure it, accompanied by two Indian chiefs, and it was found to be in the possession of a man lying at the point of death, who had purchased it from the Indian thief. The relatives of the dying man were unwilling to give up the tomahawk as their custom required that it be buried with him; but at length, on the second day, they consented to do so, on receiving a handkerchief and two strands of beads from Drewyer and a horse from each of the chiefs, the horses to be killed at the funeral, in accordance

with their custom, and the tomahawk was finally delivered to Sergeant Floyd's sorrowing father.

On September 4th, at noon, they reached Floyd's Bluff, and found that the Sergeant's grave was half uncovered. It had been opened by the Indians. They filled it up and, after resting, proceeded on their way. Captain Clark notes in his journal that there were some flourishing black-walnut trees near Floyd's grave, the first they had seen on their return trip. The expedition party arived at St. Louis at noon on September 23d, 1806, where, upon firing a salute, they were heartily welcomed by the whole village.

Floyd's grave is marked on Clark's map of 1814, and also on Nicollet's map of 1843. Writing of his trip in 1839, Nicollet says: "We stopped before night at the foot of the bluff on which is Floyd's grave; my men replaced the signal, blown down by the winds, which marks the spot and hallows the memory of the brave sergeant who died here during Lewis and Clark's expedition."

The finding of Sergeant Floyd's journal has been, as Professor Butler expresses it, "like a fourth gospel to them," for in almost every case he has been more minute than either of the Captains or Gass, and has preserved information that would not otherwise have been obtained. In matters upon which the Biddle account and the Gass journal are at variance, the Floyd journal acts as a balance to adjust them to the truth, agreeing now with one and now with the other. Its discovery was a mere accident upon the part of the present Secretary of the Wisconsin Historical Society, as he was in quest of other material, and stumbled upon it.

The Missouri River is constantly changing its course, and in 1857 it was found that the grave of Sergeant Floyd was being washed away by the water; in fact, the coffin in which he was buried was projecting out of the side of the bluff, and some of the bones had dropped into the river. His remains were re-buried on

May 28th, in a coffin made from the wood of the black-walnut trees that grew near his grave. The matter of erecting a monument to the memory of Floyd had for some time been seriously discussed, with the result that on August 20, 1895, appropriate exercises were held in Sioux City, in which Dr. Elliott Coues, of Washington, who, in 1893, published a new edition in four volumes of Biddle's "Lewis and Clark's Expedition," took part, as did also Professor Butler of Madison, Wisconsin, Hon. Charles Aldrich of Des Moines, and Dr. S. P. Yeomans of Charles City. When the matter was first brought up for discussion, the exact place of Floyd's burial was unknown, as all marks had been destroyed, and, when finally located, there were only left of his remains the skull and the bones of one leg. The skull was taken out of the grave and has been photographed, and a cast of it was made for the Scientific Association of Sioux City. The remains were placed in a burned-earth urn, sealed, and again buried in the original place. A marble slab, three feet wide by seven feet long, properly inscribed, was laid on the grave on August 20th, when a movement was put on foot to secure an appropriation for a monument.

MRS. STEPHEN B. ELKINS.

PROMINENT WOMEN IN WASHINGTON'S SOCIAL WORLD. I.

By JULIETTE M. BABBITT.

AMONG the new Senators' wives none will be more welcome to Washington than Mrs. Stephen B. Elkins, of West Virginia. She was one of the most popular of the Cabinet ladies while her husband was Secretary of War during the last eighteen months of the Harrison administration, and no one held larger receptions. She was no stranger, for she had made many friends while her father, Hon. Henry G. Davis, was Senator from the State which big, genial Stephen B. Elkins now represents; and her sister, Miss Grace Davis, was one of the most popular girls in Washington society.

Mrs. Elkins is tall and graceful, with a beautiful complexion, dark, wavy hair worn turned back from a well-shaped forehead, gray eyes and the prettiest dimples which come and go as she speaks. She has charmingly natural and unaffected manners, and is so girlish in appearance that strangers used to stare when her step-daughter — who was married soon after the family left here—called her "mother."

Four big, hearty, handsome boys and one lovely six-year-old girl can call her mother, in the fullest sense of the word. Little Katherine, the image of her mother, whom she adores, was such a wide-awake, busy little body that she kept everyone on the *qui vive* for what she might do next. She wanted to do whatever her brothers did, and it was a pretty sight to see her going out with them on her pony, Daisy, with whom she was on very good terms. One day, she concluded to take part in one of her mother's receptions, so slipped down into the dining-room and made herself very agreeable to the guests, until her mother, hearing of her unexpected assistance, had her sent to her room, greatly to Miss Katherine's disgust, for she was having "such a lovely time!"

The home of the Elkins family, "Halliehurst"— named for Mrs. Elkins — at Elkins, West Virginia, is one of the most beautiful summer homes in this country, and it is a pity they can't pick it up and set it down in Washington, for occupancy during the session.

MRS. STEPHEN R. KLEIN.

A MIDLAND POET.

By,VERNE S. PEASE.*

IN a recent article on contemporary versifiers an Eastern journal classes Mr. Nixon Waterman as one of the three best known and most widely quoted newspaper poets. The dilettante in verse-making might regard any rank in the class, "newspaper poet," as questionable praise, overlooking the fact that he who writes acceptable songs for the millions that read the great journals of the country stands very close to the great warm heart of the people.

To whatever position the critics assign his genius, it is certain the whole people love his verses. But if Mr. Waterman feels any pride in his good standing with the public he modestly conceals it, for he declares his readers love him for what he has *not* written.

Although a Western man by birth and in sentiment,—and if he has ever betrayed any partisanship in his writings it has been for this section of the country,—his verses have been nowhere more appreciated than in the East. The Eastern papers and other periodicals have been the most eager bidders for his writings, and on the 1st of June he went to Boston to edit the literary department of a popular journal.

He is a thorough lover of nature, appreciating all her sweet forms, the flowers, the birds, the brooks, the grass, the arching sky,—and his verses are often the expression of a close and genuine sympathy. But he seldom writes wholly on the beauties of nature, for the philosopher seems to dominate the muse. His favorite form of expression is to touch upon some one of the myriad beauties of nature and then, philosopher like, to take the case in hand and teach or suggest a wholesome moral lesson therefrom. A good illustration of this point is seen in the little verse entitled:

LOVE AND BEAUTY.

The lily's lips are pure and white without a touch of fire;
The rose's heart is warm and red and sweetened with desire:
In earth's broad field of deathless bloom the stateliest lives are those
Whose thoughts are like the lily and whose love is like the rose.

Though a poet of sunshine, yet he is one who seldom paints the literal gray of dawn, the effulgence of noonday, or the golden sunset, but rather the sunshine of the human heart.

The keynote of his song is located about midway between a smile and a tear, and always immeasurably distant from a sigh. He is never pessimistic, and a line of satire was never formed by his pen. Yet his optimism is not of that blooming sort to invite the green-goods and gold-brick sharper.

Perhaps the most appreciated feature of his verse is his beautiful illustration of the law of compensation. Angels unawares, blessings in disguise, are frequent subjects for his muse. Like,—

The gifts that to our friends we hold
Are brightened by our losses;
The sweetest joys a heart can hold
Grow up between its crosses.
And on life's pathway many a mile
Is made more glad and cheery,
Because for just a little while
The way seemed dark and dreary

It is too bad to prejudice Mr. Waterman's case by saying he is almost without a personal enemy. It seems incredible that a bold, bad, good, vigorous, lazy man can live without exciting animosity or jealousy; yet so perfectly is his heart attuned to all the good, and so broad and unaffected is his charity for all the weaknesses of humanity, that one could scarcely be found who bears him malice.

Although somewhat a slave to his muse he is wholly free from the moods and

*Mr. Pease, of Chicago, won the prize in the Original Story Competition of July 1st. His prize story, "Captain John Heycell," November, will appear in the December MIDLAND.

humors that so often afflict men of genius; and, whether in the spirit for writing sentiment, pathos or humor, he is always thoroughly alive, and, as his utterances indicate, he is really glad of it.

His latest contribution to *Puck* fairly exemplifies his fine sense of nonsense:

A SPRING IDYLLE.

Oh, the gentle grass is growing in the vale
and on the hill;
We cannot bear it growing, still 'tis growing
very still;
And in the Spring it springs to life with gladness and delight;
I see it growing day by day. It also grows by
night.

And now once more as mowers whisk the
whiskers from the lawn,
They'll rouse us from our slumbers at the
dawning of the dawn;
It saddens my poor heart to think what we
should do for hay,
If grass instead of growing up should grow
the other way.

Its present rate of growing makes it safe to
say that soon
'Twill cover all the hills at morn and in the
afternoon;
'Twill carpet plain and meadow, common,
park and dale and lea
In fact 'twill cover all the land not covered
by the sea.

If it keeps growing right along it shortly will
be tall;
It humps itself through strikes and legal
holidays and all.
'Tis growing up down all the streets and
clear around the square;
One end is growing in the ground—the other
in the air.

If earth possessed no grass, methinks its
beauty would be dead;
We'd have to make the best of it and use
baled hay instead.
I love to sing its praises in a way none can
surpass,
And girls everywhere are warned to "Please
keep off the grass."

Mr. Waterman was born in Kendall County, Illinois, a little more than thirty years ago, and when quite young moved with his parents to Creston, Iowa. Here, while working in the business department of a country daily, his talent for versifying was first discovered, even to himself. The paper on which he was employed became engaged in a controversy with its competitor, which controversy was carried by the latter into the realm of doggerel. An answer along the new line of

NIXON WATERMAN.
(Of Chicago and Boston.)

attack was imperative. Without knowing his power,—for to that time he had never written a verse,—Waterman undertook the reply. His first effort proved a success, and gave him a local reputation that subsequent writing has carried into every household of this country. Most of his life has been spent in the mid-West, where he has passed through all the experiences and adventures of an ambitious newspaper man.

It has been well known to his most intimate friends for some time that Mr. Waterman has in contemplation, and perhaps well under construction, a more serious work than has yet been published from his pen. With more relief from the grind of everyday work, and with thoroughly congenial surroundings,—such as his present position affords,—the completion of this or some other solid piece may be expected. But if this promise is never realized, the name of Nixon Waterman will live as the writer of beautiful songs — songs that touch the heart, songs that appeal to our best sentiments, songs that the whole people love, songs that will live.

MIDLAND WAR SKETCHES.

XIV. A STRAY BIT OF HISTORY — THE BRAVE GENERAL CROSS WHO FELL AT GETTYSBURG.

By J. A. SMITH.

THE other day I was requested to make an affidavit regarding the death of a man who had been a faithful Union soldier, serving humbly as "high private." He was a member of the Fifth New Hampshire regiment — the glorious "Old Fifth" that went down to the first battle of Bull Run 950 strong, came out of the Chickahominy campaign in command of a lieutenant and was the first regiment sent back home to be recruited — and was recruited three times before being attached to the Veteran Reserve corps. As I wrote out, in the formal style demanded by the pension department, an account of the death of Private John Ross, in order to help his aged widow obtain a pension,

GENERAL E. E. CROSS — WHO FELL AT GETTYSBURG.

and in writing remembered how John came home from Gettysburg with a leg broken by the feet of horses stampeded by that fearful charge of Pickett's, the thought awakened recollections a third of a century old.

Aside from the newspaper stories of that day, a slight allusion made by Albert Sage Richardson, in his "Beyond the Mississippi," and an even more vague reference in the *Century Magazine* some ten years ago, history is silent regarding this remarkable military organization and its commander.

The colonel of the "Fighting Fifth" was Edward Everett Cross. His native town was Lancaster, a small village nestled among the White Mountains in New Hampshire. He learned the printing trade there as a co-worker with Charles F. Browne, better known as "Artemus Ward." He was a reporter on the staff of the Cincinnati *Commercial Gazette* with Browne and afterward worked with Lewis, who became famous as the humorist of the Detroit *Free Press*.

Browne and Lewis were true Bohemians. Cross was molded from different metal. He was named for one of his grand old ancestors and with a later thought of Edward Everett Hale, a scion of the same stock as that Nathan Hale whose death as a spy on a British gallows is still regarded by every true American as the crowning of a martyr.

When Fort Sumter was fired upon, Edward Everett Cross was acting secretary of the new territory of Arizona. His desultory newspaper work had been so good as to secure him this political preferment.

His precarious surroundings and the odd positions in which the pioneers of that day were placed could not be better illustrated than by the story of the famous duel between Cross and Lieutenant Maury, of the U. S. Engineering Corps. The *casus belli* was the stealing of the clapper from the bell of the Catholic mission at Tucson, which was charged up to the account of Cross, as being in keeping with his general reputation for mischief and dare-deviltry. The act was bitterly resented by the Mexican population, and Maury espoused their side as against Cross. The result was a challenge to a duel with rifles, the principals to enter a large tract of timber from opposite sides and hunt each other down in Indian fashion. Cross got the first fire and "winged" Maury in the shoulder. Maury, by the way, joined the Confederate army and became chief of its signal service corps.

When the War broke out, Cross resigned as Secretary of Arizona and hurried home to join his brothers in the active service of raising Union troops. His brother Nelson had already recruited the First Long Island regiment, and another brother, Dick, went out with Ed. as major of the Fifth New Hampshire, and Frank, a boy in his early teens, went to the front a little later.

I cannot attempt, in this sketch, to follow the fortunes of the Fifth New Hampshire. While it possessed no better blood than the older regiments of the State, New England or the West, it had grand opportunities to prove of what stuff it was made.

It was at Seven Pines that Phil. Kearney, who had lost his left arm at Chapultepec during the Mexican War, having led his division in a gallant charge, is reported to have said to Ed. Cross, who, with his regiment fresh, asked where he should go in: "Oh, go in anywhere, Colonel; there's lots of good fighting all along the line."

I shall always remember a splendid piece of horseflesh that Colonel Cross "captured" at the battle of Fair Oaks. It was a thoroughbred sorrel mare. How he managed to "confiscate" it I never exactly understood. He was a splendid

horseman and had learned all the tricks of the Comanches, in Arizona. He could, when mounted on this mare, drop a handkerchief in the road, wheel her and pick it up while at full speed.

Colonel Cross' heart was almost broken "that foul night at Chantilly," when Kearney met his death from an accidental bullet. He loved Kearney, as he did Howard — O. O. Howard, the "Christian soldier" from Maine. Kearney a Catholic, Howard a staunch Protestant, Cross skeptical, though not atheistical — that was a combination of comrades tried and true. It was at Seven Pines that Howard, with his right arm shattered and faint from the loss of blood, had witnessed Kearney's charge and so admired its gallantry that he rode with his staff to Kearney's line and greeted Phil. with the cool remark, while exhibiting his undressed wound: "General, I suggest that hereafter we buy our gloves together."

The Fifth did not miss an important battle in which the Army of the Potomac was engaged before Grant took command in 1864. Many hundreds yet living can tell, with hushed voices, the fate of their husbands, fathers, brothers, sons and lovers in that terrible massacre known in history as the "Devil's Den," at Gettysburg, where Kelly's and Cross's brigades were sacrificed. Cross had been brevetted by Meade brigadier-general, for bravery on the field that terrible third of July, 1863, the setting sun of which witnessed the quenching of one of the bravest lives that has record in the history of our country. Then and there Edward Everett Cross yielded up the life he had risked a hundred times for his country and her cause.

It would seem that the sons of Ephraim and Abigail (Everett) Cross were born soldiers. The oldest, Nelson, who was a lawyer in Brooklyn when the War broke out, raised the first regiment on Long Island. The third son, Richard E., was in the regular army in 1861, but procured a discharge and went out as a lieutenant with the Fifth New Hampshire under his brother Edward. At Gettysburg he was lieutenant-colonel of the Fifth, and when Edward was given command of a brigade he acted as colonel, and upon Edward's death was duly commissioned. For some years past, Richard was a member of the treasury guard at Washington, and was "relieved by death" September 14th of last year. He was buried with military and civic honors beside his brother Edward in the old Lancaster cemetery.

MIDLAND WAR SKETCHES.

XV. SHILOH'S FIELD BY NIGHT—A PICTURE. "THE HYMN OF THE HORNET'S NEST BRIGADE."

By D. Ryan.[*]

ALL DAY long the battle had raged. Night spread her broad wings over the field. Darkness ended the day's battle. The two armies, about equal in numbers, had covered the field "thick with other clay." No field in modern history can tell such a tale of carnage. No battle of the War of the Rebellion bought victory at such fearful cost.

It was Easter Day, A. D. 1862. The Army of the Tennessee on the western shore of the river, between swollen, flanking streams, had pitched their tents. The rains and clouds of yesterday had disappeared. Heaven's blue dome, pure and bright, bent above them; the sun shone out in splendor. Above the heads of that great army, birds sang their sweetest music amid the branches of the teeming forest. Trees were putting on Spring's vestments of green. Buds and blossoms, everywhere bursting into new life, fit emblems of the Resurrection Morn, laded the air with delicate, sweet perfumes.

"But hush! Hark! A deep sound strikes like a rising knell!" Well out, and at the front 'tis heard repeated again and yet again. Who could guess that a great battle has begun! No, 'tis but artillery practice. Hark! "The heavy sound breaks in once more." This time, amid their deep intonations, is heard the rattle of musketry. Nearer and nearer upon the air is borne the "long roll" of the rattling drums and the bugle call "*To arms!*"

"And there was hurrying to and fro." The approaching sound of conflict told but too plainly that the surging tide of the first fierce onset was sweeping before it the Union arms. Stubbornly they held their ground. Fiercely fighting, they contested every foot of ground, falling back. Now, under arms, the whole army "to the rescue" hastened to the front. Then, "swiftly forming in the ranks of war," the tide of battle was arrested. Here, front to front, every available man of the two armies grappled in the struggle. All day through, the battle raged, surging backward and forward, now losing ground, now regaining; struggling, writhing and bleeding, hilt to hilt, like two giants contending in deadly combat.

From the "morning gun" till the "evening gun" how changed! Heaven's blue dome is shut out by the smoke of battle, hanging black and low like a pall. The sun, no longer "pure and bright," has, like the field it shone upon, taken on a redder hue, wrapped in its sable and battle-smoked mantle. It sinks out of sight, as if refusing longer to witness the work of human slaughter. The songs of the birds have given place to the whistle of bullets and the screech of shells. Blossoms and flowers have taken on a deeper dye. The sturdy oaks are torn and shattered as when a tornado in its course leaves the forest rent and strewn.

[*] Judge of the Ninth Judicial District of Iowa.

Night separated the combatants. The armies, exhausted and bleeding, withdrew to bivouac on "gory beds" till the morrow's sun would light them again to battle.

Between the lines, mingled one with another, lay thousands of killed or wounded, here one in blue, there one in gray.

Night drew on. Oh, that long and dreary night! Oh, that night of horrors! From the gaping and bleeding wounds of thousands, the unstaunched life-blood was ebbing in blackest darkness. With none near but those disabled or cold in death, the wounded lay all night on that horrid field.

The noise of battle had given place to the confused sounds of bivouacking armies, seeking position for a night's repose, doubtless the morrow's line of battle.

The night was well spent ere the armies slept. Hushed was the roar of battle and, in its stead, cries of the wounded were heard, broken only by the loud roar from the gunboats, whose shrieking shells at short but regular intervals all night long were hurled upon that field. The aim of the guns was directed, as well as might be, at the lines of the bivouacking enemy; but, with seemingly fateful certainty, they fell among the helpless wounded on the field.

But hark! what is that new sound that breaks in on the ear? Is it the sound of awakening guns, or do reinforcements signal to us — *or to them?* Ah! see the red lightning "painting wrath on the sky," and hear the loud thunder resound! It is as if Heaven's batteries replied to earth's feeble ordnance. Quick flashes scarce divide the loud peals of thunder. The storm, full of wrath, bursts with sudden fury, making blacker still, but for the lightning, the blackness of that black night.

When the night was well advanced, before the storm came on, out beyond and in front of the position held during the day by "The Hornet's Nest Brigade," and where the carnage was the thickest

on that field, a voice was heard singing. Striking contrast! Strange place! Sweet voice! Dear soul! Hark!

> "Jesus, lover of my soul,
> Let me to thy bosom fly!"

With this strain the voice ceased, as if the last expiring breath were expended in a dying effort. What to him now was yesterday's battle! What of to-morrow's dread conflict to come!

> "He has slept his last sleep, he has fought his last battle,
> No sound can awake him to glory again."

Short was the interval before the same inspiration, that lifted the singer above the field of battle to other realms, was caught up and this time two voices were heard:

> "Jesus, lover of my soul,
> Let me to thy bosom fly!
> While the nearer waters roll,
> While the tempest still is high!"

With the bursting of the storm, and while the tempest still was high, the song ceased. At length the storm spent its fury and was gone; but the wounded soldiers, now drenched with the rain that had cooled their fevered flesh, were still there. With the disappearing storm again arose from that field of the dead and the dying the sweet melody, — this time sung by a chorus of voices:

> "Jesus, lover of my soul,
> Let me to thy bosom fly!
> While the nearer waters roll,
> While the tempest still is high.
> Hide me, Oh! my Saviour, hide,
> Till the storm of life be past,
> Safe into the haven guide,
> Oh, receive my soul at last!
>
> "Other refuge have I none,
> Hangs my helpless soul on thee.
> Leave, Oh, leave me not alone,
> Still support and comfort me!
> All my trust on thee is stayed,
> All my help from thee I bring,
> Cover my defenceless head
> With the shadow of thy wing!"

The soldiers of the North and the soldiers of the South — their voices blended! There went up from that battle-field the sure promise of a glorious Union — one religion, one kindred, one country, one flag!

When morning came, some of those voices were hushed. In the darkness of night the icy finger of death had touched the parched lips, and tongues that had sung so sweetly the night before were forever still! The refuge of which they had sung had been attained! Others were rescued by comrades who in yesterday's battle had fiercely, savagely fought, but who now, with touch as tender and gentle as that of a loving mother, bound up the wounds and ministered to the wants of comrades. Possibly some who sung there that night are here to join hands and voices with us now. This hymn is, and of right ought to be, "The Hymn of the Hornet's Nest Brigade." *

*Read by Miss Cora Mel. Patton at the reunion of the Hornet's Nest Brigade at Newton, Iowa, August 21, 1895.

AUTUMN.

WHEN Summer follows
    The summer swallows
Where Song and Summer pass not away,
    Then Autumn, smiling,
    The world beguiling,
A bold new-comer, makes holiday.

    Her garb, with mellow
    Or argent yellow
And crimson glowing, is brave and fair ;
    And while she ranges
    The hues she changes
Till all is showing her colors rare.

    She paints the apple
    A golden dapple
Or red ; and dashes the wood receives
    From careless brushes ;
    And fiery flushes,
Bright random splashes, on shrubs she leaves.

    Then dancing, singing,
    And garlands flinging
Where'er she wantons, she moves along
    As if no sorrow
    Could fill the morrow
Despite her glory, despite her song.

William Francis Barnard.

The Midland's Fiction Department.

"A OUTPOURIN' UV DE SPERET."

A CHARACTER SKETCH.

By BELL BAYLESS.

GOING toward the kitchen last Monday morning, I heard what I knew of old to be a wordy scuffle between Uncle Israel and Aunt Cindy, the cook.

Israel was a Methodist,—a pillar of the church,— and his shiny bald head served as a reflector in the "Amen corner," where he always sat, while Aunt Cindy was a Baptist and one of the sisters who occasionally gave vent to her religious fervor by shouting in meeting; so the two kept up an unceasing war, egged on by Fanny, the house-maid, herself a Baptist but one of the younger generation.

I could hear their voices, raised to anger pitch, as I opened the door. There stood Cindy, with her dish pan of water, in the middle of the floor, while Israel had turned half 'round in his chair, neglecting his breakfast.

Quiet at once reigned but for the usual greeting, "Mawnin', Miss Kate," from the three. Cindy slammed the pan on the stove and began to put wood in the fire with unusual vigor. The old man hitched his chair a trifle farther away from her and resumed his meal.

"What is all this fuss about?" I asked.

"Nuffin but dat fool nigger a-airin' hees mouf too much in my kitchen, Miss Kate," explained the irate cook.

"Jes heah de ooman talk, now," jeered her enemy *pro tem.* "I's thes a-sayin' how dem Baptis' niggers ac' lack dey uz plum crazy 'estedy mawnin' at de baptizin'. Laws a mussy, ma'm, yo'd ortuh seed 'em!"

"What did they do?"

"O, dey'd sing an' shout an' go on lack a passel uv fools," — with a vindictive look at his opponent.

"Shet up, mon!" from her.

"Yassum, dey did. Dey all walk intuh de watah, 'ith dey han's on one nu'r's shouldahs, an' de preacha, he'd teck one at a time an' cross dey han's on dey bres', lack dis, an' den say, 'I baptize yo' in de name uv de Fadder an' uv de Son an' uv de Holy Gose'; den snatch him by de scruff uv de neck an'— swash —he'd sock him unda. De sinnah, sometimes he heels fly np an' he ha'uth be duck down 'gain, so de debble be all drownded out, an' when he come up de folks ud holler, 'Is yo' sins done wash away?' Am yo' sabed?' an' de oomans "— waving a hand toward angry Cindy—"ud holler an' shout, 'Glory! Glory! Bress de Lamb! Hallaluyah!'"

"Sich er racket ez dey kep up! Ole Levi Tanah, he jined, an' when de preacha put him unda, dey all squall out, 'Swash him unda 'gain!' An' when he come up dey say,—'I'm — he sutiney uz a *bad* un. Does yo' feel de change uv haht, bradduh?'"

"Lordy! Lordy!" -- breaking into a chuckle--" when he

reach de bank, dem oomans thes grabbed him an' hugged him, an' dey beat him an' dey kissed him tel he uz plum wore out."

"Was it down at the creek?" I questioned.

"Yassum, down tuh Two Run, raght by de Barrett Mill fo'd. Yo'd oruth a gone tuh see de show, honey."

"Heah, yo' shet up an' git outiv my kitchen, ur I'll bust yo' hajd wide open 'ith a stirk uv stove 'ood!" Thus threatened Aunt Cindy, unable to contain her wrath.

"Mighty po' cookin' dat. I see I bleeged tuh sen' my ole lady 'roun' tuh show yo' what cookin' rally am, Miss Kate." With that, he prudently retreated to his own realm, and I followed to the back porch to tell him to bring my horse around in an hour. On returning, I asked the cook what caused the trouble.

"Dat ole man Izul jes a takin' on dat a way cuz I diden' hab time tuh hot hees brekfus up 'gain when he late fur hit. He'sa mightylow down nigger, anyhow."

After some necessary orders had been given, she, eager to free her belief from Israel's ridicule, remarked,—"We sutiney hed a gloeyous outpourin' uv de speret yeste'd'y. A heap uv folks uz baptize an' p'fessed religeon."

"Did they! How many?" Those are great events among the negroes and I wanted her description.

"Twenty-seben j'ined yeste'd'y an' we 'cided tuh cahy on de pr'tracted meetin' fur nutha week; we done hed hit thee weeks a'ready."

"And so you got old Levi, did you?" He was a noted old rascal.

"Yassum, we did," In a delighted voice. "He J'ined right down at de watah, de vehy las' minit. Tell yo', we give him de raght hand uv fellowship good fashion!"

"You bet dey did," remarked Fanny, coming in from the dining-room with a tray full of dishes. "I liked to have died laffin', Miss Kate, when he come up on de bank wavin' his hat — he done 'fused tuh teck hit off when dey 'mersed him —

a shoutin', 'Dey done baptize Tanah ; glory, glory, dey got dis nigger; dey done baptize Tanah!' All de wimins grabbed him an' hugged him an' kissed him —"

"Yo' shet yo' mouf, gal," interrupted Cindy.

—"An' beat him. Grashus! Me an' Beckie an' two boys uz settin' on de rocks 'cross de creek, an' we could heah it. His cloze uz raght wet an' when dey hit him a lick it ud pop most loud as a gun goin' off.

"Miss Kate, it uz too funny! Johnny Johnson's heels flew up two times, an' he strangled when he come up 'til de preacha had tuh beat him on de back to meck him ketch his bref. Then Lizzy Kandy she shouted, 'Oh Lawd, my s-o-u-l,' ez soon ez she come to de top, an' churn de watah raght white, an' so did Tempy Goah. She grabbed de preacha roun' de neck an' neahly choked him. Te-he-he—" and Fanny wound up with such a giggle as only a colored girl can give.

"Yo' 'have yo'se'f, gal! Quit talkin' so light minded," reproved "Sissa" Whitehead.

"Well, dey did. An' Miss Kate, Mandy Davis's little Lily Estel was de sweetes' little thing I ever saw in de watah."

"That child join the church! Why, how old is she?"

"Eight yeahs old; an' she nuver strangled a bit, or even put her little han's to her face when she 'rose clense' from sin. Jes stood dar fur him tuh wipe her eyes. She looked Jes ez pretty!"

"An' Aunt Linde, she shouted," added Fanny, turning around on her way to the dining-room.

"I thought she was baptized a year ago," I remarked. Old Linde was the funniest character in our vicinity, and I will always regret not seeing her immersion.

"So she was, but she got happy an' sloshed 'round in de watah lack a toad-frog, a hollerin' an' jumpin' 'round de converts. Ef anybody ever ketches me a shoutin', I wants 'em to teck me out an' beat me good.''

"Yas, you' talks a heap," began Cindy, when Fanny interrupted :

"Aint I ez much Baptis' ez yo is, Aunt Cindy? Aint I been baptize'? Aint I pay my fifteen cents a month to de preacha?"

"Yas, but yo' aint nuver been baptize' 'ith de speret uv truth an' rishusous-ness, un all yo' young gals an' boys udn't jump up on de benches an' peer 'roun' an' laf ef some ole sista gits full uv de glory uv Gawd an' hit ovahflows tel she gits to shoutin'. Yo'd artuh be dealt 'ith, de last one uv yo', an' I'm gwine speak tuh br'er Ledbettah."

"I t'ought dat ud settle her," said Cindy in an extremely satisfied tone and with as much of a smile as she felt to be consistent with her profession, as Fanny departed.

"You wouldn't report them to the church, would you, auntie?" I asked in my most wheedlesome tone, for such a punishment is considered very severe and is most effectively held over the heads of all members.

"Course I udn't, I's jes a talkin'. De gals am too skittish nowadays."

Soon Israel drove up to the door and, as we started to town, he sniffed toward the kitchen and muttered something not very respectful about "dat nigger ooman." Then,—

"Miss Kate, yo' knows ole Cindy Whitehead, she ax yo' fur li'l kerscene lle tuh fill her lamp an' rub her rumatix 'ith. I tells yo' what she do 'ith it. She grease her feet tuh meek 'em limbah so she kin jump an' dance 'roun dat Baptis' chu'ch. She do prance scandlous! "Ef my ole lady uz tuh do dat away I'd whup her, then weah a hick'ry out on her."

Poor old Cindy! She always limped and groaned about her feet hurting her all day long in the kitchen. Could it be possible that all those aches were caused by her excessive zeal at church? I asked myself this question, but did not encourage Israel in making further disclosures, for I liked her in spite of her crabbed ways.

WHEN THE SUMMER SAID GOOD-BYE

OVERHEAD the sky was blue,
   But, about the distant rim,
   All the setting light was dim
From the haze it filtered through ;
   Yet the day seemed loth to die
When the Summer said good-bye.

Yellow all the flowers that showed
   In the meadow by the lane ;
   Yellow, too, the ripened grain
In the field beyond the road ;
   And the Golden Age seemed nigh
When the Summer said good-bye.

On the hill the corn was still ;
   Not a motion anywhere,
   Not a breath disturbed the air ;
But the evening's breathless chill
   Told us perfect days must die
When the Summer said good-bye.

Will F. Brewer.

"THE TRAGIC TREES."

A TALE OF MOB LAW.

II.

By MARGUERITE CHAMBERS KELLAR.

THE Hunter household was kept in order by one servant — an old negro woman fifty years old.

Aunt Milly was black and loquacious— one of the few left of the old-fashioned Southern negroes who wear the turban and who comb their kinky locks with "cotton cards."

"Its mighty cur'us," said Aunt Milly one afternoon, as she sat on her doorstep vigorously carding her hair.

"What is curious?" asked Miss Ruth, who happened to be passing.

"It's cur'us ter see niggers usin' combs. Freedom kin do a sight of good, an' it shuly do make a mighty change, but it beats me how it kin make nigger wool straight 'nuff ter use combs. Look at dis head. Freedom haint took er single kink outen it! Gim me de cyards, ebbery time." And she looked approvingly at the old toilet appliance.

"You wear your turban, Aunt Milly, and you'll look better than anybody."

"Chile, I's got too much rale pride ter hev my har unkivered; aldo it do look ez well ez enny of dese upstarts dats pretends ter use combs."

"Do you think it pretense, Aunt Milly?"

"Makes no difference what I think; but it 'pears ter me, chile, dat ef de Lawd had er meant fer us ter use combs, like white folks, he would made ha'r fer dat purpose. 'Stead uv dat, look here; jist look at dis!" With that she gave her head a savage raking over.

"I'm sure, Aunt Milly, your hair is nice, without that rough treatment," said Miss Ruth, smilingly.

"Honey, dat aint too rough; ter my 'pinion a rale good curryin' off wid de cotton cyards makes ebbery nigger's head feel better. It's dar natural comb, an' I

aint gwine ter lie 'bout it. I nebber did keer much 'bout freedom, cause, honey, I hed such a massa; I didn't hab no 'casion ter keer. But Lawd, Lawd, I use ter fu'rly pray fer white skin an' straight ha'r."

She called Miss Ruth "honey" and "chile," and recalled the old days by loving and ruling her alternately. A relic from a Southern plantation, she had strayed away from home just after the War. Her son Ike was alone left her of twelve children. She called him her "wah baby," because, she said, "he wuz bawn in de soun' ob de cannon."

"I 'low ter raise him up arter de patte'n ob de good ol' days,"— although he was already "raised." "He mus' work, too, aldo he is free, an' he orter git somethin' outen books."

But Ike failed to appreciate the blessing of freedom and did not take kindly to learning. He was good-natured and honest, but worked only when rags or hunger compelled him.

When Milly said, contemptuously, "Ike looks like er skeer crow," Ike worked. After a brief spell of industry, he would come up, with a broad smile on his face, and wearing a second-hand cunt of doubtful quality and still more dubious pattern —the only certainty being the pronounced inadaptability of its numerous folds to the contonr (?) of Ike's back.

But Ike did not mind that. In fact, he was in great part an unconscious disciple of Diogenes; though, if to the latter's tub and sunshine a goodly-sized "hunk" of corn bread be added, Ike might have been considered a mugwump in the camp of the epicureans. He began, all unconsciously, to usurp the place of the community in Miss Ruth's considerations;

and the combination seemed much more satisfactory. For, if the reconstruction of Ike's grammar was a hopeless undertaking, it was not a painful one, to an enthusiastic person who, in her childhood, had slyly played teacher to the one-garmented little darkies of the "Quarters."

So Miss Ruth persevered, although Milly said pathetically, "Spite uv all de pains and keer you takes wid dat boy, he exists in talkin' jes' like er Ginny nigger."

Lazy, honest, good-natured and faithful, none bore malice towards Ike. Children went to him in trouble, and he was the special kite maker for the juvenile population of the town. No kite flew so high, or sailed so fast, as one made by him; hence it happened that only in kitetime was Ike regularly employed. He possessed all the amiable traits of his race, without its vices.

The faithful service of Milly and the amiable indolence of Ike were pleasant to Miss Ruth, who still cherished the memory of the troops of half-employed lads, about other homes, under different conditions.

Occasionally Milly would protest about Miss Ruth's manner of "spilin' dat boy, ontwil he's no yearthly 'count." But the sight of Ike, reclining against the back fence, picking a chicken for dinner, only made Miss Ruth feel more at home.

The little household was in this state of domestic satisfaction when Mr. Hunter left for a week's absence.

The very next day after his departure, Milly came rushing into Miss Ruth's room, her eyes wide with fear and the tears rolling down her black cheeks, as she cried, "Oh, Lawd hab mercy! it come — it come; de day ob tribulation is 'pon me; de las' ha'r is laid on dis po' ol' back to break it, now. It's come, an' I's got no strength ter bar' enny mo'! Seven chillen scattered to de ends ob de yearth, an' now dis las' po' baby gone!"

"Good Heavens, Aunt Milly, what's the matter?" questioned Miss Ruth, startled out of her senses by the strange sight.

"Dey's got Ike. Oh, Lawd!"

"Who have?" asked Miss Ruth, quickly.

"De men, de perlice; dey's takin' him ter jail. Oh, Lawd! send fer Marse Charles 'fore it's eve'lastin'ly too late!"

"Hush! Tell me what Ike did."

"Nuffin', nuffin'."

"Aunt Milly, if Ike is arrested, he must have done something. What was it?"

"He only jis' hit er white boy, an' dey tuck him ter jail de nex' minute; dey jis' grabbed him, an' dey'll mob him, sho!"

"No they wont; that is never done now," said Miss Ruth firmly.

"Honey, you don' know dese white folks; you fergits whar you is."

"I know you are a frightened old goose," Miss Ruth reassuringly said. "Do try to tell me the worst."

The old creature was in such a paroxysm of terror, it seemed impossible to get the truth.

"He hit him wid er knife."

At this information, Miss Ruth turned pale, and said hurriedly, "He did not kill him?"

"No'm, he jist hit him; dey wuz quarreling, an' dey bofe hed knifes."

"Who was the other boy?"

"Dat no 'count Lige Gage; er low down, triflin' white trash from 'Possum Range. I tol' Ike, time an' ergin, not ter 'sociate wid him; nuffin' 'bout him like white folks, 'ceptin' his skin, an' dat wuz mos'ly kivered wid dirt. Showed he warnt no 'count hy his always 'sociatin' wid er nigger." For a moment she lost sight of her trouble, in contempt for "po' white trash," that peculiar class so especially abhorred by the Southern negroes.

Miss Ruth essayed to comfort her, saying, "Ike will come out all right; everybody likes him."

"Dat don' make no difference; taint like de good ol' days when we hed our own white folks ter keer fer us. Dar's always somebody ter peck on us. What de Lawd made us black fer, I don' know."

"There are laws to protect both white and black," said Miss Ruth.

But Milly gazed helplessly at her, and muttered, "Dey will hang my po' boy, an' dat Lige will be de cause."

"Oh, I'm sure Lige is not badly hurt; let me go out at once."

She hurried over to Mrs. Mathes', and learned the following facts:

It was a street brawl; the two boys were playing a game of marbles "for keeps"; had quarreled and, in the excitement, had drawn their pocket knives, and Ike had used his too effectively for his own or for Lige's good. The latter had been hauled home in a wagon, to die, so report said.

Miss Ruth returned to Milly much troubled. If the fellow died it would go hard with Ike. Lawyers' fees in the beginning, and more trouble in the end. A sad fate for "de wah baby."

Suspense was brief for, within the next hour, news came that Lige was dead.

Miss Ruth went to the kitchen to comfort Milly, whom she found rocking to and fro, groaning in a pitiable fashion. "Dey will hang him, sho!" was the burthen of her cry.

"Aunt Milly, he must have a trial before anything can be done to him," said Miss Ruth.

"De trial will be mine, honey."

"Aunt Milly," tenderly continued the patient mistress, "try to understand that Ike must be tried for murder, and, if he killed Lige in self-defence, he will be acquitted. Remember, that is the law, and nothing can change it."

"It may be de law, but it aint de practice, chile. You is mighty smart, mighty nigh ez smart ez you is good, an' when I says dat, I 'lows you ler stan' purty nigh to de angels; but honey, smart an' good ez you is, you don' know ez much 'bout de ways here ez ole black Milly."

Knowing Milly's habit of perpetual motion, after once getting under way, Miss Ruth changed the subject, saying, "Hurry now, get supper, and let us go to the jail."

"What mus' I git?"

"Oh, something nice, and we can take Ike some."

An old-time delicious supper was the result of this vague order. Tender waffles, broiled chicken, eggbread and amber coffee. None but an old Southern negro cook can give the particular flavor to these viands, and serve them with the caressing, deferential manner so dear to those who knew it in the old days, and who, having known it, can never forget. A retinue of trained help may be efficient, but fails in the homely care, the patronizing devotion, found only in the dusky servant of the old South.

The memory of it is passing away; the present generation knows it only by tradition. To the negro lad of the present, the gentle, courteous demeanor of his parents is an example to be shunned, as if it were only the badge of slavery, and, in shunning it, he too often adopts rudeness instead.

The modern white youth passes carelessly by the old Aunty whom his parents loved. He has no memory of long Sunday afternoons, when the greatest treat was a rummage through "Mammy's chist"; nor has he ever tasted such delicious cakes baked on the sly; nor ridden on strong shoulders in quest of muscadines; nor engaged in wild romps with the little darkies at "the Quarters."

With freedom began race antagonism, which is gradually sweeping away, not only sentiment, but often justice. The kindly feeling that existed so generally, between master and slave, has not been transmitted to the present generation. It is no longer master and slave, with certain ties and sentiments; but it is white and black, with hatred and contempt on one side, fear and distrust on the other.

The supper was a sad one, and Miss Ruth dispatched it hurriedly. With her own hands she arranged Ike's supper on the tray, putting on a double quantity of his favorite dishes. She was a foolish old maid, no doubt, or she would have felt indignant instead of sorry.

Milly took the tray, balanced it on her head in some mysterious way and the two women hurried to the jail — a substantial stone building a short distance away.

The jailer conducted them to the cell where Ike was confined, and Milly silently set the supper down, while great tears coursed down her cheeks, and Ike himself looked gray with pain.

"What does this mean, Ike?" Miss Ruth asked, seriously.

His good natured face was changed to an expression of horror; his hopeless eyes looked up, and he exclaimed, "Miss Ruth, I swear he tried ter kill me fust."

"He struck first?" she asked.

"Yes'm, I kin prove it."

"Who were present?"

"A lot uv boys, white an' black; dey seed it all."

"What caused the quarrel?"

"He cheated me an' cussed me. I didn't keer 'bout de cussin', but," here he looked down, "he wuz 'bout ter git all my marbles, pures an' all, by his raskifly cheatin'. Den, when I 'cused him uv it, he whipped out his knife an' hit me."

"How often have I told you that playing marbles for keeps was gambling, and gamblers are apt to be punished in some way."

"Yes'm, an' de minute I seed dat Lige wuz hurt, I 'membered you, an' 'bout dat same minute de perlice grabbed me."

"Oh, Ike," said Milly, speaking for the first time, "ef you hed only minded me, an' kep' away from po' white trash, dis trouble would not be."

"Ef de Lawd gits me safe outside, I *will* mind. I'll nebber fergit my prayers, an' you shant nebber pump ennudder bucket er water, en' Miss Ruth's fire shant nebber die out,—an' I'll men' my ways, even ter talkin'," he concluded solemnly.

Miss Ruth's heart was getting softer and warmer every moment toward the poor creature who looked appealingly at her and continued, with that garrulity so remarkable in his race:

"I wish I hed minded you an' not played fer keeps; but when I seed him er cheatin' me outen my fine agates an'

pures, I wuz bleeged ter say somethin'. Miss Ruth, dey do say dis is er case dey call bailable. Please try ter git me out."

"Certainly, Ike, we will soon have you free. Keep up your courage until Mr. Hunter comes home; but remember, it is an awful thing to kill a human being, and is only excusable in self-defence." After a moment, she said, gently, as she turned to leave, "Good-bye, until you come to make my fire again."

Standing outside, in the hall, talking to the jailer, she heard Milly beseeching Ike to pray. "Pray wid all yo' heart, chile. Bress de Lawd fer prayer. De Lawd kin hear, no matter whar you is, an' He is yo' hope dis night. Put not your trust in men, but in de Lawd. Pray widout ceasin'. Good-bye, my po' little wah baby."

"Cheer up, cheer up, Aunt Milly," said the old jailer. "Cheer up! Ike is all right."

But Miss Ruth, obeying the instincts of her alert, eager soul, sought out the sheriff, who laughed at her fears, saying, "Ike will be out in no time, on bail. He was justifiable."

"But," said Miss Ruth, "Aunt Milly is half crazy about a mob."

"Not a bit of danger. If I thought so, I'd guard the jail. Oh, you can trust me in this, Miss Hunter," as he noticed her anxious, doubting glance. "The boy will not be troubled. The community is well rid of that fellow, Gage, anyway."

Shocking as was this view of the sacredness of human life to the troubled and perplexed woman, she returned with a lighter heart, saying to the sorely tried old negro, "Go to bed, Aunt Milly, your boy is safe."

But Milly looked at her solemnly and said, "You don' know de folks like I do."

"I know you to be a foolish old woman, not to believe me."

"Chile, ef it rested wid you, an' dem like you, dar would be no doubt; but dar is jist ez much difference twixt folks as twixt white an' black skin; an' I swar 'fore de Lawd dat de folks in dis God-fersaken lan' is de bloodiest minded on de face ob de yearth. I 'low some day dey will wipe each udder clar out; an' a good thing dat would be. Dese folks is needer Norf nor Souf, but jis' *mean*. Lawd, I kin 'member when po' fool niggers down Souf 'lowed dis state wuz de aidge uv de lan' uv promise; de Mount Nebo ob Scripture. But gib me de ol' plantation ebbery time; fer I nebber see such awful doin's dar ez I see here. Honey, take yo'self fer er patte'n. Ef you hed been bawn here you would be er different creetur, to my 'pinion. You sholy would not be de angel you is. De Norf an' de Souf orter stop 'busing each udder, an' club togedder to chain de debbil dats loose in 'munities like dis, dat is needer one nur de udder, only jis' middlin'; 'cept in meanness, den dey go de whole hog. 'Deed, chile, you don' know dese folks, an' I's feard, I's feard!"

"Well, stop talking. Go to bed, and be up early with a good breakfast for Ike."

But Milly slowly shook her head, and an impatient expression clouded Miss Ruth's face, as she began to fear she was dealing with a spoiled, self-opinionated old woman. It was clear to anyone that the elements of a mob were not in apathetic Bourbonsville.

Disturbed somewhat in temper, but with fears at rest, she was not long in settling herself to an evening's reading. Her book was Tolstoi's wonderful "Anna Karenina," and she forgot Bourbonsville, Ike's danger and Milly's trouble, until the town bell, ringing out twelve strokes, hurried her to bed, where she was soon dreaming that the beautiful, misguided Anna was a happy wife and honored woman. Then, with the curious perversity of souls in dreamland, Miss Ruth became the guest in Count Tolstoi's house. Instead of the bare floors she had expected to see, her feet sank into luxurious carpets, and the great author, instead of being dressed in peasant's garb, wore the rich costume of a king. Nothing answered to the description she had read. Perplexed and irritated, she attempted to reconcile the contradictions, but no one would assist her. On the contrary, hordes of ridiculously small demons conspired to puzzle and harass her.

With the strange incongruity of dreams, a Russian prince was presented to her, dressed in a coarse blue blouse, while the smell of the hay-field floated to her senses. Presently he was transformed into Milly, wearing a crimson robe, ermine trimmed, with a striped cotton handkerchief wound about her head. She was on her knees, sobbing out that Ike had been sent to Siberia for life. Her sobs grew loud and oppressive, yet no one noticed her, and Miss Ruth was beginning to think Tolstoi a heartless old man, when she awoke, suddenly, hearing Milly's voice in reality, and in tones of terror.

"Miss Ruth! Miss Ruth! For God's sake, wake up!" and her knocks thundered on the door.

Springing out of bed, Miss Ruth opened the door. The next moment Milly was in the room, on her knees, clinging to her. The bright turban was gone from her head, and the gray hair shone strangely in the half-lighted room. It looked weird and unearthly,—a high white crown over her dark brow; her eyes, wild and despairing; her poor black face drawn in agony.

"What is it, Aunt Milly?" asked Miss Ruth, when speech came to her.

At that instant a sound broke on her ears, making her very flesh afraid. It was the awful clamor of frightened men. Let those who have never heard it be thankful.

"What is it?" she asked, as she stood, shaking from head to foot.

"De mob! De mob!" moaned the poor heap on the floor.

"God of heaven, is it that?" and she involuntarily covered her ears to shut out the sound.

"Dey's beatin' de jail do' down, don' you hear?"

Yes, she heard. Blow after blow fell on the door and, above all, rose the wild cries of the helpless prisoners.

The shrieks of despair were borne out on the night air until even the babes in Bourbonsville must have awakened in terror.

Artists have won fame by putting on canvas the faces of men in agony; but no written or spoken word has ever adequately portrayed the human voice, under the certainty of an awful fate.

"Murder! Murder! God help us!" And ringing out, clear and distinct from the rest, came, "Miss Ruth, fer de Lawd's sake, come!"

It was Ike's voice.

Miss Ruth was not brave in its proper meaning,—readiness to meet clearly defined peril; but great excitement destroyed in her all sense of danger. So, that at the sound of Ike's voice, pity and ungovernable rage possessed her. She started to the door; she would save the poor fellow; she would control the maddened crowd and return unharmed and successful. It was not danger but victory she sought. "Come!" she cried, "Hurry!"

But Milly's voice, hoarse and frightened, yet determined, answered, "Not fer yo' life!" Her strong hand pulled her back. The great, faithful heart, with the instinct of early habit, took heed to the beloved mistress. The slave spirit of self-abnegation returned to her in that supreme and awful moment, as she remembered that fiends, not men, were outside. What was she; what was hers; what was anything, compared to this sweet, delicate "chile," exposed to the vulgar, brutal, midnight marauders.

"Stay here; I'll run fer de sheriff!" And, before Miss Ruth could understand her intentions, she had taken the key, rushed out and locked the door on the outside and was gone, leaving her mistress a prisoner.

Miss Ruth went to the window and looked down in helpless despair. A knot of men were on the street, talking in low, excited tones; they came and stood under her window.

"Go, help them! Arouse the sheriff!" she cried.

Someone answered, "We can't do anything; there's a hundred men in that mob."

"Oh, my God, try to save Ike!" she implored, leaning far out of the window, and reaching her hands down in a pitiful way.

"It's Ike they are after, and we better not interfere."

She was wild and intemperate, no doubt, when she cried out in answer, "Oh, you cowards and heathen, come and help me out! I can save him!"

"Umph! Your life wouldn't be worth a cent. A woman don't count for much on these occasions. They stopped Milly; she will never find Hogan."

"But you can find him. Go! Go, for God's sake do something!"

"Miss Hunter, you know nothing about these affairs. Get back from the window. There, they have got him out now."

Miss Ruth could do no more.

The crowd was coming by her door. Baffled at every point, she threw herself down on the bed and buried her face in the pillows, sobbing hysterically. She knew they were dragging him to his death; that the stars would witness, and the innocent maple trees become again the instrument of, a crime. Yet she would not despair. She got up, shook her door frantically and called aloud, forgetting the emptiness of the house.

If she could only get out, she would yet save Ike.

They would not dare touch a woman! A woman? They would lay hands on an angel, if one stood in their way. God only could soften such hearts! With that thought she prayed, as she had never prayed before, for God to save the good-natured boy who would not wantonly hurt the smallest insect. Her last desperate petition, born of utter helplessness, was "Let me not know!"

The cries of the helpless, the low curses of the mob, came nearer; and again Ike's strong young voice, wild with fear, called, "Miss Ruth! Miss Ruth!"

She answered that, like a spirit of mercy; her voice, instinct with power and passion, rang out in a last despairing appeal to the men who held him, and a fiend's words came to her shocked ears, "The damn nigger shall swing!"

And then a pitiful God gave her oblivion.

When she recovered consciousness, Milly was sitting by her bedside, rubbing her hands; the room was filled with the odor of camphor, and the doctor was present. The gray light of early morning was struggling through the window, mingling with the blaze of the still burning lamp.

"What is the matter?" she whispered.

"Hush, honey. Go to sleep."

The old doctor stepped softly to the bed and said, "You have had a sudden illness, but you are all right now."

"Ah, it is all a dream, then. Where is Ike?" It all came back to her, even before Milly's trembling voice answered:

"He is wid de Lawd."

No race find in religion the prompt and full compensation for trials that the negroes do. It is much more than an ideal faith; and Milly possessed this in superabundance. Added to this was the lifelong slave training, which gave her character the same element of strength that mental discipline gives the scholar. Her habit of self-repression, and her fervent piety, calmed her grief; but the sad old face was pitiable.

The next week the Hunters left Bourbonsville, taking Milly with them.

A month later, in their Southern home, Miss Ruth received a letter from Mrs. Mathes, containing among other items the following piece of news:

"A terrific storm devastated this section, last week; houses were destroyed and the lightning blasted those three sugar maples you thought so beautiful.

"The negroes, however, with their foolish superstition, say 'de ghosts hab done it at las.'

"This reminds me to tell you, it was all a mistake about that boy, Lige Gage. He got well. I saw him in town to-day."

A FADED FACE.

IT IS no longer debonair,—
    This picture in the antique case;
    Why, you can barely mark the face
Which once with beauty shone so fair,
    And wore a seraph's gentle grace.

A child's sweet face! Ah, now you see
    A dash of little ringlets brown
    Which once enraptured all the town,
When, 'neath her spell of witchery,
    The boy-god cast his weapons down.

She reigns to-day, a child no more;
    In cap and frill of spotless white
    She greets the children as the light
Of even fades on sea and shore,
And kisses one and all "good-night."

T. C. Harbaugh.

"A HOME O' ME OWN."

SKETCHES FROM LIFE IN LABOR'S WORLD. II.

By Eugenie Uhlrich.

THE offices of Mr. Charles M. Scanlan, lawyer, were on the sixth floor, high enough above the noise and dust of the street to be comfortable. The suite was furnished with a substantial elegance that indicated the successful man. The thick carpet of the outer room permitted no footfall to disturb the conferences of Mr. Scanlan and his clients in the private office. This morning Mr. Scanlan was out, and the typewriter was busily writing out sundry petitions, demurrers, etc., undisturbed by thought of interruption. Suddenly the subtle current imparted to the atmosphere by a presence made her look up with a start. The building in which Mr. Scanlan's offices were located was very satisfactorily regulated. Beggars, book agents, etc., were strictly prohibited, so she had no opportunity to be familiar with figures such as the one confronting her. Mr. Scanlan's specialty is corporation law and his clients are well dressed, easy mannered, confident business men. To these she was accustomed to say, with a regretful smile at the untoward circumstance which inflicted any inconvenience on them, that Mr. Scanlan was engaged, or out, or had left word so and so,—asking them to be seated, tendering them the morning paper, etc. In accepting these little natural courtesies from Mr. Scanlan's neat stenographer and occasionally chatting with her pleasantly, they were conscious of no particular condescension. Her attire was simple and becoming, her language well chosen,—probably due to the effect of the continual copying of Mr. Scanlan's forceful rhetoric,—her wit keen ; they even sometimes enjoyed it — in the office, of course.

This time her ready smile congealed on her lips, leaving her mouth rather stupidly open, as she stared at the man in front of her. No wonder he came in noiselessly.

He could hardly have been expected to walk on his almost soleless shoes with the firm, self-conscious tread of the prosperous frequenters of Mr. Scanlan's office. He stood now, resting uneasily on one foot, turning a greasy slouch hat in his soiled fingers, while he looked at the girl, his throat throbbing under the stress of his embarrassment. Once, twice, he opened his mouth to speak, but each time closed it again with a convulsive gulp. His thin coat had a new look, suggesting some recent "raise." Otherwise his clothes were soiled and worn into a dingy indefiniteness of color, but had not yet reached the buttonless dilapidation of the tramp. His striped woolen shirt was dirty with the wear of many days, but there was a black tie knotted under the collar. There was still hope for him. The creases in his neck were outlined in black, his face was dark with a stubby growth of beard, and it struck her disagreeably that his mouth was slightly open, as if held so habitually. But he had thick dark hair and his blue eyes were fixed upon her in the struggle for speech with the pleading, helpless look of a dumb animal. Perhaps she was partial to dark hair and blue eyes ; at any rate, to her credit be it said, after the first hasty survey, she smiled again as affably as to the most influential of Mr. Scanlan's clients.

"Do you wish to see Mr. Scanlan ?"

The soft voice and pleasant smile acted like a charm. He became as garrulous as he had been dumb.

"Yis, Oi wanted to shpake to him." It had not needed the broad brogue to show his origin. "Ye see it wor this way. Oi cum up from Omaha where Oi've been tryin' for worruk these three month past, with niver a dacent job."

"Nothing at all ?" she asked.

Oh, yes, he had had a half-day here and another there, possibly enough for a good day's work in a week. A man had promised him work right along and he thought it meant a place of a couple of weeks perhaps, and then he found that it was only a little cleaning up that took him about a day and a half. But the man meant to be good to him, bring he was one of his own race, and gave him a letter of recommendation to show that he was an honest man. The work he had done for that man — Sullivan was his name and he was a lawyer — was the last work he had done for three weeks.

She interrupted him. "Have you no trade?"

"Yis, that Oi have. Oi do paint houses. But who's after wanting houses painted in these toimes? Oi havn't had a dacent turn at me thrade these four months or more. It's been nothing but a dab here an' a dab there, and they kept saying as how this wor such a loively place, Oi thought Oi'd come up here an thry me luck."

"When did you come?"

"Last night." She forbore to ask him how he came. She was sure it was not by leave of the ticket office nor on a pass granted by the president of the road.

"Oi had a card from Father Meagher last noight that got me lodgin' down here." He said this as if trying to impress upon her his claim to respect.

"Why didn't you go out into the country?"

"The plantin' is all over and harvest is still a long while off."

All the time he had been fumbling in his inner pocket and now produced a type-written letter, — dirty, broken at the corners and almost worn through in the creases, — and handed it to her.

She looked at it gingerly. Possibly the contrast between her own crisp sheets and his letter struck him and he said, apologetically, "It's moighty dirty, but how's a man goin' to keep things clean, knockin' round in his pockets."

She smiled and began to read the few words of recommendation, signed by the name of a man with whose standing and reputation as a lawyer she was familiar.

"You know the man?" he asked eagerly.

"I have heard his name."

"Then you know Oi'm all right."

She nodded, and gave him back the letter. He folded it carefully and replaced it in his pocket; then he turned to her with more dignity than he had yet shown.

"Oi've only been seven months in this country, so Oi didn't have any papers of enny koind, an' Mr. Sullivan wor afther thinkin' this leither moight help me, seein' as there wor a poor show fer a fellow wid no one to wrote him a character."

"Why did you come to this country, anyway?" To her keenly practical sense the motives that would induce the being before her to take the chances of an alien land had the fascination of the incomprehensible.

"They did say, mum, that ivery mon has a chance over here, — a harrud chance mebbe; but there's not even that for the loikes of me in the ould counthry, an' then there wor a colleen over there that Oi wor moinded to bring over to a home o' me own some day, an' settle down an' — an' marry."

Under the tan and grime of the face in front of her a flush crept up to the forehead. She dropped her eyes, shrinking with innate delicacy from gazing on his confusion, lowly as he was. With no elaboration of words or emotional effects he had voiced the hope and the woe of all life, and the expression appealed to her as something giving him a kinship she had not before recognized. Against the background of common human suffering the latent possibilities of the man's life stood out in a light that gave him a new dignity. It was not much he asked — merely the right to work, to earn a little spot somewhere, a home, amply paid for by the work of his hands. There were thousands, — she knew many herself, — with incomes that would have seemed princely to this man, whose aspirations did not go as high.

She spoke again, with more seriousness than previously. "What did you want of Mr. Scanlan?"

He explained that the lawyer had given him Mr. Scanlan's name as that of a man who would be apt to give some consideration to a letter from him and also, being of Irish antecedents, probably more inclined to generosity in this case than he otherwise might be.

"Oh, yes," the girl said, "he is always liberal. Come back again at 3 o'clock. Meantime you might look around. Have you been to the packing houses?"

"Faix, mum, it's turnin' away men they're doin', instid o' takin' 'em on."

"To the foundry?"

"Indade, mum, at the foundry an' at the car shops. Iverywhere I wor this mornin' they're layin' off the men, an' where they nade help, they're takin' back ould hands." She looked preplexed, for she knew his statement was but too true.

"They do tell me," he resumed, "that there's a hrick factory up here on the river that's been hirin' men. Could you kindly be afther tellin' me the best way to get there?"

"Oh, yes," she said, eagerly, delighted to think of the possibility of work for him, for by this time she was convinced that he was honestly looking for it. An indifferent stranger could not have acquired such familiarity with the names and places in so short a time. She glanced at the clock. Why, it was only 9:30 now! She rose and went to the open window with its fluttering awnings to direct him to the works. The outlook was over the lower part of the city, seamed with railroad tracks and black with the smoke of locomotives and factory chimneys. The man nervously followed her, as she pointed out quickly the marks by which he would know the way.

It led him over the black tracks, over which, even at this hour of the day, quivering waves of heat seemed to hang, down along the crescent of the distant river. Everything in the landscape intensified the heat. The rolling hills in the distance were a parched, greenish yellow line against the sky, hard to separate from its ecru edge. Even the patches of the rank, vivid yellow-green growth, which filled the soggy ground on the edge of the banks riff-raffed against the greedy river, seemed a species of glaring flame. The hot, heavy wind whipped the sand on the bank in the center of the churning river. In the far distance the railroad high bridge hung like a fretwork in the air. Away beyond this she directed him.

"It's about five miles from here," she concluded briskly.

"Ten moiles to get back here?" he asked. A pitiable lonk came into his face. A sudden thought struck her.

"Have you had any breakfast?"

"No, mum, me ticket didn't call fer breakfast. Oi'd been thinkin' Oi'd be loike the early birrud," he said with a smile and a weak attempt at a joke. "But if Oi axed for it now onnywhere Oi might be run in an' that ud be the end o' me, to'be sure."

She went and got her purse. There was a solitary quarter of a dollar in it, along with some car fares. It was all she had.

She handed him the quarter and, to avoid his thanks, continued talking to him. "Mr. Scanlan will surely have some sort of encouragement, so if you don't get anything come back this afternoon."

———

At 3 o'clock the girl was filing some papers in the inner room. Mr. Scanlan was at his desk. There was a hesitating step in the outer room. The girl looked out and smiled encouragingly — behind Mr. Scanlan's back. The man's face, she noted, was red and hot, as if from a long walk. He came in and stood in a corner of the room. The girl slipped out. She somehow felt her benevolence submerged in a sudden fear of ridicule, as she looked at the hesitating being waiting for Mr. Scanlan to deign to turn and speak.

"Did you want to see me?"

"I come to see if you couldn't help me to get worruk. Oi've a letter here," fumbling for it, "that'll show ye Oi'm all

right. Oi haven't had a turn of worruk
for three weeks, an' if it would plaze yer
honor to help me a bit —''

He cut him short with ''I have to work
hard every day to keep my own affairs
and a family, and nobody helps me. If
I waited for any help from others I'd
starve and go in rags, too.''

He drew himself up in his chair and
looked scrutinizingly over his glasses at
the sorry figure in front of him.

The girl in the other room was thunder-
struck. This was not what she had
expected from Mr. Scanlan, but —, well,
helping a poor devil make a man of himself and heading a subscription list for a
fashionable charity are two different
things. She stole a glance at the man.
The crushing effect of Mr. Scanlan's
remarks seemed lost on him, however.
He was frantically searching his pockets,
his face full of a piteous despair. Then
he stepped back and said to her: ''Oi
can't find me letter, mum, an' Oi haven't
had that letter out since Oi showed it to
ye this mornin', mum?''

His appeal to her annoyed her as the
evidence of a sympathy she did not now
care to admit.

''I saw you put it back into your
pocket,'' she said stiffly.

She was Mr. Scanlan's clerk, and it
did not become her to set up a different
standard of morals and courtesy in his
office than his own — even if she had the
courage to do so.

The man looked at her, — a beaten,
hopeless look. He had lost his last, cherished badge of respectability and he
seemed dazed, unable to move or speak.
He only stared at her in an aggravatingly
expectant way. She had been so sympathetic in the morning, it seemed impossible to him that she could not suggest
something now that would help him overcome this last dreadful blow. But she

turned coldly to her work, ashamed, yet
too weak to do otherwise. Mr. Scanlan
had resumed his work several minutes
before.

———

The afternoon papers of the next day
contained among the police court reports
the following :

''Thomas McGuire, found sleeping
among box cars. Arrested for vagrancy
and ordered to leave town within twenty-
four hours.''

The girl read it with a sigh. The fate
he had dreaded had overtaken him. The
great edict had gone forth to ''move on,''
and he was marked henceforth, — a
pariah. ''Move on'' would follow him
wherever he went. In furtive snatches
only would even the earth and the sky be
his, for every footstep would be guarded
by the forces of organized society.

''MOVE ON !''

STORY OF A GIRL'S VENGEANCE.

By Charles A. Kent.

THE summer was nearly over. The fierce rays of the August sun twisted the sky line on the far sand hills, and drove the lizards and "rattlers" to seek the scant shade afforded by clumps of leaden sage-brush. A cluster of "devil tongue" cacti stood brushing the side of the sod house when the wind blew, tracing a quadrant on the crumbling wall.

But to-day everything was still. A locust mounting the air flew away singing, and with the coming of eventide crickets issued from beneath the clapboards that stripped the roof of the "shanty." All else was silent.

This shanty, which to Jack Gundall was "home," had three rooms, bedroom, kitchen — which did duty for pantry, parlor and "sittin' room" — and Lede's room.

"Lede," or Orleana, as she was properly called, was the only child of Jack Gundall and his wife. She was a suntanned, rollicking girl of seventeen, the one rich gift of their prairie home. And although Mrs. Gundall, as a teacher "back East," in her school life had acquired a polish of manner belonging to kindlier surroundings, Lede had never so much as seen a city and, save her Saturday evening ride of five miles to the nearest "post" for the papers, there were but few persons or places included in her acquaintance.

With one exception.

A trip down the valley earlier in the summer, to where the Champion River pours its waters into the greater Republican River, stands out as a bright spot in Lede's life. One bright morning in June Mr. Gundall hitched up to the wagon and drove his wife and Lede to a camp-meeting where the rivers meet.

Parson Crago preached a long sermon on "Doomsday" or some equally terrible subject, and Lede remembered at least the voice and appearance of the parson as he announced in a ponderous way, his text: "Vengeance is mine: I will repay, saith the Lord."

The novelty of this camp-meeting was the wonder and joy of Lede for many days thereafter. She liked to remember the hymns heard that day, and wondered what the people meant when they sang at the last, "God be with you till we meet again." Her untutored soul drank in all of that day's gladness, and she dreamed of Parson Crago, of his wonderful text, and of the sweet songs of Zion, wishing that the time to "meet again" might not be so far away. She was hulling beans this afternoon, sitting in the kitchen, talking with her mother in the next room. You could hear their sharp Kentucky voices a long way off on that still afternoon. The father had gone that day on horseback to look after their tree-claim, which lay north of the Champion River, on the higher valley known as "second bottom." The sun was nearing the western horizon; the prairie dogs in their "town" over on the hill had ceased their barking and betaken themselves to their holes. Looking through the window, Lede glanced down the slope and across the valley. There was a cleft in the hills on the other side, Coyote Notch they called it. "Daddy," as Lede familiarly called him, was working in there and the girl knew it must be time to expect him home. The sun slid down behind the hills; the owls swept to and fro in the purple gloaming; and Lede and her mother were still waiting. The house, which had been closed during the day to shut out the sun, was now opened, and mother and daughter sat in the doorway. But Lede was tired of waiting. Her father had been gone so long.

"Mother," spoke up the girl at last, and the prolonged scream of a coyote

447

CHARLES A. KENT.

down in the canyon added to the loneliness of the place, "Mother, I'll git the pony and go and meet daddy."

The mother did not answer at once. She hesitated at the prospect of either being left for a time alone or waiting longer for her husband's return. Then she said: "You may go, child, but be careful. I think I can trust you."

"Well, you git the blanket, Mother, and I'll go over and see what daddy's doin'. Git the whip over the door and I'll buckle the blanket on Old Nolan."

The desert darkness whispered its tales to Lede as she sped away on the sanded trail, for the wilds of the prairie hold many wonders to him who cares to listen.

But she heard not yet the darkest tale that night to be revealed.

The air was warm or chill as she traversed the plain or descended to the valley. The cuts given Old Nolan by the thong in Lede's hand were unheeded. Now and then the horse would plunge forward, impelled by an unfriendly thrust from a cactus spine brushed by his lean side.

At last the girl reached the canyon.

The low whinney of her father's horse, tied to a young ash at the corner of the claim, drew her on. How terribly silent it was there! She listened; no sound. She hallooed softly, but her voice was so multiplied by the echoing canyon that she was too terrified to shout again. She went on. Leaving Old Nolan to forage on the buffalo grass, she followed a winding trail to the grove on their claim.

There was her father, sitting on the ground, leaning against his saddle which he had taken from the horse.

The moon had pushed her silver horn high over the hills till the whole canyon was bathed in her soft rays. But Lede could not see her father's face, for his head was bent forward and hidden by the brim of his hat.

"Daddy!" Her voice pierced the painful stillness. "I come to see 'f you was ever comin' home. I brung you a blanket, Daddy, 'f you want to stay all night. Why didn't you come home a good while ago, b'fore you was clean fagged out?"

He did not stir. A puff of cold wind came racing down the hills and, striking her breast, made her shiver. A bright star, shooting across the zenith, lit up the scene, only to leave her in a lonelier darkness which the moon could not fully melt away. She stepped nearer and shook him.

"Daddy, wake up! You'll git your death o' cold sleepin' out in the night this way. And here maw an' me's been watchin' an' waitin' for you hours, till our eyes an' patience is clear give out an' I've come fur you. It's kind o' mean of you, Daddy."

She shook the form again. This time the head fell back. The paleness there was not made by the moonlight alone.

"Heaven help us! Daddy! Daddy! Why don't you wake up?"

She felt the face,—cold now! The touch chilled her very bones. She placed her hand over his heart; no life was there.

"Daddy! Daddy!" The whole canyon heard her piercing, lonely cry,—"My father! He can't be—dead!"

A lizard tumbled from a rock near by. An owl—sentinel of the deserted silence—gave a muffled hoot, and the coyotes down the canyon set up their hideous barking.

Lede with great effort stifled her anguish; her feeling of fear and loneliness was only overcome when, hearing again the chorus of barks down the canyon, she determined to save the body of her father from the jaws of the hungry coyotes.

"I'll take you home, Daddy! They *shan't* get you, now!"

Her breath came easier as she spoke. Grasping the form at her feet by the shoulders, holding the body off the ground as much as possible, she dragged it to the place where her horse was feeding. Rolling the body to a projecting rock and leading Nolan to the edge, she succeeded finally in strapping it to her blanket. Then turning it over, the back was thrown fairly into the moonlight.

She saw a streak of blood down the shirt, and at the top, near the shoulder, a bullet hole. With a shudder she let the body fall. There was blood on her hands and dress! Her eyes took on a livid greenness. Her lips grew nervously pale as she muttered between her teeth one word, "*Indians!*"

But she clutched at the lifeless form which, though having fallen squarely across the back of Old Nolan, now, under the unsteady pose of the horse, was shifting toward her and would fall to the ground.

They had murdered him, then! And he had died at his post of duty! Her eyes shot up the canyon with an awful gleam. Her clenched fist was poised in air.

She fastened the body securely across the back of Old Nolan. Taking his rein she mounted her father's horse and led the way down the shadowy canyon, across the river, and up the hills again,—home. Her mother was still up, and hearing at times the coyotes, the owls, and now the sound of hoofs, she came to the door.

"Is that you, Lede? Where have you been? And did you find your father?" she asked all in one breath, for she was weary with waiting.

The girl leaped from her horse and made her way to the door, where her mother stood.

"O, Maw! Maw!" cried the poor girl, "they've killed Daddy! The Indians have killed him!"

It was later in the autumn, and the sagebrush was stripped by the colder winds, its leaves scattering over a lone grave beyond and below the shanty.

Lede was again in Coyote Notch, on the claim. As she rode along she was repeating, in a low but determined voice, something she had heard somewhere before: "I will repay—*repay!*"

"It's strange they're so scarce, them redskins. Mebby they're waitin' for us to move back to Kentucky again. They'll wait — for — *vengeance!*"

With a significant emphasis upon that last word her eye dropped and rested on something in her hands that gleamed along the cliff. It was her father's rifle. A locust swung out from a tuft of bluestem skyward; a swallow darted from a crevice across into the shades on the other side of the canyon and watched her from the safer distance.

A dark form stole out from the upper canyon and stood on the rocks still higher. Lede was not startled now, but a smile almost of triumph overspread her countenance. A face limned with paint and surmounting a chest decked with eagles' talons shone full in the evening sun. The eyes saw not the pale, smiling figure below; and well they might not see it! A glance along the shining barrel showed the swell of a bronze-hued breast. A shadow crossed the figure; a cloud flecked the sun and was gone; a bat darted between, scudding away to the canyon's depths, for it was barely sunset. Lede wondered at the creature's flight, but grasped her rifle still closer. The left hand went forward a little. The form before her straightened. The forefinger of her right hand pressed the trigger. A sharp report, and the bronze-hued figure fell lifeless.

"Vengeance is mine. I will repay,—" cried the girl, exultantly.

AUTUMN DAYS.

ALONG the meadow's summer walk
    The withered tufts of daisies nod,
And trembling on its russet stalk
    The gray plume of the golden-rod
Awaits its doom. And on the ground
The blighted grass is wound around;
And where the violet bloomed beside the way,
    Its leaves are turning gray.

Upon the fence-row, where the vine
    Was green, a rusty creeper shows;
And on the briar, like drops of wine,
    Red berries tell where bloomed the rose;
And here and there some vacant nest
Remains deserted by its guest;
The alder stalk has dropped its leaves and stands
    With naked, outstretched hands.

The summer corn, that waved its green,
    Now rustles, brown and dry and dead;
And where the marks of frost have been,
    The sumach leaves wear streaks of red;
The first ones touched have loosed their hold;
The pumpkin wears a coat of gold;
The broad gray fields are turning deeper brown,
    And weeds are drooping down.

The hardy jay, with his blue hood,
    Is looking out his winter home;
And high above the lowland wood,
    Where lazy herds in summer roam,
The wild geese, calling, southward fly,—
A dusky arrow through the sky,—
While from some tree-top, through the cloudy day,
    The crow calls them to stay.

The woods are bare. The autumn wind
    Has swept the foliage round and round,
Until in places 'tis so thinned
    The rabbit's foot scarce makes a sound.
And each tall tree a lone monk stands,
With outstretched arms and pleading hands,
Until the leadened skies, asked not in vain,
    Send down the autumn rain.

Edward Arnold Lee.

A RHYMING ROBBER.

By Frances Roberts.

A SMALL Dakota town stretched itself across the prairie. The hot summer sun glared fiercely on the small frame houses, drawing the rosin in sticky drops from the unpainted, pine boards. The long, tender, prairie grass was burnt to lifeless, brown threads. The wind blew the dust in eddying gusts down the main street, — avenue it was called in the circular generously distributed in Eastern cities, with a hope of some day finding a capitalist, with more money than caution, to lift Siste Viator from the bankruptcy into which she had fallen and start her on the road to fame and fortune. In the opinion of the natives, Siste Viator — pronounced by them Sistyvator — had never had half a chance. Handicapped in the beginning by a name "no fool could spell, let alone pernounce," she had been thrown on the prairie, seventeen miles from a railroad — in the circular she figured as a railroad center and seriously considering bids for water-works and electric lights, not to mention rapid transit through her "broad and spacious avenues lined with palatial mansions ; having once seen Siste Viator tourists found it impossible to leave." The latter clause was the only truthful statement in the circular, for the tourist who drove from Jamestown, seventeen miles, in a rattling, old, spring wagon, generally had an interest in the town to the extent of three or four lots, presented to him for a slight consideration by the very gentlemanly young man who attended to the affairs of the syndicate that owned Siste Viator, in an Eastern city. Once there the tourist stayed, waiting in hopeless anticipation for the time when the water works and electric lights would become a bright reality. Few of the inhabitants of the United States were aware of the existence of Siste Viator save the gentlemanly agent — when it was recalled to his

mind by a possible purchaser — and the state central committees who remembered in times of political excitement that "our dear voting brothers of Siste Viator were in need of a little instruction." For the last four years the only visitors in town had been representative Republicans and Democrats on an educational tour through the country teaching the young idea how to vote. Two weeks before the first Tuesday after the first Monday in November they appeared, riding on the front seat of the mail wagon, covered with dust and humility. Hungrily the voters listened to the discourse on silver, tariff and the pension bill, but as the politician talked on and no mention of Siste Viator and an advance in the price of town lots appeared, their interest flagged, though they politely listened to the end and then as politely escorted the speaker to the wagon waiting to convey him to other towns in as hopeless ignorance as Siste Viator. As Hank Jobson, one of the original settlers, said, "We haint no time fur politics. We didn't intend to make a corner on this 'er reel 'state but seein' we did, its got to be looked after."

Siste Viator was still a collection of weather-beaten houses, each one more desolate than the last, set on the windy, treeless prairie with no communication with the outside world save by the old spring wagon, and no water fit for household purposes in the length and breadth of its townsite.

As usual, the entire male population was gathered in front of the handful of stores that composed the business portion of the town, anxiously awaiting the arrival of Swante Johnson. The mail was fifteen minutes late and bets were freely offered and taken as to the cause of the delay. All eyes were turned to the brown thread that led straight across the prairie. A cloud of dust proclaimed that Swante was in sight. As he drew near they saw that he was not alone. A young man occupied the seat beside him,—a man in a natty suit of dark blue with a sailor hat pushed back on his handsome head.

"Gosh!" exclaimed Jobson, dropping his feet with a bang. "There's a passenger! Aint it early fur politics?"

"Politics don't bloom till the second week in October," said Larson, excitedly, "an' politics al'ys wears a stovepipe. Some fool's been buyin' lots."

"Yhi, thar!" called Swante as he drew the horses in with a practiced hand. "Sistyvator still here?"

"It aint rapid 'nough to move very fast, worse luck! What's the news in Jimtown?"

"Thar's been another rob'ry," said Swante solemnly. "A man held up No. 2, tied the 'spress man to the door and went through ev'ry dam thing."

"Land o' Goshen!" whistled Jobson, "who's the lucky devil?"

"That's the best part," laughed Swante, he tied the men to the doors an' writ over thar heads—le'me see,—it went like this,—

Receive the thanks, my friends, of Jones.
He took your money but spared your bones.
Do you give thanks, my friends, to Jones,
It would have been as easy to take the bones.

"Quite a poet, aint he?" admiringly.

"Well, if that don't beat the Dutch! Writ it right over ther heads, you say?" said Hoskins in astonishment. "What's he like, Swante, young feller?"

"I guess they don't rightly know," said Swante, feeling in his pockets for a paper which he slowly unfolded. "Here's a bill they want stuck up on the post-office. Catch, Hoskins?"

"What does it say, Tim?" asked Larson, as they all crowded around the postmaster.

"Get away, will you," he growled, "so's I can see the thing. It says, 'REWARD,' that's in big letters at the top. TWELVE HUNDRED DOLLARS REWARD.'"

"That's a heap o' money," interrupted Jobson. "I wouldn't mind catching the man myself."

"Would you give him up for twelve hundred dollars?" asked the stranger whom they had overlooked in their interest in Swante's news.

"Fur less'n that," said Jobson cheerfully. "I tell you, stranger, a dollar looks like a cart-wheel to most of us."

"Twelve hundred dollars reward," read Hoskins loudly with a reproving glance at Jobson, "fur the body of man named Jones. He is about six feet tall, slightly built, with dark, curly hair. Wanted fur highway rob'ry committed at Jamestown, North Dakota, July ninth. John Anderson, Sheriff."

"Might suit most any of us," laughed the stranger; "your sheriff aint very ac'rate."

"I'd like to see you measure a man 'xactly and tell what color eyes he's got when he's holdin' a pistol to your head an' goin' through your pockets. He'd get mighty little in mine," with a cheerful slap at the empty pocket.

"Well, Hoskins, how long 'ev we got ter wait fur th' mail?" asked a sneering voice.

"You'll wait, Jim Blabin, till I get good an' ready to give it ye," said the postmaster with great dignity as he took the flabby mail-bag from the driver's hand and walked slowly into the store.

They all trooped in after him and waited with ill-concealed impatience while he unlocked the bag and took out half a dozen letters. "Ther's a big mail for Sistyvator to-night," he said impressively.

"Your town's got a mighty queer name," remarked the stranger, leaning carelessly against the potato barrel.

"The idiotic syndicate called it that," said Jobson, sitting down on a soap-box, "an' its entirely too highfalutin for every-day use. The last Republican—no it must have been a Dem'crat, fur I rec'lect he talked low tariff—said it meant ' stop, stranger,'—Latin, ye know. It's been easy 'nough fur the stranger to stop but its ben mighty hard fur the syndicate to get the stranger."

"Bl-a-b-o-n," slowly spelled the postmaster. "You don't deserve it so soon,

Jim," reproachfully. "It's from your sister in Marysville,—I can't make out if its Indiany or Illynois."

"It aim none o' your business," said Blabon, pocketing the letter.

"Shut up, Jim!" said Larson, "don't be meaner'n you hev to."

"Here's another fur Nancy Hanks," said Hoskins, "from Yankton, in a man's writin'. Did any o' you hear of Nancy's gettin' a beau when she was away last winter?"

"Le's see," and Jobson reached over the counter that divided the post-office from the grocery store.

"No ye don't, Job. Uncle Sam don't let no one handle this mail but me. I swore a cast-iron oath to keep the secrets of this office."

"You keep them well," said the stranger, admiringly, as the postmaster laid the letter down.

"Wall, stranger, come out ter look up a likely site fur a thirteen story office buildin'?" asked a long, lank man, stopping in his perambulations up and down the store to help himself at the cracker barrel.

"That's what," and the stranger showed a row of firm, white teeth. "Where's your hotel?"

"Hotel?" echoed the lank man, delicately cutting a thin piece of cheese. "We aint got no hotel. We take turns lookin' after strangers. Hoskins, who was landlord last?"

"I'll hev to look it up," and Hoskins took out a long, thin book, and opened it at the first page. "Mason," he read, "entertained the Honorable James Treeman, Republican, last October. It's Pastone's turn. Will you write in the vis'ter's book?"

"I don't care if I do. I've got an uncommonly queer name; maybe some of you can help me spell it." "Greene Smith," he wrote in a bold, firm hand.

"I hope you don't live up ter your name," laughed Jobson. "Yer in luck to get to Pastone's; he's got one of the nicest places in town, an' Mame's got a mess o' green pease 'bout ready to pick."

"I've had pease for a month," said Smith, carelessly.

"I wish I was in your shoes. We feed on can goods. I'd forgot what peas looked like, till I see Mame's."

"I don't see how she does it," grumbled Larson. "She don't hev no more water 'n the rest of us."

"It's 'conomy; she don't waste a drop."

"Seems to me you're a mighty savin' people if you hang on to water," said Smith. "Aint the supply equal to the demand?"

"You bet it aint," said Jobson, earnestly. The water cart comes from Jimtown three times a week, an' it takes tall squeezin' to make it last."

"Great Scott! I wouldn't live in such a country!"

"Yes you would, my friend, if every cent you had in the world was salted in town lots. Hello! here comes yer landlord," as the door closed after a thin, weazened man in a suit of dirty, blue jeans.

"Howdy, neighbors," he said, with a broad smile. "Any mail, Hoskins?"

"Nary mail," said the postmaster, with as much interest as if he had not answered the same question in the same way ever since Pastone had been in Siste Vistor, "but here's a boarder fur you."

"It aint my turn," said Pastone quickly.

"Prove it by the books. Mason had the last, an' we take 'em alph'bet'-cally."

"All right. It don't make no difference; I didn't want to take him away from anybody else. If your comin' with me, Mr. Boarder, you'll hev to get a move on you. I want a pound o' sugar, Hoskins."

"Goin' to hev them pease to-night?" asked Hoskins, as he tied up the sugar.

"Seems to me you fellers are takin' an all-fired interest in them peas. Might be well to watch 'em nights."

"I was jes askin' fur Smith; he's too bashful to speak fur himself. You want to look out for Pastone, Smith; he'll talk you to death."

"That's right," said Jobson, "he sits on a corner an' talks to the moon when he can't get no one else."

"Oh, shut up," laughed Pastone. "So long!"

"What's the principal business of Sistyvator?" asked Smith, as they walked down the dusty street.

"Killin' time," said Pastone. "Ther' aint no use startin' more stores till some-one comes to buy. Old Hoskins gives us credit, an' the wholesalers give him credit; so we get along."

"Queer way of doin' business. Looks like rain."

"It may rain and then again it mayn't," said Pastone, looking at the sky, where the dull, leaden rain-clouds covered the fiery face of the sun. "It's mighty hard to calc'late on anythin' in Dakota 'cept wind. Where's your home?"

"Nowhere in particular. I'm a cosmopolitan."

"H·u·m. What did you come to this God-forsaken hole for?"

"I was goin' to invest in Sistyvator lots, an' thought I'd look them up before buyin'."

"That's easy done! It's right before you; an' when you've seen the site for the oprey house an' the palatial hotel an' the street-car root you've seen it all. Here we are. My house aint very big, but it's big 'nough fur me an' my friends."

The small, frame house stood back from the street, the paint blistered and cracked by the sun. A row of pea-vines clambered up strings tied to the front of the house. A young girl stood touching the tender green pods with loving fingers. Her slender form was clothed in a neat dress of blue calico with white ruffles at the neck and wrists. The wind blew her golden hair in loose curls and deepened the tender carmine in her cheeks. As the gate closed she turned. "Well, Daddy," she called, waving her hand.

"Well, Mame," responded Pastone. "I'm in time, aint I? An' I've brought a boarder."

"A boarder!" And Mame's blossoming face wore a perplexed expression as

visions of the usual supper of bread and milk floated before her eyes.

"I hope I don't intrude, Miss Pastone," said Smith, with an admiring glance. "It's too bad to make you any trouble, but it's all the fault of the alphabet."

"It aint any trouble, Mr. ——"

"Smith, Mame," put in Pastone. "Smith of Cosmopolis, didn't you say? Come on, le's go in to supper if it's ready."

"It's ready," said Mame, following the men into the house, "what ther' is of it."

That night Smith was awakened from a sound sleep by the pattering of rain-drops and the low muttering of thunder. A moment later there was a timid tap at his door. "What is it?" he called in alarm. Was the old man sick or had the house been struck by lightning as he lay asleep.

"Are you awake, Mr. Smith?" called Mame. "Would you please put your wash-basin and pitcher outside the door. It's raining, an' we want to catch all the water we can."

With a muttered anathema Smith rose to do as he was asked. The anathema was made a trifle stronger as he stubbed his toe against a rocking chair and struck the corner of the washstand with his elbow. "Damn this alkali hole," he said softly, as he placed the bowl and pitcher in the dark hall and gently closed the door.

"Here they are, Daddy," whispered Mame. "Did you put out everything,—the bowls and dishes?"

"That I did, Honey. Now go back to bed like a good girl; I'll watch for awhile."

"Indeed I won't! You'd be sure to fall asleep, and we need the water."

"Don't slander your daddy, but get to bed."

"Will you promise to empty everything as soon as it's full? Every dish and cup?"

"I'll make the rounds every five minutes."

"Well, I'll trust you this once. Be sure and call me the minute you feel sleepy. Good-night."

For hours, it seemed to Smith, he heard Pastone clattering in and out, emptying the water into the big hogshead that stood beneath his window, cheerfully whistling "Annie Rooney" with a perseverance that threatened to drive sleep forever from the premises. The rain ceased as suddenly as it began and, with a final slam to the door, Pastone climbed the stairs still interested in "Annie." It was the last thing that Smith heard that night, and the first thing in the morning, when he came down stairs in answer to a thunderous rap at his door and found his host on the steps enjoying the fresh morning air and his own music.

"Mornin'," he said cheerfully, "fine mornin'."

"Isn't it lovely after the rain?" asked Mame, coming out of the kitchen with rosy cheeks. "Everything's so fresh and cool. Come to breakfast or the bacon will be cold."

"And bacon is one of the things that improves with heat," said Smith, with an admiring glance at his hostess as he followed her into the kitchen, where the table was spread for breakfast.

"I hope we didn't disturb you las' night," said Pastone, as he helped the bacon and potatoes. "Wouldn't hev made much difference if we had. Can't stop for a little thing like that when water's to be had for the pickin'."

Smith established himself firmly in the affections of Siste Viator. The children adored him, which won the hearts of the mothers; his unfailing good nature, many accomplishments and disposition to treat made fast friends of the men. He could tell a story that they had not heard before, beat any man in town at checkers, and with a revolver he could do wonders; no mark too small for him to hit, square in the center. With it all he was so modest and unassuming no one could feel aggrieved at his superior qualities.

"Don't you ever play poker?" he asked, as with Pastone he sauntered to the store to have a game of checkers before mail time.

"We did — once. A man came here five years ago, jes' before my wife died, an' he taught us to play poker. We didn't larn very fast, an' it was kinder 'spensive, fur Scoopem won everything. We liked it purty well, but the wimen got together an' said our money'd have to stay in town; sorter put a tariff on poker, an' we aint none of us dared to try it sence. If you've got to live with wimen its best to do as they want you to. So we haint done nothin' since but play checkers and damn the country."

"I'm with you in the last," said Smith, as they joined the loafers at the postoffice, where the huge poster, "REWARD, $1,200," flapped to and fro in the wind.

"Snakes! You don't know nothin' 'bout snakes in this country," Jobson was saying as they drew near. "When I was down in Tusc'rora County, Texas, we had snakes. They was so thick they was al'ys in the way; you couldn't put your foot anywhere but you'd strike a snake, until we hired a snake-charmer to take 'em over to Brown County, and then Brown County went and sued us fur trespass.— Hello! how do ye like Sistyvator?" moving over to make room for Smith to put his feet on the same stump.

"Middlin'," responded Smith. "It's a trifle dusty and — dry. Won't you take something to keep the dust out of your throat while we wait for Swante?"

"You bet we will!" said Jobson, emphatically.

"Your treat, Smith?" asked Hoskins, carelessly.

"If the gentlemen will honor me."

"Ther aint no doubt 'bout that. I jes' wanted to be sure, fur these fellers hev used up ther credit in that d'rection. Necessaries they can still get, but no luxuries. I've got some prime whisky."

"After you, gentlemen," and Smith pointed to the door.

With a crash the feet all came to the floor and made for Hoskins.

"There's Swante now," said Jobson, wiping his mouth, as he heard a hoarse — "Whoa thar, whoa!"

"Ah, there!" cried Swante. "Still

here?" with an air of surprise, as his eye fell on Smith.

"How's your robber, Swante?" asked Johnson.

"He's a durned fool," said Swante, savagely. He got away safe 'nough, but he's taken to writin' letters to the sheriff. It's sure to catch him. I hate to see a promisin' young chap throw away his life like that. They got a letter yes'day from Omaha an' the day before from Deadwood."

"What's in them?" asked Pastone, shaking the ashes out of his well-colored clay pipe.

"More o' his po'try. I larned it t' say t' you; you seemed ter like that other. It's mighty hard work to larn po'try so's it rhymes. The one from Omaha went like this,—

> Mr. Sheriff, have no fear,
> When you want me I am here.
> Just come on an' have a toot,
> Your friend Jones can knock you out.

"An' the one from Deadwood said,—

> Mr. Sheriff, would you sell fur money
> The human life God loans
> To the soul of your friend Jones?
> In your Bible you will find
> That's a curse on all mankind.
> Put that in the days of Adam.
> Everybody since has had 'em:
> Mr. Sheriff, would you be so bad
> As to take Jones fur the sins o' Adam,
> his grandad?"

"Bravo! bravo!" cried Smith, as Swante finished his laborious recital.

"What did ye mean, stranger?" asked Swante, with a fierce glare. The others looked at him suspiciously.

"There's but one thing to mean," said Smith quickly," "you said those poems like a James tickler."

"Oh!" And Swante heaved a sigh of disappointment. "I thought it might be some French swear word, an' Swante Johnson never passes an insult."

"You wear that on your face," said Smith. "I'm proud to be your friend. Will you try some of Hoskins' whisky?"

"Will I? Well, I should smile." And again they all trooped into Hoskins', and Smith drew the voters of Siste Vistor still closer to him.

As he sat in his room next day carefully studying a piece of paper that bore

the plan of some building with copious notes as to the exact position of bells, windows and watchmen, a cry caused him to go to the window.

"Oh, Mr. Smith!" called Mame in dismay. "Won't you come down?— the grasshoppers are coming — oh, hurry!"

"Where are they?" he asked as he joined her in the garden.

"Can't you see?" pointing impatiently at a dark cloud that hovered over the yard. "Take this an' beat as hard as you can," thrusting a tin pan and a stick into his hands. "Oh, my peas, my lovely peas!" beating fiercely at the pan she held. Smith followed suit with all the strength of his arms, banging and pounding lustily.

But their pounding was all in vain ; the grasshoppers slowly settled on the garden that had been the work of all Mame's spare moments.

"It's too bad," said Smith, sympathetically, "can't you do anything?"

"Not after they're here," sobbed Mame. "Nasty things! They won't leave a leaf — an' I was goin' to hev 'em fur dinner to-morrow."

"Never put off till to-morrow what you can do to-day," quoted Smith, solemnly.

"Oh, but I hate this country!" cried Mame passionately. "Don't I wish I could leave it forever!"

"You can — and in a way that will bring heaven to one person," said Smith, significantly.

Mame blushed vividly. "I — I didn't mean that," she stammered.

"Mr. Smith! Mr. Smith!" called a boy in breathless haste, "thar's a special d'livery letter at the office an' Hoskins says ter hurry!"

"Damn Hoskins!" said Smith impatiently. "Mame, will you—"

"Aint yer comin'?" interrupted the boy in astonishment. "Hoskins says to hurry."

"All right, johnny," and with a wistful look at Mame he followed the boy.

Mr. Hoskins stood inside the counter surrounded by half a dozen curious men. "No, ye can't look at it," he said decidedly. "It's fur Smith an' you haven't any right ter other people's mail. Here, Smith, take it,"—with a sigh of relief, "I've held tight hold of it ever since it came. We never had none o' those things afore since I've been postmaster."

"That's all right. Much obliged," and Smith thrust the letter carelessly into his pocket.

"Aint you goin' to open it?" asked Hoskins in astonishment.

"It isn't anything," said Smith decidedly, "Just a letter from my mother."

"It aint treatin' me right, Smith, when I've had all the responsibility of takin' care of it. It aint right."

"You bet it aint," echoed the bystanders.

Before they had reached this conclusion — for the mind of Siste Viator works slowly — Smith had slipped away. He found Mame where he had left her. She flushed crimson as he appeared.

"I've got to go to-night, Mame," he said hurriedly. "Will you go with me?"

"To-night! Well, I guess not," and Mame nervously plaited her handkerchief with trembling fingers. "You might've known better'n to ask on such short notice."

"Oh, Mame! And I thought you cared for me. It's good-bye forever, then."

"Do you mean it?" faltered Mame.

"Did you think I was jokin'?" began Smith passionately.

"If you really mean it," whispered Mame with downcast eyes, "I — I s'pose I'll go."

"Mame, you darling!" And he caught her in his arms.

"Oh, not here!" she cried. "Some-one'll see."

"Let 'em see. I aint ashamed, if you are. Remember, Mame, ten o'clock and mum's the word."

Next morning Siste Viator saw Pastone rush up the street as fast as his rheumatic legs would carry him. He burst into Hoskins' store. "Say, hev you fellers seen anythin' of Mame or Smith?" he demanded breathlessly.

"What d' you mean?" gasped Hoskins. "You don't think —"

"Durn it! I *do* think," cried Pastone savagely. "They aint ither of 'em been in the house all night, and Mame's best dress an' hat's gone an' Smith's things."

"Well, I'll be blowed!" And Hoskins dropped the half-filled measure of molasses he held in his hand. "So that's what Smith's been hangin' 'round for."

"If we hadn't been such blamed idiots we might a-known. It would'nt take so long ter look at land," and the injured father helped himself to a half ripe banana. "Look out, Tim, you'll get in the 'lasses. What beats me is how they got away."

"Smith bought my old mare yes'day," said Jobson. "Didn't I tell you? Gave me twenty-five dollars for the horse and cart."

"Better put it down to your account, Jobson," said Hoskins quickly.

"Not if I know myself," said Jobson, decidedly. "It was a purty good price. The mare wasn't worth takin' to the bone-yard. I didn't think she'd carry Mame off."

"Nor more did I," said Pastone with a deep sigh. "I'd like to know when they did their courtin'. He never spoke to Mame afore me,—not but what she aint a good girl."

"Best in Sistyvator," exclaimed Hoskins and Jobson — the latter adding, "You'r sure to get a letter to-night tellin' all 'bout it."

"Here, Pastone," said Hoskins, "I cut a new cheese to-day. Let me do you up a poun' an' some crackers; they'll cheer you up."

As Jobson predicted, Swante brought a letter. A larger crowd than usual waited for the mail. The steps and boxes were covered with men who tried to disguise their curiosity by an air of careless indifference.

"I'll d'liver yours first, Pastone," said Hoskins, sympathetically, as he took the bag, glanced hurriedly over the mail and drew out a long thin envelope. "Here it is; shall I open it for you?"

"No you don't! I guess I can open my own letters if my daughter has 'loped.'" Pastone fully realized his importance and was willing to make the most of it.

"Dear Dad," he read slowly. "Mame and I will be married as soon as we find a minister. Awfully sorry we can't invite you to the wedding. I had a dandy time at Siste Viatur; it was a refuge in my hour of trouble. Remember me to everybody. Mame sends love. I forgot to say my name aint Smith.

With love to father-in-law Pastones. From son-in-law and daughter Jones."

"Thunder turtles!" exclaimed Swante, "the Jimtown robber."

"Jes' my luck," grumbled Jobson. "Twelve hundred dollars lost from carelessness. Come in, fellers, an' drink to a lot o' blame' fools."

HOME THEMES.

SOCIETY AND DRESS.

By Lucia B. Griffin.

"Hark! The rustle of a dress stiff with lavish costliness!
Here comes one whose cheek would flush but to have her garments brush
'Gainst the girl whose fingers thin wore the weary 'broidery in.
Bending backward from her toil, lest her tears the silk might spoil.
In the midnight's cold and mirk stitched her life into the work."

Would life be worth the living had we no other ambition than to be mere ornaments to society — to shine — to be admired? Because we are women must we go on everlastingly with the one thought uppermost in our minds — "How do I look?" "Is this becoming?" Is that the latest?" Shall we continue to spend our lives and our means on frills and flounces, while millions around us are struggling for mere existence? Can we afford to spend days and weeks and years to "make ourselves beautiful," when there is so much to be done? All well and good to be neat and tidy — there is no excuse for slovenliness in man or woman — but it is certainly a waste of time and energy for women to wrap themselves up, body, heart and soul, in the subject of wearing apparel. This seems to be the besetting vice of the virtuous.

How often the woman who hasn't so much as a dollar to help some worthy cause along will appear at church on Sunday morning in costly robes and jewels rare!

More people are socially ignored because they can't afford "up to date" raiment, than for lack of genuine worth of character, intellect, or culture. Fashion[5] gilded lady with her hurtful gossip and time-killing frivolity has been handling the reins for centuries. Everybody feels this, and the sensible are demanding a change of drivers.

Now for wear new Shakspere to "arms"
And write a tragedy on human clothes.
Touching the danger of spending so much
On ribbons and furs and jewels and such!

In Maggie Mitchell's great play "The Cricket," Fanchon says to Mother Fadet — "Give me the coarsest clothes — let 'em be ever so plain, but do not let me go in rags." Says Grandma, wisely shaking her head, "'Tis right enough as it is — 'tis right enough; vanity brought your proud mother to ruin and your father to the grave. Wear your rags with patience, Cricket. It is better that they scorn than ruin ye, my girl."

Some very good women seem never to have been taught that to act a lie is as much a crime as to tell one. People who wear better clothes than they can afford to pay for, must, in the very nature of things, create a false impression. Yet we will try to believe that with most people this habit of spending other people's money, is an "error of the head and not the heart."

The introduction of the bicycle is helping to pave the way for plainer, simpler, and more sensible suits for business women. The society woman and the actress have reasons best known to themselves for studying the monthly fashion plate instead of the Bible. Christ's teachings put into practice will always make life easy.

Women are by nature less charitable than men. This indisputable fact is probably due to their having been shielded from the rough edges of the business world. Living in a rut they have been forced to think in a rut. Hence instead of being practical and far-seeing, they move by impulse and emotion. Then they worry too much about other folks' opinions of their doings — they lack independence. "Faint Heart" and "Much Afraid" have greatly hindered women's advancement. And yet I do honestly believe that the numberless anxieties, the countless cares that overwhelm her in these tedious times, will seem like toy troubles — like bubbles light as air, when she has settled the dress question once and for all. Then she can find time to think and know and learn what life is.

This is not a kindergarten; we are living a real life in a real world. "He who is always helped remains a baby always." Effort makes self-reliance. Then women should learn to think for themselves and do for themselves, especially in matters that concern themselves only.

MISS GRIFFIN.

In a recent conversation with Colonel Robert G. Ingersoll, his views of the "Woman Question" were freely expressed, including the subject of bloomers, bicycling, horseback riding, the extermination of the side-saddle, etc. Said Colonel Ingersoll to me: "Let us get down to business and look the question square in the face. You would not think of riding your wheel sideways, would you? And whoever heard of a person trying to walk with one leg when he happened to be fortunate enough to possess two! Why not ride astride, and if you have two feet put one in each stirrup; and why not wear the most sensible garb while riding? Women in some of the Oriental countries cover all but their eyes, — a most heathenish idea. But custom has made slaves of them. It's the same in this country. Yet, after all, women make themselves slaves; that's what's the trouble.

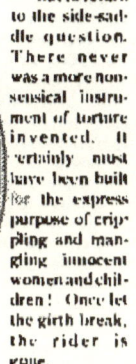

"But to return to the side-saddle question. There never was a more nonsensical instrument of torture invented. It certainly must have been built for the express purpose of crippling and mangling innocent women and children! Once let the girth break, the rider is gone.

"Miss Weeks was recently thrown from her horse, and the skirt of her riding habit caught in the horns of her saddle. The horse dragged her along head downwards and finally trampled her under its feet. If Miss Weeks had been riding in the only rational way and wearing the only safe and convenient dress for riding, her horse could not have thrown her, her dress could not have caught in the saddle, and she could not have been dragged along under the horse's feet.

"However don't hate those people who laugh at your advanced ideas. Don't hate them — they don't know any better. They can't help it. They can't help what they don't know. Never blame a man for what he doesn't know, but go about it in a systematic, sensible way, and teach him that it is folly to cling to old ideas and follow rules and regulations laid down by people dead and forgotten. In this enlightened age we have better things to think of. The average person is afraid of genius and of new ideas. While he admires, he invariably suspects that something is wrong. Was there ever great good come to us without opposition?

"Did you ever see a horse shy and jump when he saw a bicycle? Now after he gets used to it he'll make friends with it. He's got to find out first that this mysterious metal machine won't hurt him. People are the same way. They make a great fuss over new notions, but they get over their scare by and by. Just give them a little time. Don't try to hurry them or they will 'balk.'"

Can it be possible that we are nearing the day of common sense in dress? Comfort is a blessing, simplicity a jewel, and beauty is simplicity unadorned.

We can make our lives simple and beautiful as well as useful if we will. It is no longer a small band of noble women who are fighting their way to the front in this reform. O! they are gaining ground, their swords of truth are clashing against the weapons of slavish custom. Their victory is certain. It is now only a question of time. God speed the victory!

MOTHER-THOUGHTS.

From out the deeps of anguish, whose cold
    wave
Washes the border of the Vale of Shade,
I toiled, and found within my hand was laid
A pearl, that for my sorrow rapture gave.

Love's promise all fulfilled, my vague alarms
Were stilled; and, nestling there so close and
    warm,
Mystery that was, a tiny, breathing form,
My precious babe lay in my willing arms.

Within my darkened chamber came the
    sound
Of Spring; from pools, a piping shrill and
    fine;
From fields afar and faint, the low of kine,
And roll and cry of wild birds northward
    bound.

Four happy changeful Aprils came and went;
Four jeweled years wherewith to deck the
    chain
Of years to come, heavy with grief and pain.
That God foreknew to claim the pearl He lent.

I cry for comfort to the empty air;
My stricken heart refuses still to feel
That death can all my loving trust make steal,
And that she needs no more my tender care.

I know her little form within the grave
Will dust become. But to what region flown
Is that pure soul, through radiant eyes that
    shine?
"The spirit shall return to God who gave."

To Him who gave! O words in mystery dressed!
Has death for us life's holiest meaning found?
How oft our feet profane tread holy ground,
And bring to Love's fair altar gifts unblest!

To Him who gave! 'Twas from His hand
    there sped
The spark that lit our little lamp of clay,
It is jewel graced our setting for a day,
It is child and ours! O heart, be comforted!

Juliet Older Carlton.

CONSOLIDATED HOUSEKEEPING —PRACTICALLY CONDUCTED BY A HOUSEKEEPER.

BY MRS. C. F. McLEAN.

FROM all over the country we hear complaints about the inadequacy of the present household arrangements for giving domestic comfort and domestic peace. The problem of help (the old New England word seems to best fit the case) is not yet satisfactorily solved anywhere. Women in stately mansions as well as those in humbler dwellings feel the burdens of home-keeping so great, that in constantly increasing numbers they hasten to hotels and boarding houses, and give up, with the pleasures of living at home, the too heavy cares of housekeeping. Various have been the remedies proposed, many the rules laid down for the treatment of those hired to do the work of the house, which take a range from the most severe, cast-iron regulations to a sort of half-adoption into the family, with separate sitting-rooms, small libraries, supervision of wearing apparel, and other equally charming pictures to secure good work and to make "good servants." The trouble that stands ever in the way of solving this problem is that we fail to recognize the fact that what is needed at this time is not a little change here and there but an entire readjustment of old ways to new ideas. It is with no lightness, or no lack of earnest consideration, that the statement is made that for relief from domestic inadequacies and infelicities of which we as housekeepers can and do complain, we must look to no surface reformation, but to a revolution in both the principles and practice of the science of domestic economy.

The essential notion which underlies the possibility of making successful the present domestic arrangement of having the work of the house done by others is the obtaining of service from another human being not related by ties of blood or friendship. By service is meant that unquestioning compliance with the orders of others, which makes one person the thinker for the other. Domestic service implies that ; and yet, on the other hand, when it becomes desirable to the thinker to lay aside her rôle, then is demanded on the part of the one who serves an amount of personal responsibility which comes to the individual only through a great degree of independence in thought and action.

We complain that those we engage to do our work will not do as we tell them, nor do they know how to do it. The notion of implicit obedience of one person to another is in every relation of life,— domestic, social and political.— fast passing away. Most of us give to our children a reason with every command ; we do not put our minds under the spiritual guidance of any religious teacher without our reason accords. No church now commands.

Just here the reader is perhaps saying, "If we cannot get anyone to do what we want, there is no use trying to keep house." It has not been affirmed that we cannot get others to do the work we wish done in a house, but that we can no longer successfully accomplish that with the underlying principle of service. There was a time when every poet as well as every blacksmith was, in reality as well as in name, the "most humble servant" of some one else. Surely we will not claim that either blacksmithing or poetry has degenerated since both have become a profession.

I have at last reached the word which I consider the keystone in the new arch we shall rear, which is to uphold our

domestic affairs in a manner eminently satisfactory to all parties concerned, and which will bring about the revolution in fact which has already taken place in thought. We must replace our demand for domestic service with a requirement for professional knowledge and skill. That such knowledge and skill will come at the requirement we know by experience in other relations of life ; but to prove just how they will be brought about requires a wider discussion of psychological and social phenomena than would be in place in this article. Yet in other countries, much of that knowledge and skill in various branches of domestic requirements, and which we desire for ourselves, have come. We must however not forget that such knowledge and skill come by specializing them. We ought not to expect in the work of the house, more than in work outside, skill in half a dozen occupations, when skill presupposes concentrated attention to one and constant practice in it. We are too apt to want our "help" to be a good washer Monday, a good ironer Tuesday, a good baker Wednesday, a good sweeper Friday, a good general polisher Saturday, with a complete evenness of liking, and of moods and tenses thrown in,— especially for Sunday.

What we ought to strive for is, first, to specialize household work ; secondly, to have all that can be done outside the house, thus attended to ; to have much that is done in a most expensive manner outside, attended to periodically inside the house.

It should be plainly stated at once that it is not coöperation that is here advocated. Coöperation presupposes that all concerned must know each other and act together. Not even the most ardent socialists have encompassed the possibilities of coöperation which the future holds in store, yet they are in error who believe such possibilities will become realities through any form of force. As the stones of the kaleidoscope fall into forms of dazzling beauty, so will differing interests group in perfect shape for themselves, and in complete harmony with all others. That will come, however, when the fundamental wrong of private ownership in land will disappear, and equal right to natural opportunities will give all a free chance for development untrammeled by the necessity of fighting for a chance to sell to others the ability and labor which should, and would then, have unlimited chance to develop without fear or favor. Until that time does come, all attempts at coöperation must be trammeled and incomplete.

There is a transition stage, however, which, if we look about us, we see now taking huge shape in the business world. To most it is a word of terror, but to those of calm faith and hope in the future, it is the assurance of the coming and better evolution which could not take place without it. That stage is consolidation. The best example of the necessity of consolidation as a formative step to coöperation in business is the Bon Marché store of Paris, which, beginning as a consolidation of business activities under the direction of a single individual, is to-day the greatest of monuments to the success of coöperation, as well as to the enlightened philanthropy of its founders.

By consolidation in housekeeping is meant that the work of a number of homes should be done by a certain number of people known necessarily to those for whom they do the work, but that those for whom the work is done need not know each other. The living in apartment houses is in fact bringing consolidated housekeeping in many of its features into actual practice to-day. It is the evident tendency of the times, and the wise woman is she who is ready to direct and increase the impetus of those tendencies when she sees plainly that they are in the right direction. How to successfully accomplish this it is hoped here to demonstrate.

— —

Let us first consider wash-day. It is not my intention to long dwell on the sorrows and horrors of that day ; there are, however, two thoughts that will persis-

tently intrude on a consideration of wash-day as it yet holds its place in domestic arrangements, and these are, first : that too often the men of the family spend for their wash-day dinner down town, away from the hubbub at home, a sum that, added to the household expenses, would bring wash-day to a point of endurance for the women of the family ; secondly : that it would be worth while for a debating society to discuss and decide the following : " Resolved, That the girl who has her company Sunday evening is on wash-day more amiable than the one who goes to bed early and rolls out her tubs in the middle of the night." If women would only count the exact cost of having washing done at home, including fuel and loss of temper, and then see, if by being one of several giving the washing to one person (who on her hand could secure all the help needed), they could not have it done as economically as at home, they would decide on neighborhood consolidation for their washing. It does not require that those entering into this plan should know each other in order to banish wash-day from the household vocabulary.

Let us next consider baking. There is no reason whatever why bread and pastry baked in large brick ovens should not be as good as, and even better than, bread and pastry baked in household stoves and ranges ; it is only necessary to insist on having them thus supplied,—and at a reasonable price, too,—to banish baking-day along with wash-day. Then again, there is no reason why we should not have in our cities, and even in small towns and villages, the same facilities for roasting meats as are enjoyed everywhere in France. For a few pennies over the price of the raw article, at the very moment desired for the table, the housekeeper there can have brought to her door fowl and meats roasted far better than would be possible at home.

As to the work of cleaning house : many persons worry along without a second girl, finding the additional interruption and work to the members of the family less than doubling the trouble by increasing the number of help. Two good girls — and in spite of all our complaining let us acknowledge that there are such even now — could together thoroughly clean all the rooms of say from five to ten houses, by going to each for a day, or half a day every week. They would then leave leaning out of the window to talk to "the butcher, the baker, the candlestick maker" till they reached home. If the work were regular and the pay certain, they could do it for a price not possible for occasional cleaning. They would also thus learn to do their work quickly and thoroughly.

Were we to oftener require results without insisting on our own way of attaining them, there would be a decided gain for all parties concerned; whereas now it is too often the case that whenever a girl changes her place, she must undergo a complete change — but alas! not always reformation in her way of doing things. With washing and baking banished from the house, and the cleaning done periodically by those thoroughly capable of attending to it, the labor of housekeeping is reduced to a minimum. In one respect we are even now away ahead of our grandmothers. Even in our villages it is no longer necessary for a woman to secure her standing as a housekeeper by taking a stick in hand and beating carpets. Let us be thankful for all progress. In connection with housekeeping there is one profession we should make, viz.: that of the man who appears at times to repair all furniture without the expense of having it hauled away to be hauled back again.

We are groping to a realization of the fact that the better the individual the better the work he is able to perform, no matter of what sort it is. Certainly housework ought not to be considered an exception to the general rule. Even a small amount of leisure, even a little education brings an unrest, a desire for better things; these have made American girls flee from domestic service as it is to-day; they prefer to enter factories and other establishments where they earn less. If

we reason on the subject we shall readily see that it is the freedom they possess for even a small part of the twenty-four hours — the feeling that when the door of the factory closes, until it swings open again, they own themselves, which makes them prefer less money and even less comfortable surroundings than they would gain by domestic service; in proportion as they are self-respecting and capable of better things do they dislike the house of a "mistress." Whether this is a right feeling or not is no more worth discussing than the question of the improvement or non-improvement of the condition of the colored race in the South through the abolition of slavery. The fact is indisputable, and the only way to better any condition of affairs is to frankly accept facts and endeavor to work with them.

Let us work then with the fact that American-born girls do not want to go out to service; that at present they shun the work of the kitchen and the laundry. That they would cheerfully go into either to do a portion of the work, if they were free to do as they pleased when the work is done, is confidently believed. There should be homes for girls who are ready to go into houses or apartments and clean them; who are willing to wash and iron away from the houses of those who have the washing done, managing the work themselves, and assured of an amount of work sufficient to give them fair pay. There are girls who are happy when baking; there are those who even delight in washing; the girl who likes to bake ought to be able to bake every day; the one who prefers to wash should have washing as her regular occupation. If women of wealth and leisure would see that such homes were started, they would soon become self-supporting. The girl who had not enough work outside could pay her board by doing a part of the work of the house until she could obtain the kind of labor for which she is peculiarly fitted. The matron of such a home could receive the applications of those who wished a certain kind of housework periodically done, and then send the proper one to do the work; this law would be made happy in having her special liking gratified in her work.

Then the possibilities of bettering the physical, mental and moral well-being of the girls in such a home are positively dazzling. There, lectures on the care of children, on the nursing of the sick, on all subjects which are properly branches of the general subject of cookery, on sensible dress for working women, on the care of beautiful things, would be given with the certainty of reaching those whom they would most benefit, and who would most diffuse the benefits they had derived. Nor would there be a better place for giving those entertainments whose only object is to improve and elevate those who enjoy them, for we cannot too often repeat that what elevates the individual improves the work of that individual. Such central homes for working women would (except always for the hopelessly incapable) make of each occupant, instead of a servant not knowing any one kind of work thoroughly, a self-respecting and respected woman, secure in knowledge, raised to the dignity of a calling, capable of earning an excellent living, and giving full return for the money earned.

The heaviest drudgery in all kinds of work is being reduced, almost eliminated, by labor-saving devices. In front of the furnace register, or the coal elevator outside the window, and before the water faucet in an apartment in the tenth story, the term, "hewer of wood and drawer of water," becomes only historic. What we want in our homes now are cooks who know that acids left in tins create poisonous substances. We need nurses who have been taught that a child's health may be permanently ruined by a fright. We want those who clean our rooms to know the value of a Satsuma vase, the necessity of careful handling of silken draperies. How will they know those things if we do not teach them? We come back, therefore, to the original proposition: that the time has come when even

with no better feeling than that of enlightened selfishness, we should recognize the fact that the notion of service, or servitude, should be relegated to the musty past with the belief in the divine right of kings; that for our modern life, aided by the ameliorations to labor which the inventive genius of man has created, we need persons educated to the degree of professional skill in all the requirements of the work of a home, that by raising the standard of household work to the dignity of a calling we can obtain better results for ourselves with the consciousness of helping others to improve themselves; that we can best reach such results by specializing the work required. That that can be accomplished by establishing and organizing central homes for women who are to be trained in the various branches of such labor; that these places shall be not only homes for those who do the work, but bureaus of distribution of such work, where those who desire help specially trained can obtain it by application, without entering into all the labor and detail which would be necessary in carrying out any plan of coöperation in household affairs.

Here is a new field for the organizing forces of the modern woman in comfortable financial circumstances and with a little leisure to devote to bettering the condition not only of those who are to labor for their daily bread, but also of those for whom the work is done. Boarders in hotels might with excellent results take an interest in those who do the work there. If they would but suggest to the proprietor that they would be pleased to learn that the dormitories of the help were comfortably heated, that there was a sitting-room for them when off duty, so that they had another choice for spending their leisure hours than that offered by a cold sleeping-room and the street, such comforts would be supplied them. There is little doubt that they would result in an improvement in the girls themselves, and as a consequence, in the work required of them. The interest of the boarders might, without the expenditure of a penny, be extended to supplying the sitting-room with the papers and books they no longer desired.

We must, in our present stage of civilization, recognize to the fullest extent the solidarity of the human race. The breeze that is wafted to us from the tenement house many blocks away may bear upon its waves to our homes the breath of the Angel of Death; the garment with which we wrap our idolized one may hold within its folds the seeds of a disease which poverty and hunger and wretchedness gave to the one whose wasting fingers fashioned it. Therefore, if in any plan of change that is offered there is held out a benefit to the several classes concerned, it ought to meet with greater favor from all right-thinking people. That claim is made for consolidated housekeeping.

There is therefore presented a new demand for those talents for organization which, it has been proved, are so conspicuously possessed by the women of to-day. With those talents are united so great an amount of philanthropy and good sense that there is nothing good, which any one proves as such, that the women will not endorse and successfully accomplish. To them, therefore, with hopeful anticipations, are presented these claims for the plan of consolidated housekeeping.

THE FOUNTAIN OF YOUTH.

A beautiful mind is the one possession that age cannot wither nor custom stale. Its charm increases with years and experience, even as the glass found in old Assyrian monuments has been invested with a thousand delicate tints and beauties by the wonder-working hand of Time.

It is only through his highest affections and aspirations that a man can hope to retain the freshness of youth. Without these the human spirit grows old and blasé long before the hair is white. However broken with years and sorrows, the moment the nobler faculties assert themselves, behold! he finds the petition of Mignon granted,—

"Make me again forever young."

In this fine spiritual charm lay the perennial attractiveness of Madame de Sévigné. Beloved and admired by all who knew her, she hastened, like the wise woman that she was, to lay up for herself imperishable treasures. At forty she wrote: "Youth is in itself so amiable, that, were the soul as perfect as the body, we could not forbear adoring it; but when youth is past, we should endeavor to supply the loss of personal charms by the graces and perfections of the mind. I have long made this the subject of meditation, and am determined to work every day at my mind, my soul, my heart, and my sentiments."

It was no mere physical charm which secured to Madame Recamier the admiration of her contemporaries down to three score years and ten. Old and blind, with her figure slightly bent and her youthful bloom gone, she still seemed lovely and attractive as in the days of her youth, for the beauty of her soul was only the more apparent through the ruins Time had wrought in the earthly house which inclosed it.

In these ever-growing lives is to be found the secret of true beauty, the fountain of youth Ponce de Leon sought so long in vain.

Mrs. Lillian Monk.

A MEMORIAL HALL FOR IOWA.

By S. H. M. Byers.

NEXT year is Iowa's semi-centennial. What is the great State going to do to fitly commemorate the occasion?

Iowa is no longer a half-inhabited prairie of the West. It has become a great noble State, with a proud history.

In what conceivable way can Iowa better celebrate its fiftieth birthday than by establishing a Memorial Hall fitted to contain its history, its souvenirs of the past, its pictures and busts of the men and women who have made it great. Why cannot Iowa have a Walhalla of its own—a grand Memorial Hall that shall be the pride of every citizen of the State?

In any event Iowa must shortly build a house suitable to contain the splendid historical collections now grown to proportions not dreamed of twenty years ago. This grand collection of records, histories, autographs, and relics of a fast-receding period, is stowed away in dark rooms in the basement of the Capitol. This is a shame to the State, and speaks little for the intelligence, culture, and wisdom of past legislatures.

Of course, many of our people have no knowledge or comprehension of what the State of Iowa possesses in the great Aldrich Collection at the State House. Travelers have pronounced it scarcely second in importance to some of the most famous collections of its kind in Europe. Such collections elsewhere have cost hundreds of thousands of dollars. Iowa got hers as a precious gift. When Charles Aldrich and his wife laid the foundations of this collection in Iowa's Capitol they showed themselves true benefactors of the people. That was in 1882. Since then, year by year, Mr. Aldrich has patiently toiled, adding to and building up this monument to Iowa's honor.

He has traveled everywhere in search of everything that could add interest or value to the State's literary and historic treasures. His wide acquaintance with notable men and women in this country and in Europe, his constant zeal, his untiring interest in this one great object, enabled him to secure gifts for the State that are of extreme historic value.

Here are collected autograph letters, papers and manuscripts of the great men and women of all countries : kings and queens and generals, poets and sages, painters and sculptors, statesmen and presidents. It is remarkable how complete and distinguished an assembly of reminders of the world's great, the State of Iowa possesses in this collection. Days do not suffice for a full examination of the manuscripts there that enchain the interest.

The time is rapidly approaching when Iowa will be the envied of all the states for the historical record she possesses of great people and great things.

It is safe to say that were the Aldrich Collection for sale to-morrow some of the older states would give a quarter of a million dollars to possess it.

Ordinarily it requires centuries of time and large expenditure of money to secure for a state or city a collection such as Mr. Aldrich has put into the lap of Iowa as a loving gift.

Let us hope that our legislators will show their broad-mindedness, their love of extended culture, their pride in the State's history, by building for this historic exhibit a house fit to contain it.

Let it be a temple beautiful. Iowa can afford a Memorial Hall that may in architectural beauty, and fitness for its purpose, rival the memorial halls of other states. It will be adding one more historic monument to the list we have just fairly commenced.

It is said that a people's intelligence may be measured by the monuments it builds to its benefactors.

Iowa, in its fifty years of growth, has been making history. We have statesmen, dead and living, whose names have never been put in bronze or marble by the State they served.

The monument to our soldiers is at last nearing completion. It is a just, but yet feeble, recognition of what they did and of what they sacrificed.

There are single manuscripts in the Aldrich collection worth a thousand dollars. There are letters and papers that can never be duplicated. Think of being able to look upon and take in one's hands an original of Holmes' "Last Leaf," of Smith's national song "America," of verses of Queen Victoria in her own handwriting, of Sherman's original report of the "Siege of Vicksburg." of pages of Victor Hugo, of letters of Abraham Lincoln, of letters and portraits and papers of a thousand others of the world's great.

And all this we have been permitting to hide away in the basement of the Capitol! That collection contains the history and progress and greatness of Iowa's own past that must be brought out to the daylight, where every Iowa man and woman can see it and be proud.

Who would not thrill with gratitude to look upon the sword of Donelson, the battle-torn hat, red with Dodge's blood in the contest for Atlanta, the swords of Williamson and others of our War-time heroes!

The place is filled with relics like these that speak of Iowa's heroism and honor, relics of our pioneer days, of our early struggles to make a state. Let no niggardly hand or voice be raised against the effort to perpetuate them for our children's glory. The lifelong persistency and patriotism of one man made it possible for us to possess them. Let no mistaken economy prevent their preservation in a fitter form.

But where are the monuments to our great civilians, our Kirkwood, our Grimes, our Wilson, our Allison and the scores of other great men who have conferred honor on the State in these fifty years?

Let the Memorial Building be a hall of records and a temple of honor. Let it be placed where all men can see it, that it may be a "thing of beauty and a joy forever." On its walls let shine the medallions and portraits and names of men and women who have made Iowa great. Let the building be the one great keeper and protector of Iowa's name and honor. Make it a Pantheon of the State's distinguished dead, and a temple of honor for its living benefactors. Fill it up with all the noble collection now waiting a fit hiding place. Make it an honor so great to be in some way represented there that every high-minded citizen will strive for a place within its portals. Put its building and adorning in the hands of competent and cultured non-partisan men and women, and let there be a high commission who shall calmly and conservatively determine what name and what thing shall be thought noble and worthy enough to be placed inside its walls of honor. When this is done, then can great Iowa point with pride to a monument worthy of her aspirations.

It is a satisfaction that the press and many public spirited men of the State are already urging action toward the building of this Memorial Hall. It will be a lasting honor to the legislature that shall push this movement to a successful and worthy conclusion.

This coming semi-centennial year is the time to lay its corner stone. Let it be a landmark of the fifty years of our existence and progress.

Who knows what lies history will tell of our time if we put nothing of our own record in manuscript and in bronze and marble? After a thousand years the memorial buildings of Greece and Rome tell as truly the story of their people as do the books of all the ages. If a people have a history that is worth preserving, he is recreant to his kind who does not care to aid in making it imperishable.

EDITORIAL COMMENT.

STORY, the sculptor, painter, poet, novelist and critic, whose recent death has turned public attention anew to the man's remarkably versatile gifts, has been charged by most of the obituary writers with the crime of scattering his powers and so failing to produce the best results. The moral drawn from this many-sided career is that success in life consists chiefly in doing some one thing better than the rest of us can do that one thing ; and that, failing to concentrate sufficient talent or working force for the accomplishment of that one thing, the whole course of one's life is turned aside and loses the name of action. But is this the whole truth? Are there not many phases, and as many definitions, of success? Casting about for a general definition, covering both the one-idea man or woman and the general purpose man or woman, how will this answer?

Real success in life is the attainment of one's ambition, provided that ambition be worthy of one's powers.

What to William Wetmore Story in his last days would have been the satisfaction of having left behind him only a statue surpassing any ever before wrought, compared with the retrospect in which he was able to indulge, the pictures full of those delightful alternations from poetry to painting, from the still life of the studio to the throbbing life revealed to him in books,—"from toil to rest, and joy in every change!" To the great Angelo, also, was given that farther ranging soul that was not satisfied with one immortal achievement, but found pleasure in poetry, painting, sculpture, the sciences and the mechanic arts. What matter to him that Raphael was the greater painter? Or that he could not expect to rise to the poetic heights of a Dante or a Petrarch? He left much unfinished work, but it is said of him that even his fragments have educated many. His greater career was really not as successful as Story's, because

to him were committed godlike possibilities, many of which failed of fulfillment, while to his Nineteenth Century successor a much smaller measure of genius was given, enabling him to fully utilize his gifts in the work that delighted him most.

*   *   *

THAT rare gem, the character of Imogene, more beautiful because of its somber setting, the tragedy of "Cymbeline," has an ardent admirer in Julia Marlowe Tabor. This latest successful interpreter of the great master prefers the role of Imogene above all others of Shakspeare's women. This preference, of one who has succeeded as no other American actress has since Mary Anderson queened it on the stage, reveals the high ambition of the artist and points anew to the reserve of power in Shakspeare undreamt of by the surface student of the drama. Among the many general admirers of the great dramatist, few have even read "Cymbeline."

*   *   *

WHILE New York and Boston are disputing one with the other through the daily press and in the magazines as to the relative strength of their rival claims to literary supremacy, the great Middle-West is waking to consciousness of literary powers and possibilities undreamt of ten years ago. The time has not yet come for boasting, however. And when it comes, we'll not need to boast.

*   *   *

Current Literature and kindred periodicals are, by their selections from the editorial pages of our great dailies, revealing the gratifying fact that the newspaper press of this country is developing a decidedly literary flavor. The September number of *Current Literature* reprints a well considered leader from the Indianapolis *News*, which it heads "The Degeneracy of American Magazines," the point of which is that our once great reviews and pictorial magazines are sac-

468

rificing everything to "the fetich of time-
liness." Made-to-order papers on some
theme of the hour by one who is most
prominently named in connection there-
with,— as for instance Croker on Tammany, Wilson on the tariff, Dunraven on
how not to do it, Corbett on slugging as
a manly art.— are taking the place of
papers of real value by authors who are
in position to judicially consider themes.
This sort of thing belongs to journalism,
but not to magazine literature. The magazine should know its place and keep its
place.

* *

Now that the weather is cool, the
rhymesters who mistake mere rhyme
for poetry might drop such easy rhyming
as love, dove, above, mine and thine, etc.,
and attack foemen worthy of their steel,—
might practice on such words as month,
monthly, silver, liquid, spirit, chimney,
warmth, gulf, sylph, music, breadth,
width, depth, honor, iron, echo.

* *

"Our alumni seem to be afraid of us,"
said a college president recently, alluding
to the smallness of the number who attend
commencements and class reunions. A
suggestion worth considering on this
point comes from *The Cornellian*. Speaking of the number of subscription papers
habitually passed around among the visiting alumni at commencement time, it
says : "This may be a good way to satisfy
present needs but it discourages our
alumni in making such visits and in the
end is a loss to the college and its friends,
and should be discouraged."

* *

We are glad to note that Mr. H. E.
Wells in his recent scholarly translation
of Cervantes' great work pronounces
"Don Quixote" as it is spelled, and declares that the pronunciation Ke-hó-ty is
pedantic. There is too much quibbling
over the small change of literature and
too little search for gold.

* *

The time for weddings is come and the
old question of wedding presents is revived. The question is not as difficult of

practical solution as it was ten years ago.
Time was when an invitation to a wedding
was practically — though not so intended
— an invitation to send a wedding present,
and was to the mere acquaintance, as to
the friend in straightened circumstances,
a serious embarrassment. That time is
happily past. The mere acquaintance
and the general friend can now attend a
wedding, and even examine the presents,
without feeling at all uncomfortable over
the non-appearance of their names in the
bride's list of presents. On the contrary,
they would have reason to feel decidedly
uncomfortable were they conscious that
their gifts had imposed upon the bride an
obligation which, to say the least, was
unexpected. A present now rightly presupposes personal or family intimacy.
The one embarrassing question remaining
is as to the costliness of the gift. This
question should never arise ; but, alas, it
will — and it will not down ! As helps to
the practical solution of this question a
few points are worth considering.

1. Where the question of cost arises,
give modesty the benefit of the doubt.
Let it not with truth be said that less
might have been expected of one no more
intimate, or nearly related, or finan-
cially "well fixed," than yourself.

2. When the question of cost arises,
give your creditors the benefit of the
doubt, if you are in debt.

3. When the question of cost arises,
give your real feelings all the room you
can within these limitations.

4. Where the question is not one of
cost but of choice between a showy or a
modest present, give modesty the benefit
of the doubt.

5. Dismiss as far as possible the question of cost, and with it all thought about
how your gift will look alongside the
rich gifts of the near related and the
wealthy. Enter as far as possible into
the true spirit of present-making at weddings. Try to make your gift mean something to the recipient, not in grains or
pennyweights of silver or gold, not in
obtrusive house furnishings which may
embarrass, but in considerate regard for

the tastes of the prospective bride, or for the plans and purposes of the two who are about to be wedded, or in delicate expression of some subtile bond of sympathy between them and yourself.

You have, doubtless, been behind the scenes and heard the inevitable comment following a wedding. Recall the trend of remarks made by intimate friends, each on the other's gift, and you will have the whole philosophy of present-making. Have you not seen the radiant delight of the bride over some piece of handiwork which aged hands have wrought, and only general expressions of pleasure in the rich presents which cost less of personal sacrifice. The lamp-mat knit by a loving Sunday-school scholar means more to her teacher than the solid silver tray from the rich man of the town. The measure of the gift is the measure of affection which accompanies the gift. Where the heart element is wanting, the very costliness of the present makes the absence of the essential thing the more conspicuous.

* *

THE plea of an Iowa woman for Iowa girls, and boys as well, urging that the "Age of Consent" be raised by legislation from fourteen to eighteen years (see our Contributors' Department), is one which should be heard by every legislator and would-be legislator in the State. The good work in this direction, inaugurated by Helen H. Gardner, in the *Arena*, has roused the whole country on the subject. Are Iowans aware that their State is on Mrs. Gardner's black list? It is, but, we trust, it will not be there long. We confidently expect that the next legislature of Iowa, soon to be convened, will compel Mrs. Gardner to melt up that plate with its black line under Iowa, and cast a new one in which the State shall appear in fairer lines, correctly representing the real sentiment of its people on the subject.

* *

LITTLE did we think as we read Professor Boyesen's "Novels of Romance and Stories of Real Life," in the October *Cosmopolitan*, that this vigorous and stimulating bugle-blast for realism in

fiction was our last word from that inspiring source! Death came to the strong man in the midst of his work. It found him full of ambition both to do and to teach. Happily combining the romanticism of the old world with the realism of the new, the rich color of continental speech with the strength and directness of the English, he was a consummate master of that broader English which by its power is conquering the world. Refusing to be bound by the narrow interpretation which Andrew Lang and the rest would fasten to his literary creed, this realist, or "veritist," along with Garland and others, blossomed out, in story and verse, in beautiful flowers of fancy, never forgetting, however, that these flowers require earth and sun and dew and rain. It is a pity that such as Hjalmar Hjorth Boyesen should thus die, in the young manhood of their mental powers. There must be a mistake somewhere when one so well equipped for work, one physically and mentally so strong, should thus suddenly come to a standstill, the enginery of his physical life having abruptly ceased to move.

* *

ON the opposite page is given an interesting facsimile of the newly discovered diary of Sergeant Floyd, who accompanied the famous Lewis and Clark expedition to the Northwest in 1804, and who found a grave on the east bank of the Missouri River near the present city of Sioux City. This diary has thrown a flood of light upon that historic expedition, and is one of the most valued documents in the possession of the Wisconsin Historical Society. Through the courtesy of the Sioux City *Journal* we are able thus to supplement the historical paper by Mrs. Brooks, entitled "Sergeant Floyd's Grave," in the present number of this magazine.

* *

MAJOR S. H. M. BYERS, one of the foremost literary men in the country, and one of Iowa's most highly esteemed and honored citizens, makes an eloquent plea in THE MIDLAND for a Memorial Hall at

A Journal Commenced at River Dubois — Monday

May 14th 1804 Showery day Capt Clark set out at

4 oClock P m for the Western expedition the party

Consisted of Serjeants and 38 working hands which moved

the Batteaux and two Perogues we Sailed up 25 miles and

6 miles and Encamped on the L. S. 6:30 of the River

Tusday may 15th 1804 Rainey morning finished the

Latter part of the day Sailed 6 oClock and Encamped on

the S. side some from Clarke the Banks very bad —

Wensday may 16 1804 Set out early this morning pleasant

arrived at St Charles at 2 oclock P m one Loure Leveé

"first number of French people to me the Boat

Be this place is an old French village 88 Roman

With Permission of the Sioux City Journal.
FACSIMILE OF A PAGE FROM SERGEANT FLOYD'S DIARY OF THE LEWIS AND
CLARK EXPEDITION.

the State Capitol — a plea which will not be lost on the next legislature. Iowa is accumulating a wealth of historic material which cannot be estimated in money, cannot be covered by insurance. Thanks to the indefatigable and well directed labors of the curator of the Historical Department, the Hon. Charles Aldrich, the accumulation is rapid, and without any diminution of the quality of the material collected. Space is needed, and not mere space alone, but also facilities for systematizing the storage with a view to free public access to these stores, and to a suitable exhibition of the statuary, paintings, engravings, rare books and prints, etc. The several other departments of State work housed in the Capitol are constantly reaching out after more room, and in a very few years at the longest some provision must be made for more room for the Historical Department also. A separate Memorial Hall should be erected near the State Capitol, thus realizing the dream of those who preferred such a building rather than a soldiers' monument, and at the same time including far more of usefulness than was dreamt of in the minds of those who first urged a Memorial Hall. Readers of this magazine have not forgotten the eloquent pleas of Hon. George H. Parker, consul at Birmingham, England, for a suitable commemoration of Iowa's semi-centennial in 1896. What could be a more fitting commemoration than the laying of a corner stone for a building to be erected for the purpose of preserving the memorials of the State's historic past!

* *

THE type of Midland Beauty presented in this number is Miss Harriet Wright, a prominent young lady in Des Moines society.

AMONG THE MAGAZINES.

The New Bohemian made its first appearance in Cincinnati in October. It is a well-printed and illustrated magazine of forty pages and its price is one dollar a year. It bears no editorial name and is issued by the Bohemian Publishing Company. Its frontispiece is a well-drawn portrait by Harry O. Landers, of "Amber," Mrs. Martha Evans Holden, "Queen of Bohemia." Its initial story, "Saunders' Story," cleverly told by "Falcon," if taken as a type of the forthcoming fiction of the magazine, gives promise of a new outflow of erotic literature. Let us hope that the bad promise may be broken. The first poem, "In Bohemia," by Elgin H. Roy, rather confirms the promise. It calls —

"A truce upon old times and days:
A truce upon convention's ways:"—

It will be a sad day when literature and life are released from the restraints of conventionalities. But no one need fear; that day will never come. The sketch of "Amber," by Leroy Armstrong, is, barring a few extravagancies, a delightful eulogy. Mr. O'Malley, an Indiana poet, evidently thinks he has dealt Veritism a telling blow, though the veritists will doubtless smile at the man of straw he so vigorously flails. Mr. James Knapp Reeve, editor of *The Editor*, Franklin, Ohio, contributes an excellent talk with young authors. "A Night in Bohemia" (unsigned) has a strong smell of stale beer and tobacco smoke. The cigarette-smoking soubrette pictured is alone enough to make one weary of this particular "Bohemia," before reaching the concluding rhyme — which ends with, "Right good cheer, cigars and beer." The editorial departments are abundant in promise.

Peterson's Magazine dropped to ten cents but was so hurt by the fall that it soon after expired. The *American Newsman* attributes the failure to bad business judgment, and too small capital to meet the fierce competition at the metropolis.

"The Pursuit of Happiness," pictured by José Cabrinety, and filled in with reading matter by Elizabeth C. Cardozo, —the filling not sufficiently packed, though the type is large and the paragraphing absurdly frequent,—has leading place in the October *Cosmopolitan*. The illustrations, the real subject matter, are strong. The allegory sounds so like something heard before that one can't help wondering if Olive Schreiner hasn't passed on her gift to Elizabeth Cardozo.

To-Day says : Variety in covers seems to be a periodical fad just now. Publishers have the notion that the eye alone is to be appealed to, and in many cases literary worth is sacrificed to a striking exterior.

The *Century* magazine was twenty-five years old in October. It is the greatest magazine in the world and one of the most notable successes of the century.

In the regulation newspaper notice of the October *Cosmopolitan*, the last of Kipling's "Jungle Stories" for boys is thus pathetically alluded to: "The curtain is drawn over one of the most charming conceits in literature." We are just dull enough to be glad for the *Cosmopolitan* that the word "forever" can be applied to its "Jungle Stories" series. These fables are, to us, the silly "conceits" of a great genius — as great as he is fitful and uneven. Questioning our own judgment in the matter, we asked an omnivorous magazine-reading boy what he thought of these "Jungle Stories." "I skip 'em," he answered. "The pictures is all that's good in 'em."

GOSSIP ABOUT AUTHORS.

It is gratifying to note that the great Carlyle found his first publisher and his first audience in America, and that our Emerson was his sponsor. "Sartor Resartus" was first published in Boston. The first money Carlyle's "French Revolution" brought him came also from the States. Mr. Smalley says, in this connection, that Browning had an assured public here before he found it in England, that Tennyson was and is read more here than in his native country, and that Spenser had already founded a school of philosophy in America when Gladstone asked, "Who is Herbert Spenser?"

It is as gratifying to note the indebtedness of England's really great thinkers to American discoverers as it is humiliating to see the American public's eager acceptance of anything English which comes labeled "fiction," stamped with the name of any well-known publisher. Many a book of English origin has been rushed upon the American market, with shrewd accompaniment of newspaper sketches and portraits of the author, and had a large sale among that extensive and growing class with whom novel reading is a fad, when the better work of our American novelists, full of the thrill of our richer American life, has found comparatively few appreciative readers. Just at this time there are a half-dozen or more clever journalists and professional men hovering about London who are enjoying the benefits of the American popularity of two or three others of their countrymen, who by their talents have won fame in this country. Once it was said that no good thing could come out of Nazareth — an injustice none the less apparent than would have been the reverse of the proposition, namely, that nothing but good could

come out of Nazareth. Because "A Widow of Thrums" is a refreshing picture of Scottish village life, and "The Men of the Moss Hags" is the most vigorous pen-drawing of the old Covenanters since the time of Scott; because Hall Caine and Conan Doyle and Ian McLaren and Anthony Hope and the rest have respectively done some good work, it does not follow that everything is good which comes from Barrie and Crockett and Doyle and the rest, and that a new book from any of these or from any one of their clever imitators should shelve the work of our Mary Wilkins, Alice French, Amelia Barr, Howells, Garland, Stockton, Davis and other American authors who are doing much for the making of American literature.

Let us be sincere in dealing with authors as in every other relation. The musician instinctively detects the false note of admiration from one who only affects a love of music. The painter sees through the meaningless generalities by which the person devoid of the artistic sense seeks to impress upon others his fondness for art. There is, but there shouldn't be, a fashion in literature.

"I want the 'Prisoner of Zenda,'" said a young lady in Brentano's recently. Her friend asked her if she had read "Pembroke," adding, "I think you ought to read the really great novels of our own time and our own country before taking up novels wholly outside the range of your own experience and observation." The young lady responded: "To be just frank with you. 'The Prisoner of Zenda' seems to be all the go, and when I get to my cousin's I'll want to be able to talk knowingly about the book." The elder lady smiled and said, "Of course, if you buy books as you do hats and wraps, I've nothing more to say."

There are books you can't like if you try. Why not say so. If you can't see as far into "The Inferno" as Lowell can, frankly admit it. If "Hypatia," save for a few chapters, either drags or seems inartistically horrible, why not tell the truth about it? If Conan Doyle's best selling books don't seem to you to have in them the breath of real life, nobody is going to think less of you because you refuse to rave over them. If Miss Wilkins tires you; if Miss Murfree seems at times to play with words signifying nothing; if any book you read impresses you otherwise than as it impresses some critic who writes so well about books that you are disposed to distrust your own judgment entirely, hold on to your own independent judgment. Hold on to it unless the critic throws a flood of light upon the book which shows you he is right and you were wrong. His dictum alone, or the first judgment of the public, should not compel your assent to views thereon to which you do not inwardly subscribe. The critic and the public may come around to your way of thinking, or may not; but, having come honestly by your judgment hold on to it until convinced you were wrong. Thou shalt not bear false witness either against or for thy neighbor's book, and in literature all who come within touch are our neighbors.

Mr. E. V. Smalley maintains that a comparison between the *Atlantic Monthly* of 1895 and the first issue of that magazine in 1857 reveals the decadence of Boston as a literary center. In that first issue appear contributions from Motley, Longfellow, Emerson, Holmes, Lowell, Harriet Beecher Stowe, Trowbridge and Rose Terry—a brilliant galaxy, surely. But bear in mind that the first *Atlantic* appeared thirty-eight years ago, and that the glory round about most of these names was not as luminous then as it is now. Emerson had not the assured place he now has. His well-known series of essays, "Conduct of Life," also his "Society and Solitude" and his volume of poems came later. Lowell's best work also came afterward. The author of the "Biglow Papers" was known to the many because of that "timely" verse; but the history had not then been made which inspired Lowell's greatest poem, his "Commemoration Ode." "Under the Willows," "The Cathedral," "Heartsease and Rue," and all that vast wealth of prose writings embodied in "Among My Books," "My Study Windows," and other valuable works, then had no being, except possibly as phantoms of the brain waiting the creative touch. Motley, the historian of the Dutch Republic and the Netherlands, was as little known then outside his coterie as is now the promising young author of "Lincoln as a Lawyer" in the last MIDLAND. Longfellow had an assured place as a popular verse-maker, but his "Courtship of Miles Standish," "Tales of a Wayside Inn," "New England Tragedies," "Hanging of the Crane," "In the Harbor,"—in fact a half-dozen of his most popular collections of poems were not yet dreamt out. Trowbridge, always clever, was never great. Parke Godwin was only a talented and highly educated journalist with a fondness for art. Rose Terry (Mrs. Cook) was at her best not the equal of a dozen short-story writers of our time. The only one named

who had then reached the far height secure is Harriet Beecher Stowe. Though "Uncle Tom's Cabin" may have been surpassed by some of Mrs. Stowe's later work, yet that book alone made its author a unique figure in American literature, a potent force in our politics, a historic character. To make the comparison good, one must view the Boston coterie that rallied to the support of its home magazine, not in the present full light of their finished work, but in the uncertain light of that early day.

But even now, while the *Atlantic* contributors are in the midst of their life work and therefore cannot be measured as to their relative place in literature, we may safely put alongside the great ones of thirty odd years ago such names as Thomas Bailey Aldrich, John Fiske, Elizabeth Stuart Phelps, Mary J. Wilkins, Margaret Deland, Susan Coolidge, Louise Imogen Guiney, Sarah Orne Jewett, Horace E. Scudder, and others of the newer New England school of writers. But no pent-up New England now confines any magazine's powers. Mary Hartwell Catherwood of Illinois, Maurice Thompson of Indiana, Kate Douglas Wiggin of Minnesota, Mary Hallock Foote of Idaho, Virna Woods of California, Mary N. Murfree of Tennessee, Alice French of Iowa, and other stars in our western firmament have been reflected in the *Atlantic* during the past year or two. The fact is that the country has grown so great during the years that measure the life of our oldest and most historic literary magazine that a dozen periodicals may surpass the old *Atlantic* in circulation and in the number of great names attached thereto and yet leave ample field, material and talent for the pioneer magazine.

Speaking of Emerson—there will never be another Emerson. There need never be. Great as was the influence of the Sage of Concord in his time, and quotable as he is to-day, it would be impossible for an Emerson to repeat the successful literary career of the great maxim-maker. The period before the War was an era of maxims and aphorisms—and Emerson was preëminently the writer for that era. His was a period of reaction from the extreme puritanism of the last century and from the tyranny of dogmatism. Emerson reverently voiced the Christian theism of the time, and men bound hand and foot by a relentless dogma heard him gladly. The echo of Emerson's creed of reverence, dutifulness and cheerfulness is now heard in every Christian convocation, and the old abstractions of the theologians have little more than a historical significance. Much that Emerson then presented with the utmost gravity, and which was received by his following as oracular, has since become common property as proverb; we might almost call it platitude. Over against the philosophic thought of the Emerson era may be placed the practical forces at work to-day —agencies working for the better government of cities, for the amelioration of the condition of the poor without weakening the fiber of their moral nature, for placing education in the mechanic arts and in the liberal arts within the reach of all, for giving the public access to all books and enjoyment of the representative art of all ages and countries and for the substitution of mutually helpful co-operation for wasteful individualism.

Some time ago a contributor for *The Critic* stirred the women writers of the country to lively discussion by the assertion that no woman had ever invented anything useful to the world. The discussion is recalled by the story Mrs. Brown tells, in the present number of THE MIDLAND, of Mrs. Ada Van Pelt's ingenious invention,—a lock-box with 3,000 combinations and with self-closing apertures, water and dust excluded, and gravity doing the work instead of springs.

We recently received a manuscript of 155 pages which came all the way from the seaboard at an expense of $1 for coming and returning, and in the very first page of the manuscript the nominative "we" was placed as the object of the preposition "to." This writer needs a thirteen-weeks' course in grammar. Opening by chance at the fifty-second page, we find the following: "As the real business of the story is to commence in the next chapter, it will be presumed that the foregoing is sufficient introduction of the commonplace individual who clutches the pen." Quite so.

Speaking of Conan Doyle's "White Company," we must have "gone wrong" in our estimate of the book, for that all-knowing critic, Andrew Lang, fairly warms to it! Our consolation is that in literature there is no absolute standard—not even Andrew Lang's judgment — by which we may determine who has and who hasn't gone wrong.

Mr. Charles A. Gray, whose attractively illustrated paper on "Newspaper Illustrating" has first place in the present number, is on the *Times-Herald* force of artists. His specialty is portraits in pen and ink, in which he has few if any

equals. This we learn from unprejudiced sources. But the reader has only to turn to the etching from Mr. Gray's pen-drawing of Gladstone on page 392 to see for himself that this work could not well be surpassed.

Max O'Rell (Paul Blouet), the irrepressible, having worn out American and English audiences, by making fun of them to their faces, will next attempt a drama.

Hon. Henry Sabin has an able paper in the September *Educational Review* on "The Rural School Problem."

Albert Shaw's "Municipal Government in Continental Europe" will soon appear.

Leonard W. Volk, whose statue of Stephen A. Douglas stands at Thirty-fifth street near the lake in South Chicago, and whose statues of Lincoln and Douglas adorn the capitol at Springfield, died recently at his summer home in Wisconsin.

Mr. J. A. Smith, whose sketch, "The Hegira of the Elk," appeared in the August MIDLAND, and whose sketch of General Cross appears in the present number, learned the printer's trade in the Vermont office in which General Cross and "Artemus Ward" learned the trade, and personally knows of the vagaries of those well known men.

The *Critic's* first prize of $25 for bicycle poetry was awarded to Robert Clarkson Tongue, Middleton, Conn.; the second prize, to Eben E. Rexford, Shiocton, Wis., author of the prize descriptive paper, "The Island of Mackinac," in the September MIDLAND.

Max O'Rell, Ian McLaren, Hall Caine and other European lovers of American dollars are headed toward us, purposing to lecture us, for a consideration.

Miss Eugenie Uhlrich,—whose character sketch, "A Home o' Me Own," in the present number, is the second of THE MIDLAND series of "Sketches from Life in Labor's World,"— is assistant editor of the *Northwestern Chronicle*, St. Paul.

RECENT events have developed patriotic poems from three poets of national reputation. James Whitcomb Riley's poem adds nothing to the Hoosier's great fame. Frank L. Stanton, the Georgia poet, rises to a higher level than before attained. Major S. H. M. Byers, the foremost poet of Iowa, gives splendid promise of what the public may expect from his forthcoming long poem on Sherman's historic march.

The *Chap-Book* accuses Conan Doyle of writing his "Stark-Munro Letters," his latest fiction, "to the sapping of all intelligence in the reader," the plot hanging upon "a pale and anæmic love affair and a marriage."

Maurice Thompson thinks he finds an "unbroken strain of man-harrying Amazons marching through history."

Hamlin Garland's poem "Wagner," in the October *Chap-Book*, is a real poem standing out in an era of clever rhymes. It begins:

"A faint, far horn was blown—
I listened   and the hollow north
Grew thunderous and sweet with sound!" *

CONTRIBUTOR'S DEPARTMENT.

A BIOGRAPHER OF JOHN BROWN DEFENDS RICHARD REALF— COLONEL HINTON REPLIES TO MR. COPPOC.

I had already written Mr. Coppoc after reading his article on "John Brown and His Cause," but a re-perusal compels me to ask of you space in your next issue in order to say why I am sure that Richard Realf did not betray John Brown's movements. Even his evidence in the January following the attack, given before the United States Senate Harper's Ferry committee, told nothing not already known to the slavocrat politicians. It did give the facts as to John Brown's movements in a more consecutive fashion. That's all. The charge of treachery was made by James Redpath in the heat of events. I was with him, assisting in preparing the life of John Brown (1860), and urged upon Redpath the injustice of the accusation. He persisted then, but in a later edition withdrew it.

Richard Realf may have been weak, but he was noble in his purposes. He was not treacherous. In the design of my book, "John Brown and His Men," I did not enter into many details more directly relative to others who were not present at Harper's Ferry. If I had, perhaps, it might have fallen to my duty to have made more clear my own humble actions. It certainly would have obliged me to make clear Richard Realf's connection. That I shall do in my memoir of him, when his poems are published by me.

Let me say then, as to Realf, these facts: He went to England in June, 1866, in good faith. He failed in his efforts to raise money. Ere returning, after lecturing in the Channel Islands, he crossed over to France and visited Paris. Returning to Havre, he sold a pair of revolvers and some other things for money to take a cheap passage to New Orleans on a cotton ship. His idea was to see something of slavery for himself and work his way up to Kansas by

way of the Mississippi River, and on the voyage he read a work by some casuist on "The Responsibility of the Human Will." It upset him on the question of the right to attack slavery by force. At New Orleans he got some slight employment on one of the dailies and fell in with Catholic priests. He was baptized by the name of "John," was then sent to Alabama to a seminary, but he soon left and wandered off lecturing on Shakspeare, Keats, Poetry, the Working Classes, Intemperance, etc. He never disguised that he had been on the Free State side in Kansas, but he never attacked slavery.

At the time of the blow against Harper's Ferry, he was in Texas. He kept still, but after awhile his name and personality attracted marked attention. Those familiar with the period know that the slavocrat politicians sought to use the John Brown raid against the Republican leaders and to hasten the tendency to civil war. To that end a Senate Committee was authorized, with Jefferson Davis as chairman, and William Mason of Virginia as a member, to investigate. Suspicion became certainty as to Realf, and the Texas mob wanted his blood. Adroit men, chiefly inspired by Judge George W. Paschall, of Austin, Texas, I think, who desired, first, to save Realf's life and, second, to prevent the political evil that would have resulted from his mob-murder, persuaded the people that he was more valuable as a state prisoner than as a victim of lynch law. Judge Paschall was within two years after a Unionist fugitive. In Washington he several times told me the story of his acquaintance with Realf. His purpose was to get the young man to Washington to save his life. He succeeded. Texans thought that they now had the key to all the conspiracy and guarded him as a precious jewel. Under Paschall's advice, Realf looked mysterious and said nothing. He was guarded to Washington as a witness. When there, he also said nothing of any moment. On being discharged, he made his way to Northern Ohio. The $600 he was paid as witness fees was divided, as to half of it, between two of the fugitives who escaped Virginian savagery.

Senator Henry Wilson, I recall, for one, and Representative Anson P. Burlingame, for another, telling me over and over again that Realf's testimony did no harm. Ex-Governor Amy, of Kansas, did not think he did any mischief. Indeed, there was none to do. The carpet-bag captured at the hill-side school house with its contents, put together by Governor Wise's shrewd lawyers, as aided by extended detective work, had unraveled practically all there was in the John Brown movement. Realf did not confess, convey or betray any information hurtful to Captain Brown or the friends who aided him. Major George L. Stearns, who was in the largest peril, never thought, certainly never expressed such charge. Realf was not faithless, though faulty, keeping his connection up by writing, or at least by formally withdrawing as Luke F. Parsons did.

RICHARD J. HINTON.
Bay Ridge, N. Y., October 4.

AN APPEAL TO IOWA WOMEN.

To-day the women throughout the United States are working, each in her respective state, to raise the Age of Consent laws. Where is Iowa? What is she doing? Simply nothing. When the bill asking that the age be raised to eighteen years was defeated, it plainly showed the class of men who rule our state. Noble men were there who honored their manhood, but more were there who cared more for the votes of men than for the protection of their daughters.

And now I appeal to the women, to the mothers. Will you not join hands and remedy this wrong?

Iowa is a grand state — a state of which we are all proud. Let us lead her forward with the others that are advancing. Is there not a woman in Iowa who will take up this cause for the good of all humanity?

Helen H. Gardner should be honored throughout our land for her work in this direction. Wherein lies the justice of this age at thirteen, fourteen or fifteen? What is the girl but a child? Our laws say she has not judgment to protect property at that age; would she have judgment to protect her virtue? Ah, no.

"We must protect our boys," it is said. Does not the law protect them — the law which punishes them for ruining a girl?

Put the age of consent at eighteen and our boys will be better protected than they are to-day, better than society will ever protect them — the society which closes its eyes and says, "sowing wild oats." Colorado, Nebraska and many other states have made the fight and won. Shall we not try?

LELA MOORE.
Randalia, Iowa.

TALKS WITH CORRESPONDENTS.

I have decided to devote my entire time to literary pursuits, and poetry seems to be my forte, though I have written some few prose articles. I wish to find a market for my productions, and thought I would apply to you first as you are located in my own state. They will be all equally as good as the enclosed sample. This is a subject which has seldom, if ever, been treated in the form of poetry, or if it has, has not come under my observation, hence, if it possesses any merit, must be entirely original. I can furnish you with one or more pieces every month, including a humorous piece once in a while, if you like that kind of literature.

1. Before deciding to devote your entire time to literary pursuits, try your powers and see if they be of the winning and the staying kind. Many are inwardly called, but few are chosen. 2. You will find no regular market for your poetry, etc., as the dairyman finds a market for his butter. 3. No poet who has accurately measured his powers is able to say that his productions are all equally good. The great newspapers buy "piece-work" regularly, but they buy only the work of contributors who have learned the trade of writing and have a reputation for good work. There are only a few magazine editors left who dare stipulate in advance that they will regularly publish any man's writing.

The young writer should reflect on the difference between literary pursuits and other callings, and how much is implied by the adoption of authorship as a profession. Unlike news-gathering, unlike editing the news after it is gathered, the career of an author presupposes either genius transcending knowledge or knowledge not possessed by others, or experiences unique and interesting in themselves, or rare powers of revealing the workings of the soul, the operations of society or the secrets of nature. To most writers it is quite enough that they are able to occasionally contribute something which interests or benefits or blesses others, increasing the volume of work or, better yet, improving the quality, as experience strengthens their powers and their hold on the public.

This is my first attempt to have my writings published. I am very anxious to succeed in literary work and would much like to write for your paper if my work will please you. If you have any "subjects" you would like written I would be glad if you would send them to me and will see what I can do with them.

1. The sad fact in this connection is that, in justice to the readers of the magazine, a writer's anxiety to succeed cannot be considered by the editor. If that kindly disposed individual, the editor, could only attach to a weak contribution a note something like this : "Don't judge the contribution severely ; this is the author's first attempt," all might be well. But, alas ! the public expect an editor's best selection and refuse to pay for the immature author's schooling in the rudiments. 2. In a world of many writers, happily the editor doesn't need to send subjects around among writers for them to practice upon. The best contributions to current literature are not given out ; they are born of experience, observation, thought or emotion ; then they grow in the mind and finally they are delivered — and some portion of the great reading world recognize a something in their lives and thought which was not there before.

My story is a fine one and founded on fact.

1. Better to let the story speak for itself. 2. The phrase "founded on fact" cannot make a story one whit more true

to life than it seems to the reader to be. It rather begs the whole question as to whether the story be good or poor.

What is the object of a poem ? To carry out the poetic idea in the best manner possible, or to arrange the lines so as to contain the exact number of poetic feet ?

Primarily, to carry out the poetic idea, and secondarily to arrange the lines so as to make them rhythmical. The quotations our friend makes from Longfellow's "Haunted Chamber" only prove that Longfellow, like all the other great poets, did not always keep his ideals in mind. One can find among the great poets vindication for all sorts of sins against rhythm and rhyme, just as one can find isolated passages in the Bible that convey all sorts of unbiblical impressions. In studying the history of poetic style one should take the poets at their best, not seek to catch them nodding.

My writing is poor, grammar imperfect, composing good. Do I stand any show in the competition ?

If your grammar is imperfect, your composing can't be good and your show in the contest would not be good The judges in any competition for a prize in composition have a right to assume that all competitors have at least mastered the art of expressing themselves grammatically.

THE MIDLAND BOOK TABLE.

Mrs. Julia C. R. Dorr's sketches of English travel, under the historic title of "The Flower of England's Face," have been recently published by Macmillan & Company in a dainty volume, the cover of which is appropriately starred with roses. We have no sketches of the byways of England similar to this charming book except Mr. Reuben Goldthwaite's "Our Cycling Tour in England," or Mr. William Winter's "Shakespeare's England." Mrs. Dorr went upon no ordinary quest when she traveled in Europe during the summer of 1897 — a half dozen of our great writers bidding her Godspeed and giving her instructions as to the most delightful untraveled haunts. Oliver Wendell Holmes wrote with a hand tremulous with age : "Take this hurried letter of mine with you, and show it if you will, and it will be a kind of letter of introduction." Mr. Edmund C. Stedman sent her to Conway Castle, and another writer to the Caledonia Canal where, on one gala day she explored its hidden recesses, when every Scotch man and woman wore a sprig of the

heather and many were clad in full Highland costume.

One can scarcely tell which chapter is the most interesting, but the reader who desires to learn about "the heart of England" will prefer "In the Forest of Arden," a chapter which not only gives some unhackneyed glimpses of Stratford-on-Avon but also describes most delightfully Leycester hospital, founded in the sixteenth century by Lord Dudley, the Leicester of Queen Elizabeth. This hospital was built for the perpetual maintenance of twelve old impoverished English soldiers, who have, to this day, an annual income of eighty pounds, and a historic home decorated everywhere with the Bear and Ragged Staff — the coat of arms of the founder

The lover of Charlotte Bronte will perhaps prefer "At Haworth," while those interested in that form of philanthropy which educates the artistic sense of the poor will enjoy "At the Peacock Inn."

The whole book reveals the secret of that subtle charm which binds the New Engleader of to-day, notwithstanding many national differences, to the historic old England of the past.

MARY J. REID.

Most sonnets have the life squeezed out of them by the mold in which they are cast, but Herbert Bashford's little book, "Seadrift,"* includes several sonnets which seem as naturally adapted to the ancient form as though they themselves had made the fashion. The one beginning with, "Can I forget that glorious autumn night," is especially worthy of mention.

The fame of Elizabeth Stuart Phelps is well beyond the power of any one story to seriously injure it, and yet we confess to having taken up the latest work of this favorite author with a fear of finding therein a suggestion of loss of power. The serial completed in the October *Atlantic*, and since published in book form, entitled "A Singular Life,"† far from giving evidence of waning strength, is a series of surprises, both in the delicate humor of much of the character sketching and scene painting and in the intensity of the tragedy. Emanuel Bayard is a rare creation, and yet always recognizably human — a delicate organization possessed of a moral courage that cheerfully faces death for duty's sake and, better yet, unflinchingly accepts a life of continual sacrifice in the spirit and service of the Master. He feels called to preach the Word of Life to souls that most need the Word, and yet he will not be trammeled by the severely mathematical plan of salvation taught in his school of theology. He ardently loves the daughter of a professor of theology, Helen Carruth by name. His love approaches adoration, and at times seems to him sinful, it is so sweet. Helen's love for him is tender as a mother's, and yet of a very practical old-New England sort, a trifle severe on the surface sometimes, but ever strong and deep and full of the spirit of helpfulness. Helen's wit is a foil to Emanuel's seriousness. The droll characters and drolleries of speech freely introduced are a happy relief to the intensity of the main current of the story. The eye-opening effect of a great love upon the life-work of the preacher is vividly portrayed, revealing to the man's astonished soul that "something else than consecration is needed to do the best and greatest thing by the human want or woe that leans upon us," — namely, human experience.

*Herbert Bashford. Tacoma, Wash. †Houghton, Mifflin & Co., Boston and New York. $1.25.

Elizabeth Stuart Phelps has strengthened her strong hold on readers of books and has done humanity a service by putting forth "A Singular Life," a story primarily entertaining and secondarily healthfully stimulating.

The lover of good literature knows no sectional lines, no nationality. He condemns the hot-house productions of certain Eastern publishers, not because they are Eastern, but because they are hot-house productions. He protests against the present American craze for English books, not because the books are written by Britons, but because it is a craze and therefore undiscriminating as between wholesome and unwholesome fiction, and as between real novels, in which the people live and move and have being, and those which are made after the journalistic yarn-spinning fashion of the time. Invigorating as a trip to Scotland after confinement in a London hotel is an escape from the hot-house atmosphere of London fiction to the moss-hags of Scotland, where the men are men and the women are women, and life is real and earnest and love is true, and marriage is the end and not the beginning of childish follies. S. R. Crockett, in his "Men of the Moss-Hags,"* reaffirms his claim to permanent place in literature. Though his narrative drags at times, as does Scott's, yet in the main it is interesting, at times intensely interesting. It peoples the moss-hags with Covenanters and kings' men so real in all their strength and weakness that the reader feels the life of two hundred years ago as never before. The simple home-life of the Scotch, the practical wisdom and thought of the women, the virility of the men, the vitality of the religion they professed, the strength of their love of religious liberty, the depths of their affection, all are reflected in these pages with marvelous clearness. William Gordon, odd compound of courage and cowardice; Sandy, his brother, rough, brave, dull, true; Jean, Sandy's wife, "just inordinate for preachings and prophesyings"; Wat Gordon, gay, dashing, handsome, brave even to rashness; Maisie Lennox, shrewd, helpful, faithful, loving, self-denying, the noblest Scotch woman in literature since Jeannie Deans, — these are the principal figures in the narrative. We use the term "narrative," for no other word seems to fit this realistic story, which purports to be "a history of adventure taken from the papers of William Gordon

*Macmillan & Co., publishers. New York. $1.50.

of Earlstoun, in Galloway, and told over again by S. R. Crockett." Nothing could be more real than the Richard Cameron who incidentally enters upon the scene as he preaches the gospel to the hill-folk, and as he leads his forlorn hope "in the last charge at Ayrsmoss." The picture given in the last chapter of Maisie Lennox riding without rein, the people opening a lane that she might save her William from execution by the pardon she has obtained, though conventional in general conception, becomes intensely real as one reads on to the end. "Very pale was her face, the sweetest ever the sun shone on. Very weary were the lids of her eyes, that were the truest and the bravest which ever God gave to woman. But when they were lifted up to look at me on the scaffold of death, I saw that through the anxiety, which drew dark rings about them, they were joyful with a great joy!"

Shakspeare found "sermons in stones," and if he had lived in our time he would have found sermons in verse; not texts for sermons, but sermons. "Plymouth Vespers," by Rev. Dr. A. L. Frisbie, of Plymouth Church, Des Moines, is chiefly made up of three short long poems, or long short poems, which were read by him from his pulpit on three different evenings. They are respectively entitled "The Easter Story," "Storm and Peace," and "The Shepherd Lord." They are written in various measures well fitting the subject-matter, and they'll all "scan." They abound in rare imagery and religious suggestion. The most poetical of the three is "Storm and Peace," a vivid picture of the storm on Lake Genesaret. The burden of the thought is that—

" In all nights, on every wave,
    In every gale, however high,
  The Lord is walking, strong to save,
    And saying, 'Fear not. It is I.'"

As we were about to close this department for the month, came "Beatrice of Bayou Téche,"* and along with her came the odor of magnolia blossoms, the fragrance from "blossoming hedges of roses," and myriad other suggestions of the "colonnaded forests" in the romance land of Louisiana. With those who read

the story as it first appeared in THE MIDLAND how vividly remains the picture of the child dreamer of dreams and seer of visions; the spiritually passionate young woman, her soul beating its wings against the bars of caste; the friend, the lover, the artist, the banished victim of distinctions of society's own selfish creating! The pathos of the story is intense. The humor is exquisite. The character sketching is so delicate that its artistic strength is a continual surprise. Its gifted author, Alice Ilgenfritz Jones, has but yielded to the wishes of her friends and the many admirers of her work, in publishing the story in book form. It makes a pretty little volume of 386 pages.

Anticipating the question in the minds of many MIDLAND readers, "To what extent has the story been revised?" we find the only revision materially affecting the story itself is in the twenty-sixth and the closing chapter. The re-writing of these chapters has greatly strengthened the book. It dignifies Burgoyne, presenting him no longer as the weak youth, idly trifling with a great love, and at the last perversely marrying the wrong woman; but, rather, as the victim of a mistaken sense of honor in marrying an unworthy woman he did not love. The final consciousness that she had really been loved by Burgoyne lifts Beatrice above the dead level on which the first draft of the story left her, fires her soul with new ambition, and imparts to her life a new meaning. Those who read the story before will be glad to have it in book form, and they who haven't read it will find rare pleasure in it.

OTHER BOOKS RECEIVED.

Potomac Series, No. 5, Club Number, Potomac Series Co., Washington, D. C. Price 25 cents.

Stenotypy, or Shorthand by the Typewriter, by Rev. D. A. Quinn, Providence, R. I.

"A Son of the Plains," by Arthur Paterson. Macmillan & Co., New York, $1.25.

"The Wise Woman," a novel, by Clara Louise Burnham. Houghton, Mifflin & Co., Boston, $1.25.

"Wild Rose," a tale of the Mexican frontier, by Francis Francis. Macmillan & Co., New York, $1.00.

*A. C. McClurg & Co., Chicago, publishers. Sold by the Lathrop-Rhoads Co., Des Moines. $1.25.

Photo, by Brewer, Alloa.

TYPES OF MIDLAND BEAUTY. VI.

THE MIDLAND MONTHLY.

VOLUME IV.   DECEMBER, 1895.   NUMBER 6.

THOMAS NAST AND HIS WORK.

By LEIGH LESLIE.

WHO that read *Harper's Weekly* in the dark and troublous days of the Civil War can ever forget those powerful emblematic pictures on its pages, rich in originality and in vigor, which bore the signature of Thomas Nast? What inspiration was in those pictures! How they thrilled the heart of the weary, foot-sore soldier! How they roused the enthusiasm of the loyal citizen!

Thomas Nast's soul was *en rapport* with the spirit of the North, and his pencil gleamed like a sword. President Lincoln publicly acknowledged that Nast did more than anyone else to inspire patriotism and to recruit the army. Others high in public station paid similar tribute to his genius.

It was in that period, too, that Nast's first great political caricatures appeared. It may be said that the publication of these cartoons marked an epoch in the history of pictorial satire. The work of the young artist increased in audacity and in importance until Nast came to be regarded as a master of the satirical grotesque.

In the creations of pictorial satirists of all ages rarer humor or more far-reaching suggestiveness can nowhere be found than in the works of Nast. To his cartoons must the historian turn for the popular reflection of many political notabilities.

In the great uprising in New York City against that arch-corruptionist, Tweed, and his "ring," Nast employed his pencil to excellent purpose, doing more, it was conceded, to expose the nefarious methods of the "bosses" who for so many years had been misruling and robbing the municipality, and to rouse public sentiment against them, than did all of the other reform agencies combined. None of his cartoons was without sharp point. One of them represented Tweed as a money-bag, suggesting to the public what was afterward absolutely proved,— namely, that the notorious leader had comprehended a great fortune for himself through corrupt political practices. That famous money-bag caricature directed public attention so strongly to, and crystallized public sentiment so clearly on, this proposition, that Tweed himself attributed to it the disruption of his forces.

Before the Republican National Convention of 1872, the coterie of great journalists who sought to discredit the administration of President Grant, and to prevent his renomination for the presidency, winced under the keen thrusts of satire from Nast's pencil. In the political struggle of that year Nast achieved the greatest triumphs. That skill of grotesque suggestiveness with which he is so richly endowed was thrown into his combinations with an *abandon* that challenged admiration. His works sorted well with the strong party feeling of the time, and wielded a prodigious influence. The absurd positions assumed in that memorable campaign by Greeley, Sumner and other of the former republican leaders were a source of constant inspiration to Nast. Each cartoon was a mirror in which these distinguished personages were enabled to see themselves in grotesque attitudes, as the public saw them.

Many of Nast's symbolic creations, as, for example, the great Republican Elephant, the Democratic Donkey, and the Tammany Tiger, are as securely established in American politics as are the Lion and the Unicorn on the escutcheon of John Bull. It is noteworthy, too, that the Republican Elephant never went down in defeat in a national campaign until Nast temporarily retired from the field. The result of the election of 1884 might have been otherwise if the editor of *Harper's Weekly*, George William Curtis, had not seen fit, for obvious reasons, to dispense with Nast's services on that journal.

But Thomas Nast is possessed of distinct genius for more serious art than that with which his name is most intimately associated in the popular mind. Already he has given us several great oil paintings

haps the choicest of his historical paintings. It is regarded as one of the best of the paintings relating to the War of the Rebellion. It represents with striking effect the scene of Lee's surrender to Grant at Appomattox. His masterly treatment of the great culminating scene in the gigantic struggle has won for the artist warmest encomiums from many critics.

While abroad last fall Mr. Nast met Mr. Hermann H. Kohlsaat, the well-known journalist, now editor and publisher of

THE IMMORTAL LIGHT OF GENIUS.

of historical association, and there is rich promise of even better work from his hand. His resolute determination to apply himself to great subjects augurs the highest success. Nast has a mind capable of grasping the loftiest conceptions, and he is daring, original, fertile in resource, ever aspiring after the highest forms of excellence. In range of subject, as well as of method, his art is comprehensive.

"Peace in Union," upon which he put the finishing touches last April, is per-

The Chicago Times-Herald. Nast and Kohlsaat spent some time together in London, and, before they parted, the editor and publisher had engaged the artist to execute this painting. Nast was given *carte blanche.* After diligent research and study, he shut himself in his studio and took up his brush. For months he labored assiduously, his interest in and love for the work growing with the development of the figures on the canvas. On April 9th, the thirtieth anniversary of the surrender, the picture was finished, and on April 27th, the seventy-third anniversary of Grant's birth, it was formally presented by Mr. Kohlsaat to the historic old town of Galena (which was Mr. Kohlsaat's home when Grant was an obscure clerk there in a leather store), Nast himself and many other distinguished men witnessing the unveiling.

For the better understanding of this historic painting, let me briefly recall to the

HEADQUARTERS ARMIES OF THE U. S.
8 P. M., April 7th, 1865.

GENERAL R. E. LEE,
    Commanding C. S. A:

The results of the last week must convince you of the hopelessness of further resistance on the part of the Army of Northern Virginia in this struggle. I feel that it is so and regard it as my duty to shift from myself the responsibility of any further effusion of blood by asking of you the surrender of that portion of the Confederate States Army known as the Army of Northern Virginia.

    U. S. GRANT,
    Lieutenant-General.

Copyright by Thomas Nast.
THE DEPARTURE OF THE SEVENTH REGIMENT, OF NEW YORK, 1861.

reader's mind, the events leading down to the surrender.

On Palm Sunday, April 9th, 1865, at Appomattox Court House, Virginia, the War of the Rebellion virtually terminated in the surrender of General Robert E. Lee, commanding the Army of Northern Virginia, to General Ulysses S. Grant, Commander-in-Chief of the Union Army.

Under date of April 7th, 1865, Grant wrote the following letter:

Lee's answer to this letter was as follows :

April 7th, 1865.

General:—I have received your note of this day. Though not entertaining the opinion you express on the hopelessness of further resistance on the part of the Army of Northern Virginia, I reciprocate your desire to avoid useless effusion of blood, and therefore before considering your proposition, ask the terms you will offer on condition of its surrender.
    R. E. Lee,

LIEUT.-GENERAL U. S. GRANT,   General
    Commanding Armies of the U. S.

To this unsatisfactory letter Grant made the following reply :

APRIL 9th, 1865.

GENERAL R. E. LEE,
Commanding C. S. A :

Your note of last evening in reply to mine of same date, asking the condition on which I will accept the surrender of the Army of Northern Virginia, is just received. In reply I would say that, peace being my great desire, there is but one condition I would insist upon, namely: that the men and officers surrendered shall be disqualified for taking up arms against the Government of the United States until properly exchanged. I will meet you, or will designate officers to meet any officers you may name for the same purpose, at any point agreeable to you, for the purpose of arranging definitely the terms upon which the surrender of the Army of Northern Virginia will be received.
U. S. GRANT,
Lieutenant-General.

The correspondence between Grant and Lee continued up to April 9th, when Lee requested the personal interview with Grant which resulted in the surrender of the Army of Northern Virginia. In his "Memoirs" Grant relates that Sheridan's troops were fearful lest the communications of Lee were only a ruse. "But," Grant goes on to say, "I had no doubt about the good faith of Lee, and pretty soon was conducted to where he was. I found him at the house of a Mr. McLean, at Appomattox Court House, with Colonel Marshall, one of his staff officers, awaiting my arrival. The head of his column was occupying a hill, on a portion of which was an apple orchard, beyond a little valley which separated it from that on the crest of which Sheridan's forces were drawn up in line of battle to the south. I had known General Lee in the old army, and had served with him in the Mexican War; but did not suppose, owing to the difference in our age and rank, that he would remember me; while I would more naturally remember him distinctly, because he was the chief of staff of General Scott in the Mexican War." The story of the surrender is thus told by General Grant :

When I had left camp that morning I had not expected so soon the result that was then taking place, and consequently was in rough garb. I was without a sword, as I usually was when on horseback on the field, and wore a soldier's blouse for a coat, with the shoulder straps of my rank to indicate to the army who I was. When I went into the house I found General Lee. We greeted each other, and, after shaking hands, took our seats. I had my staff with me, a good portion of whom were in the room during the whole of the interview.

What General Lee's feelings were I do not know. As he was a man of much dignity, with an impassible face, it was impossible to say whether he felt inwardly glad that the end had finally come, or felt sad over the result, and was too manly to show it. Whatever his feelings, they were entirely concealed from my observation; but my own feelings, which had been quite jubilant on the receipt of his letter, were sad and depressed. I felt like anything rather than rejoicing at the downfall of a foe who had fought so long and valiantly, and had suffered so much for a cause, though that cause was, I believe, one of the worst for which a people ever fought, and one for which there was the least excuse. I do not question, however, the sincerity of the great mass of those who were opposed to us.

General Lee was dressed in a full uniform which was entirely new, and was wearing a sword of considerable value, very likely the sword which had been presented by the State of Virginia ; at all events, it was an entirely different sword from the one that would ordinarily be worn in the field. In my rough traveling suit, the uniform of a private with the straps of a lieutenant-general, I must have contrasted very strangely with a man so handsomely dressed, six feet high and of faultless form. But this was not a matter that I thought of until afterward.

The moment when, with clasped hands, they stood looking earnestly into each other's face, has been seized upon by the artist to portray Grant and Lee. The short, slightly-stooped, carelessly-dressed figure of the one is in striking contrast with the tall, erect, carefully-dressed figure of the other. Behind the modest warrior in blue stand Colonel Parker, Colonel Merritt, General Rawlins (chief of staff), Captain Seth Williams, Colonel Porter, Colonel Ingalls, General P. H. Sheridan, Colonel Badeau, General Ord, Colonel Bowers, Colonel Dent and General Custer. Behind the haughty general in gray stand Colonel Charles Marshall, a member of his staff, and Colonel Orville E. Babcock, the Federal staff-officer deputed by Grant to act as Lee's escort to the place of meeting. None of the figures are cold or languid; there is life and earnestness in every one.

Nast went to his studio superbly equipped for the execution of this splendid work. He had visited Appomattox and obtained an accurate description of the room in the McLean house wherein Grant and Lee met, and of the table whereon the articles of surrender were drawn. Colonel Frederick D. Grant had sent him the hat, the blouse and the top-boots worn by General Grant on the occasion. (To the boots there still clings some of the red soil of Virginia.) With all of the officers whom he was to picture on the canvas he had met and conversed. Of many of them, including Grant, he had contemporaneous portraits.

As the work progressed, he received many helpful suggestions from Miss Lee, daughter of the Confederate chieftain, from Colonel Grant, from General Horace Porter and from Colonels Parker and Marshall.

This wealth of material, joined with his high conception of the subject, with his strong power of drawing, and with his fine technical skill, has enabled Nast to enrich American art with a historical painting that, for vivid realism and for nice discrimination of character, is indeed remarkable. The figures are life-size. The canvas is nine by twelve feet. It hangs on the east wall of the public library room in the government building at Galena.

The largest of Nast's other historical paintings, "The Departure of the Seventh Regiment of New York, 1861," was executed in the time of the war, and it hangs in the regimental armory at the metropolis. The canvas is seven by nine feet.

Nast was an eye-witness of the scene he has so graphically portrayed on canvas. "I was there at the time," he tells me, "and sketched the picture on the spot." In some respects this is one of his best

performances; it is notably accurate and particularly strong in power of action.

The *New York Herald* of April 20th, 1861, describes the departure of the regiment in this wise:

With the band playing the national airs and the regiment's quick-steps; with the police relieving each other by turns, in frantic efforts to clear a way for the soldiery; with the line broken by the crowd, which surged backward and forward like an ocean, the march began. Through a crowd so dense that it seemed to block up the way impassably; through walls of human beings, close, compact, unshrinking, as if the police, like a modern Moses, had parted the sea of people into living walls; under a perfect canopy of flags, gilded by the sun with a glory as bright as that which they have always won and deserved; with cheers rolling along like enthusiastic thunders; past buildings whose fronts were covered with flags, and above doors, windows, stoops and balconies were jammed with people; with handkerchiefs, waved by fair hands, and as numerous as the forest leaves which the winds rustle, saluting the gallant volunteers; past Major Anderson, who reviewed the regiment from the balcony of Ball, Black & Co.'s building, and, by his presence, reminded them of war's dangers and of its glories; with bayonets brightly gleaming in the sun; with step firm; with bearing proud and erect, as befitted the men and the occasion, the Seventh Regiment marched down Broadway. Never was a popular demonstration more brilliant and more enthusiastic.

The young artist, his heart aglow with the patriotism and with the enthusiasm of the time, caught superbly the spirit of this scene.

As exquisite a performance, both in conception and in finish, as has yet come from Nast's hand, is "The Immortal Light of Genius," which is owned by Sir Henry Irving, the great English actor, who sent an order for it by cable last summer. This dainty work represents the little room at Stratford-on-Avon in which Shakspeare was born. From the famous bust of the poet which occupies the place of honor in front of the quaint and crumbling old fireplace there appears to radiate a lurid, mellow light, which illumines everything round about. Bowed before the illuminated bust, and offering to the bard tribute of laurel wreaths, are two spirit forms, one representing Comedy as the "Jester," and the other representing Tragedy in the garb of an old Roman.

"Sherman's Marching Through Georgia" is the title of one of Nast's strongest war pictures, and "The Halt" is that of another. The latter represents a familiar scene on the march.

Nast is in receipt of orders for still other historical pictures, one of which will represent President Lincoln's entry into Richmond. This will doubtless be one of his best efforts. The subject is a noble one, and it is not to be questioned that he will treat it faithfully.

These great historical paintings by Nast will become more and more interesting and valuable with the lapse of time. They have all been done with rare fidelity. The artist puts his whole soul into his work. He is earnest, purposeful, painstaking. While he was executing "Peace in Union" he had scarcely a thought of anything else. "Every morn-

THOMAS NAST.

ing," he says, "before taking my bath I would go and take a look at it. Now there is only a blank wall in its place."

———

Thomas Nast is by birth a Bavarian. He was born September 27th, 1840. His father, who had been a musician in the Bavarian army, quit Germany before the outbreak of the revolutionary struggle which culminated in 1848, and came to this country, bringing his son with him. Young Nast early exhibited remarkable talent for pictorial art, and, after a little home practice and a six months' course of instruction under Theodore Kaukmann, he began to furnish sketches to Frank Leslie's illustrated journals. At the age of twenty-one he was assigned to go to England to make illustrations for the *New York Illustrated News.* So successfully did he do his work in England that in a short time he was instructed to go to Italy to join General Mazzini in the famous campaigns in which Garibaldi freed Sicily and created the Kingdom of Italy. From Italy he also furnished several other papers, among them English and French journals, with war pictures of great power. He returned to America in February, 1861, just before the breaking out of the War of the Rebellion. Soon afterward he began in *Harper's Weekly* that series of pictures which gave him so great fame.

In the great collection of pictures, books, armor and curios which adorns his home at Morristown, New Jersey,— a home to which the visitor is always heartily welcomed,—there is nothing else for which Nast cherishes so tender a sentiment as a beautiful silver vase bearing this inscription: "The members of the Union League Club unite in presenting to Thomas Nast this token of their admiration of his genius, and his ardent devotion of that genius to the preservation of his country from the scheme of rebellion — 1869."

Next to this splendid trophy the artist prizes a canteen-shaped vase on which is represented in strong relief America decorating Nast in the presence of the Army and the Navy, and on the reverse side of which is this inscription: "Presented to Thomas Nast by his friends in the Army and Navy of the United States in recognition of the patriotic use he has made of his rare abilities as the artist of the people; the gift of three thousand and five hundred officers and enlisted men in the Army and Navy of the United States."

Nast is a many-sided man. As a caricaturist he has no superior; as a historical painter he is scarcely less successful than as a pictorial satirist; as a public lecturer (he has made several lecture tours of this country), he is instructive and entertaining; as an observer of events he is alert and intelligent, and as a conversationalist he is delightfully interesting. He possesses to an extraordinary degree those qualities which are so potent to cultivate friendships,—which attract men and lay hold upon their hearts. He is gracious, generous and sympathetic; these endearing qualities have made him the idol of his friends. He has traveled widely, has read much, and has met and conversed with most of the great painters, sculptors, actors, writers, preachers and statesmen of his time. It is safe to say that no one has the friendship of more men and women of distinction than he.

Nast is a well-preserved, plain-looking man; his figure is short, his well-shaped head is set squarely upon good shoulders, and his beard, hair and eyes are dark. His bearing is that of the modest, cultured American gentleman.

AMONG THE CHICAGO WRITERS.

By Mary J. Reid.

THE visitor who knew Chicago before the World's Columbian Exposition and the great strike, the Chicago of Mr. Opie Read's "Colossus" and Mr. Henry B. Fuller's "The Cliff Dwellers," who thought that the Lake City could make but one response — the response of business — to the many appeals of art and humanity, will note to-day a marked change in the spirit of the people. Now and then one will meet an old-time braggart, a mere business machine, like Kirkland's Zury or Mr. Opie Read's George Witherspoon; but the new Chicago is the Chicago portrayed in Mr. Fuller's "With the Procession,"[*] governed by a Jane Marshall, a Susan Bates, a faithful Brower, and (it is a pity that one must say it) a Truesdale Marshall, the last type being a blot on the scutcheon of Chicago and every other city in America; for, struggle as we will, none of us can get beyond Walt Whitman's view of American life in "Songs of Parting."

How America Illustrates birth, muscular youth, the promise, the sure fulfillment, the absolute success, despite of people — illustrates evil as well as good.

When the evil predominates, Chicagoans reëcho Mr. Francis F. Browne's pessimistic poem of † Retrogression:

Opposing forces up and down
Shall sway us till the end of time;
These fit us for an angel's crown, —
Those drag us backward to the slime.
And still must rage the horrid feud
Inherent in our being's law:
The artistry of God and Good
By wager of the tooth and claw.

But the cry of Chicago is more frequently optimistic than pessimistic. Professor Triggs, of the Chicago University, may be said to have voiced it when he wrote:

‡ Have you marked the dominant, ever dominant note of hope of American speakers and writers? Have you read the message of Whitman in its entirety? At this moment the people are confronted by as momentous a question as has come to any nation, a question which is resolving itself into one of industrial war. But light-hearted, nothing daunted,

We take up the task eternal, and the burden
and the lesson.
    Pioneers! O pioneers!

And again Professor Triggs says, speaking for the large army of law-abiding citizens:

America has, I believe, one great and abiding passion, — to make the reason, the soul of man, and the will of God to prevail.

The divine hopefulness of the Chicagoans, their spirit of toleration, their passions for art and for philanthropy strike with wonder the stranger who has expected to find them wholly given over to materialism. Perhaps this marvelous growth may not be observable to the New Yorker or the Bostonian, but it is certainly noted by every intelligent sojourner from San Francisco, St. Paul or Kansas City; and in England Chicago has found a zealous advocate in Sir Walter Besant. It is also a singularly receptive city, not alone to European and Eastern ideas but the talent of the West, of the South, of Canada, is taken in Chicago at its full valuation, and frequently finds its first recognition there.

The greatest signs of progress, however, next to the University of Chicago and the Art Institute, are the vast collections of manuscripts, rare old books and costly specimens of the bookmaker's art, which have been imperceptibly accumulating in the Newberry, the Cretar, the Public, and the University libraries to such an extent that few Chicagoans are aware of the literary hoards therein contained, — hoards "heaped up" as Mr. Fuller expresses it, "with the pillage of a sacked and ravaged globe." In the

* Harper Brothers.
† "Volunteer Grain." Way and Williams.
‡ "Browning and Whitman, a Study in Democracy." Macmillan & Co.

Newberry Library, for example, (particularly distinguished by having the poet, Mr. John Vance Cheney, for its librarian,) one may spend days in examining its ancient and modern treasures — from the *Djami* or *Jami Yusef ve Zulukha*, captured at Mooltan in 1489 (a manuscript still kept in a bag which was slung over some Persian student's shoulder) to one of the costliest books produced in our century, the *Portraits de Personages Historiques* collected and painted in water colors by Rauderval. The latter work is a wonderful study of French types, and displays better than any other modern book the actual value of ideal illustrations to the student of history. The Newberry library also contains one of the best collections of rare old Bibles in the United States, among which may be mentioned the *Biblia Sacra Latina Venetius*, 1476 ; the Great Bible, 1539 ; Cranmer's Bible, 1541, and the *Bibliorum Sacrorum Vulgatæ Versionis* (on vellum), 1788. At the University of Chicago the impulse that President Harper and Professor Moulton are giving to the study of the Bible as literature, the University Extension lectures, and the large army of able professors bringing exact scholarship to a busy metropolis, are all surrounding the smoky city with a clearer atmosphere of learning.

There is nothing more charming in Chicago than the absence of jealousy among its writers and artists. They all stand by one another. But it cannot be denied that the crying want of that city is the cohesion of its literary and artistic elements. At the present time each journalist, author, professor or artist works solely within his own circle or club, and is apt to be known simply by reputation to the *literati* outside that circle. Practically there are but three meeting places in Chicago where the circles may be crossed. One is the Woman's Club. There I was fortunate enough to hear one of Dr. Sarah H. Stevenson's witty papers and to meet Miss Harriet Hosmer, the sculptor. Another is the house of Mrs. Linden Bates. In her pretty home one may chance upon Professor Louis Block, — the poet-linguist, — Mr. Eugene Field, Mr. Hamlin Garland or Mr. Francis F. Browne, the scholarly editor of the Chicago *Dial.* Nor must one forget the "Saints and Sinner's Corner" at A. C. McClurg & Company's publishing house where divines and actresses, Bohemian journalists and women of fashion, poets and politicians meet upon an equal plane.

It was here I heard from Mr. Millard (Ye olde booke man of McClurg's) a story characteristic of three Chicago writers. On one occasion Messrs. Eugene Field, Opie Read and Stanley Waterloo went fishing with Mr. Millard. Mr. Field paid no attention to the fishing, but "ran down" some very valuable first editions of Whittier and Lowell ; Mr. Read dawdled a

MARY HARTWELL CATHERWOOD.

SAINTS AND SINNER'S CORNER AT McCLURG'S — MR. MILLARD IN THE BACKGROUND.

little with the fishing, but spent most of his time in searching for elemental types, the first editions of men, while Mr. Waterloo stuck close to the fishing with the pertinacity of a true follower of Izaak Walton. The last time I heard from ye olde. booke man he was engaged in another kind of sport, fishing for ancient books in London for the Saints and Sinner's Corner.

Classifying roughly, Literary Chicago may be divided into the journalists, the author-professors and the professional authors.

The most noted journalists, many of whom have written books, are Messrs. Eugene and Roswell Martin Field, Mr. Stanley Waterloo, Mr. Opie Read, Mr. Upton, Dr. Oliver Nixon, Mr. Elwyn Barron, Mr. William Armstrong, Mrs. Mary Abbott and the young editor, J. Percival Pollard.

The professional writers are best represented by Mr. John Vance Cheney, Mr. Henry B. Fuller, Mrs. Mary Hartwell Catherwood, Mrs. De Koven, Miss Harriet Monroe, Mr. Ernest McGaffey and the new writers, Miss Lillian Bell and Mr. Chatfield-Taylor.

There are also the University author-professors, such as Professors Shorey, Von Holst, Moulton, M'Laughlin, Triggs, Starr and Herrick.

The Chicago *Dial* editors can scarcely be classed with the journalists since that periodical is in some respects a unique one, no other periodical in the country giving such a large space to the contributions of university men. Mr. Browne has been for years one of the educational forces in Chicago. A tall, reserved man belonging to a type which was often seen during the War-generation, but is now fast dying out, — an American type which has always possessed "a golden store of scholar's lore" and once found its highest exemplar in this country in William Cullen Bryant. While Chicagoans may grumble at Mr. Morton Payne — the literary editor of the *Dial* — because of his slow recognition of Western authors, when recognition from his pen comes, the author feels that he has surely put amateur work behind him and has become a master in what Ben Johnson calls "the craft of making." Mr. Payne is not a "name-hunter." No matter how obscure the writer, when his work reaches a certain standard of excellence it is favorably noted in the *Dial*. A recent case where the *Dial* stood practically alone in its advocacy of a poet was that of the late Professor Perkins of the University of Iowa.

In the purely literary field, those who understand best "the craft of making" in Chicago are Mr. Fuller, Mr. Eugene Field, Mr. Cheney, Mrs. Catherwood and Miss Monroe. To this list the Mid-West always adds the names of Messrs. Opie Read, Stanley Waterloo and Hamlin Garland, rightly estimating their vivid studies of real life as an equivalent for any lack of constructive power they may evince.

The first author whom I met was Mrs. Catherwood. It was an ideal day in May when the meadows were dotted with violets that I took the train to Hoopeston, for in this little city, not quite near enough

OPIE READ.

to be a suburb of Chicago, were composed nearly all of Mrs. Catherwood's stories: "The Romance of Dollard," "The Story of Tonty," "Old Kaskaskia," "The Lady of Fort St. John," and "The Chase of Saint Castin and Other Stories of the French in the New World."[*] Here she has a charming home among her husband's kith and kin. Yet it is not too costly for her to run away from it when she wishes to take a trip to France, to Canada or to the South-Mississippi States for the collection of material. No one knows the Mississippi Valley better than Mrs. Catherwood, but she loves best the region around the Illinois River. She has a fine photograph of Fort St. Louis of the Illinois, where the Illinois Indians made their last stand, and her uncle had a ranch of ten thousand acres bordering on that river. His home was one of the old French seignory houses, which she has described in "Old Kaskaskia." They were all built upon the same general plan — the lower floor was used for cattle and stores, on the second floor were the living apartments, and the third floor was a ball-room where the tenants were in the habit of assembling for a dance. A duel was fought in old French days in her uncle's seignory house, and the blood spots on the hearth could never be washed out. The legend was that these blood spots always quivered at midnight. "The Beauport Loup-Garou," "The Windigo" and "Pontiac's Lookout" show that Mrs. Catherwood is very fond of the weird and terrible. She told me that while she cared little for poetry, she enjoyed one of Victor Hugo's novels or one of Miss Wilkins' ghost stories better than anything else. Sometimes when she goes to Chicago, Mr. Waterloo, the president of the Press Club, and Mrs. Catherwood amuse a small coterie by trying to outvie one another in telling weird tales. In such a combat "The Windigo" was born.

It is a great treat to hear Mrs. Catherwood tell a story. She tells a story much

---

[*] Houghton, Mifflin & Co.

better than she reads one. In the narration, the little artistic touches are never forgotten, nor the grouping of apparently incidental circumstances which finally lead up to the development of the plot. She is also very fond of the picturesque, even knowing how to use the bizarre effectively. But it is noticeable that her touches of the bizarre never reach the blood-curdling point, which Mrs. Gertrude Atherton is fond of touching in her descriptions of Spanish life. Mrs. Catherwood never forgets that she is an artist, and while she considers herself at liberty to use any color upon her easel, no matter how barbaric, the picture itself is always a work of art. In a very subtle manner are the comic, the fantastic and the weird commingled in "Old Kaskaskia" and "The Lady of Fort St. John." One must go to Victor Hugo for a more fantastically horrible death than that of D'Aulnay de Charnisay, caught in the quicksand, and the little woman-dwarf sitting by, ruthlessly naming the galloping waves which cover his head after the French Huguenots whom Charnisay had foully executed.

It is quite a study in the art of phantasy to compare some of the scenes in these novels with Mr. Fuller's "The Chatelaine of La Trinité," and "The Chevalier of Pensieri-Vani."[*] That scene, for instance, where the chevalier feels the high disdain of the old Etruscan warrior, who has defied time for three thousand years, but who crumbled to dust when his crown was but borrowed. Or that strange spectacle in the cathedral where the chevalier improvises "a vast fantasia of thunders and lightnings, of tumult and terror, of shrieks and curses and condemnations," till, to the art-loving Italian hearers, the music suggests "the vengeance not to be stayed" of Michael Angelo's "Last Judgment" and Dante's "Inferno."

Just as we owe to Mr. Fuller some phases of Italian and Swiss life, so we owe to Mrs. Catherwood the resurrection of the old French emigré,—La Salle,

[*] The Century Company.

STANLEY WATERLOO.

Father Jogues, Tonty, Marie de la Tour, Colonel Menard, Angélique Saucier and her tante-gra'-mère. But still more wonderful is her conception of the lights and shades of the Indian character. No other woman in the United States with the exception of Miss Mary Alicia Owen, the student of Indian folk-lore, knows the Indians better.

In a knowledge of Indian types, the sculptor, Mr. Edward Kemeys, who has but lately established his "Wolf Den" at Bryn Mawr, Chicago, exceeds them both, his manhood giving him an advantage; but Kemeys' busts of Indians are wonderful creations, particularly the bust of Wild Hog, a famous Indian fighter, who even in his captivity put his foes at a disadvantage.

Mrs. Catherwood has some rare old French books, but the books she showed me with the most pride were presentation copies from Eugene Field with some of his verses written on the fly-leaves in his fine, exquisite hand,—the capitals and illustrations illuminated as in a mediæval manuscript.

Miss Harriet Monroe also possesses some beautiful specimens of Eugene Field's handiwork. Mrs. Catherwood remarked to me: "You will find that Miss Monroe is physically a dainty little creature; she always makes me think of a piece of fine china." And these two gentlewomen are indeed a contrast,—Mrs. Catherwood giving the impression of native force and character, and Miss Monroe, a force naturally springing from generations of culture. Mrs. Catherwood has a vigorous physique, a strong face and a searching blue eye. Her most marked feature is her nose, about which there is a certain elegance, such as Balzac has described in his characterization of Madame Claës. Miss Monroe is a small, slight woman with a brunette complexion, brown eyes, brown hair and a flexible, expressive mouth. More than any other poet of her time, she makes me think of Mrs. Browning; not in the quantity of her work, nor in the carelessness of her versification, but in the largeness of her conceptions which rise above the prejudices of race and sex. Song is not dead among us when a poet can carry us upward to the

HARRIET MONROE.

height of the following sonnet upon Shelley.—a sonnet sent to her brother with a copy of Shelley's poems:

*Behold, I send thee to the heights of song,
My brother! Let thine eyes awake as clear
As morning dew, within whose glowing sphere
Is mirrored half a world; and listen long.
Till in thine ears famished to keenness throng
The bugles of the soul — till far and near
Silence grows populous, and wind and mere
Are phantom-choked with voices. Then be strong
Then halt not till thou seest the heaven's flare,
Souls mad for truth have lit from peak to peak.
Haste on to breathe the intoxicating air —
Wine to the brave and poison to the weak —
Far in the blue where angels feet have trod,
Where earth is one with heaven and man with God.

The study of types is particularly interesting in Chicago. Professor Moulton is of a pleasing English type—a polished scholar wholly opposed to the crude, popular conception of an Englishman.

Professor Starr has the scientific curiosity and some of the remorselessness of an anthropologist, joined to an ingenuous, almost boyish, manner,—a manner which doubtless aids him in his studies of primitive peoples.

Professor Von Holst is rather unapproachable, but he represents the learned German, wholly absorbed in his work. While Professor Moulton is an ideal lecturer, leaving the mind at the conclusion of a lecture stimulated rather than exhausted, Professor Von Holst's concentrated style, added to his rasping voice and unsympathetic face, makes his lectures (until one gets used to his mannerisms) far more exhausting than the perusal of his books. He holds his students with a tense, unnatural air, as if he were the Czar rather than the father. He has fairly conquered the English language and has a rugged and concise style,— not that dry, labored expression which is ordinarily associated with conciseness, but one which is intense and vivid with an element of picturesqueness in it.

* McClurg & Co.

Professor Crow, one of the woman-professors, is a charming lecturer and makes a pretty picture as she leans upon her pulpit-like desk, discoursing upon Shakspeare and the Elizabethan Era. She is about middle height, has dark brown hair, gray eyes, and a high forehead which makes one think of Chaucer's lines:

But sikerly she had a fair forehead.
It was almost a spanne broad I trow.

Her manner is very agreeable and I fancy that the average student learns more from her careful, exact training in the best methods of assorting and collecting literary facts than from a great lecturer.

President Harper has so much individuality that one would surely pick him out of a crowd. He is below the medium height; has a broad brow and an enormous head, strong features, strong

HENRY B. FULLER.

chin and alert, peculiar eyes. In looking at him I was reminded of one of J. R. Green's sentences descriptive of Henry II.: "His practicable, serviceable frame suited the hardest worker of his time." President Harper's manner is a little abrupt, quick and decisive. He gives you five minutes and all is over.

No one could be more unlike President Harper than Mr. Opie Read. The latter is a purely Southern type, a giant in stature who personally impresses one with a sense of reserve power greater than that conveyed by "The Colossus" and "Len Gansett." At the base of his forehead he has a very heavy wrinkle which smooths itself out in his earnest moments. Gray eyes, which are set rather far back in his head, shine with a

kindly, humane light and somewhat relieve the darkness of the heavy eye-brows and black hair. His voice is musical with a melancholy cadence in it, and his manners are the outcome of his kindly, sympathetic nature. Next to Octave Thanet, I know of no author who gives one a better idea of the typical Southern manner. I was particularly struck with his ideas upon words. I had asked him if he and Mr. Waterloo were not striving to describe life with absolute simplicity and sincerity of expression, for those qualities seemed to me to be the main characteristics of "The Kentucky Colonel" and "A Man and a Woman." He answered in the affirmative, and during a little discussion upon the relative value of Anglo-Saxon and Latin words he remarked : "Words seem to me to have color, to shine with a red, blue or green light. There are words which are white with heat, and those that are as cold as ice, so that I want to drop them as quickly as possible. Others bristle with ruggedness. There are warmth, color and vigor in Anglo-Saxon words, but conscience words are Latin."

In respect to his views as a novelist, Mr. Read said : "Mr. Garland and I have had many a discussion upon realism. I am not *always* a realist. I do not believe in drawing everything that one sees. The artist must choose his material. I lived with the gypsies for a while, but I should never think of depicting gypsy life. Beauty, more than absolute realism, appeals to me. I like to paint the rose, but I leave out the toad unless it is necessary to complete the landscape. Mr. Garland has force and strength in describing the humble, tired woman or the powerful man, but the fact is, he thinks a woman's nature is just like that of a man. Women are finer and nobler than men. There is something wrong in

WILLIAM MORTON PAYNE.

his conception of woman, for he has never been able to draw a fine one."

The last remark recalled to mind the saying of another realist : " Somehow Mr. Garland always draws a woman with a tarred stick." Mr. Read prefers Octave Thanet's work to that of any other western writer, while Mr. Waterloo's ideal writer of the West is Mrs. Catherwood. I met Mr. Waterloo by appointment at the Press Club in a most Bohemian way, and saw the portraits of the various presidents of the club, and the lounge which is always reserved for Mr. Read. Mr. Waterloo slyly remarked that upon that lounge Mr. Read had told stories enough to fill several volumes. He also spoke of Mr. McGovern as a luminous pessimist, and of Mr. J. Percival Pollard as one of the cleverest young writers of Chicago.

At the Press Club, in the Saints and Sinner's Corner, and at a ladies' lunch I heard the remark iterated and reiterated that Mr. Fuller was a scholarly gentleman who gave everything he touched an artistic finish, yet he held himself so far aloof from the life of Chicago that his latest novel, "With the Procession," must necessarily give a narrow view of the city. No remark could be farther away

FRANCIS F. BROWNE.

JOHN VANCE CHENEY.

me long or completely, but 'The Chatelaine' pleased me longest and most completely."

I do not know if Chicagoans have noted that Mr. Cheney and Mr. Fuller have the same type of face. Not that they are in any respect doubles, as Lafcadio Hearn and Pierre Loti, William Morris and Charles Edwin Markham, or Mrs. Catherwood and Mrs. Jean Blewitt are said to be. As a matter of fact, intellectually Mr. Cheney and Mr. Fuller are contrasts rather than doubles; one being a poet and essayist, in one degree modern, yet with a leaning towards the literature of the past; the other a novelist, modern in every sense, except as an architect, with a keen ear for music, but no ear for song. Yet each possesses what in America we consider the typical intellectual face.

Mr. Cheney, Professor Moulton and Professor Triggs quite fairly represent three schools of criticism. Mr. Cheney belongs to that school of which Matthew Arnold was the greatest light

from the truth. There is no question as to Mr. Fuller's reserve or his avoidance of crowds and large assemblies. But the byways of Chicago, the artists' studios, the minor libraries and the houses of the old residents are familiar haunts to him, and no writer, except Miss Alice French, is watching with greater interest the steady growth of literature at the West. Like Octave Thanet, he does not believe in drawing characters directly from life. All the people who inhabit his books are types, drawn from at least half a dozen different sources, or are idealistic studies. Chicago may think she has the monopoly of the characters in "The Cliff Dwellers" and "With the Procession." But many western towns which Mr. Fuller has not visited since he was a boy hold their counterparts. When asked why he did not continue to write such idealistic stories as "The Chatelaine of La Trinité," he answered:

"I am not the same man I was when I wrote 'The Chatelaine.' An author cannot be expected to stand still in order to please his audience; but," he added, shaking his head in a way peculiar to himself, "none of my books has pleased

JOHN McGOVERN.

in England and Mr. Edmund C. Stedman in the United States. It is a form of criticism classified by Professor Moulton as the "criticism of taste." Professor Moulton has popularized *scientific* criticism while Professor Triggs voices the democratic spirit of the people. No works which these three critics have published better exemplify the difference in these three schools than Mr. Cheney's "Golden Guess," [*] Professor Moulton's "Shakspeare as a Dramatic Artist," [†] and Professor Triggs' "Browning and Whitman, A Study in Democracy." [†] The best essay written upon Matthew Arnold in this country may be found in "The Golden Guess." Mr. Cheney proclaims Arnold to be "the keenest and wisest critic so far adorning English literature." His view of Tennyson is no less sympathetic and the essay upon "Who Are the Great Poets" is in the same line with Professor Moulton's efforts to teach the historical and poetical value of the old Hebrew writers. Mr. Cheney has inherited from his father, the late Simeon Pease Cheney, not only a love of instrumental and vocal music but also of Nature's music. One of his latest labors has been to edit a work left unfinished by his father, entitled, "Wood Notes

[*] Lee & Shepard.
[†] Macmillan & Co.

J. PERCIVAL POLLARD.

Wild." [*] In 1848 the father wrote : "I have become sure there is nothing so wonderful on earth as the birds and their music." Those readers who have marveled at Mr. Cheney's quaint revelations of nature's secrets in the poems of "Thistle Drift" and "Wood Blooms" will no longer marvel when they find that to his father "the voices of the wood and field were as familiar as those of his own family."

To the young student of Shakspeare, there is no work more helpful than the discussions of character-development, character-grouping, the main-plot and the under-plot, to be found in Professor Moulton's "Shakspeare as a Dramatic Artist"; and, next to the interpretations of Mr. John Burroughs and Mr. Arthur Stedman, the reader will find no more sympathetic work upon Walt Whitman than Professor Triggs' "Study of Browning and Whitman."

At the moment of correcting the proofs for this paper, there came the startling announcement that "the Angel with a Wreath of Rue" had silently entered the home of Eugene Field, carrying away "when the world was fast asleep" that restless spirit, who but yesterday enlivened the Chicagoans with his witticisms or moved them to tears with a pathetic poem.

His sister-in-law told me an odd little story about him, which seems, now that he is gone, worth repeating. One night he awakened her out of a sound sleep in order to read to her the first draft of a touching little poem. As he read the last stanza a tear trickled down her cheek. When he saw it he laughed quite like a boy, and said : "You are a gauge by which I can measure other people's feelings. I thought there was something in these verses but I could not rest until I knew how they would affect you."

An evening with Eugene Field was an event not only on account of his witty sayings, his command of dialect and his out-of-the-way learning, but also because

[*] Lee & Shepard.

ROSWELL MARTIN FIELD.

he was a great mimic and had a face so flexible that it could be transformed into almost any shape. Mrs. Bates told me that at her table he seized two fern leaves and placing them behind his ears whispered in a funereal tone, "Dante." His face was such a mock semblance of the famous Florentine that the room itself seemed to shake with laughter. Alas! he has met Alighieri and the Horace he loved so well on the other side of the "misty Stygian Sea."

Mr. Field had accumulated a library upon the singular theory that books should either be the work of masters or of fools. He had one case devoted entirely to the fools. But this was simply the fantastic side of his nature. Like Goldsmith, whom he somewhat resembled in character, he was one of the masters of simple expression. His child-songs are the sweetest and quaintest in our language and will still be the favorite rhymes of the hearth long after many a stately building in Chicago has crumbled away.

His brother, Roswell Martin Field, has a fine, strong intellectual face and is the author of "In Sunflower Land," a most

delightful series of humorous stories depicting life in Kansas. While R. M. Field lived in Kansas City, his column entitled "The Faultfinder" in the Kansas City *Star* was eagerly read all over the South-west. The two brothers have paraphrased Horace in a work entitled "Echoes from the Sabine Farm."[*]

Mr. George P. Upton has been for years one of the musical authorities of Chicago. He is author of "[†]Women in Music," The Standard Symphonies, Operas, Oratorios and Cantatas and various translations from the German, as the "Life of Wagner." The fame and success of these works mark the musical progress of Chicago. For many years, Mr. Upton was musical critic of the Chicago *Tribune* and he is now upon its editorial staff. About seventy of the letters of "Peregrine Pickle" were published in the *Tribune*. If Chicago is now more truly a musical center than any other Western city, it is largely due to the pioneer efforts of Mr. Upton, whose musical works belong to the standard literature of the country.

[*]Scribner's Sons.
[†]McClurg & Co.

GEORGE P. UPTON.

The dramatic criticisms of Mr. Ellwyn Barron are considered by the Chicagoans to rival those of Mr. William Winter.

One of my pleasantest remembrances is a visit to Miss Lilian Bell, author of "The Love Affairs of an Old Maid" and "A Little Sister to the Wilderness."[*] On the top floor of her home she has a little retreat where she writes and entertains her most intimate friends. It is very simply furnished with but one case of books, a large writing-desk, a table, a Japanese screen, three or four easy chairs and a few pictures. The occupant of this bright room, where the sun streams in unmolested, is a tall, slender girlish looking woman with black hair and black eyebrows which set off her fair complexion. She is full of literary enthusiasms and is to her very finger-tips a Chicagoan. At my request she read to me one of her unpublished dialect stories "Lizzie Lee's Separation." She reads her stories most charmingly without any attempt at rhetorical effect, and speaks the negro and South-western dialects with much fluency. We had a little chat about some of the Chicago writers, but I can recall nothing

[*] Stone & Kimball.

HOBART C. CHATFIELD-TAYLOR.

except her remarks upon Mr. Garland, which I cite, because they were in the main a reëcho of what I heard in many different quarters. "Mr. Garland," said Miss Bell, "is an earnest, talented fellow. Here in Chicago we care nothing about his theories. We accept him for what he is himself. But he does not know the society woman at all. He hates society and takes no pains to learn anything about it."

While it is true enough that there are certain types and some phases of civilization which never appeal to Mr. Garland, yet no other novelist has described the monotonous scenery, the treacherous climate and the average man of the Northwest with a like fidelity to nature. In "Jason Edwards" the very genius of the whirlwind seems to have inspired Mr. Garland in his description of the cyclone. In the same manner the intense cold of the Dakota blizzard is a living reality in "A Little Norsk." But "Jason Edwards" and "A Little Norsk" are not great stories. Notwithstanding their vivid pictures and local coloring they lack the balance of parts and the technical harmony of Howells' "Silas Lapham" or Mr. Fuller's "With The Procession." Our realists are too apt to forget that a great novel is as much a work of art as a symphony or a mediæval abbey. Figuratively speaking, a novel has its buttress, its "arch within arch" and its "archivolt and fretted moulding" just as we find them in some pure Gothic cathedral, created by the cunning of a master architect.

It is in "Main Traveled Roads" that Mr. Garland reaches his highest mark. In fact, I think, he is so much of an impressionist in literature, is so fond of an instantaneous effect of light and shade, that his short stories will always be his best. To use his own words applied to impressionism in art, "The modern picture takes up and relates at a stroke the impression of a dramatic moment."

From Mr. Garland to Mr. Hobart C. Chatfield-Taylor is a long step. Chicago has never been able to take Mr. Chatfield-

Taylor seriously but he has planned for himself some serious work amidst Spanish scenes and life. His ancestors are from New England and Western New York. He was mainly educated abroad, partly under a tutor. His boyish life was one of perpetual change as he attended many foreign schools while his mother was traveling. He was graduated at the University of Cornell, thus following the good old custom established by John Quincy Adams of spending one's university life in one's native land. Mr. Chatfield-Taylor's first venture was a newspaper, which was finally merged into the Chicago *Record*. He tells a funny story in respect to the origin of his novels. His sister-in-law had often told him he had no imagination. To prove to her that he had imagination he wrote his stories. She denied the gift to his first and second stories but was quite enthusiastic about "Two Women and a Fool." But now that he has proved to his sister that he can write a novel, he intends to apply himself to more serious literary work to please himself, as he says his novels seem outside of himself and are wholly opposed to his own theories of art. He does not care for the modern novel. He sometimes reads it as a study of methods and construction, but never for pure pleasure. He would rather write a good drama than anything else, for while there are dozens of good novelists in this country there are but few good playwrights.

The author who studies art with the most seriousness is the young poet, William Francis Barnard. While I was one of the editors of the *Literary Northwest Magazine* I noted the strength, originality and spontaneity of his sonnet upon "The West." He has subjected himself to a severe mental training, studying the English classics with ardor, and taking Matthew Arnold, Mr. Edmund C. Stedman and Mr. Mabie for his critical guides. He has a love of art and beauty which is almost pagan. In fact he thinks that there is a trend in Chicago towards pagan ideals and his theory is that Beauty as an end cannot lead us far astray. Mr.

L. J. BLOCK.

Barnard's contributions to THE MIDLAND are among the best which have yet appeared in its pages.

Professor Louis Block's poems are imbued with German mysticism and are popularly esteemed as unmodern, but the spirit of the new Chicago is to regard classic and modern lore as coëqual. In the odes to Dante, Goethe and Plato, one will often find the spirit of a writer condensed into a line, as when Plato is styled the "finder of the serene and permanent." If these poems lack spontaneity and are occasionally almost as rugged as those of Walt Whitman, the thought is always noble and inspiring. But, unlike Walt Whitman, the audience whom Professor Block addresses must of necessity be a scholarly one. As Miss Monroe is ever appealing to the pure spirit of Truth, so in these metaphysical poems, the old ideas of the masters in respect to nobility of character are recast in a modern mold as in the following melodious verse:

He only wins his freedom truly,
Who daily wins it fresh and fair,
He only ever rises newly
Into the regions of the purer air
Who falters not for blame nor praise,'
But lives in strenuous and victorious days.*

* "The New World," Putnam's Sons.

LILIAN BELL.

I have thus tried to picture a few of the leading writers in Chicago. It was a disappointment to me not to meet Mrs. Elizabeth A. Reed, Mrs. Mary Abbott, Mrs. De Koven, Doctor Gunsaulus and several other well known Chicago authors, who are helping to make their city famous, but this article simply claims to be a record of personal impressions.

The record would scarcely be complete, however, if it failed to note the stirring passions which are driving the people of this great city forward. The World's Columbian Exposition aroused in them the art-passion, and the sufferings of the poor people who were stranded among them, the humane-passion. The architect, Mr. Henry Van Brunt, in his "Greek Lines " * complains that although the art of the architect is not more technical than that of the musician, few novelists and poets, except Sir Walter Scott and Victor

*Houghton, Mifflin & Co.

Hugo, have understood the language of architectural forms. Herein I think the Chicagoans are making rapid strides, for the language of painting and architecture is beginning to be a common language which the poorest mechanic who makes his weekly visit to the Art Institute may understand. It is also well for the city that she has such an art-interpreter as Mr. Fuller, to whom architecture and music are under-studies hardly second in his regard to the art of the novelist. And while most of us still prefer Corot, Troyon, and Millet, to Monet or Hassam, it cannot be denied that Mr. Garland has pleaded the cause of the impressionists with sympathy and insight. The social question as to the adoption of Old World races, which Mr. Fuller has discussed with apparent lightness, and yet with sound common sense in the informal talks at the "Consolation Club" is the most difficult one which Chicagoans must answer. But they are meeting it with a hopefulness which no calamity can daunt. They believe in themselves and the future of their city. There is, however, another question which must be answered, before long.

I have watched several periods in the history of San Francisco when it seemed as if Western literature would find a permanent home in that city. Through lack of encouragement the young literary plants found the soil too barren and were transplanted. Will it be so with Chicago, or will she have strength and vitality enough to support her own writers at home? If she will rise to the conception that Chicago is to be not alone the business center but the literary and artistic center of the West, her future need trouble no one. It can no longer be questioned that there are writers enough to successfully establish a literary center in Chicago, but where may be found the leader to crystallize their work into a harmonious whole!

LULLABY.*

BIRDS in their nests are softly calling,
    The dew is falling, the day is done.
Over the hill come night winds creeping,
    To lull thy sleeping, my little one.
Far in the sky gleams the golden crescent,
    With motion incessant she swings on high,—
A golden hammock for angels' swinging,
    While softly singing a lullaby.
            Then swing slow, sing low,
        Droop little head in thy slumber deep;
            Breathe low, breezes, blow,—
        Zephyrs that bring on drowsy wing
                Sweet sleep.

Down in the grass, the folded clover,
    With mother-leaf over, lies warm and deep.
Stars in the blue that lightly hover
    Shine brightly over, to guard thy sleep.
Come happy dreams, from your home in heaven
    This midsummer even, and hover nigh,
While baby and I in our hammock are swinging
    And softly singing a lullaby.
            Then swing slow, sing low,
        Droop little head, in thy slumber deep;
            Breathe low, breezes, blow,—
        Zephyrs that bring on downy wing
                Sweet sleep.

                                Grace Mitchell.

---
* Awarded the Original Poetry Prize in THE MIDLAND's October competition.

JAPANESE WOMEN OF THE PAST AND PRESENT.

By Lucetta H. Clement.

ONCE again in the land of Japan — the land of mists and shadows, as well as of radiant sunshine. As I pass along, familiar scenes and familiar sights greet the eye and ear. The delightful novelty of a first visit to this dreamland comes back to me through the vista of years, and once again I am under the irresistible charm of life in the Orient. The same Japanese sun with its soft witchery pours its beams upon me from a sky of wondrously luminous blue, so translucent that one almost unconsciously seeks to penetrate to the mysteries of the beyond, and yet the magical effect of distance makes the sky seem at such great height that the gaze is lost as in infinite space. But even after the delusion vanishes, the enchantment still remains.

The strange fascination of this people may be ascribed to various causes. No doubt the originality of the thronging masses of people, the picturesqueness of the streets full of strange devices that seem to smile or grimace alternately, — from the backs of the laborers, on signboards, door-posts, or wheresoever the Japanese and Chinese ideographs meet the eye, — all go to make up an alluring picture.

And then in a greater degree, perhaps, the simplicity and kindlier impulses, the courtesies and innocent superstitions of the common people add much to the interest the visitor has in them.

But even this indescribable charm is not potent enough to dispel the shadow that rests upon the social life of the Japanese, and which extends to a certain extent to the life of foreigners whose residence is in this otherwise favored land. No European or American can remain long in Japan without being pained at the deplorable position of woman in this country. Even the little that can be learned of her inner life is sufficient to show the subordinate place she occupies socially and intellectually even now, after

AN OLD-STYLE SCHOOL.

THRESHING RICE.

a score of years of Christian enlightenment.

Notwithstanding Japan's marvelous opening to the world of her arts, manufactures, commerce, and the opportunities given to study these; rich as she is in ancient records of all that pertains to her external affairs; abounding in traditions and legends of her famous warriors and heroes — all that we may know which relates to women is very meager. It is difficult to obtain reliable information of their public or private lives in the past, or trace the various gradations through which they have come to be what they are in this Nineteenth Century. Enough can be gleaned, however, to show that several important epochs have marked their lives, and we find the varying light and shade of barbarism and civilization running through the ages. But it appears quite certain that none of the strict moral code and precepts, or laws of education, regarding women of later days seem to have existed, or at least to have been in force, in the days of antiquity, nor even down to historic times.

For, be it said to the credit of the nation, in the early centuries, and away back in the legendary period, women were highly educated and greatly esteemed by men, and were considered the equals of husbands and fathers. In courage and bravery they ranked with heroes, were very influential and played conspicuous parts in the annals of their country.

Leaving the Divine Ages, when gods and goddesses ruled the land, we come down to the so-called Human Ages, and we find that women assumed the reins of government and sat upon the throne even of Dai Nippon (Great Japan). And it is said they ruled the empire with wisdom and justice.

From ancient records we read that ten women became sovereigns, reigning during the Sixth, Seventh and Eighth Centuries; although two of these Empresses held the crown when the actual power of government was in the hands of the Shogunate.

The most celebrated of these female sovereigns was one who did not assume the regal title, although she exercised all the powers of an empress, and as such her name has gone into history. Chroniclers place her in the last of the legendary period. This woman was the Empress Jingu. She was said to have been

endowed with extraordinary gifts of
nature, was of a strong masculine character and of unusual administrative ability,
which made her seem born to command.
She may be called the Jeanne D' Arc of
Japan, for, like the Maid of Orleans, she
was distinguished for simplicity, modesty and piety. Like her, also, she had
divine revelations and felt that divine
voices called her to go and fight for
the conquest of unknown lands to the
Westward. When she made known to
her husband the divine command she had
received, he regarded her story as a
strange hallucination, and refused to listen
to her. But she insisted that the message
was from the gods, and began forthwith
to organize an expedition for the conquest. Recruiting and shipbuilding began at once, she continually appealing to
the gods for aid. When all was ready
she donned male attire, took her white
banner, and, with a sword and other
warlike equipments, she put herself at the
head of her army and bade her ships set
sail. The gallant expedition was favored
by smooth seas and gentle breezes, and
the fleet ran safely over the water until it
touched Southern Corea. Tradition says
that "even the fishes swarmed in shoals

about their keels and carried them on to
their desired haven." Here they found
a king and a people to receive them,
who without any battle or struggle were
ready to tender allegiance to the con-
querers, and also loaded them with vast
wealth and treasures. The expedition
returned with these, as spoils of a blood-
less victory. Thus was Corea conquered
for Japan.

This episode is of double significance
just now, when, after an interval of over
six centuries, Japan is again seeking
supremacy in Corea. Not as then peace-
fully, but through fierce conflicts and the
sacrifice of the blood of her valiant soldiers.

For many hundreds of years women
seem to have wielded a powerful political
influence with government, and we might
with justice add other illustrious names
of those whose prudence, wisdom and
heroic fortitude have acted like a charm
through the long and warlike centuries.

Not alone in the political and military
world of this early time do we find women
conspicuous, but in the field of literature
there were many brilliant women, both
in poetry and prose. That they were
ambitious to excel is shown by their writ-

WRITING BY AN OLD STYLE LAMP CALLED ANDON.

SPINNING SILK.

ings,—a passage from one of their number is to this effect : "If it be not possible to secure the first rank, be willing to serve ; if not, be content with the second or third place." Many were well read in Japanese and Chinese literature, in history and even in the Buddhist Sutras.

One worthy of special mention is Murasaki Shikibu, of the notable family of Fujiwara, which dated back into the earliest times and was of rank about equal to that of the Emperor. She was the author of several famous works which are extant,—and are of undying fame. One of her immortal works was so learned that the Emperor after reading it observed that the authoress must have studied the *Nihonki* or "Japanese Chronicles." She was ever afterward known as the "Maid of the Nihonki." Her father often exclaimed, " O, that she were a man."

Others became distinguished for great learning. About this time the Court, feeling their power so firmly established, became absorbed in luxurious extravagance, and literature declined. But the court ladies continued to feel great pride in competing in wit and humor ; "and they not infrequently teased their gentlemen colleagues by asking such learned questions as required great erudition to answer."

One woman writer became a famous critic and wrote a treatise on the poems of the Imperial collections. Others aided greatly in the development of the Japanese language.

These ages seem surely to have been the renaissance period for women as well as for men ; and, as a Japanese woman of the present time expresses it, "they [the women] were not a whit inferior to their literary brothers."

The more feminine graces of music, painting, chirography and the art of decorating were among the accomplishments of all. Not even sewing, dyeing, weaving and cookery were forgotten, but all were practiced by the highest as well as the lowest. They mingled freely in social gatherings, where, by their grace of manner, gentleness, beauty and charming wit, they were greatly admired.

But the condition of women seems to have declined rapidly after the introduction of Chinese manners and institutions and Buddhism. The powers of State rapidly drifted into the hands of the military class, and with this dates the completion of the dual government and the feudal system which had remained in force for seven centuries,—till 1868,—a period of three hundred years.

During the Tokugawa age—the reign of the tyrant lords of Japan—the women were kept down, "for fear that their influence, which had been so powerful in past ages, might dash the whole nicely balanced structure into pieces." Her education, and all interests pertaining to her, were utterly neglected, and woman was thenceforth relegated to a condition of slavery to man.

Unlettered warriors took to the rearrangement of society,—the Confucian doctrine ("women under men") gained great ascendancy, and the teachings of Buddhism prevailed. These taught that women are greater sinners than men; that women can only be taken to Paradise by being changed to men; that they must look upon their husbands as heaven itself; that their great life-long duty is obedience to the masculine dictates. Permitting her even to live was almost a condescension. We are told that it was "the custom of the ancients, on the birth of a female child, to let it lie on the floor for the space of three days."

TEMPLE DANCING WOMAN.

From such a degraded idea of woman grew the severe code of laws which were enforced during long, weary and stormy centuries. Girls were never permitted to forget the iron grasp in which they were held, for from early childhood they were compelled to use daily as a copy-book one called "Onna Daigoku,"—a book on the system of education of girls, by one Ekken, and based upon the books of Confucius, and in which was the famous code of "Obediences for Women." The common term for education, "Shitei no kyoiku" excluded girls, as it means the education only of "the son and younger brother," in other words, only the males of the family.

With the influence of women sunk so low, who can wonder that Japan has made so little advancement in assigning to woman her proper place in the Empire! But with the Restoration of 1868, began the period "Meiji"—"Enlightened Rule" of the Emperor Mutsuhito. With this will come also the "Revival of Letters," and, let us hope, the emancipation of women from the oppressions of feudal times. The leaders in civilization have learned that they cannot raise half of a nation and let the other half act as lodestones to drag them back to barbarism. The existence of such laws proves the necessity of legislation prompt and strong. Not a few, however, of the bolder women have braved public opinion and stepped out from their cloister-like lives, and nature, which is stronger than man, has in their cases proved that women are amply qualified to compete with men.

As yet, prejudice and custom are but little overcome. Even in 1890, Professor Chamberlain said, "The greatest duchess, or marchioness, in the land is still her husband's drudge. She fetches and carries for him; bows down humbly in the hall when my lord sallies forth, and waits upon him at his meals and eats not with him. The

woman may still love and serve,—
she is not expected to know."

About the same date I was a
daily spectator of such scenes as
this quotation suggests. I was living directly across the street from
the residence of the Governor
of —— province. Every morning
His Excellency's carriage—a large
barouche and a span of spirited
horses, with coachman, body-serv-
ant and footman, all in livery—
drove to the Executive Mansion.
Instantly the entrance doors slid
aside and then, kneeling at the
right were the wife and daughter,
while on the opposite side were
three or four servants. As the
sound of the Governor's footsteps
came through the house, every head
went to the floor and remained
there till " my lord " was seated in
his carriage. Not until he had
passed out of the gate could the
kneeling servants rise. The same
performance was gone over when
"Okaeri," the signal of return,
rang out through the air. Four
times a day was this repeated, and
with a lordly air the husband and
father passed out and in without so
much as a nod of recognition to wife or
daughter.

COUNTRY MAIDEN.

This man was a Liberal and progres-
sionist ; but, such was the power of tradition and custom that kindness, even, was
lost in the love of himself, as *man !* Yet
when " the foreigners " were invited to
his house, both wife and daughter were
allowed places at the table with them and
the daughter even took her share in
entertaining them by music on the *Koto.*

The wife of a peasant or merchant is
much nearer to her husband's level than
is the wife of the Emperor or Prince. No
great gulf is spread between the farmer
and his wife. Side by side they till the
soil, side by side they push and pull at
the same cart—she with blue trousers
on, and tucked up skirts, identically like
the man. But when evening comes, the
mother and the baby are put into the cart

and the father draws them home. The
father, too, will even assist at the evening
meal. Such little attentions as these
make the woman much happier than the
wife of a noble, who spends her life in
the seclusion of her home, with no companions but her retinue of ladies-in-wait-
ing and servants,—never the sharer of
her husband's cares or duties and seldom
of his love. She must ever be ready
cheerfully to receive his concubine into
her house, and to adopt the children of
such, who often outrank even her own
children. By the same law, the real
mother is thenceforth no more to her
child than the other servants of the
household, and never sees it until the
thirtieth day, when she goes with them
to pay her respects to her master.

A law, however, has been recently
promulgated which, if enforced, will in
time eradicate this evil. By it, no child

EMPRESS HARU KO.

of a concubine can succeed to a noble title; and the heir to the throne must henceforth be the son not only of the Emperor, but of the Empress as well. Thus the light of a better future is beginning to dawn for the women of Japan.

Another and more significant fact is that with the promulgation of the Liberal Constitution in February, 1889, the Emperor publicly placed his wife upon his own level, when in a grand procession through the streets of His Imperial City, he allowed the Empress for the first time to ride at his side in the coach; also to sit at the same banqueting table with His Majesty!

This was a very gracious act on his part, and these old feudal bars of oppression once let down can never be put up again. During the last twenty or twenty-five years schools for the better education of girls of all classes have been established. The first and most notable epoch of this kind, however, was the opening of Mission Schools by Christian women from America and Europe. These were as an entering

GEISHA—DANCING WOMEN.

HOUSE SALUTATION.

wedge into the old manner of educating girls. The Christian doctrine of the worth of women as mortal and immortal beings, and the self-sacrificing lives of these consecrated women, awoke a like ambition in many Japanese women, and they set themselves to study how they could enlighten and elevate their own sex. Assisted by government they secured an education, some of them abroad, and they are now occupying places of trust in the native schools, as well as in medicine and in business. A former court lady is at the head of the Peeresses' School, which is a large and flourishing institution.

But, amid all this galaxy of reformed, and reformers of, Japanese women, there are none more noble, none more beautiful and lovely in character, than the Empress herself. She is the patroness of several schools, visits them, offers prizes for higher scholarships and encourages every step in the advancement of her sex. She speaks several foreign

MODE OF WASHING.

languages, is a fine artist and a poetess of much merit. Hospitals for the poor have been built and equipped by her own munificence. By self-denial and strict economy in her own personal expenses she has bestowed upon the Tokyo Charity Hospital the liberal sum of over 8,000 yen. This hospital is free to all the lowest classes. In her frequent visits to the children's ward, she takes with her toys, which she distributes among them with her own hand. In this way and many other ways she has endeared herself to her people and found a home in the hearts of the poorest of her subjects.

Since the opening of the war with China, she has gathered her court ladies around her and with them she has spent much time in preparing lint and bandages for the supply of hospitals for wounded soldiers.

Thus we see the Empress Haru Ko eminently fitted to be the leader of her country-women to far greater achievements in the fields of art, science and literature in the bright future that is opening to them through Christian civilization.

AN EARLY TIME.

HAVE you forgotten, dear, the bright hearth's glow,
    In days we planned our life in hopeful smiles?
Don't you remember, love, the suns were low,
And cold December blasts were at their wiles,
And sledge-bells tinkled forth their silv'ry tune.
And soft blue wraiths of smoke trailed high above
The maples and the willows near the rune
Whereby we romped and first avowed our love?

Does recollection bring all back to you,
And wake your mem'ry with that fragrant day
When your sweet lips were fresh and crisp as dew
Upon the nut-brown clovers in the hay?
Noons of sunshine! Nights all laughing stars!
And all the earth entrancing with the strain
Of faint, wild harmonies, attuned in bars
Of Autumn zephyrs, playing through the grain?

As Time re-echoes fondly back that joy
Of our glad summer in that early time,
When you were "Doe" and I—well I the boy
Who often led you through the mint and thyme,
Just as the sun in glory kissed to life
A rare June day—of Daphne, fair, begot?

I ask: "Do *you* remember?"—you—*his* wife!—
For *I*—if I remember—have forgot!

Harry Wellington Wack.

A PATCH OF BARBARISM.

By Samuel B. Evans.

IN a paper contributed to the International Congress of Americanists at Paris in 1890, the author of this sketch made some observations as to the persistency with which races of men adhere to certain inborn qualities. "There are races of men," he said, "inimical to civilization, and in this Nineteenth Century are struggling against its approach as they have been from the time history was carved in stone or imprinted on the cylinders of Babylon. The ancient Eastern civilizations perished, but the barbarians remain, preserving with fidelity the rude customs of their forefathers, and warring still against the ideas which their ancestors fought with a persistency that speaks well for that quality, if for nothing else, that is theirs. If one should search for the marks they have made on the earth's surface, the search would be vain; their mission is to destroy, not to build; to burn, not to create; they made no monuments in the past; they are making none now; they never will make any; it would be as reasonable to expect that coneys would grow into dam-building animals like beavers, as to believe that a child of the desert would, of his own free will, develop into a builder of cities." The same stubborn persistency in the ways of nomadic life belongs to the American tribes. The European has known them nearly four hundred years, and with slight variations, brought about by abnormal conditions, they preserve the traits they displayed when Columbus first encountered them. An example is brought to mind: A fragment of a tribe holds a reservation in the midst of a populous state, where four hundred individuals of the race

are surrounded by the appliances and inventions of the age; and yet, with all the influences that contact with high civilization affords, these lingering relics of a barbarism that once held a continent within its folds adhere rigidly as they may to the customs, religion, modes and superstitions of primitive life.

It is of these people and the patch of barbarism they maintain that this paper is written, and it is a strange fact that less is known of them than the general reader knows of some of the tribes of interior Africa. An occasional newspaper paragraph appears that alludes in a mere perfunctory way to the Musquakie In-

MA-TAU-E-QUA
The old Chief of the Sac and Fox Tribes, 85 years old

515

dians; but the business, literary and social world is ignorant of a state of things existing in Iowa that is an anomaly in the history and development of civilization and a most striking illustration of the strength and potency of inherited barbaric traits.

In the southern part of Tama County, about four miles from Tama City and near the same distance from Toledo, there are over four hundred and fifty Indians, four hundred of whom are of the once powerful Sac and Fox tribe, and known locally as Musquakies. These Indians do not live on a reservation proper, but reside on lands purchased with their own money and held in trust for them, some by the Governor of Iowa and some by the United States Indian Agent. They own nearly three thousand acres of land, acquiring their title by purchase from settlers, and their rights to such land were confirmed by a special act of the Iowa Legislature, and their location was approved by the Indian department. In 1842 the Sac and Fox confederation ceded their lands in Iowa to the United States government, and in part consideration were given a reservation in Kansas. Some of these Indians became dissatisfied with Kansas, and returned in groups to Iowa and by the year 1855 had squatted along the Iowa River in Tama County. In 1856 the Legislature enacted a law permitting these Indians to remain within the State so long as peaceful, and in July, 1857, they purchased eighty acres of land. From time to time thereafter they added to their original purchase until they now have about three thousand acres. In 1867 they were ordered by the Secretary of the Interior to go to their reservation, but they refused, rightfully maintaining that the State had given them permission to remain, and in 1867 Congress provided that it should be lawful for them to receive their annuities in Iowa, and the independent fragment has since been recognized as a part of the Sac and Fox tribe. The more powerful branch of the Sac and Foxes of the Mississippi remained on the Kansas reservation until 1842, when they were ordered to the Indian Territory by the government, where they have received lands in allotment, one hundred and sixty acres to each family, besides their annuities. The agent in his last report says that they have shown marked progress in the improvement and cultivation of their lands, building houses and fences and planting orchards and manifesting greater interest in making their homes more pleasant. The census of 1894 enrolled 512 Indians in that branch of the tribe.

It is, however, to the less progressive members of the tribe that we turn with greater interest, to see how their intense love for the land of their nativity led them to brave the orders of a powerful

MUSQUAKIE SQUAW AND PAPOOSE.

SHOWING FRAMEWORK OF A WICKIUP.

government and refuse to abandon their old homes. It is impossible to obtain details of the strategy that was employed by these primitive Iowa patriots to secure their purpose, but it is certain from results accomplished that they were led by a diplomacy of no mean order. Their councilmen, unlettered and unskilled as they were in civilized arts, adopted the best means to gain a foothold; and the policy, rude as it may appear in contrast with the methods of white men, was effective in establishing the Musquakies on Iowa soil with a title and rights as well secured by law as any community of Iowa farmers.

Tama County is situated not far away from the geographical center of the State. There are few acres that are not enclosed and adapted to the use of agriculture; the twin cities of Toledo and Tama are situated but two and one-half miles apart, connected by an electric railway. Trunk lines of railroads extend through the county, and two important roads have right of way through the lands of the Indians. The county is populous, the people partake of the culture of the cen-

tury; school-houses and churches are at all convenient places, and yet, surrounded by these evidences of civilization, there is maintained within the domain of the Musquakies a semblance of savage government, with the modes, customs and superstitions peculiar to them one hundred years ago.

The little patch of barbarism is situated on the banks of the river. The Indian requires wood and water convenient and is moved to his choice by a natural desire for the picturesque and beautiful, and yet his childish thoughtlessness and necessities have caused him to destroy great trees, by skinning them for the purpose of procuring bark for his wickiup.

A visit to the locality during the recent summer was made under the guidance of Mr. Rebok, the United States Agent. It was but a step from civilization to barbarism, as we crossed the track of the Chicago & Northwestern Railway with its splendid equipment, passed through a gate and encountered the small plats of growing corn, the stalks of which were then heavy with the rich and milky "roasting ears." In the midst of one of these truck patches was a rude shed covered with bark, and beneath the shade was a group of squaws and naked children surrounding a boiling pot, and on a primitive hammock reclined a lord of the forest. The squaws were engaged in drying corn, which was spread out on mats made of rushes that grow in the vicinity. This was not a permanent place of abode, but a place where the corn is dried and made ready for winter use. It was about the noon hour, and the presence of the head of the household is explained by his desire to eat something, for after his stomach is filled with succotash he soon returns to the village on the other side of the river, where he will doze away the afternoon in the cool shade of a rude veranda, erected in front of his wigwam. There is a labyrinth of roads winding through truck patches

and in each one of these small gardens are similar groups of squaws and children, the former industriously drying corn or cooking succotash, brewing strong coffee, or baking bread yellow with saleratus.

Between the fields of corn and the summer villages is a body of forest trees and brush and scattered through this growth are the bent poles of last year's wickiups erected in this sheltered locality to escape the fierce blasts of winter. When the leaves have fallen and the first biting frosts of November have come, the squaws will be busy for a few days in preparing the wickiups, which will be the abodes of themselves and families until spring. The wickiups are covered with bark and matting and meet the Indian idea of comfort by being made small, oval in form, 10 to 16 feet in diameter, and about ten feet in height. When the mats are spread upon the ground, the various articles of Indian equipment packed closely around the inner walls, an open fire blazing in the center, with the smoke struggling to escape through a hole in the roof, the winter residence of the Musquakie will be complete.

Crossing the river at a shallow ford, we saw a squaw arrayed in the most exaggerated and aggravating style of Bloomerism emerging from a pool of water, and one unaccustomed to Indian habits would be led to believe that she had been taking a bath on that hot, summer day; but this was not the maiden's whim or purpose. She was fishing for pearls in company with a number of her sex and they had cast off what little superfluous clothing they had. The bright turkey-red hue of the garments, spread out over the bushes on the bank of the stream, gave a picturesque bit of color to the scene.

Pearl fishing is a pleasing and sometimes profitable industry carried on by the squaws and young men, and the agent says that a few pearls of beauty and value have

MA-PELLA-EA.
Member of the Musquakie Council

been found and sold to Eastern jewelers. The pearl is found within the shell of the lowly mussel, and occasionally one is discovered that will sell for as much as fifteen dollars, and then there is indeed rejoicing in the family of the fortunate fisher.

The river is crossed in order to reach the two straggling villages on the plain, that lie immediately south and west from the stream. On this plain or valley the summer wigwams are erected, and these seem to be permanent dwellings. These differ from the winter wickiups in being constructed of, first, a frame-work of poles set firmly in the ground, covering a space of twenty-five by thirty-two feet, and the height of an ordinary one-story building of the whites. This rude frame-work is covered with the bark of trees, and the wigwam covered with the broadest strips of bark is accounted in Musquakie circles as the most aristocratic!

The inner economy is Indian-like and unique. There are platforms of boards and puncheons extending each side of the wigwam, raised about four feet above the level, and these are covered with mats of woven rushes and grasses, and then with blankets. Here the family sleep or repose. An adult Indian in good health may easily climb to the platform, but, for the convenience of the aged or infirm and for the children, notched poles are provided, almost identical in pattern with those found in the abandoned cliff-dwellings of the Southwest, and by the aid of these primitive ladders the Skinneway and Sunkisee ascend to their resting places. On these platforms and next to the wall are convenient places for depositing all the trumpery and accoutrements of Indian economy. There will be found an occasional valise purchased from cheap clothing houses or picked up in barter, and these seem in odd contrast to the primitive and genuine

Indian packing-case or bundle, made of matting or skins, embellished with the peculiar hieroglyphics or picture writing of primitive peoples. Two, three and sometimes four families live in one of these structures.

Leaning against any convenient wall or platform we see papooses, or infants, strapped to boards, where they must stay until they have reached the age when they can walk. The cradle-board was invented by an Indian a long time ago, who thus early was impressed with the maxim that "as a twig is bent, the tree inclines." As the board is supposed to compel the young Indian to be straight in his cradle days, so will he be straight during his lifetime. In one of the larger wickiups in the village we found a lone, sick Indian, his squaw being absent drying corn, and he very ill, his head covered with a blanket and he quite despondent. It was found that he was one of the principal men at a big dog feast the day before; he had exercised violently in the dance and had eaten too much dog. Dances and festivals of a character similar to this are frequent during the summer, especially in the time of green corn, and immediately after the payment of annuities.

This leads me to speak of the singular case of Muck-Qua-Push-E-To, who claims to be the hereditary chief of the tribe and whose place is usurped by the present ruling chief, who is known as Push-E-To-Neke-Qua, who acquired his title and place through a quiet sort of revolution. Muck-Qua-Push-E-To is therefore sullen and disdains to draw the annuity to which he is entitled. He is a sort of Count de Chambord, who might have been King of France had he accepted the tri color of the Bourbons.

There is a curious belief among these people that when death occurs to a member of the tribe, the spirit wanders to and fro, without definite object, subject to

every breeze that blows; it has no resting place and can have none until the ceremony of adoption is performed by surviving members of the family. Any person, a member of the tribe or even Indians of other tribes may be "adopted" by the family, to take the place of the deceased. So soon as adoption is accomplished the spirit of the dead is released and its course is directed westward and to a point where two roads diverge. If the Indian has been good, according to the Indian standard, the spirit is directed to a road that leads to where the sun goes down. This is the Indian paradise. On the other hand, if the Indian has led a wicked life, the spirit is forced to take a broad road that leads to a place of punishment. The graveyards of these people present a weird, uncanny sight. There are two of them, situated on a hillside half a mile apart. The grave is made from one to three feet in depth and then earth is heaped on above the surface until it presents the appearance of an oblong mound somewhat similar in shape to the

A TYPICAL WINTER RESIDENCE.

M'SH-E-TO-BSES-QUA,
Chief of the Musquakie Indians.

graves of whites. Over this mound is either a pile of logs or a rude structure; in a few instances a wickiup is built over the remains, or a stockade of roughly-hewn boards or slabs. In each grave there are deposited articles used by the deceased during life,— a pipe, strands of beads, a bowl, ornaments, etc.

The presence of Indians from the Sac and Fox reservations in Indian Territory and from other tribes is of itself suggestive. These wanderers go to the Musquakies to escape the restraints of civilization that are laid upon them in the reservations elsewhere. Here repair renegades from the Winnebagoes and

Pottawattamies, to indulge in the license and liberty of barbarism; where they may clothe themselves in Indian toggery and dispense with hats; where they can go naked if they choose, and paint their bodies as their ancestors did, one hundred or five hundred years ago; where they may dance to the monotonous music of the tom-tom or the rattle of gourds; where the wild, free life of primitive man is preserved and the right to enjoy all these things is most jealously guarded.

It will be in place now to introduce the reigning chief, the traditions of his tribe and its internal polity, and I gratefully acknowledge the aid of Mr. Horace M. Rebok, the agent of these Indians, whose intelligent and humane efforts to better their condition will, I hope, be crowned with success. I gather from him the following facts.

But two Indians of the tribe have adopted the citizen's dress and these sometimes appear with blankets in the winter time. Of the whole tribe probably about 250 wear some essential feature of citizen's dress. There are but two or three who habitually wear hats.

There are probably not more than six of these Indians over twenty-one years old who can read the English language at all, and that to a limited extent. About thirty or forty of the men and women under that age can read and write a little, and a few of them fairly well. These Indians have a written language of their own, and the officers of the tribe keep their accounts in the native language.

The tribe is ruled by a council of ten, at the head of which is a principal chief whose name is Push-E-To-Neke-Qua. However, nearly all of the business of the tribe is conducted by three men, and rarely do more than five take an active part in the deliberations of the council. The chief is a shrewd politician and a diplomat of no ordinary ability, who always puts his ear to the ground to hear the wishes of his people, but his word is law. With him thoroughly enlisted, no cause would fail in his tribe, but he is shrewd enough not to unnecessarily cross

the wishes of his people. He h an orator. He frequently delivers addresses in the council in rounded and polished periods.

The oldest member of the tribe is a woman 100 years old. She had two sons in the Black Hawk War, and has two grandsons here who are past middle life. One woman died during the past winter whose age was 112.

The one who in his time has been the blood and iron man of his tribe, is old Ma-Tau-E-Qua, who still abides among his people and is now eighty-five years of age, but has given the exercise of his power almost wholly to Push-E-To-Neke-Qua. Ma-Tau-E-Qua has been the one who has most sternly resisted all encroachments of civilization upon his tribe. His nearest concession to civilization was made last spring when, talking in council about the erection of a school building, he said, "May be,—after I am dead."

The secretary of the tribe is Ash-E-Ton-E-Quot, more familiarly known as George Morgan, who was given the advantage of some education by Agent Davenport, who sent George to school at Davenport, Iowa, for a short time; yet George keeps all his accounts in the Indian language, and takes no pride in knowing how to read or write English.

There are at present 117 children between six and eighteen years of age.

The tribe receives annually a little over $16,000 from the government in annuities arising from the interest on the principal, derived from the sale of lands in Iowa to the Federal government. This constitutes about fifty per cent of their subsistence.

They have cultivated this year 460 acres of corn, 12 acres of potatoes, 15 acres of beans, 31 acres of oats, 5 acres of squashes, 23 acres of millet. Their live stock consists of 100 horses, 400 ponies, 12 head of hogs, 13 head of cattle, 500 chickens and turkeys. The crops and live stock are owned individually. The land and farming implements are owned by the tribe. A few of the Indians have purchased their farming implements.

They own in all and in common nearly 3,000 acres of land, 700 acres of which are leased to whites. Out of the fund arising from the rent of this land they pay their annual taxes, amounting to about $700, and keep up repairs of their fences.

The religion of this people does not differ materially from that of other Indian tribes. It is their strong motive, and in it they seem to find their greatest happiness. The adoption and the dog feast are as sacred to them as they were to Black Hawk and his followers, and are practiced unrestricted among them. They believe in four gods, three of whom have been killed by Indians and who now preside over their destinies in the world of spirits. One resides half-way between here and "where the sun goes down," at the forks of the road,—one of which roads, the narrow one, leads due westward to the abode of the good, over which presides another of these gods. The other branch of the road, the wide one, turns to the right, leading to the place of the wicked and is presided over by the third god. Their fourth god is Ke-Che-Ma-Ne-To-Wa, the Great Spirit, whom they worship. They believe that the spirit of their dead does not leave earth until after the adoption of some person into the family from which the deceased has been taken, and hence their adoption. This adoption is merely a religious ceremony and does not imply that the person adopted actually becomes a member of the family. It is attended with a feast, sacred music and sacred dance, an address by one of the principal men of the tribe and the distribution of gifts. At these adoptions the men frequently throw aside all garments except the breech-cloth, tattoo their bodies and conduct themselves as nearly in imitation of their ancestors as possible. One of the reasons offered by the old men against education has been that it tends to lessen the interest of the young men in these religious ceremonies. The basis of their prejudices lies in their religion.

There has been maintained for many years a day school at the Agency with one teacher. It has accomplished little. The objective point to which the Indian Rights Association of Iowa is now working is the erection of an Industrial Boarding School in close proximity to the Indian land, with the purpose of teaching the rising generation the essential features of industry and the elements of education that will enable them to protect themselves against the stronger white civilization.

"We do not intend," says the agent, "to give the Indians a white man's education, but rather to educate them in the practical affairs of life that will enable them as Indians to live better in the situation in which they find themselves. The Presbyterian Home Board of Missions of Iowa erected a mission building about five years ago, at an expense of nearly $5,000, and for twelve years has maintained a mission among these people.

There are no formal marriages among the Musquakies. They marry Indian fashion, that is, they take up the married life and break it off at their pleasure. There are no formal divorces, but separation of wife and husband is very common. However, for a people living in their environments, it must be said that they are exceptionally virtuous and live well up to their standard or Indian code of morals.

They are a most peaceful people. They do not quarrel with the whites, neither do they quarrel among themselves. Complaints of this kind are rare indeed.

———

Our exploration of the little pagan country was too soon ended. There is a charm in the uncivilized life that seems to woo one back to the joys that comforted our European ancestors but a few centuries ago. The wild freedom of the woods tempts the fisherman and hunter to forego the pleasures of home and revel for a time in the indefinable felicity that savages find in their everyday lives. There is a strain of barbarism within us all that is quickened by contact with those who have preserved the taint with fanatical zeal and pride of race.

The Musquakie is a survival of all that barbarism which dominated the continent four hundred years ago, and his proudest boast is that he is an Indian still. To an educated Sioux missionary who came among them preaching the new life, this reply came from the Musquakie chief: "We have heard what you say; we understand; I hope you will be sincere in your new life and continue, but as for us, we are Indians, and will always be Indians! and so in future years when you have traveled all over this country and have seen all the Indians and then come back to us, we will show you by our lives what you were when you were an Indian."

What shall we do with such a people? The answer seems plain: Help them to live in comfort on present lines. Quails and antelope do not thrive in captivity nor would the Musquakies be happy if their tribal relations were dissolved and they compelled to adopt all the white man's ways. Better a group of four hundred living in wickiups on the Iowa River than four hundred more idlers turned loose to live in squalor and sin in the slums of cities, or to become vagabonds and tramps begging for charity over the face of the earth.

IOWA STATE NORMAL SCHOOL.

By Sara M. Riggs.

THE Normal School in the United States is of comparatively recent origin, for it is less than sixty years ago that the first institution of this class was established. Since that time more than a hundred such schools have been founded and maintained by the different states, thus showing that this sort of education met an actual need. Not until 1876, however, could Iowa boast of such an institution. At that time, the buildings of the Soldiers' Orphan Home at Cedar Falls were given for the use of the school and it was opened, enrolling about one hundred students the first year.

The school is not in the heart of the city, as one might suppose, but a mile and a half from the business portion. In fact, it has been in the country until recently, when its grounds and the immediate vicinity were incorporated with the city. There is no sightlier place in the county than the hill upon which the buildings stand. It commands a wide view — characteristically Iowan — of gently undulating prairies diversified by groves. The eastern horizon is bounded by the Cedar River, whose banks are skirted by a wealth of trees ever lending beauty to the landscape, whether clad in the varied greens of spring; the red, yellow and brown of autumn; or, stripped

of their foliage, standing bare and gray, merely outlined against the sky.

In consequence of the distance of the school from town, there has arisen in the vicinity a considerable village, "Normalville," as it is familiarly called. This is composed principally of boarding houses and halls. Several of the professors have made their homes here, too, thus removing to some extent the boarding-hall aspect that the hill might otherwise assume. The President's cottage, a handsome brick building, adorns the campus on the north. There are at present but two buildings devoted to the use of the school; a third will be ready for use next term. North Hall, the "old building," is devoted to the training, and to the preparatory department, as well as to recitation rooms; Central Hall, the "new building," to library, museum and recitation rooms; South Hall, to recitation rooms.

The purpose of the school is a technical one — that of educating teachers. It seeks to give such training, both scholastic and professional, as will fit the graduates to go back to the country schools or to the graded schools of our cities and raise the standard of elementary education. To prepare for the higher ranks of teaching is not the chief aim, but that it

HON. HENRY SABIN.
State Superintendent of Public Instruction and Chairman of the Board of Directors of the State Normal School.

does so is demonstrated by the fact that in many of the high schools of our state are found Normal graduates who, in the character and efficiency of their work, hold equal rank with college-trained teachers. But I do not need to eulogize the Normal School, or plead its cause; its reputation is established; my object is rather to give a picture of its student life.

To one whose actual experiences date back into the early eighties, the present shows many changes. There was then but one building, and one course of study; there were no laboratories for work in Physics, Chemistry or the Natural Sciences; there was no Athletic Association, no Military Department, no Christian Association. With three buildings, six courses of study, and various societies and associations for culture and development, there is not to-day a more earnest, painstaking spirit than was seen in the old days of fewer opportunities. The changes have been gradual, and yet, to any "old student" who has

Hon. E. B. Moore,
Professor D. S. Wright.
Hon. L. J. McDuffie.

Hon. J. W. Beresheim,
President H. H. Seerley.
Hon. J. W. Jarnagin.

Hon. W. W. Montgomery,
Professor M. W. Bartlett.
Hon. E. Townsend.

THE PRESIDENT, HEADS OF DEPARTMENTS AND BOARD OF DIRECTORS OF THE IOWA STATE
NORMAL SCHOOL.

not watched them, the Normal of the present would hardly seem like his Alma Mater.

The students of to-day are met by a reception committee, who, although strangers, prove indeed friends in aiding the new-comers to find boarding-places, and in initiating them into the ways of Normal life. That bugbear to the students of long ago, that barrier to all happiness until it was passed,—examination for entrance,—is now almost unknown, for this is secured through certificates from the county superintendents or through graduation from a high school.

The student having entered, what next awaits him? Work, work, work ; yes, and plenty of it. He now begins to realize that the Normal School is not designed for play nor to give merely a smattering of the subjects presented upon its curriculum. Normal Schools everywhere are proverbial for doing a great deal of work in a short space of time, and the Iowa Normal is not altogether an exception ; yet, although such is the fact, the thoroughness and excellent quality of the work cannot be questioned. Hand

in hand with the imparting of the subject matter goes that of method. Right here in justice it should be said that no attempt is made to kill the individuality of the would-be teacher ; on the contrary, effort is made to develop that individuality, to guide it according to correct pedagogical principles rather than to supplant it by a "machine method."

The dominating spirit of the Normal student is work,—earnest, faithful, downright hard work. , One often feels inclined to ask if he cares for amusements at all, so thoroughly imbued is he with this spirit ; but it takes not a very close

MEMBERS OF THE FACULTY OF THE IOWA STATE NORMAL SCHOOL.

observer to discover that, like his college friends, he knows that "all work and no play makes Jack a dull boy."

And opportunities for amusement are not lacking. Athletics have never been very conspicuous, for, in fact, until within a few years no attention was given them. In 1892, not to be outdone by its college neighbors, the Normal organized an athletic association, under whose direction the usual games are provided. This next year there will be four departments,—baseball, football, gymnasium and track-team. Three annual field-days have been held and several inter-collegiate baseball games have been played. An interest has thereby been aroused, which, it is safe to predict, will not soon die out. Under the direction of the tennis association, courts and apparatus have been provided, and in spring or fall the campus is enlivened by groups of merry players engaged in this popular sport. In winter, the hill furnishes a fine opportunity for coasting.

The military department provides exercise, if not sport, for every male student. This is a comparatively new feature of the school, having been organized and put in charge of an officer only three years ago. Since that time, the department has steadily gained both in favor and in the character of the work done. The girls do not, as at Ames, take part in the military drill, but get exercise, and rest from the routine of study, in the physical culture classes, which are also in charge of a special teacher.

There is little opportunity for social life,—a fact greatly to be deplored, since as teachers the students will need the culture that can be gained in no other way than through the medium of society. There has, however, been a marked improvement in this respect, and efforts are being made to provide means whereby the social nature may be cultivated. In this, the school must depend largely upon its own resources, for the distance of the school from town creates a barrier between the two,—a barrier, nevertheless, destined to disappear when the two are connected by an electric railway. Then,

it is safe to say, a better state of social life will develop. One of the pleasantest features of each term is the reception given by the Christian associations to the new students. After the rendering of a short program, all give themselves up to having a "good time," to greeting old friends and forming new ones. The ice is broken now, and the "new student" feels at home. An innovation of recent origin is the extension of social courtesy among the literary societies. The "Aristos" set the fashion by giving a banquet to the "Shaksperians." Like all other fashions, it was soon followed,—the "Alphas" entertaining the "Philos," while the "Philos" capped the climax by entertaining all the others. Such social events are bright spots in the otherwise somewhat humdrum life of the Normal student.

The school, through its lecture association, furnishes several good lectures each year, thus keeping in touch with outside thought and broadening its culture. In this connection, too, there should be mentioned the public programs of the various literary societies. During the year each society gives one, at which time every energy is bent to score a grand success. As these are intended to be indicative of the actual work done, the program consists usually of essays, orations, debates and recitations; occasionally, however, it is enlivened by the production of some scene from Shakspeare or a costume drill by members of the physical culture classes.

Although the Normal student has usually had the reputation of being a law-abiding one, it is possible that, could one be found who would divulge secrets, he might give some very interesting accounts of other, but not so legitimate, amusements. Upon the whole, however, there has always been a comparative freedom from the pranks in which students are wont to indulge. This is no doubt due to the fact that the Normal student, expecting to be a teacher, feels already the dignity of his future office creeping upon him.

34

INTERIOR VIEW — THE LIBRARY AND READING ROOM.

THE NEW CENTRAL BUILDING.

The feeling between classes is of the kindliest. There is none of the unpleasantness so frequently prevalent in colleges. To be sure, the senior has sometimes an "I know-it-all" air, as with the confidence begotten of his long residence midst Normal scenes, he sees some "new student" wandering about trying in vain to find the recitation-room in which he is next to recite. But the over-confident air is pardoned, as the senior steps up quickly and helps the "new student" out of his difficulty.

The State Normal School had a share in the "Bahama Expedition," of which an interesting report was given in the article on the State University in the February MIDLAND of 1894. Professor Arey of the Natural Science department accompanied this expedition and, as a result, a museum has been started and an interest awakened in biological research. A direct outgrowth of such interest is the M'Arey Natural History Society, founded to promote the study of nature and to provide means of becoming acquainted with what has been done in that field of knowlege.

Every student is obliged to do rhetorical work. The high school graduates and all other students above the first year are eligible to membership in the literary societies, of which there are eight — five admitting women; three, men. Although some rivalry exists among these, it is never a bitter one. Occasionally, inter-society debates are held; thereby is aroused a kindly rivalry, which stimulates each to do its best. The work is under the supervision of a special teacher; hence the best possible results are secured.

These gatherings in society are among the pleasantest of our recollections of Normal life. Saturday evening was a gala night, for then all the cares of the week were laid aside. The society bell meant not a call to some new task, but a call to a feast — a literary feast where were served up in the best of style the substantial food of essay, oration and debate, the lighter food of parody, soliloquy or prophecy, while the whole was spiced with song and quotation.

Religious life is phenomenally active. Strong organizations of the Young Men's and Young Women's Christian Associations are maintained, and under their direction are held semi-weekly prayer-meetings, where much interest has been shown. Such influences can but lead to higher living, can but fit better for their work those who have come to prepare for the great task of teaching. The world needs true Christian workers; with such in our schools to set the example of pure and noble manhood and womanhood the result must inevitably be the rise of similar workers from whom an untold influence will radiate. Sunday is the busiest of days. In early morning the Bible classes meet; in the afternoon, service is held in the Chapel; following this service is Sunday-school, and in the evening, prayer-meeting. No one is compelled to attend any of these, but such is the interest that comparatively few of those in "Normalville" ever stay away.

Journalism is not altogether neglected. The "Normal Eyte" is published weekly under the direction of the Normal Publishing Association, representing four departments — the Alumni, Y. M. C. A. and Y. W. C. A., Athletic and Exchange. The editors are elected by the societies and the contributions are secured from the students.

Six courses, besides three special courses, are now open to those who come to Normal halls. Effort has been made to suit these to the varied needs of the students, and to present a thorough course of instruction combined with method. Four of these courses are open to high school graduates; two to all that secure entrance. The special courses comprise a professional course for college graduates, and two for primary teachers, one giving especial attention to such kindergarten work as may be adapted to the public primary school system.

Two degrees are granted — B. Di., Bachelor of Didactics, and M. Di., Master of Didactics, the latter being secured by four years of study, the former by three. A year's credit is given to all high school graduates; hence they secure these degrees by two and three years' study respectively. The seniors of the third and fourth year spend a portion of the last year teaching in the training department. This gives them a practical knowledge of school-room work and enables the faculty to estimate, to a certain extent, their value as teachers.

The rapid development of the school and its present high standard of efficiency are due largely to the wise direction, untiring energy, broad culture, scholarly attainments and strong personality of its president, H. H. Seerley, who was called to this office in '86. In his work he is aided by a corps of well-qualified, efficient teachers, to whom also the school is greatly indebted for its prosperity, since only through good teachers can any school attain excellence.

The Normal School is still in its infancy, and yet it has already sent forth an army of graduates nearly a thousand strong, most of whom are engaged in the profession of teaching. Besides these, there are many others who have attended a term or more, and have gained something of the spirit and method of the school. What the State needs is a larger force of well-trained, thoroughly equipped teachers; not but that there are enough who call themselves such; there are too few of the right sort. That the Iowa Normal has done and is doing much to supply this need cannot be questioned by those who have had the opportunity to test the work done by its graduates. With only limited resources it has already done much to raise the standard of education in Iowa. Greater things even are in store for the State when a higher standard is made possible through better equipment and stronger support.

DECEMBER.

THE Storm King flings snow fleeces down;
*   Star-eyed December, drawing near,*
*   Accepts the tribute without fear*
And bares her brow for Winter's crown.

*   She whirls the russet leaves aside*
*   With trailing garments dull and gray.—*
*   A shadow steals across the bay,*
*   Then sweeps the night through portals wide.*

"And bares her brow for Winter's crown."

Gaunt watchmen guard the wind-swept hill,
*   And point with ice-clad fingers down*
*   Where twinkling lights reveal the town,*
Then whistle warnings weird and shrill.

*   A rabbit, startled, hears the cry*
*   And leaps the hedge with fleeing feet ;*
*   A babe awakes from slumber sweet*
*   And moans, though mother-love is nigh.*

*   December bends her to the storm,*
*   Nor heeds Old Winter's wrack and wrath ;*
*   Though shade or sunshine flood the path*
*   She is content,— her heart is warm.*

Clara Adele Neidig.

MRS. JOHN W. FOSTER.

PROMINENT WOMEN IN WASHINGTON'S SOCIAL WORLD. II.

By Juliette M. Babbitt.

MRS. Mary McFerson Foster, the new President-General of the Daughters of the American Revolution, is one of the most popular women in Washington, where she and her distinguished husband, the Hon. John W. Foster, have resided for many years, when not abroad on diplomatic missions or traveling for pleasure. Mrs. Foster has much executive ability, rare tact and dignified and pleasing manners, and makes a very capable and charming presiding officer. She is a charter member of the society, and a "lineal." One great-grandfather, Daniel Read, was a commissioned officer under Washington. Another ancestor, Colonel John Brown, of Massachusetts, fell at the head of his troops, and a third, Captain Silas Clark, died from wounds received at Monmouth. Her mother's father, Ezra Read, was one of the earliest and most prominent settlers of Urbana, Ohio. Her father was the Reverend Alexander McFerson, of Salem, Indiana, Mrs. Foster's birthplace. She was educated chiefly under the watchful eye of her uncle, Doctor Read, a professor of languages and a noted educator of the young for many years; and to him, no doubt, she owes her proficiency in languages which has been of great advantage to her abroad, and is a pleasure to foreigners who meet her here.

She accompanied her husband to Russia, Spain and Mexico, when he went as Minister to those countries. She made many warm friends while he was Secretary of State, during the latter part of the Harrison administration. No Cabinet receptions were as large as hers. She is a perfect hostess and entertains handsomely, in official or private life.

Mrs. Foster is of medium height and good figure, with a charming face. Her hair is slightly tinged with gray. She has a pleasing voice and most engaging manners. She has two daughters, Mrs. Lansing and Mrs. Dulles, whose homes are in Watertown, New York, and has several pretty little grandchildren of whom she is very proud.

Mrs. John W. Foster.

The home of Mr. and Mrs. Foster, on I street, a few doors from the Mexican legation, is filled with valuable and pleasing souvenirs of their wanderings. Among the paintings are fine modern ones and several from old Mexican churches and convents which are either works of old Spanish masters or excellent copies. There are quaint old mirrors, bits of pottery, idols from various countries, curios from Alaska and Zuni, tiles from the Alhambra, a handsome Moorish desk from Granada and fine old embroideries from different countries, those from China and Japan being especially attractive. Last year, a large music room was added, and among the many things upon its walls are several handsome panels set with precious and semi-precious stones in beautiful colorings and quaint designs, which, like all Japanese pictures, tell interesting stories to those able to read them.

Mrs. Foster has one of the finest collections of fans in this country — some of them three or four hundred years old — and some of the loveliest combs in tortoise shell, ivory and silver, finely carved and ornamented.

Her collection of china, old and new, is beautiful and very valuable, many a bit being worth its weight in gold to the connoisseur.

The library in the Foster home is full to overflowing with interesting volumes in many languages, Spanish predominating. A good many quaint old books, bound with skin and tied with leathern thongs, were found in Mexico. An odd old "Catechism," with annotations in an exquisitely fine hand, came from the Convent Del Carmen, at Toluca, and there are many manuscripts, yellow with age, but well preserved, whose fine and regular lines were penned by hands which have long been dust.

NOT UNAWARE.

SHE treads, apart, the paths of care,
    Nor from them knows release;
Yet her calm eyes forever wear
    The beauteous light of peace.

In others' weal or woe she lives,—
    No thought of self has she;
Her days, like One divine, she gives
    To loving ministry.

Her tenderness is wont to heal
    The rudest earthly stings;
Who rests in her can not but feel
    Enfolded as with wings.

To passing eyes her brows are lit
    By her soft silver hair,—
Love ever sees, in place of it,
    A halo shining there.

Julia W. Albright.

TWINKLE AND THE STAR.

A CHRISTMAS STORY FOR CHILDREN.

By James Clarence Jones.

Chat on, sweet maid, and rescue from annoy
 Hearts that by wiser talk are unbeguiled;
Ah, happy he who owns that tenderest joy,
 The heart-love of a child!

Away, fond thoughts, and vex my soul no
 more;
 Work claims my wakeful nights, my busy
 days,
Albeit bright memories of that sunlit shore
 Yet haunt my dreaming gaze.
 —Rhyme and Reason.

Once upon a time, I do not know when, and once in some place, I do not know where, there lived a little boy named Twinkle. His hair was golden, his eyes were blue and his teeth were pearly. His proper name was Harold, but his father and mother called him Twinkle because his eyes twinkled so with laughter and merriment One afternoon his mother told him it was nearly Christmas time. He asked if it would be "after the next Sunday," but his mother said "No." Then he asked if it would be "after the Sunday after the next Sunday," and she said "Yes, it will be the Thursday after the Sunday after next Sunday." "That seems a very long time," said Twinkle. "It will not seem so long when it has passed," said his mother.

Later in the day when he went to drive with his father he noticed that the shop windows were decorated with evergreens and that there were many grown people hurrying out of the shops with mysterious paper packages under their arms. Through a hole in one bundle he was sure he saw the end of a drumstick.

When evening came and Twinkle had been put in his bed and left alone to go to sleep, his head was crowded with Christmas thoughts. He made a plan to buy some beautiful things for his father and mother. He felt he could buy a great deal because his red bank was nearly

filled with pennies. He so enjoyed thinking about these things, and his bed was so warm and soft, that he determined to lie awake all night and think. A little while after this he concluded the night must be rather long to lie awake in, so he decided to watch himself to find when he went to sleep. Now if you have ever tried this you know it is a very hard thing to do. Twinkle thought two or three times that he had caught himself, but he had not, for he found he was really awake every time.

Finally he turned to look out of the window and there he saw a beautiful, bright star shining down upon him through the upper part of the window. He was very much delighted at this, so he roused himself at once and began watching the star to keep himself awake ; "for," said he, "when I cannot see the star I will know that I am asleep, and then I will catch myself."

So he lay a long time gazing up into the sky, and the star twinkled at Twinkle, and Twinkle twinkled at the star.

At last a strange thing seemed to happen, so strange that Twinkle forgot all about watching himself. The star rolled over and over in the air and came right down towards the window, growing larger as it came. It stopped when still some distance away, and on the side towards Twinkle a little door flew open and from the door there shot forth a ray of light that fell upon his pillow. Then there stepped forth a little, old man with a long staff in his hand and a bundle under his arm. He had a smooth face, bright eyes and a pointed nose and chin, and Twinkle noticed that he held between his lips a small sprig of evergreen. This looked strange, for he seemed to have no teeth. The little, old man walked down the ray of light, which made a golden pathway, until he came near where Twinkle lay. Then he stopped and made a bow profound and with a grave manner asked Twinkle if he would not attend the Christmas Tree in the star that night.

"There must be some mistake," said Twinkle. "Christmas will not come till the Thursday after the Sunday after next Sunday, so how can you have a tree to-night?"

long staff in one hand and the bundle under his arm. As he ducked his head to catch the falling twig he turned into a puff of smoke and the night wind blew him into the outer darkness.

Now, of course, Twinkle wanted to see that Christmas tree in the star. He was afraid, however, that the golden pathway would not bear his weight. While he

"At last a strange thing seemed to happen."

"Tut! Tut!" said the little, old man. "That's the way you do down here. Tut! Tut! It is different up in the star: it is Christmas there to-night."

It seemed difficult for him to keep the sprig of evergreen in his mouth when he said "Tut! Tut!" and at the end of the sentence he nearly dropped it, nor could he help himself much because he had the

was wondering whether to try it or not, a little boy stepped out of the door and came bounding down the golden way, which Twinkle noticed was so springy that the child had only to touch his toe upon it, when he would fly along for some distance without having to touch his foot again. As the beautiful boy came half tripping, half floating, down the golden pathway he sang a strange song Twinkle had never heard before, and at last he stopped on the pillow and made a bow profound and said, "How do you do, Twinkle? Come up to the Christmas tree in the star to-night."

Twinkle was just going to ask how to walk on the golden pathway, when the little boy turned into a rose-bud and the night wind blew him into the outer darkness. So Twinkle got up and commenced to climb, and found that the golden way held him very well and was much wider than he had supposed.

He had not been climbing long when a little girl came out of the door in the star and descended towards him. As she came she waved a garland of roses about her head and her light feet kept time to a song she was singing:

> May you have a Merry Christmas!
> May your cares for this year be
> Light as gently falling snowflakes
> And as softly rest on thee!
>
> May all the cares that come to thee,
> In thy future's store of years,
> Blow away like downy snowflakes
> Long before they melt to tears!

As she passed Twinkle she threw a garland of roses about his head and said, "Come to our court to-night, Twinkle! Come to our court to-night."

Twinkle wondered more than ever, but before he had time to ask any questions the little girl turned into a spray of lilies of the valley and the night wind blew her into the outer darkness, and there was only a sweet fragrance left behind to remind him that the beautiful maiden had passed on the golden way.

Then he turned and journeyed upward towards the star. He walked, and he walked, and he walked, but the further he climbed the further the star seemed from him, until at last he began to cry, for he was getting tired and he knew it was too far for him to go back to his pillow that night and the night wind began to blow fiercely about him.

At last it occurred to him to talk to the star, but he was afraid it would not understand him, for he did not know what to say, until suddenly he remembered some verses from a book that had been given him the Christmas before, so he began to say them:

> Twinkle! Twinkle! Little star;
> How I wonder what you are,
> Up above the world—

Suddenly he stopped in amazement, for the star was talking to him. And this is what it said:

> Twinkle! Twinkle! Little Twinkle;
> How I wonder why you wrinkle
> Up your nose and when you cry,
> Climbing upward to the sky!

This made him laugh. So he went merrily on and soon reached the door, which he entered. He found himself in a new world of cities and towns and farms and animals and forests and flowers. All the ways were golden ways like the one he had ascended. From one town to another he half walked, half floated in a dreamy delight as he touched his toe from time to time upon the golden paths. The air was soft and perfumed. The birds were bright and songful. The houses were clean and golden. He walked on, and on, and on, through city after city and town after town, until at last he saw coming towards him the little, old man with the sprig of evergreen in his mouth. As he drew near he shouted out in a busy kind of voice, "Heigh-ho! Twinkle! Heigh-ho! ho! ho! Twinkle! How do you do?"

"Very well, I thank you; but where do you come from?"

"I hasten and hasten from pillow to pillow," said the little man. His extremely small size had the effect of making him appear very busy, even though he was not doing much of anything.

When Twinkle strolled slowly along the golden way, the little man by his side sputtered, and swung his arms, and stretched his legs, and blew out his cheeks, and bulged his eyes, but really got over the ground very slowly. When they stood still with nothing to do but look at each other, he seemed as busy as ever as he leaned upon his long staff with one arm and held his cloak over the other and munched away at the sprig of evergreen, which was always in his mouth. When you think of it, it does not seem much of an undertaking to nibble away at a green twig, but it gave the little man an appearance of being extremely busy as he stood tapping his toe on the ground.

"May I ask who you are?" Twinkle ventured to inquire.

"I am the Chief Staff Officer of the King and Queen of Dream-land Court," was the answer. As he said the word "staff" he shook his long cane so violently that it broke in two pieces and fell on the ground before him.

The little man seemed delighted, because it gave him something to do. He sat down quickly and began to mend it with a piece of his shoe-string.

"Where are the King and Queen?" asked Twinkle.

"Would you like to see them?" inquired the Chief Staff Officer.

"If I may, please."

The words were hardly out of Twinkle's mouth when the busy little man exploded with a bang and turned into a puff of smoke which the wind blew away.

"Dear me!" said Twinkle. The explosion seemed to be a signal to the King and Queen, for he at once heard in the distance the musical rumble of approaching wheels, and soon there came in sight a beautiful golden carriage drawn by four black horses decked in golden harness. As the vehicle approached, he recognized the King and Queen as the boy and girl he had met on the golden way. Behind them on a lofty seat, with his arms lightly folded over his breast, and his body held very straight and stiff, sat the little old man, very busy with his sprig of evergreen. As the carriage stopped the King and Queen asked Twinkle to get in and ride with them. This he did. For a time he cast frequent glances at the Chief Staff Officer, who was so busy sitting up straight and stiff that Twinkle feared he would explode again. He did not, however, and soon he forgot all about the small footman, as he listened to the talk of the King and Queen of Dream-land Court. They seemed to know just what Twinkle liked to talk about. They spoke of picture books and toys and candy and dogs and cats and soldiers and guns and boats and fish and lemonade and drums

and many other things, and they knew all of Twinkle's friends by name. So he had a lovely visit, as the golden carriage bowled softly along the golden roads, past brooks and lawns and trees and flowers.

Finally he reminded them he was looking for the Christmas tree which the King had told him of at the foot of the golden way, and that he had searched diligently for seven days and seven nights but had not yet found it. "And now," he said sorrowfully, "I fear it is too late."

"Not at all," said the King and Queen, "it is Christmas here all the time."

"How delightful!" said Twinkle. "But where is the Christmas tree?"

"Every tree that grows here is a Christmas tree," they answered.

Twinkle looked quickly to the fields and saw that all the trees were evergreens covered with beautiful ornaments and hung full of mysterious looking bundles. Through a hole torn in one package he felt sure he saw the end of a drumstick.

"There are presents on the tree for all who want them," said the Queen.

"Is there one for me?" asked Twinkle.

"Certainly."

"I would like to get it, please," he said.

The horses were at once drawn up, and Twinkle got out and ran to the nearest tree and, taking down the first bundle he came to, he carried it to the roadside and began to open it, while the King and Queen looked on. He was surprised to find the package addressed to "Master Harold Twinkle." It took him some time to undo the numerous pieces of string, and remove the many wrappers folded about the present. Finally he opened the last paper, and there, lying in the center of the package, was the little old man with the evergreen twig in his mouth. He laughed merrily up at Twinkle and said, "Heigh-ho-ho-ho! here I am again!"

"How disappointing!" said Twinkle, "I supposed this package held a present for me."

"That's all right," said the little man, "I have your present in my pocket."

"What is it, please?" asked Twinkle.

"What do you want?" was the answer.

"I would like a drum," said Twinkle.

The Chief Staff Officer put his hand in his pocket and pulled out a drum larger than himself and handed it to Twinkle with a bow profound, and at the same time inquired, "What more do you want?"

"I would like a dog," was the answer.

"Candy, wooden or alive?" asked the strange little man.

"Alive, please."

"Large or small?"

"Very large, thank you; but not cross."

The little man put his hand in the same pocket, and drew out a dog much larger than Twinkle. The handsome creature ran to him and put his head in his lap and looked up with his large, beautiful eyes, as though he wanted to say, "Twinkle, I am your dog; please pat me on the head."

So Twinkle patted him on the head.

"Do you want something more?" asked the staff officer.

"I believe I have all I can manage, thank you," said Twinkle, as he took the drum in one hand and grasped the dog by the ear with the other.

Just then the King and Queen bade him good-bye, saying they had many other guests to look after, and drove away, leaving him alone with the little old man. Twinkle was getting more and more curious. At last he ventured to inquire, "Can you be in more than one place at the same time?"

"Time has no power over me," said the Chief Staff Officer of Dream-land Court. "I can be in as many places as I wish at the same time, and I can turn myself into any shape I please. Do you want to see me do it?"

"Do you have to explode every time you make a change?" asked Twinkle.

"No, I can slump," said the Staff Officer.

"Will you please slump into a Griffolif?"

That was the name of an animal in one of his favorite fairy stories, and he wanted to see what it looked like. The little man at once began to fall apart slowly, and when the pieces came together again, behold there was a Griffolif! Then the Griffolif fell apart, and, when the pieces came together again, there was the little man with the evergreen twig in his mouth.

"I think you had better explode next time," said Twinkle.

"I can change as fast as I please," said the little man, and, without waiting to be asked, he exploded into more than a hundred different shapes a minute, so fast that the astonished Twinkle could hardly catch a glimpse of each, and at the end there stood the little old man with the evergreen twig in his mouth.

"That's enough, thank you," said Twinkle.

"I can not only be in more than one place at the same time," said the Chief Staff Officer, "but I can give you the same power. You are both here and in your bed at home," said he, pointing through the door of the star down the golden way.

Twinkle looked and, sure enough, saw himself lying in his own bed at the foot of the golden way.

"And what is more," he continued, "I can lift you out of the power of time. How long do you suppose you have been here?"

"Seven days and seven nights," said Twinkle, "and this is the morning of the eighth day."

"You have been here," said the little old man, drawing out his watch and looking at it carefully,—"you have been here just thirty seconds. And now it is time for you to go. Off with you down the golden way."

"But I don't want to go yet," answered Twinkle.

"Heigh-ho-ho-ho! you must, you know! Off with you!"

But Twinkle began to struggle with the little man. The Staff Officer was surprisingly strong for his size, however, and slowly pushed him towards the sloping way. Just as he felt himself slipping,

slipping, over the edge of the doorway, he threw both his arms tightly about the little man and held him, and together the two slid rapidly down the golden way, passed through the window, and landed with a bump in Twinkle's bed. He held the Staff Officer fast and called for his mother to come and see. They were still struggling when his mother entered the room.

"Look! Look! Mamma, at this little old man," said Twinkle, squeezing his arms tightly together.

Just then the Staff Officer seemed to turn very soft and to lie perfectly still.

"My dear," said his mother, "what makes you hold your pillow so tightly?"

"Dear me!" said Twinkle, "he has slumped again." He looked out of the window and saw the star shining down upon him, but the golden pathway had been withdrawn.

"Have you been asleep, Dear One?" asked his mother.

"I've been to Dream-land Court," said Twinkle.

He slept soundly through the rest of the night, and rose the next morning, and slept again the next night, and rose the morning after,—and so on, and on, and on, until he had slept and risen for more than sixty times three hundred and sixty-five nights and mornings, but he never visited the star again. When he grew up he had children to whom he often told the story of the golden way. When his children grew up and had little boys and girls of their own, who were Twinkle's grandchildren, he would tell them stories whenever they asked him. Sometimes when they gathered about him he would lean forward in his chair, and rub his hands together, and say, "Well! Well! What story shall I tell you now?" When he said that, they would always answer, "Tell us the story of the Chief Staff Officer of Dream-land Court."

After a long time Twinkle died, and his children and grandchildren buried him in the churchyard near his bedroom window, and the star still twinkles over his grave.

A VISION OF LIFE.

I SAW a mighty caravan with slow
   Steps move across a bare and wind-swept plain;
   As wave crowds wave upon the tossing main,
So each his brother drove with threat and blow.
Far in the west the mist hung thick and low,
   Yet on they moved, and none turned back again;
   Eastward, from purple shades swept on the train—
Whither or whence no watching eye might know.

Long gazed I on the soft and shrouding mist
   Which wavered, thinned, and almost drew aside,
With hues which changed from gray to amethyst,
   And portals which held fast the living tide.
Nor knew, until I felt its folds touch me,
That I was one of that strange company.

Ninette M. Lowater.

Captain John Reycliff, Moonshiner.

By Verne S. Pease.[*]

lived, "Redcliff," after the old family home in North Carolina. He had acquired all the book-learning — commonly called education — that the limited curriculum of the country school afforded; was the acknowledged master of debate for miles around, and gave promise of being the one who should lead his family out of its social and intellectual darkness back to that high plane which the force of heredity made it possible, almost necessary, that it should occupy.

All things considered, John Reycliff was looked upon as the most promising young man in the neighborhood, and it was regarded somewhat natural that he should love Hester Markham, the prettiest girl in all those parts. Her family was of Puritan stock and came, several years back, from some New England state to the hill country, where her father sought the health-giving air and waters of that blissful middle climate and, rumor had it, a refuge from the complications that often follow business disaster. From the first the Markhams had been well received, and Hester's pretty face and frank, independent manner won the admiration of the whole community. Her voice led the choir in the old log church at Laurel Ridge, and, as she had received in early life unusual advantages in schooling, she was made teacher in the little school attended by all the children for miles around.

Even here slavery was, at that time — early in the year 1861 — the absorbing topic of conversation and controversy; but as no slaves were owned, except in Lawrenceburg, the county seat, it was a

IN HIS early manhood John Reycliff bore some marks of good breeding. Down in the hill country of Middle Tennessee, where he was born and reared, he was called aristocratic; not that he carried a higher head than his associates, but because he seemed by nature to possess in a bountiful degree those indefinable yet unmistakable qualities that bespeak gentility.

His appearance, on first sight, was not prepossessing. His erect carriage and determined manner — characteristics not often seen among the inhabitants of that section — came so easy and natural as to attract no notice, and did not even serve to draw attention from his homespun suit and slouched wool-hat. But a more careful study of his features and habits discovered in the frank blue eye, — not flashing but steady and meditative, — the square-set jaw, the resolute, well considered step, a character of inflexible and predetermined purpose.

His family came more than a century ago from North Carolina, a thriftless offshoot of an ancient cavalier race, which through generations of poverty and inaction had come to represent that most deplorable estate of humanity — quality gone to seed. The only shred of that once lofty ancestral pride that had escaped moral dry-rot found expression in calling the little valley in which the Reycliffs

[*] Awarded the Story Prize in The Midland's July Competition.

matter of sentiment or principle rather than of personal interest, and consequently reached no very high state of excitement. The two factions were about evenly divided, old Silas Reycliff leading the slavery sympathizers while Samuel Markham was the recognized exponent of the free-soilers. Both were well grounded in their respective beliefs, from rearing rather than convictions, and each was armed with the stock arguments and scriptural quotations of his party. But these differences of opinion and sentiment led up to no breach of friendship, so long as their parties confined the warfare to words, and all looked forward to a lasting union of the families by the marriage of Hester to John Reycliff. The fond parents on both sides had planned that this marriage should be celebrated at an early day and that the young people should settle down upon a small patch of land, about midway between the parental homes, and continue the quiet life of the backwoods farmer.

But this arrangement was summarily modified, for John Reycliff had already felt the inspiration of long-buried hereditary ambition and had determined to make for himself, and his bride to be, a better place in the material outside world. He knew little of the turmoil of the busy world, yet he longed for a place in its very vortex. The sheer, rock-faced bluffs, that encompassed the narrow valley in which several generations of Reycliffs had lived and died, seemed to press in upon him until his swelling heart could scarcely throb between their narrow limits. The red, rebellious soil of the steep hillsides, with its stunted growth of corn and tobacco, but prolific in cankerous sedge, promised little to his reaching ambition in worldly affairs. The simple habits of his people, their very lack of wants, and the compensatory absence of cares and responsibilities, depressed him. Poor soul! He did not then know that his very surroundings exemplified the Utopian songs of poets for centuries past.

In this purpose he had the sympathy and encouragement of Hester, who longed for a wider field of usefulness, and perhaps more responsive surroundings for display than the narrow bounds of their social environment afforded. Her girlhood dreams of marble halls, elegant turnouts, rich dresses, social dominion and other accompaniments of material greatness had solidified with her maturity into consuming desire.

Accordingly John made preparations to go to the city to begin his new career and become a citizen of the world. He was to start Monday morning. Sunday evening he spent with Hester as usual. It seemed the sweetest of his wooing. Again the well-conned plans of their future were gone over. The picture had no dark spots, no uncertain lines. It stood out as bold as bas-relief upon the dark background of purposeless life with which they were surrounded. They could trace his rise step by step, through numberless successes, until he had fully regained the once proud eminence of his now degenerate race. His determination was at fever heat and he could scarcely await another dawn to begin his undertaking.

The parting said and once outside the Markham cabin his courage faltered for an instant. He felt for the first time the pangs of separation, and, to heighten the agony, came the realization that this separation would drag through days into weeks, weeks into months and perhaps years. He felt certain that his passion would conquer his purpose and that his fine project would end in failure more dismal and spectral than the worthless lives of his immediate ancestors. But the vision of his success came back and he went buoyantly homeward, chagrined at the weakness that had allowed him to waver for even a moment. With Hester it was quite different. The parting had caused her pain, but her swelling ambition had not, even at the moment of parting, permitted her sentiment to obscure the purpose of their enterprise.

Before dawn John Reycliff stole quietly from his father's house, fearing to risk another formal leave-taking, and hurried down the valley to the devious old ridge road, on his twenty-mile walk to the nearest railroad station, where he was to take a train to the great city. The towering bluffs, enveloped with gray clouds of rising mist that spanned the little chasm of a valley like a heavenly bridge; the pale, opal water in Resurrection Creek that rushed down past his father's house; the delicious fragrance of the pink honeysuckle, with which the air was fairly burdened; the voices of a hundred songsters and the echoing melody of the mocking-birds,—all struck him with a new beauty, like the unveiling of a new universe. Had his life been surrounded by these thousand charms, and had he weighed them only in the narrow scales of utility? he asked himself. How strangely the every-day beauties of nature and character, which compass our lives, are passed unappreciated, unnoticed even, and rush in upon us like a revelation at the hour of parting!

A mile down the road, as the first gray of dawn appeared, he stepped aside a few yards to a slight elevation and cast a long, wistful look at the old log house, with its shake roof and rock chimneys, the home of his Hester. Farther on he paused by an old rail fence that enclosed the neighboring burying-ground where, he had been told, lay the dust of his ancestors, in graves profaned by neglect and marked by rude, unlettered stones. Even the mounds were depressed to the level of the little plain. Would his life be so aimless, his fame so meager, that it could be amply proclaimed by a few tufts of grass and a mystifying rock, such as his feet had trod in crossing the creek?

With the early summer of 1861, in Tennessee, came the culmination of the secession controversy. It was but the inevitable, foreseen by all, but put off through months of agony by those who, in utter despair, had hoped for some averting accident. History is the record of inevitables, with a very small percentage of accidents. Fate had decided that Tennessee should secede,— not the fate of fatalism, but the cold, unchanging law of cause and effect.

Resisting or retarding the operation of this law to its natural fruition had kept the state in a turmoil for months. It had caused the holding of innumerable primaries, mass-meetings, conventions, and, finally of two popular elections, the first of which strongly favored loyalty to the Union, but the last was overwhelming for secession. The governor had issued his proclamation formally severing the ties that had bound the State in the Federal compact.

The turmoil of the campaign was followed by political chaos. There was perfect union of sentiment, but the structure of political sovereignity had not yet been reared. In the cities bands of music paraded the streets day and night. One orator followed another on the public square so that speaking went on almost without interruption. Strangers met, shook hands, conversed, and parted with a sincere exchange of Godspeed, like old friends. All was excitement,— not happy and expectant, but sullen and apprehensive. Military companies were formed from counting-rooms, stores and offices. Public schools became places of military training; the college, a fortress; the campus, a drill ground.

John Reycliff was one of the first to answer the excited call for home guards. His few months of city experience had disappointed his expectations. The uncommercial training of his early life had placed him at a great disadvantage in the sharp struggle for advancement. His determination had been good, his wit ready, but he daily felt the lack of such previous contact with different phases of the world as was necessary to bring the latter quality to a proper edge and make it readily useful to his purpose. So that John Reycliff's patriotism for his native state, like many another brave soldier's, was not entirely unmixed with personal disappointment. He was assigned to duty in a squad of sharpshooters attached to the —th Artillery,— one of the first regiments to report to the Confederate

States of America to fight under the Stars and Bars.

For two years he followed faithfully the wavering fortunes of his people, and rose to the command of his squad, with the rank of lieutenant. A further promotion was promised,—in fact, daily expected, and with it a furlough of ten days in which to visit home and see Hester. How proudly he would go back with a captain's commission, and that earned by bravery on the battle-field! But before the commission arrived came an engagement, unexpected and terrific. His army was routed; his comrades fell on every side; the enemy called on him to surrender, but he answered with a defiant yell and another shot from his musket. A volley from the on-coming horde and he sank to the ground with a dangerous wound in his leg. In place of his furlough came a hospital certificate.

For weeks he lay between life and death with a minie ball in his thigh. As he began to amend, he thought more of home with its perfect peace and simple abundance, and he resolved to set out as soon as he could walk and spend the period of his convalescence amid those quiet, helpful surroundings.

With great effort and suffering he dragged himself over half the distance, his craving for home and for the attentions of loved ones impelling him to redoubled exertions.

One day he stopped at a row of cabins that flanked a fine country place in the richest agricultural region of Middle Tennessee, to ask a morsel of food from the generous negroes, who were friends in war and peace. Having finished his meal, and with a bountiful supply tied in his handkerchief against the uncertainties of the barren country that was before him, he set forth again on his weary journey, when his attention was drawn to a young child in the arms of its old negro mammy. He was struck with its peculiar beauty and, half from admiration, half to gratify the easy pride of its nurse, remarked, "What a pretty baby!"

"Ya-as, sah; dis is Mis' Hester's baby boy. Dey calls 'im John. Some folks says he named fur Mis' Hester's sweetheart she had 'fore de wah begun."

"But, Mammy, where did your mistress come from?" asked John with quickened interest.

"O, Mis' Hester she come from up de hill country, not very 'ristocratic place, though she's a mighty fine lady. Her folks was all kilt out, an' dere house burnt by de g'rillies, I think dey calls 'em. Some good white gem'men fetched her to D— an' put her in a boa'din' school, case she hadn't no place to live at. 'Twar thar dat young marster fust knowed her, an' sot out to makin' love to her. He war struck all to onct. He 'peared strange, an' we niggers 'lowed 'twar de misery come back in his wound, fur Marster war shot in de 'ginning ob de wah, an' war home gettin' well. But when we seed him pickin' flowahs in de garden ever' day, an' ridin' over to'rds de school, we knowed suthin' else war de matter. Well, sah, hit seemed like he would ride down erry las' hoss on de place, totin' flowahs to dat school-house; till fin'ly Mis' Hester mahried 'im. Sence den, he 'mended mighty fas', till now, 'pears like he well 'nough to go bark to de wah, but I don' reckon he will leave Mis' Hester an' de baby. They's mon-st'us happy, an' Mis' Hester has hosses an' cerriages, an' fine clothes, an' is de grandes' lady in dese parts."

The truth came to him with a shock, and he could hear no more. With a word of parting he dragged himself on.

Hester had been faithless. She had not even called on him in her affliction! But, he had been weak; his life, so far as she knew, had been an unsuccessful struggle. Perhaps she had not heard that he was a captain. What man, in the eyes of woman, is so weak as he who has made a failure in life? So he might have expected this termination of his love affair; possibly he deserved it. At all events, it was better than for him to have led her into the perdition of his life of disappointment and material shipwreck. Now all her dreams of splendor were realized. She was in all probability happy.

But his parents, his home — that home to which he was journeying with so much expectancy — were they safe? His neighborhood had become embroiled in that fierce guerrilla warfare that raged along the borders of the war field, more cruel and furious than the relentless struggle of organized forces.

Four days of tedious tramping, in which the agony of suspense precluded rest or refreshment, brought him again to the old ridge road that he had traveled so expectantly only three years before. He stopped again by the old graveyard fence, but could see no new graves in the Reycliff corner. Had one of the few amenities of war spared his parents, or one of its countless atrocities forbidden them a Christian burial? He noticed the old road, once so well beaten, now nearly overgrown with grass and weeds. Houses, that had been landmarks since his first memory, all gone! He looked for the Markham cabin; a pile of crumbling stone in the vacant field was the only sign of previous habitation.

With the energy of despair he turned up the narrow valley that led to his father's house. Every foot-stone in the creek was as familiar as his own name. The winding road was overgrown with vegetation. The opal creek ran and murmured as before. The prodigious trunks of the poplars and master oaks stood just as when he saw them last. The frowning bluffs, with gray rocks and red soil, stood unchanged. Everything in nature was unchanged, but all traces of human habitation were gone. How transitory is man, how fleeting the kingdoms of man by the side of undying nature! These same crags and bluffs had looked down on primitive man and through succeeding ages on races, kingdoms, principalities, as they appeared on the scene, played their little parts and vanished from the earth.

As he hastened up the valley, a rising mist like a gray pall enshrouded his old home. Rounding a sharp turn in the bluffs his father's farm spread out before him. The giant oak trees in the front yard, the stone spring-house, and the two massive chimneys of his father's house, standing like gaunt specters, were all he saw.

There was no home.

Far up Resurrection Creek, above Redcliff, after many curves and angles, the valley, narrowed to a chasm, turns squarely to the left, spreads out over a little oblong space and heads abrupt and precipitous. The entrance to this area is up the bed of the creek, which rolls boisterously between sentinel cliffs that stand out like giants at the door of some mysterious grotto. The creek comes forth from cavernous fissures in the rock at the head of the valley, after having been buried for hours in the earth, which receives it, a mile above, — the ridge, a veritable mountain, standing an apostrophe in its course.

On the east, Resurrection Hill rises sheer to a dizzy height, its many seams and fissures hidden by an impenetrable growth of laurel and red cedar. And when, on the west, the oaks and poplars of Oblivion Bluff stand out, gaunt and spectral against the wintry sky, like emblems of death and oblivion, Resurrection Hill remains serenely perennial, in calm defiance of threatening dissolution, a pledge of eternal life.

Nowhere in nature are the conflicting miracle of life and mystery of death more grandly portrayed. Over against the rising sun the one adds its undying testimony to the daily proclamation of light and life, and to the parting day the other joins its dire omen of inevitable death and gloom. When this glorification was enacted is beyond human speculation. Years have come and gone, centuries have rolled into ages, ages into cycles, and still the miracle of life and the mystery of death have stood in opposing transfiguration.

Here, shut out from the world, shut in from heaven, except from an occasional star that blinked above the gorge, like an eye of the Eternal prying into the secrets of his craft, Captain John Reycliff had for years conducted his still. The times were practical. Chivalry had passed away. The devastation of war had been replaced by new settlements, indolent and shiftless, but more practical and calculating than the civilization that had been swept away. Swords had been beaten into plowshares, which were doing ungallant but heroic service in the struggle for bread. Resurrection Creek — the artist of this picture — that, through ages of persistent industry had carved all this beauty from the insensate rock, had finished its work and laid aside the habiliments of art. Why should not it, too, be turned to practical use? Captain Reycliff had caught the infection and, while deploring the loss of the old, resolved to keep in touch with the new order of things. Accordingly, its current was made to turn a wheel that furnished power to stir his mash; its freestone water made the best possible mixture for the beer, and the cold stream flowing over the "worm" induced that slow distillation necessary to produce good whisky.

Through all the years since the close of the War, Captain Reycliff's still had flourished unmolested, although he had failed to go through the formality of taking out the license and paying the tribute exacted by the Federal government for the privilege of conducting such business enterprises. He believed his business honorable and could not understand the justice in, or economic reasons for, taxing it while the mill that ground his meal went free. He was equally steadfast in his moral grounding, and daily strengthened his position with scriptural quotations of more or less relevancy. Then, too, he had great confidence in his inaccessible location. The barrier hills were impassable, the creek entrance dangerous, except with the most practiced pilot. No one of his neighbors had ever visited his retreat; but, had the way been as familiar as their own roads, they would not have

directed an expedition against him, for Captain Reycliff was never known to have a personal enemy.

The greatest indifference prevailed regarding the still. How the liquor was made, or in what quantities, no mortal outside the gorge knew — none cared. How it found a market was equally uncertain, for man had never seen the meal going to or the liquor coming from the still; yet every bar for miles around had a full stock of "Captain's Red." Whenever sickness invaded the cabins, a jug was found on the front step, with a tag attached, bearing this strange epigram, "Free whisky for the sick; jugs cost money; empty and leave outside." And the empty jug would disappear as mysteriously as it had come.

Captain Reycliff seldom left his still. He was known to make occasional trips into the valley country, in the neighborhood of D—, but, whether his mission was one of charity or business, nobody knew. His life was so lonely and melancholy, perhaps he took these little excursions into the outside world to break its dismal monotony. Whatever the impelling motive, he returned in a more cheerful frame of mind; and, in his musings, which had come to be almost habitual, he was heard to mutter, over and over again, "It's right; it's better so."

The Captain had been so long unmolested by the authorities that he began to feel himself secure, and for a time neglected those measures of caution maintained for a score of years. They were a source of some expense, and his still-house yielded very meager profits; and at times he seriously considered the idea of abandoning the business entirely. But what could he do? His farm had grown up to underbrush; he was too old to apply himself to a new trade or a profession. Then, too, the material problems with which he had wrestled early in life had thrown him so mercilessly that he could not rally his crushed ambition to give them a new encounter. He could not think of becoming a public charge: he would not accept private bounty, although any cabin in the country would have given him a hearty welcome for the remainder of his life. But either of these alternatives would have given him less pain than to have to forego the means of practicing those mysterious benevolences that brought the only pleasure to his melancholy life. His friends often advised him to marry, and several eligible spinsters and widows were pointed out; to which suggestion, whether made in jest or in earnest, he had one good-humored, but rather melancholy, reply, "Two things I aim a-hankering for— them's love and war."

The federal authorities knew, in a general way, that an illicit distillery was in operation near Laurel Ridge Church, and, from the persistence with which it was maintained, and the ineffective efforts that had been made to suppress it, they judged that it must be in the hands of a desperate man. They were sworn to maintain the peace and dignity of the United States, yet here was a man "manufacturing and selling spirituous liquors without license," which the letter of the law declared was "against the peace and dignity of the United States." A new administration was coming in. A show must be made towards keeping the ante-election pledges that were believed to have contributed to its political success. The usual series of petty abuses was scheduled for reformation. A larger, more flagrant, but less conspicuous, series of abuses was tacitly scheduled to be winked at. Accordingly, as Captain Reycliff's still had achieved undeserved notoriety, it headed the list, which meant early annihilation. The lumbering wheels of justice were set in motion, and, as its victim was a gentle, disheartened man, too poor to place the usual and convenient obstructions in its course, he was doomed to be crushed beneath the Juggernaut.

Among the deputy marshals appointed was a young farmer from the lower section of Middle Tennessee, a recent graduate of a military academy. His charge was over the hill country, with instructions to stamp out moonshining, at whatever cost. He had been a good student, and was deeply learned in theoretical manslaughter; but had never witnessed any of the inhuman scenes of carnage to which he was educated.

It was early May.

The rising sun was gilding the tops of the oaks and poplars on Oblivion Bluff. The heavy clouds of mist shut out from the valley a portion of the reflected day, protracting the morning with a long, dreamy dawn. The breeze that stole slowly up the creek was laden, almost to lassitude, with the entrancing fragrance of the wild honeysuckle. The birds, strangers to one another for months, set the somnolent air a-quiver with their happy songs of reunion and home-building. It was a scene that forced reverie. To Captain Reycliff it was more—it was the anniversary of his home-leaving, more than a generation ago. He sat on the rough bench before his still-house in deep reflection, smoking his morning pipe. In his reverie he lived again his parting with Hester and saw once more the bright picture of his future. Again he stole silently from his father's house, lest the leave-taking would unman him, and hurried down the valley to the highway. He took the last look at the Markham cabin, leaned against the fence at the burial-ground and hastened on to the great city.

The scene changed. A cloud passed over his immobile countenance His pipe dropped from his hand and smouldered on the ground at his feet. He passed again through countless struggles and disappointments. Then came the War with its sufferings and horrors—the last battle—his comrades falling on every hand—the enemy calling on the remnant to surrender before he was wounded—

"Surrender!" came a sharp voice from the entrance to the valley, as three horsemen, with muskets leveled, rode up the creek bed. Was he in battle? Were these horsemen intruders on his privacy or was it the enemy calling on him to surrender? In the delirium of fancy he sprang to his feet and reiterated his defiant battle-cry,—

"I never surrender!"

A flash in the dim half-light and the report of a musket echoed in quick reverberations from cliff to cliff.

They raised the prostrate form of the Captain and laid it on the bench. There was a small jagged hole in his flannel shirt-front, above his leathern belt. He breathed heavily. At last he opened his eyes. "So you're not Yankee soldiers — only revenue hunters! I reckon you've

got shet of this still." Fixing his eyes on the deputy marshal, he said, faintly: "I know you. You other fellers 'scuse us and stand aside."

They withdrew a few yards. Then, taking the hand of the deputy, he said with great effort: "Captain, it mought bring your mother some misery if she knowed her son shot John Reycliff — you'll narry tell her? — Swear it!"

His eyes closed again, and he murmured a few incoherent words, which showed his last mortal vision was on the scenes of his early hopes and love,—and then was silent.

THE CURSE OF JUDAS.

By Frank A. Wilder.

I.

ALEC LAPOINTE was slowly walking along one of the great business streets of Chicago. It was midwinter. To this bore witness the heaps of snow along the walks, the cold wind sweeping down from the north, and the brilliantly-lighted store windows filled with holiday attractions Lapointe crossed the river from the North Side, and went on toward the south. The multitude thronging the street hastened past him as he sauntered aimlessly along. Evidently he had no definite purpose in view. It was too cold to stand still, and it was easier to walk with the wind than against it. After a time he paused on a corner and looked around, and then sought shelter by leaning against the side of a great building. The snow whirled in eddies at his feet, lay for a moment in little drifts, and then was scattered over the pavement to be packed beneath the feet of the hurrying crowds. At short intervals great revolving sweepers rumbled along the cable lines, but they hardly disappeared before the tracks were again covered with snow. As darkness came on the storm increased and the cars on the street became more and more infrequent. Shop girls and clerks

gathered on the corner and waited patiently. Some were thinly clad and the wind was sharp and penetrating. In spite of the cold and storm every one seemed cheerful.

Three little cash girls were looking in at the great show window near which Lapointe stood. It was a jeweler's store and the window was brilliant with precious stones set in rings and necklaces. On either side a bronze figure of a boy held out a cluster of incandescent lights. In the rear stood a figure of Father Time with his sickle, bearing on his back a great clock, the pendulum of which swung slowly back and forth as though time were the most deliberate thing in the world.

"Do you know what I would do if I had that?" said one of the girls, her black eyes dancing as she pointed to a brilliant solitaire. As she stood there in the bright light that came from the window, with her laughing face and her black hair almost concealed by the shawl she wore over her head, she looked like a bit of sunny Italy which had somehow strayed to this land of snow.

"I know what I'd do," exclaimed one of the others. "I'd sell it and get a hundred dollars, and then I wouldn't have to work any more or have Mr. Barnes to scold me."

"I'd buy a fur coat and give it to mama for Christmas," said the third.

"I'd wear it in my hair. This way,—see," said the first. She took the shawl from her head and held it out till she caught a great snow-flake that came drifting down by the side of the building. Then she held the shawl above her head and shook it till the snow-flake fell in her hair, a great scintillating diamond.

They all joined in a chorus of childish laughter, and then ran off to catch a car which came rumbling along the street. Lapointe followed them and saw that they were safely on board, and then returned to his place by the window.

The number of those who were waiting increased steadily till about 8 o'clock Almost every one carried a parcel of some sort. A burly German sought shelter for a moment by the side of the building. He carried a great wicker basket full to the brim, so full that the covers would not stay fastened. From one side projected the handle of something. "For mein sohn," he said with a hearty laugh, and then ran off to catch a car which came rumbling along the street. Lapointe eyeing his load. "A shovel. He can all day dig in dat snow." Having recovered his breath he went on elbowing his way through the crowd.

Soon a woman with a thin, worn face came to the window and unwrapped a parcel. It contained a leather case,—a little sewing case in which were needles and a pair of scissors and a silver thimble. Her face lighted with pleasure as she looked at it. She took the thimble from the case and put it on her finger, but as she did so someone crowded past and the thimble fell to the pavement and was buried in the snow. Lapointe was on his knees in an instant and soon recovered the lost treasure. He was richly rewarded by the look of gratitude on the woman's face.

"These are for my daughter," she said, after thanking him. "She has wanted them for so long, and then to

think that I almost lost the thimble, because, like a child, I couldn't keep from looking at them! I'm so anxious to get home. She is a little girl and I have been away all day. I wonder what is the matter with the cars."

"Do you go south?"

"As far as Fiftieth Street."

"Then you had better take the elevated."

Again the woman thanked him and went on down the street.

By this time it was apparent to all that the cable lines were hopelessly blockaded. Those who were waiting sought the elevated roads, or started to make their way through the storm on foot. Soon Lapointe was left almost alone.

He was a tall man and well built. His features were regular, almost handsome. His complexion was swarthy, due partly perhaps to exposure to inclement weather, but it harmonized well with his black mustache and the black hair which cropped out from under his slouch hat. His clothes were of the proper style and fitted him well, and though they were threadbare, gave him an air of a gentleman. They told a story of better times. His shoes, though badly worn, were not coarse. He had no overcoat.

The crowds waiting at the corner for the cable cars had been some company for him. When they moved away he felt lonesome. He went to the store window and looked at the clock. It was half-past eight. Once more he started down the street.

II.

The various factors that had entered into Lapointe's life and had tended to make him what he was were readily traceable. His parents were simple French people, and still lived in the little interior town of Canada called Laplaisance, where he was born. He knew of no one else from Laplaisance that had ever strayed so far into the world. The boys who had recited the catechism with him to Father José were farmers about his native town, or lumbermen who spent the winter in the woods and came back to the old home in summer. He often wondered at the difference between his life and theirs. It was all due to Father José, the spiritual and intellectual head of the village. The Father knew every one in the town and had baptized them all, save a very few old folks, for he had been in Laplaisance ever since he came from France fifty years before. Laplaisance was then but a mission station among the Indians. He taught the parish school, and it was there that he first became interested in Alec Lapointe. He was such a little fellow to come so far to school, especially in winter, over the hills and through two miles of the big forest where the snow did not melt till late in the spring, that the Father took the boy to stay with him.

"You are to be a priest, my son," Father José said to him again and again, as, hand in hand, they walked through the woods after school hours.

"That will I, Father," the boy invariably replied.

In those days Father José was his ideal. In a shady nook on the edge of the forest, beneath the great pines, he used to lie by the hour and think of the time when he would wear a long black gown and have long white hair and smile and speak kind words to the people who should take off their hats as he passed by. Such were his boyhood dreams.

When he grew older, Father José took him into his library. It was a quaint little room, with a low ceiling, in which were chests of oak, and one great bookcase as tall as the room, with heavy doors which locked with an iron key. This key the Father had been in the habit of keeping in a drawer in his own room. But not a month had passed after the day when the boy was first admitted to the library before it was left in the door.

"I can trust you, my son," he said one day when Alec told him that he was forgetting the key.

For a year the boy spent all his odd moments over the Latin which he found in the quaint leather-covered volumes. His greatest delight, however, was in the sand heap in the corner of the yard to which he had given the name of Palestine. It was a shady corner, and here Father José used to tell him of his pilgrimage to the Holy Land. They spent many days in building the city of Jerusalem, the priest sitting in his arm-chair and giving directions while Alec piled the sand to represent the hills of Moriah and Zion, and put pine cones around for the city walls. He built the temple on Mount Moriah with wooden blocks, and connected it with Mount Zion by a bridge. On other days he leveled the city with a more ruthless hand than did Herod of old, and made instead a map of Palestine. Judea and Samaria and Galilee he bounded with white string. He dug the Jordan valley with a piece of tin, and filled the Dead Sea and the Sea of Galilee with water and made beautiful falls in the Jordan which were not in the original. He located Jericho and Nazareth and Bethlehem with bits of paper and built the roads that led thence to Jerusalem. When he was tired he would lie at Father José's feet and listen as he told him stories from the Old and New Testaments.

He often wondered what the world outside of Laplaisance was like. Father José was the only one he knew who had ever been far from the village, and that was many years before. He had heard vague accounts of the great towns in the provinces to the east, but he could conceive of them only as larger villages made up of the same sort of people he saw around him. Boyhood passed into youth and youth was merging into manhood before these notions were changed.

They were walking in Father José's garden between the house and the church when the Father told him that he was to go to Montreal. "See how great is your opportunity," said the Father, looking down at the boy thoughtfully. "That is given to you which has never before been given to a boy in our village. Think how your parents and myself and every one in the village will watch for your return. Many prayers will be offered for you. But the city is a great place, and its dangers are many. I was there myself many years ago, and it has grown since. Remember, my son, what I have taught you, and hold to the truth."

It was a proud day, the proudest in his life, the Sunday before he left Laplaisance for Montreal. He wore his new clothes for the first time. His mother had made them, for there was no tailor in the village. The cloth had been bought of a peddler, and was considered finer than anything that could be had at the village store. Every one knew that he was to go away on Monday and that he was to wear his new clothes to church the day before.

Father José seemed to speak especially to him that morning. After church the people gathered around the door to shake hands with him and say good-bye. Father Jose walked home with him and took dinner at his father's cottage that day—an unusual honor. As they went through the big woods they talked about the city to which he was going and the life he would lead there.

The ride to the railroad station was a long one, and long before sunrise his father had yoked the oxen which in winter he drove in the logging camps, and loaded on the wooden box with its leather handles in which were all of Alec's possessions. His mother wept and the boy tried to comfort her by telling her that in a few years he would come back a man and they should all be proud of him. He never thought of crying himself till the sharp crack of the lash started the oxen and the journey was actually begun. But as the little cottage, with his mother still standing in the doorway, grew smaller and smaller, and the road spun out longer and longer beneath the slow-turning wheels, he took out his handkerchief and wiped his eyes.

The long railroad journey was not a bit tiresome, and he was almost sorry when he reached the city. He had expected someone to meet him at the station, but, after waiting for some time, he took the advice that Father José had given him in case of such an emergency, and asked a cabman to take him and his box to Father Lewis's house. As he passed through the noisy, crowded streets, lined on either side with tall buildings, he felt as though he had entered another world.

Of course the new life brought with it new influences. In the first place, there was Father Lewis, to whose care he was entrusted. Father José, who had known him years before, forgot that some men change with time. He himself had not changed. If there are no wolves wearing the shepherd's cloak, there are at least careless shepherds. The boy missed the kind words and the watchful care he had known in the village. Yet in the city he needed them more. A little care during this transition period might have kept him true to his early training. As it was, this sudden revelation of a new world with its wonderful activities and its great possibilities fascinated him and led him to think that all his former life had been narrow and limited. He did not lose his old beliefs, but they lost their vitality. He had thought that the calling of the priest was the highest. It had been so in the village of Laplaisance. He now saw that there were others which the world ranked as high. He had thought that the truths which Father José had taught him were undisputed. He found that there were men who questioned them. His conception of life was changed, whether for better or worse he could not say, but it was changed. At the end of the second year at the University it seemed plain to him that he was not fitted to become a priest. To those at home he sent word that he could no longer accept aid, since he must disappoint them in their plans. At least, he was thoroughly honest.

Then he began life for himself. At the University he had shown himself to be a good companion, though a poor scholar, — poor because he was careless. Through the influence of friends he had made since coming to the city, he secured a temporary position on one of the great

Drawing by C. A. Cumming.

"Seeing no vacant seat Lapointe leaned against one of the great pillars which supported the gallery."

daily papers. At the same time he kept up some of his studies. Thus a third year passed. At the end of the fourth he had fairly earned the title of "Lapointe, the best reporter on the *Recorder*."

Then his wanderings began. It was simple restlessness, for the proprietors of the *Recorder* were satisfied with his work. On one of the smallest of the sailing vessels that venture across the Atlantic in midwinter he embarked for France. Landing at Havre he wrote a graphic account of his voyage, which yielded him funds to continue his travels. For two years he wandered in Europe, sending reports of his adventures to the

Recorder in the form of weekly letters. Then the Columbian Exposition opened. Having succeeded in getting himself appointed as representative of various foreign papers, he embarked for America with no more money in his pocket than when he left it.

III.

Lapointe was not the only man who had neither work nor money on this winter night. During the busy days of the Exposition the city had been crowded with newspaper men. Many, like himself, had been improvident and found themselves without employment in the midst of a period of unusual financial depression.

"Hello, Lapointe! Great Christmas weather, and a delightful Christmas season for us fellows, isn't it? Got anything to do yet?" The speaker, who came up behind Lapointe, was so thoroughly wrapped up in his great coat, the collar of which almost touched his hat, that only his eyes were visible. Lapointe recognized the voice, for he hardly turned to look at him.

"As much as usual," he answered.

"I had a trifle of luck with a little Christmas matter to-day; got the *News* to take it."

Lapointe stood still for a moment.

"Where do you stay now?" asked his friend.

"At The Friendship."

"Whew! You deserve better luck than that. Aren't you going any farther? It is too cold to stand here."

"No, I must go back. I've forgotten something. I'm glad I met you though, Richardson, for you've given me an idea that I'm going to work out."

As Lapointe spoke, he turned and started up the street. He had gone only a block when he came to the Grand Pacific Hotel. Pushing open the storm-door, he stepped in, swept the snow from his shoes and then surveyed himself hastily. The result was hardly satisfactory, for he still hesitated. He shook the snow from his coat, however, and turned down the collar that had been pinned about his neck. Then, with the air of one familiar with the place, he walked across the brilliantly-lighted lobby to a cozy little room where a number of men sat about small tables on which they were writing busily. On his way the clerk saw him and nodded slightly. In order to keep up appearances Lapointe had asked that he might have his mail addressed in care of the hotel. In this way they had become acquainted. He took off his hat and hung it on a rack near the door and then sat down at one of the tables. For half an hour he sat with his head on the back of the chair and his eyes closed. Two or three men across the table glanced at him curiously

without interrupting their work. He then took paper and pen and was soon the busiest man in the room. The hands of the great clock over the door indicated in turn the hours,—9, 10, 11. One after another the others arose, sealed and pocketed the letters they had been writing and left the room. But Lapointe wrote on. He glanced at the clock and saw that it was five minutes of 12. Then he placed the written pages in his inside pocket, buttoned his coat, and once more went out into the storm.

He made his way slowly along the street till he crossed the river to the West Side of the city. Walking was now difficult, for the hour was late and there were few persons on the street to trample down the swiftly-falling snow. He kept on until he reached a region of cheap lodging-houses. When he came to The Friendship he stopped. Looking through the large front windows, on which the name of the place was conspicuously painted, he saw a dozen men dozing in rough wooden chairs in the waiting-room. He entered. Paying 20 cents to the clerk, he secured the best quarters the place afforded,—a small box-like apartment containing a rude bed. On this he threw himself without undressing and was soon asleep. He had eaten no supper.

He arose before daybreak the next morning. Hardly a person was moving when he crossed the waiting-room and opened the door to the street. The snow lay in an unbroken sheet on the sidewalk, save for a narrow irregular path which had been broken by a patrolman. Lapointe glanced at his shoes and then plunged boldly into the drift that blocked the door. Though the hour was early he wondered why there were not more persons stirring. Then he remembered that it was Christmas morning.

He went directly to the hotel he had left so late the night before, and seating himself at one of the tables took the roll of manuscript from his pocket and began to write. As the morning advanced, elegantly-dressed men sauntered into the room from the breakfast table and sat down to dispose of the day's correspondence. Lapointe did not notice them. He seemed to have forgotten that he had eaten no breakfast. His pen ran rapidly over the paper, and page after page was added to the manuscript prepared the night before. At 10 o'clock he stopped, laid down his pen with a sigh, rubbed his hands together, leaned back in his chair and closed his eyes. After resting thus a few minutes, he sat up again, arranged his papers carefully, and then arose and left the room.

IV.

Christmas was no holiday for the staff of the *Advocate*. That enterprising factor in public opinion had seized the occasion as an excuse for an extra edition. It was well understood by every member of the *Advocate* force that the editors of the other city papers were to awake on the 26th to the fact that they had been thoroughly outdone. At 10 o'clock the forms for thirty-six pages were up. Ten pages had been allowed for advertisements. At 10:30 the editor received word from the composing room that a half-page more of matter was needed. He began to look through his desk for more copy.

The paper already contained Dickens' always available Christmas Carol entire, an interesting article on Christmas in Iceland, a learned discussion of the origin of Christmas by the Rev. Dr. Holstze, and half a score of short Christmas stories by popular writers of the day.

At 11 o'clock Lapointe entered the editor's room. He closed the door behind him and without hesitancy walked to the editor's desk.

"I have written something which I should like to have you look over, sir, and it will be a great favor if you can do so at once." Lapointe spoke without embarrassment. The editor, who had not looked up when he entered, wheeled part way around in his chair and gave him a searching glance. Then he let his eyes fall on the manuscript which La-

pointe had placed on his desk. The title attracted his attention. It was "The Myth of Myths." The editor glanced hastily over the first page.

"I do not know whether I can use this. It is just possible that I can. Call this afternoon or to-morrow morning,—better to-morrow. I don't know anything about it, you know,—it is seldom that we can use matter of this sort," he added, as he saw the expression of relief on Lapointe's face.

"It will be a great favor if you can advance me a dollar on it, sir." Lapointe spoke in a low tone, and in spite of his effort did not wholly succeed in controlling his feelings.

The editor looked at him with an expression of surprise. "This is not business," he said, as though he were making an apology to himself, as he took a dollar from his pocket and held it out to Lapointe. "But I will make an exception. This is an exceptional day.— Christmas. From what I read of your article, though, it seems that you don't think so. I have no more time now. Call to-morrow. Good-day." And the editor turned once more to his desk without waiting for a reply from Lapointe who, knowing that none was expected, did not make any.

As soon as he heard the door close, the editor took up the manuscript and began to read. "Humph," he said after reading busily for some time, "it sounds like Renan, smooth and readable. It seems quite plausible, too."

He pulled a rope which connected with a bell on the floor above and presently the foreman of the composing room entered.

"This copy will fill up that space, Jim," said the editor as he held out the manuscript Lapointe had just left.

"It's late, sir, and the men were hoping for a bit of a holiday to-day, sir," said the foreman.

"We make altogether too much fuss about Christmas, Jim. Read that copy and you'll think so, too. Take part of it yourself and give the rest to Jackson and Walker."

V.

The scene in the composing room was a busy one. Twenty men were standing before tall racks which were laden with type fonts, some engaged in setting copy, others correcting their work according to the proof sheets spread out before them. To two of the men the foreman gave parts of the manuscript that had been handed him. "That is good, clean copy, boys. Hurry up with it," he said as he turned away.

Walker, to whom the last part of the manuscript was assigned, took up a page and began to work. With wonderful rapidity paragraph after paragraph was set, and at noon he was half through. When he left the room for luncheon his face, usually cheerful, wore such a scowl that Jackson, the man who worked behind him, noticed it.

"What's the matter, Walker? No holiday to-day, eh?" he said with a laugh.

"These fellows are getting things down pretty fine when they rule out Christmas. Soon it will be work every day. No fun —just a steady grind," said Walker in a surly tone.

Walker's feelings will be best understood by giving a portion of the "take" assigned to him. It read as follows :

It was midnight of a sacred Jewish Sabbath, a Sabbath made doubly sacred by its occurrence during the great feast of the Passover. All Jerusalem was silent. Not one of the thousands of pilgrims who had come to the feast was stirring. Even the guards that watched at the tomb of the Nazarite, who had been crucified three days before, were dozing. But the city was not all asleep. Six men were at this moment passing through one of the small gates in the wall which was called "the Needle's Eye." They approached the Nazarite's tomb without hesitation, which showed that they were not Jews of any of the stricter sects. They surprised the sleeping soldiers and, after binding them, rolled away the stone from the sepulchre. On a rude bier they laid the body and covered it with a coarse, linen cloth, having first taken the precaution to remove the grave clothes and leave them properly folded in the tomb. To touch a dead body would have shocked a Pharisee, but the followers of the Nazarite were Galileans.

Through the darkness they made their way to the Vale of Jehosaphat and the tombs of the kings. On the east Mount Olivet rose like a dim shadow in the darkness. On the west rose Mount Moriah and the Temple, —the temple which the Nazarite had promised to destroy and raise again in three days. In a natural cave they laid the bier and its burden and hastened away.

So ended the career of this man of mystery, who, from his birth at Bethlehem to his death on the skull mound of Golgotha presents the strangest character that the world has ever seen.

VI.

After leaving the office of the *Recorder*, Lapointe hastened down the street, intent on finding a chop house where he could break his fast of twenty-four hours.

"Merry Christmas, Mister !" shouted a grimy-faced little boot-black who adopted this method of calling attention to his trade.

Lapointe did not hear him.

"I say, there, you feller with the long face,— it's Christmas ; so take a reef in yer fiz !" shouted the boy, forgetting the purpose of his first salutation in the pleasure that he found in playing the wag at the man's expense.

Lapointe bestowed on him a savage look, and the urchin took to his heels. The incident, however, turned Lapointe's thoughts from the meal he had been anticipating. Forgetting for a time his hunger, he began to review the article he had just written. Father José would be surprised at the use to which the instructions received from him had been put, he thought. After all, Lapointe had no profound convictions on the subject of which he had written. The thought of Father José called up the whole history of his boyhood. He saw the tall, pine forest as it was in summer time when they had strolled together in search of wild flowers, about which the Father knew a great deal. Then it changed to a winter scene, with the pure white of the snow broken only by the great tree trunks and the dense clumps of bushes bent down with their burden of snow, every twig forming an arch for the snow roof,—a veritable fairies' palace fallen in ruin, with chinks and holes in roof and wall. And these snow mansions were not without tenants, for well-beaten paths led up to many of them. They were the homes of the wild rabbits. As his thoughts dwelt on these boyhood scenes, the feelings he had known in youth came crowding on him. At first they were vague and ill-defined. Soon, in fancy, he was walking hand in hand with Father José as they climbed the little hill behind his house and, after reaching the top, looked down on the town below. In fancy he heard again the kindly voice of the priest. The farmers were working in the fields below, and he knew them. They were good, ignorant folk, who already looked at him with awe, because he was going to be a priest.

"See to how many of these good people I am the light," said Father José. "Their life here is hard and plain, but I tell them of God and the hereafter and they are happy and contented. What else have they? And they look to me as the one who brings to them their bests gifts. The joy that awaits you, my son, you can never know till you have carried to some village like this the light of the truth that I have taught you." Then together they descended the hill to the house, where the Father took a favorite volume from the library and together they sat under the pine tree between the house and the church and read till evening.

Then Lapointe thought of the church with its quaint windows and its little steeple which had once seemed very tall, and the bell which sometimes he had been allowed to ring, and the beautiful ivy that climbed to the very top of the roof. The picture of the church suggested Christmas. How brightly the light had shone from the windows, when, long before daylight on Christmas morning, he had come to the church with his mother. There was the altar, with the tall candles all lighted, and a stable with a manger, and, hanging above, a gilded star, to represent the scene at Bethlehem.

How far he had walked he did not know, when he was aroused from his revery by the sound of music. With the mood which these thoughts had created still on him, he turned and entered the church from which the music came.

The vast edifice was crowded, and, seeing no vacant seat, Lapointe leaned against one of the great pillars which supported the gallery. The light that came through the tall, stained windows was subdued. At first he could not see the other end of the church, but as his eyes became used to the light he noticed the great organ with its gilded pipes and the white robes of the choir boys.

When he entered, the choir was singing a part of the *Messe Solennelle*. His ear caught first the pleading, tender notes of the *Benedictus*. The voice of the singer was pure and unusually sympathetic. Lapointe's physical nature was strained to just the tension which made it most responsive to any emotion. He listened intently to the solo, and when a hundred voices joined in the chorus, he trembled with excitement.

After a brief interval the choir began the *Credo*. Lapointe was familiar with the Latin and, in addition to the pleasure he derived from the music, he found a charm in the classic words. He was engaged in mentally translating, when his attention was suddenly arrested and directed to the thought in the words sung.

"*Crucifixus*," sang a single bass voice. The notes were inexpressibly sad.

They were taken up by a single singer for each part in turn, and then softly, very softly, repeated in unison. "*Crucifixus, etiam pro nobis, pro nobis sub Pontio Pilato.*" It was like the lament of the few disciples who had left all to follow their Master,—had left the happy fisherman's home on the shore of Galilee where the first rays of the sun came dancing over the water inviting to a day of healthful, hearty toil; had left the wife who waited at sunset for the fishing boat, and the laughing children who had climbed over the boat's side the instant its keel had touched the pebbles of the shore,— had left all, seeking the Master's Kingdom, the pearl of great price, only to see that kingdom, their hope, their all, perish with its Lord upon the cross.

"Crucifixus, Crucifixus!" sang the chorus. It was no longer the lament of a few, but a deep, universal wail.

"Crucified, crucified," murmured Lapointe, his thoughts echoing and re-echoing the words. He heard again the sad story of the scene at Calvary as he had heard it from Father José's trembling lips. He saw the crosses and the two thieves on either side and the angry crowd. He saw the cloud which wrapped the sacred city like a pall, and felt the awful darkness. He heard the agonizing cry, "My God, my God, why hast thou forsaken me!"

An intense silence fell upon the place. Even the most thoughtless were moved. For Lapointe the suspense was agony.

Suddenly the whole chorus joined in a song of triumph. "On the third day He rose from the dead." The very walls of the church vibrated in response to the deep tones of the organ. Lapointe felt as though he were being borne on irresistibly by this flood of melody,— borne on and on through hosts of singing angels, till suddenly the hosts parted and he saw in their midst the risen Christ who held out his hands to him.

As the anthem died away, the aged rector rose and with trembling lips repeated a single line : "For as in Adam all died, so in Christ shall all be made alive."

"Resurgam." Strong and full came the answering chorus. "Gloria in Excelsis!"

VII.

For a few moments Lapointe's mind wandered. His long fast and the strain he had undergone were beginning to to make themselves felt. When he came to himself the great congregation was moving. His knees trembled as he passed down the church steps. Looking at nothing, as a man in a dream, he hurried on as fast as he could go, till once

more he reached the *Recorder* office. Taking the elevator he went at once to the composing room on the fourth floor. He entered and stood for a moment just inside the door looking keenly around. On three hooks he saw parts of his manuscript. Jim, the foreman, noticed him, but gave him no further thought. An instant later Lapointe stood at his side and was tearing into bits the copy which he had snatched from the hook. Before the foreman realized what was taking place, Lapointe had destroyed the portions of his manuscript which had been assigned to Jackson and Walker. Walker had just finished his task. The galley which contained the matter he had set lay upon the proof rack. Lapointe saw it and threw it upon the floor. Then he hurried to the office before any one could stop him.

"Here is your money, sir," he said to the astonished editor, as he threw the dollar on the desk. "The article I left with you is not for sale,— not at any price."

Before the editor could answer, Lapointe was gone. His footsteps could still be heard in the lower hall when the foreman entered and told of what had taken place on the floor above. "It is time to go to press, sir, and we can set up no more matter," he added.

The editor was thoughtful for a moment. "Run the advertisement of the Lake Shore Improvement Company again, and I will take my chances on getting something for it," he said at length.

As he turned once more to his desk his eye fell on a card which lay on the floor. On picking it up he found that it gave Lapointe's name and address.

That evening, after wandering hopelessly all day, Lapointe received the following letter from the clerk of the Pacific Hotel :

Mr. A. Lapointe:

Dear Sir,- I shall be pleased to have you call at our office to-morrow at ten. The matter which I wish to present has no reference to the affair of yesterday. I take it that you want work. I think it probable that I can find something for you. At any rate, a man should not be any the worse off for having a conscience. Sincerely yours,

A. E. Yorxo,

Managing Editor *Recorder*.

MIDLAND WAR SKETCHES.

XVI. THE PASS OF JOHN FORBES.

By C. H. Robinson.[*]

Provost Marshal's Office, Columbus, Ky., July 8th, 1864.

John Forbes has permission to leave Columbus and pass the pickets.
Issued by Albert Tengler.   Good for one day.

Description: Hair .... eyes .... height ...., peculiarities

BEFORE me on the table lies a strip of paper very much like the above, which I found to-day in an old pocket book wherein are kept my commission, discharge and a few other army papers. On the back of it with the prodigality of flourishes and capitals so characteristic of the military headquarters of that day, —and of this day also so far as I know,— was written:

"Approved By Order of W. Hudson Lawrence, Col. Com'dg Post. Chas. E. Sinclair, 1st Lt. & A. D. C."

That strip of paper carries my mind back to the sultry, scorching July day on which it is dated. As Second Lieutenant of Company C of my regiment, I had that morning been detailed to command the picket post at the foot of the bluff southwest of the town, at the point where the principal wagon road leading to the agricultural country lying back from the Mississippi River crosses the track of the Mobile & Ohio Railway. The reserves for that post remained with me while the relief on duty was stretched out to the right and left at intervals of a few rods until they reached to those of the next post on each side. There was no part of the regularly organized force of the Confederate Army in our immediate vicinity, but Forrest with his command of guerrillas hovered around the state line of Tennessee, and the woods and swamps were more or less populated with bushwhackers.

Columbus was at the time regarded as one of the most important places on the river, and was occupied by a force of several thousand men. Besides my own regiment I now recall the One Hundred and Thirty-second Illinois Infantry, the Second Illinois Battery Light Artillery, the Tenth Minnesota and the Thirty-fourth New Jersey Infantry. Colonel William Hudson Lawrence of the last-named organization was commander of the post.

Two large forts, Halleck and Quinby—the former manned by colored troops, the Fourth United States Heavy Artillery, I think, with their immense Columbiads, Parrotts, and other siege artillery peering over the parapets, *en barbette*, or peeping from the heavy embrasures — frowned ominously at all boats passing up or down the river, which their elevated position enabled them to command for many miles both up and down; while a number of similar guns, protruding toward the open country in the rear, had a tendency to warn off all intruders from that direction.

So well fortified was the place, and so many were the troops stationed there, that we had no fear of an attack; but, notwithstanding this, a continuous line of chain pickets was kept posted day and night just back of the town and forts, from the bank of the river a mile or more above Fort Halleck to the river at the bluffs below the town at a point commonly known as "The Whirlpool." Boats also patrolled the river. All this made guard duty pretty heavy, and the remarks made by the boys concerning the same would, for artistic profanity, have largely discounted "our army in Flanders."

[*] Major Robinson is U. S. Pension Agent for Iowa and Nebraska.

This chain picket was rendered necessary by the fact that the Confederacy, then almost upon its last legs, was making desperate efforts to secure a supply of quinine and other medicines for the treatment of the sick, and to procure gun caps and other articles for military use which were not manufactured in the seceded states, and which could only be procured from blockade runners or by smuggling. As they were reported to be willing to pay its weight in gold for quinine, and about as much for gun caps, there were a good many enterprising citizens within our lines who were willing "to turn an honest penny" by supplying their necessities. Smuggling was as profitable as it was dangerous; but our chain pickets, while they did not entirely prevent the traffic in contraband articles, did act as a great restraint upon the smuggling business in general.

No person, man or woman, was allowed to leave the city without a pass, nor could they take out any articles of merchandise whatever without a permit in which the articles to be removed were fully described; and the officer in command of each picket post had daily orders to send in to headquarters under guard any one who should attempt to take out of the lines any article, however trivial, which was not mentioned in the permit or the bill of items thereto attached.

This was the situation about the middle of that July afternoon. The writer was lying in the shade of a freight car which had been thrown from the track at that point, his sword, sash and other insignia of rank hanging with his coat against the side of the car. The men, except those on duty, were lounging about, smoking, writing letters, playing cards, asleep,—all putting in the time in the usual manner of the soldier waiting for his trick on guard, when a man in citizen's dress approached the line from the direction of the town, and, when halted by the guard, presented the pass, a copy of which is given above. The corporal brought him to me, and, having found his pass to be correct, after

examination of his clothing for articles contraband of war and finding none, I waved my hand to the guard to permit him to pass through the lines. He was a small man with red hair and a carroty red beard some two or three inches in length. There was nothing striking in his appearance, but a circumstance which soon after occurred fixed his features indelibly upon my memory.

He left the wagon road at this point and walked briskly up the railroad track, finally disappearing in a cut and curve a few hundred yards distant. Scarcely was he out of sight, however, when a commissioned officer and a squad of colored troops came down over the bluffs from the direction of the forts. The officer asked me if any one had passed out recently, and when I gave him a description of the man who had just gone up the track he said, "That's our man, boys. Right shoulder shift arms; forward, double quick—march!"

Not long after their disappearance a volley and some scattering shots were heard in the direction in which they had gone, and in about two hours they returned, the officer saluting without remark as he passed in with his men. But two of the men were a few paces behind the squad, one of them having a soldier blanket gathered in a loose bundle under his arm, and, when I asked him what he had, he turned back a fold of the blanket and showed me the bloody, ghastly head of the man whom I had passed out a short time before as John Forbes. When I asked why they had killed him, I was told that the man was a guerrilla captain who had been guilty of murdering colored soldiers after they had been taken prisoner.

The head was taken to the fort and put on a pole at the gate, but as soon as Colonel Lawrence learned of the matter he ordered that it be at once taken down and buried.

My orders were to turn over all passes at headquarters when relieved from duty, but this time I ventured to disobey orders so far as to retain the pass of John Forbes.

CHRISTMAS BELLS.

COLD and still is the midnight,
  Still and cold is my heart;
Stars are gone and the darkness
  Holdeth my life apart.

Chiming I hear the Christ-bells
  Gladdest evangel proclaim,—
"Glory to God in the highest!"
  "Peace on earth," the refrain.

Mary A. Kirkup.

Wonderful story of angels,
  Of shepherds so lowly, of stars,
Showing His love and His glory
  Shining through prison bars.

Lift up your heads, O ye mourners!
  Put off the sorrow that mars,—
Peace and good-will from our Father,
  Angels and shepherds and stars!

Drawings by Florence Young.

MERCY HOSPITAL

By Mrs. A. L. McGrew.

IT WILL detract nothing from this new and noble institution in Des Moines if we go back for a brief period to its parent in Davenport.

In the autumn of the year 1868, a young surgeon, looking with favor upon the fair young city and surrounding country, located in Davenport and identified himself with the best interests of the city of his adoption. Full of ambition, he verified the adage "It is pluck and not luck that weaves the web of life." He saw the pressing need of a hospital, and decided that one must be erected as early as possible. He became enthusiastic upon the subject. "Hospital" was his constant theme. He wished to have one which would reflect credit upon its founders and merit the blessing of every sick and afflicted inmate; and, furthermore, he decided that it should be placed in charge of the Sisters of Mercy, for he held tender memories of their nursing and gentle ministrations. In the time of our Civil War this young surgeon was one among the many who heroically faced danger for duty. A severe wound took him to the door of death, but the careful nursing of the Sisters of Mercy brought him back to health. This surgeon was the lamented Dr. W. F. Peck.

Having enlisted the services of the pioneer priest, Father Palamorgus, the two called to their aid Father Borlando of Baltimore, and together these three philanthropists surveyed the situation. The outlook was not flattering. Huge difficulties seemed in the way, but, with such perseverance as built the pyramids on Egypt's plains, they soon reduced seeming mountains to mole-hills. They secured a building remote from the city and in no way suitable for a hospital; but it was a beginning. They sent to Chicago for the Rev. Mother Baromeo and an assistant Sister to inaugurate the work of fitting the building for patients. The county loaned the Sisters $2,000, to secure its speedy equipment. Wards were provided for the incurable insane of the county, and for the insane whose friends did not wish them taken to the State hospital. Success crowned every effort. The excellent management of the hospital and the ability of its medical staff were heralded far and wide, and patients came from the far West, and even Canada. From so small a beginning, how great has been the growth! Step by step the hospital has gained, until to-day it has an

THE LATE W. F. PECK, M. D.,
Founder of the Mercy Hospital, Davenport.

invested capital of over a quarter million dollars. On the 8th of December, 1894, they celebrated their twenty-fifth anniversary in an appropriate manner.

Doctor Peck was the president of the institution, and was a pillar of strength until his death, which occurred December 12th, 1891. He was known through-

to her memory by the medical staff of the institution. One by one the founders of the hospital have passed to the "home beyond," but the memory of their lives crowned with good deeds is like the lasting fragrance of the rose.

But their mantle of usefulness has fallen upon willing shoulders. The noble work

MERCY HOSPITAL, CARRYING OUT THE ORIGINAL PLANS TO FULL COMPLETION.

out the Middle-West for his ability and sterling worth. Life to him meant no idle game, but was as full of duties as the sky is of stars. He believed in noble aim and earnest work. His dying words were of Mercy Hospital. A large portrait of the lamented doctor occupies a conspicuous place in one of the halls. Mother Boromeo, who was head of the institution, has finished her work also, and sleeps near the stately edifice, where she labored so long for the cause of humanity. A neat monument was erected

continues, and the citizens of Davenport speak with just pride of Mercy Hospital.

On the 28th of November, 1893, a delegation of the Sisters of Mercy from Davenport arrived in Des Moines to inaugurate the building of a commodious and well-equipped hospital, of which the State Capital was greatly in need. Assured of success by leading citizens, they immediately began a search for temporary quarters A building was secured, which was formerly the handsome home of Major Hoyt Sherman.

The deft hands of the Sisters soon converted this dwelling into a hospital, with
the end in view of a new building as
early as possible. In a short time they
had all the patients that their twelve-
room house could accommodate. On
the third day of July, 1894, ground was
broken for the new hospital on Fourth
and Ascension Streets, and on the
20th of February, 1895, the Sisters
moved into their new home, which was
formally opened on the twenty-third day
of April following. It was an auspicious
event. Hundreds of people viewed the
beautiful edifice, which is built of red
pressed-brick and finished throughout
with Georgia pine. It has every modern
convenience, is a place of real comfort,
and everything about it is calculated to
aid the patient's recovery. It stands on
a high bluff, and the view is grand, look
which way one will. From the east
windows the Des Moines River and the
high bluffs beyond and the State House
and the Soldier's Monument can be seen,
also the entire east side of the city; from
the north window, Oak Park and Highland Park and Highland Park College with
its adjacent halls, can be seen. To the
south and west, one can look down upon
the busy West Des Moines, but its noisy
traffic is too far removed to disturb the
inmates of the hospital. Every room in
the building is light, airy and inviting.

Wards and private rooms were ele-
gantly furnished by the following individ-
uals and companies: Bishop Cosgrove,
Doctor McGorrisk, Doctor Cokenower,
Rev. Father Flavin, Mr. and Mrs. Fire-
stone, Younker Brothers, Younker
Brothers' employes, American Daugh-
ters of Isabella, Mrs. M. Kennedy, em-
ployes of the Des Moines & Kansas City
Railroad Company, employes of the Des
Moines and St. Joseph Division of the
Chicago & Great Western Railroad
Company, the Des Moines Insurance
Company, and a large ward furnished by
the Ancient Order of Hibernians of Polk
County.

The operating-room of the hospital has
perfect light and is furnished with every
modern appliance. A glass operating-
table was donated by the medical staff,
also a large brass sterilizer, the finest
west of New York. There is a large
dispensary where the Sisters compound
their medicine, a registry-room, a recep-

Photo by Poynore, Des Moines.
THE OPERATING ROOM, MERCY HOSPITAL.

Dr. T. F. Kellogg, President. Dr. F. E. Storr. Dr. William Van Werden.
Dr. J. W. Cokenower. Dr. J. L. Wells, Secretary. Dr. H. C. Eakins.

THE REGULAR BOARD, MERCY HOSPITAL.

tion-room, a parlor and the chapel, each complete in its appointments.

This beautiful hospital, dedicated by the Sisters in charge to the use of the afflicted, is worthy of all that can be said in its favor. The name, "Sisters of Mercy," is a synonym for incomparable nursing. The entire lives of the members of the order are devoted to the work. Living apart from the world, they have not the world's atlas to carry upon their shoulders. Their mission is —with gentle hands and loving care— to soothe the sick and dying, to provide dainty nutriment, to encourage the despondent.

Many people have erroneous ideas concerning a hospital, and at the mention of one their thoughts become coffin-shaped; but a visit to Mercy Hospital would speedily dispel the illusion. It is a non-sectarian institution. The religious belief of every patient is respected, and each has the privilege of inviting the pastor of his church whenever he may desire spiritual consolation. The physicians and surgeons who compose the regular staff and the consultants are gentlemen standing high in their profession — none higher — and patients coming from a distance are assured of as good medical attendance as the State affords.

None are exempt from disease or accident, for the angels of Joy and Sorrow walk the earth together. A peal of laughter, a wail of sorrow, a groan of pain, float upon every passing breeze. Our cup of joy is running over to-day; to-morrow, perchance, we drink to the dregs the cup of sorrow. Grateful recog-

nition should be given the noble army of men and women, our physicians and nurses, who with moral heroism face danger in many forms, ofttimes going into the midst of pestilence to relieve pain and to rescue from the grave.

The managers of Mercy Hospital invite all who need their care to come to their pleasant retreat, and those who enter will not find "*Memento Mori*" written upon its walls, but, will find instead, the soul-inspiring word, "Hope."

HOME THEMES.

THE MOTHER LOVE.

Beloved, can it be that thou art dead?
Thou wast, but yesterd'en, within this room,
Sat close beside me when the daylight fled
And watched with me the stars shine through the gloom;
Thy little hand that nestled in my own
Was pulsing warm with happy love and life,
Thy low, sweet laugh rang out in silvery tone,
Unmarred by time, untouched by pain or strife.

But when again the stars to-night do shine,
I stand alone and watch thy dreamless rest;
My sweet child wife, thy tiny babe, and mine,
Close clasped in death, lies on thy pulseless breast.
That little life that lingered but an hour,
Then, wailing, passed into the land unknown.
Dear, could it be there was some subtle power
Taught it to know and claim thee for its own?

And did it pause, in its lone flight to Heaven,
Holding its tiny, helpless hands to thee,
Pleading thy gentle love and care be given?
And, seeing, thou couldst not resist its plea,
But, filled with new, sweet mother-love and yearning,
Softly thy playing soul did speed away,
And, from earth's hopes and joys forever turning,
Bore thy sweet child to realms of endless day?

Think not, dear love, that I do chide thee, ever;
No love like mother-love was ever known;
That wond'rous tie our life nor death could sever,
No dear to thee that unseen life had grown.
But when at eve the stars do shine, to-morrow,
And I thy new-made grave shall stand beside,
Help me, Oh God, to bear the bitter sorrow
That, while I live, will in my heart abide!

Maggie Walker Parsons.

EDUCATION.

Next to a fine character, the acquisition of knowledge is the best thing in the world. To grow old, like Solon, in the pursuit of learning is certainly one of the most satisfying pleasures of existence.

Considered in its finest relations to human life, education has failed to do its perfect work unless it has brought the young impressible mind into living contact with the great masters of the poetic and the ideal. "Blessed are they," says

Matthew Arnold, "who have heard such voices in their youth; they are a possession forever." By such fine companionship hard, prosaic natures are softened and refined, while delicate souls are inspired with the courage which struggles and fulfils.

Some one has justly said that genuine education and culture mean increased sweetness, increased light, increased life, increased sympathy,—in a word, the uplifting and upbuilding of the entire man. The finest satisfactions this world can offer belong to him who is at once intellectual and spiritually minded.

To know, to grow, to carry safely down through all the days of our years the heart's best and freshest impulses and join them to the maturity of age is the end of all true education, and the real preservative of human life.

Mrs. Lillian Monk.

It stood on a sunny slope with the graves of the dead clustering around it, lifting its arms to this western sky, the cross of a crucified Christ. I wondered for a moment if I was not living in Jerusalem nearly nineteen hundred years ago. So strange it seemed, that cross with its burden, looking down upon corn-fields and meadow-lands. So near it seemed to bring the words, "And I, if I be lifted up, will draw all men unto me." Dying long years ago in a far-away land, such a pitiful, terrible death, could His eyes, ere they closed, foresee that that cross of martyrdom would shadow all the world to-day? Would stand forth in the light of this latter day glory, preaching its wonderful message to human souls?

Mary E. P. Smith.

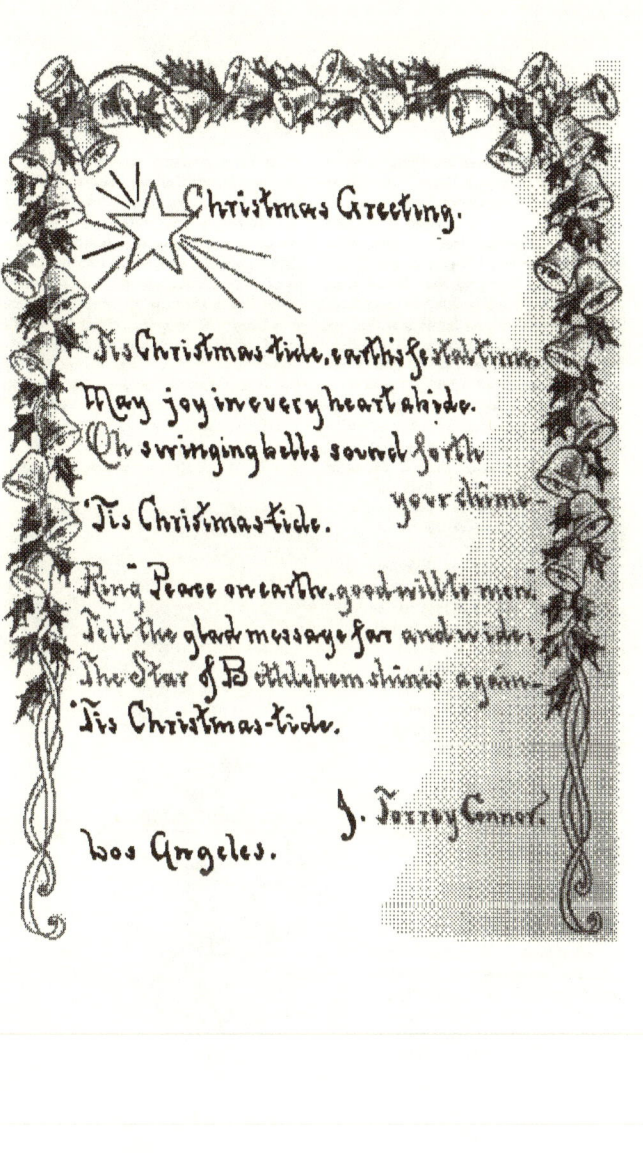

Christmas Greeting.

'Tis Christmas-tide, earth's festal time.
May joy in every heart abide.
Oh swinging bells sound forth
                              your chime—
    'Tis Christmas-tide.

Ring Peace on earth, good will to men,
Tell the glad message far and wide,
The Star of Bethlehem shines again—
    'Tis Christmas-tide.

                        J. Torrey Connor.

Los Angeles.

FRANKLIN WELLES CALKINS.

A BIOGRAPHICAL SKETCH.

By F. F. Willard.

AS a rule those persons living west of the Mississippi River who have attained any considerable reputation as writers of fiction have been men and women of decided individuality, who have been deeply impressed by certain phases of the early pioneer life of their youth and have endeavored to reproduce its spirit and color, so far as possible, by means of the printed page. This life — which is so recent as to seem almost like current history, but which in reality is even now a thing of the past — will receive more attention from the historian a few years hence than it does to-day.

Among the better known of these writers, whose stories may be likened to kodak flashes upon the scenes of early pioneer life on the Western prairies, Mr. Frank W. Calkins holds a place peculiarly his own. In depicting the earliest phases of pioneer life in that region about the Upper Missouri, including Northwestern Iowa, Nebraska and South Dakota, before the days of town-meetings and court-houses, and while the Indian still contested his title to the country, Mr. Calkins has been practically alone in the field. Although his work has been addressed in the main to juvenile readers, and has been published chiefly in the *Youth's Companion* and *Golden Days*, it is none the less realistic and valuable in its character.

Mr. Calkins was born in Iowa County, Wisconsin, shortly before the Civil War. His parents are of old New England stock, and inherited those qualities of character, of sturdy strength and intelligence, which have made New England famous for nearly three centuries.

He is a descendant in the eleventh generation of Hugh Calkins, who came from Wales to Massachusetts in 1638, and who, in after years, represented Gloucester in the Colonial legislature. Hugh Calkins was the progenitor of a large family of descendants, who took an active interest in the affairs of the times in which they lived. They were among the founders of Hartford, New London and Sharon, Connecticut. Mrs. Calkins, mother of the author, traces her ancestry back to the old Sprague and Ross families of Rhode Island. Thus on both sides the stock is thoroughly American. Ancestors of Mr. Calkins have proven their

FRANK W. CALKINS.

569

patriotism by fighting for their country in every war of our history, from King William's to the War of the Rebellion.

At the outbreak of the Civil War, Mr. Calkins' father enlisted as a member of the Twenty-third Regiment of Wisconsin Volunteers. After its close the family removed to Clay County, Iowa, in May, 1866, where their home has been nearly ever since. Clay County was then a part of the extreme frontier, and far removed from railroad connections. The experiences and vicissitudes of those early pioneer days still furnish the first settlers with never-ending themes for interesting reminiscence.

The son, Frank, had entered the public schools of Wisconsin in his sixth year, and had made so good progress in his studies that at the age of nine he was able to enter an academy, where the next youngest pupil was five years older than himself. He had already outstripped the district schools of Iowa when his parents removed there, and his education henceforth was nearly all self-acquired from books and magazines. He early manifested one of his most marked characteristics — that of an omnivorous reader. At nine years of age he had read the Bible, Glick's Fairy Tales, Abbott's History of the Rebellion, and many other books. Thus his taste for good literature was early developed.

In his new home, despite the lack of suitable school advantages, the standard authors, Harper's Monthly and the Youth's Companion served to keep his mind active, and to furnish an intellectual recompense for the rather monotonous aspect of things upon a flat, treeless prairie. A lady who moved to the frontier village of Spencer in 1870 loaned him the back numbers of Harper's, from the very beginning of the magazine up to date. This great quantity of reading matter, thus opportunely placed at his service, was devoured en masse. An active memory served him well in holding to that which was worth remembering, and his mental development was rapid. It was, as he himself says, a

process of "soaking in knowledge," and he gained at the same time ideas of style and literary form. He spent some time at the Iowa Agricultural College at Ames, where his rapid, plunging manner of going through books did not accord well with the strict requirements of the curriculum.

Although still a young man, Mr. Calkins' experiences entitle him to speak with the authority of personal knowledge concerning the subjects that in the main constitute the themes of his stories. In the summer of '75, he visited many parts of the West which were then wild and practically unknown to civilization. The man and the fitting experience fortunately met. Keen perceptive faculties, which had not failed to note much that was picturesque and peculiar to life on a flat stretch of weather-beaten prairie, added greatly to the mind's store of literary material.

He traveled by wagon train with several companions, and was among those who in August of that year ran the government blockade upon the Sioux reserve, and succeeded in reaching the heart of the Black Hills country. He and his companions were among those who founded Custer City, and "pre-empted" the first mining claims on French Creek. Their adventurous schemes were, however, nipped in the bud. A squad of United States cavalry, under the command of Captain Benteen, gathered them in and escorted them back to the Missouri, setting them free with the admonition to keep off the reserve until the government should be able to come to an agreement with the Indians. The country was thrown open to settlement a few days afterward, but the party did not return.

This trip furnished Mr. Calkins with the material for his first sketches. Fragments of personal experience, vividly narrated, and addressed to the Youth's Companion, Golden Days and other young people's journals, met with immediate success. Thus encouraged, he devoted the greater part of his atten-

tion to literary work during the following seven years. Sketches and serial
stories followed in rapid succession.
A good living was earned with the pen,
and in addition the means for further
travel and research. The name of the
hitherto unknown country lad suddenly
became known to thousands of interested
readers, and appeared prominently on
the announcement pages of the most
widely circulated of juvenile weeklies.
During this period he visited many of the
states and territories of the West and
Southwest. He camped, tramped and
hunted over a wide stretch of country
between the British possessions and the
Gulf of Mexico, the Great Lakes and the
western slope of the Rockies. In these
journeyings he mingled with all sorts and
conditions of frontiersmen, and gained
that intimate and varied local knowledge
which characterizes his Western sketches.

During more recent years Mr. Calkins'
attention has been diverted largely from
the field of his earlier successes to business
pursuits. He spent two years in the
study of law, and later did an extensive
business in real estate. The financial
crisis of '93 taught him, and many others,
that fortune, while constant in one field
of activity, may be fickle in another, and
his friends are pleased to note his present
expressed purpose to henceforth devote
his energies solely to the profession of
literature.

Mr. Calkins has been a careful student,
not only of current fiction and poetry but
of the whole range of English and foreign
literature. He has accustomed himself
to regular habits of study, and it is a rare
thing for the light in his room to be
extinguished before midnight. His studies have not been confined to literature
alone, for few men, other than specialists,
are better informed along the lines of
history, science, art, and even politics.
In fact he has always taken a lively

personal interest in politics, and is in
demand for forceful and telling campaign
speeches. He is, however, a man of
broad and liberal views in politics, as in
everything else. His spirit is optimistic
and cosmopolitan. The free atmosphere
of the Great West, in which the incidents
of most of his stories have their setting, is
the atmosphere in which the forces of his
life and character have had their development. They are conditions which
produce activity, independence and freedom of thought.

Mr. Calkins' literary style is what one
would expect from a knowledge of his
character and habits of thought. It is
direct and earnest, lucid and forceful,
harmonizing perfectly with the nature of
his favorite subjects. Had he devoted
his entire attention to literature of late
years, instead of turning to it only occasionally as a diversion from other labors,
it is confidently believed that he would
to-day be recognized wherever our current literature is read as the leading
exponent of those peculiar phases of life
of which he writes. As it is, he stands
without any living superior in depicting
scenes and incidents of the frontier
life in that section of the Northwest
which he has made his special study. In
1884, a competent and well-known literary critic writing from Boston, said:
"We have come to regard him [Calkins]
as truly the representative of the Great
Northwest in literature, as Cable is of
Louisiana, or Craddock of the Tennessee
Mountains."

Mr. Calkins has only just entered upon
the prime of life. In the ordinary course
of events, he still has a whole generation
of active usefulness before him. He has
produced some of his best work within
the past year and, if he shall adhere to
his present expressed purpose, the literature upon which his reputation is eventually to rest is yet to be written.

EDITORIAL COMMENT.

SHARING the general sorrow over the death of Eugene Field and feeling the deepest sympathy with those who mourn a husband and father gone, we do not also share the profound regret which many express in that the literary career of Eugene Field, the poet, is closed. That career was already rounded out into completeness. Already our keenest critics had pronounced this poet incapable of anything surpassing his few best and best known verses. Already the growing bent of the poet's mind toward Latin verse had given little promise of real flesh and blood poetry in the immediate future. If it is true that he had reached or was nearing the outermost limit of his powers, then — from a purely literary standpoint — it is best as it is. What real admirer of our Middle - Western poet would have him linger on, his power gone, the spell of his name a fading memory! We recently came across a bit of trivial summer verse written by one who thirty odd years ago was one of our most popular poets. This same poet a few months before had sent THE MIDLAND another bit of verse which jingled like poetry but was only clever rhyming—only the re-threshing of old Virgilian straw. Our Middle-Western poet, had he lived on, might not thus have written himself out of the fame of his middle life. But this we know : Eugene Field had sung himself into the hearts of children and of fathers and mothers whose lives are close to the children. Is not that enough? What a gift was his! What a full and rounded out success was his! How the crest-hunting rich and the wealth-seeking wearers of inherited honors and the popularity - seeking and place - hunting politicians whom their promoters half satirically style "great" dwindle when compared with this man, who with a few simple little heart-songs had won the love of children, had found a place in the hearts of those who mourn and had entered the home and made it the happier and better for his presence !

* * *

CHRISTMAS DAY is fast nearing. Like Twinkle in one of THE MIDLAND's Christmas stories, children everywhere are counting the intervening weeks and days, wondering how they can possibly wait so long for its coming. To us children of larger growth it is far easier,— this lesson of waiting. But with some — perhaps many — grown-up men and women the coming of Christmas - time brings anything but eagerness. Instead there is a terror — purely of one's own creating — and all because of undue anxiety over the annually recurring problem of present-making. Vanity and vexation of spirit ! This undue

From Photo by S. L. Stern, Milwaukee, with permission.

EUGENE FIELD.

anxiety robs the Christmas-time of all its old-time religious significance. It makes the exchange of Christmas presents an enormous social clearing-house affair — so much for so much. It fills the mind with vain imaginings as to what others may or may not do, and embarrassing speculations as to how best to keep up the exchange of presents without giving so little as to seem mean or so much as to seem lavish. What a burden many make of it — this annual round-up of giving and getting!

* * *

"THE DOOM OF THE SMALL TOWN."

"THE Doom of the Small Town," is the question-begging title of a strangely pessimistic paper which appeared in the April *Forum*. It was written by Mr. Henry J. Fletcher, of Minneapolis, author of a number of economic papers which have recently appeared in the *Atlantic Monthly*. Mr. Fletcher was for years a resident of Maquoketa, Iowa, and in the course of his reasoning he draws a picture of the changed conditions in the river counties of Iowa within his own recollection and coming under his own observation, the inference being that the gloomy picture he has drawn illustrates the prevalent condition of the small towns in the entire State, and in all the other states of the Middle-West. He writes pathetically of "the silent tragedy" being enacted in a multitude of small towns in Ohio, Indiana, Illinois, Iowa and Michigan, "the richest and best watered region in the United States," the tragedy referred to being the continual sapping of their township population to feed the rapacity of railroad corporations and to further the abnormal growth of the large cities. After presenting a truthful picture of the natural advantages of these midland states, this writer adds:

"Yet in these rich states, empires of themselves, and in the finest counties of each, forces are at work to check the growth and stifle the vitality of nearly half their townships."

Before we accept as fact the existence of these alarming forces here mentioned,

let us see for ourselves whether the conditions described by this writer do actually obtain.

Mr. Fletcher declares, on authority of the last United States census, that in these five states, from 1880 to 1890, there was gain of population in 3,003 townships and loss of population in 3,744 townships. The showing is to him conclusive evidence that railroad discriminations against intermediate points have sealed the doom of the small town, and consequently "there is no prospect for the latter but gradual extinction."

It is not necessary in this connection to point to the changed conditions of labor following the invention of machinery which has made the old diversification of village industries a thing of the past. Mr. Fletcher himself has done this. He vividly pictures the almost total absorption of several of the village trades and the total obliteration of others by the use of machinery and the consequent concentration of manufactories in the cities. This of itself is enough, one would think, to account for all the depression to which the census of 1890 points. But, instead of recognizing this potent force, at work upon small communities everywhere, as largely responsible for this decadence, he sees in the figures chiefly the consequence of one great first cause — namely, the all-grasping policy of the railroads.

To this writer it goes for nothing that railroad rates have been forced down and down, until the railroad question of the day has come to be a legal one — namely: "What constitutes a living rate?" It is nothing to him that the railroads have extended their lines into every county in Iowa and nearly if not quite every county in the four other states he names. Lost on him is the evident fact that the "gradual extinction" of the small towns would be a "silent tragedy" to the railroads themselves and to the people living in those towns, and therefore cannot be the purpose of the roads.

If the major premise of the *Forum* contributor be correct, then is our faith in the Middle-West vain, and the sooner we emigrate the better for us all; for, with only one overwhelmingly large city to which the towns of the Mississippi Valley are tributary, the "doom of the small town" speaks the general doom of all that region stretching all the way from Chicago to the Missouri and from St. Paul and Minneapolis to St. Louis. But, happily, Mr. Fletcher's major premise is not correct.

In the first place, Mr. Fletcher groups five states and labels them decadent when only two of the five give even this surface indication of decadence. His tabular statement shows that between 1880 and 1890 Ohio lost population in 755 townships and gained in 529; and that Illinois lost in 800 townships and gained in 579; but that Indiana gained in 496 townships and lost in 482; Iowa gained in 893 and lost in 691, and Michigan gained in 306 and lost in 416. Why advertise these states as "decadent" when the census shows only growth in general and movement of population?

But showings by townships are misleading. Suppose ten townships indicate a loss of from one to ten inhabitants — say a loss of thirty all told. Now, suppose the adjoining townships together show a gain of thirty to fifty inhabitants — say a gain of a hundred — does the showing prove decadence? No; it only proves a redistribution of population.

After reading Mr. Fletcher's doleful tale of decadence and startling prophecy of extinction, the reader finds himself wondering how it happened that with this policy of gradual extinction in full operation, there should nevertheless have been actual growth in a very large minority of the towns of Ohio and Illinois and in a majority of the towns of Michigan, Indiana and Iowa.

Mr. Fletcher finds that Iowa with its two million population has more miles of railway than New York with its six million. And yet, right here where the railroad corporations reach into every county in the State, there was during that decade of readjustment and redis-

tribution of population a gain in population in 893 townships and a loss in only 720!

But this *Forum* contributor selects a few counties in Iowa as especially bad examples of this "gradual extinction" policy. Let us follow in the track of this devastation and see what there is of the startling report rendered. The counties selected are those lying along the Rock Island Railroad between Des Moines and Davenport and those lying along the Mississippi River. Here Mr. Fletcher finds the "evil influence" especially marked. That influence he finds to be none other than the inequality of transportation charges. Now, we are not attempting to argue the freight-rate question with Mr. Fletcher. Doubtless there are unequal rates that should be remedied and other wrongs that need righting. The point we make is this: Assuming, for the moment, that the railroads are so unwise as to seek to kill by slow starvation the goose that will lay golden eggs for them when sufficiently nourished, how can Mr. Fletcher explain the persistency of the goose in living on, and growing, despite this alleged gradual extinction policy? If his answer be that the small towns live in spite of the railroads, then his declaration that they cannot live and that their time on earth is short, is, to say the least, unfounded. " But," the reader may say, "you, too, are begging the question. You are assuming growth, when Mr. Fletcher produces figures to show decadence." The criticism is just. We therefore proceed to fortify our assertion.

In the Eastern Iowa counties he finds the strongest exemplification of his theory. Ignoring the enormous growth of the western half of the State, he follows the track of the devastation from Des Moines to the Mississippi and then up and down the river, only to find business dwindling and industries starving, "until dilapidation seems their natural condition and public spirit dies away."

Then, to substantiate this finding, he

reports the losses not by counties but by straggling townships—14 townships in Polk, 14 in Jasper, 13 in Poweshiek, 15 in Iowa, 19 in Johnson, 11 in Muscatine and 14 in Scott. Turning to the official sources quoted in the *Forum*, we find that Polk County in 1880 had a population of 42,395, and in 1890 its population was 65,410. "But that growth was in Des Moines." Yes, but Des Moines is not a terminal point of the railroads; it is at the mercy of the roads same as the other towns along the trunk lines. And, again, the value of every farm in Polk County is enhanced by the growth of its county seat. In those ten years of readjustment Jasper's population fell off from 25,963 to 24,943. Poweshiek fell off from 18,936 to 18,270. Iowa County dwindled from 19,221 to 18,270; Johnson, from 25,429 to 23,046. Muscatine increased from 23,170 to 24,504. Scott increased from 41,266 to 43,164. Is this a bad showing for the four counties between Polk and Muscatine? Let us look closer. We find by the State census of 1885 that the loss in Poweshiek occurred from 1880 to 1885 and that from 1885 to 1890 there was growth! Growth also from 1885 to 1890 in Iowa and Johnson! At this rate of "gradual extinction," when may we look for the end?

Let us follow the line of devastation along the Mississippi River. Starting off with Lee County and ascending the river, we find that county gained 2,856 in population in those ten trying years. Des Moines County in the same time gained 2,223. Louisa lost 1,269. Muscatine gained 1,334. Scott gained 1,898. Clinton gained 4,436. Jackson (Mr. Fletcher's former home) lost 1,000. Dubuque gained 6,852. Clayton lost 2,096. Allamakee lost 1,884.

Here certainly are some suggestions of Mr. Fletcher's dream of "gradual extinction." But, fortunately, another census has been taken since this pessimistic wail was voiced in the *Forum*. The State census of 1895 effectually disproves the misleading and damaging utterance of last April, and proves beyond any remaining question that—whether with the help of the railroads or despite the railroads, matters not so far as our present purpose extends—this great Middle-West—vast aggregation of small towns as it is—is rising superior to all obstacles and fast fulfilling its destiny. We have waited for the official returns to verify our position, and the figures are now before us. Take these same counties—alleged to be steadily and gradually nearing the point of total extinction!—and what do they show?

	1890.	1895.	Gain.
Polk	65,410	72,999	7,474
Jasper	24,594	25,061	946
Poweshiek	18,304	18,524	220
Iowa	18,270	18,064	*206
Johnson	23,082	24,303	941
Lee	37,715	39,520	2,205
Des Moines	35,324	37,620	2,296
Louisa	11,873	12,286	413
Muscatine	24,504	25,130	626
Scott	43,164	45,869	2,705
Clinton	41,199	43,108	2,199
Jackson	22,771	23,171	400
Dubuque	50,869	61,172	10,339
Clayton	26,754	26,670	*108
Allamakee	17,907	17,984	74

*Loss.

This, then, is the latest official showing of "gradual extinction" in the counties especially selected as the best—that is the worst—examples of the destruction of the small towns. If an objection be made that the growth is mainly in the larger cities, we answer: "Yes." If you call our Iowa cities large; but "mainly" is the word, not altogether. In several of these counties the cities have not grown as fast as the counties they are in. But this objection does not explain away the growth of the smaller counties alongside the larger—such as Jasper, Poweshiek, Iowa, Louisa and Jackson—the last-named presumably the point from which this writer drew his harrowing picture of ruin and decay.

But, why linger in one portion of the State selected as "meetest for death?" We could fill pages showing growth of the unlooked for small towns of Iowa—and that, too, during a period of great general business depression, and we have thus far learned of less than a dozen small towns of Iowa that have not grown during the past five years.

Hastening to a conclusion of the subject, we have only to point to the grand total of population in Iowa,—a State with no overpowering great cities, a commonwealth made up of small towns, —to totally undermine the whole argument of the *Forum* article, based as it is upon an assumption of facts which do not exist.

In 1880 Iowa's population was 1,624,615.

In 1890 it was 1,911,896.

In 1895 it is 2,057,250.

•₊•

THE sixth Type of Midland Beauty presented in this magazine is the work of Dawson, the Albia photographer, engraved by Binner, of Chicago. The modest little beauty who sat for the picture is Miss Melissa Katherine Taylor, of Albia, Iowa, a young lady who gives abundant promise as a vocalist.

THE MIDLAND BOOK TABLE.

A true poet, possibly our greatest poet, is Thomas Bailey Aldrich. A pretty little book entitled "Later Lyrics," * selected from Mercedes, The Sisters' Tragedy, Wyndham Towers and Unguarded Gates, gives the reader new proof of Mr. Aldrich's power. These lyrics reveal more tenderly than ever before the poet's deep sympathy with nature. They all have that undertone of sadness ever to be found in the song of those who turn to nature for companionship. The coming of Spring is to this poet an inspiration. At sight of the first crocus he sings:

"A sudden tremor goes
Into my mind and makes me kith and kin
To every wild-born thing that thrills and blows."

In the same poem, "A Touch of Nature," he claims to share—

"The tremulous sense of bud and briar
And inarticulate ardors of the vine."

In "Threnody" occur the lines—

"Unvexed by any dream of fame,
You smiled and bade the world pass by."

Equally exquisite is that voice of sadness, "A Mood," in which the poet acknowledges the spell of—

"Some vague, remote ancestral touch of
sorrow or of sadness;
A fear that is not fear, a pain that has not
pain's insistence."

Not easily forgotten are the lines from the poem on Sargent's portrait of Edwin Booth —

"That face which no man ever saw
And from his memory banished quite."

"Casa Braccio," † by F. Marion Crawford, has come out from *The Century* and taken its place in the now good-sized collection of Mr. Crawford's novels. It appears in two pretty green and gold covers with numerous exquisite illustrations by that master of the engraver's art, Castaigne, whose recent work in *The Century* has done much to raise the standard of magazine illustrating. "Casa Braccio" is Mr. Crawford's twenty-fifth novel. It is "affectionately dedicated" to the author's wife. Just why this novel should have been thus signally honored does not yet appear; for it cannot be that even the most partial reader of the twenty-five novels from this author's pen is likely to say that it is best of them all.

"Casa Braccio" is a connecting link between Rome, the scene of the author's most popular novels, and New York, the city in which his new work finds local habitation. Gloria Dalrymple may be said to be that link. She is a New York girl connected with the coterie of rather common-place aristocrats, introduced to the reader in "Katherine Lauderdale" and to be passed on through "The Ralstons" to the forthcoming next of the series. The atmosphere of a Roman convent pervades the story, and in the shadow of old churches and of narrow streets and passages the traditional dagger of the Italian assassin gleams. Intrigue and crime involve Angus Dalrymple and his daughter Gloria and her husband, the artist, Paul Griggs, in whom the followers of the Ralston family's fortunes have already become interested. Above all this wickedness a sweet, sad face is seen,—that of the unwisely-loving nun, Sister Maria Addolorata. Through all the after-misery moves the passionate Donna Francesca. The story is a tragedy, the blackness of which must impart a borrowed intensity to the otherwise not very startling follies of the Ralstons,

* Houghton, Mifflin & Co., Boston. Sold by J. R. Aldill. Des Moines. $1.02.
† Macmillan & Co., New York. $2.00.